PUCKING SWEET

ALSO BY EMILY RATH

PUCKING SWEET

EMILY RATH

Kensington Books
kensingtonbooks.com

Tropes: Hockey romance, workplace romance, unplanned pregnancy, "it's a love triangle until it's not"

Tags: MF, MFM, MMF, MM, hockey romance, enemies to lovers, friends to lovers, it's a love triangle until it's not, the OG emergency contacts, double bingo, stick your pretty dick in me, there's nothing accidental about these roommates, worst-kept secret, unplanned pregnancy, listening at doors, I'll try anything once, hand job wizard, forever running from my feelings, can I taste it, third act freakout, groveling, that micro trope where the MMC who hates cats gets a cat and he's miserable but slowly learns to love the cat and by the end he'd die for that cat

I make no apologies for how long this book is, but I will apologize in advance to anyone who has ever worked in PR for an actual NHL team. This will not be accurate, but I promise it'll be fun.

Content Warnings: This book contains themes that may be distressing to readers including homophobia, patriarchal gender norms, judgmental parents, narcissism, gaslighting, history of a past abusive romantic relationship (verbal and emotional, cheating), and history of child abuse (verbal, emotional, physical, neglect). There are several medical emergencies depicted including two graphic on-ice injuries (blood/open wounds and sudden cardiac complications). A character experiences debilitating claustrophobia, to include hyperventilating and panic attacks. A character also suffers from anxiety.

A main character experiences an unplanned pregnancy. She drinks alcohol while pregnant (only while she is unaware of the pregnancy). She goes into preterm labor, but there are no complications for parent or child. The delivery is not shown on page.

Aside from the above, this book contains detailed MF, MFM, MMF, and MM explicit sex scenes that include elements of public sex, voyeurism, dirty talk, cum as lube, cuckolding, bondage/restraint, impact play, anal play, toy use, praise, and mutual masturbation.

Author's Note

Welcome back, friends! This is the third book in the Jacksonville Rays hockey romance series. Book One, *Pucking Around*, is Rachel's story. Book Two, *Pucking Wild*, is Tess's story. It's finally time to read Poppy's story. Are you ready to travel back in time?

Pucking Sweet starts at the beginning, even before Rachel arrives in town. We have a lot of ground to cover, so buckle up! I left a ton of Easter eggs for Novy, Poppy, and Morrow across the pages of the first two books (and the HEA novellas). Did you catch them all?

If you want the best, most comprehensive version of all the Jacksonville Rays characters and their universe, I recommend reading all three of the main books in order (and don't forget the spicy prequel that started it all, *That One Night*).

XO,

E Roth

Meet the Rays

PLAYERS
*Compton/Price, Jake (#42): defenseman
Davidson, Tyler "Dave-O" (#65): backup goalie
Fields, Ethan (#94): forward
Gerard, Jean-Luc "J-Lo" (#6): defenseman
Gordon, Sam "Flash": rookie, non-starter
Hanner, Paul (#24): defenseman
Jones, Brayden "Jonesy": rookie, non-starter
Karlsson, Henrik (#17): forward
*Kinnunen/Price, Ilmari "Mars" (#31): starting goalie
Langley, Ryan "Langers" (#20): forward
Morrow, Cole (#3): defenseman
Novikov, Lukas "Novy" (#22): defenseman
O'Rourke, Patrick "Patty": rookie, non-starter
O'Sullivan, Josh "Sully" (#19): forward, Captain
Perry, David "DJ" (#13): forward
Walsh, Cade (#10): forward
West, Connor "Westie": rookie, non-starter
Woodson, Chris "Woody" (#51): defenseman

COACHES
Andrews, Brody: Assistant Coach (defense)
Denison, Nick: Assistant Coach (offense)
Johnson, Harold "Hodge": Head Coach
Tomlin, Eric: Goalie Coach

TEAM SUPPORT
Gordon, Jerry: Assistant Equipment Manager
Jones, Cody: Equipment Tech
*Sanford/Price, Caleb: Assistant Equipment Manager

MEDICAL SUPPORT
Avery, Todd: Director of Physical Therapy
Jacobs, Hillary: Team Nurse
O'Connor, Teddy: PT intern

Price, Rachel: Barkley Fellow
Tyler, Scott: Team Doctor

OPERATIONS/MANAGEMENT
Francis, Vicki: Operations Manager
Ortiz, Claribel "Wednesday": Social Media Manager
St. James, Poppy: Public Relations Director
Talbot, Mark: Owner and Interim General Manager

*Jake, Ilmari, and Caleb are listed with their unmarried and married names as this book crosses timelines with books one and two in the series.

STAR SIGNS
POPPY: Libra (air): strategic, compassionate, indecisive
LUKAS: Scorpio (water): intuitive, calculating, guarded
COLTON: Leo (fire): passionate, playful, loyal

PUCKING SWEET

1
POPPY

"*H*ey, Poppy, I think you're gonna want to see this..."

I look up sharply over my laptop screen, eyeing the cellphone my social media manager extends my way. Claribel Ortiz was my first official hire in my new position as public relations director for the Jacksonville Rays. She may have all the charm of an angry black crow, with her goth girl eyeliner and dyed inky black hair, but she's a genius. Besides, she works behind the camera, not in front of it.

Personally, I like her fierce attitude. These days, marketing on social media is like battling a hydra. Each time you slay the algorithm and start seeing success, the darn thing grows three new heads, and you have to start all over.

Enter Claribel.

This girl is quickly becoming the Rays' own personal Hercules. She's sharp and inventive with content creation. Nothing feels boring or overdone. She teases trends rather than beating them dead. In a matter of weeks, her team took all our fledgling NHL accounts and turned them into content machines. Our views are climbing, and our followers are growing—just in time for the first game of the season.

In the past few months, I've learned Claribel only has two expressions: lifeless and loathing. To see a third on her face is a little unsettling. In this moment, she looks almost... amused?

"What is it?" I say, warily reaching for her phone. "Oh heavens, please don't tell me this is still about those gosh darn balloons."

"It's not about the balloons."

"Thank goodness for small mercies."

Last week, we used two large balloon arches outside the new practice facility to decorate for our inaugural training camp. Within hours, every climate change group in the city descended to declare the Jacksonville Rays an environmental scourge. Claribel's team has been working overtime across our social media accounts to showcase all the environmentally friendly features of the facility.

But this is definitely not about balloons.

"Oh, no." I flick the screen with my thumb. My frown deepens with each picture I scroll past. Most of them are grainy, but there's no mistaking what I'm seeing—dancing women in bikinis; glassy-eyed, lounging men; and lots of free-flowing alcohol. I huff, flicking my ponytail off my shoulder. "Seriously? These look like stills from a Pitbull music video."

Claribel raises a dark brow. "Latin crunk doesn't seem like your vibe, boss."

I eye her over the phone. "Don't let the pearls and polish fool you, Miss Claribel. I'm a woman of the world."

You have to be tough to work in public relations. You have to be even tougher to work in a male-dominated field like the National Hockey League. I may look like a kitten, but with the St. James name and the reputation of a major international PR firm behind me, I'm a tiger.

Claribel is one of the only people who isn't intimidated by my family connections or my cutthroat business style. Just one more reason why I like working with her. She crosses her arms, her long black nails tapping her forearm as she surveys me. "Let me guess . . . you were a sorority girl?"

I smile, glancing back at her phone.

"Yeah, I bet you ran circles around those frat boys," she teases.

My smile falls when I realize the same man is in almost every photo. I'd know his stupidly handsome face anywhere—that sculpted jaw, those serious eyes, the confident smirk. It's Lukas Novikov, star defenseman for the Jacksonville Rays. He has tousled, light brown hair and a soft spray of freckles across his pale cheeks and nose, a nose that has been broken at least once judging by the little lump in the bridge. His colorfully tattooed arm drapes casually over the shoulders of girl after girl. In every picture he looks bored and cocky, downright unobtainable.

But I know the truth: the man is *too* obtainable.

Lukas Novikov is a walking PR nightmare—the constant parties, the endlessly rotating roster of girls, his surly post-game interview tactics. If he weren't one of the top-ranked players in the League, he'd probably be unemployed by now. But I've seen him in action. He hits like a freight train and fights like a bear. It'd be easier to dismiss him as a mindless bruiser if he wasn't one of the top defensemen scorers. Not only can he assist with goals, he makes them too. He's worth the seven million dollars a year the Rays pay him . . . *on* the ice.

Off the ice, he's nothing but a thorn in my side. The season hasn't even started, and I already wish we could trade him away. But that's above my pay grade. I don't get to pick the cards I'm dealt. I just have to find a way to win with them.

Novikov is my wild card. When the Bruins announced his trade to the Rays, their PR manager sent me a file on him an inch thick. She'd slipped a pink sticky note inside the manilla folder that said, "He's your problem now." I'm sure she laughed her way to the nearest bar and bought everyone the first round of drinks to celebrate.

As if I don't have enough problems! I'm trying to build the reputation of an international men's hockey team from scratch. Do these players really think it's so easy? In the current political and social climate, sports teams are under a microscope every hour of the day. If the city is willing to pick up their torches and pitchforks over a balloon arch, what will they do to our whiskey-guzzling manwhore of a star defenseman who spends every moment he's not on the ice with his hands on a different puck bunny's cleavage?

I glance up at Claribel. "When did these post?"

"Last night. More this morning," she adds. "Novikov rented a rooftop bar over at the beach and threw this little private party."

"When will these guys learn?" I hand the phone back to her with a tired shake of my head.

"Learn what, boss?"

"Nothing is ever private anymore."

"It can be, if you know how to be careful," she hedges. "Novikov clearly doesn't . . . or he just doesn't care."

I close my laptop and push away from my desk, slipping my feet back into my patent leather Saint Laurent slingbacks. "Okay, Clary-B. Give it to me straight. What's the fallout?"

"Pretty much what we expected. They're calling the Rays a bunch of party boys and players. The fan groups are split between wishing they were invited and wishing the team was setting a better example for the city."

I stand, slipping into my heels like armor. "Did Novikov post any of those photos to his own social media?"

"No, he hasn't posted anything since he announced his trade."

That's a relief at least.

"You know, Angela Whitney over at the Bruins warned me about him," I say, stuffing my laptop into my purse. "The moment they announced, she was in my emails asking for a call. I'd hoped he'd at least wait until the season started before he pulled this crap here."

"Maybe it's a one-off. Just letting off some end-of-summer steam before the season starts."

"Yeah, and maybe he's a party-loving pretty boy with more charisma than sense, determined to make my job here impossible." I sling my heavy bag over my shoulder, clutching my buzzing phone in my manicured hand. Whoever they are and whatever they need, they're going to have to wait.

Claribel watches me round the desk. "What are you gonna do, boss?"

"I'll tell you what I'm *not* gonna do. I'm not giving Novikov the long leash he had up in Boston." I snatch my facility access pass off the hook by the door. "He thinks he can behave here the way he did up there? I intend to educate."

"You gonna tug on his leash a little, Pop?"

I slip the lanyard around my neck. "If I have to."

She leans against the wall by the door. "You gonna call him a 'bad boy?' Make him crawl?"

"I'm not above treating these grown men like naughty children," I say, freeing my ponytail from under the lanyard. "Athletes crave structure. Sometimes they just need a firm hand."

"Kinky. Can I watch?"

I step past her and shrug. "Sure."

Her expression brightens just a little. "Can I record it?"

"No."

She shuts my door and follows me down the hall. "What about just audio?"

My heels click as I head for the elevator. "No, Claribel."

"What about a picture?" she says at my shoulder. "Trust me, boss, there's nothing hotter than seeing a man who deserves it get reprimanded by a female superior."

I laugh, jabbing my thumb on the elevator's shiny silver down button. The elevator doors open and we both step inside. I hate elevators, but it can't be helped. I am simply not climbing four flights of stairs every time I need something from one of the players.

As the doors close, I smile. "Fine. One picture. We look at it, then we delete it."

Her eyes are already back on her phone, but I see her smirk. "Consider it done, boss."

1
LUKAS

Well, hot goddamn. I am on fire. Training camp is going exceptionally well for me. Thanks to my grueling summer cardio routine, I'm as fast as I've ever been out on the ice. Strong too. At twenty-six, I'm seven years into my NHL career, and I'm in the best shape of my life. I feel like a bull only just hitting my prime.

As if I need the affirmation, the next words out of the physical therapy intern's mouth are: "You've been looking great out there, man."

"Thanks."

"Seriously, you're really fun to watch." Teddy O'Connor stands at the end of the massage table, my feet cupped in his hands as he gently jiggles my legs. It always helps me to get some of the lactic acid moving before I hit the ice.

I groan, tipping my head back as his strong fingers massage my left calf muscles. "God, you're good at that." I feel my body go slack. "What will it take to convince you to come to my house and do this every night?"

Teddy stills.

"Novy, stop propositioning my interns," Doc Avery calls from the next table over. He's busy working on Langley, one of the flashy young wingers. I don't know why, but Avery always makes me grit my teeth. The guy is a fucking asshole.

"Don't listen to him, Teddy Bear," I tease. "You know I'm totally loaded, right? I'll make it more than worth your while." I flash him an obnoxious wink that Langley and Avery can both see.

Teddy laughs. "Sure, Nov. Why don't I just move in for the season? I can kip on your couch and make you oatmeal in the morning too."

"Sounds like a plan."

He grins. "Cool. My going rate is a thousand dollars a night."

I huff a laugh that comes out part grunt as he digs his thumb into my soleus muscle.

"Hey, you just said you're loaded, right?"

"Don't even tempt me, bud. You're that good. You've got way better technique than old Hotdogs-for-Hands Avery over there."

Avery grumbles something under his breath while Teddy puffs out his chest a little, pleased with my compliment. "Okay, man. That's about all I can do," he says, lowering my leg. "Hit the bike for fifteen to twenty minutes when you get off the ice. Keep it loose and casual."

"Loose and casual? Did you memorize my Tinder bio?"

"I can help you stretch after if you need me," he offers.

"Hey, there are twenty-two other guys on this team," Avery calls over to him. "Time to crawl out of Novy's ass, kid."

Sitting up, I swing my legs off the side of the table.

"Good luck out there today," Teddy says, his voice lower now, his smile falling.

I hop off the table and flash him my most confident grin. "Like I need it."

He's right to wish me luck though. On a regular team, training camp is typically used to decide which farm team guys will fill out the twenty-three-man roster. But this is year one for the Jacksonville Rays. No player's position is guaranteed, not even mine. All the rookies are hungry for a chance to shine, and the older guys are desperate to stay relevant. Hopefully, Coach Johnson is about to announce that I'll be the starting left defenseman this season.

I think the only holdup at this point is deciding who will skate at my right. There are a few good prospects. Jean-Luc Gerard is a legend. Jake Compton is definitely solid. We've been chasing each other in the League rankings for years.

But I've got my hopes set on Cole Morrow. Methodical and confident, he's like a cannonball on the ice. He's knocked me on my ass more times than I can count over the years. And we already have a shorthand we can dust off from the time we played together back in the Western Hockey League. It was only for one season, but when we started together on the Seattle Thunderbirds, we were a well-oiled, two-man machine.

Langley hops off the other table. He's only an inch or two shorter than my six-foot-two frame, but he's a forward and I'm a defenseman. He's lean and fast, while I'm built like a tree. "You ready for another exhibition game?"

"I was born ready."

"You're from Thunder Bay, right? And you played in the WHL?"

I eye him carefully. "Did you google me, Langers?"

"Might have done."

I press a hand to my chest. "Aww, I'm touched. You wanna know my star sign too there, bud? My favorite food?"

He laughs. "Don't pretend you didn't look up my stats just as soon as they announced the full trade list."

"Of course I did. Gotta know your enemy, right? And my star sign is Scorpio by the way—not that you asked."

"So, I'm your enemy now? You really want to start the season with an enemy on the team?"

"Hey, they traded you in from Montreal, Langers. I was a Bruin. You do the math. Besides, everyone loves a good enemies-to-lovers trope."

"Spare me, tough guy. I know you're a marshmallow under all that angry muscle. And it doesn't matter where we came from. We're both Rays now."

"Rivalries die a slow death," I intone.

He just shrugs. "Not for me. I don't like to dwell on the past. Tell you what, the first game we play in Montreal, we'll find a great dive and split an order of poutine. My treat. Then I'll have to beat you away with a stick." He holds out a hand, intending for me to shake it.

I glance down at it. "Oh, so you think it's that easy to woo a Canadian? A little poutine and I'll just forget about how you smoked us during the last playoffs?"

"It worked for me before," he replies, still holding out his hand. "If poutine's not your thing, I'll just shake a box of maple candy at you. Either way, we'll both be dressed in the teal and white of the Rays. Boom. Best friends forever."

Okay, I officially like Langley. I laugh as I reach out my hand, but the sound dies as I take in the sudden look of panic on his face.

"Uh-oh." He drops his hand to his side. "Dude, watch your six."

I hear the soft click of heels coming from directly behind me and my shoulders stiffen. "Oh shit . . . PR Barbie?"

"Yep."

"No."

"She's clocked you, man."

I groan. "Exactly what color is her pencil skirt?"

"Uhh . . ." He glances surreptitiously around me to check. "Black."

"Fuck."

Black means no nonsense. Black means it's about to be someone's fucking funeral.

He claps me on the shoulder. "She's hungry for it, man. Total blood in the water."

My gaze darts around, noting all the exits. I feel it when her eyes lock on me. "Can I still escape?"

"Not a chance. Sorry, man."

I grab his arm as he tries to step past me. "Goddamn it. Don't leave me."

He twists his wrist, wrenching away from my grasp. "If I stay here, she'll drag me into whatever mess you're in, and I'd rather keep my balls attached, thanks."

"You are dead to me," I hiss. "*This* is how we become enemies."

Langley laughs, ducking around me like a rabbit fleeing from a fox. Only in this case, the fox stands at all of five-foot-two and has pink manicured nails for claws.

"Good luck ever becoming my lover now, you fucking Judas," I rasp at his back. He uses Teddy as a human shield, darting away from our approaching director of public relations.

"Yoo-hoo, Lukas," Poppy calls. "Honey, do you have a minute to chat?"

Teddy looks wide-eyed at me while, behind him, Avery just smirks. Arrogant fuck. I hate him. I take a deep breath, filling my chest with air as I spin around.

Fuck me. Why does the biggest ball-buster I've ever met have to be so gorgeous? She marches toward me in her kitten heels, that devilish black pencil skirt hugging the narrow curve of her hips. Her blazer is unbuttoned, revealing a silky blouse underneath that hugs her perky boobs.

Fuck—don't look at her boobs.

My gaze darts up to take in the pointed features of her face instead. Her bright blue eyes are narrowed at me, while that curly blonde ponytail swings from side to side with each step. "Poppy St. James, as I live and breathe," I say at her approach. "To what do I owe the pleasure?"

"Spare me the sass, Lukas. We need to talk. In private, if you please," she adds, her gaze darting over to the PT staff. Behind her, Wednesday Addams deadpans me, her phone clutched in her pasty hand capped with pointed black talons.

Avery just chuckles and walks off in the direction of his office. But sweet Teddy doesn't take the hint. "Good morning, Ms. St. James," he says brightly.

She turns, blasting him a megawatt smile. "Teddy, honey, haven't I told you to call me Poppy?"

Sure, for *him* she coos like an angel.

He gives a nervous laugh. "Right. I'll remember one of these days."

"Am *I* allowed to call you Poppy?" I ask.

She turns back to me, her every feature sharpening. Fuck, it's terrifying how she can just turn it on and off like that. "That remains to be seen. Shall we?" She gestures with her free hand, daring me to walk ahead of her toward some private location. But I've seen this all before. This is the moment in the horror movie where the jock boyfriend named Jason goes down into the cellar alone. No way. I'm not dying like that.

"I'm good right here," I dare to say, crossing my tattooed arms. I lean my hip against the massage table. "There's nothing you could say to me that you can't say in front of my good friend Teddy."

Poor Teddy glances between us, looking like he'd rather follow Langers out the nearest exit. At Poppy's shoulder, Wednesday smirks.

Fuck.

I see the flash in Poppy's eyes as she steps forward, pressing right up in my space. "Alright then. Here it is." She plops her heavy bag down on the empty massage table and turns her back on Teddy, glaring fiercely up at me. It's so cute how she has to crane her neck. I'm at least a foot taller, even when she's in her heels. "Stow the smile, Lukas. This isn't a courtesy call. It's a formal reprimand."

Am I smiling? I think I must be. I clear my throat, wiping the smile from my face as I drop my arms to my sides. "Of course. Give me a second to warm up first, yeah?" I bounce on the balls of my feet and roll my shoulders. "Right. I'm ready. Lay into me. Just not the face, okay? Gotta look pretty for my roster pictures later."

"Everything's a joke to you, isn't it? You can't take anything seriously—not your career, not your reputation, certainly not the reputation of this team."

I stiffen, my good mood souring. "I'd argue that you don't know me—"

"Oh, I know you, Lukas Novikov. I've known cocky showboats like you my entire life. You think I haven't been following your career—on and off the ice? You think I didn't do extensive research on every player on this team, every member of the support staff? I have a dossier on you back in my office. You want to know what the top page says?"

"Enlighten me."

She squares her shoulders, ready to fire her sharpest arrow. "It's a personal note from your last PR manager that says, 'he's your problem now.'"

Shit. Not gonna lie, that fucking hurts. It shouldn't. The Bruins PR team were a bunch of no-fun Nancys. But hearing Poppy say the words feels like taking a cross check to the chest with no protective pads.

"Is that what you're going to be, Lukas? Are you determined to be my problem? Because I have to tell you here and now that if that's what you want, you will be sorely disappointed."

Something dark and heavy roils in my gut. "Before you tear me a new asshole, why don't you back up a step and start by telling me what great sin I committed?"

She raises a brow, obliging me by backing away. "Fine. Claribel?"

Wednesday steps in on her left, flashing me her phone screen. She swipes with her thumb, and I see pic after pic of me from the party last night. Gotta be honest, the details are a bit fuzzy. All I remember was being bored at home around nine o'clock and calling some of the guys out to that rooftop bar. None of the married guys came, of course. It was just me and some rookies who all quickly got shit-faced and left me with the bill.

All around, it was a pretty shitty night.

I laugh. "Seriously? That's what you're so mad about? It was just a private party—"

"That every single bunny in attendance photographed to kingdom come," Poppy cries with a dramatic wave of her hand. "And posted all over every social site and fan group. Now the city is calling you all a bunch of playboys and party animals."

"Wow." I drag a hand through my short hair. "I didn't take this team's management for a bunch of prudes. You know we're allowed to have a little pre-season fun, right? We're allowed to have private lives too—or is that banned in the contract I signed?"

"Private implies just that," she counters. "You think I care that you flounce around from bunny to bunny every night?"

"Hey, I don't flounce. I wouldn't even know how to flounce—"

"You think it bothers me one iota that you drink and party and otherwise waste away all your free time in the dark corners of seedy bars and clubs? I don't care, Lukas. It's your life. Do what you want with it. Just keep it off the front pages of the gossip rags and fan sites."

"What do you want me to do? I can't stop the bunnies from taking pictures—"

"Yes, you *can*," she insists. "This is simple PR. You want to throw a private rooftop party? Fine. But make it *private*. Have security at the stairs and confiscate phones. They can't post the pictures they don't take. As for your constant dalliances, all this 'take a number' like you're a one-man deli counter has to stop. There's this nifty little device called an NDA. Have all your lady friends sign them—preferably *before* the miniskirts come off. If your lawyer doesn't have a template ready, I can provide one my clients have used in the past."

I blink down at her, my anger fizzling. "Wait—what are you doing?"

She leans away. "What do you mean?"

"I thought this was a reprimand. Are you seriously advising me on how best to throw a private rooftop orgy right now?"

She does me the courtesy of blushing, but she brushes it off with another wave of her hand. "I just told you, Lukas. I don't care what you do. I only care *how* you do it. If you're determined to make it your job to party every moment you're not on the ice, then as your PR manager, it's *my* job to ensure you do it with as little damage to your reputation as possible."

I glare down at her. "Why do you care so much about my damn reputation?"

"Because you're a Ray now."

I bristle again. "Oh, and it's as simple as that?"

"Yes, it's as simple as that."

I glance from her to Wednesday to Teddy, who still looks like he'd rather be anywhere else.

Poppy sighs, leaning her hip against the massage table. "Look . . . I don't relish this part of my job, okay? I don't want to come off as the morality police. It's not about that. I'm sorry if, in my frustration, I sounded like a prude just now . . . or made you feel like you should be ashamed of your behavior."

"*If*?" I press with a raised brow. "Poppy, you may as well have sprayed me down with disinfectant. Are you sure you wanna stand this close to me? You never know, my proclivity for promiscuity might be catching. I'd hate for you to become afflicted. Don't they take your pearls away when you join the 'bad girls club?'"

A heavy moment of silence hangs in the air between us as she doesn't take my bait.

"Are you finished?" she asks.

Goddamn it, the pink of her lipstick matches her nails. Why does that turn me on? I don't want to be turned on by this harpy of a PR manager. I want to be *pissed*. When I signed up to play professional hockey, I didn't know I'd receive this constant policing of my behavior. *Don't be too slutty, Lukas. Don't chirp the competition, Lukas. Don't pull pranks, Lukas.* It's fucking exhausting. What does it matter what I do *off* the ice so long as I dominate *on* the ice?

But it's been like this on every team in every league. It's like they expect us to behave like goddamn choirboys. I'm tired of getting my nose swatted with a rolled-up newspaper for daring to live my life on my terms. I've done enough of living under the rules and restrictions of others. Lukas Novikov is his own fucking person. If I want to fuck and drink and party my way into an early grave, that shouldn't put my PR manager's pink frilly undies in a twist. I do my job, and I do it better than practically everyone in the League. So, PR Barbie can just get off my fucking back already.

I only *think* all this, of course. I don't actually say any of it out loud because I've been doing this dance for years. Instead, I grit my teeth and say, "Yeah, I'm done."

Reaching over, she pats my thigh. I stiffen, my gaze darting down to where her hand is touching me. She moves it away too soon. And then she's moving away entirely. "Let's start over," she says, flicking her ponytail off her shoulder. I bet when that hair is down, it nearly touches her perky butt—

Shit—don't think about her butt.

I grunt something that may be the word "okay" or may just be a sound like "harglumph."

She offers me a weak smile. "I don't want to be your enemy, Lukas. And I *really* don't want you to be my new problem. Between the balloon arches, and the fundraisers, and the whole 'newest team in the NHL' curse I'm trying to break, I have my hands more than full right now."

"I don't want that either," I hear myself admit.

She checks on her buzzing phone, sending the call to voicemail. "So, then let's find a new way forward. Right, here's what we'll do. Lukas, I want you to work with Claribel."

Okay, shoe fucking drop.

I push off the massage table. "What?"

"Yeah, what?" Wednesday echoes.

"Claribel possesses the skill set you lack," Poppy reasons, stepping between us to fetch her massive bag. "She'll coach you in the art of living your private life *in private*."

Wednesday looks like she'd rather be torn apart by wild dogs. "I already have a job, boss. And I don't do charity work."

"Yeah, and she sorta scares the shit out of me. No offense," I add.

"It's fine," Wednesday deadpans. "Actually, I take it as a compliment."

Now it's Poppy's turn to huff in frustration, juggling her bag and her still-buzzing phone. Our new PR director is clearly in high demand. "Heavens—fine. Lukas, I suppose I'll just have to deal with you myself."

Deal with me? Why am I perking up at this? I should definitely still be annoyed, right? Affronted even. And she'd clearly rather sky-dive into a volcano than waste more of her precious time talking to me.

That's probably why I'm excited . . .

God, I'm such an ass.

I smirk. "You're gonna be my new sexual sensei? You'll teach me the art of hush-hush hookups? Why, Ms. St. James, you surprise me. They really *are* gonna take away your pearls—"

"I already said to stow the sass, Lukas." She slings her heavy bag on her shoulder, nearly hitting me with it, her eyes locked on her phone. "Be in my office Monday morning at ten o'clock."

"I have a better idea," I tease, my mood brightening at the thought of wasting her time. "Let's make this an evening affair and say we meet at seven o'clock over at Neptune Beach. I'm thinking the fish camp. Candles on every table. Very intimate . . . and delicious. Are you a raw oyster kind of girl?"

She lowers her phone and glares at me. That little pointed nose of hers looks so cute when she's annoyed. "This is not a date, Lukas. This is business. Be in my office Monday morning, or I *will* assign you to Claribel and watch as she runs you over with the Zamboni."

I flash her my most asshole-ish smile. "It's a date."

3
POPPY

"Ugh, that man is infuriating! Everything is a joke to him. Nothing is serious. You'd think he didn't even care that this kind of behavior could get him traded . . . *again*." I march down the fourth-floor hallway back toward my office, heels clicking. "He's nothing but a big . . . a big butt!"

At my side, Claribel snorts. "A butt? Is that the best you can do?"

"Hey, don't laugh," I say, eyes on my phone as I shoot off another text to the ticket office manager. "If you grew up with my Nana, you'd be afraid to curse too."

"Were you looking at his butt, boss?"

"Of course not."

"There's no shame if you were," she teases. "Hockey butts are some of the best butts around. I think it's all the squats they do. And the lunging. They lunge a lot—have you noticed that?"

I release a weary sigh. "Claribel, *please* stop trying to make me picture the players' butts. These men are our work associates now. They are hard-working professionals. We are to treat them with respect, and not ogle their . . ."

"Juicy hams?"

I pause, frowning at her.

"I was just trying to fill in your blank," she says, raising a hand in surrender. "Gluteus maximus? Is that better? More technical . . . sounds sportier, right?"

I turn on my heel and keep walking. We have to duck around a painting crew doing touch ups to the fancy new wall mural, sidestepping their buckets and trays.

Mark Talbot spared no expense in designing this new facility, but it's taken a couple acts of god—and more than a few extra checks—to have it ready on time. I'm still without internet or a working phone in my office. And the overhead lights keep flickering . . . something to do with glitching backup generators. But so long as the ice stays frozen for the team to practice, the rest of us are expected to just suffer through these initial growing pains.

This is fine. I love running a public relations department from my cell phone . . . incurring roaming charges because of the terrible reception inside this bunker of a building . . . while I sit alone in the dark. It's all going to be just fine.

I can hear my old Division 1 track coach's voice inside my head. *Mind over matter, Poppy. Winners never quit.*

Paint cans rattle as the workmen shuffle out of our way.

"Boss, I can't make the ten o'clock," says Claribel, both thumbs feverishly tapping out a message on her phone. "Dale is having some kind of crisis down at warm-up. I need to get down there."

I pause again. "Wait—what's at ten o'clock?"

"The meeting with the new Barkley Fellow. You wanted me to get some content for the socials. 'New Doc on the Block' and all that—"

"Oh, sweet goodness," I gasp. "That was today? For some reason, I thought she was flying in tomorrow."

"Nope, her flight got in yesterday."

I flick through my calendar to make sure there's nothing else I'm missing. "I swear, the closer we get to the start of the season, time is losing all meaning for me."

As we stand there, Caleb Sanford comes wandering out of one of the office suites. He's one of the lead equipment managers for the team. He gives off a broody, "don't look at me" vibe, which I'm sure just lures all the ladies in faster. Too bad he backs up the looks with an even grouchier personality. He'd be social media gold if Claribel could just get him to cooperate for the cameras. But so far, the man has proved to be more slippery than an eel.

"Is the new Barkley Fellow coming in today?" I ask him.

"Rachel? Yeah, she's in there with Vic now," he replies.

"She's here?" I cry, my excitement bubbling. After going two rounds with Lukas Novikov downstairs, this is just what I need to put my day back on track.

"Pop, I gotta go," Claribel says at my shoulder.

"Well, come right back," I say with a distracted wave. "I want us to dive in with her announcement. All the socials. Static posts and video."

"Got it," she calls, slinking away between the painters.

I step past Caleb, letting myself into Vicki's office. She gives me a smile in welcome, but I hardly notice. Dropping my heavy bag to the floor, I only have eyes for the beauty sitting in the chair opposite Vicki's desk. I've seen pictures of her of course, mainly in trashy tabloids and airport fashion magazines. But she's even prettier in person—the dark hair, the pouty lips, the mocha chocolate eyes. She looks effortlessly cool, even in her scrubs.

"Are you our new Barkley Fellow?" I say in welcome.

She stands and holds out a hand. "Yes, hi. Doctor Rachel Price."

I wave her hand away as I step forward. "Oh, sweetie, here in the South, we hug." I wrap her in a quick embrace, noting the sweetly spiced scent of her perfume. "I'm Poppy St. James," I say, letting her go. "Head of PR for the Rays. And can I just say that I am *so* excited to have our team participate in the fellowship program this year? I mean, who doesn't love good press? And when I learned that you were going to be our new fellow? Well, I just about died!" I laugh, glancing from Rachel to Vicki.

"I mean, it's enough that you're gorgeous and *so* deeply talented," I add breathlessly. "But then I found out about your family. I mean, nothing goes with hockey quite like rock and roll, right?"

Her smile falters and she leans away.

Okay, maybe I *am* laying this on a little thick. I didn't just "find out" she was Rachel Price and connect the dots to her famous dad. She's Rachel Freaking Price! She's practically American royalty. She grew up in the spotlight—concerts and movie premieres, fashion weeks, awards ceremonies.

My family is rather established too. We're just part of the East Coast old money set. We live quieter lives, much less public. Think DC dynasty-makers, not LA icons. But Rachel and I are about the same age. We even share some mutual acquaintances. I followed all her escapades over the years—the brief modeling career in Paris, the wrecked yacht on the Amalfi Coast, the whirlwind engagement to that smarmy fashion photographer.

And those were just her teen years.

But now she's a doctor. Her wild child days are behind her, and she's got a bright, shiny career in sports medicine ahead. With that pretty face, and her famous father, she'll be public relations gold for us this year.

Time to lean all the way in. "Say, do you think your daddy might be interested in coming out for a game this season?"

Her smile flickers and disappears. "Umm . . . you know, I'm not really sure of his schedule," she replies noncommittally.

Vicki glances between us. "What are you two talking about?"

I turn to her. "Oh, hadn't you heard? Our talented new Barkley Fellow has some added star power. Her daddy is Hal Price from The Ferrymen!"

Poor, sweet Vicki looks completely clueless. She must have missed the gossip train. We've all been humming with the news for the last two days. "Is that a band?" she asks.

I feign a gasp, clutching my chest. "A band? Vicki, they're only one of the biggest rock bands of *all* time!" I turn back to Rachel, my hand lightly brushing her arm. "I swear, when I told my brother, he nearly fell out of his chair."

"That's great—"

"Say, does he ever play the national anthem?" I press. "You know, like Hendrix? Oh, wouldn't that be amazing, Vic? The Ferrymen in our arena! Can you imagine?"

"That would be really great," Vicki replies with a nod.

It would be more than great. We'd be able to ride the good press of that for weeks.

Rachel shifts uncomfortably. "Yeah, you know, I can ask."

Okay, fine. I've tortured her enough for this first meeting. I turn to the business at hand. Digging inside my bag, I look for the press events calendars, pausing to shoot Claribel a text.

POPPY: Get back up here. We need pics of Rachel.

She responds in seconds, my phone buzzing in my hand.

CLARIBEL: Can't. Rookie tripped over camera cords and almost chipped a tooth. Coaches chewed us out. Moving cords now.

I huff in frustration, tugging out the folder marked with Rachel's name. "Sorry." I nearly drop my phone as I right myself, folder in hand. "I've got, like, three press events this morning, and I'm trying to hunt down Claribel. I wanted her to get a few pics of Rachel in action—*oh*—do you mind if I call you Rachel?"

Yeah, I just said all that in one breath. Rachel looks at me wide-eyed, like I'm about to pop into a cloud of pink confetti. Honestly, I'm not entirely convinced I won't. I'm wound so dang tight right now. As soon as I get off work, I need to go for a run . . . or drink a whole bottle of bubbly champagne . . . or have a back-breaking orgasm.

All three.

Preferably in that order.

Behind her desk, Vicki laughs. "Poppy, honey, *breathe*."

I pause, taking a deep breath. She's right. I can't do this job if I'm wrapped up in a ball of jitters. Everything will work out. I'll have a desk and lights that stay on. I won't have to fight the players or lock them up in towers to make them behave.

It's all going to be fine.

As I think it, the lights overhead faintly flicker.

I let out another shaky breath.

This is all perfectly fine.

"Thanks, Vic, I needed that."

Rachel is still eyeing me like she's not sure what to make of me.

"I'm sorry," I say at her. "I'm just a big ole mess these days. I think it's all this stress leading up to the first game day."

"We're all a little on edge," Vicki assures me.

I step forward, handing Rachel her folder. "I promise I'm not always like this," I say with a laugh. "I can be normal. You'll see. Hopefully once the season starts, we'll all find our rhythm."

Rachel relaxes a little, taking the folder. "Of course." She glances down at the calendar, quickly scanning each row. "What's this?"

"That's a schedule for some upcoming public relations events," I explain. "With a new team, we can't leave it to just the players to help put the Rays on the map."

Her eyes go wide as she takes in all the colored dots. It's jam-packed, I know. But we're going with the "shock and awe" approach here. She glances up at me. "I'm attending all these events?"

I don't know why she looks so concerned. Her schedule is light. I had to leave room for her to do her actual fellowship hours too. "Yeah, don't you think it will be great? We've got the coaches hitting the town too, the players, even staff. Like I said, it's all hands on deck."

For a brief moment, she looks like she might hand her access pass back over to Vicki. Is Rachel Price about to disappoint me? Seeing as she's a doctor now, I was hoping that she'd come ready to work. The last thing I need is another diva on this team. I already get enough of that with the players.

I mentally bat away the image of Lukas Novikov that floats in front of me. Claribel's wrong if she thinks I was looking at his butt earlier. It's those devilish caramel-colored eyes that threaten to make me melt.

"I really hope you're a team player," I press, ignoring the repeated buzzing of my phone. "Because we mean to win this game."

"Which game?" she asks, tucking her calendar back inside the folder.

"*The* game," I reply. "The only one that matters."

She searches my face like she's confused.

I smile, hefting my portable office back onto my shoulder. "Sports at this level is never just about the sport, Rachel. It's about everything else. Our most important game this year won't be played on the ice. It's about winning the hearts and minds of the people of Jacksonville. We need to let the hockey world see that the Rays are here to play, and we're here to stay."

That's my job this year, to put the Rays on the map. That's why Mark hired me. And I can't fail him. If I do, he won't be renewing my contract next year. I have exactly one year to show this team and this city what I can do.

One year.

No distractions. No mistakes.

Let's do this, Poppy. Winners never quit.

4
COLTON

My heart races as I skate into the corner, chasing after the puck. There's only two minutes left in this exhibition game, and my team is winning—not that the points actually matter. We're all just out here showing the coaches what we can do. I beat Walsh to the puck, elbowing him into the boards. Then I slap the puck behind the net over to Novy and he bats it out of the corner. As one, we dig our toe blades into the ice, launching back toward the blue line.

Gripping my mouth guard between my teeth, I slide to a stop, surveying the action. Our forwards are clumped around the net, looking for one last score. *Good luck.* Mars Kinnunen is a two-time Stanley Cup-winning goalie. As I watch, he easily catches the puck in his glove, stopping the action. It gives me a moment to breathe and assess.

Hockey is a highly technical sport, which is why I love it so much. It's about input and output. My body is my machine, and each input and output helps it to work at peak efficiency—nutrition, exercise, hydration, sleep. Everything is flowing today, and I'm feeling great. Muscle memory is good. My legs are strong. Lungs and heart are working in rhythm. My recovery time between shifts feels well-regulated. This is definitely the best I've felt in years, and it's showing. I'll be shocked if the coaches don't start me.

The game ends, and Novy skates over to me, grinning around the blue mouth guard hanging out of his mouth. "If that doesn't secure us starting spots, I don't know what will."

"Compton and J-Lo are skating well too," I hedge, glancing to the bench where Jean-Luc Gerard, our most senior defenseman, is chatting with the equipment manager. Jake Compton skipped this game altogether, but he doesn't have to worry. He's flashy and strong and well worth the millions the Rays paid to trade him in.

"I bet they take second pair," says Novy. "No way the coaches don't pair us up. We're dynamite together. Just like old times, eh?"

I shrug. Nothing is sure in this sport. I'm playing, and that's all that matters. Whether I'm first pair or third, I know I'll be on the ice for another season, and I'm grateful. "Hey, great assist," I say. "That's gotta feel good, eh? Scoring on Kinnunen?"

"Nah, Mars was distracted," he replies. "Doesn't count if the tendy lets you have it."

"Well, you can guarantee the Canes won't let us have a damn thing next week."

I follow him off the ice and back to the dressing room. It's noisy and high energy as we all get changed. Metallica blasts through the speakers as I shrug out of my gear, handing off the pieces that need to go to the laundry to one of the waiting EMs.

"Hey Sanny, where's your DLP?" Novy calls from the stall next to me. The stall on the other side of him belongs to Compton. All his gear is stacked neatly inside, untouched.

Caleb Sanford, our assistant equipment manager, just shrugs, taking my practice jersey. "DLP" stands for "domestic life partner." It's what all the guys call Compton because of how close they are. "No idea," he says. "He was supposed to be back from the DMV already."

"Hey, we should all hang out this weekend," says Novy. "Let's grab dinner or something, celebrate the end of training camp."

"The team is going to Rip's tonight," I reply.

"Yeah, I'm saying *we* should still celebrate," Novy replies. "You know, just us?"

"Who's us?" Davidson asks from the other side of me. He's the backup goalie and he's weird as fuck. The guy always eats these crunchy, everything-flavored bagel crisps, giving him permanent bagel breath.

"Not you, Dave-O, that's for damn sure," Novy replies. "This is a D-man only invite."

"Sanny's not a D-man," Davidson says, unbuckling his pads.

"Yeah, but he's Compton's emotional support friend, so we gotta invite him to all the barbecues," Novy replies, making Sanford smirk.

"He shouldn't be on all the group chats either," Davidson mutters.

Novy digs in. "Aw, you jealous there, bud? Well, how 'bout this:

Prove you can grow a personality better than you can grow that lip lettuce on your face, and we'll add you to the blue line group chat. Deal?"

Davidson glares at him before shuffling off.

I give Novy a wary look and he shrugs. He likes to joke, and he loves to chirp. But sometimes he doesn't know where to find the line, and he skates right over it into full asshole zone.

Most of us are in the changing room attached to the showers when Coach Andrews pops his head in. "I wanna see all the defensemen in my office before you leave," he calls out. "Gerard, Compton, Novikov, Morrow, Hanner, Woodson—let's go!"

"Compton's not here," says J-Lo.

"Find him," Andrews shouts as he walks away.

The mood in the room quiets as we all glance at each other.

"Well, here we go, boys," Novy says. "Moment of truth." He claps Gerard on the naked shoulder. "J-Lo, no hard feelings if I take the left-side starting spot over you, eh?"

Gerard tugs on a shirt and punches Novy in the arm. Novy just laughs, leading the way out of the room. We run into Paulie and Woody in the hallway. Once we enter Andrews' office, I see Compton is already there, leaning against the desk. He's smiling from ear to ear.

"What the hell happened to you?" J-Lo asks.

Compton spreads his arms wide. "Just call me Buddy the Elf because I'm in love, and I don't care who knows it."

Gerard sinks into the chair by the door. "Lord, help us."

"Don't tell me you've already fallen for Hot Doc," Novy says, perching his ass on the arm of Gerard's chair.

"Oh no. What happened to the girl from Seattle?" Woody asks, snagging the other chair.

Compton mimes zipping his lips, his eyes flashing with barely contained glee.

"Bud, wake up," Novy says at Woody. "The Seattle girl was fictional."

Compton bristles. "She wasn't fictional, asshole."

"Yeah, I gotta admit, that always sounded a bit too good to be true," says Paulie. "It's good you're moving on, man." He pats Compton consolingly on the back.

"Wait—who's Hot Dog?" Gerard asks.

"Hot *Doc*," Novy corrects. Leaning in, he cups Gerard's ear with his hand and shouts. "Doc, as in doctor. Jeezus, J-Lo, get a hearing aid there, bud."

"The new Barkley Fellow," I add over the guys' laughter. Then they all start talking at once.

"She's a total babe—"

"Did you see her tattoos?"

"Hey, asshole, she's a doctor. She's *our* doctor now—"

"Is she married?"

"I thought she was a physical therapist—"

"She's a smoke show," Novy says, leaning around me to show Woody a picture of her he snapped on his phone earlier.

Woody's eyes go wide. "Whoa."

Paulie leans in too. "Okay, yeah . . . ten outta ten. Do we know, is she seeing anyone?"

Compton snatches Novy's phone. "Dude, stop taking pictures of our doctor."

"She wasn't our doc yet," he teases. "She was just 'woman at coffee cart.'"

"Well, now she is and you're gonna knock it off," Compton warns. "And I'm deleting these."

"Easy there, Jakey." Novy snatches back his phone. "She doesn't need you playing bodyguard. Besides, she's so far out of your league—"

"Let me know when you're all done playing *Gossip Girl*," Coach Andrews calls from behind his desk. "Then maybe I can tell you who's gonna start this season."

That settles us down real quick. We all look to Coach and wait.

He stands behind his desk, hands pressed flat to the surface. "Right, fellas, here's how it's gonna be. Hanner and Woodson, you're paired third."

They look to each other and give a curt nod. Paulie makes a great grinder, and Woody is a useful enforcer. Solid players, both. I certainly won't complain when it's time for a shift change.

"As for you four," Coach goes on, gesturing between the rest of us. "Look, we all know the Rays are still in a period of settling—"

"Oh shit." Novy's mask of humor flickers.

"I don't want any bruised egos here, guys," Coach says. "You'll all be getting plenty of ice time. And no one is getting punished here," he adds, looking directly at Novy. "We're just not locking down the first and second pairs quite yet—"

"But someone's gonna start next week," says Novy.

Coach nods. "For game one next week, we want to see Gerard and Morrow on the ice first. Compton and Novy, that makes you second pair."

Holy shit, I'm starting. In the first game the Jacksonville Rays play in the NHL, Colton Morrow, the Black kid from Canada who everyone bet against will be the starting right-side defender. Given what's it taken for me to reach this point, I can't help but smile . . . and send up a little prayer of thanks.

Gerard reaches around Novy to pat my arm. "First on the ice. We'll make a great team, eh?"

Compton crosses the room to his hand outstretched for me to shake. "Well done, Morrow. Between you, me, and Paulie, we'll have a strong right side this season. Let's leave it to these other assholes to pull their weight on the left."

"That's the team spirit I'm looking for," Coach says. "Now, make sure to check in with PT before you leave for the day. Good work this week, boys."

I shake Compton's hand, making room for Paulie and Woody to step out behind me. "You sure there's no hard feelings?"

"None at all," Compton replies. "Hey, let's celebrate. We'll let Cay pick the dive, and I'll take the check. Nov, you're coming too."

Novy just shrugs.

"Gotta count me out, boys," says Gerard. "The missus and I have plans this weekend. Last little getaway before the season starts."

"We never counted you in," Compton teases. Then he drops my hand. "Right, fellas. I'll have Cay send a message in the group chat with the time and place for dinner. Let's make it Sunday. For now, I gotta go see a girl about a number." He ducks away without a backward glance.

Coach Andrews follows him out, leaving his office door wide open.

I look to Novy. "Hey . . . you good?"

Novy stands, flashing me a smile that doesn't quite meet his eyes. "Always."

I don't even realize I'm reaching for him, but my hand brushes his shoulder. "Hey, man, you know you don't have to—"

"Cole, I said I'm good," he says, shrugging away from my touch.

His use of my name has me dropping my hand to my side. I don't think I've ever heard him say it, even when we played together.

"Come on, let's get outta here." He ducks around me. "Hey, wanna help me pull a prank on the new Hot Doc?"

I follow him into the hallway. "What kind of prank?"

He fishes his phone from his pocket. "How hard do you think it would be to rent an inflatable ball pit on short notice?"

I pause in my steps, looking at the back of his head. "Do you really wanna get fired that bad, Nov? You just got here."

He laughs, eyes still on his phone. "We can't let Compton have all the fun. Let's go see a girl about a number."

I laugh, shaking my head. *This* is the Lukas Novikov I remember from my days on the Thunderbirds: Prankster, chirper, competitive asshole, constantly wheeling multiple girls at once.

It's oddly comforting to know some people really do never change.

5
COLTON

My phone buzzes on the kitchen island and I know it's Novy texting me to hurry up. I'm running so late. My mom called for her Sunday chat as I was hauling in groceries, and I couldn't get her off the phone for almost an hour. Now I'm still wet from my shower, T-shirt tucked into the top of my shorts, letting my body air dry as I hunt around this tiny apartment for my wallet.

"Aha." I find it sitting beside the bowl of seashells on my coffee table, along with my lip balm. I slip both in my pocket and glance around.

Unlike most of the guys, I'm still living in the team's temporary housing. This apartment is just an efficiency unit—two small bedrooms, a laundry stack in the kitchen, a little balcony barely large enough for three people to stand on. But hey, I've lived in much worse dives over the years.

With all my family drama, I barely made it to town in time for the start of training camp. Most of my stuff is still in suitcases in the bedroom. I'm lucky I even found a clean T-shirt to wear tonight.

But I can't think about that now. I pass through the kitchen. Grabbing my buzzing phone, I answer the call as I slip on my slides. "Nov, what?"

Loud bar sounds echo around him. "Where are you? We said seven."

"Yeah, and it's only just now seven," I say, juggling the phone to my ear as I snag my keys.

"Well, we're all here waiting—"

"Jeez, I'm on the way. I'm in the car."

"No, you're not, asshole."

I pause. "How the hell do you know that?"

"Because I synced our contacts with the Find My Phone app."

I groan, pinching the bridge of my nose. "Why did you . . . you know what? Fine. Forget it. I haven't left the house yet. But I've got my keys in hand, and I'm leaving right now. Just order me a beer, and I'll be there in like ten minutes."

"Well, what kind of beer do you want? They have like thirty on tap."

I drop the phone to the counter, switching it to speaker so I can shrug into my T-shirt. "Nov, we've only been friends for, like, ten fucking years. You know what I like."

"A double IPA, right? Something pale and extra hoppy? Hey, they have Space Dust—"

"Sounds good. Hanging up now." I tap the red circle before he can respond.

Double-checking my pockets, I step out onto the fourth-floor apartment landing. I lock the door and spin around, headed for the stairs, but I don't take two steps before I nearly topple into someone.

There's a sharp squeal as a pair of small hands grab my forearms. "*Ahh*, Colton."

I latch onto Poppy St. James, keeping her from falling over. "Shit, sorry."

"Heavens, honey, you scared me," she says with a laugh, dropping her sporty headphones down around her neck. She takes a step back, neck craning as she smiles up at me. I'm six-foot-three and she's barely five feet tall. "Where are you going in such a hurry?"

I let myself look at her. She's usually wearing those sexy business outfits. Everything is always covered, always professional. Now she's standing in nothing but a pair of blue runner's micro shorts and a hot pink sports bra. I can see *every* curve of her fit body. Her chest and arms are slicked with sweat, her tanned skin is flushed, blood pumping. Her pretty blue eyes are bright with exercise. She searches my face, still smiling.

Shit, she asked me a question.

"I . . . out," I manage to say. "Dinner."

"Fun," she chimes. "You meeting some of the guys?"

I'm distracted by the little rivulet of sweat that is inching down her collarbone, threatening to disappear between her breasts.

Speak words, Cole.

"Yeah."

Perfect.

I groan inwardly. "I'm meeting Novy, Compton, and Sanford," I add. "Sanny found a dive he wants us to try. Just some bar food and music."

Her smile flickers as her eyes flash with annoyance. "Be careful with Novikov. Don't let him throw any parties tonight . . . or any punches. That man is trouble. You're in charge, okay?"

"Yeah, we'll watch him. No parties and no punching. Just a few beers and a good cheat meal."

She relaxes, propping her hands on her hips. "Well, it's so good to see you, Colton. I feel like we haven't gotten any chances to talk since you arrived in town. And here we are, neighbors sharing a wall. Small world, huh?"

I like the way she's calling me by my full first name. Not Cole, not Coley, and definitely not Morrow. And she pronounces the "T" too. I fucking love that. Each time, it parts her lips and I see a little flash of her teeth, like my name alone is enough to make her smile.

"Yeah," I say for the third time. "Small world."

Hockey *is* a small world. The smallest of worlds. There are only thirty-three teams in the League, so the chances were high I would know at least a few of the people who got transferred to the Rays. Poppy and I were both at the Washington Capitals when the new team was announced. Mark Talbot worked quickly to snap her up, naming her head of public relations even before he'd announced a single player.

The timing felt perfect for me too. I got to negotiate a new contract with excellent terms, giving myself some job security. But there's no denying the added incentive I felt to accept the trade. I came because I knew she'd be here. Hell, let's face it: I followed her like a lovesick fool. Poppy St. James—Queen of NHL Public Relations . . . and my poor, busted heart.

I'm not crazy; I know this is just a crush. She's beautiful and smart. But I don't know a real thing about her. She's always been a dream, a mirage I could hold at a distance and pretend to chase while I focused on my career.

But the universe clearly understands the concept of give and take. It took something precious from me, and now it's giving me this chance. I share an apartment wall with Poppy St. James. I get to learn new things about her. I get to see her outside of work. The door is open to more if I'm bold enough to step through it.

I search her face, ignoring my buzzing phone. "Hey, would you ever want to—"

"Oh, my goodness," she says on a breath. "Oh, Colton—here I am making small talk about sharing walls, and I haven't even offered you my condolences yet." She steps in, her hand brushing down my arm. Her sun-kissed skin still looks pale against my forearm. "Honey, I'm so sorry. That should've been the first thing out of my mouth."

I go still. I haven't been able to escape this reality for months. My dad died. It happens. People get sick, then they get sicker, and then they die. I was ready for it, and so was he. We said our goodbyes. We buried him in the ground the day after I signed my new contract.

The Rays have been great, offering me extensions and delaying my move so I could be there for my family. That's the reason all the other guys have flashy beach houses and bachelor pads and I'm stuck here in temporary housing. I couldn't be bothered to plan for the future when I was so focused on the present, on being there for my mom and sisters.

Poppy's head tilts, her smile softer now. I hate it. "How are you doing, honey?"

"I'm fine."

Sensing my stiffness, she drops her hand away. "I lost my Nana two years ago. She was as close to me as a parent could be. I understand how hard it is. If you ever need anything, I'm just a wall away."

"Thanks." In my hand, my phone buzzes. It's Compton calling this time. They must really be getting restless.

She glances down at my phone, then back up at me. "Well, I don't wanna keep you from your dinner. And if I stay here any longer, I'll start to smell like a stinky possum," she adds with a laugh. She gives me a little wave, then she's turning away, our moment over.

I feel frozen. So long as she's out here sharing air with me, I don't want to move. I take in the profile of her lithe body as she inserts her key into her front door lock. I watch as she turns it. I hear the click.

Moments. That's all I get with Poppy St. James. These little moments that are nothing. But to me, they're everything.

Her door squeaks open. "Hey, do you like granola?"

I blink, pulling my eyes away from the narrow curve of her hip. "Hmm? Granola?"

"Yeah, I just made a big batch before my run. It's cooling in here on the stove," she adds, pointing inside her unit. "If you want, I'll give you some. You know, as a 'welcome to the neighborhood' gift."

"Uhh..."

"It's delicious," she goes on. "It's my Nana's recipe. She made it for me all the time during my competitive running days. It really packs a protein punch. It's got some maple syrup, slivered almonds, pistachios, pepitas, dried cherries, cranberries..."

My stomach grumbles loud enough for us to both hear it and we laugh.

"Yeah, it sounds fucking amazing," I say. "I like granola, Poppy."

Fuck, I just said her name. I don't know if I've ever actually said it out loud. It's so pretty. It fits her so well.

Her smile widens and her face brightens like she's got particles of light trapped beneath her sun-kissed skin. She's fucking breathtaking. "Great. Well, I'm a bit of a night owl, so just give my door a knock when you get back and I'll have it ready for you. Have a good dinner, Colton."

With a last wave, she disappears inside her unit, and I'm left standing here, staring at her closed door. My phone buzzes in my hand again. This time it's Sanford, and I know I'm in trouble. Twenty bucks says the guys threaten to take me off the group chat and replace me with Davidson as soon as I sit down.

In this moment, I really don't care. I just learned four new things about Poppy St. James:

Close to (and still grieving) her dead grandmother.

Former competitive (now occasional) runner.

Likes to bake.

Night owl.

That's four things I didn't know before. Four things that make her real. A mirage can't make homemade granola. A mirage doesn't fill my senses with the sweet smell of her athletic sweat. A mirage can't touch my arm, offering me the condoling caress of a friend.

Poppy is real, and she's here.

I was a chickenshit in DC, too focused on chasing my own career to bother with actually chasing *her*. But Dad's dying put so much of my life into sharp perspective. I don't want to look back on my death-bed and realize I only ever had my career to keep me warm. I want a partner, a friend, a lover. God willing, I'll have a family too. I want something that lasts when I'm gone. I want something *real*.

I want Poppy St. James.

This is my second chance. I've been chasing the idea of her in my dreams for so long. Now it's time to man up and chase the real thing.

6
LUKAS

"Novikov?"

My feet go still on my exercise bike. I watch as Doctor Price strolls out of her exam room, tablet in hand. Compton steps out after her, bouncing on his feet like he's walking on a damn cloud. The fool must really have it bad for her.

Hot Doc glances around the gym again. "Lukas Novikov? You're up next!"

"Dude, that's you," Paulie says from the bike next to me.

"Okay," I say under my breath. "Go time, Nov." I've got a multi-part prank planned for today, and it all hinges on this moment. I slip off my bike and wave my hand to get her attention. Pulling a Poppy, I call out with a, "Yoo-hoo! Doc, over here!"

Paulie and Woody snort, miming my wave as I saunter over to where Doc Price waits.

"Hey, Novikov." She tucks her tablet under her arm and offers me her hand. "I'm Rachel Price. Nice to meet you."

I shake her hand, winking over at Compton just because I can. The asshole glowers at me, so I step in a little closer. "Nice to meet you too, Doc. And you can call me Novy. Everyone does."

She gestures for me to go into the exam room first. My gaze darts around as I search for my prize. Right there, resting on the counter next to her coffee cup, is a set of keys.

Bingo.

She keeps the door open as she follows me in. "Okay, so this is just a routine hip and knee checkup. We'll do some range of motion exercises, and I'll test your flexibility, making note of any pain or worry spots you may have."

"Righto."

"Doctor Tyler said you tripped and fell off a treadmill last week. Banged up your knee pretty good, right? Do you mind showing me which knee?"

God, that was fucking embarrassing. Hit both elbows too. And my hip. I manage to huff a laugh and wave her off. "Oh, that was nothing. I feel fine."

"Mhmm. Hop up on the table for me, Novy."

I do as she asks, and she sets the tablet down next to me. Without preamble, she places both hands on my left knee and presses in lightly with her thumbs on either side of my kneecap.

"Ow—fuck," I all but squeal, jerking away from her.

"But you're fine, right?" she says, clearly unimpressed.

I mutter a curse, rubbing the sore spot.

"I think it's likely you may still have some intramuscular bruising from the fall. Rate your pain for me on a scale of one to five."

"Uhh . . . yeah, like a one," I say with a shrug.

She looks up at me. "Do you want me to squeeze the knee again?"

I hold her gaze. "It's a two."

She nods. "The most I want you doing today is a leisurely walk on the treadmill. Otherwise, you're on the RICE regime for the rest of the week. Rest, ice—"

"Compression and elevation," I finish for her. "Yeah, I know the deal."

"Good. Because we want you in top shape for the season starter. No weights, no high impact. Doc Tyler did your initial checkup after the fall," she goes on, picking up her tablet. "And he says here that he's confident there'll be no lasting damage so long as you rest, ice, compress—"

"And elevate. Yeah, I got it."

She surveys me for a second before nodding. "Good. And hey, Novy?"

"Yeah, Doc?"

She holds my gaze. Fuck, she looks as serious as Poppy. "Within the four walls of this practice center, you can call me Doc, Rachel, Doc Price, or Doctor Rachel Price. What you will *not* call me is Hot Doc. Agreed?"

I nod. "You got it, Doc."

"Good. You will also not lie about pain or minimize your injuries. I'm on your side, Novy. Your pain is my pain. Tell me the truth. That's how we keep you on the ice longer. Agreed?"

Searching her face, I give her my truth. "My hip hurts from the fall. It's still a little bruised . . . worse than the knee. I've been popping ibuprofen like candy."

She smiles. "Thank you, Novy. That's very helpful. Now, lie back on the table, and let's do these range of motion exercises. I promise to be gentle as a lamb. And I'll check that hip while we're at it."

Ten minutes later, she's tapping my shoulder. "Okay, you're all good to go. Stick to the RICE regime, like I said. If anyone from strength training gives you any problems this week, direct them to me."

"You got it," I say, sitting up and swinging my legs off the table. "Hey—do you mind if I wash my hands in here before I duck out?"

She's got her eyes back on her tablet. "Be my guest."

Cool as a cucumber, I saunter over to the sink and make a show of turning the water on and noisily pressing the soap dispenser. Then I reach out and gently pluck her keys off the counter. Quick as I can, I tuck them in my pocket. "Ooookay," I call, jerking a few paper towels out of the holder. "Thanks for everything, Doc."

"Yeah, just make sure you double-knot your shoelaces from here on out, okay?"

I spin around and give her a lame-o salute. "Right you are, Doc. I'll just see myself out, eh?"

She follows me to the door and I duck out as she calls for J-Lo. He's ready and waiting, flashing her that endearing, toothless smile. As soon as she steps into the exam room with him, I snap my fingers at two of the young farm team guys. "Patty, Flash Gordon, on me."

"Yeah, boss?" says Flash.

"I need your help with something top secret. Can you do it?"

Their eyes brighten. God, rookies can be so easy. These two can't be a day over nineteen.

"Yeah, anything you need," says Patty.

On principle, I hand the keys to Flash Gordon, starting with my own. "Okay, here's the deal," I say, lowering my voice. "I need you to go down to the parking garage and find my truck. In the back, you'll find a ball pit's worth of colored balls tied up in black garbage bags. You both with me so far?"

Flash nods, taking the keys. "Truck, bags, balls. Got it."

Fuck, these guys get to vote in this country.

"Okay, I want you to take all those balls and move them into *this* truck." I hand him the second set of keys. "Can you do it?"

Patty the Brainless nods while Flash glances down at the second set of keys held flat in his palm. "Whose truck is this, Nov?"

I puff out my chest a little. "It's Mr. Novikov to you. And that information is above your pay grade. Can you do it? Yes or no. Don't make me find more willing rookies."

"We got it," says Patty, snatching the keys out of Flash's hand.

"Good boys." I slap both their shoulders. "You have fifteen minutes. Go."

The two of them dart away just as Morrow saunters up behind me, munching on some granola. His walnut-brown eyes lock on me. "Do I dare ask what you're doing?"

"Plausible deniability would say no, but I'd stick around this afternoon for the show."

He raises a dark brow. "The show?"

"Yeah, around four o'clock, I'm thinking. We're meeting down in the parking garage. Spread the word." I try to reach my hand into his granola bag, but he bats it away, the greedy fuck.

"And until then? What are you gonna do?"

I glance around the gym, looking for my other mark. "Well, right now, I'm gonna go nurture my tender little sprout of a prank idea and just hope it grows fruit."

He pauses, mid-chew. "What the fuck are you talking about?"

I just laugh and step past him. I slip my shirt off, stepping up onto the open treadmill next to where Langers is lifting weights. This Judas, he thought it was soooo funny to leave me alone with Poppy. Let's see how he likes it when the tables are turned.

"Hey," he pants, dropping his weight bar down with a clank.

"Hey," I say, making a show of tugging my shirt back on now that he's looking. "Just finished my physical. You do yours yet?"

"Nah. I'm up in, like, ten. Just wanted to finish this set before she calls me in."

"Well, don't get too sweaty," I warn. "You'll get the table all sticky when you take your clothes off."

"Gotta finish my set," he grunts, lifting the bar up again.

Doc Price calls out. "Kinnunen, you're up next!"

I feel giddy as I press my treadmill's "on" button.

After a minute or two, Doc Price walks up behind me. "Hey, have you seen Kinnunen this morning?"

I glance around and shrug. The Bear is pretty damn hard to miss. He has the look and build of a Finnish Thor. "Maybe his practice ran long," I say. "I'd just skip him, Doc. He'll show up eventually."

She sighs, checking her tablet. "Langley, you're up!"

The weight bar clangs as Langers drops it and sits up. "Great," he calls in that cheery tone. "Yeah, Doc. I'll be right there!"

I watch as they walk away, parting for a moment as he heads into the exam room, and she goes into the little broom cupboard of an office. I slam the red button on my treadmill, stopping it. Compton walks up, leaning in with both arms on my machine. "You mind telling me what the fuck you're doing?"

I laugh. "Just wait."

"Nov—"

"Watch and wait," I say, hopping off my machine. I grab him by the shoulders and turn him to face Doc's office.

Morrow steps up on Compton's other side. "Novy, what the hell did you do?"

"I told Langers it was a full physical."

They both glance sharply at me and Morrow sighs. "Nov—"

"Hey, I owed him one. He left me to the wolves last week. I got cornered by Poppy, and now I'm in private remedial PR lessons. Oh!" Doc Price emerges from her office and steps into the exam room. I sling an arm around Compton, holding my breath. "Here we go . . ."

The three of us stand still, waiting.

"Ohmygod," we hear Doc shriek from inside the room. "What the hell are you doing?"

"What's happening?" says J-Lo, standing with Karlsson and Teddy.

"I convinced Langers to get naked for his knee check," I say. "Just wait . . ."

"Oh, fuck those guys," we hear Langers shout from inside the room. "I'm gonna kill Novy!"

In moments, Doc Price steps out, clutching her tablet, and we all burst into laughter. Her eyes find me at once, glaring from me to Compton.

"See somethin' you like in there, Doc?" I call.

Her eyes flash with mirth, even as she tries to keep on her mask of annoyance. "Who are you hazing here? Him or me?"

Langley comes barreling out of the room, tugging his shirt down. "Fuck you, Novy," he shouts. "You guys are all jerks!" With pink blooming in his cheeks, he ducks back into the exam room.

"Please tell me he stripped totally naked," I say, tears in my eyes.

"No, he didn't," Doc replies. "And just for future reference—the first guy who gets naked in my exam room is gonna get benched for a week. Bad idea to piss off the person who signs your medical releases."

"What's wrong, Doc?" I call. "Can't appreciate the male form?"

Morrow shoots me a warning look.

"Oh, I appreciate the hell out of a fine male form," she teases right back. "I just like to have finished my damn coffee first."

Compton joins in. "So, you *would* want to see us naked . . . just later in the day, after you've finished your coffee."

"Yeah, it's all a matter of timing," I add with a nod.

"Noted, Doc," he says with a grin.

"We could try again after lunch," calls Walsh.

From somewhere over by the exercise bikes, a few of the guys start singing the chorus of "Afternoon Delight" and we all crack up again.

"You're all twelve," says Doc, turning back to her exam room.

"And you love our dumb asses!" I shout, the whole gym howling as she closes her door.

"You are so gonna get traded," Morrow mutters. "Or fired for harassment."

"Nah, Doc Price is cool. Way cooler than Avery the Ass. And I promise all my other pranks will involve everyone's clothes staying on."

Both Morrow and Compton turn.

"Other pranks?" says Morrow.

At that moment, my phone buzzes in my pocket. I pull it out and read a message from Flash.

FLASH GORDON: Huston, we have a problem!!!!

The asshole spelled "Houston" wrong. And there's a video. I tap the play button, groaning as I watch Patty stumble around the parking garage, trying to catch all the colorful plastic balls tumbling from one of the broken trash bags. "Motherfuck—" I take a deep breath. "Must I always do everything myself?"

"What's wrong?" asks Morrow.

"What's wrong is we need another flood," I say, shoving my phone in my pocket. "Only this one needs to target incompetent rookies." Turning on my heel, I march away.

"Hey—you better not be pranking Poppy," he calls after me. "Novy, I'm serious. Leave her alone!"

I just wave over my shoulder. "Sorry, I've gotta go bust some balls."

Before Doc notices her keys are missing.

7

POPPY

Florence & The Machine pulses through the sound system of my little sports car as I pull into the practice center parking garage. I bop my head to the beat, flipping my sunglasses up onto my head. For once, I had a nice, relaxing morning. I get better internet back at my apartment, so I took a series of important fundraising calls from my lanai. I also treated myself to a proper homemade breakfast: avocado toast, a poached egg, and two cups of caramel iced coffee. I even squeezed in ten minutes of breathing meditation.

My afternoon, however, is stacked with in-person meetings downtown. I wouldn't have even come to the office at all today, except I told Lukas Novikov to meet me here at ten o'clock. That flashy showboat somehow has the ability to ruin my day without even trying.

I blink in the sudden darkness of the garage, slowing my car to a crawl as I look for a parking spot. With a gasp, I pump the breaks, both hands tight on the wheel. "What the . . . ?"

Speak the devil's name, and he shall appear. Lukas Novikov and two of the rookies are standing in the middle of the garage. They spin around, eyes wide. They look like I've just caught them in the act of moving a dead body.

I gasp again. "Oh my . . ."

Clutched between them is something large and lumpy, wrapped in a black trash bag.

"Oh, sweet heavens, I do *not* get paid enough for this," I hiss, jerking my car into park. I fling open my door and pop out the side. "Honeys, *please* tell me that is not a human body! Or an animal body!"

Lukas lets out a laugh that echoes in the empty concrete space.

"Seriously, Poppy? Do you really think we're down here moving bodies?"

"Well, I don't know," I cry. "Why do y'all look so suspicious then?"

"Maybe because you rounded the corner and flashed your lights at us," he replies.

I take a breath. "Okay that's good because I cannot be a witness to a murder this morning. My goodness, can you even imagine?"

"Uhh, boss . . . what do we do now?" the tall one mutters.

Lukas stands upright, still holding his side of the lumpy trash bag. "We greet the nice lady, Patrick, and we let her go on her way."

I glance around the garage. "If you're not moving bodies . . . then what *are* you doing?"

"Just hauling some gear," Lukas replies. "You know—sticks and pads, some smelly jocks. Nothing to interest you."

"Mhmm." I cross my arms, still peering around.

"I think there's some open parking spots down that row," says the raven-haired cutie, pointing to the sunlit corner of the garage.

I level my gaze at him. This is the one. He'll break for me so nicely. Lukas is a steel vault, and the tall blond is a brick wall. But Raven Boy? He'll crack like an egg.

I leave my car in park, the headlights shining on their malfeasance, and saunter forward. My stiletto heels click softly on the concrete. I give my hips a little sway in my camel pencil skirt, feeling the flip of the fabric against my calves. I shift my long hair off my shoulder with a practiced flick of my wrist and stand before him. "What's your name, honey?"

"Don't tell her anything," Lukas mutters.

Raven glances between us, lips slightly parted. "Uhh . . . Flash. Flash Gordon . . . ma'am."

I smile, batting my lashes. "What's your *real* name, sweets?"

During my time in the professional hockey world, I've found the players' constant use of nicknames to be clever shields. Sure, it creates a sense of camaraderie, but it also helps these men hide who they really are. Which is why I'm out here like a perky, blonde Rumpelstiltskin, collecting names, growing in my power. I widen my smile, encouraging him to spill.

He shifts his weight, distracted by the death glare Lukas is no doubt giving him over my shoulder. "It's uhh . . . Sam, ma'am. Samuel Gordon. It's why they all call me Flash. You know, 'cause it's for Flash Gordon, like the superhero."

"Fuck," Lukas mutters.

Cracked, just like a sweet little egg.

"Samuel." I hum. "Now, what are you doing, Samuel?"

"We're moving the balls from that truck into this truck," he replies.

"Moving the—" I glance around to where he points. "What balls?"

"The ball pit balls," says Big Blondie. I didn't even need to give him the eyes and he's cracked by association.

I slowly turn to face Lukas. "Do you want to fill in the blanks, here? Or should we all just keep playing rookie mad libs?"

He sighs. "We're pranking Doc Price by putting ball pit balls in her car."

I raise a brow at him. "We?"

"Me," he admits. "I'm pranking her. These two proved to be completely useless."

"Hey, we moved like half the balls without you," Samuel retorts.

"Yeah, we had it under control," Big Blondie adds.

Lukas turns on them, his tattooed arm flexing as he still holds the trash bag. "Then why did I get a text from Flash saying 'Houston, we have a problem' and a video of *your* dumb ass chasing the balls all over the damn parking garage?" He rounds on Samuel. "Oh, and Houston has two 'o's by the way, Flash."

The three of them bicker about the spelling of Houston until I step forward and place a hand on Lukas's shoulder. "Why don't we leave these two to finish this good work alone? Lukas, you and I can go ahead and get an early start on our meeting. Sound good? Good."

I walk over to my car and pluck out my purse and keys. Walking back over to the ball boys, I hold out my keys to Samuel. "Park my car and finish moving your balls. Then I expect to have my keys *and* Rachel's keys returned to their owners. Do you understand me?"

"Yes, ma'am."

Next to me, Lukas narrows his eyes. "Wait, you're gonna let us finish the prank?"

"Yes, I am."

"Why?"

I glance over at Rachel's rental truck. I can see the mess of red, green, and yellow balls already filling her backseat. "Because this prank is utterly benign. And if I don't let you do it, you'll just do something else once my back is turned again, and it will likely be even worse . . . like putting a dead fish in her air vent . . . or gluing her shoes to the floor."

He smirks, and I know I've just given him two fresh ideas for future pranks.

"Move your balls, and then bring me my keys," I say at the rookies. "Lukas, let's go. I'm moving up our meeting to now."

I drop my keys into Samuel's hand and turn on my heel, not waiting and not looking back. I know Lukas is following me. I know because I can hear him cursing at me under his breath.

8
LUKAS

I follow Poppy into her fourth-floor executive office and frown as I glance around. It's a drab place, with white walls, discount furniture, an L-shaped desk, and a pair of gray metal filing cabinets. "You don't even have a window in here," I say, sinking onto the only rickety chair in front of her desk.

She sits behind the desk. "Only the outer offices have windows."

Is that a drip I hear? My frown deepens. "You should spring for an office with windows. I mean, this is just sad." As I say the words, the overhead fluorescent lights flicker ominously.

Poppy's shoulders stiffen. "It's fine."

"Yeah, maybe add a pop of color or something."

"Sure, a pop of color should do the trick." She turns to her desktop computer, clicking the keys with her manicured nails. In seconds, the screen lights up. A few more clicks of her mouse, and she's muttering something that sounds like, "At this point, I'd settle for some internet service."

I scoot the chair forward on squeaky wheels. "Wait—you don't even have internet in here?"

"It's fine," she says again. "They're working on it. Steve down in IT assures me of that every day."

I glance at the office phone perched on the corner of her desk. No lights glow from the screen. "And the phones?"

"I'm sorry. Are *you* from IT?" she snaps. "You wanna fix my flickering lights and connect my internet and hook my phone up to an actual jack? Be my guest, Lukas. I won't stop you."

I lean away, eyes wide.

She takes in the look on my face and deflates. "Oh goodness, I'm so sorry." Her hand flutters over her chest. "That was uncalled for. I'm just . . ." She takes a deep breath. "You know, I'm just *really* tired of running my department from a cell phone."

I nod, settling back in the uncomfortable chair. "You should talk to Talbot."

She pulls out a manilla folder, setting it on the desk between us. "I'm not going to bother the team owner about a few flickering light bulbs. Maintenance is on it. And IT is dealing with the phones. It's all just growing pains. It'll be dealt with in a timely manner."

Is she trying to convince me or herself?

"No, I mean you should talk to him about moving you out of this coffin," I say.

She straightens in her chair, her blue eyes wide as she looks at me. "What coffin?"

"Poppy, you're the director of public relations for a major international sports team. You can't be sitting in the dark with no internet and no phones with this janky-ass furniture. I mean, *look* at me. I'm, like, two hundred and twenty pounds, and I think I'm about to break this shitty chair."

"Well then stand up," she cries. "God, I only have the one in here, Lukas. I can't have you snapping its little matchstick legs the first time you sit down."

I roll my eyes. Of course she's choosing to miss my point. "I'm not gonna stand for this meeting."

She huffs, crossing her arms. "Well, then just sit very carefully."

I jerk the chair forward with another squeak. "You know, this is starting to feel a bit like a hostile work environment."

Her eyes go wide again. "Lukas, what—"

"Yeah, since I came in here, I've felt nothing but devalued and demeaned by you. I'm too unqualified to fix your internet, too heavy to sit in your chair."

She knows I'm joking now, and her shoulders relax. "You *are* unqualified to fix my internet."

"And we both know the only reason I'm here is because you're taking preemptive disciplinary action against me."

"That is not what this is about!" Oh, she's rising to my baiting beautifully. The pink is glowing in her cheeks. I like her like this, angry and indignant.

"Maybe if I knew there was just *one* thing you actually liked about me," I say with a dramatic wave of my hand. "One thing that made me a human worth knowing in your eyes. I think that would be enough."

She searches my face. "Is that really how you feel?"

"Hard not to," I reply, crossing my arms over my barrel chest. It's a good look for me. I've got great arms—and a great chest. I know this angle makes my biceps pop. And girls always swoon for my colorful ink. It stretches up both arms from my wrists, under my T-shirt, and over my shoulders.

"Fine. You want to know one thing I like about you?"

"One thing is certainly a good start," I say with a solemn nod.

She purses those pretty pink lips, her eyes searching my face.

As her silence stretches, I huff, leaning back in the squeaky chair. "Seriously? It's really taking you *this* long to name one single thing you like about me? Should I just tunnel my way through this wall over to an office with a window and leap out?"

"You've got nice eyes," she says at last.

Oh, shit. This is actually working? I lean forward and bat my lashes. "What, these eyes right here?"

She hides her smile.

"What do you like about them?"

"I like the color," she replies.

"What color are they?"

She raises a brow. "You don't know your own eye color?"

"I'll admit, I don't look at them much," I say with a shrug.

"Interesting. With the way you were crossing your arms trying to get me to notice your rippling pectorals a moment ago, I would've thought your full-body mirror was your most prized possession. My only question would be does it stand along the wall, or is it mounted to the ceiling over your bed?"

"Trick question," I tease. "I have *two* mirrors."

"Of course you do."

"But don't stop now. You were saying you like the color of my eyes. What color are they, Poppy?"

She searches my face again, her gaze softening a little. "They remind me of salted caramel."

"Mmm, sweet and delicious . . . and soft," I tease. "I'd say I'm more of a hard and spicy rock candy, wouldn't you?"

"During the holidays, my Nana used to make salted caramel sauce by the gallon," she goes on. "She made so much, we couldn't give it away fast enough. And the kitchen always smelled like caramel for weeks after."

Shit, that was a deeply personal answer. I wasn't expecting it. Time to deflect. "I remind you of your grandma?"

"Only your eyes," she clarifies. "And it's a compliment, Lukas. It's the only one you're getting today. Take it, and let's change the subject."

I cross my arms again and puff out my chest, just because I can. "Sure. Why don't you tell me something else you like about me?"

"Still fishing for compliments? I never would have pegged you as insecure."

"Try curious."

She sighs. "You know you're attractive, Lukas. You're not as beautiful as Ryan, obviously. But then, what man can be?"

My chair squeaks as I roll forward again. "Wait. Who the hell is Ryan?"

"Langley. You know, Ryan Langley? Star forward of the Rays?" The minx practically purrs his name.

Why do I suddenly feel the urge to track down Langers and punch him in the head? "Seriously? That pretty boy? He's all hair. Please tell me that's not your type, I beg of you."

"I never said he was my type," she replies. "I'm simply saying he sets a standard for male beauty that even Adonis himself would fail to meet."

Okay, this game is officially over. "Keep talking about Langley like that, and I may just turn green."

Reaching up, she tucks a few loose strands of her blonde hair behind her ear. "No need for any jealous fits. You're handsome too, and you know it. You've just got that 'jock pretty' look."

I raise a brow. "Jock pretty?"

"Yeah, you know, the kind of pretty where you can tell all the conventional attributes of a handsome man are present—strong jaw, proud eyes, imposing profile—but you've also been knocked one too many times in the head, so it's all starting to go a bit hazy."

I bust out a laugh, surprising myself with the honesty of the sound. "Ain't that the truth. This poor face has taken a real beating over the years. Broke my nose twice." I point to the noticeable lump in my bridge. "And look." I flash her a crocodile smile. "Four of these teeth aren't real. Bet you can't guess which ones."

She leans away with a laugh of her own, reaching for her phone. "I'm good, thanks."

I settle back in my chair, feeling more relaxed. "Yeah, I've got a great dentist. You have to if you wanna play hockey at this level."

She slides over the manila folder one-handed, still balancing her phone in the other. "Is this how you bag all those bunnies? Flashing them your fake teeth?"

So, we're getting down to business then? I cross my arms again. "You want me to show you how I bag puck bunnies? I thought *you* were the teacher in these sessions. Don't rip the fantasy away now."

She lowers her phone, meeting my gaze. "The fantasy?"

"Yeah, you know . . . you on that side of the desk in your pencil skirt looking all 'bad teacher' as you instruct me on how to keep my hookups secret? You gotta admit, Pops, it's hot."

She sets her phone down and flashes me a seductive smile. "Wanna play a game? A little teacher-student role-play?"

Well, color me the fuck intrigued. I mirror her body position. "I fucking love games."

"I thought you would," she coos. "Okay, here it is. You ready?"

I grin. "Always."

Her gaze hardens with her tone. "Be serious for three minutes together, and I'll buy you a pretzel from the lobby cart."

I sigh, my sex drive coasting back to neutral as I stretch back in this janky chair. "Sorry, Pop. No can do."

"You can't stay focused and professional for three minutes?"

"A typical shift in hockey is only like sixty seconds long. That's all the serious I can give."

"Impressive."

I shrug. "What can I say? I'm a well-programmed machine."

"Shall I set a timer on my phone? We can take stretching and snack breaks in between."

"Sounds like a plan."

She opens the manila folder on the desk and pulls out a thin stack of stapled documents.

I pick it up and instantly note the legalese. "What's this?"

"It's a boilerplate nondisclosure agreement. I've used it with clients in the past who found themselves in your situation."

"My situation?"

"Show it to your lawyer and your agent, let them approve the language and make any necessary tweaks. Then I want you to have all your intimate partners sign it, preferably *before* the deed is done. Send a copy to your lawyer and keep a copy for your own records. If you feel comfortable doing so, you can even send a copy to me."

My heart stops. "You want me to send you signed gag orders from all the women I fuck?"

"I prefer the language of 'NDA' to 'gag order,' but yes. As head of public relations, it's my job to protect not only the image of the team and the overall brand, but the individual players as well. I can assure you that my staff and I will operate with the utmost discretion. But we can only be as well-armed as you make us. Every signature, Lukas. Just think of it as a legal condom. I assume you know how condoms work?"

I blink at her before dropping my gaze back to the stack of papers in my hand. "So, what do you expect me to do here? I just make copies of this and stuff them into my pockets before I head out to the club? I suppose I can just hand them out like business cards. That'll really make sure I never have sex again."

"Don't be ridiculous. You have a phone, right?"

I eye her across the desk. Is this the flirting again or still business? "Are you asking for my number, Poppy?"

"I already have your number."

I grin. "Eager, are we?"

"It's in your personnel file. Along with your new roster photo . . . which looks like a mugshot, by the way. Is it really so difficult for you men to smile?" She pulls it up on her phone, flashing me the new picture of my broody face.

"Impossible," I tease. "I can't let the other teams know I'm actually a nice guy. Besides, I like to save all my smiles for you."

She goes still, searching my face.

Fuck. Too far. Dial it back, Nov.

She sets her phone down. "Does all this bravado actually work on women?"

Seriously, are we back to the harmless flirting? I can't tell. "Usually, yes. But I think my software isn't compatible with your current operating system. That's a little IT talk," I tease. "See, you underestimated me before about the phones and internet."

There it is, a real smile.

Fuck, she's pretty when she smiles.

She clears her throat and it's gone. "As to your question regarding logistics, that's just a paper copy for your records. I've already sent you the PDF as well. Have all your intimate partners sign electronically. You can send them in batches if that's easier."

"Perhaps we can establish a weekly deadline," I offer. "Like homework for teacher. My signed sex contracts are due to Ms. St. James every Sunday night at 8 p.m. If I'm late, you'll make me write lines on Coach Johnson's whiteboard."

"I don't think we need to be that dramatic. But if you'd prefer to set a scheduled time for me to mark the receipt of your contracts each week, I'm amenable to that."

I can't help but shake my head, staring at her in wonder. "You're serious. You really expect me to get women to sign this, fuck them, then send the signed 'we fucked' contracts over to you?"

"It's a standard practice with public figures who find themselves in this position—"

"This *position* being philandering manwhore. Just say it, Poppy."

She stiffens. "Lukas, I swear this isn't a trap. I'm not trying to trick you or reprimand you or judge you. I'm trying to *help* you. You can send the contracts to one of my male staff members if that will make you more comfortable."

"Fucking hell," I mutter.

Before either of us can say another word, there comes a sharp knock at the door.

"Knock, knock," says a deep voice. "Hey, Poppy, I just wanted to— *oh*—Novy, hey."

I glance over my shoulder to see Morrow standing in Poppy's doorway, holding a plant.

"Hey, Colton," she says brightly. "Lukas and I are just finishing up. Can this possibly wait?"

He looks from me to Poppy, and fuck if I don't know that look. Is Morrow seriously about to get territorial with me over our public relations director? "There's nothing I needed other than to just drop this off, a little 'thank you' for the granola." His smile falls as he glances around. "But now I see there's no window in here so . . ."

I stretch out my legs, making a show of getting comfortable in the only chair. "Pathetic, right?"

"Excuse me, but I happen to like this office." As Poppy says the words, the lights overhead flicker.

Morrow is still looking around with a frown. "Not to be rude but . . . why?"

I snort.

Poppy casts me a pointed glare before looking over my shoulder to Morrow. "Thank you, Colton. This was so sweet of you. Tell you what—why don't you take the plant home with you for now, and you can drop it off at my apartment later?"

He brightens, clutching the plant like it's the last one on earth. "Yeah, sure. That works."

My gaze darts between them. "You know where she lives?"

The asshole grins and Poppy laughs. "Well, he better, seeing as we share a wall."

Okay, what the actual fuck?

I spin around and glare up at Morrow. Goddamn it, why does he have to be so handsome? He's rocking the whole biracial heartthrob look with his stupid cool haircut that fades up the sides, and his perfect stubbled jaw. His medium brown skin has a bronze glow from our time at the beach this weekend. Meanwhile, I'm this pasty white Canadian asshole who can't tan. I just burn.

I glance between them again. "You're neighbors?"

He smirks down at me. "Yep."

"It's only temporary," Poppy says. "Colton just needs to get with a realtor so he can scope out some places. Oh, I was meaning to ask you, honey. Do you need help with any of that?" I know she's not talking to *me* in that sweet tone. No, I'm just Novy the fuckup. Novy the pig with the sex contracts she has to scold and sigh at and suffer through.

"You want to help me?" Morrow asks.

"With finding a realtor," she clarifies. "I don't want to cut in or anything. I just wanted to offer since . . . you know." Her tone changes, more somber now, and I glance between them again.

"Well, *I* don't know," I say into the void.

"It's not important," Morrow mutters, keeping me firmly locked out of what now feels like a private conversation. Which is frankly a bit annoying, seeing as *I* was the one in her office with the door mostly closed when he charged in here carrying that stupid fucking plant. "I'll just see you at home, Poppy," he says. "Sorry I interrupted, and thanks again for the granola."

"You're welcome, honey," she calls as he ducks out, leaving the door cracked.

I give the air in the room a moment to settle. We had a lead balloon vibe in here I was quite happy with. Morrow had to go and ruin it with his positivity and general goodness. "So . . . when's the wedding?"

Poppy looks up from her phone. "What?"

"You and Morrow." I hate myself for putting the idea into her head, but apparently that's not going to stop me from diving in with both feet. "I sensed a little something there just now."

"Don't be ridiculous."

"Oh, I'm ridiculous? You make him granola and he buys you office plants. Tit for tat."

"He's just being nice."

"Nice? I'm nice, and I didn't bring you an office plant."

"You're calculating," she retorts. "There's a difference. Colton does favors just to do them. You would only ever do me a favor as part of your carefully calculated exchange program. Tit for tat."

Well, fuck me. That felt a little too on target. "So, what's next? You gonna find him a realtor?"

"Probably," she says with a shrug, eyes still on her phone.

I hate that I'm losing her attention. She's done with me, moving on. Pretty soon, I'll be as useful to her as the damn filing cabinet.

I sit forward in this stupid squeaky chair. "Okay but be warned that he's gonna demand to take you to dinner as a 'thank you.' Before you know it, you'll be exchanging sexual favors with your new wall buddy, likely up against a wall. From there, it's just a short walk down Sex Friend Alley before he'll be down on one knee as you're pulling a diamond ring out of a chocolate lava cake while you're on a couple's vacation in Aruba. Then it'll be all babies and buying a bigger house until, at last, you're arguing while he's on the road about whether you'll spend the offseason in Jacksonville or Jackson Hole. I've seen it all a hundred times before."

She just stares at me. "Wow. You've painted quite the picture. You're just missing one important detail."

"Am I?"

"Mhmm."

"Lay it on me."

"Colton and I are *friends*. We knew each other from before."

I raise a brow. "Before?"

"Before the Rays. We were both up at the Washington Capitals. We were friendly then, and we're friendly now. You know why?"

"Why?"

It's her turn to lean forward. "Because Colton Morrow is *friendly*. He knows how to have a relationship with a woman and not make it more—or less, in your case."

Everything tightens in my chest as I stare at her. "Does he now?"

"Yes, he knows how to be sweet to a woman and not expect anything in return. Not everything in life is a transaction, Lukas. Not everyone is out to get you, or hurt you, or use you. I wanted to give him the granola because I had enough to share. Simple as that. Now, can we please finish our meeting? I really do have a lot to do today."

I narrow my gaze at her. "You mean our meeting about my transactional love contracts?"

She purses those damn lips again. "Hmm, do we really want to use the word 'love'?"

"Fine. Transactional *sex* contracts."

"Better."

Fuck me. How did this entire exchange go so completely off the rails? We were flirting, and that was fun. I've always been a heavy flirt. Hell, I could flirt with a cereal box. But I'm also selfish and emotionally closed off to an almost pathological degree.

Women can only get two things from me: sexy banter—the wittier the better—and, if they're lucky, an unforgettable lay. I don't do feelings. Ever. I don't question the motives and meanings of every word in a conversation either. When you make it a point to never be serious about anything, you never have to be taken seriously. It's pure freedom.

So why the fuck is Poppy looking at me like that? Why does she look like she fucking cares? I swear to god, I think she might even feel sorry for me.

This can't happen. This whole exchange was a mistake. No more flirting with Poppy St. James. I'm not out here trying to reveal my dark sadness to my goddamn PR director.

I stand, every part of me feeling coiled tight. "Don't worry, Poppy. I never forget to use a condom, latex or legal. You can expect my first batch of signed sex contracts on Sunday night."

I can't let her have the last word. I don't think I could bear it after seeing the way she lit up for Colton fucking Morrow. I escape the room as fast as I can, leaving her sitting alone under the faintly flickering fluorescent lights.

9
COLTON

It's nearly nine o'clock at night, and I'm standing outside Poppy's front door, trying to remember how to breathe. It's a pretty basic human function. I do it all the time without even thinking. So, why am I standing here under this ring of yellow light feeling like my lungs won't inflate?

Oh, that's right. Because I'm twelve years old again, suffering under the weight of a hopeless and inappropriate crush. Truly, this is embarrassing. I don't have this problem with any other women. What can I say? I'm a consummate Leo. I like parties and clubs. I like dancing and karaoke. I like to flirt. I like to date. I like to pamper the women I'm with and get pampered in return. It's all very cool and casual. What are the kids calling it these days? Rizz?

Yeah, I've got a lot of rizz.

And yet, here I stand, staring at Poppy's front door, noting the chipping paint around her peep hole. Fuck me. I have zero fucking rizz. Not with Poppy St. James. Why else would I be holding this potted pothos plant?

Oh god, I even know what it's called. I asked the guy at the shop. It's a golden pothos. Low sunlight needed. Water once a week. What the fuck am I doing? I should throw this plant over the balcony and just go home.

No, you're doing this. Lift arm, make fist, knock on door.

Fuck, I really *am* doing it. I just knocked on her door.

Oh shit. Back up and act cool—

The door swings inward six inches, and Poppy's there, wearing nothing but silky pink sleep shorts and a matching top with straps as thin as dental floss. Her blonde hair is plaited in two thick braids, the ends trailing down either side of her chest.

"Hey, Poppy. I—"

She puts a finger up to her lips and pulls the door open all the way, revealing that she's holding her phone up to her ear.

"I can come back." I barely get the words out before she snags the front of my T-shirt with her free hand, tugging me over the threshold into her apartment.

"Uh-huh," she says into the phone, inching around me to close the door. The close proximity has her brushing up against me. I can smell the herbal scent of her shampoo, rosemary and mint. It mixes with the rich, chocolatey smell of fresh baked cookies that's filling her apartment.

My senses don't know what to focus on. They're pinging around inside me like a bunch of pin balls. She steps away and that helps . . . and hurts. Then she's smiling up at me in welcome and I'm slipping my slides off, leaving them next to her tiny blue running shoes. I follow her down the narrow hall into her kitchen.

"Uh-huh," she says again, rolling her eyes at me in a knowing way. Then she lifts a hand and mimes someone yapping.

I smile down at her, and she turns away, moving over to the living room to perch on a blue ottoman. My eyes go wide as I take in the chaos of her kitchen. Baking sheets are spread across every surface in various states of cooling. I see at least three different kinds of cookies. The rest of the granola sits in a large glass jar on the counter.

Does this woman ever stop baking? When does she even find the time?

"Yeah, Mom, listen—" She sighs, giving me another long-suffering look. "Yeah, I know. You already told me that. No, I'm just saying you already told me—"

I set the pothos down on the only spare patch of counter I can find, over by the sink. Poppy hops off the ottoman, stepping back into the kitchen on bare feet. She comes up next to me and plucks a chocolate and marshmallow cookie off one of the trays. She hands it wordlessly to me and walks away.

She and her mom exchange a few more sentences as I take a bite of the cookie and groan. Oh god, it's still warm. The chocolate is melty, and the marshmallow is gooey, and the cookie batter tastes like graham crackers. It's a s'mores cookie, and I'm dead.

"Okay, well I gotta go. No, I have to—" She huffs. "Mom, my neighbor just came over. He needs to borrow something, so I gotta go. I'll see you and Daddy for lunch next week, okay? Yep, I love you too. Byeeee." She drops the phone from her ear with an exhausted sigh. "I am *so* sorry about that."

"Not a problem," I say, sucking the sticky marshmallow off my thumb.

"And if my mother ever asks, you came over here in desperate need to borrow something."

I don't love that my role in her life can be summarized down to "the neighbor," but that's what I'm here to try to fix. "We'll say I was out of laundry soap."

"Perfect." She sets her phone down and picks up a creamy cable-knit sweater. "Ugh, you really saved me, you know?" She pulls it on over her head and lets it settle at her hips. It's two sizes too large, hanging seductively off one shoulder. But at least it covers her perky breasts, hiding her firm nipples under that silky pink—

I swallow the rest of my cookie. I'm getting hard in her kitchen right now. I'm eating her cookies, and thinking about her breasts, and getting hard. I turn away quickly, using the sink as an excuse to wash my hands.

"If you hadn't knocked when you did, I'd be on the phone with her for another hour at least," she goes on behind me. "How did you like the cookie?" Her hand brushes my arm as she reaches around me, plucking another cookie off the tray. "It's a new recipe. My sister-in-law sent it to me." She takes a bite of the cookie and moans. "Oh, my goodness. Okay, I know I'm biased," she says through a full mouth, "but this is *really* good." She catches the rest of her cookie before it crumbles, and looks up at me, those blue eyes holding an unspoken question.

I drop the dish towel down to the lip of the sink. "Oh. Yeah. No, they're really good. They're fucking amazing, Poppy. Best cookie I've ever tasted, honestly."

Her smile lights up her whole face. "Do you like caramel?"

"I . . ."

She spins away before I can answer. "I was in the mood for salted caramel today," she says over her shoulder. "So, I made some sauce from scratch and added it to my trusty chocolate chip pretzel cookies. Tell me what you think." She hands me another cookie.

I look down, noting the swirls of thick caramel mixed with the crunchy pretzel pieces and gobs of chocolate. She watches me take a bite. I'm ready to control my sound effects this time. "Fuck. This might be even better than the s'mores cookie," I admit.

Her smile brightens again, and I add something else to my running list of facts about Poppy: *lights up when praised.*

Very useful fact to know.

I hide my smirk, finishing the cookie in two bites. "You made caramel from scratch today?"

"Just like Nana taught me," she replies. "It's really not that hard. There are only four ingredients. I can give you some if you want. I have a couple jars cooling in the fridge."

I glance around again. "How did you have the time to do all this? Didn't you work a full day today?"

She laughs and waves the question away, swaying around the kitchen bar to fetch her glass of rosé. "I bake when I'm stressed. It's how I cope with this crazy thing we call life. That, and running."

"What are you stressed about?"

She looks at me over her wine glass. "Oh, you know, this and that."

Even as the question came out of me, I knew it was dumb. What *doesn't* she have to be stressed about? She's the head of public relations for a brand-new international sports team. She's living in a new city, working with new people, and we're a week out from the start of the season. I'm stressed, and I'm just playing the game. She's one of the maestros orchestrating the show of it all. I'm like the backup dancer to her Beyoncé.

"Sorry, that was a stupid question," I admit. "Of course you're stressed. How could you not be?"

She smiles again, taking a sip of her wine. "You must be feeling it too. I heard you'll be starting against Carolina. Congratulations. First Ray in history to skate on the ice."

"Well, one of six," I reply.

"First right-side defenseman."

I grin. "That's true."

"Jake didn't try to twist your ankle in the shower?"

I laugh. "No, he was actually really cool about it. Odds are he'll skate first next game. It's not really a competition to me."

Her eyes go wide at this admission. "It's not? I thought all you hockey boys were as competitive as they come?"

"I mean, sure, I like to win," I say with a shrug. "But more than winning, I like to play. I can only be grateful I have the chance at all."

"And you're not nervous?"

I lean against the counter, relaxing a bit. This feels easy. I'm talking to Poppy, but we're talking hockey. I can talk hockey all day. "I wouldn't say I'm nervous. This isn't my first game. I'm excited more than anything. I want to see what the Rays can do when the points actually matter."

She nods. "What do you think of the team so far? Of the chemistry?"

"Well, Mars is as solid as they come. We don't have to worry about him. I wish the backup tendy wasn't such a sieve, but he'll only get in the net as a last resort—"

"A sieve?" She tips her head to the side. "What does that mean?"

I blink, running back what I just said. "Oh." I laugh again. "Sorry, hockey slang. Uhh . . . it just means he's kind of useless. Like he's full of holes. The pucks just go right through him."

She giggles. "Not very flattering."

"Yeah, it doesn't help that Dave-O's an odd bird off the ice too. He's always eating these weird bagel chips that make his stall smell like garlic and onion."

Her nose scrunches. "Ew."

"Yeah, avoid close contact unless you want to breathe in some serious bagel fumes."

"Noted." She sets her wine down, crossing her arms to mirror my stance in her too-large sweater. "Well, what about you, honey?"

"What about me?"

Her expression softens and I know exactly where she's going. "How are you doing?"

"I'm fine," I say quickly.

She nods. "You haven't told the guys?"

"I don't know what they know."

"You haven't told Novikov. He's the one you're closest to on the team, right? You skated with him before?"

"Yeah, we skated in the Juniors together."

"And he doesn't know why you were delayed in moving down here?"

I sigh. "No, he doesn't know."

"Is it a secret?"

At this, I look up, my chest squeezing tight. I suddenly feel irrationally angry. I drop my hands behind me, holding tight to her counter. My mind flashes with pictures of my dad lying in the hospital bed, his skin so pale, his body so weak. "No, my dad's death isn't some dirty little secret, Poppy. He was alive, then he got sick, and now he's dead. There's nothing secret about it."

She nods again, tears rimming her eyes. "Poor choice of words," she says softly. "I meant do you want it kept private? Would you prefer your teammates not be informed?"

I cross my arms again, wishing we could go back to talking about cookies and hockey. "Why would they need to be informed? What business is it of theirs what happens in my personal life?"

She steps around the bar, moving closer. "Colton, these things have a tendency of bleeding over from the personal into the professional. And you know hockey is both anyways," she adds. "This team, these guys, they're not just your work colleagues. They're your family. They need to know if you're not okay. They need to know whether to give you space or fill the void. You can't keep them all at arm's length. Not about something as big as this."

"I don't like talking about it," I admit. "I'm not—I don't have the words yet, okay? It's still too fresh, and some days it's all I can do just to get out of bed and show up for practice."

She nods, eyes glistening again. "Okay."

"I'm not ready to sit on the therapy couch and spill out all my sadness to the whole team, okay?"

"Okay," she says again.

Fuck, I need to get out of here. I turn away, crossing her kitchen in two strides.

"Colton." Her hand brushes my arm as I pass. She's not holding me back, but it's a clear invitation to stay.

I stand there, not looking at her, feeling her standing next to me.

"Can I ask you to do one thing?"

I slowly turn, gazing down at her. She looks up at me with such openness—no doors, no guile. "Anything," I hear myself say.

Her hand grazes up my arm to my shoulder and she gives it a gentle squeeze. "Tell one person, okay? Just one. Let them be there for you. Let them know to check in. Let them see when you're hurting and help you stand when you feel like all you can do is fall."

I search her face, memorizing the pattern of the summer freckles dotting her cheeks. She's so beautiful. Holding her gaze, I cup her face with my large, calloused hand. I know I don't deserve to touch her. I don't deserve to hold her like this. I can't be soft right now. I can't be gentle.

She leans away, eyes wide, her back pressed up against the kitchen counter. She wraps her hand around my wrist. "Colton," she says again, enunciating the "T."

"I told you," I say, my voice low.

The energy between us turns on a dime as her grip on my wrist tightens. My face lowers on its own. I just need to be a little closer, need to breathe her in. I brush my thumb against her cheek, feeling how it's tanned and warm from running in the sun. She leans into the stroke of my thumb, eyes fluttering shut.

"You're my person here, Poppy. My one. I told *you*."

A moment stretches between us, pulled tight like the string of a kite caught on a gust of wind. Her eyes flash with need, and then I'm pressing my lips to hers, tipping her head back with urgency, desperate to taste all of her. Both her hands are at my shoulders, and she's pulling me closer. Her mouth slants with mine as she returns my kiss.

My kiss.

I'm kissing Poppy St. James.

With a desperate groan, I drop my hands to her hips and lift her right off the floor. The cookie trays rattle behind her as I put her up on the counter, stepping between her spread legs. She welcomes me in, her ankles hooking behind my knees as she makes room for me to press in with my hips.

"Oh god," she says on a breathless sigh.

Fuck, she's so soft, so supple. And yet, she knows what she wants. Her hands push and pull at me, stroking the nape of my neck. Her lips part and her tongue flicks. She's so fucking eager. And she tastes so sweet, like wine and caramel. We keep kissing like we'll die if we stop.

I need to feel her. I need more. My hands are still at her hips. I slip them both under the hem of her baggy sweater, my thumbs stroking over the impossible silkiness of her little pink camisole. She makes the perfect whimpering sound in my mouth as my thumbs stroke over her ribs. She arches into me, inching closer with her hips. Any closer, and she'll feel how hard I am for her. My fingertips brush the bare skin under her arms, and I press in—

She jolts, gasping for air. "Colton, we can't."

I groan, my hold on her going from coaxing to claiming. "Please," I beg, determined to brand myself on her lips.

"Colton, wait," she pants, her hands now pushing at my shoulders. "*Stop.*"

That one little word hits me like a bucket of ice water poured down my back. I instantly lift both hands away from her, spreading my arms wide. She reels from the loss of my support, her hold on me tightening. Her ankles brush the backs of my thighs as we rebalance ourselves.

I press my forehead lightly against hers, eyes shut tight. "I'm sorry."

"No, it's fine," she says in a small voice, still holding onto me.

I inch back, my hands kept well away from her. "No, Poppy, I'm so sorry. I had no right."

She's trembling. Fuck, did I scare her? In her eyes, I see heat and passion. No fear. *Thank god*. But there's hesitancy too. I step back fully. Her hands brush down my chest as I pull away. I drop my hands to my sides in defeat. Slowly, she lets her hands fall too. She sits there on the edge of the counter, her bare legs dangling. Her parted lips are still wet with my kisses. Her blue eyes watch me, always searching my face, always trying to read me.

"I'm sorry," I say again, taking another step back. My hip bumps the corner of her fridge.

"Colton, it's okay," she says, slipping off the counter to the floor. "We just—we got caught up. It's late, we're both tired, and you're grieving. It happens."

Her list stops there. That's why she kissed me? Because it's late and she's tired and she thinks I need sympathy? I brush my fingers over my lips. That sure as fuck didn't feel like a sympathy kiss. "Well, it won't happen again," I hear myself say. "You're safe with me, Poppy."

She inches closer. "Colton."

I drop my hand back to my side. "I need to go."

She swallows and nods. "Okay."

"The plant." I gesture to where it sits over by the sink. "Don't overwater it. The guy said that's the big mistake most people make. Only water it once a week."

"Okay," she says again.

"And it doesn't need much sunlight, but definitely more than what you have in your office at work."

She smiles weakly. "I'll take care of it, Colton. Thank you. It was thoughtful and lovely."

Thoughtful and lovely. Two words I want to add to the list of real things I know about Poppy. St. James.

"Can you text me the numbers for those realtors?" I say, backing toward the front door.

She nods again. "Yeah, I'll do it tonight before I go to bed."

She doesn't try to follow me. Whether it's me she doesn't trust, or herself, I can't be sure. But I can't stay here, not when I still have her taste on my tongue and the scent of her clouding all my senses. "Goodnight, Poppy," I manage to say.

"Goodnight."

I turn away, breaking the static charge between us. I'm in such a rush to leave, I forget to put on my damn slides. I don't notice until I'm back in my own unit with the door shut.

Whatever. Fuck it. She can keep them.

10
POPPY

My phone buzzes on the dresser, and I know it has to be Claribel. We've been doing a social media strategy session for the last hour via text message because Little Miss Too Busy can't just call me back. Well, *I've* been texting. She's been sending one-word responses and inappropriate GIFs. I swipe my phone off the dresser and read her text with narrowed eyes.

CLARIBEL: Boss, it's Sunday night. Clock out *wine emojipeace sign emoji***

I huff, tossing the phone on the end of the bed. Of course I know it's Sunday night. I've only been counting down the hours and minutes for months. Tomorrow, the NHL season officially starts. At 8 a.m., this rocket is blasting off. Then all we can do is fix problems as they arise—and hope we don't come crashing back to earth.

No pressure, Poppy.

It may be Sunday night, but the work still has to get done. In the last two hours, I've been on the phone with five other department heads. All the while, I've been whirling around my apartment like a tornado, feverishly packing. I'm about to spend two weeks traveling up and down the East Coast with a professional hockey team. It's less than ideal to do so much travel at once, but necessary.

For all the money and influence Mark Talbot has in this city, he's not actually god, and he can't change the fundamental laws of concrete pouring. Which means construction at the brand-new arena isn't finished. As a result, the first six games the Rays play will all be away. Three this week. Three next week. That's six cities with six different climates. Six different social and professional atmospheres.

All this to say, Poppy is bringing the big bag.

My largest piece of luggage is currently flipped open on the bed. Inside, I've stuffed everything from business separates to formal wear, to club wear, to running gear. Because, while the team has six hockey games, I have six games, eight dinners, five lunches, four charity events, and eight sponsorship meetings. Yeah, my PR team is perhaps a little *too* efficient when it comes to time management. We've stacked practically every minute of the next two weeks.

There's only one little break in my schedule for the day we're in DC. I close my eyes, clutching a pair of beige Yves Saint Laurent platform sandals. *Lunch with family.* That's what will occupy the only blessed break in my grueling schedule. At my mother's insistence, I'll be attending family lunch at The Hay-Adams.

Don't get me wrong, I love my parents. I am eternally grateful for the life they've afforded me—the first-rate education, the travel and business opportunities. They set out a shining golden path for me, and all they ever asked was that I walk it without question.

Mother knows best.

And, god help me, I tried. For years, I only ever did what she wanted. I went to the schools she liked and studied the subjects she deemed appropriate for me. I dated only the boys from her approved list. I wore the clothes she wanted me to wear and made friends with the "right set" of girls. But at some point, children have to be free to live their own lives, right?

Three years ago, I did just that. I looked my St. James destiny in the face, and I said no. I walked away. Now, I'm Poppy the disappointment. Poppy the wayward lamb. My mother has a lot of euphemisms to describe the gaping hole I left in her heart. It seems like no amount of success I achieve on my own can ever erase her disappointment over the destiny I denied, the hope I squandered.

Poppy the unfaithful. Poppy the ungrateful.

I drop the sandals into my suitcase, blinking back tears. Taking a couple deep breaths, I rub my face with tired hands. "Oh, goodness. Girl, get it together."

I don't do this. I don't wallow. I made my choices then, and I would make them all again. *Life is all about choices, honeybun.* I hear my Nana's sweet voice saying the words as if she were standing before me.

I've been making some surprising choices here recently—like choosing to wrap myself around my neighbor like powdered sugar on a donut. Yeah, that happened. Colton was grieving, and I thought it was a good idea to stick my tongue in his mouth.

"Oh, god."

Seeking any distraction, I hurry over to my closet and jerk out a couple more blazers. I clumsily fold them and place them atop the mounting pile in my suitcase. There's no way I'm getting this thing closed without an industrial press. I stand there, staring at it, hands on my hips.

Colton hasn't said anything about the kiss. We've both been so busy this week, I've hardly seen him. Part of it feels like some kind of fever dream. I was so swept up in stress baking and cleaning, then my mom called. Perhaps it was all in my head. Perhaps I just imagined that a handsome hockey player came over late at night and pinned me to the kitchen counter.

No, it definitely happened.

My stomach does a little flip as I remember the feel of his strong hands on me, the taste of his lips, all warm and chocolatey. Heavens, but he knows how to kiss. I'd be lying if I said I hadn't thought about kissing him before. The man is simply undeniable. He's confident, but not cocky, driven but not dominating. And he's so beautiful I could literally cry. With those broad shoulders and the high cheekbones, it's no wonder he lands modeling endorsements. Did I mention the way his warm brown skin gets this golden glow?

Seriously, it's not fair that god made a man that beautiful and perfect and then put him firmly out of my reach. He's out of reach because I don't date the players. *Ever.* It was the one rule I made for myself when I started working in PR for professional sports. I see and manage too much of these men's messy personal lives as it is. I don't ever want to become part of the personal life getting managed.

No, Colton Morrow is a dream I get to dream from afar.

And I *have* dreamed about him. Many times. Last night in fact. I blush thinking about it. Let's just say I got to know whether he was that talented with his tongue everywhere . . .

"He is your colleague, Poppy." I point a finger at my reflection in the mirror. "You will not ogle him, and you will *not* think about him naked."

My eyes go wide as new images flash in my mind: Colton running down the beach at sunset, Colton striding out of the surf, Colton stepping out my shower and handing me a towel—

"No!" I rush into the bathroom and start feverishly packing my toiletries and makeup.

Out on the bed, my phone pings. I have a new email.

I step back into the bedroom and pick up my phone. The new email is from hothockeyhunk22. The subject line says in all caps: URGENT—SEX CONTRACTS—HIGHLY CONFIDENTIAL.

Lukas.

I check the time. 8:01 p.m.

"Seriously, is everything a joke to this man?" I sink down onto the end of the bed and tap the email open. The body just says, "As promised." Holding my breath, I check the attachments.

There are seven.

"Seven contracts? It hasn't even been seven *days* since our meeting! How the heck does he even find the time?"

Clearly, I'm in no mood to deal with Lukas Novikov's sex contracts, but I tap open the first one. My eyes skim the first few lines until I get to the paramour's name. My heart stops. It's right there in blue ink, laughing up at me: Minnie Mouse.

"What the . . .?" I close it out and tap open the next one, only to find it signed by Natasha Romanov. I scoff "Black Widow? Seriously? Someone thinks rather highly of himself."

I open the next three contracts.

Snow White.

Diana Prince.

Leslie Knope.

I glare down at my phone. "I am going to *kill* Lukas Novikov."

Aswarm of excited energy hums inside PNC Arena, home of the Carolina Hurricanes. Game one of the season is officially here. It's warm-up time, and the stands are already filling fast. I breathe deeply, taking in the chemical smell of the freshly sprayed ice, the hot buttery popcorn, and the detergent-fresh scent of my new warmup jersey.

God, I fucking *love* hockey.

And there is nothing better than game one of a new season. Everyone is excited to see the Rays take to the ice, so this game is sold out. Eager fans are already standing right behind our bench, cheering and waving homemade signs.

I give them a wave and a smile as I glide up. Then I catch Sanford's attention, beckoning him down the bench. He gives a nod to Wednesday and Doc Price and heads my way. "Trouble?"

"My blade feels funny. It's loose or warped or something."

He's all business as he turns to the blade box perched behind him. "Which foot?"

"Left."

He rattles around in the box. "Put it up."

I lean over the boards on my elbows, and prop my left foot up on the bench. "Hey, don't trip," I shout at J-Lo as he skates past.

He gives me a laugh and a gloved middle finger. I've been teasing him since we left Jacksonville, just little things about tripping or forgetting his socks. Sure, he's starting over me, but I'm not actually *that* big of a sore loser. He's just easy to chirp. He's so good-natured. If you're his teammate, nothing gets under his skin.

"Lukas, we need to talk."

"Jesus—*fuck*." My stick rattles away, and I nearly topple over as Poppy "Silent Mode Activated" St. James appears at my shoulder.

"Hey," Sanford says behind me, his grip tightening on my skate. "Hold still, you wobbly fuck. These blades aren't made of rubber."

"Sorry, Sanny," I say, slowly turning with my upper body to gaze down at our director of public relations.

I knew she was on this trip. I watched her board the plane, climbing the steps of our chartered jet looking like a supermodel in her black shades and slinky black dress. She looks very on brand tonight too. She's sporting a Rays' teal business suit. The color is loud, but she pulls it off. Her blonde hair is swept up in a long ponytail. That's one thing to be grateful for, I guess. I don't have to pretend her skinny little pencil skirt isn't driving me fucking crazy as I talk to her.

But—oh, this is perfect. She looks *pissed*. I brighten immediately. My dick is practically twitching in my hockey pants as I take in the glint in her eyes. "Poppy St. James," I croon at her. "I get the feeling you need something."

"I *do* need something," she replies, one hand on her hip. "I need to know where you find the king-sized audacity."

From behind me, Sanford chuckles. "He buys it in bulk at Costco."

"Eyes on your own work, Sanny," I say at him. Then I turn back to Poppy. "Could we maybe do this later? Sanford and I were kind of having a moment."

"No, we can't do this later," she counters. "Because this may be the only chance I have to hold your attention for more than sixty seconds."

"Bold of you to assume you have my attention now," I say, faking a wave at someone out on the ice. Stupid fucking Walsh. He sees it, and now he's looking over his shoulder and waving back, confused. I snort a laugh.

"I just need to know if you have any respect for me at all," she goes on.

I turn to her, smile falling. "Poppy—"

"Really, I do. I need to hear you say that you respect my role here as director of public relations."

I blink, noting the stiff silence coming from Sanny. The asshole is terrible at pretending not to listen. "Poppy, I respect you—"

"Well, I don't believe you," she replies, crossing her arms.

"Well, that's too damn bad." I lean over until my sweaty face is level with hers. "And I don't think *you* respect *me*. If you did, you wouldn't be crashing down on me like a fucking tsunami right now when I'm supposed to be getting my head in the game. Bad form, Poppy. You could cost us our first chance at a W. Then how would you live with yourself, eh?"

She points out to the ice. "You were just out there skating around with your stick between your legs, riding it like a broom! That's not 'head in the game' behavior to me, Lukas. That's more like head up your butt!"

Behind us, Sanford snorts. "Get him, Poppy."

I glance over my shoulder. "Are you nearly finished?"

"I *am* finished," he replies.

I lower my leg to the mats. "Good. Then get lost, Sanford."

Now it's his turn to cross his arms in his long-sleeved Rays staff shirt. "Try again."

I sigh. I can't possibly take them both on at once. "Look, give us a minute, and I'll buy you dinner for the next week."

"You're still missing something." He raises a brow, waiting.

"Please," I grit out.

With a nod to Poppy, he walks away, leaving me alone with this feral puma in a pantsuit.

"Well?" I say at her.

"Well, what?" she says back.

I face her, arms crossed. In my pads and skates, I tower over her. *Good*. I have a feeling I'll need the extra inches. "You were about to explain how saying my head is lodged up my ass is proof of you respecting me. Go on, I'm listening," I say with a wave of my gloved hand.

She glares up at me. "Where are the contracts, Lukas? That's all I came to ask."

Behind her, the fans cheer and slap the glass, trying to get my attention. But all I see is her—the point of her chin as she holds my gaze, the determined look in her eyes. She's wearing more makeup tonight. Her eyes look dark and smoky, which just makes the blue of her irises pop more. They're like sea glass, all shiny and reflective under these bright arena lights.

Fuck me. She's devastating.

And a real fucking ball-buster.

"I sent you the contracts on Sunday night," I reply. "I wasn't sure if you got them, seeing as you never responded. I think the proper form is to provide an email as proof of receipt. But then, what do I know? I'm just a dumb horndog hockey player whom you don't respect."

"See?" She waves erratically with her phone-wielding hand. "This is *exactly* what I'm talking about. You're not taking any of this seriously. By extension, you're not taking *me* seriously. I'm trying to help you, Lukas. But you're refusing to accept my help, and instead you're turning everything I say on its head, making yourself the victim."

Okay, now she's getting under my skin. "I sent you the contracts," I say again. "You wanted signed sex contracts? You got them."

"Oh, really?" Her indignation in this moment could fuel a small city. It's certainly giving me life. "You expect me to believe you had sex with Diana Prince this weekend? In what universe do you really think you could ever pull Wonder Woman?"

"Hey, I thought you said you weren't here to judge me," I snap back. "No questions either. It's *my* sex life, Poppy."

"It's your *delusion*," she hisses, those blue eyes narrowing as she steps closer. "And for your information, Snow White was canonically fourteen years old, which makes you a *pervert*."

And now I'm laughing. "What do you want me to say, Poppy?"

"Admit the names are fake," she cries.

"Of course they're fake."

"Then give me the real contracts!"

I shrug indifferently. "There are no real contracts."

She blinks up at me, eyes wide. "What?"

I crouch, getting myself right in her face. "There are no contracts," I say again, enunciating each word.

Her mood shifts as she leans away. I watch her slender throat as she swallows. "You didn't? I mean, you . . ." And now she's blushing. God, it's fucking precious.

"Didn't fuck a rotating door of nameless, faceless women this week?" I finish for her. "Nope. Sorry to disappoint. I was a little preoccupied with, oh, I don't know, my job? Season starters are no joke, Poppy. We were about to spend two weeks on the road, and I needed to conserve all my energy for the ice. Sorry I couldn't indulge your twisted curiosity about my sex life."

She gasps, pressing a hand to her chest. "*My* twisted—"

"I promise, I'll have *loads* of sordid contracts for you to peruse this Sunday," I say over her. "Hey, perhaps I'll even get lucky tonight." And just because I can, I glance around her, waving and winking at the crowd of fans pressing in behind the plexiglass. Most of them are women, and they squeal and shout my name.

Poppy fumes as she looks from them back to me. "Go ahead. I don't care. But know this, Lukas: You stick your pretzel in any of that cheese dip, and all you'll get is herpes!"

With that, she stomps away. I laugh, letting the sound trail after her as she disappears down the chute back toward the locker room.

Morrow skates up to the boards behind me, one gloved hand on my shoulder. "Hey, what the hell was that about? She looked mad."

I huff, unsurprised that her savior is ready to swoop in and rescue her. "Oh that? I just proposed and she said yes. Wanna be my best man?"

"You—*what*?"

My laugh deepens. God, he's too fucking easy. "Relax, bud. She'd never marry me in a million fucking years. Not that I'm asking," I add quickly. "She's a ball-busting harpy witch—"

"Hey," he growls. "Be professional. She's our colleague."

"She's a pill," I counter. "And you can have her." I try to push all thoughts of Poppy St. James from my mind as I gaze out at the ice, watching the Canes sink pucks into an empty net. "Tonight, I only care about getting lucky."

12
POPPY

I'm still fuming as I part with Claribel down in the tunnels. She'll stay near the ice to get some behind-the-scenes footage. Meanwhile, I have to hike to the top of the arena to sit in a stuffy suite and chat up industry reps. I've got to get my head on straight. I'm about to spend the whole of this first game schmoozing a bunch of potential brands, looking for more endorsement deals. But all I can think about is Lukas Novikov and his stupid caramel eyes!

Oh, he thinks he's *sooo* funny sending me those silly contracts. And positively charming . . . and devilishly handsome. How could he not, when the collective universe seems ready to bust through a thick wall of plexiglass trying to get to him?

What is his problem that he refuses to take any of this seriously? Clearly, he doesn't know about the email I received from Mark Talbot's office on Friday, asking for a rundown on all the press related to each player. I wouldn't be surprised if Mark is doing early calculations for the upcoming trade window, trying to decide who to keep.

Well, I'm no expert in hockey stats, but from the PR angle, Lukas Novikov screams trade. The folder we're putting together on him is a hot mess of articles about his constant partying, the on- and off-ice fights. The man has been banned from *two* Vegas casinos. Oh, and he once pulled a prank that resulted in a small arena fire and a totaled Zamboni.

Rachel's truck full of balls is starting to look like child's play. Luckily, she was a good sport about it. She's a really cool girl. Nothing like what I expected. I've met some musicians' kids before, and they're all a bit too "the moon is in the ninth house, let's do 'shrooms and talk about the multiverse" for me. But Rachel is smart and funny.

For the most part, she ignores the players who try to get too flirty with her.

Except for Jake Compton. That man is making no mystery of the Olympic-sized torch he carries for her.

Okay, this is actually helping. Don't think about Lukas and his Texas-sized ego. Think about sweet Jake Compton, and his inappropriate crush on his doctor . . .

I stop in the middle of the concourse, gripping tighter to the strap of my leather shoulder bag. "Oh, sweet cheese and crackers."

Jake Compton has a wildly inappropriate crush on his treating physician, an internationally famous rock star's daughter. If that gets out—or if they start fooling around in secret and *that* gets out—it's going to be a PR nightmare.

I take a deep breath. "One crisis at a time, Poppy."

For now, Lukas Novikov remains my primary PR concern.

FIRST period is well underway, and the Rays look amazing! They're skating hard against Carolina. We've had a few good shots on goal, but nothing has gone in yet. The crowd is electric. There's a sea of teal jerseys swaying and cheering as all the new Rays fans practice the wave. It's really wonderful to see the way the guys are being embraced by the League.

I'm distracted from chatting up the Bauer rep when I hear the screams and boos of the Carolina fans. "What happened?" I sit forward in my seat, nearly tipping my gin and tonic off the ledge.

"Carolina just got a penalty," someone replies from the row behind me.

"Is Number Three okay?" the woman next to him asks.

My heart leaps in my throat. "Number Three" is Colton Morrow. My gaze darts from the Jumbotron back to the ice. I exhale as I watch Colton get to his feet. Then I watch the replay footage, shrieking as he takes a nasty hit into the boards from behind.

I don't know enough about the penalties to know what just happened, but a Canes player is going to the box, and they're setting up for another face-off. Colton and Jean-Luc leave the ice and Lukas and Jake skate on.

I've never been so grateful to know the players have instant medical care. Rachel is behind Colton in a flash, one hand on his shoulder as he nods, taking the water bottle offered by Sanford.

"He's okay," I whisper to myself, sinking back in my seat.

The puck drops, and Josh O'Sullivan, our center and team captain, gets possession. He quickly bats it back to Jake, who shoots it across the ice to where Lukas is already waiting. Lukas just barely catches the puck on the tip of his stick as he surges forward, darting around a charging Hurricane.

"Shoot it," the Bauer rep next to me yells.

"Pass it," someone shouts behind me.

I'm on the edge of my seat again, watching as Lukas dances around his pursuer. The slot is a mess of players. All our forwards are jammed up by the Hurricanes, trying to get clear for a pass. Lukas darts right with the puck and takes the shot. The whole arena seems to hold their breath for the span of the two seconds it takes for the puck to fly across the ice and slip right between the goalie's skate and the post. The cherry lights up, and the Rays fans go wild.

Rays—1. Hurricanes—0.

Lukas Novikov, a mouthy defenseman with anger issues and caramel eyes, just scored the first goal in Rays history.

The team descends on him, cheering and patting his back. He breaks free, smiling ear to ear as the music changes. The chorus of Daft Punk's "Get Lucky" plays over the sound system as the Jumbotron zooms in on Lukas's confident, smiling face. Finding the right camera, he turns, looks straight down the lens, and winks.

My cheers die in my throat as I drop to my seat. I snatch my gin and tonic off the ledge and take a sip, trying to drown the stupid, girlish fluttering in my chest. Even if no one else in this arena knows the truth, Lukas knows . . . and I know it too.

He was winking at me.

13

POPPY

Claribel and I are two of the first people on the plane after the Hurricanes game ends. Leaving her up with the rest of the media team at the front, I make my way to the back. Now I'm just sitting here, foot jiggling, anxiously waiting for the flight attendants to close the boarding door. If I was thinking straight, I would be the last one on for each flight. Then I wouldn't have time to let my anxiety build.

For better or worse, I have a serious fear of closed-in spaces. Blame my brother, Rowan. When he was eight and I was five, we were playing hide-and-seek, and he shut me in a hope chest in our Nana's attic. Then the jerk forgot about me and left me up there all afternoon. No one could hear my screams because it was the attic. Our Daddy whooped him for it, but the damage was already done.

Twenty-two years and three therapists later, I'm still a bit of a mess. Planes, elevators, tanning beds—basically, if it's got a lid or a sealed door, I'm counting the milliseconds until the torture is over.

"Gosh, what is the holdup?" Peering up the aisle, I see Mars Kinnunen is out of his seat, saying something to Rachel. I'm too far away to hear, but it looks animated. After a couple minutes, she stands, snatching her stuff out of the seat. Then she follows Kinnunen up the plane to his row and sits with him.

Hmm . . . I knew Jake Compton was carrying a torch for our dear Barkley Fellow. Could it be that our two-time Stanley Cup-winning goalie is also a smitten kitten?

As Rachel and Mars sit farther up the plane, Colton stands.

Oh my . . . was she just sitting with him? He's not interested in her too, is he?

A flash of jealousy sparks through me, and I feel a primal urge to go hiss the word *mine* at her. It must be my anxiety gummy talking.

Colton Morrow is not mine. He's allowed to sit by whoever he wants—and kiss them too.

We make eye contact and I gasp, sinking back in my seat.

Colton's coming this way. He's walking right down the aisle toward me. A wild image flashes in my mind of Rachel trying to flirt with him. No doubt, she offers him a taste of her better, sexier granola, but he throws the bag in her face, vowing he'll never eat anyone's granola but mine. Then he kicks her out of his row, banishing her to the death seats in the middle of the plane.

Sure . . . I bet that's *exactly* what just happened.

I groan, trying to make myself as small as possible. This crush is getting really inconvenient. I don't want him to see the way I'm blushing, so I bury my face in my phone.

"Poppy?"

The surprise in his tone has me looking up. Heavens, he's gorgeous. He got his haircut since I last saw him. Now the sides have a sharper fade. All his stubble is gone too. His dark cheeks are silky smooth. I trace the line of his angular jaw with my eyes, following it down to his full lips.

"Poppy," he says again. I watch his mouth form the word, his lips curling in slightly to pronounce the "P."

I pull my gaze from his mouth and meet his dark eyes. "Yeah?"

He glances around. "What are you doing back here?"

"Sitting," I reply lamely.

"Managers usually sit up front with the coaching staff," he says, pointing over his shoulder. "Back of the plane is for interns."

"Wow, really feeling the love, Morrow," says Teddy in the row across from me. He's sitting with Max, my favorite social media intern.

One of the flight attendants walks up behind Colton and taps him on the shoulder. He's a tall, Black man wearing clear-frame glasses. "Mr. Morrow, you need to find your seat, please."

"Yeah, just give me a minute to hit the head," he replies.

"No, now," says the attendant. "The lavatory will be open again as soon as we reach our cruising altitude."

"Fine." I gasp in surprise as Colton plops himself down in the empty seat next to me. "There. I'm sitting. Are you happy?"

"Buckle your seatbelt, and I'll be ecstatic," the attendant deadpans.

Colton grapples for the pieces of his seatbelt, clicking them together. "Happy now?"

The corner of the attendant's mouth twitches. "I'm dancing on the inside." He saunters off, calling the all-clear to his crew.

Oh, heaven help me. Now that Colton's sitting, I can smell his cologne. It's the same one he was wearing the night he kissed me, all warm and woodsy. I detect notes of leather and bergamot, a hint of orange. Smelling it again puts me right back in my kitchen—my legs wrapped around his hips, my hands on his shoulders, my tongue teasing his perfect lips . . .

I lean as far away as possible. My shoulder is pressed against the window. "Colton, what are you doing?"

He gestures to the seat. "I'm sitting."

"You're sitting by me," I clarify. "I thought players don't sit with staff."

"Doc Price is sitting with Kinnunen," he says with a shrug. "Compton is sitting with Sanford. Apparently, the Rays don't obey the time-honored laws of hockey travel."

I glance his way, trying to keep my tone uninterested. "Yeah, what was that about?"

"What was what about?"

"I saw Rachel talking to Mars . . . and she was sitting with you?"

He huffs, pulling his earbud from his ear and returning it to its little case. "Oh, Doc Price is just learning about the ins and outs of hockey superstitions."

"What do you mean?"

"Well, Mars is a goalie," he explains. "If there's one thing goalies crave, it's routine. And she was sitting with Mars on our flight out, right? Well, then he played a shutout game, and she tried to move seats. Mars wasn't having it. He made her move."

"He made her move? Why?"

"Because he needs to know."

"Know what?"

"Whether she's lucky."

I go still. There it is again, that word. *Lucky*. Lukas teased me with it earlier—

I wince as the plane hits a bump. Dropping my hand down, I hold tight to the armrest. We're about to take off. This is always the hardest part for me. But Colton is here, and I'll take any distraction. "So, umm, he thinks he played a shutout game because Rachel sat next to him on the plane?"

Colton chuckles. "Probably not. If we lose the next game, he'll likely let her go. Right now, she's his unwilling hostage."

So, not a love connection. That simplifies things for me. I don't have to worry about spinning anything if their relationship doesn't go beyond her warming an airplane seat.

I glance up at him. "What about you?"

"What about me?"

"Do you believe in luck?"

He smiles. "Of course I do. I wouldn't be here right now if the universe hadn't granted me at least a little bit of luck."

"By 'here' you mean on a chartered jet, playing professional hockey?"

His expression heats as he leans in. "I mean sitting here talking to you."

Okay, if he keeps looking at me like that, I'm going to kiss him again, and the interns *cannot* catch me kissing a player.

The plane bumps and rattles as we take off, and Colton moves with the motion, dropping his elbow down so it brushes mine on the armrest. "I can smell your perfume," he murmurs, his voice all low and rumbly. It's doing unholy things to me to feel his warm breath at my ear. "You were wearing it when I kissed you. What is it?"

I swallow, heart in my throat. The plane tips up, up, up as we start to climb. "Umm . . . it's Chanel. Gardénia."

The plane dips and his nose brushes against my temple. He lifts a hand, his fingers trailing lightly down my arm. "You smell like summer and sunshine. It's intoxicating, Poppy. I can't get it out of my head."

Oh god, I really am going to kiss him again!

"Do you want some granola?" I all but shout at him. Diving forward, I dig under the seat and pull out my quart-sized baggie of homemade granola. I right myself, holding it up between us.

He's smirking like he knows exactly what I'm doing. Of course he does. I'm being as subtle as a foghorn. He laughs. "Sure, I'd love some."

I pry open the bag, nearly dropping it as the plane jolts again. "Oh—*Jesus*." One hand grips the armrest as I all but tip the granola into his lap.

He catches it with his quick reflexes. "Poppy, are you . . .?"

I shut my eyes tight as the whole plane bounces like a rock skipping on a pond.

His hand covers mine and he gives it a gentle squeeze. "Are you afraid of flying?"

"No," I say with a forced, squeaky laugh.

"Then why are you clinging to this armrest like we'll drop from the sky if you don't?"

I open my eyes wide. "Ohmygod. Why would you even say that?" I cry, slapping his arm.

He chuckles, popping a handful of my granola in his mouth.

"Colton, the universe can hear you. You can't talk about planes falling from the sky while you're *on* a plane *in* the sky! God, I thought all you hockey players were superstitious."

"I didn't say I was superstitious," he replies, crunching on my granola. "I said I believe in luck. Two very different things."

"Oh yeah? How so?"

He leans down with a smile. "Well, if I was superstitious, I might think the only way I'll ever get you to kiss me again is to wait until you're stress baking and show up at your door with a new potted plant."

"Colton—"

"But I believe in luck," he goes on. "I know if I'm patient, it's just a matter of time before the conditions will be right, and you'll give in to your desires again."

"Oh, yeah?"

"Yeah, that's pretty much my plan. Patience and luck."

I cross my arms. "So, you think I have some kind of insatiable desire, a fire burning in me that only your sweet lovin' can quench?"

He laughs, placing the half-eaten bag of granola in my lap. Then he dusts off his hands and turns to me. Cupping my face, he leans in, his woodsy scent enveloping me once more. He lowers his voice. "Let's put it this way, Poppy. Just the thought of my lips on yours has you letting go of all fear. You're not thinking about this plane falling from the sky. You're thinking about my hard dick brushing against your inner thigh."

I gasp, leaning away. "You're a poet and you don't know it."

He laughs again. "That's what had you pulling away in the

kitchen, right? You wanted me then, like you want me now, and you're just too afraid to admit it." He nods down at my chest. "And you crossed your arms just now so I wouldn't see your hard nipples through that silky shirt."

"Colton," I cry, outraged at his impertinence . . . and so turned on I'm fighting the urge to squirm under his intense gaze.

His dark eyes sparkle. "Go on, Poppy. Make my fucking night. Tell me I'm wrong."

Heart racing, I lift a hand, placing it over his on my cheek. "I don't date my players," I say, my tone solemn. "Colton, I'm so sorry. It's my one rule."

He just smiles, his thumb brushing my cheek. "I'm not asking to date you. I'm just letting you know that you need to be kissed more often, and I'm willing to be the man to do it." He drops his hand away from me, leaving me reeling. "Any time of the day or night. You need kissing? You come to me. Understand?"

Somehow, I find myself nodding, my hands settling back on the armrests.

The seatbelt sign dings, and he immediately unbuckles. "Not to force an early end to this moment, but I really did come back here to use the lavatory. And I need to get back to my seat for when they serve dinner. But you just remember what I said, okay?"

Which part? The part where he called me intoxicating? The part where he admitted he pressed his hard dick against me in my kitchen? Or the part where he said I need to be kissed every day and he wants to be the man to do it?

All of it. I'm going to remember everything he just said. I'll be adding it to the ever-lengthening list of reasons why Colton Morrow is my dreamboat. This man I can't let myself have is quickly becoming the only thing I think about.

And I teased Lukas earlier about living in the land of delusion?

Gazing up at Colton, I just nod again.

"Have a good night, Poppy." He moves away down the aisle, leaving me clutching the armrests for a reason we both know has nothing to do with my fear of flying.

14
POPPY

$\mathcal{S}$omehow, I survive two weeks on the road without any major public relations disasters from the players or staff. The guys have all been perfect gentlemen, using their time off the ice to try various coffee shops and restaurants. It turns out Jake Compton is a social media gold mine. He meticulously documents almost every meal he eats. He even managed to snag a few shots of Caleb Sanford looking like the surly eye candy he is.

I'm pleased to say he seems to be keeping Lukas out of trouble too. The men dine together most nights, along with Colton and Jean-Luc. So long as the most seductive photos they post are of the soy sauce dripping from their sushi rolls, I'm a happy PR director.

Honestly, for most of this trip, the team and I have felt like two ships passing in the night. I've attended all the games, making some good inroads on future endorsement deals, but I've also been hard at work in each of the cities, attending various meetings and charity events.

Mark Talbot has a vision for his philanthropy beyond what he can accomplish with the Rays. It's my hope that as the charity end of things grows, I might transition away from PR and into more of a philanthropic foundation role. But I have to prove myself first. Mark isn't going to trust me with his legacy if he can't trust me to handle basic PR for his hockey team.

At the moment, public relations and philanthropy are the furthest things from my mind, because I'm sitting in the back of a cab, heading over to The Hay-Adams hotel for my obligatory family lunch. Standing a literal stone's throw from the front steps of the White House, the hotel boasts of having one of the swankiest restaurants in the capital, The Lafayette.

My dad is Hank St. James. In this town, they call him "The Kingmaker." He's deep in the pocket of virtually every lobbying group and politician in town. He's the kind of man-in-the-shadows who can say, "Get me the president on the phone," and a secretary will actually call the sitting president. He often takes working lunches at this hotel with power-hungry senators and bored billionaires.

By extension, my mom sees herself as a modern-day Jackie Kennedy. She's tried to raise us girls to be just the same. Behind every powerful politician, there's a good woman in pearls ready to help him shine. She attends weekly afternoon tea here at The Hay-Adams with her society friends.

My phone buzzes in my hand. I glance down to see a new message from a number I don't have saved:

UNKNOWN: Did you get my contracts?
POPPY: Who is this?

I smile, watching the three little dots dance at the bottom of my screen. Yes, Lukas sent me a fresh batch of contracts on Sunday night. I have to hand it to him, he's getting more inventive. This time, he had a ménage à trois with Marie Antoinette and Miss Piggy—both of whom are also *way* out of his league.

Despite my better judgment, I save his number in my phone.

LUKAS: Are you asking me for nudes, Poppy? A bit forward don't you think?

I laugh, typing back a response.

POPPY: Is that the only way women can recognize you? Probably because there's not much happening in the face department, right?
LUKAS: Ouch. Your wounding words always cut the deepest.
POPPY: Walk it off, Lukas. And lose this number. I never gave it to you.

There's a bit of a delay before his answer buzzes in my hand.

LUKAS: Seriously? I could be having a PR crisis right now. I could be in jail, Poppy. Don't you want me to have a way to contact you if I land myself in jail in a foreign country?
POPPY: Foreign country? We flew from Philly to DC last night. You're still in the United States.
LUKAS: Yeah, but I'm Canadian. So, no matter where I get arrested, it will still be a foreign country to me.

Shaking my head, I type out my response.

POPPY: In that case, you have my email.
LUKAS: YOU NEVER ANSWER YOUR EMAIL!

I laugh, feeling a lightness in my chest that wasn't there a few moments ago.

LUKAS: For your information, I was texting to invite you out to a post-game dinner with the D-men. Very private. Very delicious. But now that you've just told me to lose your number, I guess you can lose my invite too. Tit for tat.

"Oh, no you don't," I mutter, tapping the call button and lifting the phone to my ear.

He picks up on the second ring. "Poppy St. James, are you calling to beg for your invitation back? I do love a little groveling."

"No, I'm not calling for an invitation. I'm calling to *cancel* your reservation."

"What?" His indignation drips hot and heavy though the phone. "You can't do that! We're allowed to go out if we want, Poppy. You can't just—"

"Now ask me *why*, Lukas," I say over him. "Ask me why I might have a problem with the bulk of my star players heading out to a *private* dinner tonight of all nights."

He's quiet for a moment.

"Fuck," he finally mutters.

"Yeah, fudge is right. I used a lot of favors to get that reservation at Club 7, and I *need* you there, Lukas. Consider this an official team event. There will be press outside when we arrive, and select fans have been granted VIP access. You don't have to stay forever, but *please*—I'm begging here, Lukas. Are you happy? I'm actually begging. Just stay for one hour."

"Fine!" he barks. "God. You know, usually I love the sound of a woman begging, but when you do it, I feel like my insides are being twisted into a knot."

I can barely contain my relief as my cab pulls up at The Hay-Adams. "Oh my goodness, really? You'll come out tonight?"

"I said it's fine. This restaurant has two Michelin stars and a three-month wait, but it's fine."

"Thank you, Lukas. I promise, I'll find a way to make this up to you. Hey, I can be your wingwoman tonight! Maybe we'll finally get you a real name to put on those contracts."

"No fucking thanks. I can wheel my own dates, Poppy."

I'm smiling wide now. "Hmm, would we call them dates?"

He sighs into the phone. "Fine. Hookups."

"Better."

"Hanging up now."

"Not if I hang up first," I chime, tapping the little red button to end the call.

The moment I do, a valet opens my door. "Good afternoon, ma'am. Welcome to The Hay-Adams."

I take a deep breath, slipping my phone inside my green Gucci Marmont mini. What's that expression? Out of the frying pan, into the fire.

"MY Poppy girl!" Mom stands from the table the moment she sees me enter the dining room. She holds her arms out wide, welcoming me into her loving embrace like I'm the prodigal daughter returned.

I step into her hug. "Hey, Mom."

"Why didn't you wear the Chanel?" she says in my ear. "You always look so pretty in Chanel."

I sigh, letting her go. I wore this Dolce & Gabbana floral print dress and sweater set because last time she complained I was wearing too many block colors. "It's good to see you," I say, forcing a smile.

She cups my face and pinches my cheek. "Oh, honey, you too."

Behind me, Dad stands waiting. "Don't I get a hug?" I turn, giving him a warmer hug. He melts into it like he might just be genuinely happy to see me. "Good to have you home, Princess."

"Thanks, Daddy."

"And look," Mom says. "Rowan and Deidre are here. And your sister even managed to get away from all those books to come join us."

I move around the table, giving quick hugs to my brother and his wife and my older sister, Ivy, before taking the empty seat between my parents. There's one extra seat between Ivy and Deidre. "Is Vi coming?"

My younger sister Violet currently works on the Hill. Daddy got her the position using his many connections.

Mom laughs. "Oh, no. She simply couldn't get away."

A few knowing smirks are passed around between the other three. Am I missing something?

Meanwhile, Daddy's oblivious. He refuses to wear cheaters, so he's got the menu pressed to his face like he's trying to decipher a magic eye image. "I hope you all came hungry."

"Starved," Deidre replies. "It's so sweet of you to treat us all, Annmarie."

"Nonsense. We're happy to do it. This is a day for celebrating," Mom assures her.

"What are we celebrating?" I ask as the waiter comes over with a round of mimosas for the table. He starts reading off the day's specials, but dad stops him with a wave of his hand. *Oh, here we go.* Classic Hank St. James, always needs to be in control of everything—even our food order.

"We'll have a round of the soup du jour to start," he says. "Then the poached pear salad and the seared bass. You can bring those out together, Ed."

I set my water down, smiling up at the waiter. "Actually, I'd like the chicken. And an order of the potatoes—"

"The bass is better," Dad says over me. "Get the bass."

"I don't want fish."

"She'll have the bass," he says, handing the waiter our menus. "Oh, and add in a couple orders of the crab cakes for the table. That's not fish," he teases.

Across from us, Ivy finishes her first mimosa and taps her glass for a refill. She's got the right idea. I pluck my champagne flute off the table and take a long sip. I'll likely pay for it tonight with a pounding headache.

Worth it.

Five minutes later, the first course of autumn squash soup is placed before us.

"So, Pops," my brother says. "How's your little communications gig going?"

I pause, spoon halfway to my lips. "Well, the 'gig' isn't so little. I'm the director of public relations for a major international sports team. It's actually a pretty demanding job."

He smirks, buttering his bread. "Huh, I assumed it was just a lot of party planning and fundraisers. Right, Pop?"

Ass. He knows exactly what I do, and he knows I'm darn good at it too. He even asked me for season tickets when I worked for the Capitals. He's just resentful because I did what he never could and walked away from our father.

His wife bats at his arm playfully. "Oh, don't tease her, Ro. It sounds fascinating, Poppy."

Next to me, Dad hums in agreement.

Wait—who is he agreeing with? Rowan or Deidre?

I pat my mouth with my napkin. "It's a little more than party planning. In fact—"

"Oh, Poppy, honey." Mom leans in, hand on my arm. "Did you hear about Ivy's good news?"

And, just like that, we're done talking about me.

I glance across the table. "Is Ivy who we're celebrating?"

Ivy is older than me by eight years, which means we've never really been close. She's a tenured professor over at Georgetown in the Art History department. With her stylish glasses and tweed blazer, she looks like she's ready to stand up and give us all a lecture on Picasso's Blue Period.

"Tell her, Ivy," Mom presses.

"I've accepted a one-year visiting lecturer position at the Sorbonne," Ivy declares.

"Hey, that's great, Ivy."

Mom sighs. "Poppy, your sister will be teaching at the famed Institute of Art and Archeology in Paris. Every day she'll be strolling through Luxembourg Gardens and touring museums along the Seine. Can you imagine?"

"It's *really* great," I correct, taking another sip of my mimosa.

"I don't think Pop is very impressed, Mom," Rowan teases. "Hey, don't they call Jacksonville the Paris of Florida?"

I hum my agreement. "Mhmm, just like they call *you* the funny one in the family."

He snorts.

"Deidre, honey. You're not drinking your mimosa," says Mom. "Do you want something else?"

My brother's wife smiles. "Oh, no, I'm fine."

"Really, you can order whatever you want. Spritzer? Bloody Mary?"

"I'm fine—"

"She's not drinking, Mom," my brother says over her. "Take the hint already."

I glance up to see the grin on his face. He eyes me across the table and winks. Everyone turns to stone momentarily as the news sinks in. Mom is the first to break. "Oh my—Hank," she shrieks. "Hank, she's—they're pregnant. Are you pregnant, Deidre?"

"The whole restaurant can hear you, Mom," Ivy warns, reaching over to steal Deidre's mimosa.

"*Yes*," says Deidre, placing her hands on her stomach. "We're expecting again."

"Oh, goodness," Mom cries, hurrying around the table to hug them both. "My third grandbaby! I thought you kids were going to let me go gray before I ever got to hold another baby."

Dad stands too, shaking Rowan's hand.

"You'll just have to wait until next spring," Deidre assures her.

"We've quite given up on Ivy," Mom goes on. "And we had hope for a minute there with Poppy, but we all saw how that turned out. Now it's all down to you and our sweet Violet."

Right, Ivy the academic spinster and Poppy the disappointment. I raise my mimosa in silent salute. Ivy just smirks.

At that moment, the waiter steps in and serves our entrées. I frown down at my portion of fish served on a dollop of creamed parsnips. The waiter places a last plate at the empty seat between Ivy and Deidre. "I thought you said Vi wasn't coming," I say, surreptitiously sliding the plate of crab cakes closer.

"She's not," replies Dad.

"Then why did they bring an extra plate of fish?"

The mood at the table shifts again. Rowan, Deidre, and Ivy are now all inordinately concerned with inspecting their seared bass.

I set down my fork. "Someone please just tell me what the rest of you already seem to know."

Mom leans a little closer. "Well, honey, Violet *really* wanted to be here to tell you her special news in person."

"What's her special news?"

"I think we'll just see if we can get her on the phone." She dials my sister and turns the phone on speaker, holding it up between us.

Violet finally answers on the fourth ring. "Hey, Momma! Y'all at lunch?"

"Yes, honey, we're all here!" Mom is speaking much louder than she needs to.

"Is Poppy there?"

"She's right here." Mom pats my arm. "She's waiting to hear your big, exciting news!"

"Hi, Poppy," my sister gushes. "I'm *so* sorry I'm missing lunch. Hey, maybe we can grab drinks later tonight. Will you still be in town or—"

"Your news, Vi," I say over her, not sure I can take much more of this suspense.

"Oh!" She laughs. "Yeah, well I really wanted to do this in person but . . . I'm engaged!"

I sink back in my chair.

"Isn't that wonderful?" says Mom. "A baby *and* an engagement all in one day! My heart is fit to burst."

"Wait—who's having a baby?" my sister says through the phone.

"Rowan and Deidre," Mom replies. "They just told us."

"Number three," Deidre chimes.

"No way! Oh, that's so amazing," Violet cries. "Give them a hug for me."

"We will, honey," Mom assures her. Then she looks sharply at me. "Poppy, don't you have anything to say to your sister?"

I sit forward, mind racing. "I . . . well, I guess I didn't even know you were seeing anyone, Vi."

The mood on the other side of the table gets, if possible, even more arctic. No one will look at me. Oh goodness, is she pregnant too? Out of wedlock? That would kill our mother.

"We've actually been dating for a while," says Violet. "We were just keeping it hush-hush because we didn't want to ruffle any feathers."

"You've both been very respectful, Vi," says Mom with a solemn nod. "And we're all so thrilled for you. Aren't we, Hank?"

"We're very pleased," Dad echoes, more concerned with finishing his salad.

"I'm sure you'll be pleased too," says Rowan, breaking the silence on that side of the table.

At this point, I feel like I'm about to pop an ulcer. "Violet, *who* are you marrying?"

"Now, don't get mad at me," she says through the phone. "You promise? You're the last one I'm telling because I don't want you to be mad at me. But just keep in mind that you had your chance once, and you blew it. This is *my* chance, and I'm not gonna blow it. Right, Mom?"

"You're a match made in heaven, Vi. Everybody says so," Mom says, positively beaming with pride.

Oh no, this is not happening . . .

"Ahh—here he is," Mom sings, turning in her chair to wave down someone at the door. "Vi, your beau has arrived!"

Heart in my throat, I slowly turn, already knowing exactly who I'll see behind me.

And there he is, striding into The Lafayette dining room like he owns it, waving at my mother and flashing her his million-dollar smile. Anderson Montgomery, heir to one of the largest architectural firms in the southern United States.

Anderson Montgomery, the man my mother handpicked for *me* to marry. Together, we were meant to forge a new political dynasty: an empire-building king and his dutiful, loving queen.

Anderson Montgomery, the man I left at the altar three years ago.

The man who is now engaged to my spoiled baby sister.

15
POPPY

*A*nderson strides up to our table looking like a million bucks, so confident knowing he's worth easily fifty times that. He wears his hair with that deep side part, casually flashing his grandfather's heirloom wristwatch as he waves.

Dad and Rowan push back their chairs and stand to shake his hand, welcoming him to our little family lunch. Mom stands too, wrapping her arms around him with the same warmth she just showed me.

From over her shoulder, he looks down, locking eyes with me at last. His piercing blue gaze roots me to my chair as the corner of his mouth tips. "Hey, Poppy. Good to see you again."

I shiver. I haven't heard that voice in three long years. It feels like my heart hasn't beat for almost a full minute. It sputters to life, and I exhale through parted lips. "Oh, this is *not* happening." I slap my napkin down on the table, rattling the silverware.

"Told you she'd take it poorly," Rowan says, scooting his chair back in.

"You all knew?" I search their faces, first Rowan, then Deidre, then Ivy. "You knew they were together this whole time?"

"Violet asked us not to tell you," Deidre explains, her worried eyes wide.

Furious, I push back from the table and stand.

"She didn't want to hurt you, Poppy," Deidre goes on, desperate to placate me. "She just wanted to give you time to grieve and move on. It didn't seem right to tell you."

I turn away from them to face my mom, who's still standing with Anderson. "How long?"

"Poppy, please don't make a scene," Mom says, glancing all around the dining room with a fake smile on her face.

"Sit down, and eat your fish," says Dad from behind me.

"How long?" I say again, looking up at Anderson.

"About two years," he replies.

My heart drops right through the floor. *Two years.* My family has been sneaking around and lying to me about this for *two* freaking years? My sister is too much of a social butterfly to keep something like this quiet by herself. How many people helped her? Who else smiled in my face and made me look like a fool?

Mom wraps a hand around my forearm and leans in, voice stern. "Poppy, you will sit down and hear Anderson out. It's not his fault you called things off—"

I wrench my arm away from her. "Not his fault?"

Her eyes flash with malice. "Sit down. *Now*."

"The fish is getting cold, Princess," says Dad.

I spin around. "Oh, Daddy, I fucking *hate* fish! I hate it, okay? So, you can take that plate of seared bass, and shove it up Rowan's ass!"

"Poppy," Mom cries, reaching out with both hands like I'm a wild horse loose in the dining room.

Dad's fork and knife clatter down to his plate as he glares up at me. Normally, that face would be enough to have me bursting into tears. But in this moment, I feel only rage.

"Poppy, sit down," he says.

I take a step back, looking around the table. "You all knew. You kept this from me, you lied to me, and then you manipulated me to get me here so you could spring this on me like—like *what*? God, this is like the world's worst intervention!"

"A little decorum right now would go a long way," Mom urges.

I glare at her. "And Anderson, Mom? Seriously? After everything I said?"

Now it's Anderson's turn to step in. He towers over me. "Go on, Poppy. What lies are you going to tell your family about me now?"

My hand drops limp to my side as I see the way they're all watching, waiting for me to respond. Do they really believe him over me? They must, with the way they all greeted him so warmly just now. Mom said they're all thrilled for this union.

A match made in heaven.

Those words make my stomach churn.

"I have to go."

"Oh, don't be silly. You haven't even touched your fish," says Mom, trying to lead me back over to the table. "Just sit down now. That's my sweet girl."

I go with her, but only so I can retrieve my clutch from the back of my chair. I pick it up by the delicate gold chain, slipping it on my shoulder.

"Poppy, don't you dare leave this dining room," Dad warns.

"I've gotta go," I say again, my voice eerily calm. My motions are robotic as I check my clutch for my phone, lipstick, and credit cards.

Mom steps in closer. "Poppy, if you leave—"

"You'll what?" I say, snapping my clutch shut. "Lie to me some more? Belittle me? *Disown* me?"

She crosses her arms. "Well, your Nana certainly didn't leave you that trust fund for you to go around acting like this, now did she?"

I glare at her. Our Nana was an heiress. She left each of us kids with a trust fund of ten million dollars. Once we turn thirty, we can start drawing on it. At five percent a year, that's five-hundred thousand dollars a year over twenty years. Ivy and Rowan are already drawing on theirs.

I've always been smart. I haven't been planning on that money as a need, but heavens what a blessing. In a few short years, I could have real options. I'll have a safety net, travel money, and guaranteed retirement. It's cruel to think my own mother would rip that away.

"You wouldn't dare touch Nana's money," I say at her.

"I am the guarantor of her estate—"

"She wanted me to have that money, Mom."

She smirks, knowing she has me. "Well, if you're going to be an embarrassment to the family, I think we'll have to rethink the terms, won't we?"

I search her face, heart sinking. "How can you be so cruel?"

She blinks twice. Then she changes her manipulation tactic as smoothly as an F1 driver changes gears. "You're being hysterical right now. This was clearly a lot for you to digest, so allowances will be made. Anderson warned us that your feelings for him might not be completely gone—"

"Ohmygod!" I throw up my hands and stalk away from the table.

"Poppy, come back," Mom cries.

"I've got this Mrs. S.," I hear Anderson say.

Oh great, the master manipulator is letting herself be manipulated!

My heels click as I march through the doors of the restaurant into the empty hotel lobby.

Anderson follows close behind me. "Poppy, wait—"

"Go away."

"Will you just slow down? Give me two minutes to explain."

"I'm not interested."

"You know, this is completely unfair, and I don't deserve it. *You* dumped *me*, Poppy. Remember?"

I stop, chest heaving as I try to breathe.

Anderson steps in behind me, and I can just barely smell his expensive cologne. It unlocks so many memories. "You left me the night before our wedding," he goes on. "I had to wake up and find the ring and that pathetic fucking note. You bailed, and I moved on. Now you're gonna crucify me for it?"

I spin around, my rage burning white-hot. "You moved on with my *sister*! Are you freaking kidding me, Anderson? There wasn't a single other woman in the whole wide world you could rebound with?"

He glares down at me, that sweep of dark hair framing his brow. "You don't think I tried? You think I wanted this?"

"Well, you can't have tried very hard now, can you? The population of metro DC alone is, like, what? Five million people? If we assume half of those are women, and even just a quarter of those women would be willing to consider marrying an egotistical, entitled *ass*, that still leaves over half a million women you could've dated before you crawled into bed with my sister!"

"Poppy—"

"Did you date half a million women in a year, Anderson?"

"No, but I—"

"Did you at least float them your nepo baby resumé that just says 'M&H Construction' at the top?"

"God, you are such a fucking *bitch*," he shouts. "No wonder you're still fucking single."

I can't hide my flinch as I try desperately to rebuild my walls of slipping sand. "Anderson, please, let's not do this here—"

He leans in, glaring at me. "I've waited three goddamn years to say this to you, Poppy: I thank my lucky stars every day that I was spared being yoked to you for the rest of my fucking life. I already wasted three good years on you. I'm not wasting anymore. You're insufferable and you're gonna die alone."

A moment of silence hangs heavy in the air between us. Slowly, I nod, blinking back my tears. It's true, we dated for three years. In that time, I gave him my heart and my body. I told him I loved him again and again. I told him until I started to believe it too. I tried so hard to be what he needed and what my family expected.

And they had such beautiful dreams for us. We attended every society function, blazing our trail straight to the peak of Olympus— state senate runs, then the governor's mansion, maybe even one day the White House itself. Anderson would be the star, and I would be the one who helped him shine.

St. James & Montgomery, the merger of the century.

That was my path . . . until I stood at my mirror the night before our wedding and took a long hard look at my reflection. I didn't even recognize the woman looking back at me. Who was Poppy? I didn't know anymore. I'd spent so much of my life following the rules and living up to other's expectations. I twisted myself inside out again and again. First for my family, then for him.

Anderson dismissed my dreams and belittled me in front of our friends, so I made my dreams smaller. He was unfaithful, and I looked the other way. He was controlling, and I corrected my behavior to better meet his exacting standards. All the while, our families looked on with pride. *A match made in heaven.* Mom used to say that about us too. I close my eyes tight, catching my tears before they fall, ashamed I can't hold them back.

Anderson heaves a tired sigh. "Why do we do this, Pop? Why do we make each other so crazy?"

"Because we're all wrong for each other, and always have been." I gaze up at him. "Just . . . tell me you love her. Tell me you're different with her. Tell me you're faithful. Tell me you listen to her. Tell me you care."

He rubs the back of his neck. "Poppy . . ."

"*Please*, Anderson."

His gaze heats as his frustration mounts again. "What the hell do you want me to say here? I mean, come on, Poppy. You know what this is. You know how this game is played. You used to play it better than anyone."

For the third time today, my heart drops. "You're just using her. You're using my little sister?"

He scoffs. "Of course I'm using her. I'm using her like she's using me—like *you* used me."

I shake my head again.

"Oh, don't act so holier than thou." He levels a finger in my face. "You used me for my name and my family and everything that came with it. You wanted to be queen of the fucking universe. Admit it."

"No. I didn't, Anderson, which is why I gave back the ring and left."

He sighs, dropping his hand to his side.

I look around at the opulence of this grand hotel lobby, steeped in so much history and significance, and I feel nothing but a deep, aching emptiness. For so long, I chased this. I chased belonging in a place like this, belonging to people like Anderson Montgomery, and for what?

"This life is done for me," I say. "I'm done, and now I'm leaving." I turn away, and Anderson grabs my hand.

"What now, Poppy? I marry into your family, and you'll just be a ghost? For the rest of our shared lives, you'll just be somebody that I used to know?"

I gently twist myself free of his grasp. "I gave my sister all the warnings I can give. If she's still willing to choose this life, then she deserves it . . . and you. Goodbye, Anderson."

Squaring his shoulders at me, he throws his last sharpened dagger. "If there's one thing we both know, it's that family always comes first for you, Poppy. I'll be seeing you again, most likely at the wedding. I'll be the one standing at the altar." He takes a step closer, lowering his face to mine. "And you'll be standing one step behind your little sister, holding her bouquet, watching as she claims the destiny that was always meant to be yours."

With a last devastating smirk, he turns on his heel and walks away, back toward the dining room. Back to my waiting family.

*S*omething's wrong with Poppy. She appeared during warmups and stood behind the glass in our VIP section, chatting with some industry reps, but her hand motions were too animated, and her smile didn't meet her eyes. I even made an ass of myself and did a few groin stretches on the ice right in front of her. Nothing. No eye-rolling. No pursed lips. She had *no* reaction to my assholery.

Yeah, something's definitely wrong.

But this isn't my business, right? We're not friends. At best, I'd say were hostile coworkers. I don't have to care about this. And I definitely don't have to investigate further. It's done. Out of sight, out of mind.

I rattle my gear down piece by piece in the dressing room, handing off the stuff that goes to the laundry to a waiting equipment manager. I strip off all my upper layers and drop my hockey pants, sitting on the bench with a tired sigh. Once my skates are off, I pop a couple pain relievers and lean back against my stall, eyes closed as I just take a second to catch my breath.

I mean, a friend would probably investigate, right? Even a teammate might show casual interest. But Poppy's not my teammate. She's my PR rep. She's a corporate suit—

God, why did I have to think about her in a suit? That high-waisted skirt and white blouse combo she's rocking tonight feels very "the headmistress will see you now."

No, I can't care about her suits or her moods. She's not my problem. I'm pushing her from my mind, starting now—

"Right, so I've made a reservation at Club 7 for 11 p.m.!"

Fucking hell.

My eyes flash open to see Poppy standing in the doorway. Balancing in those sky-high heels, she keeps a hand over her eyes, blocking her view of our various stages of undress. Her gloomy shadow, Wednesday, stands at her shoulder, eyes on her phone.

"The VIP area is all set up," Poppy goes on.

A couple of the guys groan.

"You only need to stay for an hour," she assures them. "First round of drinks is on the house. And don't forget to snap those pics!"

"You got it, Poppy," Langley calls after her retreating form.

Stupid fucking Boy Scout. I hate him.

I turn to Compton. "Hey, you're going tonight, right?"

"Hmm? Waszzit?" He only vaguely registers that I'm speaking. He's got his eyes locked on Doc Price standing over in the corner.

I wave a hand in front of his face. "Hello? Earth to Compton."

He blinks and leans away, slapping my hand down. "Don't be a dick."

"Don't be so obvious then."

"I'm not being obvious . . . am I?"

"Bud, the only person in this whole building who *doesn't* know you have the hots for Doc Price is the night janitor, but even she suspects something."

"Keep your fuckin' voice down," he says, elbowing me in the ribs.

"Jake, it's not a big deal," says Morrow from my other side.

Compton turns on me like I just slapped his dick. "Oh great. So he knows too?"

"We all know," says Morrow.

"Yeah, and in case you haven't noticed, she's totally into you too," I add with a grin.

He glances back her way with a dopey smile on his face. "Oh god, do you think so?"

Morrow and I both laugh. This asshole is too damn earnest.

"Just don't go fooling around until you clear it with HR," Morrow warns. "She's not a bunny, Jake. She's part of the team. You gotta respect that for all our sakes. We need her."

I go still, my smiling falling. She *is* part of the team. The medical staff are as essential to what we do here as the coaches and the equipment managers. We can't play without Doc Price there to catch us when we fall.

Poppy is part of the team too. She may move behind the scenes, but she's the one putting butts in seats so we can keep playing the game we all love so much.

Jake heads off toward the showers and I turn to Morrow. "Hey, have you talked to Poppy today?"

He glances to the open doorway where she just disappeared. "Nah, she showed up after I was already out on the ice for warmups."

"What's going on there?" I dare to ask. "Is this another Compton situation? Do I need to alert the night janitor?"

He ducks down and suddenly becomes very concerned with fiddling with his skate laces.

I lower my voice. "You can tell me, you know. If there's something between you—"

"There's nothing." He sits up, glancing around the room before he turns to me. "Poppy is cool. She's smart, and beautiful, and kind, and . . . we're friends, alright?"

A heavy weight sinks in my chest, even as I force a smile. "Yeah, and I'm Bruce Banner."

"We are, Nov. We . . ." He heaves a tired sigh. "She doesn't date hockey players, okay?"

My eyes narrow. "So, you asked."

"Let's just say she volunteered the information."

Sneaky fucker. What is he hiding? "She turned you down flat, eh?"

"She's focusing on her career, and I can respect that."

"Yeah, she turned you down flat," I tease, feeling a little lighter.

He punches my arm and stands. "I'm hitting the showers. You going to the club tonight?"

As he talks, I hear the click of heels out in the hall. Poppy walks past the open doorway, phone up to her ear, still working for us even though the game is done.

"Yeah," I say. "I'm going."

OH, I'm going straight to hell is where I'm going. That's where they send men who have depraved thoughts about their coworkers, right? Poppy St. James just stepped off the hotel elevator wearing a curve-hugging, electric-blue mini dress. Her blonde hair tumbles down her back in a mess of curls. She did something different with her makeup too. It's darker, edgier.

I'm just gonna say it inside my head: *She looks positively fuckable.* I've never said that about a PR director before. It's an odd sensation, but not wholly unpleasant.

She strides across the lobby like she owns it, walking in a matching pair of strappy blue heels. Doc Price walks at her side, looking just as gorgeous in a black jumpsuit with a plunging neckline. Behind me, a couple of the guys let off wolf whistles.

Compton is already on his feet, moving straight to Doc's side. I don't even realize that I'm standing too. I follow Compton, letting him step around me with Doc on his arm.

Poppy is looking at her phone, tapping away with both thumbs. "Okay," she calls to the lobby. "Ubers are a minute out!" With her head still down, she nearly walks right into me. "Oh! Sorry, honey, didn't see you." She finally registers that it's me and her lips part in surprise. She looks me up and down, those sky-blue eyes wide. "Whoa. Lukas, you look . . . *good.*"

Is this a trick? Why am I suddenly second-guessing everything about this outfit? It's just a white V-neck shirt and a pair of navy dress pants, but the shirt is tight, and I'm built like a house. I mean, I *know* I look good, but I still brush a self-conscious hand over my chest. "What's wrong with what I'm wearing?"

She huffs. "Nothing. That's why I used a superlative."

"Kind of a lukewarm one," I mutter. Her eyes flash with annoyance, and I breathe a little sigh of relief. Maybe she's fine.

"What do you want me to say? I usually only see you in a hockey uniform or workout wear. Forgive me, but tube socks and sandals don't really scream 'fashion icon.' Now, take the compliment, and take a hike. I'm not in the mood to spar with you tonight."

"Yo, Poppy," Sully calls. "Ubers are here!"

I offer my arm, mirroring Compton's smooth move. To my surprise, she only hesitates for a second before she places her hand on my arm and lets me lead her toward the doors.

"Okay," she calls out again. "Everyone pick a car. And remember, the press *will* be waiting when we arrive."

Three sleek SUVs idle by the valet attendant. I follow Compton and Doc to the first Uber, helping Poppy get in. Langers edges his way past Morrow to snag the front seat. Morrow drops back, giving me a nod before piling into the next Uber with Sanford and the forwards. Does he know something's up with Poppy too?

I step around to the other side and get in. Poppy and Doc are already mid-conversation, and Compton is just leaning back, eyeing Doc like he's gonna eat her. From the front seat, Langers calls out for any music requests. The car rolls forward, and I settle in, pretending I'm on my phone. Really, I'm watching Poppy.

Let's walk this back. I saw her at the hotel's buffet breakfast this morning and she seemed fine. Granted, it was from the other side of the room, but she was her normal, bubbly self. I don't think she drinks coffee in the morning. I only ever see her go for the water or juice. She likes grapefruit with cottage cheese and yogurt parfait, I know that too.

So, sometime between breakfast and our game, her day took a serious turn. She's from DC, right? Shit, maybe it's a family thing. Maybe I shouldn't pry. Family shit is definitely none of my business.

I don't have long to ponder because we pull up at the club in minutes. A scrum of press is waiting. The sidewalk to either side of the entrance is packed with people trying to get in.

"Okay, here we go," says Poppy. "Smiles everyone." I don't even get a word in before she's out the door. The music hits me, along with the flashing of the camera lenses, and I'm momentarily stunned.

Langley is already out too, one hand on Poppy's lower back as he waves and smiles. Oh, fuck that. I launch into action, exiting the car and stepping around to join them. I move through the crowd, catching up with Langers and Poppy. I step right in at his back and say in his ear, "Sully wants you for a forward line pic."

Gullible Langers just nods and drops back, leaving me with Poppy. I replace his hand with mine, steering her into the packed club. As we get our wristbands, I look around. This is a big club. There are some burlesque cage dancers, and a small stage up at the front for the DJ. I feel the beat kicking in my chest. Something about the vibrations soothes my tense mood, and I relax. Next to me, Poppy does the same. Her hips sway to the beat as she stays by my side, unbothered that my hand is still on her back.

I lean down, all but pressing my lips to her ear. "Do you want a drink?"

She turns her face, her lips brushing my jaw as she says, "The bartender should be ready for us. First round is comped. Let's go!" Then, surprising the shit out of me, she weaves her fingers in with mine, leading me over to the bar.

I follow close behind her, my eyes taking in her sway as she walks. That dress is doing sinful things to her ass. She's petite, so I just assumed she didn't have much happening in that department. Either way, her little blazers always tend to cover it. Now I can see *everything* and it's fucking perfect. There's definitely enough there to take a bite.

Okay, fuck me, what is happening?

I slip my hand from hers. Flirting is one thing. Flirting is harmless fun. But have I just spent the last fifteen minutes genuinely lusting after Poppy St. James? I mean, she's gorgeous, but she's a fucking pill. She's a PR princess. A ball-busting, no-fun Nancy, who lives to ruin my good time. She's got me terrified to even hook up with random strangers anymore because I don't want to have to fill out a form after. Lukas Novikov doesn't keep receipts. You can't be hurt by someone if you don't even remember that they happened.

As I'm thinking all of this, she leans over the bar, bracing herself on her elbows and popping that sweet little peach in the air. She says something to the bartender, an edgy chick with dyed pink hair and lots of face piercings. I can hear Poppy's high, pealing laugh from here. Palms flat on the bar, she glances over her shoulder, looking around. Spotting me, she smiles and waves me over.

I cross to her side, and she hands me a cocktail. She's got a matching one in her hand. "What's this?"

She takes a sip of hers with extra cherries floating in the ice. "It's called a Jax Ray. Tina made it." She flashes another smile at the bartender. "It's basically just a Jack & Coke. But fruitier. Try it!"

I take a sip of the cocktail and nearly gag on the sweetness. "Is that grenadine?"

"Mhmm. And a splash of bitters."

"So basically, it's an old fashioned ruined with Coke." I take another sip. "Jeezus, Pop. This thing is strong."

"And it's gooood," she hums.

"You better pace yourself. A girl your size could get drunk off the fumes."

"Don't patronize me, Lukas." She takes another sip. "Okay, so I promised you a good time tonight. Wingwoman Poppy is officially on duty." She gives me a cheeky little salute.

"Not necessary, Pop. But thanks for the offer."

"What, *no*," she cries, her eyes getting all wide and sad like a hurt squirrel. "Come on, I'm a great wingwoman. I don't want you thinking I'm some kind of HR stiff who can't appreciate the value of carnal connections."

"Carnal connections?" I repeat.

"Lustful liaisons? A passionate pounding?"

I snort into my cocktail. Fuck, why am I still drinking this?

"Sex, Lukas," she says louder. "I'm talking about you getting some good old-fashioned bodies pressing, hearts beating, physical intercourse."

"Jeezus."

"I wouldn't dare call it lovemaking," she adds with a wink. "I know that would send you running for the hills faster than me shouting 'who's available for a TikTok challenge'?"

Okay, and now I'm laughing. "I think I'll just keep passionately pounding drinks tonight. But not this," I add, taking a half-step away to set my cocktail down on a nearby table.

"Come on," she says again. "It's been what, two weeks since Little Lukas last saw any action? That can't be good for your health. It's certainly bad for the reputation."

I round on her. "Okay, first, he's not so little. Reach your hand down there and check if you don't believe me."

"Hard pass." She makes a show of stirring her cherries into her ice instead.

"And second, let's just turn this spotlight around, eh? How long has it been for *you*? Since you know so much about me, let's hear more about you, wingwoman."

She drains the rest of her cocktail and looks me dead in the eye. "Three years." Stepping around me, she discards her empty glass and takes mine.

Three years? Poppy hasn't had sex in *three* fucking years? Please god, tell me that doesn't include masturbation. I don't think I ever go longer than three days without jerking one out. And don't tell me a woman as hot as her hasn't had plenty of opportunities. She could have anyone in this club—guy or girl—with a curl of her finger. What the hell is she waiting for?

I'm about to ask just that, but we're interrupted by the arrival of the rest of the team. Things get crazy for a few minutes as all the Rays descend on the bar. We laugh it up about how disgusting our signature cocktail is before most of us switch to craft beers.

Poppy is standing between Morrow and Langers when she calls out, "Our VIP section is upstairs. Just flash them your wristbands. Have a great time!"

A few of the younger guys peel away, already eyeing dance partners. The rest of them make their way toward the stairs. Morrow leans down and says something in Poppy's ear that has her smiling and shaking her head. She points over her shoulder at the bartender as she talks, taking a seat on a vacant stool. He invited her upstairs and she said no. She wants to stay down here to chat with the bartender. They must know each other. Poppy *did* live here not that long ago . . .

Fuck, so did Morrow. Has he been here before? Have they been here together? Oh god. Now my mind is filling with images of them out on that dance floor, fucking with their clothes on, his hands in her hair. He leads her down the dark hallway to the bathroom. She pulls him into an empty stall, and he's inside her within a minute, pounding her into the wall—

Oh, goddamn it.

Now I'm getting hard—and pissed. I'm standing here alone like a total fucking asshole, beer in hand, picturing my PR manager fucking my teammate over a toilet.

No, she just said she hasn't had sex in three years. She also told Coley she doesn't date the players. Poppy St. James is a proper lady. She's not hooking up with hockey players in dirty bar bathrooms. I bet she only does missionary, and only if the sheets are Egyptian cotton. I bet she doesn't even take her bra off, too embarrassed to be seen fully naked. Who was the stiff who last got a taste? Probably a pastor's son . . . or an investment banker with a limp dick.

Now, I'm smiling again.

Morrow crosses over to me. "You comin' up?"

"She staying down here?"

He nods.

"Should someone stay with her?"

He glances over his shoulder. "Nah, Tina will keep an eye on her."

I take a sip of my beer. "They're friends?"

He looks at me, the obvious question in his eyes. "Are you?"

17
COLTON

ovy holds my gaze, and I can tell he's trying to decide what to say, a joke or the truth. I know the instant he lands on joke. He flashes me a grin that doesn't quite meet his eyes and laughs, wrapping an arm around my shoulders. "Nah, bud. The day Poppy and I become friends will be the day the Sabres finally win the Stanley Cup." He clinks our beer glasses together, taking a sip.

Seriously, what's his problem? Always deflection. Always guarding his true thoughts and feelings. He's a good enough guy, and a ton of fun to be around, but these iron walls and constant dodges make it hard for me to see him as anything other than a teammate.

"Come on. Let's go." He leads me away like I don't know exactly what he's doing. If he's not staying down here with Poppy, apparently neither am I.

When did this happen? I knew he liked to tease her, and he flirts with her all the time, but Novy flirts with everyone. He flirts with Sanford to get him to change his skate blades first. He flirts with the PTs to get more massages. Hell, he even flirts with the coffee cart guy for extra shots of espresso. The man could flirt paint off the wall.

That's all this is, harmless flirting . . . or so I thought. But when I turned around just now, and he saw me laughing with Poppy, there was a glint of fire in his eyes. He didn't like it.

Well, the feeling is mutual, asshole.

I shrug away from his touch and lead the way over toward the VIP stairs. We pass Compton dancing with Doc, and I can't help but flash Nov a smirk over my shoulder. He leans in against my back, shouting to be heard over the music. "I bet you a thousand dollars we'll find them together in a bathroom stall within the hour."

"No bet," I reply, showing the bouncer my wristband.

Novy shows his too, and we're waved through.

The stairs are quieter. Darker too, lined only with two strands of lights that glow at our ankles, illuminating each step.

"Come on," Novy says. "Why won't you bet me? I'm bored."

"Then go find someone to dance with. Better yet, go find someone to lure into a bathroom stall for yourself. You're so damn tense these days, it's giving *me* anxiety."

"Wait—are you volunteering, Coley?"

I roll my eyes, even if he can't see it. "In your dreams, Nov. I don't fuck desperate men."

"I said I'm bored, not desperate."

"Well, I don't fuck bored men either."

"Got it. So, the next time I find myself perfectly balanced on the scale between boredom and desperation, I'll tap your number, which I already have saved for emergencies—sexual and otherwise—and you and I can have the most moderately exciting sex of your life. Sound good?"

I stop at the top of the stairs. "You have me saved on your phone? What are we, then? Boyfriends?"

"No, but you're my emergency contact."

I raise a brow at him. "I'm your what?"

"My emergency contact. You know how Vicki made us fill out all those forms when we signed our contracts?"

"Yeah."

"Well, I needed to provide an emergency contact so . . ." He shows me his phone screen, tapping the "Emergency SOS" tab. Right there, saved as his primary emergency contact, I see my name and number. "Why do you look so weird?" He searches my face, lowering his phone. "Did I need to ask you first or something?"

"No." I take a sip of my beer. "I guess I just assumed you'd pick a family member. You know, someone who might actually *like* you and want to keep all your organs attached."

He laughs.

"'Cause if you leave the decision up to me, I'm donating everything," I warn him.

It's his turn to roll his eyes. "Hey, if we're to the point where they're even asking about organ donation, just unplug me, okay?"

"Nov—"

"I'm serious. I'm in great shape, no health conditions. Give it all away, even Little Lukas." He points down to his dick.

I turn away, heading over to the VIP area.

He follows right behind, still talking. "They're doing some amazing stuff with penis transplants these days. He's got some miles on him, sure, but he deserves to help make other people happy for as long as he can."

"Fucking Christ," I mutter. "This is why you need to pick someone else," I say over my shoulder. "I don't want to make medical decisions about Lukas *or* Little Lukas."

"I don't have anyone else."

I stop, waiting for the joke. But no, the silence stretching between us could fill an ocean, even in this noisy club. Slowly, I turn. "Nov—"

"But it's fine." He shrugs past me. "I'll change it if it's that big a deal—"

"No." I grab him by the shoulder. He's tense under my hand, but he doesn't pull away. "Keep me on the forms. I'll be your emergency contact." I let him go, and he doesn't turn around. He doesn't say another word. He just walks off, like we didn't just share our first real moment of true friendship in ten years.

"What were you assholes whispering about over there?" J-Lo says as we walk up to the VIP table.

Giving Novy's shoulder one more squeeze, I step around him and claim the empty spot by Sully. "Novy wants to donate his dick to science."

This gets the guys going, leading to a hilarious and morbid conversation about the ins and outs of penis transplants. All the while, I keep glancing across the table at Novy. I watch the casual, aloof way he interacts with the other guys. All his careful little walls are securely back in place.

18
POPPY

Alcohol hums through my body, loosening the tension in my muscles and making me feel all floaty. Club music thumps as colored lights flash pink, blue, and green. I lean over the bar, palms flat against the polished wood, and finish my story for Tina. I have to yell to be heard. "And then he told me he'll be seeing me at the wedding, holding my sister's bouquet, watching as all her—meaning my—dreams come true!"

Tina pauses in the pouring of a third glass of merlot. Her face is a mask of shock and horror. "Shut up. He did not."

"He did," I say, taking another sip of my third Jax Ray.

Tina sets the wine bottle down. "These people, man, I swear to fucking god. Well, you are *not* going to that wedding, Pop. Period."

I roll my eyes and finish my drink. Tina knows me, perhaps better than anyone. We grew up together. It's a charming, All-American story of the personal chef's troubled kid bonding with the lonely middle child of the millionaire political lobbyist. Christina and her mom lived in the apartment above our garage for eleven years.

Our lives were always destined for different paths, but we keep in touch as much as we're able. I was so glad I was able to get the Rays in here tonight. As part-owner of this club, she gets the good publicity and the packed club, and I get some wholesome press coverage, showing off the fun side of the team.

I'm extra glad she's here tonight after that lunch today. She knows *all* my family drama. She was even a witness to some of it—like the time my brother pushed Dick Cheney's grandson into a pool, and we all thought Mom was going to get in a slap fight with Lynne.

Tina delivers the merlots down to the end of the bar and comes back.

"How can I not go?" I shout, clutching my now-empty glass. "Tina, she's my sister."

She grabs a quartet of shot glasses and lines them up, pulling out a bottle of tequila. "Yeah, she's your spoiled little witch of a sister who slept with your ex for *two* fucking years and didn't tell you."

I sit up a little straighter on my stool, anger coursing through me, making my body feel like it's vibrating. "Yeah."

"Yeah," she echoes, filling the shot glasses.

"Heck yeah."

"*Fuck* yeah!"

"I'm not going," I declare.

"Good." She slides the shots over to the guy on my left, who passes them around to his friends, leaving her a generous tip.

"I'm serious, Tina. I'm not going to that wedding. Vi will just have to find someone else to hold her stupid bouquet!"

"Damn fuckin' straight." She hurries off to fill a few more drinks, leaving me with my glass of ice and cherries. I pop a few bar peanuts in my mouth, enjoying the salty taste. When she returns, she picks up a rag and begins wiping down some glasses. "So, what was it like to see him again?"

"Tina!" The hipster-looking bartender waves her down. "I could use a little help over here!"

"Give me a minute," she shouts back.

Meanwhile, I'm shaking my head, popping a few more peanuts in my mouth. "Tina, it was awful. I heard his voice, and I got literal chills." I run my hands down my forearms, remembering the feeling. "He touched me, and it took everything in me not to flinch."

"I can imagine," she says, her pierced lips pursed.

"I can't believe I ever actually considered marrying him."

"You dodged a bullet, Pop."

I look down at the little silver dish of peanuts. "He told me I was gonna die alone."

Tina slaps down her bar towel. "No."

"Yeah, apparently I'm insufferable, and I'll be alone forever."

Her dark eyes flash with rage. I know if Anderson were here, she'd knee him where it hurts. "That's ridiculous. Poppy, you're a catch. Any man would be lucky to have you."

I just shrug, popping a few more peanuts in my mouth. "Well..."

Tina leans over the bar. "I mean, you've moved on, right? Oh please, Poppy, tell me you've moved on—"

"Ohmygod," I cry, leaning away. "Of course I have. Are you serious? Tina, I moved on from that relationship while I was still freaking in it. I was like a zombie by the end. Seriously, I think 'Thriller' was playing when I escaped the house and climbed in that getaway car—thanks for the keys, by the way."

"You're welcome." But she's not distracted by my humor. "And you know that's not what I meant—"

"Tina!"

She growls and spins around. "Darius, if you can't man the bar without me for *two* fucking minutes, I'm gonna fire you and hire a waiter robot, and I'm gonna dress it just like you in those stupid fucking glasses, and I'll call it Better Darius!"

He grumbles but turns away.

I sink back on my stool, sliding my empty glass over to her. "I can't keep distracting you while you're working."

She grabs my wrist. "No, Pop, hold on a sec." I lift my face to look at her. Always a mistake. Christina Renoux can read me like a book. "You've moved on, right? By that, I mean you've been with other people since Anderson...right?"

Oh, goodness. Am I about to cry in this club? I shake my head, pulling away from her.

She sighs, letting me go. "Oh, Poppy. *Why?*"

I blink back my tears. "I guess he just made me feel so awful by the end, like it was a chore to love me, and like I wasn't any good at it anyway." I tuck my hair back behind my ears. "I've just been, you know, handling it myself."

"Oh, Pop."

I look up to see tears rimming Tina's eyes and a surge of frustration races through me. "Don't you 'Oh, Pop' me!"

"For three years, Poppy? You've been feeling this way, and you didn't tell me?"

I slap both my hands down on the bar and lean forward. "*Yes*, okay? I'm sad and lonely and damaged, and I'm running out of new ways to give myself pleasure. Happy, Miss Nosey?"

"I swear, I am gonna *kill* that guy."

"Don't bother. He's marrying my sister. Vi will be torture enough for three lifetimes."

We both smile, then we're laughing. It takes us a minute to recover.

"Alright, new game plan." She grabs a shot glass and fills it with tequila. "You're gonna take this, you're gonna down it, and then you're gonna go out there and find something pretty to dance up on." She points over my shoulder out to the dance floor.

"Tina, no—"

"Yes. Time to clean off those cobwebs, girl."

"Tina!"

"You are gonna have sex with a man. Tonight."

I look down at the little shot of tequila, heart racing. "Tina, you're crazy. This is a work function. My players are here. I can't do this now—"

"Do you wanna die alone?"

I go still as stone. Oh, she did not just go there. Slowly, I lift my gaze to glare at her.

She raises a pierced brow. "Too soon?"

I just shake my head. "You're a real bitch, you know that?"

She grins. It flexes her cheek piercings, making the little diamonds glint in the strobe lights. "Just think of me as your shoulder devil. Now, drink the shot, Poppy."

Something new is buzzing in my chest. Oh god, is this excitement? Am I really doing this? No, this is crazy. I am *not* having sex with a stranger tonight. Period.

Oh, yes, I am.

Tina's right. It's time to move on for real. I'm done living in the past. I'm done hiding and being scared. "Fuck it." I snatch up the shot glass.

"Down the hatch!"

I shoot the tequila, slapping the glass down with a gasp. "Ooh, it burns!" I slide the glass over to her. "I'm doing this."

"You're doing *him*." She points over my shoulder.

I turn around to see a pretty blond guy chatting nearby with a few friends. He has a millennial feel, like he may be corporate level, but at a firm where they believe in "open walls" and "fostering a hive mind." He's not really my type, but does that matter for a one-night stand? He's pretty and he's here and, if he's willing, for one night only I'm saying yes.

Screw it. I am saying *hell* yes.

I swivel back around, nervous excitement surging through me. Grinning at Tina, I slide my clutch across the bar. "Hold my purse," I shout.

"Go get 'em, tiger!"

Hopping off the barstool, I quickly adjust my dress, checking to make sure everything is where it should be. God, I haven't approached a man like this since college. Do I even remember what to do? I flick my hair behind me and roll my shoulders. No thinking. No second-guessing. Tonight, I'm just doing.

I turn for one last nod of approval from Tina. "Right, I'm gonna go get my body slammed."

She cackles as I turn away. "That's my girl. Go knock his socks off. And don't forget to use a condom!"

19
LUKAS

Oh shit. We should bring Doc Price out to the club with us every night. I'm sitting in our VIP booth next to Morrow, watching as Doc climbs into Sanford's lap and starts telling off some blonde bunny-looking chick. This girl is not having it, and the mood is fucking tense.

"What am I watching?" Morrow asks.

On his other side, Sully says, "That's Sanford's ex. She's a total ring-chaser. Dumped Sanny the minute he got his injury. I think she's up here trolling."

"Batten down those hatches, boys," J-Lo warns from across the table.

We all shift uncomfortably. Karlsson goes so far as to cover his drink with his hand, holding it in close to his chest.

Listen, we don't mind the bunnies. In fact, they can be a ton of fun. Some of my best times after a game have been spent laughing and joking around with the puck bunnies. But there are puck bunnies looking for a good time, and then there are the predator bunnies. It happens across all professional sports. We're talking full Monty Python, go-for-the-jugular type bunnies.

Yeah, I said it. Women can prey on men too—especially some of these teenage rookies cashing big fat NHL checks who still don't know their asses from their elbows. These bunnies will pick your pocket for your room key. They'll follow you to the bathroom. They'll find your favorite coffee shop and camp out. It's exceptionally rare, but it happens.

And it only needs to happen once for a player to learn to take it seriously. I've had a couple stalkers in the past. I even had a woman corner me at my car, trying to get inside. One more reason I prefer no names, no numbers, and no repeats. You can't get attached with a one-and-done. Call me crass, but safety first.

The blonde has her arms crossed, glaring down at Rachel still sitting in Sanny's lap. "Whose girlfriend is she really, Cay?" she says loud enough for us all to hear. "Compton's? Novy's? It's sweet of them to loan her out to you so you don't have to look pathetic in front of your ex. But really, honey, I got that message a long time ago!"

Rachel is still as stone in Sanny's lap. Oh shit, it's like the moment of calm before a lightning strike. I can just barely see the side of her face as she smiles. "What was your name again? Apple?"

"Aspen—"

"Yeah, whatever," Doc says with a wave of her hand. "Look, sweetheart, this is just sad, okay? We all know you didn't wiggle your way past the bouncer by offering him a handy just to come up here and reconnect with your old college flame."

The blonde makes a face like she just smelled dog shit. "Bitch, you don't know me!"

A few of the guys gasp.

"I *do* know you, Asphalt."

Fuck, Doc is funny . . . and brutal.

"I've known girls like you all my life," she goes on. "Caleb broke his knee, and you took him out with the trash. Well, lucky for him, hitting your curb is the best thing that could have ever happened to him. Because now he has *me*."

Doc leans forward in Sanny's lap, going in for the kill. "You had your chance with a great guy, and you blew it, Asteroid. He's gone, and he's not coming back. You're so far off his radar now, you may as well be lost in space. And don't for one second think he's going to waste his breath introducing you to any of the great guys sitting behind us either!"

"A-fucking-men," says J-Lo, clinking his beer glass against Karlsson's.

"Should we break this up?" Morrow says at my shoulder.

"*Shh*. It's just getting good." I wave him back, glancing over at the other guys. "Did any of you have to offer a handy to get up here?"

"No, but I'll *give* a handy to the first guy who gets me out of here," Sully mutters. "I'm beat, and this is just getting sad."

"Control your girl, Cay," the blonde shouts, her voice cracking. "She needs a muzzle and a leash!"

Fuck, the balls on Sanford must be ginormous right now. He keeps rubbing up on Doc, his hands roaming as he says, "That's not a bad idea. You'd look good with a leash, Hurricane. Something with spikes."

"Oh, daddy, don't tease me," Doc replies with a sultry smile.

"God, you're both psychos," the blonde shrieks. At long last, she stomps away, muttering curses as she goes.

"Bye, Avocado!" Rachel calls after her.

Our table explodes with laughter.

"Later, Alligator," J-Lo shouts.

"Bye, Asteroid!" calls Sully.

"No bunnies allowed!"

Morrow taps my shoulder, and I slide out of the booth, still laughing.

Langers comes rushing over with Doc's drink. "Hoooly shit. That was the single hottest thing I've ever seen. That was like an *Animal Planet* shark attack, but with heels and hair flipping."

"You destroyed her," I tease.

"We bow to the master," says Morrow, making a fake bow.

I elbow him, sloshing his beer. "It's *mistress*, jackass."

He elbows me back, and I bump into Sully.

"Hey, make me spill the rest of this beer, and you're paying for my Uber," he warns.

"You heading out?"

"Yeah, I'm wiped." He drains his glass and sets it down on the table. "We've got an early call time for the busses."

I turn to Morrow. "You heading out too?"

He glances over toward the railing and back to me. He doesn't need to say a word. He wants to go find Poppy first. But he also didn't miss my not-so-subtle diversion tactic from earlier. He doesn't want me getting cozy with her any more than I want her cozy with him.

Shit, how the hell did we get here?

"Hey," Rachel calls over to me, wedged between Sanford and a very territorial looking Compton. "Keep an eye on Poppy! Switch her to Shirley Temples at midnight!"

Fuck, is Poppy still down there draining cocktails like they're water? Screw our alpha-posturing bullshit, Morrow and I need to go check on her, maybe get a cheeseburger in her. I look down over the railing, searching for her at the bar.

"Bust a move, Sanford," Morrow calls from my side, waving the trio off.

"Yeah, have fun, Snuffy," says Langley.

A few of the other guys laugh, watching as Doc Price hurries away with Compton, dragging Sanford behind her.

"Okay, a thousand bucks says we find all *three* of them in a closet within the hour," I say at Morrow.

"No bet."

I squeeze his shoulder. "Come on, let's go get Poppy—"

Just then, one of the young rookies comes rushing up from behind us and tugs on Sully's arm. "Hey, man. I think you need to come. DJ is lookin' pretty bad."

All three of us snap to attention. "DJ" is David Perry, one of our forwards.

"Where is he?" says Morrow.

"Out back in the alley, spilling his guts," Westie replies. He looks glassy-eyed. Shit, he's drunk as a skunk too. "I, uhh . . . he drank a lot of those Jax Rays things. Like, a lot."

Sully groans, dragging a tired hand over his face. Heavy is the chest that wears the captain's *C*. "I'm getting too fucking old for this shit." He turns to Morrow. "Will you help me?"

Morrow gives me a long-suffering look before he nods. He's too damn nice to turn down a direct ask from our captain. "Sure, yeah." He puts his hand on my shoulder and leans in. "Pay my tab?"

"It's done," I say with a solemn nod. "I have all the tabs," I assure Sully too. "Just go get that asshole before any of the press get pictures of him sitting in his own vomit."

I follow them toward the back corner where a set of utility stairs must lead down to the alley. I nearly run into Morrow as he grabs the railing, glaring down at the dance floor. "Holy shit."

I peer down too, my gaze locking instantly on Poppy. The lights flash purple and blue, reflecting off the angles of her face and golden hair. The music thumps a heavy beat as she sways, her hips pressed up tight against the crotch of some blond dick in khakis. He's got his hands all over her. She leans her head back against his shoulder, her eyes shut tight, lips parted, like she's a few seconds away from coming.

My heart stops. "What the actual fucking fuck?"

Next to me, Morrow grips tight to the rail. "Will you please go take care of her?"

My eyes narrow on the dead man grinding behind her. "I got it."

He grabs my arm as I turn away. "Hey—and by 'take care of her,' I mean get her safely back to the hotel."

"What, did you think I was gonna dump her in the fucking Potomac? I said I'll take care of her, Cole." I give him a shove. "You go deal with your drunk teammate. I'll deal with mine."

With one last look, he storms off, following the urgent calls of Sully and West. They disappear into the utility stairwell, and I take off for the main stairs, ready to track down my PR director.

20
POPPY

The feeling out on this dance floor is carnal. I'm letting the music and the mood move me. My limbs all feel loose, and my body is heating up. I sway and bounce to the beat, tossing my head back, running my fingers through my hair.

Behind me, Kyle the investment banker dances like a frat boy. He's not clumsy, but he's not skilled either. But he's sweet and friendly and he smells really good. That's about all I can ask for in a one-night stand, right?

He cradles my hips with his hands, rocking to the beat with me. His thumbs brush little circles on my hip bones as his fingers inch perilously close to my bikini line. A little more to the left, and this man will be cupping my pussy over my dress.

I want this, right? What did Tina say? I am exorcising this freaking demon.

His hand inches closer and I gasp, spinning around to face him. I'm more comfortable with the idea of his hands on my ass than my pussy. Bending at the knees a bit, he brushes my hair back and says in my ear, "Want to get out of here?"

Oh, god . . .

I have to leave with him! To have sex with this man, I have to get in a car and go to some other location. Why does the very idea make me want to run to the nearest wall and pull the fire alarm? There is no way I'm leaving here with a stranger. No sex is worth that anxiety. I don't care how good it is.

I guess we could have sex here . . . maybe in the bathroom? *Ugh*, no. That's not happening either. Poppy St. James does not have hookup sex in dirty bar bathrooms. But if we're not having sex in the bathroom, and I'm not leaving here with him to have sex anywhere else, that doesn't really leave us a lot of options.

Kyle tips my face up. "We could go to my place. I rent a little studio over by H Street."

Sure, except the "H" now stands for "How 'bout not, and say we did?"

Poor Kyle. It's not his fault I can't even do a one-night stand right. I'm all twisted up in my head, thinking through every scenario. I haven't showered since last night, and I've been running around all day. With everything I had to drink tonight, I don't feel particularly sexy at the moment anyway. In fact, I'm feeling kind of bloaty and—

"Poppy."

A large hand clasps down on my shoulder, pulling me backward. I spin around, following the colorful spray of tattoos up the forearm to see Lukas standing there looking murderous. The music changes and the lights switch to red and orange, the colors dancing like flames on his face. I swear, he looks like a sexy devil glaring down at me.

My heart beats with instant relief. "Lukas—"

"Let's go," he says, extracting me from Kyle's embrace.

But Kyle doesn't let go. "Hey, pal. Take your hands off her. Poppy and I were just about to leave."

On instinct, I grab a handful of Lukas's shirt. He glances down, a question in his eyes. I answer with a pleading look of my own. His jaw tightens as he wraps his tattooed arm around my shoulders. He raises his free hand toward Kyle, pointing a finger in the air. "First, I am not your pal. Second"—he flicks up another finger—"Poppy isn't going anywhere with you, now or ever. You had a nice dance, and now it's time for you to go."

Kyle huffs, alcohol and embarrassment fueling him as he glances around. "I'm sorry, is she your girl or something? Because I've been rubbing my dick up on her for the last twenty minutes, and you've been nowhere to be seen, asshole—"

"Lukas, *no*." I press my hands against his chest and push him back. I think he was just about to punch this investment banker in the face.

Lukas keeps his arm around me, even as he tries to step in on Kyle. "Say that again to my fuckin' face, you khaki-wearing, limp dick motherfucker!"

"Do *not* touch him." I push on his hard chest again. "Lukas, let's go."

"Keep your girl on a tighter leash next time," Kyle shouts. His friends have sensed the disturbance and they're edging closer, hackles raised in alarm.

Oh, this cannot happen. My hot-headed hockey player is not getting in a fight over me in the middle of this club. "Lukas, *please*," I beg again, pressing my whole body against him. If he's going to fight Kyle, he'll have to physically remove me first to do it.

Lukas glances down at me again, his hand bracing my hip. There's a fire in his eyes like I've never seen before, and it's not just this sultry light show. He looks like he's ready to peel his skin off and morph into a dragon. It's hot and scary and my brain feels like jelly as I take any opening I can find. I reach up, cupping his face with both hands. "Lukas, honey, *look* at me," I all but shout. "Look only at me. He doesn't matter, okay? He's gone. He's leaving."

His hand tightens on my hip, fingers splayed wide as he pulls me closer. My hips press in against his thigh. I'm practically straddling his leg and—

Oh my—is he hard right now?

My heart races faster. Something about all this is turning him on. I know it can't be me. I drive him crazy. Every other word out of his mouth seems to be a teasing joke or an expletive. And most of the time the only physical response I can elicit from him is a long-suffering eye roll or an annoyed huff.

But I'm pressed up against him now, his arm around me like he's Tarzan and I'm Jane, and he is definitely feeling some kind of way about it. I lower a hand back to his chest, pressing my palm over his heart. Oh god, it's racing too. A muscle in his jaw is ticking. He's like a bomb ready to explode.

I brush my thumb over the stubble on his cheek, right where I know a dimple hides. "Lukas, take me back. I want to go back to the hotel now. Please."

Behind us, Kyle's friends are pulling him away. The tension dissolves, and dancers start to press back in around us. Lukas keeps his hands on me, his body stiff as he peers over my head, eyes narrowed.

"Let's go," I say again.

"Not yet. That douche and his friends are leaving. I'm not taking you outside until I know they're gone."

"Well, we can't just stand here." I glance around, noting the way people are still watching us. "Lukas, *please*." I brush my hands down his arms, following the corded muscle until I reach his hands on my hips. I turn around in his hold so we're back to front. Lacing our fingers together, I step forward, pulling him behind me.

He lets himself be led, his fingers wrapping possessively around mine as he stays in step with me. I head over to the far end of the bar, finding a solitary open stool. Lukas helps me onto it, his front pressed against my back as he braces the bar with his hands to either side of me. Angry, possessive Lukas was really working for me, but it was all a show to get Kyle to go away. "You can drop the act now," I call over my shoulder. "I'm in no danger from Lord Khaki Pants."

"They haven't left," he replies. "They're down at the other end of the bar paying their tab."

I lean forward and peer down the length of the bar. Kyle is standing at the end between two of his banker friends. He's giving me a heated look, one part angry, two parts yearning. He raises a brow, gesturing with a nod toward the door as if to say, "Still wanna meet me outside?"

Behind me, Lukas literally growls like an angry bear. He saw it too. Dead Kyle dares to toss me a wink.

"Oh, for Pete's sake." Swiveling around on my stool, I grab Lukas by the shirt and pull him closer, my mouth near his ear. "Do me a favor and pretend we're kissing or something. This guy is just not getting the memo."

Lukas pulls away, searching my eyes for a split second before he cups my face and kisses the heck out of me. His mouth presses to mine, and I feel the warmth of his tongue. I taste the hoppy notes of beer on his lips. He unleashes himself, pressing me back against the bar, his fingers tangling in my hair.

I fight to hold back a moan as my knees part, giving him room to step in closer. I'm still just holding to the front of his shirt, helpless to do anything else as he kisses me. His fingers dig in at my nape, giving my hair a little tug that has me letting off a soft moan.

Just as soon as it starts, he's cursing against my lips and pulling back, leaving me swaying on the stool.

"Well, that was pornographic."

I glance over my shoulder to see Tina standing there, her pierced dimples on display as she grins at me. Untangling myself from Lukas, I swivel back around. "Is he gone?"

"Who? Dancer Boy?" She rolls her eyes. "Yeah, he and his friends just left. Gave me a shitty tip too." She turns her attention to Lukas. "Hi there." She leans across the bar, offering her hand. "Tina Renoux, Poppy's best friend and shoulder devil."

He laughs. "Shoulder devil, huh? I'm Lukas Novikov, Poppy's regular devil." He leans over me, his chest pressing against my back, and they shake hands in a swirl of colorfully tattooed forearms. His are all in the Neo-traditional style, clearly planned out to cover and flow. Tina's arm is a hot mess of styles, evidence of her long hours spent in a tattoo shop letting various friends and lovers practice on her blank canvas.

"So, are you the new candidate?" she says, flashing me a wink.

"Candidate?"

"No," I shout over him, patting his arm—which is still around me, by the way. "Nope. Tina, he's my, well, Lukas is my . . . player." What am I supposed to call the man who just had me seeing stars with his tongue in my mouth? My work associate?

"Hey, you're a Ray," she says with an appreciative nod. "Forward or D-man? You're too cocky to be a goalie. All the goalies I've known are total adorable weirdos."

Lukas laughs again. I feel it against my back because that's how dang close he's standing to me. "I'm a defenseman. Best damn defenseman in the League."

"Well, that tracks." She flashes me another excited grin.

I give her a look like I'm gonna murder her and her cockatiel, Sammy. She totally ignores it. "We actually just came by to grab my purse," I shout. "We're going back to our hotel." The span of two seconds pass as Tina turns away to get my clutch before I'm all but throwing myself over the bar to add, "To sleep—and *not* together!"

Tina comes back with my clutch, still grinning like a little pink-haired witch.

"We're going back to the hotel together because we're both staying there," I explain. "But he has a room, and I have a room, and we'll each be going to those separate rooms to sleep."

"Yeah, I think she's got it, Pop," Lukas teases. "I bet your friend knows how grocery stores work too."

"Actually, I do," Tina says.

Aaaand now they're both conspiring against me. Time to go before they make up a secret handshake. I slip off my stool. "Well, this has been fun. Let's do it again never, okay?"

She cackles, offering my clutch. I reach to take it, but she holds on, giving it a pull until I'm practically folded over the bar. "He's perfect," she whisper-shouts. "Have a great night. I slipped a mint and two condoms into your purse."

"I hate you," I hiss.

"Go get some." She blows me an air kiss and lets go of the clutch, sauntering off to help more customers.

I right myself, cheeks burning, and turn to face Lukas. "Should we maybe find some of the others? Save money on an Uber?"

"I'm an NHL superstar, remember? I can afford an Uber." Slipping his arm around my waist, he leads me toward the front door. "The others will all find their way back when they're ready."

I know he's right. I just don't know if I'm strong enough to ride in a cab with him alone. Not when I have the taste of his kiss on my lips. This has been a topsy-turvy kind of day, and all my careful shields are down right now. I can't even blame the alcohol. That's been wearing off for hours. No, I think I'm just too tired and emotionally spent to keep holding them up.

I want someone to see me. Not the Poppy I carefully curate all the time. Not the clothes and the accent and the curls. Not the business savvy and the constant, clever strategizing. I want to feel like someone could see *me*. Just Poppy.

More than that, I want them to *want* me.

And I'm tired of feeling so alone. Is Anderson right? Am I truly so insufferable, destined to be alone forever?

Lukas leads me out of Club 7, his phone in his hand as he orders the Uber. "Two minutes out," he says, his arm still casually around my waist. As soon as the little blue sedan arrives, he's opening the door, letting me slide in the back seat. I scoot all the way over, and he gets in. The driver pulls us into traffic. "Electric Feel" by MGMT plays softly on the stereo.

"Mmm, I love this song," I murmur, resting my head on the cool window glass. The quiet of the car after the noise of the club is almost disorienting.

"Your friend seems cool," Lukas offers after a minute of silence.

I smile. "Yeah, she's great."

"How do you know each other?"

"Her mom was my family's private chef for eleven years. They lived over the garage."

"Jesus. Silver spoon much?"

"Oh, please, darling." I channel my mother's haughtiest voice. "Silver was reserved for public use and that unmannerly Bush boy. The family always ate with 24-karat gold."

He chuckles.

I glance across the dark car, my mood sobering. "It's true. My family is rich. I don't apologize for who I am or where I come from. It's my story, just like your story belongs to you."

He holds my gaze, searching my face. "Fair enough."

I turn to look back out the window.

"What did she mean by 'the candidate'?"

I go still, hand clutching my little purse. "Nothing."

"Poppy . . ."

"Hmm?"

His gaze is molten, the caramel flashing gold with each streetlamp we drive under. "Why were you wasting your time dancing with that asshole?"

I look pointedly away. "Kyle was being a perfect gentleman until you showed up. And I'm allowed to dance with whoever I want, Lukas. It's a free country."

"Of course his name is Kyle. And what was going to happen between you and Limp Dick Kyle if I hadn't walked up when I did?"

"Nothing."

"Really? Because *he* seemed to think he was taking you home tonight. Is that because he was your chosen candidate?"

"Lukas—"

"Your candidate for what, Poppy?"

Pulse racing, anger rising, I turn to face him again. "Do I really have to explain it? You of all people should know how a one-night stand works."

He's still as stone as he glares at me across the car. "You were gonna fuck that guy?"

I look quickly away. "No."

"You're saying if I hadn't walked up exactly when I did, you were gonna let that whiny little wannabe golf pro take you to his home and fuck you on his Tommy Bahama bedspread?"

"No," I say again. "I wasn't going to go through with it, okay? I mean, I *was* for like a minute—but I couldn't. I just . . ." I drag both my hands through my hair. "God, I chickened out, okay? But you already know all this. You read the room the moment you walked up, so why are you pushing me right now? Just ask what you really want to ask."

"Why?"

"Because I want to know," I cry. "I want you to be real with me for *two* freaking minutes. Is that too much to ask? Drop the bravado, drop the bullshit, and just be a person with me, Lukas. Why are you pushing me on this?"

He just shakes his head. "No, why were you going to have sex with him tonight? That's the question I really want to ask."

I'm not going to hide from this man. What would be the point? He has the uncanny ability to see through me anyway. I look back out the window, watching the city flash past. "Because I'm tired," I admit. "I'm tired of holding it all together on my own. I guess I just wanted to feel something other than hurt and alone tonight, even if it only lasted for a moment."

Silence hangs in the air between us.

"I was jealous," he says, breaking the tension with the swing of a hammer.

Suddenly, I feel like I can't breathe. I don't dare look at him. "What?"

"I knew what you wanted from him. I saw it from the balcony. I saw your face, all lit up by the strobes. You looked like a fallen fucking angel, and I knew what you were chasing . . . and I was jealous. I almost tripped down the stairs trying to get to you."

"Why were you jealous?"

"Because take however tired and lonely you feel and multiply it by about twenty-seven years. Add in a dash of abandonment issues and a sprinkling of abuse, and you'll have some idea of what it feels like to go through your entire life wanting things you can't have."

Tears sting the corners of my eyes as I search his face. He's only showing me the profile. Any more might be too revealing for him. But his words are revealing enough.

"I wasn't jealous just in that moment," he goes on. "Jealous is my natural state of being. It comes from having to fight for every single thing you earn, watching while the rest of the world is casually handed things." He turns, looking me dead in the eye. "That shitty asshole didn't do a goddamn thing to earn you. He didn't put in the work. He didn't have your trust. Hell, you were inching the fuck away from him half the time. But he was going to know what it feels like to be inside you? I couldn't let that happen."

"Shouldn't it be my choice who I sleep with? Not yours?"

"Yeah, well, I'm an imperfect fucking person. But you already knew that."

From the front seat, the driver awkwardly clears his throat. "Uhh, guys. We're here."

I sigh, leaning against the door as we pull up at the valet parking stand of our hotel. As soon as the car stops, I get out. I feel like I can't breathe. This day was already a disaster. Now this night is shredding me at the seams. Lukas is shredding me. What the heck is he even saying? He wants me? All this time, he's wanted me? He just knows he can't have me.

I'm sure there are reasons why that's true. Good reasons. But for the life of me, in this moment, I can't remember a single one.

He follows silently behind me into the hotel lobby. The concierge greets us. Otherwise the lobby is empty. It's late. I don't see any other Rays, and I'm definitely looking. My heels click as I make my way over to the elevator bank. Lukas follows.

I take a deep breath, readying myself as much for a ride in an elevator as sharing it with this man who keeps hogging all my air with a look and a touch. I press the silver "up" button and the mirrored doors open. The back of the elevator is mirrored too, and I get a full look at Lukas and I together as we step in.

Sweet heavens, he's so handsome. I mean, I always knew he was, in a rough-around-the-edges sort of way. But now the lumps and scars tell the story of his life—his injuries, his fight to earn his way to the top of his sport. He works so hard. And, like me, he's tired. And he's alone too. We're alone because it's easier. It stops us from getting let down, getting hurt.

We turn as one, away from our reflections. "I'm on five," I say, pressing the button.

"Six," he says from behind me.

I press the number six and the car rattles upwards, the wall panel beeping with each floor we pass. So long as we're moving, I'm fine. It's when elevators stop that the panic sets in. I watch the numbers glow and change as every fiber of me feels pulled to the man standing behind me.

We pass the fourth floor, and the words come tumbling out of my mouth. "Lukas, you can have me."

11
POPPY

"What did you just say?"

Behind me, I can feel the tension rolling off Lukas in waves. I don't dare turn around. "You think you can't have me, and I'm saying that you can. I mean, if you—only if you want to," I finish, tucking my hair behind my ear.

The elevator stops at floor five and the doors whoosh open.

Lukas shakes his head. I see the reflection of it in the steel wall panel. "Just get out, Poppy. You're still drunk. Go sleep it off."

I spin around, eyes wide. "I'm totally not. Look!" I stand on one leg, wobbling a bit as I tap my nose with my left finger, then my right. "That's just the heels," I say defensively, lowering my foot to the floor.

He grins, crossing his arms as he leans against the elevator wall.

"Hey, *you* try to flamingo in heels."

"Try it in skates, and I'll try it in heels."

The doors shut behind me. "Oh, *shoot*."

If he's really going to turn me down right now, I need to be able to make a quick exit. I slam my thumb on the "door open" button and step out. Holding the door with my hand, I give this one last try. "Okay, look, I'm tipsy, but I'm not drunk. I'm tired and lonely and sad and yeah, let's face it, I'm pretty much a hot mess. But I'm also horny, and for one night only I am saying yes. So, if you want the universe to hand you something without you having to fight for it for once, then here I am. Now, are you in or out?"

He searches my face, those caramel eyes unraveling me. Then the corner of his mouth twitches with a smirk. "Show me the flamingo again."

"Goodnight, Lukas." I let the door go, spinning away. "Hope the elevator doesn't crash," I call over my shoulder.

He laughs, following me out. "Poppy, wait." He wraps his hand around my wrist.

I try to tug free. "Let me go."

He weaves his fingers in with mine, holding on as he follows me down the long, narrow hallway. "Pop—"

"I've had enough emotional battering for one day, and I really can't bear to be teased by you right now. So, *please*, just go back to the elevator—"

"I never said no."

I glance over my shoulder. He's still holding my hand, his grip steady, calm as a rock. I search his face, taking comfort in the familiar gold flecks in his pretty caramel eyes. "Then what *are* you saying?"

Lukas sighs, glancing around. "I'm saying, if we do this, we both know it will be a terrible mistake."

"Huge," I whisper, heart in my throat.

His hand brushes along my shoulder and down my arm, raising gooseflesh as he goes. "I mean, it's me." His hand starts trailing back up, and I think I'm going to melt into the floor. "And it's you . . ."

I lean into him, my free hand resting on his hip. "I'm well aware that you're an obnoxious, egotistical ass."

He cups my cheek, his fingers smoothing my hair back as he wraps his hand around to hold my nape. These points of connection feel magnetic—his hand in mine, my fingers brushing the curve of his hip. Neither of us can pull away.

"And you're a ball-busting harpy witch," he assures me. "But you're also so gorgeous you knock the air out of my chest when you walk in the fucking room."

I tip my head back. "And you make my tongue feel like it's too big for my mouth."

"And that's—" He blinks, pulling away slighting. "Wait, is that a good thing?"

"Apparently." I slip my hand under the hem of his shirt, my fingers brushing the bare skin of his side.

He jolts. In a blink, he's cursing and backing away from me, nearly hitting his hip on the little decorative side table holding a tacky gold lamp. "Fuck, we need ground rules." He drags both hands through his hair, which just puts his tatted biceps on display, flexing those chest muscles in his too-tight shirt. "Come on, you're the rule-maker here. Tell me what I can do. Better yet, tell me what I *can't* do before I lose my fucking mind."

"One night only," I say.

"Obviously."

"And no one can know."

"Duh. Do you have any idea what this would do to my reputation if it got out? No good-time bunny would ever look at me twice again."

"Why?"

"Uhh, *hello*." He waves a frantic hand at me from head to toe. "Look at you."

I brush a self-conscious hand down the front of my dress. "What's wrong with me?"

"You're a total boyfriend girl. The bunnies will all think I've moved on. They'll think I'm suddenly looking for commitment. The news will spread that Lukas Novikov is finally ready for the house and the kids and the dog. That cannot happen. Do you understand?"

"No one will know," I say again. "One night only. *Please*, Lukas. I just want to feel something. Please, can you help me with that . . . as a friend?"

He sighs, looking me up and down one more time. "Fine. On one condition."

Hope blooms in my chest. Oh god, is this really happening? Are we doing this? "What?" I ask, trying not to sound too eager.

Those caramel eyes flash with hunger as he takes a step away from the wall. "Kiss me again."

My heart stops. "What?"

"Show me what it feels like when you're not pretending for the sake of some handsy douche. Kiss me because you actually want to, because you wanna kiss *me*." Lukas stands there, holding his vulnerability in his hands, asking me not to break it. Just like me, he wants to be wanted. He wants to feel seen for exactly who he is.

Oh, we are so doing this.

I cross to his side, my clutch dropping to the floor as I wrap both my hands around his neck and pull him down to me. Then I kiss him because I want to. His mouth slants over mine, and his hands are on me, first bracing possessively at my back, then sliding down to my hips.

He groans, his tongue dancing with mine. Then he spins us around, pressing me up against the wall. "Can I touch you?"

"Yes," I pant. "Please god, *yes*—"

"Where?"

"Anywhere. Everywhere. Please, just don't stop."

With a feral sound, he wraps both hands around me, cupping my ass. I love the strength of his touch. He lifts me off the floor, pressing me against the wall with his hips. My little blue dress bunches at my waist as my legs wrap around him. I graze my nails over his shoulders and kiss his neck.

"Oh, fuck." He braces me with one hand as the other dives into my hair.

"Do I pass the test?" I say in his ear. "Can you feel how much I want you? If not, there are other places you can check besides my mouth."

"Such a goddamn fucking tease," he growls, sucking on my neck. The sensation lights me up inside, turning my core from flickering flames into molten lava. "If you're about to tell me you keep busting balls even when a guy is balls deep, we're gonna have to find something to do with this smart mouth."

I laugh, wiggling my hips until I find what I want. "Oh *god*." His hard dick presses against my pussy, and I'm flying. "Please. Please, *please*, don't make me wait."

"Fuck," he says again, one hand roughly cupping my chin. "Say you want this." I move my hips against him, and he presses me harder against the wall. "*Say* it."

"I want this."

"Say it again."

I tip my head back. "I want you, Lukas. Now, stop second-guessing and stick your pretty dick in me."

His hand slips down between us and he cups me hard, practically pinning me to the wall by my pussy. "Listen to me, you spoiled fucking princess. I am going to fuck you in this tight little cunt until you scream." He rubs his hand up and down, stimulating my clit until I'm moaning. "You've gone three years without sex, right?"

My heart races as I nod.

He kisses me again, hard and fast. "Good. From this moment

forward, I can guarantee you won't go three fucking minutes without thinking about how hard I made you come. This can be for one night only, and no one ever has to know . . . but *you'll* know. Won't you, Princess?"

I nod again. "Yes."

"Tomorrow, we'll go back to trading chirps and annoying the shit out of each other, but you'll bother me knowing *exactly* what my dick can do to you." He shifts his hold on me, his fingers brushing my inner thigh. "You'll know how it feels when I come inside you, and you'll know *I* know how this sweet pussy feels squeezing my cock as you shatter."

"Lukas, please," I say on a whimper, my entire body coiled tight, ready to burst.

"Tell me one more time. You want this, Princess?"

My hands tighten on his shoulders, my nails pinching in. "Call me 'Princess' again, and I'll knee you in the balls."

He grins, dropping me to the floor. "Where's your room?"

"507."

He ducks down and picks up my discarded clutch. I weave my fingers in with his and lead him down the hall. We stop in front of the door, and I drop his hand to rifle in my clutch for the room key. He presses in at my back, hands on my hips, kissing my neck. "Was that asshole hard while he was dancing with you?" he asks in my ear.

"I hardly noticed," I reply, distractedly flicking through my thin stack of cards again.

He flips my hair off my other shoulder and kisses his way up to the spot behind my ear, his tongue teasing. When he starts to suck, I sink against him with a little moan. All the while, his hands stroke up and down my sides, his fingers brushing the underside of my breasts then dancing away.

"You're gonna make me drop this clutch, and then we'll have to start this all over."

He hums a laugh, pressing in with his hips as he finally cups my breasts.

"Oh, god." I tip my head back as he massages me. I feel the rumble of pleasure in his chest as my nipples peak under his palms.

"Did you let him touch you here?"

"No," I whisper.

He drops a hand down, cupping my pussy again. "Did he touch you here?"

"No—*ah*—" I stumble forward, catching myself with one hand on the door, palm pressed flat. He slips his hand up under my dress, and now he's grazing a finger over my pussy lips. There's another hum of approval when he feels how damp my panties are.

"Were you wet for him too, Poppy? Or is this all for me?"

I flash him a smile over my shoulder, pressing back against him with my hips. "Wouldn't you like to know—" I gasp as he digs his fingers into my hair. He speaks right in my ear, his voice hoarse as he holds me possessively by my pussy.

"One thing to know about me is I don't fucking share, Poppy. Did I not just tell you I'm a jealous person? I don't care if there's been other men. Fuck a thousand other men. But when I ask you if there are others, you will tell me no. Understand?"

I nod, wholly turned on by this possessive side of him. It feels good to feel this wanted, this desired. And Lukas would never hurt me. I know if I said "stop" right now, he would back away and bid me a goodnight. I move my hips against him, ready to soothe his worry. "Put your fingers in me," I whisper, still braced against the door. "Do it, Lukas. Feel how wet I am for you. Only you."

He shifts my panties aside, letting his finger glide between my wet pussy lips. I whimper, moving my hips with the motion of his hand. "So wet," he praises me. Then he sinks his finger in deep, dropping his other hand to brace at my hip. Head tipped back, I ride his hand. "Such a good fucking girl. You're so ready for my dick, aren't you?"

"Please," I say again. "Please, I want it so bad."

"Yeah, you fucking do. But first, I'm gonna lay you out on that bed and bury my face in this needy little cunt. You don't come on my dick until you've come in my mouth. Understood?"

Okay, I need this door open. *Now.*

I push off the door, digging in my clutch again, looking in earnest for the key. All the while, Lukas teases me, his hip grinding as he pumps his finger inside me. I bite my bottom lip to keep from moaning again.

"Open the door," he says in my ear.

"I'm trying to find the dang key," I say on a frustrated huff.

"That purse is the size of a deck of cards. How hard can it be?"

My shoulders stiffen. He's right. "It's not in here."

Behind me, he goes still, slipping his finger out of me. "What?"

My panic sets in as I check for a fourth time. "It's not in here, Lukas. The key is—oh god, did I lose it? Did I forget to even put it in before I left?" He steps back and I drag a frustrated hand through my hair, checking everywhere on the floor. "I'm gonna have to go down to the front desk and get a new one. They'll see we're still together. Oh god, this is so embarrassing. Why do I always do stuff like this?"

Snatching my hand, he leads me down the hall. "Come on."

"What are you doing?" I pull on his hand. "Wait, the elevator is the other way—*Lukas.*"

He shoulders open the door marked "Ice Room" and pulls me inside. The auto lights blink on, the fluorescent bulbs flickering as the industrial-sized ice machine crackles and hums.

"What do you think you're doing?" I cry. "Lukas, I am *not* having sex with you up against an ice machine!"

He laughs, spinning me around and walking me back until I'm up against the side of the machine. His lips descend once more to kiss my neck as his hands roam.

I'm stiff as a board, pushing uselessly against his shoulders. "Absolutely not. Lukas, anyone could come in here. Hell will freeze over first—*ahh*—"

He presses two thick fingers back inside me with a satisfied hum, watching as I melt, my body turning to jelly. "There it is," he teases. "Is this your goddamn 'off' switch? When that brain won't stop whirring, and the mouth won't stop talking, I'll know to do this." He wiggles his fingers and I cling to his arms with both hands. I couldn't even tell you where I dropped my clutch now.

"Don't stop," I beg, my head tipped back against the machine. "Please, don't stop."

"Can I take a look at these perky breasts, Pop? I'd like to have one in my mouth when you come all over my hand."

I nod, eyes shut tight, lost to the sensations coiling deep in my belly.

He peels the strap of my dress down, stretching the fabric until my breast is exposed. My nipple tightens into a little bud at the feel of the exposed air. "So fucking pretty." He brushes over it with his thumb.

The sensation jolts through me, zapping me right in the clit. Feeling bold, I squeeze my pussy tight around his fingers.

"Fuck," he groans. "Do that again."

"Take your shirt off, and I will."

He kisses my lips, a single hard press, and then he's pulling back, leaving me reeling. He strips off his shirt, dropping it to the floor, and I get the first real effect of a shirtless Lukas Novikov. This man is a work of art, and I'm not just talking about the tattoos. They paint their way up his arms on both sides, ending in swirls of patterns and colors over his shoulders. He has a few more tattoos dotting his sides and ribs. One sits low on his left hip, a red heart outline with black letters inside spelling FREE.

Aside from the tattoos, the man is in peak physical condition, with hard pecs and washboard abs. A sharp "V" lines either hip, disappearing into his navy dress pants. "Like what you see?" He teases me with a flex of his pecs.

"You're beautiful," I admit.

He steps in, cupping my face with both hands. His caramel eyes feast on me, darting to take in all my features. He looks like he's trying to memorize them, every line, every freckle. "So are you," he says, voice low.

I brush my hands up his naked sides, smoothing them over his hairless chest. "Do you wax?"

He grins. "Of course. This body is my temple. I take care of it in all ways." He leans in. "And from what I just felt between your legs, you do too."

I nod, biting my bottom lip.

"Mind if I see for myself?"

I swallow my gasp. "What? Right here?"

He kisses down my neck to my breast, humming against my skin. "Right here, Poppy. We are not leaving this room until I've fucked all this worry right out of you." Then he closes his mouth around my nipple, sucking it hard.

I swallow my cry, both hands digging into his hair. My dress fights to slip back up over my boob. With a frustrated growl, Lukas forces my hands down. Then he reaches out with both hands and jerks my dress off my shoulders, exposing my whole chest. I free my arms from the straps and wrap them back around his neck as he descends, sucking both breasts and playing with my nipples until I'm rocking against his thigh whispering, "Please, please . . ."

"Do you wanna come, Poppy?" He kisses his way up my chest to speak against my ear. "Does my good girl want to show me how well you can finish on my fingers?"

I nod, clinging to his heated skin. He drops his hands to the bottom of my dress, and I do a little shimmy as he pulls it up, exposing my pink thong. Now I'm wearing my dress like a thick scrunchie belt. Lukas doesn't seem to care one bit. He slips my thong down my legs until it snakes around my ankles. Then he's dropping down to one knee with a needy groan, both his hands wrapping around to cup my bare ass.

I wobble in my heels, hands on his shoulders as he presses his face to my pussy and breathes in deep. He's scenting me like a wildcat, and it's so hot I may combust right here and now. "Lukas, please," I beg again.

He laughs as he kisses across the tops of my thighs. "Spread these legs a bit for me."

I do my best in my heels to comply. He parts my lips with two fingers and flicks his tongue against my clit. "Oh god." My knees are already trembling, and he's barely even begun. He kisses my smooth pussy lips, parting them wider with his fingers as he probes lower with his tongue.

I practically climb onto his shoulder as I lift a leg off the floor. He helps support me with his free hand before his eager tongue is burying itself deep inside me. He groans, flicking, sucking, and teasing. I sway on one leg, pussy clenching. He replaces his tongue with his fingers, and then his mouth is back on my clit.

"*Oh!*" I throw my head back so hard it bangs against the ice machine. Behind me, the machine hums and cracks, releasing a fresh collection of ice. He keeps working me over, spinning me tighter with every taste and touch. "Lukas," I whimper. "I think I'm gonna—"

I'm like a lightbulb left on too long, my essence heating from the inside out until it feels like even my skin is on fire. He adds a third finger. The feeling of fullness in my pussy is the match, and his velvet tongue on my clit is the strike pad. Hands buried in his hair, I tip my head back and ignite.

He lets me ride his face through my orgasm, still teasing me with that devilishly talented tongue until I'm all but squirming to get off his face. "Oh my god," I cry, limbs shaking as I hold to the side of the ice machine for support.

Lukas stands. The caramel in his eyes are now thin rims swallowed by black. He gazes down at me like he wants to eat *all* of me. "How was that?" he asks, his lips and chin wet with my release.

I'm shaking like a leaf as I reach for him. "So good," I say on a broken sigh. "Lukas, that felt so, so good. Thank you." My sensitive nipples send little aftershocks of pleasure to my core as he presses himself against me.

"We're not finished," he warns, brushing his fingers through my hair. "Are we finished?"

I let out a breath, relaxing in his arms. My endorphins are pulsing, and my mind feels like a furry box of rattling marbles. "No," I whisper, letting my head drop weakly forward to pepper kisses across his chest.

"What do you want, Poppy?" His hand is still buried in my hair, fingers massaging the nape of my neck. God, it feels so good.

"I want more," I say, flicking his nipple with my tongue.

He grunts, tipping my head back. "You better get more specific real quick, or I'll paddle this canoe right over Kink Falls. You wanna crawl to me and call me 'master'?"

I shake my head, still feeling breathless.

"Good, because there's no room for that in here. And, either way, I'd prefer you to be wearing my collar when that happens. Now, tell me what you *do* want."

Blinking up at him, my orgasm fog lifting, I drop my hand between us and smooth it over the hard length in his pants.

"Is that what you want, Poppy?"

I nod, looking up at him with what I hope is an expression of raw, aching need.

But he's not going to make anything easy. He smiles down at me. "Use your words, beautiful. Say what you want. Be specific."

"I want you to fuck me," I whisper. "I want you to press me up against this ice machine and bury your cock in me. Please."

His gaze hardens as he fists my hair tighter. "Open my pants and take out my dick."

With trembling fingers, I lower my hands to his brown leather belt and work it open. Then I'm unzipping his pants and reaching my hand inside. I palm him over his boxer briefs, taking in the full outline of his cock. It twitches against my hand, a spot of wetness soaking through his briefs at the tip.

"Does that size work for you?" he says in my ear. "You want all those inches buried deep? Wanna ride this while I press you up against the goddamn ice machine?"

I nod, brushing my thumb over his tip. "Yes."

"Then take it out."

I tug down on his pants and briefs, not stopping until his cock pops out, fully erect, the tip glistening. I wrap a hand around it, stroking the silky length from root to tip. He groans, both hands on my shoulders. I swirl my thumb around his tip again, spreading his slick precum around his head.

I look up at him through my lashes, daring to let my walls drop with the rest of my inhibitions. "Please, take control. I don't want to think, and I don't want to make any more choices. Please, Lukas. I only want to feel."

He nods and brushes his lips against mine. "Get the condom out of your bag."

I duck down, searching the floor for my discarded clutch. I find it open in the corner, phone and lipstick scattered on the floor. I pull out one of the condoms and stand, holding it out to him. Lukas wraps his hand around my wrist and reels me in, giving me another open-mouthed kiss. He lets me go, and I place my hands on his naked shoulders as he opens the foil wrapper and slips the condom on down his hard length.

"Turn around."

I blink up at him, eyes wide. "What?"

Oh god, does he think he's going to put that monster in my *other* hole? Anderson was always asking me to do anal, but I was just too anxious to ever want to give it a try. If Lukas thinks that's what we're about to do . . .

I lean away, shaking my head. "No, I don't—can we just do it the other way?"

Lukas stares down at me, one hand slowly pumping his dick. "What, face to face?" He shrugs. "Sure, we can do that. I just thought you'd have a bit more control of how much of me you take if you're on your feet too but—"

"No, I mean about the other—" God, why do I feel so embarrassed right now? "I mean I only want *that* going in my vagina," I say, pointing down at his condom-wrapped dick.

He blinks twice. Then the asshole starts laughing. Okay, now I'm not embarrassed, I'm *angry*. This jerk is not going to laugh at me when I'm standing here, naked and vulnerable, wearing my dress like a belt scrunchie. "Lukas, if you don't stop laughing at me *right now*—"

He's still fisting his dick as he cuts me off with a stern look. "Did you really think I was about to shove this in your ass with absolutely zero prep and no prior fucking consent?"

Now it's my turn to blink up at him. "Well, I . . ."

He shakes his head, reaching for me with his free hand. "God, you drive me fucking crazy," he says against my lips, kissing me senseless. Too soon, he's pulling away. "Yes, Poppy, my penis will only be going in your vagina tonight. Would you like me to stimulate your clitoris with my phalanges again?"

"Don't be a jerk."

"Hey, you're the one who started getting all medical with talk of your vagina."

"I'm about to stimulate your scrotum with my fist," I mutter, digging my hands into his tawny hair and giving it a tug.

He grunts. "God, I *love* it when you talk dirty." He nips at my breast, flicking my peaked nipple with his tongue.

"Lukas, you have five seconds to put your dick in me, or I'm gonna walk naked down this hallway and knock on the first door I see and—*ahh*—"

I squeal as he lifts me clear off the ground, slamming my back against the ice machine. All my air leaves my chest with an unfeminine "ooof" as he wraps his hands around my thighs and spreads me open. He's all power as he holds me up like I weigh nothing, the tip of his dick prodding at my entrance. "Look at me," he commands.

My heart is racing, and my core is already spiraling tight as I look up, searching his face.

"You're gonna know this is me. I'm not just any dick for you, Poppy. That's all you wanted, right? Any dick will do, so long as you get to feel something?"

He notches his tip at my entrance, pressing in, and I hold tighter to his shoulders. "Lukas—*ah*—"

"That's right," he coaxes, his breath stuttering as he slides me down his length, filling me. "Keep saying my name."

I tense as I feel overfull, my fingers digging into his shoulders. The fullness is verging on pain.

"Relax, baby," he soothes. "Look at me—hey—Poppy, look at me, pretty girl."

I blink my eyes open, panting through parted lips as I look in his eyes again. There's a softness there, even as I feel him against me, his every muscle coiled tight.

"I've got you," he says. "I won't hurt you. Breathe out with me. Deep exhale and relax."

I do as he says, letting out a yoga breath as I sink against him. My body slides a few more inches down as I settle against his hips, his whole dick buried inside me.

"Such a good fucking girl," he praises. "Look at you, taking my cock like a fucking champ. Your cunt is so tight. You fit me like a glove, baby." His words wash over me, soothing me as he begins to move. He rocks against me, keeping his length buried. "That good?"

"Mhmm." I close my eyes, tipping my head back as I sink into the feeling of him filling me inside and out. The clean, citrus scent of his sporty cologne clouds my senses, while the heat of his skin burns into me at every point where we're touching.

"Open your eyes," he urges. "Be here with me."

I open my eyes, tears filling them. "Go faster."

He shakes his head. "I'm not rushing this. I get one night to call you mine, Poppy. You are gonna ride this dick until it rewrites your goddamn DNA." He doesn't thrust faster, but he ruts deeper, his hips driving up and in.

I hold onto his shoulders, opening myself to every sensation. My pussy tightens, and he finally ups the pace. "Yes," he pants, driving harder. "There it is, baby. Give me one more like this. Come, Poppy. Squeeze me. *Yes*—"

I cry out, head tipped back as I come. All the muscles in my core contract, and I ride wave after wave of pulsing orgasm. Lukas keeps his tempo steady, riding it out with me on a long groan. Then he presses a few kisses to my mouth and chin. "Let me finish you. Let's see fucking stars."

I nod, unable to form words.

He eases out of me and lowers me to the floor. I ungracefully un-pretzel myself, my legs like jelly as I stand in my stupid heels. "Turn around. I promise my penis will only go in your vagina," he teases, kissing the tip of my nose.

I teeter on my heels, turning around to face the ice machine.

"Hands flat. Widen your stance a bit." Lukas helps get me into po-sition, putting light pressure on my back to bend me over. "Just like that. Such a good girl. So good at taking direction."

I glare at him over my shoulder, and he laughs, smacking my butt. I gasp, hands flexing against the machine. Then Lukas is behind me, bending at the knees and sinking himself back inside me. I swallow a moan as he pulls back on my hips while he pushes forward, burying himself to the hilt. "There it is," he groans. "So fucking good. So deep and tight. You ready?"

I nod, still unable to speak.

Behind me, Lukas unleashes himself. With one hand on my hip and the other buried in my hair, he slams his hips into me. My lips part on a silent scream and I arch my back. My body lights up like a Christmas tree as he owns me from the inside out.

I only realize my cries aren't so silent when Lukas folds himself over my back, wrapping a hand around my mouth. "Shh. You gotta be quiet, baby. These sounds are only for me. How else will we both lie about this later and say it never happened?"

I moan into his hand, feeling whoever I was before I stumbled into this ice room burn down to ash and embers. That Poppy is gone.

Lukas is right. I'm going to be leaving this room as someone different, someone stronger.

I rock into his thrusts, and that drives him wild. He ruts harder, snaking a hand between my legs to massage my clit. "Come again," he commands. "One more. Give me everything this time. We don't stop until you fucking shatter."

He wants everything? He can have it. Lukas Novikov can take literally any piece of me. Closing my eyes tight, I focus on that ball of fire burning in my core, willing it to burn brighter. My body shakes, and his hand holds back my scream as we both climax. He folds over my back, digging his teeth in at my shoulder as he swallows his own shout of ecstasy. That little bite of pain is the only thing keeping me tethered to reality, centering me as I slowly float back down to earth.

"You're not alone, Pop," he says in my ear. Then he kisses the mark he left on my shoulder.

It should be a sweet moment. It *is* sweet. Lukas is here with me. His warmth surrounds me. His cool, comforting scent mixes with mine, with our sweat, our primal essence. There's something sacred about it. I feel so full of him, so blissfully at peace.

But then he's pulling out of me.

Then he's stepping away, searching for his discarded clothes.

And now I'm left with my hands pressed against the side of this ice machine, my body trembling, feeling somehow emptier and lonelier than I ever was before.

22
LUKAS

I wake up in a dark hotel room and I know without checking that it's ten minutes to six. I know because that's my fun little party trick. My body always jolts awake about ten minutes before my alarm is set to go off. I've been this way since I was a kid. It doesn't matter that I experience constant time changes, or how much I've had to drink the night before. My body just *knows*.

And there's never any going back to sleep once I'm awake.

I lie on this queen-sized bed, one arm tucked behind my head, staring up at the ceiling. Under the window, the AC unit hums, working overtime to blast cold air. I run hot, so I like the room frigid when I sleep. We're talking industrial meat locker.

Even now, I'm only under the sheet, and only to my waist, but I still feel overheated. I don't kick it off. I don't even dare turn my head. I don't want to move because I know what I'll see when I do.

Poppy St. James is asleep in my bed.

A thoroughly fucked Poppy St. James, wearing only my goddamn shirt.

After the ice machine, the combination of alcohol burn-off and multiple orgasms led to an unexpected sub drop that had Poppy feeling pretty loopy. I saw the signs immediately, the disorientation, the fatigue, the shaking. She needed some serious aftercare. I brought her up to my room, cleaned her up, and put her to bed—which led to us cuddling like a pair of teenagers—which led to me getting hard because, hello, Poppy St. James was naked in my bed.

When she felt it, she stretched behind herself, reaching for her little purse on the bedside table. She took out the second condom, sheathed me with her own goddamn hand, then tossed her leg over my hip and slid me in. We slow-fucked until we came together, me groaning her name into a fistful of her hair. She fell asleep curled against my chest with my dick still inside her.

It was . . .

I sigh, dragging a tired hand over my face.

She's lying next to me now, body bent like the letter "V," with her tight little ass pressed against my hip. I don't want to wake her, but I have to. She has to get out of here, and quick. All the guys will be waking up for our 7 a.m. flight back to Jacksonville. Once they start wandering the halls, there'll be no sneaking her out. She only had two rules: one night only, and no one else can know. That's the only reason I got to fuck her last night, because she trusts that I can hold to those two simple requests. Who would I be if I let her down now?

Bracing myself, I roll to my side, taking in the view of her asleep in my bed. The only light comes from behind the half-closed bathroom door, but it's enough. The white comforter is double-folded and piled on top of her, covering her to the shoulder. She's got one arm tucked under the pillow. The other is by her face. Her long blonde hair is a tangled mess, fanning out across the pillow.

I pick up a silky handful, rubbing the strands between finger and thumb. She has really pretty hair. It's so smooth and shiny. It smells good too, like rosemary and mint. Soft and refreshing, just like her. I dip my head, pressing the handful to my face. I breathe deep. *Fuck—* please god, just let me have this scent. I'll lock it away in the back of my mind with the rest of my memories of this night.

She stirs in her sleep, scooting closer, chasing my warmth like a greedy lap cat. Then she lets out a soft hum of contentment and I'm ready to crawl between her goddamn legs. I have to taste her again. Just one more time—

No, I can't do this. I can't bear it. She needs to go. *Now.*

I drop her hair and sit up, propping myself up with the pillows just as my phone alarm starts to beep. Next to me, Poppy wakes. Reaching over, I turn off the alarm and unplug my phone. I stretch back and pretend I'm reading something, but all my senses are locked on her.

Poppy stretches under her mountain of comforter. Then she slowly sits up like a mummy rising from a coffin. Her messy golden curls tumble down her back as she rubs her face and looks around.

"Morning," I say in a bored tone.

She shrieks, all but falling out of the bed as she stands, dragging the comforter with her. "Lukas, what are you doing in my room?"

"Try again, Princess," I tease, my chest hollow as I take in the look of shock on her face. "This is my room."

She looks around, still disoriented. Her eye makeup is smeared, giving her dark circles like a sexy little raccoon. She spies my backpack on the chair, my tablet charging by the TV. "No." She shakes her head. "No, I went back to my room. *Please* tell me I went back to my room."

"You didn't have a key, remember? Still don't."

She groans, holding her head with one hand as she clutches the comforter to her half-naked body with the other. "Oh, my lord in heaven, this pounding in my head is like hail on a tin roof."

"Blame Tina. Too many Jax Ray cocktails."

"Everything is so fuzzy," she whimpers. "Please tell me this is a dream. Am I dreaming? Did we really have sex last night?"

My shoulders tense. "You said you weren't drunk—"

"I wasn't," she cries. "At least, I didn't think I was—but I have absolutely no memory of anything that happened after the ice machine. Even that feels like this big, hazy . . . blur."

Okay, fuck this. I toss my phone to the bed. "Wow, I didn't know there was a level of so-thoroughly-fucked it causes memory loss. I guess I should add that to the 'special skills' section of my online dating profile, eh?"

She groans again. "Sure, you can add it right above 'flexing in mirrors' and 'skating into walls at high speed.'"

I flip back the sheet and swing my legs off the bed. "Well, we both agreed this was for one night only. And I already bent my iron rules by letting you stay here so—"

"Wait, you *let* me stay here?" She blinks over at me. "What the heck does that mean?"

"Well, you were all sad and desperate, begging me to fuck you last night. Remember that?"

"Vaguely," she replies, still clutching to that damn comforter. Is she trying to hide from me or herself? Either way, I'm pissed.

"Afterward, I used my room key, and I let you in here to crash— oh, a room key is this little thing, shaped like a credit card."

She glares at me. "I *know* what a room key is, Lukas, even if I no longer seem to have one."

"So, you remember that part too? Good," I say, nodding again. "Well, like I said, I generally don't let my hookups stay over, but I made an exception for a sad, desperate friend."

"Gee, thanks."

I watch her stumble, muttering under her breath as she looks for her clothes. "I realize now I never got the 411 on *why* you were so sad and desperate—"

"And you won't." She drops to one knee to scoop up her discarded dress. "What time is it?"

"Just after six."

She bolts upright, eyes wide. "What? We have to check out within the next thirty minutes!" She drops the comforter and shimmies into her dress, trying to put it on while still keeping my T-shirt on.

Oh, she wants a little modesty now? I stand up with my back to her, pretending to stretch as I just wait for her to—

"Oh my—Lukas, why are you naked?"

I slowly turn, flashing her the front too. She's standing there with her arms inside my too-large T-shirt, those cute little raccoon eyes wide as she takes me in. That she can still blush should be precious. Instead, it just pisses me off further. "Sweetheart, I've been naked," I tease. "You fucked me naked, right here in this bed. You slept next to this nakedness all night long."

"Well, it's morning now," she says, shouldering her way into the straps of her dress. "And mornings are for clothes. Find some."

"Mornings are for clothes? Is that one of your sweet little Nana's sayings?"

She gasps. Tugging off my T-shirt, she wads it up in a ball and throws it at me. "My sweet little Nana is *dead*, you jerk. Now put that on. And find some pants. I'm tired of looking at your Little Lukas."

"I'd worry less about me and more about yourself," I say, pulling on a pair of athletic shorts. "Any minute now, the doors out there will start to open, and then an entire NHL team plus support staff will be wandering the halls. Good luck getting out of here without half of them seeing how completely fucked you look right now."

She goes still, her discarded heels and purse in hand. "Why are you being like this?"

I cross my arms. "I suppose I've realized I don't particularly like being used by you."

Her eyes go wide. I sense her confusion. "Lukas, I—"

Time to burn this down. "But that's the life, right? You rich girls have staff for everything, don't you? Personal chef, personal bartender, personal fuck toy—"

Her gaze hardens. "Now, stop right there—"

"Hey, don't even worry about it," I say with a dismissive wave of my hand. "You used me, and I used you. That it was utterly forgettable for both of us is proof it doesn't need to happen again. Now, the night is over, and you really need to go." I point to the door with finality.

She searches my face, tears rimming her makeup-smeared eyes. I see the hurt there, the squashed hope, the simmering frustration. In this moment, she's actively hating me. *Good.* She can hate me all she wants. It doesn't matter. It's not like anyone can ever hate me as much as I hate myself.

"Well, I see it's true what they say about morning-after regret."

"Can I add that as a testimonial on my dating profile?"

"Oh, screw you, Lukas." She turns away, searching for her phone.

"Again? I mean, it'll be breaking all your precious rules, but I suppose, if you're on top this time and you're quick about it—"

"No thanks," she snaps, hurrying over to the TV stand to unplug her phone. Never mind that I was the jerk who plugged it in for her. "I think I'd rather sleep with a possum," she tosses over her shoulder as she heads for the door. "Don't be late for the bus. And forget this ever happened!"

"Already did!" I call after her as she disappears, closing the door with a snap.

I stand there, hands shaking, staring at the closed door. A low growl rumbles in my chest. Well, this is just fucking perfect. Classic Novikov. Whenever there's a good thing in my life, I have to go and ruin it. It's like I'm fucking Thanos, always turning beautiful things to ash.

Desperate to lean into this burning feeling of destruction, I snatch my pillow off the bed and throw it at the door. It hits with a pathetic thump. Cursing under my breath, I grab the other pillows, throwing them one after the other. I throw the remote. I throw my shoes, the TV guide, the complimentary slippers. I even throw my goddamn phone. That makes the loudest thud. As it clatters to the floor, it pings with a new message.

Hands still shaking, I cross the room and pick it up. I tap the screen to see a new text from Morrow. I read it, feeling like I've somehow reached a level below rock-fucking-bottom.

MORROW: Why did Sully and I just get Venmo requests from Karlsson saying we each owe him fifty bucks? You said you were paying our tabs. What the hell happened last night?

13
COLTON

I'm a ball of nerves as I heft my bag onto my shoulder and climb the stairs of the team bus. Novy is already on. I spot him immediately, five rows down, shades on, hat pulled low, hood up. He's leaning against the window like he's sleeping, but I know better.

Most hockey players live to nap. During the season, if I'm not playing, working out, or eating, you can assume I'm napping. But Novy doesn't nap. *Ever.* The asshole is like a hockey anomaly. He says he doesn't like the way naps make him feel. It's fucking weird.

I drop down in the seat next to him, jostling him with my bag. "Hey."

"Jeez, fucker." He elbows me hard, shifting his hold on his free hotel coffee. "Mind moving your damn bag outta my spleen?"

I drop my bag between my feet. "So, what happened last night?"

He grunts, taking a noisy slurp from his travel cup. "How 'bout a 'Good morning, Novy' or a 'You're looking exceptionally spry'—"

"How 'bout go fuck yourself, Novy. Tell me what happened."

He slowly turns to glare at me. "Nothing."

"Was Poppy okay? Did you get her back to the hotel?"

He sighs. "Look, I was a perfect fucking gentleman, alright? I saved her from the groping hands of Kyle, the wannabe golf pro, loudly proclaiming how tall you are the whole time. Then I took her over to the bar to get her purse. I met her friend—I told *her* how tall you are too. Then I personally paid for the Uber that took us back to the hotel? Okay? Now, get off my case about it. And go find a different seat. That one's taken."

"No one ever sits here."

"My ego does. You're squashing it with your stupid, giant body. Now, move."

I lean back against the seat. "So, she's okay?"

He takes another sip of his coffee, not looking at me. "You'll have to ask her."

Oh, believe me, I will.

I get settled on the plane, pulling my headphones and e-reader out of my backpack. I wrap the headphones around my neck and tuck the e-reader into my seat pocket. Novy is sitting in his own row across the aisle from me, scrolling on his phone. Langley leans back from a row ahead of him. "Hey, either of you wanna play Mario Kart?"

"No thanks," I say as Novy mutters, "Fuck off, Langers."

"They're out," he calls up the plane as the others settle in to start a game.

I put on my headphones and crank my music, nearly missing my mouth with my bottle of water as Poppy enters the plane. I drop my bottle down, screwing on the cap. Like Novy, she's wearing a ball cap, this one a crisp white. Her blonde hair hangs in a ponytail through the hole in the back. She's also wearing dark sunglasses, double fisting her phone and a travel coffee. She's saying something over her shoulder to our social media lead, Claribel.

I pause my music and peer through the seats, taking in her stylish leisure wear look. Fuck, she's so pretty. And so effortlessly cool. I'm about to be a total simp and wave at her, but that's the exact moment she trips. Stumbling forward with a shriek, her phone goes flying from her hand. She flings her arm around Langley's seat—his head with it—catching herself before she faceplants.

"Poppy!" I unbuckle in a flash and slide over to the aisle seat.

"Ow, ow, ow," she cries, sucking up the hot coffee now dripping off her wrist, staining the cuff of her white designer hoodie.

"Oh gosh, Pop. I'm so sorry," says Sully from two rows up, rising out of his seat. "My foot was in the aisle—"

"It's okay," she assures him on a breath, taking off her sunglasses and tucking them into the top of her hoodie. "Nothing bent or broken." She looks down at Langley. "Sorry, Ryan. Didn't mean to strangle you there, honey."

"I'm fine—"

"Who the fuck is Anderson Montgomery?" Novy calls from across the aisle.

Poppy jolts, nearly spilling her coffee again. Her eyes narrow as she glares at him. That's all the sign I need to know something definitely happened between them last night. My chest feels like it's caving in. But then she gasps, lunging forward. "Ohmygod, *give* me that!"

Novy leans away, arm in the air, holding up her dropped phone. "Not until you tell me why you're social media stalking some preppy douche named Anderson Montgomery. Is he your new Hinge match or something?"

"He's nobody, and my phone is *private.*"

"Seriously. What kind of name is Anderson Montgomery?"

"Lukas," she shrieks, all but climbing in his lap to get her phone.

"Langers, catch," he says on a muffled grunt, tossing her phone between the seats.

Langley catches the phone one-handed. "Let's get a look at this guy," he teases. "See if he's good enough for our Poppy."

"Oh my—Ryan, you give me that phone right now!"

He and Walsh both scroll the pictures on Poppy's feed, while Langley holds her back with his arm. "Hmm, I say nope." He hands the phone over to Walsh.

"Ryan!"

"He wears North Face zip-ups and khakis unironically, Pop. Do you really wanna pass that on to your children?"

"Yeah, and Anderson Montgomery is a total frat boy douche name," Walsh echoes, passing the phone up a row. "I bet he buys all his socks at the Izod outlet."

The other guys laugh, and just like that, now it's a game. Poppy shrieks as they play hot potato with her phone. Jake and Sanford take a look next. "Jesus," Sanford mutters. "This guy looks like he tells all his dates his favorite book is *Catcher in the Rye.*"

"I bet you a thousand bucks he says his favorite movies are *Apocalypse Now* and *A Clockwork Orange,*" Jake adds.

"Yeah, more like *A Clockwork Orgy,*" Novy calls, and they all roar with more laughter.

"I bet he has a saffron allergy," Sully teases. He fakes a pretentious voice. "Yes, excuse me, waiter? Are these mussels steamed in saffron butter? Because I'm allergic."

"He looks like he wears boat shoes without the boat!"

"I bet he tells people his dick is seven inches—"

"Hey, seven inches is perfectly respectable!"

"Try seven centimeters!"

The guys are howling as the phone gets tossed over Doc and Mars, landing on the seat next to me. I grab it and look down, too curious not to. I take in the first few images on this guy's social media feed. Fuck me, he *does* look like a douche. He's got the confident swagger of a rich, entitled white boy who's never had to work for a thing in his life.

I open my mouth to make a joke as Novy lunges across the aisle, snatching the phone from my hand. "I'm sorry, but guys named 'Colton John Morrow III' don't get to play this game."

I glare at him, but no one is glaring harder than Poppy. Her cheeks are pink, and she looks an inch from feral as she sticks out her hand. "Lukas Novikov, give me that phone *right now*, or I will push you out the emergency exit."

With one more smirk, he hands it over. The guys all cheer, the game finished.

"We love you, Pop," Sully calls.

"Yeah, we tease 'cause we care," Walsh assures her.

"And swipe left on that guy, seriously!"

She casts Novy one more loathing look before she takes off down the aisle, Claribel hot on her heels. I'm still glaring across the aisle at him as they pass.

He catches my eye and raises a brow. "What?"

"So, nothing happened last night? Is that still your story?"

He turns away, eyes locked on his phone.

Fuck.

The other guys all settle back to their music and games as we get our safety briefing and take off. As soon as I can get a stable Wi-Fi connection, I'm on my phone. I look up Anderson Montgomery. It doesn't take me long to get a good picture of this guy—bachelor millionaire architect, well-educated and well-connected with clear political aspirations. He's the goddamn golden ticket.

I pause in my scrolling when I pass a news article that looks like it only just posted this morning. It's a wedding announcement. It includes a picture of Anderson with a gorgeous young blonde—a blonde who looks shockingly like Poppy. The headline reads: "M&H Construction heir, Anderson Montgomery, to wed Violet St. James, daughter of prominent political lobbyist Hank St. James."

Wait, does this explain why Poppy was acting so odd yesterday? Does she have a problem with her sister's fiancé?

"Holy fucking fuck," Novy growls from across the aisle.

I turn to see he's finally taken his stupid sunglasses off. His eyes are wide as he stares down at his phone. "What?"

He holds up his phone, flashing me the screen. "She was engaged to that fucking guy."

My heart drops. "What?"

He unbuckles and hops across the aisle mid-takeoff. Dropping into the empty seat next to me, he shows me his phone. The article's a few years old, but there they are in a photo together: Poppy St. James on the arm of the dashing Anderson Montgomery. Christ, they look like young Kennedys. She's even wearing the pearls and the cocktail dress.

"Poppy was gonna marry this guy?" The words slip out, and I hear how defeated I sound. Is this the kind of guy she wants, rich and polished and pretty enough to impress her family? Of course he is. Why would Poppy St. James waste her time on rowdy, sweaty hockey players?

She doesn't, comes the voice in my head. She said so herself. She said it to my goddamn face. She doesn't date hockey players. She's not interested in us. She's looking for a kind of life none of us could ever give her.

But she didn't marry him. So, what happened?

Novy glances over his shoulder, peering down the aisle of the plane. "Over-under, how long d'you think she'll stay pissed at me for teasing her about this?"

I hand him back his phone. "I think it might be way worse than you think, bud."

"Why?"

I show him the article I have pulled up on my phone. "Because I think maybe he dumped her for her sister."

"What?" He snatches my phone from me, staring down at the article headline. Slowly, he looks up, his face haunted. Resigned, he hands me back the phone. "Coley, be a pal and push me out the emergency exit, yeah?"

"Nov—"

"Seriously, just kill me. She can hate my sexy corpse."

I sigh, stuffing my phone in my pocket. "Okay, what the *fuck* happened between you two last night?"

It's 8:01 p.m. on Sunday night, and my phone just pinged on the coffee table. New email alert. I don't dare touch it. Instead, I wait, clutching my glass of wine with both hands. At 8:03 p.m., the phone buzzes with a text message. There's only one person who would contact me with such punctuality on a Sunday night. But I can't deal with him right now. I take another sip of my wine, staring at the phone.

It's been three days since DC, and Lukas and I haven't spoken. Not one word. He and Colton tried to corner me as I was getting off the plane but, thank goodness, the defensive coach picked that exact moment to call for a quick huddle, and I made my lucky escape.

Three days and not a word—until now.

And I'm no fool. I'm sure those gossiping geese started looking up Anderson the moment I walked away. If they know my history with him, they aren't saying anything. Why aren't they saying anything? The news is everywhere. Mom wasted no time posting the wedding announcement far and wide. The charming Anderson Montgomery to wed the beautiful Violet St. James. The tycoon prince and the political princess. *A match made in heaven.*

I take another sip of rosé.

If you scroll down far enough, you'll see another wedding announcement featuring a different daughter of Hank St. James. But—to quote my snotty little sister—I had my chance, and I blew it. The spotlight shines on only Violet now.

I was worried her announcement would turn me into the object of everyone's pity. Poor Poppy. This was supposed to be *her* wedding. How does this feel even worse? It's like I no longer exist. I've been forgotten, erased. As a "Type A" middle child with a desperate need to please everyone, this silence feels unbearable.

Well, Lukas's silence, I understand. What did he call me again? Oh, that's right, "utterly forgettable." Stupid, tattooed, gorgeous jerk. I hate him. As if I couldn't see right through his macho bullcrap. He pushed my buttons just hard enough, so I'd be the one storming off, thus saving him the emotional labor of actually caring about someone.

And it worked. After my battle with Anderson, Lukas's pointed sting about me using him felt a little too targeted. Even now, I lift a hand to my chest, rubbing the bruise those words left behind. Is it true? Did I use him? Did we use each other?

I know what "just sex" feels like. I've used my partner to get off in the past, chasing that brief high of orgasm, only to come crashing back down. I know what it feels like to feel so wretchedly alone, even when someone is buried inside you.

But then I close my eyes and I hear his voice in my ear. Soft and sated, his lips brush against my skin. *You're not alone, Pop.* No, what Lukas and I shared was not just sex. It wasn't just orgasmic. It was . . .

I don't even have the words.

As the days have passed, more of that night has come back to me, creeping in with the early twilight hours while I'm lying alone in my bed, or slamming into my mind while I'm jogging down the wooded path behind my apartment. I feel more of him, taste more of him.

It wasn't just sex, and I didn't use him.

I *found* him.

I wipe a tear from my eye, still staring at the phone. I found Lukas Novikov, and he found me. I let him find me. I led him down the path to fill the deepest parts of me. He's in me now. The arrogant ass is right, he's in my DNA. I can't get him out.

Which is why the thought of opening this email haunts me. Were there others this week? Am I really that forgettable? Am I so completely replaceable? To Anderson, I am. He traded one St. James sister for another as easily as changing socks. All he cares about are the connections he can make through her, through my father, DC's precious "Kingmaker."

All Lukas seems to care about is having a good time. I'm sure he can find plenty of women more talented than me to do that. I just wish he'd have the courtesy to send the contracts to someone else in my office. I gave him a list. But no, he's emailing *me*. He just wants to keep pushing me away.

Heart in my throat, I swipe my phone off the coffee table and read the text message first:

LUKAS: Did you get my email? Please confirm receipt.

I set my glass down and lean back on the couch. Opening my email app, I easily spot the one from Hothockeyhunk22. Once again, the subject line is marked: URGENT—SEX CONTRACT—HIGHLY CONFIDENTIAL.

Sex contract. Only one?

Wait . . .

"Oh god." I sit up and tap open the email. He only wrote one line. No salutation, no closing, no signature. One single sentence smirks up at me:

Please sign and return at your earliest convenience.

I tap the attachment. "Son of a—"

Lukas sent me an NDA and he's requesting *my* signature because I'm now officially one of his sexual partners in need of silencing. Next to the blank signature line, my full name is already printed: Poppy Aurora St. James.

I scramble to my feet, glaring down at my phone. "How the *heck* does that jerk know my middle name?!"

25
POPPY

"**T**his is so neat, Poppy. Thanks so much for doing this." Jenni Malthus, one of the board members of Jacksonville General Hospital, walks at my side. Her colleagues—both named John—follow behind us.

"Oh, it's my pleasure," I assure her. "If we hurry, I think we'll just catch the tail end of practice."

We just spent the last two hours in the executive boardroom, finalizing all the details for our upcoming fundraiser. It's my first big charity event as head of PR for the Rays. As a little sweetener, I promised them all a quick behind the scenes tour.

"The Rays are having a great season so far," says John One.

"Early buzz says they might just make the playoffs," John Two echoes.

"Hey, you better knock on wood," I tease. "You know how superstitious these hockey players are. Mentioning the playoffs around here is like saying 'Macbeth' in the theater."

They all laugh as I lead the way down the hall toward the public atrium. Above our heads, the hallway lights flicker.

"Do they always do that?" asks John One.

"Oh, just the joys of new construction," I say with an airy wave. I tap my keycard on the door lock, and it beeps green. "Sometimes the generators fritz," I add, pulling the door open.

And the air conditioning . . .

And I *still* don't have a working phone or internet in my office.

"Are you going to bid on any of the silent auction items?" Jenni asks.

"Of course." I slip my keycard back in the pocket of my lilac sheath dress. "How can I pass up the chance to win a yacht cruise?"

"I have my eye set on that golf package," says John Two.

"You're new to the area, right?" Jenni goes on.

Before I can answer, someone calls my name.

"Poppy St. James, as I live and breathe."

My shoulders stiffen as I spin around. Lukas is striding toward us looking fresh from a shower. His cheeks are pink, eyes bright. The hair at his nape is still wet. "Shouldn't you be playing hockey?" I say. "We were just heading over to catch the end of practice."

"We finished early," he replies with an easy smile.

What the heck is he doing? The last time we spoke, we were like two angry cats in a bag. Now he's practically purring at me. Why do I feel the sudden urge to check that my purse isn't full of Jell-O?

He looks from me to the JGH reps. "Hi, Lukas Novikov, best damn defenseman in the League." He holds out a hand to Jenni first. She shakes it, and I do an obligatory round of introductions. The reps are all smiling like a trio of eager squirrels. It's maddening.

"Did you need something, Lukas?"

"I do," he replies, flashing me that crocodile smile. "I need to talk to you about the contract I sent over on Sunday. Did you get it?"

Oh, he is *not* doing this now!

"Yes, I did. Thank you," I reply crisply.

He fakes a confused look. "Hmm, I never heard from you. Best practice should probably be that you shoot me a reply, just so I'm not worrying."

I smile, gesturing to the JGH reps. "Well, as you can see, I've been a little busy this week, planning for the fundraiser."

And dodging my mother's increasingly urgent calls.

And my sister's barrage of whiny, desperate text messages.

And all my social media accounts, which are still buzzing with the news of the wedding.

Oh, and Colton, my dream boyfriend, who I now feel like I've cheated on thanks to the walking red flag standing in front of me.

"I get it," he says with a solemn nod. "You're too busy to answer emails from us lowly players. Or a text. I sent you a text too. Did you get that?"

"I got your text."

"And left me on read."

Jenni and the Johns glance between us, their eyes darting like they're watching ping pong.

"Poppy's a tough woman to pin down," Lukas says at Jenni with a wink. "Always playing hard to get."

Jenni smiles. "Well, she's in high demand."

"Ain't that the truth," he replies. "In high demand and highly demanding."

Oh god.

I step over to him, placing my hand on his arm. "Why don't we set up an appointment to go over all the particulars later this week?"

"Particulars?" He feigns confusion again, even going so far as to scratch his head. "I thought everything in the contract was all pretty straightforward. I mean, I used the template you provided. Is your name spelled incorrectly?"

"Yes, I noticed you added me." I really hope he can read the "curl up and die" message I'm blinking at him right now. The jerk just smiles wider. "And I'll be happy to be your representative on this deal." I turn to Jenni and the Johns. "Lukas just secured a lucrative endorsement deal."

"Ooh, with who?" chimes Jenni.

Lukas looks slowly down at me, still grinning. "Yeah, Pop, with who?"

I laugh, squeezing his arm tighter. "Oh, you know we can't share that quite yet, not before the ink's dry. Gotta cross all those *I*s and dot those *T*s."

"I think you got those backward, Pop," he teases.

"I know."

"You're squeezing my arm kinda tight there, Pop."

"I know. Would y'all please excuse us for one teensy moment?"

"Sure," says Jenni, looking a little crestfallen that I'm taking him away. It shouldn't bother me. She's young and single, and so is he. For all I know, she could be another willing name to add to his stack of sex contracts.

Over my dead body.

I dig my nails tighter into his arm, leading him down the hall.

"Say, have you tried the coffee cart?" he calls over his shoulder.

"Best macchiatos in Jacksonville. And the almond biscotti are to die for. Why don't you go tell Gavin to put your orders on my tab? Our intrepid PR director will be along in just a minute."

We turn the corner, and I'm seething as I open the door to a utility closet and pull him in behind me.

"Is this your new office?" he says, glancing around at the cleaning supplies and the mop bucket. "Nice. Definitely an improvement. I can see they're really paying you the big bucks—*ow!*" He rubs his bicep as I shake out my fist. "What was that for?"

"You *know* what that was for," I hiss. "What the heck do you think you're doing?"

"I think this is gonna leave a bruise."

"Oh yeah? Well, consider us even."

His expression flickers with alarm. "Wait, I bruised you? Where?"

"Are you freaking kidding me? You took a *literal* bite out of my shoulder, Lukas."

His gaze heats, and I know he's picturing it. "Oh, yeah . . . that."

"Yes, *that*. And I bruise like a peach. I couldn't run in my sports bra for days because you could see the marks from all your fake freaking teeth!"

His expression flashes with hot indignation. "Hey, not all my teeth are fake—"

"I am not trapped in this smelly mop closet with you to discuss which of your teeth are fake!"

He crosses his arms, those tatted biceps bulging. "Then why are we in here, Poppy?"

"Because you just—"

"And you're not trapped."

I blink up at him. "What?"

"This door doesn't even lock," he says, reaching over and jiggling the handle. "You could leave at any time. So, not trapped."

"I'm emotionally trapped! Lukas, you can't approach me at work about personal matters."

"I thought that was your literal job," he challenges, and gosh darn it, I know he's right. I'm being completely irrational right now, but he's standing in front of me looking so good and smelling like he did that night . . .

"You're the one who told me to have all my sexual partners sign contracts," he goes on.

"I did. But—"

"Every partner, you said. A legal condom, you said."

I sigh. "I did."

His expression flashes with triumph. "Well, you're my sexual partner now, so I'm really gonna need you to sign that contract."

"Was."

"What?"

"I *was* your sexual partner," I correct. "Past tense. It happened once."

"Pretty sure you came like five times, but who's counting?"

"I'm counting it as *once*. One sad, desperate mistake, never to be repeated," I add, echoing his words from our infamous morning after.

He glares at me, and I glare right back. He really wants to push me on this now? Between my grueling work schedule, my exhausting family, and the emotional whiplash of Anderson reentering my life, I'm at my wits-freaking-end. "Fine," I say, pulling out my phone.

He leans away, eyes wide. "Wait, what are you doing?"

I open his email and tap on the contract file. "I'm signing this contract."

"Poppy, we're in a mop closet—"

"Well, where do you want me to sign it? You wanna go out to center ice? Hey, why don't we head on over to the beach? That way, after I sign this, I can just walk straight into the surf and let a shark eat me!"

"Poppy—"

"Are you happy now, Mr. Everything's A Big Joke?" I scribble my signature on the form with my finger and tap "save," showing him the proof. "It's done. I'll send you a copy and keep a copy for my records."

He rubs the back of his neck, looking almost sheepish. "Come on, Pop—"

"And now there's nothing left for us to do but part ways, never to speak of our mutual mistake again," I say over him. I feel like if I stop talking, I'll either cry or scream. "You're free, Lukas. You have my silence, signed in ink. Trust me, you didn't need a signed NDA to guarantee that I'll *never* speak of what happened to anyone—"

He leans in closer, reaching out his hand as if he means to touch my shoulder. "Poppy . . ."

I bat him away. "And if it's okay with you, I'll ask that you send all future contracts to Jeff. I gave you his email in our last correspondence. I think it's best for the health of our working relationship that we not have direct communication regarding—"

"Poppy," he shouts, his voice so deep and loud it echoes in this small space.

I jolt. "What?"

His hands brace my shoulders now, holding me still. He looks down at me, searching my face. What is he looking for? What is he thinking? It's impossible to know. Oh god, what is he about to say? I can't bear him being mean right now. I'll shatter like glass. And I cannot cry in front of this jerk. I really will have to walk into the ocean.

He lowers his face an inch, his gaze softening. His thumbs brush my shoulders. Oh god, my body is coming alive at the memory of his confident touch, his scent, his . . . everything.

I relax in his hold, lost in the caramel of his eyes. "What do you want from me? Please, just tell me."

His face lowers another inch as his lips part. My heart is racing. Oh god, I think he's going to kiss me. "Poppy . . ." He says my name on a sigh. "I want—"

A sharp knock at the door has us jolting apart like a pair of naughty teenagers, turning to face the open doorway. The most unexpected person is standing there.

"Colton," I gasp, pulse pounding as his cold gaze darts between us.

Lukas dares to look a little guilty. "Hey, bud. We were just—"

"I don't need to know," Colton says, silencing him with a glare. He turns that hard stare on me, and I feel myself withering. "That hospital chick said you two went this way."

Something about his tone has me stepping forward, reaching for him. "What is it?"

"I came to warn you," he says.

I drop my hand to my sides, anxiety humming. "Warn me?"

He nods, his expression solemn. "Yeah. There's a cute blonde over at the coffee cart chatting up some of the rookies."

My heart freaking stops. With the way he's looking at me right now, I know he knows exactly who she is. Apparently, he cared enough to look me up. He looked up Anderson too. Colton knows. "Just say it," I whisper.

He holds my gaze. "It's your sister."

26

POPPY

"**W**ell, shit." Lukas is still standing next to me, and we're still in this freaking mop closet. He puts his hand on my shoulder, his expression serious. "Do you need a fast exit? We can go through the gym to the parking garage. She never has to know you were here."

I search his face. "Why would you help me?"

"Seriously?" He turns to Colton. "Is she serious?"

"She's serious," Colton replies with a nod, arms crossed.

"Pop, you're a Ray," Lukas explains. "And that boyfriend-stealing witch is probably only here to rub your nose in it. Well, I say fuck her. Coley can get you out of here, and I'll get the rookies to key her car."

"Oh, Lukas, enough." I shift out from under his hand. "We are *not* keying my sister's car."

"Then what do you want us to do—"

"Nothing," I snap at him. "I won't have her pranked or punk'd or whatever it is you have planned in that crazy head." I brush past Colton, stepping out into the hallway.

"What are you gonna do then?" Lukas calls after me.

"I'm going to go out there and *talk* to her like an adult," I say over my shoulder. They follow me, elbowing each other. "Don't you both have some weights to lift or pasta to eat or something?"

"Nope," Lukas replies, a fresh spring in his step.

"I'm free for the rest of the day," Colton echoes.

"Well, if you think I'm introducing you to my sister, think again," I warn them.

"Don't even worry about it," Lukas replies. "I can introduce myself."

I stop and spin around. They nearly crash into me. I glare up at them, hands on my hips. "I don't know what you think you know about the situation, but trust me, you're both wrong."

Lukas glances warily over at Colton, then back to me. "So, you *weren't* engaged to that DC prep school-looking asshole?"

I sigh. "No, I was."

"And he's *not* currently engaged to your sister?" says Colton.

"No, he *is*. But—"

"Did you call it off, or did he?" Lukas says over me.

My gaze darts between their serious faces. "I don't see how that's any of your gosh darn business. We are not friends." I point between the three of us. "This is not some cozy little knitting circle where I share my dark secrets, and you share your jam recipes."

"Actually, I *can* knit," says Colton.

Lukas and I both look at him. "Wait, seriously?" Lukas asks.

"Yeah, it's good for dexterity," Colton replies with a shrug. "And I've got some dementia up my mom's side of the family tree so . . ."

"Smart," Lukas mutters. "We talking crochet? You out here clicking the needles, bud?"

"Just lumpy hats and scarves."

"Sweet. Can I have one?"

"Ohmygod," I cry, throwing up my hands.

They both look down at me.

"Cool it, Pops," Lukas teases. "The man's allowed to have a hobby."

I take a deep breath and let it out. "Colton, I'm very happy for you and your lumpy hats. But if you'll both excuse me, I have to go confront my spoiled little sister in the middle of this impossibly busy workday. I've already lost precious minutes being smothered by Lukas's cologne in that supply closet." I march off down the hall, heels clicking. "And it's still not any of your freaking business, but *I* dumped *him!*"

Their shoes squeak on the polished tile floor as they race to catch up with me.

I lead the way down the hall, through the security door, and into the bright atrium. There's a two-story wall of glass that lets in all that warm Florida sunshine. A small fountain bubbles in the corner. The atrium echoes with laughter. I recognize Violet's high, pealing notes.

And there she is, standing by the coffee cart, iced coffee in one hand, gesturing in the air with the other as she tells an animated story. She's taller than me by a couple inches, and her hair is white blonde compared to my golden yellow. She's curvier too. I got the pixie body like our Nana. She has Mom's generous hips and thighs.

I take in her fresh blowout, her belted Lily Pulitzer dress and chunky Hermès Oasis sandals. She does know this is a hockey rink in Jacksonville, right? Not Worth Avenue in Palm Beach?

"And then I—*oh*—Poppy," she squeals, waving me over.

The small crowd of hockey guys standing around her parts, making way for me. Even Jenni and the Johns are there, John Two munching on biscotti.

Taking a deep breath, I smooth my hands down the front of my lilac sheath dress. Plastering a smile on my face, I cross the atrium. Violet dances forward, her free hand outstretched to wrap me in a one-armed hug. She squeezes me, and I get a lungful of Dior.

"Are you surprised?" she says, shifting her hold on me to my hand. "*Please*, tell me you're surprised. Oh! Your hair looks so pretty like this." She nods at the artfully messy braid resting on my shoulder.

"Thanks."

I know what she's doing. She doesn't want me to get away. Not before she's had her say. I glance down, noting the giant sparkling diamond on her ring finger. It's princess cut, easily four carats, with a white gold band. Anderson put it there. Did he get down on one knee? Did she pick it out herself? I can feel every eye in the atrium watching us. Oh gosh, they can't all possibly know, can they?

Keep it together, Poppy.

"Well, were you surprised?" she says again.

"So surprised," I manage to say.

"I had no choice. You're impossible to get ahold of these days," she chides, squeezing my hand. "A girl can go gray waiting to hear back from you."

Lukas appears at my side, one hand on my shoulder. "I just said the same thing." He sticks out his other hand around me. "Hi, Lukas Novikov, friend of Poppy's."

Friend? That's a bit of stretch, seeing as I'm the utterly forgettable one-time mistake he just legally silenced.

She drops my hand, and her eyes go wide as she takes him in, clearly appreciating his physique. She traces the tattoos on his arm with her gaze, and I fight the urge to step in front of him. "Are you a hockey player too?" she asks, shaking his hand.

"Sweetheart, I'm *the* player," he says with a wink.

She grins, her blue eyes twinkling.

"He's *a* player, and he was just leaving." I push on his arm. "You were all just leaving, right?" I call out to the guys.

A few of them mumble about wanting to order coffee.

"Your coffee is in your hand, honey," I say at Cade Walsh, pointing to the cup he's holding.

"Oh, don't send them away," says Violet. "I came because I wanted to meet your friends and see this glamorous new life you've made for yourself."

"Did you hear that?" Paul jokes. "Malibu Barbie thinks we're glamorous."

"I *do* have a certain panache," Flash says with a nod.

"Dude, you can't even spell panache," says Cade.

Flash elbows him as the others laugh.

Colton moves quietly around them, weaving his way back over from the coffee cart. He slips a drink in my hand, and I check the little tea tag. Green tea with lemon. How did he know? I clutch to the cup like it's a lifeline and loop my arm in with Violet's. I am not doing this in front of an audience. "Okay, time to say 'goodbye' to Malibu Barbie, fellas."

A few of them groan. Others wave.

"Bye, Barbie."

"Nice to meet you."

"Nice to meet you too!" She waves over her shoulder. "Such nice guys."

"Yeah, they're great," I mutter, pulling her over to where Jenni and the Johns are standing. "I'm so sorry about this," I say at Jenni. "My sister just surprised me and—"

"Oh, don't be. Family comes first," she assures me. "We're just glad we got to meet you in person before the event. We can't wait for Saturday."

"It's gonna be a smash," says John One.

"What's Saturday?" asks Violet, sipping her iced coffee.

"A fundraiser," I reply.

"If anything else comes up this week, we'll talk," Jenni says in parting. "Otherwise, we'll see you all over at the art museum!"

I walk them to the door, leaving Violet in the middle of the atrium. As soon as they're beyond the wall of glass, I slowly turn to face her. Most of the players are still mingling by the coffee cart, Colton and Lukas chief among them. They're watching me like a pair of hawks. What are they waiting for, some kind of signal to swoop in and shove my sister in the fountain?

"Oh, for heaven's sake." Striding forward in my Jimmy Choo pink patent leather pumps, I loop my arm back in with Violet's. "Come on."

"Where are we going?"

"Away." I lead her into the main practice rink where the temperature drops a cool fifteen degrees. Out on the ice, a mix of skating lessons are happening. A few parents sit clustered in the middle of the stands, distracted by their own conversations.

"Ooh, it's chilly in here," Violet whines.

"It's figure skating. They do that on ice." I stomp up the metal stairs, pulling her behind me. I plop down on an empty stretch of bench and tug her down next to me. "What do you want, Violet? Why are you here?"

Her pink lips part as she searches my face. For a moment, she almost looks nervous. "I just . . . wanted to see you."

"Then look at a picture of me. I'm sure you have some on your phone."

She flicks her silky hair off her shoulder. "Fine. I wanted to *talk* to you."

"Well, clearly, if I wanted to talk to *you*, I would've answered one of your many calls or texts this last week."

Her icy blue eyes narrow. "Are we seriously gonna do it like this? Can't we just talk like sisters? Poppy, we used to be so close."

False. Christina and I were close. Violet was three years younger and Mom's spoiled favorite. I clutch my cup of tea, glaring at her. "You had the last two years to talk to me, Vi. You could have told me the truth at *any* point."

"And risk breaking your heart all over again? I was protecting you, Popcorn."

Not her using my childhood nickname to twist the freaking knife.

Rowan made it up. They're the only two people who still call me that. I brush past the nostalgia with a wave of my hand. "Look, I'm not some delicate flower that can't handle the world, okay? You want to wear the crown and scale Olympus with Anderson? Fine. I can't stop you. I can *warn* you," I add with a firm look. "But I can't stop you."

"He's not all bad, Pop."

"He's worse. You're just delusional." I set my tea aside. I'm too frazzled to drink it.

"You know, he has some not-so-nice opinions about you too."

"I'm sure he does."

"And it takes *two* people to end a relationship."

"I think in our case it was more like five," I clap back. "Those are just the other women I knew about, including the stripper at his bachelor party."

"God, Poppy. That was *three* years ago."

"And yet, here we are," I say gesturing between us.

Her cheeks glow pink with a mix of the cold and her rising frustration. "Can't you at least *try* to be just a little bit happy for me? I'm getting married, Poppy. And I'm doing this for us, you know. For the family—"

"Seriously? We're not the freaking Medicis, Vi. We're not the Vanderbilts or even the Kennedys. Mom's world is fading fast. The rules are changing. We don't have to play those awful social-climbing games anymore."

She shakes her head. "You're not around anymore. You don't know what it's like—"

"I know you should marry who you want. Or heck, don't get married at all!"

She snorts. "Yeah, like that's an option."

I grab her hand, squeezing it. "It *is*, Violet. I'll admit, it took me a long time to deprogram myself from Mom's world, but I know this much to be true. The last thing on this earth you should ever do is bind yourself to a man who cannot and *will not* hold to a single vow he makes to you."

She jerks her hand free. "He's different with me than he was with you."

"No, he's really not."

"People can grow, Poppy. Are you saying we're all incapable of change?"

"I'm saying *he* is."

She huffs, crossing her arms.

"Vi, he has no inducement to change," I go on, praying she'll hear me. "And besides, do you really want to be in the business of changing people? He has to be allowed to be exactly who he is, honey. The only changing he'll ever do is the changing he *wants* to do for himself. Hard to accomplish when you already think you're perfect."

She turns away, watching the little girls in their leggings and sweaters learning to figure skate. We're both quiet for a minute. "Do you ever wish you could turn back the clock and be eighteen again?"

I watch her watch the girls spin. "Why?"

"Life just felt so much easier. I was just traveling and partying, making amazing memories with great friends. It was like one big dream."

"I can't say I relate," I mutter, snatching up my tea and taking a sip. It's sweet and soothing, a perfect blend.

Vi glances over at me. "You didn't take a gap year?"

"Mom wouldn't let me. It would've interfered with my cross country schedule. I qualified for nationals, but then I hurt my knee. Either way, I was on scholarship. You don't graduate summa cum laude if you're sailing on a yacht in the Mediterranean for a year."

She looks back out at the skaters. "We've lived such different lives."

I hum into my tea. "Yeah, we sure have."

"I'm sorry, Poppy."

I go still, not daring to look at her. "For what?"

She just shrugs. "Honestly, I don't really know. Everything? Nothing? Does that count as an apology?"

"Not really."

She's quiet for another minute. "I think I was always jealous."

"Of what?"

She tucks her hair behind her ear, still not looking at me. "Mom never pushed me the way she pushed you because she knew I wasn't worth it."

Silence meets her confession. After a moment, I place a hand on her thigh. "Violet . . ."

"Oh, come on. You know it's true." She blinks back her tears. "I mean, look around us. You're Poppy, the high-powered sports executive with the scholarships and the trophies. I'm just Violet. I'm the fun sister. The life of the party. No one expects me to amount to anything."

"Hey, come on now. You're smart and beautiful and everyone thinks the world of you."

She nods, but I can tell she's unconvinced. "I just want my life to matter too, you know? I want to do something meaningful. I want people to look at me and not see all my wasted potential."

"You're being too hard on yourself."

"Am I? Well, what do I have to call my own, Pop? What do I offer the world? I can't run Daddy's company like Rowan, and I'm not organized enough to manage nonprofits like you. I certainly can't explain the merits of Surrealist art."

"Well, who can, really?" I say with a weak smile.

Slowly, she looks down at her hand. Then she lifts it, wiggling her fingers to make the diamond glint under the arena lights. "This feels like something I can do. I can make a fabulous match. I can be a good wife who throws great parties and has impeccable fashion sense."

"Vi, you can be so much more—"

"No, *you* can be more. Poppy, you *are* more. You and Anderson were a bad fit from the start because you were never meant to be the one on his arm." Reaching up, she tucks a strand of my hair behind my ear. I lean away from the intimate touch. "I think you were so miserable together because, deep down, he knew it too."

"Knew what?"

"He knew if he married you, he'd spend the rest of his life being on *your* arm," she replies, cutting me to the quick. "Your star is just too bright not to shine, and he's too selfish to be a mirror for someone else's light."

I search her face, my heart breaking. "Well, Vi, honey, if you know all this about him, why are you marrying him?"

"Because this is how *I* shine. This is my chance, Poppy. I'm not looking for perfect. I'm just looking for a chance to matter."

"And you're sure? I mean really *really* sure this is the way you wanna go?"

She gives me a solemn nod. Her fake smile is finally gone. I can see her now. I see my sweet little sister who danced in the living room with me to *The Nutcracker* and called me "Popcorn." No walls, no masks. I see her hopes and her fears. "Poppy, I have to ask you something. Please don't hate me for it, okay?"

I take her hand, giving it a gentle squeeze. "What, honey? Anything."

17
COLTON

fter making a few more jokes about Poppy and her sister, the rest of the guys clear out with their coffees, even Novy. I can tell he wants to stay, but he has a PT meeting he can't skip. "Just . . . take care of her," he mutters, giving one last look at the double doors.

I wait for less than thirty minutes, and then I'm watching from a bench in the atrium as Poppy and her sister walk out. Poppy looks more relaxed now, which has me relaxing a little too. She also looks gorgeous. That soft purple dress is hugging her curves in all the right ways. She's got a little flower scarf wrapped around her neck, making her look like a sexy flight attendant.

She and her sister cross the atrium, heading for the front doors. I can't hear what they're saying, but they're both smiling and hugging. Is Violet staying? Maybe they're agreeing to meet up somewhere after work. Poppy nods. Then Violet is walking off into the Florida sunshine, and Poppy is turning back around. She searches the atrium as if she's looking for something. The moment she sees me, her smile falls. Then she cracks. With a sob, she flings her hand over her mouth, trying to catch the sound as she rushes away.

I leap to my feet. "Poppy!"

She tugs her keycard from her pocket and taps it on the security access panel. The door beeps and she jerks it open, not looking back.

"Poppy, wait," I call after her, ducking inside the closing door.

"Go away."

I follow her down the hall to the elevator bank. "Will you just wait?"

She thumbs the elevator button, pressing it until the car dings and the doors slide open. I slip in right as they shut. She sinks against the wall, hand still over her mouth to stifle her sobs.

I don't know what to do. Should I touch her? Not touch her? Does she need a hug? I go for something in the middle and place my hand on her shoulder. "What do you need?"

"Oh god," she gasps. "I can't breathe—"

"Just slow down," I soothe. "In and out, Pop."

She grabs my forearm. Clinging to me, she takes in a shaky breath.

"Good, that's it. Now, let it out."

She closes her eyes, shaking her head.

I brush her hair back with my free hand. "What happened?"

"Nothing I shouldn't have expected," she says, clutching her chest with her other hand.

"Tell me."

She blinks her eyes open. I hate that they're rimmed with tears. She looks at me, and I see the trust there. I'm so goddamn grateful for it. She knows I care, so she lets me in. "I was ready to cut my sister out of my life for good."

"By the manner of your parting, you clearly didn't. What happened?"

She gives a little laugh, shrugging. "I think I just agreed to be her maid of freaking honor."

Whoa. That's some Shakespeare-level drama. "You're gonna be the maid of honor at your sister's wedding to your ex-fiancé?"

She tugs at her little neck scarf like it's choking her. "Oh, great. Please, make me feel worse about this." Getting it loose, she lets it float to the floor.

"Sorry, it's just . . . well, why did you do it?" I'm genuinely curious.

"Because she pulled the face!"

"What face?"

"The Violet face," she says with a distracted wave of her hand. "You know, the sad, pathetic 'my charmed life is so easy because no one really loves me' face. Oh man, she's good. She actually had *me* apologizing to *her* by the end." She drags both hands through her hair, leaning against the elevator wall. "God, I am so spineless."

"No, you're not."

"I'm a freaking jellyfish. I'm a Poppy-fish," she says with a squeaky laugh. "I'm a pushover."

"You're not. Have you met you?"

"With my family? Yes, I am. I'm a people-pleasing, hot freaking mess!"

"Poppy—"

"No, it's fine." She fans herself with both hands. Pink blush is rising up her neck to her cheeks. "Honestly, the joke is on her because I'm just gonna plan the most boring bachelorette party of her life!"

I can't hide my grin. This is my little tiger showing her claws, threatening to plan a party badly on purpose. God, she's fucking adorable. But then my smile falls. "Wait, you're throwing her a bachelorette party?"

"The MOH always throws the bachelorette party," she says, still fanning herself. "And she only gave me like three weeks to plan it, as if I don't have enough to do running an entire freaking PR department." She looks up at me. "Why do you ask?"

"Nothing," I say quickly. "You're just . . . sister of the year."

Personally, I could never. Both my sisters are happily married, but if one of them *ever* went sniffing around one of my exes, it would be game over. Poppy should be given a medal for even considering it.

"Wait." She glances around, eyes wide. "Why aren't we moving?"

Shit, for a moment, I forgot we were in an elevator. I glance over at the control panel. "Neither of us pressed a button for a floor."

She jabs the number four with her thumb, and the elevator lurches upward. She clings to the handrail, lips moving as if she's praying to be delivered from this metal box. I knew her thing about planes, but I thought that was just about flying. It is all small spaces?

I brush her shoulder again. "Poppy, do you have claustrophobia?"

She fakes a laugh. "Don't be silly—*ahh!*" The elevator jolts. Her eyes go wide with terror. "What the heck was that?"

I glance around. "Uhh, I don't—"

The elevator shudders to a stop, making a sound like a machine powering down. Then the bright lights flicker out. The only light left is the soft red glow of an emergency bulb in the ceiling.

"What's happening?" she cries, stumbling forward to wrap her arms around me. "Why have we stopped?"

"I don't know—"

"Oh god, are we trapped?"

Placing an arm around her waist, I groan, remembering some of the chatter at practice this morning. "Yeah, so someone might have mentioned they were doing some repairs on the generators today—"

"The freaking generators?!" Her panic morphs into rage as she shoves away from me. "Are you kidding me? I swear to Lucifer, when I get out of here, I am setting those generators on fire so Mark will have to buy new ones! Maybe then they'll actually *work*, and I can do my freaking job!"

While she's busy spiraling out, I reach in my pocket for my phone and turn on my flashlight. Shining it at the control panel, I press the alarm button. Nothing happens.

Fucking perfect.

I tap all the other buttons, including the emergency call button. Nothing.

I shoot off a couple texts to some of the staff, letting them know we're stuck in here. All the while, Poppy rants, gasping for air as her panic mounts. "—just freaking perfect. Everything else has gone to crap. I may as well add plummeting to my death—"

"Hey." I cup her face one-handed, still holding my phone flashlight with my other hand. "You're not gonna die, okay? Elevators have all kinds of emergency brake systems. We're good. We're just stuck—"

"And that's supposed to calm me down? This is *literally* my worst nightmare!"

Ouch. "It's your worst nightmare to be stuck in an elevator with me?"

But she's not listening. "Oh, god. Colton, I really feel like I can't breathe." She sinks down to the floor, both hands now pressed to her chest.

"Whoa, okay." I drop to my knees too, setting my phone aside with the flashlight up so it shines on the ceiling. "Do you think you're gonna pass out? You gotta invert—"

"No." Her eyes are closed as she shakes her head. "I feel like I'm having a heart attack."

She just said the two magic words. For a panicked beat, my own heart stops. I grab her wrist, checking her pulse. "Walk me through your symptoms, Poppy. What are you feeling right now?"

"I can't breathe—heart is racing—" She grabs my hand and places it over her chest.

"Are you experiencing any pain across your shoulders, your arms, or your back?"

"No."

"Does your chest feel weighted, like there's an elephant sitting on it? Or compressed like someone has it in a tight fist?"

She shakes her head. "No, I don't think so."

I move my hand from her chest, feeling along her throat. "Any pain in your jaw or neck?"

She blinks up at me, eyes wide. "What's with the twenty questions? Are you secretly a doctor or something?"

"No, but my mom and both my sisters are." My quick examination done, I relax a little. "Poppy, look at me." Tipping her chin up, I can clearly see the fear in her eyes. "I don't think you're having a heart attack, okay? I think this is just a panic attack. Still scary, but we can breathe it out."

"How the heck would you know?"

"Because I've had three."

"Three what? Panic attacks?"

"No, three heart attacks."

Her eyes go, if possible, even wider. I can see she doesn't believe me. Why would she? Few do unless they've seen my medical records . . . or my scars. Balancing on my knees, I rock back on the balls of my feet and tug my Rays tech shirt off.

She gasps. "Colton, what are you—"

"Look," I say, tossing the shirt aside. There's not a lot of light in here, so I take her hand in mine and run her fingers over the mess of scars on my chest. "Feel it?" I stroke her fingers down the middle of my chest over the thick, raised scar. "This one's from the sternotomy I had when I was six years old."

"Oh." Her fingers are gentle as they explore.

"And this one is from a thoracotomy when I was eight," I say, showing her the shorter, thinner scar on my left pec.

"Oh, Colton . . ." Her breathing slows as she brushes her fingertips over each one. "I didn't know." She glances up, her expression soft in this odd light. "Are you . . .?"

"Fit as a fiddle," I reply with a reassuring smile. This is calming her down, so I keep talking. "I was born with a weak heart. I practically lived in hospitals. But since we finally got the repairs I needed, I've been making this ole pump earn its keep and then some."

"And they let you play hockey like this?" She blinks twice, lowering her hand away. "Wait, I'm sorry. That was rude."

I laugh. "No, it's a fair question. Trust me, the League wouldn't have signed me if I couldn't play. This is all in my past. I spent the first ten years of my life thinking I'd be unable to play sports at any level. No running, no jumping, no skating down the ice."

"What was wrong?"

I shrug. "A few congenital defects with long names and low probabilities. Basically, it all meant my heart couldn't pump my blood properly. Low oxygenation led to fatigue, weakness, shortness of breath. But I fought my fight and won. Now, every day that I get to keep playing hockey is my little victory lap. Honestly, it's why I still play. Lord knows I don't need the money. And my knees would probably thank me if I retired early," I add with another smile.

I've clearly surprised her. "I had no idea. Why aren't you more vocal about it? I could help you." She sits forward, her eyes brightening. "Oh! We could do a campaign. Heart health is such an important topic—"

"Whoa there." I raise a hand to stop her. "This is why I don't tell people. Especially not media-minded people like you."

"Why?"

"Because I don't want to be anybody's poster boy. I don't want to be driving to the beach and see a big billboard with my face and the word BRAVE in all caps. I get enough tokenism being one of only a handful of guys in the entire League who isn't white. I support my causes privately, and I make my appearances at the cardiac wing of my hometown hospital every time I'm home. My doctors all have season tickets for life. That's enough for me."

She nods. "I understand. You want people to see you as an athlete first, not as a heart patient."

I consider her words for a moment. Is that what I've been doing all these years? I've spent so long internalizing my own identity as that of "former" heart patient. I *was* sick. Now, I'm not. Every day, I push my body to the limit again and again, showing it and myself what we can achieve together.

The rest of my family all chose medicine and academia. Dad was a chemist, Mom's a neurologist, both my older sisters are pediatricians. And then there's Colton, who always had a point to prove: my body is mine to control. Who would I be if I didn't feel this pressure to constantly make my body perform? What would I do if I actually had a choice? If I didn't have to keep proving everyone wrong?

"Colton?"

I look down, catching Poppy's concerned gaze. Leaving my phone on the floor, I stand and reach out my hand. "Wanna try standing again?"

She slips her hand in mine, and I pull her up. Her other hand goes to my chest as she braces against me. Wobbling, she fixes her shoe. Her palm presses flat against my bare skin, burning me like a brand. Now I'm the one feeling like I can't breathe. Her finger traces my sternotomy scar again. By the light of my phone, I see the questions shining in her eyes. She wants to know more about me, about my story. I want to know her too, if she'll only give me a chance. Am I too late? Did I wait too long?

Her fingers inch lower, away from my scar. Christ, now she's just touching me. There's no pity in these touches. I reach out on instinct, wrapping my hands around her wrists. "Stop."

She freezes. "Sorry."

I let her go and she drops her hands to her sides. The energy in this dark elevator feels suddenly charged. Now that she's not panicking about her sister or being stuck in this elevator, her mind that never stops churning is thinking about something else. "What is it?"

She bites her bottom lip, worry flashing in her eyes. "Umm, about Lukas—"

"Don't."

She looks up at me, and I see I've wounded her. She's trying to communicate, and I'm shutting her down. She feels like she needs to tell me about what happened between them. He's my friend and my teammate. She needs to unburden herself, but I can't fucking bear it. "Whatever you're about to tell me, I don't want to know," I say, my tone gruff.

She shrinks back farther. "Okay."

With a groan, I close the space between us. Cupping her face with both hands, I tip her chin up. "I said I don't want to know."

"I didn't say anything—"

"You're not mine, Poppy."

Her gaze hardens as her hands wrap around my wrists. "You think I don't know that?"

I walk her back until she touches the wall again. She gasps, her hip hitting the metal handrail. One hand drops down to brace against it. The other stays wrapped around my wrist, her fingers pressing against my pulse point. Can she feel the way it's racing? "Whatever happened between you and Novy in DC is your own business," I explain. "He's not talking, and I don't want you to either. You weren't mine, so you owe me nothing. Understand?"

She nods.

Fuck this. I'm done waiting for my shot with her. I'm done watching from the bench just hoping she'll notice me. Seizing this chance, I dare to go on. "But you need to know that if you *were* mine, he would never touch you again."

She blinks up at me. "If I was yours?"

I stroke her cheek with my thumb, praying she'll let me get this all out, praying she'll hear me. "I've died and come back three times over, Poppy. I know with a clarity most others lack that sometimes you only get one shot in this life. You have to be ready to take it when it comes. You have to be ready to fucking cherish it."

Her eyes trail from my chest scar back up to my face. "And what do you cherish?"

"Hockey," I reply with a smile, knowing it's not what she expected me to say. "It's all I wanted. I gave it everything I had, and I rose right to the top."

"You've had an amazing career," she admits.

"But that's *all* I have, Poppy: my career. Dad dying put that in harsh perspective for me. I was so focused on this one thing I wanted that I didn't let myself dare want anything else."

"What else do you want?"

Leaning down, I place a kiss on her forehead, whispering against her warm skin, "I want *you*. I have for years."

She leans away on a gasp. "Years?"

I nod, clearly picturing the moment in my mind. "Since the first day I saw you sweep into the practice rink in DC. You were wearing a pale-yellow dress with your hair down."

"You remember my dress?"

"How could I forget? You were like a ray of sunshine. I couldn't look away. You stopped me in my tracks, Poppy. You still do. Every day. I want you so fucking bad. Since the moment you walked into my life two years ago, I think I've been chasing this dream of you. Hell, I chased it all the way to Jacksonville. You're the reason I took this trade. I wanted to be where you are. I wanted to be ready to take my shot. All I need to know now is . . . do I have one?"

"Colton," she whispers again, pronouncing the "T" in that way that makes me feral.

"Don't," I grit out, locking my elbows to keep her from inching closer.

She leans away, confused. "Don't what?"

"Don't say my name like that."

"Like what?"

"Like you already know how I taste." I brush my thumb over her parted lips. "Like you might just give a damn about me."

"I *do*." She holds my sides. "Colton, I care about you."

"Then answer my question."

"I . . ." She goes silent, not meeting my eye.

I tip her chin up again, determined to hear her truth. She has all of mine now. It's only fair I get a little taste of hers, even if it breaks what's left of my heart. "You what? Tell me."

She holds my gaze, those blue eyes so bold and beautiful. "I want you too."

28

POPPY

I don't know who moved first, and I don't care. All I know is that I'm kissing Colton Morrow, and I never want to stop. My arms are around his waist, and his hands cup my face, sweeping back to tangle in my braided hair. We tremble with need as we taste each other. I press my lips to his again and again, my hands splayed on the muscles of his back as he pins me against the wall of this busted elevator.

Call me cured because I don't care if this car falls. I'm already free-falling right into Colton's arms.

He groans against my mouth. "Can I touch you?"

"Yes." I kiss his chin, his jaw. "Touch me. *Please*."

He smells so good, all woodsy and spiced. And he *feels* good. His beautiful brown skin is so warm to the touch. Everywhere my hand moves, he heats like a fire. It's intoxicating. He's literally burning for me, and I want to be a matching flame.

"I want you," he says, peppering kisses down my neck. "God, Poppy. You fucking kill me."

"Don't say that." I pull back, looking deep in his beautiful walnut-brown eyes. "This isn't dying. This is living."

He nods.

I drop a hand down to stroke two fingers over the thick scar on his chest. He tenses, holding himself still. I let him see in my eyes that I don't pity him. I don't see him as weak or damaged because of these scars. He's strong. He's poised and perfect, and I've wanted him for so long now, longer than I think even I knew.

He talks of first impressions? Well, he left one on me. I remember the first time we met too. How could anyone forget Colton Morrow? The Capitals practice was just finishing, and he skated up to the boards, pulling his helmet off as he slid to a stop. He smiled down at me, and my heart flipped. I remembered then thinking he was the most beautiful man I'd ever seen—and then I promptly put my fluttering heart in a box and closed the lid. I had a job to do and people to impress and I don't get involved with my players.

Always work.

Always obligations and expectations.

Well, what has that gotten me? I'm twenty-seven and alone, chasing this man in my dreams, too afraid to want him in real life. Too afraid to risk it. I press my palm over his scar, covering it with my hand.

"Tell me what you're thinking," he says, trying to get closer, looking for his way in.

My eyes trace the shape of my fingers against the dark canvas of his skin. The truth comes unbidden, and I speak it into the air between us. "I think I've been a ghost."

"What do you mean?"

I look up. "I mean I've been going through the motions of my life for so long now without actually living. Or if I *was* living, I was living for others. I was following their rules, making their dreams mine."

Hunger burns in his eyes. I've never felt so wanted before. And there are no conditions with Colton, no expectations. It's just a gift he's offering me, reflected in his every look and touch. Colton Morrow *wants* me, and he's not ashamed to admit it. "And now?" he asks.

I brush my fingers over his perfect lips. "Now, I think it's time I finally start living for myself."

He smiles, kissing my fingertips. "And how do you do that?"

I return his smile. "By doing what I want for a change, not only what's expected."

"And what do you want, Poppy?"

"I already told you."

"I want to hear you say it again."

"I want you."

He lowers his face on a sigh until our foreheads touch. "Don't say it if you don't mean it."

"I want you," I say again. "I dream of you, Colton. I have for years."

"Fuck." He kisses me, his hands roving. I bite back a whimper as he pulls away, lowering his face to my neck. Breathing me in, his tongue starts to tease, setting me on fire. I tip my head to the side, giving him more of me to taste.

"I've been chasing you too," I admit. "Too afraid to want you, but I can't get you out of my head."

He kisses up my neck to my ear, nipping the lobe. His breath is warm as he whispers, "Tell me what you dream about."

I swallow my nerves. "Umm . . ."

I've never felt like I'm particularly good at talking during sex. And I've never really *felt* sexy. Pretty, yes. But sexy requires a different energy. It's power and confidence. I think it requires the determination to *take*, and I've always been more of a giver in the bedroom.

"Talk to me," Colton says, his hands cupping my breasts as he kisses below my ear.

I cling to his arms. For him, I want to try. I turn my head until I'm the one speaking in his ear. "You kissing me like this," I begin. "Your hands on me . . ."

"Where?"

"Everywhere."

He reaches behind my back and slowly works open the zipper of my dress. With gentle hands, he peels it off my shoulders, exposing my white lacy bra. "What else happens in your dreams?"

Smiling, I free my arms from the little cap sleeves. I recall the dream I lost when turbulence jostled me awake on our last flight.

"Tell me," he commands, pinching my peaked nipple.

I gasp, fighting a shiver as he cups me with both hands, his thumbs rubbing against the lace. "Last time, we were in a bubble bath. I was in your lap, and you were so deep inside me, thrusting so hard, we spilled water all over the floor—"

My words end on another gasp as he kisses me, his tongue dancing with mine. We chase and claim, kissing like we were always meant to do. He pulls away to look in my eyes. "How often are you dreaming of me?" I see the pride there, the joy and excitement. This is turning him on.

I flash him another smile. "Enough that all my toys are tired of hearing me cry out your name."

He grins. "Keep going."

"Enough to wake up wet and wanting you almost every morning," I say on a sigh, pressing in with my hips as his hand teases over my pussy. "Sometimes, I even reach for you . . . but you're never there."

His face glows with triumph. "I'm right here, Poppy. I'm in your arms, and I'm saying yes. Now, what are you gonna do about it?"

Heart racing, I shimmy out of my dress, letting it slip past my hips. "I'm saying yes too."

"Yes?"

This is crazy. We're in an elevator, and those doors could open at any moment. But, for the second time in a week, I'm taking what *I* want, and damn the consequences. "Wild horses couldn't stop me," I say, dropping my dress to the floor. "Fuck me, Colton. I'm yours."

"*Yes*." His hand wraps possessively around my throat as he pulls me to him. I arch my neck, heart beating wildly as I wait for the squeeze. But he holds his pressure firm, his other hand dropping to palm between my legs again. We both groan as he feels how wet I already am through my panties. "We don't have a lot of time to play and explore," he says in my ear. "What does my queen like? What gets you off?"

I shiver at the use of his endearment. Queen? I've been called "baby" and "sugar" before. Lukas swooped in and teased me with that ill-advised "princess." That's what Daddy calls me. No lover can call me by the same pet name as my father. I wasn't joking; I would've punched him in the balls if he said it again.

But "queen?" I like the sound of that. *A lot.* I tremble in his arms, ready for anything he'll give me, aching for it. Seeing the mirrored look of need in his eyes, my confidence surges. I wrap my hand around his at my throat and squeeze. "I may look sweet, but I like to get fucked, Colton. I want it hard and fast. I want your cock buried deep so I feel you the next morning. I want to be owned."

He growls his approval as he moves his hand down my chest and presses a sucking kiss to my neck. "We'll have to get a little creative because I don't have a condom—"

"I'm on the pill," I say, cupping his hard dick through his athletic shorts. "Oh!" My eyes go wide as I feel his impressive length. This perfect cock will more than fill me. I'm not even sure it will fit. My pussy is already weeping at the chance to try.

"Are you sure?"

I nod. "Yeah, I've . . ." I try to work around how I can say this. "Umm, I've only been with one other person in the last three years—and we used a condom," I add quickly. "Both—I mean—all of the times . . . we used a condom."

Colton's eyes narrow. Signing Lukas's NDA means I can't *officially* name him, but we both know what I'm saying without me saying it. He swoops in, kissing me again until I'm left swaying in my heels and breathless. Pulling away, chest heaving, he grabs a fistful of my braided hair and jerks my head back. I cry out, loving his tight hold on me. "I am going to burn the memory of him from your soul. Do you understand? When I'm done, there will be nothing left of him but a fucking echo."

Wild with want, I nod.

"Good girl," he praises, pressing one more kiss to my lips. "Now, you said you want me to own you?"

I nod again.

He leans closer, rasping in my ear. "Then get on your knees and get your pretty mouth on my dick. I want it wet with you before I shove it in your cunt." His eyes are two pools of night as he glares hungrily down at me. "You want me buried deep?"

I nod for a third time. "Yes, please."

He grins. "Perfect. Because I want to fill you with my cum. I wanna watch you stumble out of this goddamn elevator with me dripping down your thighs." He cups my pussy again, rubbing my clit with his palm until I squirm. "You're gonna feel me in this pretty cunt and know exactly who owns you. Sound good?"

"Yes," I whisper, heart racing.

"Good." He kisses me again, biting at my bottom lip. "Get on your fucking knees."

Okay, dirty-talking Colton is my new kryptonite. I melt to the floor. Whimpering with need, I pull down on his shorts, freeing his cock. It hangs hard and ready in front of my face, casting a shadow in this eerie light. I take in the size, my hands reaching out to tentatively wrap around his base. The tips of my nails don't quite touch.

Oh, my freaking god.

His hands go to my hair as I flick with my tongue, wetting his tip.

That first taste of his salty precum has me feeling desperate. Parting my lips, I take his whole tip in my mouth and suck.

"Fuck," he grunts, his body tensing, fingers digging into my hair.

I hum with pleasure, gliding my tongue down his thick shaft.

"Keep going," he urges. "Show me how much of me you can take."

I swirl my tongue around his head again. Opening my mouth wide, I swallow his hard length. I take as much as I can into my mouth, my hands wrapping around him at the base.

"You're so fucking beautiful," he says, his hands firm but gentle in my hair. "So perfect. This is my dream, Poppy. Seeing you like this, your sweet mouth on me. Your hands—*fuck*!"

I pop off him, taking a deep breath. "You've had dreams of me sucking your cock?"

He smiles down at me, hunger written on every line of his face. "Poppy, all my dreams are of you."

My core warms at the thought of him alone and wanting me all this time, like I've been wanting him. I flash him a teasing smile. "But the real thing is better, right?"

Swooping down, he grabs me by the arms and pulls me up, kissing me senseless.

"I don't know how long we have in here," I say against his mouth. "Please, Colton. Please, fuck me. I need your cock inside me. No more dreaming. Make it real."

He drops to his knees right there on the elevator floor. His shorts are around his thighs, dick out. He balances on the balls of his feet, gym shoes still on.

"What are you doing?" I swallow a squeal, nearing tripping in my heels as he jerks my panties down to my ankles. Next to him, his phone buzzes with a call. It vibrates on the floor, making the light flicker. Neither of us answer. We can't stop. We're obsessed. We're *possessed*.

Colton reels me in by the hips, and my hands smooth over his short hair. He presses his face to my pussy, making a desperate sound.

"No, we don't have time—*ah*!" I cry out as he tongues my clit, his fingers wiggling to dip into my wet pussy. "Colton, *please*." I swallow a moan as he gives my pussy a light smack.

"Behave," he growls, burying his tongue back inside me.

I ride his face, both hands gripping the handrail behind his head. He groans his approval, sinking his tongue inside my pussy. "Oh, I'm right there," I say on a gasp. "Don't stop—"

He shoves two fingers inside me, flicking my clit with his tongue until I'm squeezing him tight, my orgasm crashing over me. I cling to the handrail, grinding on his face. He groans again, and I feel the vibration against my pussy. I'm so sensitive and turned on, just the sound makes my walls flutter around his fingers in a last, desperate little wave of pleasure.

The phone buzzes on the floor again, and he leans back, his tight core muscles on full display. My god, he's beautiful, sculpted from stone. He looks up at me with those dark eyes. "Get on my dick, Poppy."

I'm delirious, still floating back into my body. Lifting a hand, I brush my hair back from my face. "What?"

He taps my inner thigh to have me widen my stance. I stand with one foot to either side of him. From this angle, I *feel* like a queen, watching him gaze up at me with such longing. A girl could get used to this kind of adoration.

"Come here."

Following his lead, I sink down, bending at the knees. He drops one hand between us, holding his hard cock ready as I notch him at my entrance. "Oh god," I whimper, my face now even with his.

"You've got this." He kisses my cheek, my brow. "Sit down, beautiful. Take me nice and slow. Ride me. Fucking own me. A queen on her throne."

Fighting the shaking of my legs, I exhale and sink down, letting him fill me inch by inch. I'm trembling as he helps hold my weight, his strong arms supporting my hips and thighs as I bury his dick inside me. "I can't," I whine, breathless and feeling the pinch and burn of being overfull.

"I've got you," he soothes, kissing my neck. "Only take as much as you want."

I nod, one hand going from the handrail to his shoulder as I let out a breath and settle a little deeper. He lifts me up, sliding me slowly back down his length. We both moan with satisfaction.

"Better?" he asks.

"Mhmm." I lift up again and slide down, feeling him unlocking more of me. "God, you're so deep." I whimper, loving the exquisite ache of this fullness.

Leaning back, he glances down between us. "You're more than halfway. Stop if it's too much."

"It's not too much," I assure him, feeling completely untethered. Another orgasm is building deep in my core, this one heavy and full of static like a storm head. Electricity tingles across my chest and down my arms. I'm empty and I'm full and I need more.

"You feel so fucking good." He sucks on my breast over the lace cup of my bra. My nipple is peaked and aching. "God, I feel all of you. Poppy—"

I cling to him, one arm wrapped around his shoulders, holding him to my breast. My other hand holds a death grip on the handrail behind his head as I grind down on his hard cock, trying to take more of him inside me.

All of him. I want all of him. Nothing else will do.

"It's not enough," I pant, dancing at the edge of delirious. "Col, I need more. Is that crazy? I'm so full, but please, *please*, give me more. I can take it. I know I can. *Please*—"

He groans again, his hands tightening on my thighs as he changes the angle of his hips and arches back. At the same time, he thrusts up, impaling me on his cock until I feel myself seated fully. I cry out, throwing my head back as he fucks me from below. I'm just along for this ride, my whole body swept up in the storm of his passion as he buries himself in me again and again.

"Fuck," he shouts, his hands digging into my hips so hard they'll leave bruises. "I'm gonna come."

"Me too." Melting against him, I press my lips to his in a searing kiss and let the super nova consume us both. My pussy clamps down on him like a vise. His body shudders as he thrusts again, his arms wrapping protectively around me as we both release.

I don't even know how much time passes before he's saying my name. Brushing my hair back. "Poppy . . ."

"Hmm?" I lift my head off his shoulder and blink my eyes open. Everything looks so bright. I wince.

"Poppy, get up." His voice is urgent. He's shifting me away. In my fog, I cling to him, not wanting a repeat of that empty feeling I got when Lukas left me against the ice machine. "Pop, the lights just came on."

The elevator buzzes. Somewhere in the shaft above us, there's a loud, alarm-like beep.

My happy pink orgasm bubble bursts as I glance around. I'm naked in the middle of this broken elevator, straddling a hockey player's lap with his cock buried inside me. "Oh god—"

"Poppy, you gotta get up. The doors could open any second."

"Help me!"

He shifts me off his lap, and I rise shakily to my feet. I snatch up my dress while Colton tucks himself away and shrugs back into his T-shirt. We both jump as a deep voice fills the elevator car. "Hey, this is Fire Chief Dale Finnick. Do we have some people stuck in this elevator?"

With an anxious look at me, Colton steps over to the control panel and presses the red phone button. "Uhh, yeah. Hey, Chief. Colton Morrow here. I'm with our PR director, Poppy St. James."

There's a moment's delay where the only sound is the mechanical whirring and that alarm buzz. I shimmy back into my lilac sheath dress, getting it up over my hips.

"You both alright?" calls the fire chief.

Colton smirks at me, his eye roving my half-nakedness. "Yeah, we're great. Little panicked at first, but now I'd say we're fan-freaking-tastic. Can you get us outta here?"

I roll my eyes, tugging my dress up onto my shoulders as I search the floor for my shoe. I had two when I walked in here . . .

"Sorry 'bout that, folks," comes the fire chief's deep voice. "We're resetting the system now. We'll have you out in a jiff."

Oh god, they're about to get us out? A crowd of firefighters is going to watch me do a walk of shame out of this freaking elevator. "My shoe!"

Colton drops to one knee and grabs my discarded shoe. I wobble on one foot as he wraps a gentle hand around my ankle, helping me slip the pink patent leather pump back on my foot.

"Oh—my panties!"

"Got 'em." He swipes my pink panties and my little silk neckerchief off the floor, along with his phone, tucking them all in his pockets.

I gasp as the elevator starts to move. "We're going down instead of up. Colton, if that lobby is full of people, I swear to god—"

"Turn around," he urges.

I spin to face the back wall, my fingers fumbling to fix my hair as Colton zips up the back of my dress. Using his much larger body, he blocks me from view. The doors open just as I'm tucking the loose tendrils of hair behind my ear.

"Hey, there," comes the fire chief's deep voice. "How we doing, folks? Everyone have fun in there?"

"Oh, yeah," says Colton, still blocking me with his body. "We had a great time."

"Poppy, honey, I'm so sorry," cries Vicki. "They started working on those dang generators, and then they blew a fuse, and it all went to hell in a hand basket."

I step out from behind Colton, a fake smile plastered on my face. "Well, it's about time y'all rescued us," I chime. "If I had to play 'I Spy' with this guy for one more minute, I was gonna lose my dang mind."

They all laugh, including Colton. It's rich and deep and warms me through like sinking into a hot bath. He makes the rounds, shaking the firefighters' hands as Vicki hurries over to me, her dark eyes wide with worry. "Poppy, honey, is everything alright?"

Oh god, how bad do I look? First stop: bathroom mirror.

"I may have had a teensy little panic attack," I admit. "But Colton helped calm me down."

"I'm so sorry," Vicki repeats. "I'm glad you weren't stuck in there all alone."

"She was a difficult patient, but I had her relaxed by the end," Colton teases.

I just smile. How the heck are we getting away with this? Surely there must be a large flashing sign over our heads that reads: "WE JUST HAD SEX."

But Vicki is still chattering about broken generators, and the quartet of firefighters is moving off, their job here done. Colton inches closer, filling my already-swimming senses with his woodsy scent and the heat of his now-familiar body.

I have to get out of here. "Well, the day doesn't end just because you get stuck in an elevator. Back to work I go."

Vicki steps over to the elevator and presses the "up" button. "You heading back up to four, honey?"

I watch the doors open and shake my head. "Sorry, Vic. For the foreseeable future, I think I'll be taking the stairs."

Colton chuckles. I cast him one more parting glance and the smooth devil winks. Only he and I will ever know that I walked into that elevator wearing panties, and I just walked out with those panties in his pocket, his cum now sticky between my legs.

29
LUKAS

"**W**ait, what are we doing?" I glance around at all the stuff Wednesday Addams and the social media interns have set out for us. Word to the wise: never say "nothing" when someone asks you what you're doing until you've *one hundred percent* confirmed their identity. I walked right into this and have no one to blame but myself.

"It's called the tortilla slap challenge," Wednesday says again.

"That tells us nothing," says Karlsson.

She glares at him. He doesn't take offense; she just doesn't have another way she looks at people. "You each take a large drink of water and hold it in your mouth," she explains again. "Don't swallow. Then you pick up a tortilla. Then you take turns slapping each other in the face with it. What's hard to understand?"

Sully glances from the bottles of water to the stack of tortillas. "Yeah, but . . . why?"

"Because it's funny and it's trending. Now, Karlsson and Sully, you're up first."

"Why do we need the water?" asks Karlsson.

"Just put the water in your mouth and don't swallow it," she says. "When Sully hits you with the tortilla, try not to spit it out."

"Hear that, Hen?" I elbow Karlsson. "In this game, you don't get to spit or swallow. You just gotta hold that shit in your mouth. Gargle it. Really give it a good soak."

He mutters something in Swedish as Sully says, "This sounds so dumb."

"It *is* dumb," Wednesday replies. "But it's trending and you all volunteered. So, pick up the tortillas and get slapping. Come on, I want to post this content within the hour."

Woody raises his hand like he's twelve and this is class.

Wednesday looks at him. "What, Woodson?"

"Yeah, uhh, I think I'd like to change my previous answer to 'I'm busy.' Can I do that? Can I go?"

Wednesday just stares him down until he lowers his hand.

"How 'bout I just watch the first round?" he offers.

She turns away from him and looks to Sully and Karlsson. "You're up first, gentlemen."

"So dumb," Sully mutters, grabbing a bottle of water. He and Karlsson stand on their marks.

"Okay, and . . . we're rolling," Wednesday calls, standing behind the phone tripod.

"Hey, y'all," Sully says to the camera with a wave. "Uhh, so we're the Rays. I'm Team Captain Josh O'Sullivan, and this here is my fellow lineman Henrik Karlsson." Always a man of few words, Hen just gives a nod to the camera. "And uhh, yeah, this is the tortilla slap challenge."

I shake my head, grinning as I watch them take big swigs of water. They hold it in their cheeks like a pair of chipmunks. Then an intern hands them each a tortilla. Sully gives Hen the nod, and Hen slaps him as hard as he can with the limp tortilla.

My eyes go wide as the tortilla makes the loudest cartoon *slap* noise I've ever heard. I join everyone behind the camera, roaring with laughter as Sully slaps Hen and they both spray water everywhere, choking as they laugh too.

"Oh my god. I wanna play," says Paulie, bouncing on the balls of his feet. "Woody, come slap me with a tortilla."

Woody and Paulie go next, introducing themselves to the camera before they take their swigs of water and start slapping. This is so fucking stupid. I'm crying, I'm laughing so hard. Holding my sides, I wheeze, tears in my eyes as Woody sprays Paulie in the face.

"Hey, what did I miss?"

I turn to see Cole standing at my shoulder, and my smile falls. I pull him back a few steps away from the camera. "What the hell? You weren't answering my calls. What happened with Poppy?"

He rubs the back of his neck. "Yeah, we sorta got trapped in an elevator."

My eyes go wide. "What?"

"Cool out. She's fine. You don't need to worry about it. Seriously, what are they doing?" He's distracted, watching as Sully and Hen join Woody and Paulie. Now they're doing a four-way slap fight with the tortillas, spraying water everywhere as the others howl with laughter.

"Oh man, water just went up my nose," Paulie says on a snort.

"It's the tortilla slap challenge," I say. "Wait, what do you mean I don't need to worry about it? Is she okay? What did the sister want?"

His smile falls as he places a hand on my shoulder. "Look, Novikov, whatever did or didn't happen between you and Poppy is finished. Find another shiny object."

Did this asshole just full-last-name me? I shrug his hand off my shoulder. "What the fuck is your problem?"

Before he can respond, I catch a whiff of his cologne . . . only he doesn't *just* smell like his cologne. He smells like rosemary and mint and a warm summer's day. And I've had enough sex to know that this fucking asshole is standing right next to me smelling like a freshly fucked pussy. My hackles rise. I bet if I lifted his fingers to my mouth, I could still taste Poppy on him.

"Trapped in an elevator?" I say with a raised brow. "That's the story?"

"Yeah, and it's a long story," he mutters, daring to move away.

I grab his arm, stepping close to speak in his ear. "Yeah, a story that ends with you three-fingers-deep inside our PR director's cunt—"

"Shut your fucking mouth," he growls.

"Well, that's why you came down here, right? To tell me you fucked her? Because you could've just left. Practice is long over, and you've got no PT. But no, you wanted to come rub it in my face first, you fucking caveman."

"I didn't come to crow over you, I came to *warn* you," he counters.

"Warn me?"

He holds my gaze, his expression dark and fucking menacing. Usually, he reserves this attitude for the ice and the opposition. "I'm only saying it once: You had your taste. Now, you're done. Poppy is off-limits."

I huff a hollow laugh. "Are you calling dibs on our PR director?"

"Yeah, I am," he replies with a solemn nod.

I stuff my hands in my pockets, my frustration rising. "Well, shouldn't that be her decision? I don't think she'd take too kindly to learn how you kicked me out of her bed."

"I'm sure you already kicked yourself out of it with your usual self-sabotaging bullshit."

Ouch. Fucker.

He leans in, that hand back on my shoulder like we're fucking friends. "Look, I know you, Nov. I know you like games, and I know your favorite game is the chase. So, I'm doing you this favor."

I shrug his hand away again. "What fucking favor?"

"Consider it a warning," he clarifies, his tone cold as ice. "I'm in the game now too."

Something dark and heavy churns in my gut. Are Cole and I seriously about to fall out over our PR director? Am I about to lose my only real friend on this team?

"Who's next?" Wednesday calls.

Clearly done with me, Cole raises his hand and calls out, "I'll play." He steps around the camera tripod, heading over to the table with the water and tortillas.

"I'm playing too," I say, shouldering past Woody.

"On your marks then." Wednesday points to the tape *X*s on the floor.

I unscrew my water bottle and take a deep swig, filling my mouth. Cole does the same. Then we're each handed a tortilla. He gives a nod, and I slap him as hard as I can. Even as the guys behind the camera cheer, he doesn't laugh, and he doesn't spray his water. Neither do I. Suddenly, this all got very un-fucking-funny.

I'm barely back on my mark before he's backhanding me with his fucking tortilla. I spit a little water in surprise, swallowing the rest. "Dude—what the fuck?"

He spits his water out on the carpet. Then he lunges, tackling me to the floor. We hit the table as we grapple, scattering the tortillas and bottles of water.

"Whoa—*hey*—this is not how you do the tortilla challenge," Wednesday shouts.

"Guys, what the fuck?"

'Hey, break it up!'

"I'm not gonna fight you," I grunt. "Getoffme—"

Cole glares down at me, his hips pinning mine down as he presses his forearm to my chest. Fuck, this guy's so strong. "You're done chasing her, understand?"

"Dude, what's your fucking problem? No chick is worth this," I say, twisting a hand free and punching him in the ribs.

He grunts, absorbing it. "She is. Now, get there faster, and I'll stop."

"Guys, knock it off—"

"That's enough—"

Two pairs of strong hands pull him off me. I blink up from the floor to see Sully and Woody with hands on him, holding him back.

"What the fuck is this?" Sully says, looking from Cole to me.

"Yeah, I thought you two were tight," says Paulie, eyes wide with confusion.

"We are," I pant from the floor.

Cole just keeps his gaze locked on me. "We're just working through a puzzle here, guys. Give Novy one more minute to solve it on his own."

As they all look down at me lying spread-eagle on the carpet, realization sinks deep.

"Got there yet?" Cole asks.

Sitting up with a groan, I nod, rubbing the back of my neck. "Yeah, I got it."

God, he's fucking right. The problem with chasing someone like Poppy St. James is that she's the kind of girl you catch to *keep*—and no woman worth having would ever want to be caught by me. Worse, I don't know the first thing about catching someone to keep them. Cole knows, and *I* know, that if I keep playing my fun chase games, I'll only end up hurting her.

And now he's in the game too, and his threat is crystal fucking clear: He will hurt me if I hurt her.

"We good?" he mutters.

I nod again. "Yeah."

He relaxes and gives a nod to Sully and Paulie. "We're good, guys. Nov and I are on the same page again."

They let him go and he stalks off, not giving me a second look.

"Someone wanna fucking fill me in?" Sully calls after his retreating form.

I just sit there on the floor next to the crushed tortillas, feeling emptier than I've ever felt in my life. Cole is mad at me, and my Poppy-chasing days are officially over. I respect her enough as my colleague, and I respect him enough as a friend, to bow out gracefully, right?

I had my little taste of heaven, and now I'm done.

This is fine. I can live with this easy.

Plenty more fish in the sea, right?

So, you tell me why, for the first time in my fucking life, I'm lying here on this floor fighting the aching feeling that *I* want to be the one who gets caught for once, but only if Poppy St. James is doing the chasing.

30
POPPY

"Uh-huh. Yeah, for nine people." I tuck my phone between my shoulder and my ear, unscrewing the cap off my chilled bottle of rosé. I've been on the phone for the last hour, making plans for a rental house and arranging activities for Violet's impromptu bachelorette weekend that I'm now suddenly in charge of hosting.

Listen, do I want to do it? No. *Should* I do it? Probably not. Am I *going* to do it? Abso-freaking-lutely. Because the more I ponder it—and trust me, I've pondered the heck out of it—the more this is all starting to feel like one big test. Like, maybe they want to see if this will be the thing that finally makes me crack. All the secrets and the lies and the sneaking around behind my back for two years wasn't enough. Let's add a little public humiliation. Let's put Poppy front and center at the "wedding of the season." Let's stick her in a bright red dress and put her right behind the bride, reminding everyone that she had her chance to matter, and she blew it.

Not enough? Then let's put her in charge of planning the bachelorette party so she can fondly remember the night of her own party . . . to the same man. The night when one of the drunk groomsmen sent her a grainy video of a stripper deep throating her fiancé.

Well, call me petty, but if this a game, I am *not* going to let them win. I'm not giving anyone from that life a reason to pity me or call me pathetic. I know, down to my bones, that walking away from Anderson Montgomery was the best decision I ever made.

I pour myself a glass of wine as the restaurant hostess rattles off a list of available dining times. "Yeah, eight o'clock sounds perfect."

A loud knock at my front door has me turning. I check the time on my stove. It's a little after ten. I'm standing in my kitchen in my silky pink shorts and a cropped tissue-thin cross country T-shirt. The neck is cut too, so it hangs off one shoulder. It might be my favorite scrap of cotton I own, but it's not exactly the right attire for visitors.

Another knock, softer this time.

"Yeah, so we're good?" I say into the phone.

"Yes, ma'am," says the hostess. "I have you down for eight o'clock."

"Great, thanks so much." I don't wait to hear her echoing "thanks" before I'm hanging up and hurrying over to the door. Glass of wine in hand, I tip up on my toes, peeking in the peephole.

I smile.

Colton is standing outside my door.

I was wondering when he might show up. We had sex in the elevator *two* days ago, and since then it's been total radio silence. It took me until midway through my lunch today to realize the only reason there's radio silence on his end is likely because he doesn't have my cell phone number. The team directory only lists my office number, which still doesn't work.

Still, he's my neighbor. He could have tapped on the wall or slipped a note under my door, something to indicate we were more than a one-and-done. All his pretty words in the elevator are starting to ring a little hollow.

He's about to leave, muttering something under his breath, and I'm still just standing here on my tiptoes, leering at him through my peephole. I twist the lock and fling the door open just as he's turning away. "Colton—hi," I say on a breath.

He turns back, his expression warming as he takes me in from head to toe. I do the same to him. He's dressed casually in a Rays T-shirt and athletic shorts. His hands are full of a bunch of reusable shopping bags, fit to burst with groceries.

"A little late for grocery shopping—"

"I was in Orlando," he says at the same time.

"What?"

"Orlando," he says again. "Helping my mom move. That's where I've been, in case you were wondering."

I smile, feeling a little lighter. "I was, actually."

"Yeah, I couldn't get out of it," he goes on, his tone apologetic. "She's moving down from Canada. I promised I'd go back down tomorrow morning too. And I didn't have your number, so I couldn't tell you."

I take a sip of my wine. "Is she retiring?"

"Nah, I think she'll retire when she's dead," he replies, shifting his hold on the bags. "She likes the work too much, and she's good at it. A hospital offered her a crazy good contract, and she was ready for a change, you know, after Dad's death."

"Fresh starts are always good," I say. I should know, having taken two myself. I nod to the bags. "Those look heavy. Why don't you go put them away and come back?"

"Actually, they're for you."

"For me?"

"Yeah, I uhh . . . I may have gone a bit overboard with this."

"Well, now I'm curious." I try to peek inside the closest bag.

"I wanted to get you stuff to make that granola again. But I didn't know what recipe you use, and I wanted it to be a surprise, so I didn't ask. I looked up seven recipes on the internet, all with really good reviews, and I got you the stuff for all seven. I figured, if it's not in one of these bags, it doesn't belong in granola," he finishes with a shrug.

Okay, I think I might cry. "You want me to make you more granola at . . ." I check the time on my phone. "Ten-thirty at night?"

"No, I want you to teach *me* how to make it," he corrects.

Heart skipping, I swing the door open wider. "You wanna come in?"

"Yes."

I step back, letting him in. He fills my entryway, closing the door behind himself. I wait as he slips out of his Rays-branded tennis shoes. Now two pairs of his shoes wait by my front door. I pad on bare feet backward into my kitchen, unable to take my eyes off him. The energy between us is charged. He follows me into the kitchen, only breaking his heated gaze away when he turns to heft the bags onto the counter. Heavens, he bought enough stuff to feed a small army . . . or a hockey team. He stays facing away from me, shoulders tense, like he's trying to decide what to do next.

Please tell me he's as nervous as I am.

I step back, my hip hitting the edge of the sink. My heart is racing. There's so much we should say first, right? Ground rules we should establish. But all I can think about is him standing here, close enough to touch, and we're not touching. Why aren't we touching?

I set my glass of wine aside. "Colton . . ."

He doesn't turn around. "What?"

"Before we make granola . . . would you like to fuck me?"

That has him turning. He reaches back to grip the counter with both hands as if it's the only thing keeping him from coming over here and ripping my clothes off. I let my gaze trail down his muscular body. I stop at his athletic shorts, where I can see the clear outline of his hard cock tucked against his leg. My eyes dart back up to his face.

Holding my gaze, he smiles. "Yes."

I let out a sigh of relief. "Oh, thank god."

We crash into each other, our lips meeting in a fevered kiss as I wrap my arms around his neck, pressing myself against him. He reels me in, hands on my hips. "Fuck, I want you so bad," he says against my mouth, all pretense of awkwardness forgotten now that I'm back in his arms. "Can't breathe for wanting you. Can't think. I could barely fucking drive here—only want to be where you are."

I whimper against his mouth, desperate for him. I do the only thing I can think to do and jump. He catches me, his hands wrapping around my thighs. I laugh as he rushes out of my kitchen.

"Couch or bed?" he asks, his lips still searing mine with hungry kisses.

"*Mmph*, bed. Left," I add, pointing over my shoulder toward the open door. I squeal as he carries me inside my bedroom, kissing me again before he drops me onto the bed.

"Get naked."

I stifle my giggle as I prop myself up on my elbows. "Eager, are we?"

He towers over me, wasting no time stripping off his shirt. "For you? Always."

I slip my silky pink sleep shorts down my legs, tossing them on the floor. My panties go next, then my ratty cross country crop top. I scoot back on the bed, unashamed that I'm fully naked, laid bare for this beautiful man.

I watch Colton's ab muscles flex as he drops his shorts to my floor. He slips his socks off last, then he's standing over me at the side of my bed, fisting his hard cock. I look up at him through my lashes, heart hammering.

"You are so goddamn beautiful." He wraps his hand around his tip, squeezing it tight. "I don't want to blink."

"You're beautiful too," I reply, taking in the sharp lines of his chest. "Do you have lube?"

I nod, pointing. "Bedside table. Top drawer."

"Touch yourself," he commands. "Show me your pussy."

Swallowing my nerves, I part my legs for him, pressing a finger to my clit. I hum, biting my bottom lip as I feel my clit warm under my fingertip, the heat spreading across my skin and coiling deeper into my core.

Colton steps over to my bedside table and rattles open the top drawer. He's such a masculine presence in such a frilly, feminine room. I didn't pick any of these decorations. I didn't pick the pale blue bedspread or the seashell lamps. I certainly didn't pick the pillow covers that look like my Nana's lace doilies. I've just been too busy to bother getting anything else.

He holds up my favorite magic wand with a grin. "Should I introduce myself, or does it already know my name?"

I smile, dipping the tip of my finger inside my pussy. "Oh, it knows you very well."

He brings the wand and the lube over to the bed, tossing them down beside me. "Deeper," he commands, his hand back to fisting his cock.

Someday, when I'm not feeling so ravenous, I think I'd like to watch him stroke himself to completion. But now I need him closer. I need him touching me. "Please," I whimper, sinking two fingers inside myself.

"So beautiful." His eyes are locked on where I'm teasing myself. His gaze travels slowly up to my face, taking in every inch of me. "Do you have any idea what you do to me?"

"Come show me."

Dropping to the floor on his knees, he grabs me by both ankles and pulls me to the edge of the bed.

"Oh my—" I shriek, fighting the urge to squirm as he laughs, flipping my legs over his shoulders, his breath warm on my thighs. After one teasing lick of his tongue, I'm digging my heels into his back and grinding my pussy against his chin. He's ferocious, his hands wrapping around my thighs to brace my hips as he growls.

"Oh, don't stop," I chant. "Don't stop—"

Colton reaches up with his long arm, cupping my breast, pinching and teasing the tight little bud of my nipple. I arch into him, arms thrown back over my head as I sink into the floaty, warm feeling of a clitoral orgasm.

"Yes," I cry. "*There*."

I drop a hand down to his head, holding him to me as I grind with my hips, not releasing him until my legs are trembling and I feel boneless. He kisses down my thigh as I sink back to the bed, my orgasm leaving me feeling like a glass of bubbly pink champagne. "You taste so good," he says.

He slips my legs off his shoulders, and I sit up on my elbows, smiling down my naked body at him. "Let me return the favor."

"No fucking way." He gets to his feet.

"But—"

"You can show me how well you swallow my cum later. Right now, I need to be inside you. Turn over. Hands and knees, baby."

I sweep my eyes up his body again. "Can you . . ." Too embarrassed to ask, I let it lie, turning over for him.

"What?"

"Nothing."

He senses my hesitation and folds himself over me, cupping my face. "What is it?" His walnut-brown eyes search my face.

Lost in those dark pools, I dare to ask, "Can you call me your queen again?"

His smile lights up his entire face as he kisses me. I melt into it, my body half-turned like a twisty pretzel. He smooths his free hand up my thigh and over my ass. His every touch and kiss are so possessive and claiming. "You wanna be my queen, baby?"

I nod as he kisses down my jaw.

"You want me to worship you? Pledge you my fucking fealty?"

"Yes," I say on a breath. His head drops lower so he can suck on my breast. He palms the other one. My breasts are small, barely enough to fill a hand, but he doesn't seem to mind.

"You like being owned, but you're possessive too, aren't you?"

My body shivers as he flicks at my nipple with his tongue. "Yes," I say again.

"Don't I fucking know it." He moves to my other breast. He didn't get to play with them in the elevator. There was no time. My bra never even came off. "My queen has sharp claws," he teases. "Fuck, I'd love to watch you shred anyone who tried to touch me. I'm getting harder just thinking about it." He takes me by the wrist and tugs my hand down, letting me feel how hard his cock is for me, how ready.

I wrap my hand around his tip. "Colton . . ."

"Yes, my queen?"

I smile, lost in my bliss. "Will you please fuck me now?"

His laugh is warm against my skin. "Yes, my queen. I'm gonna use some lube this time so you feel good, okay?"

I nod and he kisses me again.

"Perfect. Now, be a good girl, and get on your hands and knees for me. Let me show you how you deserve to be worshipped, body and fucking soul."

31
COLTON

Poppy rolls onto her stomach for me. She's stretched out naked on this bed, and I can't look away. Her every curve is perfect—the tight roundness of her ass, the soft little hills of her breasts. One orgasm has her feeling loose and relaxed. I want to pull at least two more from her before I let her sleep.

She came apart so beautifully for me just now. And she tastes divine, soft and sweet, with just the perfect hint of feminine musk. It's been two days since I last tasted her, since I last held her in my arms. The wanting her is shredding me apart. It was all I could do to not break speed limits just so I could get here by ten o'clock tonight. And I'll have to go back to Orlando in the morning.

It's not my mom's fault she picked this week to move, but damn if the timing isn't inconvenient. Instead of showering Poppy with affection, I've spent the last two days hooking up TVs and unpacking plates in my mom's new lakeview condo.

But I'm not thinking about Orlando right now. No, my every thought is centered on the naked woman in the middle of this bed. She wants to be worshipped and adored? I'm about to show her the meaning of the words.

"Like this?" she asks, glancing over her shoulder as she gets to her hands and knees.

"Perfect." I crawl onto the bed behind her, grabbing her little blue wand and the bottle of lube. I'm curious to know what other toys my Poppy might play with when I'm not here, but this will do for now. More than anything, I just need to be inside her again. I need to feel that hum of connection with her, soul to soul.

I pop the cap off the lube and squeeze some into my hand, working it down my shaft with a groan. I can't even think about this woman without getting hard. It's becoming a real problem. Hell, I was hard for half the drive up here. I had to turn on a true crime podcast just to try to get some goddamn relief.

Scooting closer, I smooth my lube-free hand over the rounded curve of her ass. She shivers at my touch, her hips moving reflexively as she backs into my hand, craving more contact. She's so responsive. I think she might be physically needy, like me. Now that I know I can touch her, it's gonna be damn hard for me to stop.

I snake my other hand between her thighs, flipping my palm up to run my lubed fingers through her wetness. "Are you ready for me?"

She drops down on a little moan, burying her face in the crook of her elbow. "Mhmm." Her hair is down, tousled over her back, and her little asshole peeks out at me between her cheeks. We're not going there tonight, but fuck if I haven't already thought about how tight she'll fit me.

I fist my cock at the base, guiding my tip between her legs. We both groan at the first slide of my shaft along her wet silk. "Fuck, you feel so good," I say, reveling in the feel of doing this without a condom.

Even now, an alarm bell is dinging in my head that I should stop and put one on. Hockey players are read the riot act from an early age: no rubber, no ride. I can count on one hand the number of girlfriends I've taken bare. In fact, I can count it on half a hand. It's a gift, and a sign of trust, and I won't be squandering it. To feel her like this, to connect with her on this level after so long of dreaming and waiting—god, I'm already about to lose my load.

She presses those hips against me, seeking more, and I know she's ready. I prod her entrance, finding the right angle. Her wet heat pulls me in as she pushes back, but I catch her, my hold firm on her hips. "Go slow," I direct. "Let me stretch you out first." I curl over her, kissing her shoulder. "I only ever want to bring you pleasure."

She pushes up onto her hands, adjusting her hips as she sinks deeper on me. Once I'm halfway, I move my hand, letting it smooth over her ass and up the curve of her back until I'm bracing her by the neck. Heat spirals out from our shared point of connection. Heart racing, I move my hips, pumping deeper into her until she's humming out another breathy moan.

"How's that feel?"

"So good," she says immediately. "Col, you feel so good."

Okay, I thought her saying my full name with that lemon twist of a Southern accent sent me over the edge. But this is the second time she's called me "Col" while I've been half a dick deep, and I'm living for that too. "I want my queen to take charge," I say, brushing my other hand over her hip. "Sit back. Take as much of me as you want. Ride me. Show me how much you want my dick."

She shifts her legs, widening her hips as she pushes against me on a soft moan. From this angle, I can hold her waist and watch as she takes me inside her tight cunt. Fuck, I'm not gonna last long.

"I want more," she pants, rocking her hips harder against me. "Colton, please. I need more."

I fold myself over top of her. Cupping her breasts with my hands, I haul her up and rock back, impaling her on my dick. She cries out, her hands slapping over mine on her breasts, head thrown back against my shoulder. I rock with her, feeling the hot glide of her pussy squeezing me tight.

"Yes—oh my god," she pants. "Oh, right there."

I grind up into her, holding the weight of her easily against me. Her hair is brushing my chest, and her nails dig into my forearms as her pussy clenches with her coming orgasm.

"Oh, I'm so close. Honey, don't you dare stop—"

I let out a joyous laugh, sucking her neck, tasting her sweat with my tongue. She's starting to tremble, her orgasm seconds from crashing into her. It's gonna hit like a wave, sweeping us both under. My god, she's exquisite like this. I can't get enough.

Don't get me wrong, I'm a huge fan of PR Poppy too. But PR Poppy is a creature of rules and routine. She's got impeccable fashion, polite manners, and an acute business savvy. She's fierce and funny, and I could fall for her in a blink. I *am* falling for her.

But this woman in my arms? This wild thing? Sexy Poppy is uninhibited and raw, taking what she wants, begging for more. I don't think she knows how beautiful she looks like this, how powerful, how desirable. I feel like I'm holding onto a beam of pure fucking sunlight. Her attention is life-giving. It's restoring. With her, I am remade.

Snatching up her fancy blue wand, I turn it on and angle the vibrating head between her legs. The second it touches her sensitive clit, she cries out, her slick pussy clamping down on me.

"Fuck yes," I pant, wrapping my arm around her chest to cup her other breast. I pull her up tight against me, her back to my front, and just hold her there, seated with me all the way inside her. Her body is ready to tip over that sweet edge. She's shaking, pussy fluttering, eyes shut tight. "Come for me," I growl in her ear. As I do, I press in hard with the wand, letting that vibrating head spark against her clit like a Roman candle.

Her mouth opens on a scream. It's all I can do to hold onto her and keep the wand in place as she rocks against me, her orgasm bursting forth from her center and spiraling outward.

"Oh my god," she whimpers as soon as she's able to speak, her body going limp and breaking our connection.

I know she has one more in her, and I know I can get her there. I fall forward with her, letting her drop down to the mattress. I turn off the wand and toss it aside. She's jelly as I roll her over, scooting her across the bed to make more room for myself between her knees.

Her arms go around me, clinging to me, desperate for my closeness. I give her a reassuring kiss, deep and seeking as her hands pull at my back, trying to make us share one skin again.

"Does my queen feel treasured?" I say against her lips.

She nods, eyes shut tight as she recovers her breath.

"Do you want more?"

She nods again.

"Do you want my cum?" I turn her head to kiss down her neck. "Do you want me to fill this sweet little cunt?"

"Yes," she hums, spreading her legs beneath me to fit me in the cradle of her thighs.

I curl a hand around her leg, spreading her wider, and sink right back inside. Every inch of me slides in until I'm settled against her hips. Once I'm in, her hands on my shoulders relax, sated knowing we're one again. Her eyes open as I rock into her. She gazes up at me with more clarity now, those blue eyes searching my face.

"What is it?" I say, kissing her chin.

"You're so beautiful," she murmurs, her fingers brushing down my cheek and over my lips. She takes in my features like she's trying to memorize them.

I imprint her to memory too. I want to always be able to picture her just like this—lips parted, the soft freckles of her cheeks not hidden by makeup, eyes bright with lust and longing. She's timeless. God help me, she's *mine*. I kiss the soft pads of her fingertips before she drops her arm over her head, arching back on the bed.

"Come again for me."

"I can't," she whines.

"Yes, you can." I'm so fucking close, and I want to feel her squeezing me as I shatter. "One more time. Come with me."

"It's too much. So full."

I let go of her leg and cup her face instead, kissing her deep, luring her back to me. She meets my kisses, her arms going back around my neck. "Yes," I pant, stroking down the column of her neck. "There she is. Stay with me, Poppy. My goddess, my fucking queen. Come with me. *Look* at me."

She opens her eyes. They're glassy with lust. I feel her starting to tighten around me again. I palm her breast, tweaking her nipple until she gasps, waking her up. "Baby, I'm gonna come," I pant.

This has her clinging to me, her legs wrapping around my hips. "Don't stop," she squeals, her nails digging into my shoulders.

I can't hold back my release for another second. I come on a shout, my hand dropping away from her breast and down to the bed as I thrust once, twice. She's trembling, her pussy clenching around my cock as she comes with me, quietly this time, sacred, like a fucking prayer.

After a few more seconds, I pull out, rolling my weight to the side so I don't crush her. She clings to me, her leg wrapping around my hip. We settle on the bed with my head tucked against her bare chest. I keep my arms around her, breathing in the softly floral smell of her heated skin.

A few minutes pass, but we stay just like this, entangled and unmoving. Slowly, she comes back to life, her hand stroking down my back. She sighs dreamily, tilting her face to kiss my forehead. "While the granola bakes, can we do that again?"

I snort a laugh, ducking my face down to kiss her breast, giving her nipple a little suck that has her moaning the first half of my name like a goddamn siren. I get the feeling now that I'm never going to survive her. Smiling, I press a promising kiss to her lips. "Yes, Poppy. I will gladly fuck you again."

And again.

And again.

32
POPPY

Riptide's Bar & Grill is chaotic tonight. It's karaoke night, the Rays are fresh off a home game win, and the autumn weather is perfect. A gorgeous, sunny day with good waves on the beach is quickly shifting to a lavender sunset. The outdoor bar area is packed, with more people wandering up from the beach to grab drinks and listen to the live music.

Mojito in hand, I make my rounds at all our tables, greeting the Rays and their wives and girlfriends. I take a few pictures and get approval to post them to the socials, but mainly I'm just here for a good time.

At this exact moment, I feel like a million bucks. Everything is set for our first big fundraiser this weekend. As a little treat, I spent three hours at the beach this afternoon, so now I have sun-kissed cheeks and beachy waves in my hair. Also, I'm wearing my favorite pair of skinny jeans that give me supermodel legs—always a feat when you're only five-foot-two.

Oh, and Colton is here, and he's winked at me twice.

After our marathon of sex and granola-making last night, he ducked out before six in the morning to drive back down to Orlando, something to do with updating his mom's security system. But in between the sex and granola, we talked. He knows how important this job is to me, and he's willing to keep what we're doing quiet. He may have a multi-year contract with the Rays, but I don't, and I won't do anything to risk my place here.

There's nothing strictly forbidden about what we're doing, but after a decade of running from the pressures of high society public life, I find I'm much happier spinning the stories, not starring in them. Colton more than understands. He wants any media focused on him to be about building a new team, not his private life.

That doesn't make it any easier to keep my hands off him. The man is sex on a hockey stick. I swear, I can feel his eyes on me even now. They burn into the back of my head, searing my skin with desire. I fight a shiver, taking a sip of my minty mojito as I glance over my shoulder—

I gasp, turning back around. It wasn't Colton I felt looking at me.

Lukas steps in behind me. "Hey, Popsicle. You singing tonight, or you too chickenshit?"

I glare over my shoulder at him, one brow raised. "Popsicle?"

He grins. "I thought it was fitting. You know, 'cause—"

"I know why you're calling me 'Popsicle,' Lukas. And I don't find it cute or charming."

"I wasn't going for charming. I was going for teasing."

"Because that's all you are. A big tease."

He laughs, not denying it. "Langers just challenged me to get up there and sing. I told him we'll flip a coin and loser takes the mic. Now, I have great luck with coin tosses, but just in case the gods curse me, what would you like to hear me sing?"

"'So Yesterday,'" I deadpan.

"Hmm, I don't know that one."

"It's by Hilary Duff. Consider it my love letter to you."

"I was thinking I'll dust off some Boyz II Men, maybe some Backstreet Boys."

I spin around, my eyes narrowed at him. I see the joke dancing in his pretty caramel eyes. "How did you know?"

"What, that the Backstreet Boys is one of your favorite bands?" He takes a sip of his beer. "Word to the wise, Popsicle. If you don't want people to know things about you, don't post them to social media. As my PR director, I assumed you were aware—"

"I haven't posted a picture of me at a Backstreet Boys concert this *millennium*, you creep! What, did you stalk my old Facebook photos?"

"The internet is forever, Pops—"

"*Don't* call me 'Popsicle.' And don't you *dare* ruin Backstreet Boys for me. I mean it, Lukas."

Chuckling, he winks and saunters away. Arrogant ass. I turn back toward the band, taking another sip of my mojito. Up on the stage, our captain's wife, Shelby, is singing "That Don't Impress Me Much" by Shania Twain. No one is a bigger hype man than Josh. He stands there clapping and singing along, throwing out the occasional wolf whistle.

They're so stinkin' cute together. And they have the cutest mess of adorable, sporty kids. Honestly, they're a PR dream. He even teaches Sunday school. I snap a few pictures with Josh foregrounded, Shelby glowing under the purple lights of the stage. I won't post these to the team socials, I'll just send them to her as a little keepsake. Everyone deserves to have evidence of being treasured.

"Hey." Colton steps in behind me, his hand on my hip. I'm wearing a little floral print, off-the-shoulder peasant top that doesn't quite skim the top of my jeans. His fingers find that barest strip of exposed skin, brushing over it quick like a kiss. But, oh god, I feel it like a brand.

"Hey."

"What was that about?"

"What was what?"

"Novikov. Was he bothering you?"

I roll my eyes. "He's always bothering me."

Colton turns to go after him, and I fist his shirt. "No—hey, what are you doing?"

"I told him to stay the fuck away from you," he growls.

"You did what?" My frustration rises as I let go of his shirt. "Colton, we work together. I'm going to see and talk to Lukas. Regularly. But I'm a big girl, and I can handle my own business. I don't need you being a jerk to him for no reason—"

"You think I have no reason to be a jerk?"

"No, you don't."

He crosses his arms.

"Lukas was there for me as a friend. I asked for everything that happened that night. I was sad about Anderson, and my family, and all of it. I didn't want to be alone. He was there, and that's it. Okay?"

He shakes his head, his gaze still on wherever Lukas is in the crowd. Then he's leaning down, his dark eyes locked on me. "I told you to come to *me* if you needed to be kissed. I told you on the plane, days before DC—"

"Well, I wasn't going to just waltz up to you and say 'Hey, remember that open invitation to kiss me senseless? Well, my ex-fiancé is marrying my little sister, so I'd like to cash that in now.'"

"Why not?"

"Because it's embarrassing. And pathetic and sad. Three words I'd rather not associate with myself when it comes to you."

His eyes narrow. "So, the sex with Novy was pathetic and sad?"

"No, it was—" I groan, fisting my mojito. "*You* told me you didn't want to know any of this."

"Well, I've changed my mind."

I shake my head. "Colton, *no*. I am not going to hurt you just because you're already feeling hurt. Believe it or not, he was good to me. It happened. That doesn't mean it will ever happen again."

"It better not," he growls.

Tears of frustration sting my eyes. "Well, maybe next time you won't sit pining after a girl for two freaking years. Maybe next time you'll make your move. You'll take your shot. Otherwise, you'll sit back and realize someone else already has!"

Storming away from him, I weave my way toward the bar, desperate for a refill on this dang mojito. I slide the glass across the bar and wait. My attention is pulled to the laptop propped on the edge of the bar, taking requests for the karaoke queue. I skim the list, my eye stopping on the name in all caps: LUKAS NOVIKOV.

"Son of a freaking bitch," I huff under my breath.

The jerk is up next to sing "I'll Never Break Your Heart" by the Backstreet Boys.

Feeling reckless, I type in my name too.

33
POPPY

I stay at the bar, clutching my second mojito. A wooden column at the end of the bar hides me from the microphone as Lukas's name is called. The Rays section cheers as he jumps up on stage, waving to the crowd. He grabs the mic, slipping it from the stand. "This song is dedicated to someone very special in the crowd tonight."

I sit forward on my stool. Oh, he better freaking not—

"Henrik Karlsson, where are you, bud?" He shields his eyes from the lights as "I'll Never Break Your Heart" starts to play.

The Rays all laugh and clap as two guys point out the handsome Swede, quietly nursing a beer.

"Hen, I'm sorry you took an elbow to the face at practice and lost a tooth," Lukas says to more laughter. "I may break your teeth on occasion, but you know I'll never break your heart."

The crowd cheers as Henrik gets to his feet and salutes Lukas with his beer. Then Lukas starts to sing. I swallow a gulp of my mojito, peering around the wooden pillar.

"Oh, goddamn it." Slapping my drink down, I shove it away.

The man has the voice of a freaking angel.

"ALRIGHT, that was awesome," the emcee says as Lukas finishes his song. "Let's hear it for Lukas Novikov!"

Lukas waves to the cheering crowd as he replaces the mic on the stand. While he was singing, I wove my way around the back of the open-air bar, trying to stay hidden in the sea of people. The last thing

I'm going to do is give him an excuse to tease me more by singing while looking longingly into my eyes. I make it to the edge of the stage just as the emcee says, "Next up, we have Poppy St. James, ready to wow us with a little Dolly Parton."

Lukas makes his way over to me. A sheen of sweat glistens on his brow. The yellow of the stage lights make his eyes shine almost golden. "I warmed them up for you," he says with a grin.

"Thanks."

As he passes, he leans in. "I sang that for you."

My shoulders stiffen. He tosses me a wink as he walks away.

God *damn* that man!

"Let's go, Poppy," one of the wives cheers from the crowd.

"Get it, girl!"

Taking a deep breath, I put on my best smile and wave, entering the bright circle of the stage lights. They switch to purple and pink, and the crowd cheers again as I step up to the mic. I reach for the dial, twisting it lower as the song starts. "Sorry, y'all. Some of us are a little vertically challenged."

The crowd laughs.

Looking out, I note all the faces of people I know. Friends, colleagues. I smile, relaxing a little. Despite all the crazy, *this* is my life now. This is where I want to belong. Not in a stuffy tearoom on a New York City boulevard or in the halls of Congress chasing down some harried senator. I want to belong here, on a karaoke stage in a rowdy beach bar in Jacksonville, Florida, surrounded by all my friends.

I focus my attention on Shelby O'Sullivan's bright, encouraging smile. Leaning in, I sing the first verse of "Jolene."

"*HEY*, Poppy, that was amazing!" Rachel brushes her hand down my arm as I pass her table.

"Thanks, girl," I return with a smile.

The great thing about "Jolene" is that it's a short song that most people know. It takes the pressure off me having to be any good if I can just hype up the crowd to sing it with me. And this crowd ate it all the way up. My good mood is locked firmly back in place as I exchange more smiles, weaving my way inside the main dining room. Once inside, I make a beeline for the restroom.

I step into the far one, noting the dingy, dark walls covered in old posters and flyers for concerts and beach events. Beyond the walls, the house music pumps, something loud and rock'n'roll. I push the door shut, shrieking as it gets blocked by a body. "Lukas—"

He slips in, shutting the door and turning the lock. "Seriously? You sang 'Jolene'?"

"God, get out. This bathroom is occupied." I move over to the cracked mirror in the corner. Desperate for something to do with my hands, I start washing them.

"Please tell me you're not still hung up on that douchey architect who is currently fucking your sister."

I glare through the mirror at his reflection, taking in his crossed arms, those tattooed biceps bulging in his tight gray T-shirt. "I'm not."

He scoffs. "Yeah, right."

"What?" I slam my palm against the soap dispenser, squirting soap into my hand. "I'm not. I don't want Anderson. I don't care about Anderson. I don't even *think* about Anderson. Look, this is me, actively not thinking about him."

He raises a brow. "Oh, yeah?"

"Well, I *wasn't* thinking about him until you stormed in here, shoving him in my face. The door is behind you, by the way."

He leans against it. "I'm not going anywhere."

"Suit yourself." I rinse off the soap under the hot water, squeezing my hands together instead of squeezing his stupid neck.

"If you're so over it, why were you singing 'Jolene?'"

"Seriously?" Shutting off the water, I tug paper towels out of the dispenser by his shoulder. "Maybe because Dolly Parton is a literal icon who just happens to be one of my favorite singers? Didn't sleuth that on my social media, did you? I've been singing 'Jolene' at karaoke since I was twelve years old!"

"Likely story."

"Ohmygod, this is so pathetic. I know why you're really in here."

His gaze heats as he glares down at me. "And why is that?"

I cross my arms, glaring right back. "You know about me and Colton—"

"Of course I fucking know," he shouts, crowding my space until I'm backing up against the wall. "The asshole only came and rubbed it in my face the moment he pulled out of you."

My eyes widen. "He what?"

"Yeah, he came and found me right after the elevator. I could still smell you on his fucking skin."

I search his face, looking for the lie. "Why would Colton do that?"

"Because he's a territorial fucking asshole! He was all 'finders keepers,' and told me I can't play the game. But now I'm all twisted up because I think I *want* to play the game. I mean—it's not a game anymore, and I get that—but I don't know how to *not* play this like a game, you know? Not when the rules are finders keepers and—"

"What's finders keepers?"

"It's you," he replies. Then he groans, dragging a hand through his short, almond-brown hair. "Or maybe now it's me. I'm not quite sure about that part. It feels like somewhere it all got twisted around."

"Lukas, you're not making any sense. Colton came to you after the elevator?"

"Of course he did," he snaps.

"And you know we . . ."

He just rolls his eyes. "Seriously? You think I don't know the scent of your shampoo?"

I stiffen.

"You think I don't know the sweet smell of your pussy?"

I gasp, shoving against his chest. "Now you're just being *rude*."

"It was wafting off of him," he says, letting me push him back a step. "Two men in one week? Impressive. How many more contracts will be stacked next to your bed by Sunday night? I hear Henrik's on the market."

Hot rage boils through me. "Slut shaming? Really? That's a new low, even for you."

"Hey, there's no shame in sex. If anything, I'm proud. Your dry spell is officially over, eh? I bet if I checked right now, you'd be wet as fucking rain."

My rage turns cold as ice. "Touch me, and I'll scream."

He grins. "If I touch you again, the only thing you'll be screaming is my name."

"God, just get *out*, Lukas. Your jealousy bores me—"

He crowds me against the wall again, his hands slamming to either side of me, boxing me in. His caramel eyes are dark and heated. "Lie to me again," he growls. "Do it, Poppy. Make my fucking week. You *love* my jealousy. It turns you the fuck on, don't even try denying it."

My heart's racing so fast, but I tip my head back. "Once again, you're delusional."

"You think I don't see the way you look at me? You think I can't *feel* it? I feel your eyes on me. Watching me—"

"Stop."

"Undressing me. On the ice, off the ice."

"Why would I bother? You were utterly forgettable, remember?"

He leans away. His gaze trails down my body. "We both know you remember every single thing I did to you. You remember my tongue flicking your tits."

"No, I don't—"

"You remember how I held you up against the side of the god-damn ice machine and fucked you senseless," he goes on. "And you remember the hotel room."

"Total blank," I whisper.

"*You* got that second condom, not me."

"Stop," I beg him.

"You wrapped your hand around my aching dick and slipped me inside your needy cunt."

I shake my head, eyes closed, trying to banish the memories from my mind.

"Then you rode my dick until you came the fuck apart."

"I said, stop."

"*You* stop." He lowers his face until I can feel the warmth of his breath on my cheek. "Stop thinking about it. Stop squeezing the walls of that sweet pussy right now, dreaming about how I filled you."

I open my eyes, looking up into his face. He's teasing me, and it's cruel. This is all still just one big game to him. What did he call it?

Finders keepers? And apparently Colton is playing too. Well, I am not a toy for them pick up and fight over like children. "Just tell me what you want, Lukas. Why did you really follow me in here?"

"I want you to ask for it."

"Ask for what?"

"Ask for more! Ask me to fill you again, and I'll take you right here against this *fucking* wall." He slaps the wall of faded posters next to my head, making me jump. "I'll pound your cunt, and grab your hair, and bury myself inside this scent." He fists a handful of my loose hair. Breathing it in, he groans again. "*God*, this fucking scent."

I'm trembling. My locked knees are the only thing keeping me standing. "It sounds like *you're* the one aching to ask for more. Is that what you want, Lukas? You want another night in heaven with me?"

His body goes stiff as he lets go of my hair. "Don't tease me."

I huff a laugh. "That's rich, coming from *you*. That's what you want, isn't it? Anything to score a point or two over Colton."

He blinks down at me. "What?"

"Well, you're both professional athletes, so I assume there must be a point system. One point for a kiss, three points if you get inside my pants? Or is it location based? He took me in an elevator, now you get points for a bathroom?"

He groans. "No, that's not what I—"

"You just said I'm nothing but a game to you! So come on, explain the rules. I wanna play too. How many points do you get for fingering me?"

He leans away. "Poppy, there's no game."

"Come on, this has to be worth a couple points, right?" I slip my hand inside the top of my tight jeans, wiggling my fingers against my clit.

Lukas's gaze locks on my hand. "Poppy, what the hell are you doing?"

"What does it look like I'm doing?" I dip two fingers inside my pussy, unashamed to find that I'm wet. This man riles me up like nothing else. Who knew irritation could have such an effect on the libido? I hum, working myself harder. "How many points do I get for this?"

Lukas shakes his head. "Poppy, there are no points."

Ever so slowly, I pull my hand free, and lift it to my lips. "What about this?"

His eyes go wide as he watches me suck my glistening fingers into my mouth. Letting out a soft little moan, I taste my own sweetness, sliding my fingers in and out like I'm sucking a dick.

"Fuck me," he says on a breath.

I pop my fingers from my mouth, my eyes narrowing. "Fuck you? I think not."

"What? No, it was just an expression—"

"God, I'm so mad, I could scream!" I shove at his shoulders again. "I am not a toy, Lukas. I'm not something you and Colton can pick up and fight over and set aside when you're done playing your little games."

"Yeah, I know—"

"And contrary to what you might think, I don't use people," I say, my voice cracking as I fight to hold back my tears. "Sex is *never* a game to me."

He groans, dragging a hand through his hair. "Okay, so I can sense that you're still mad about what I said at the hotel—"

"You called me utterly forgettable! You said it was a mistake never to be repeated. Do you remember that? Because I sure do."

"Poppy—"

"You said I *used* you. Do you have any idea how much that hurt me, Lukas? Never mind that Anderson had already thrown that exact same insult grenade at me earlier the same freaking day!"

His eyes widen with horror. "Oh shit. He did?"

"You said I'm nothing but a spoiled, rotten brat, and then you kicked me out of your hotel room. I never got my panties back, by the way," I add, hands on my hips.

"Poppy, come on," he pleads. "You know I was obviously lying."

"Yeah, and now you're obviously leaving." I point to the door. "Or I really will scream."

He opens his mouth just as there's a sharp knock at the door. He turns, shoulders tensing, like he's going to murder the first person who tries to come through.

My anger is simmering down, replaced with shame and frustration.

Now, it's all I can do to keep myself from crying, and I refuse to do that in front of him. He has to go. "Time's up, Lukas."

He turns back to me, his expression anxious. "This isn't a game for me, Pop. I swear to god."

"Everything is a game to you."

"Just admit that you want me and we can move forward."

I point to the locked door again. "I *want* you to leave."

Someone hammers on the door for a second time. "Come on, man. Get outta there!"

"In a minute!" Lukas bellows, pounding the inside of the door with his own fist.

"Lukas," I say on a broken whisper.

He turns back to me.

Tears sting my eyes as I let him see my pain. "Don't make me beg."

Without another word, he leaves, taking all my air with him. I follow him to the door, shoving on it as the next person tries to come in. I twist the lock as they knock again, cursing and pounding on it with their fist.

Pulse racing, heart breaking, I back myself away until I bump into the far wall. Hands braced against the old, faded posters, I slide down, sinking to the dirty bathroom floor.

34
COLTON

Where the hell is Poppy? She disappeared right as she got off the karaoke stage, and we need to finish our conversation. I fly out for a game first thing in the morning, and I won't see her again for two days. I really don't want to leave us like this.

Fuck, why did I have to be such a possessive asshole? I knew about Novy. He didn't say a word, even when I pressed him, and still I knew. That should've been my warning right there. Novy is never shy about talking about the bunnies he's wheeling. But one night with Poppy, and he locks up tighter than a fucking vault?

Yeah, the big red flag is waving in my face. No matter what she says, I know he's not over her. Who could be once they've had a taste?

I groan, dragging a hand over my face. Sanford is on the karaoke stage now, wowing the crowd with a Måneskin cover. He dedicated the song to Doc Price, which really got the Rays section going. I thought she had a thing for Jake, but the way she's watching Sanny play right now should come with an explicit content warning.

I pause in my pursuit of Poppy, eyes narrowing on our Barkley Fellow. People are complicated, right? Attraction doesn't end just because you decide to commit yourself to one person. Rachel can be with Jake and still be attracted to Sanford.

Attraction is raw, animal instinct. Our humanity comes in when we decide whether to *act* on that instinct. And there's attraction between Poppy and Novy. It's undeniable. What I need to know is whether they're going to act on it again.

She assures me they're done. So, why can't I just let it lie?

Worse, why do I keep picturing them together?

I groan again, shoving on the door to enter the restaurant. It's like a hot and horny nightmare playing on repeat in my mind. I can't stop picturing him with her, and it's confusing the hell out of me. Most of the time, it makes me just as hard as it does angry.

I don't want Novy touching her. I don't want him even *thinking* about her. That he tasted her before me will haunt me until I die. If I had a machine to remove all memory of her from his brain, I would strap him in it and push the goddamn button.

Instead, I get to watch her "handle him" as he buzzes around like a cocky little bee, stinging her with jokes and longing looks. This is why you don't try to date the people you work with, right? How do I set the wanting her aside and do my job? How do I stifle this jealousy as I watch him flirt with her right in front of me?

I told him to leave her alone. I told him to back the fuck off.

Great job, Cole. That backfired spectacularly.

Now he's even more interested in her than he was before.

"Fuck," I mutter, searching for a head of long blonde hair in the crowd.

This is my own goddamn fault. She's right, I shouldn't have played it safe. I shouldn't have waited. I had years to try for her with him nowhere in the picture. But I was too wrapped up in my career to take her off her pedestal and put her in my arms where she belongs. Now my girl is trading hungry looks with my teammate and lying to herself about it.

Fuck, I can't do this. I can't share her. This is too hard. I liked it better when she was a dream I was chasing, unobtainable and flawless. This real person with raw instincts and moods and needs is too powerful. She'll devastate me. She'll break me wide open. She'll ruin me and leave me for dead.

I grab Karlsson's arm as he passes. "Hey, you seen Poppy?"

He shakes his head. "Not since she was onstage."

I let him go and he walks away. Feeling desperate, I leave the restaurant and head for the parking lot. I find her car parked in one of the back rows. Where the fuck is she?

Weaving my way through the cars, I loop around the far side of the outdoor bar area, my feet sinking into the sand of the beach. The sun has all but set. Now the ocean is a pale blue gray under the half-moon. The surf rocks in and out, small whitecaps foaming in the sand. I can't hear it over the music coming from the two stages at Rip's.

A few people wander along the water's edge—a couple holding hands, teenagers with a pair of dogs. I stop, taking in the figure of a lone woman standing in the surf fifty yards away. She holds her little wedge sandals in one hand. Her skinny jeans are soaked to the knee.

"Poppy," I say on a breath, the tension in my chest uncoiling. I kick off my shoes, leaving them in the sand as I go to her. The music fades with the bright lights of the bar as I enter that realm of the in between where the ocean meets the beach. "Poppy!"

She jolts, not turning around. "Go away."

Oh, fuck. Is she crying? I run the last ten yards to her, my feet sinking deep in the sand. "What's wrong?" I reach for her, but she pulls back, splashing away from me.

"Just go, Colton. I don't want to see you right now."

That tension coils right back inside my chest. "What happened?"

"Ask Lukas," she calls over her shoulder.

That stops me in my tracks. The surf crashes against my calves, pulling at my ankles as it drags sand over my bare toes. Anger churns in my stomach, making me feel sick as I watch her walk away.

"Is she okay?"

I close my eyes, trying to control the shaking of my hands as I slowly turn. Novy is crossing the sand toward me. "What the hell did you do now?"

He stops ten feet away. "What did she say?"

"Nothing," I growl. "Except she doesn't even want to fucking see me. What did you do, asshole? What did you say to her?"

He groans. "Look, I just got a little tongue-tied."

Seeing red, I barrel toward him, ready to pound him into the sand. "I told you what would happen if you fucking hurt her!"

"It was unintentional," he says, raising both hands. "And she clawed me right back, I'll have you know. I'll need therapy to unpack all the baggage she threw at me."

"You'll need therapy and a new fucking spleen." I lunge at him.

His forearms go up to block his face as I take a swing. Then we're tackling each other to the sand. We roll, punching and elbowing. I get him under me, but the sand gives way too easy, and he frees his arm, punching me in the ribs.

"*Fuck*," I wheeze. The man hits like a hammer. "I told you to back off."

"And I'm telling you I can't," he grunts, flipping me down to the sand.

"Stop it!" Poppy appears beside us. "Lukas—Colton, *stop*. I mean it!"

The fight goes out of me as I glance over his shoulder and see the look of shock and disgust on her face. I lie flat on the sand, letting him right himself. He scrambles off me and gets to his feet in a shower of sand. I shut my eyes, throwing both hands up over my face.

"Poppy, look—"

"Don't *touch* me, Lukas."

That has me on my feet. I blink sand from my eyes as I follow her voice, moving to her side. Her lips are parted as she huffs, cheeks pink. She ran to us, leaving her shoes to be swept away by the surf. Her eye makeup is smeared from crying. Her long blonde hair is caught in the ocean breeze. Fuck, she looks devastating.

And angry.

And sad.

I made my girl sad.

All the breath leaves my chest as I sigh, looking between them. "Please, just talk to us. At the very least fill me in too, so I know why you're so upset."

She turns to me, crossing her arms. The wind sends a few strands of her hair fluttering across her face. "Tell me about the game."

"What game?"

Her glare turns icy. "The game you two made up about me. Finders keepers, right? I want to know how it works."

I glare at Novy.

"I told her there was no game," he says.

"Yes, you *did*," she snaps. "You cornered me in the bathroom, and you told me that chasing me into bed is a game you're both playing—"

"She misunderstood," Novy says at me. "That was the whole me getting tongue-tied part that really sent everything off the rails."

"Oh, and it was *on* the rails before then?" I challenge. "You chased her into the goddamn bathroom?"

"I followed her," he clarifies. "It was impetuous, but I'm not feeling quite myself at the moment—"

"Impetuous?" she echoes. "Lukas, it was borderline criminal. You don't lock yourself in the bathroom with a woman and tell her you're using her to win some creepy sex game!"

"Okay, I want to *strongly* clarify that there is no game," he says again. "Cole, *please*."

"Please, what?" I cross my arms too.

"Help me," he begs. "Tell her that this isn't a game to us. Tell her what finders keepers means, before she sets me out to sea on a goddamn boogie board."

She looks to me. I can see the hope she's trying to hide in her eyes under a thick wall of hurt and suspicion. She wants to believe I'm still a good guy. She wants to believe I'm the *right* guy. Taking a deep breath, I hold her gaze. "You're not a game to me, Poppy. Or if you are, you're the endgame. You're it. That's what 'playing for keeps' means. It means this is not catch-and-release. I catch you; I fucking keep you. I love you, and marry you, and follow you to the ends of the fucking earth."

Her eyes go wide, and I take a step closer. "But I am not going to compete with this asshole for your attention or your affection. You're attracted to him. I get that. You can't help it. I'm sure you'd probably stop if you could—"

"Okay, *ouch*," Novy growls. "I'm standing right here, asshole."

She glances between us.

"My jealousy issues are my own," I say at her. "I need you to let me work through them in my way. In the meantime, you can be attracted to him all you want. What I need to know is if you're going to act on it again. Because for as much as I dream about you and want you, at the end of the day, I want to be with someone who wants to be with *me*. Not someone who's settling for me while dreaming of someone else."

She blinks back tears. "Colton, I—"

"Wait, don't I get to say anything here?" Novy butts in. "He gets a big, long speech, and I just get to stand here with my dick in my hand?"

I swallow a growl of frustration, turning to him.

Poppy looks nervously between us, her gaze settling on Novy. I'm pleased to see the same hope isn't shining in her eyes. He's already hurt her once. She doesn't want to open the door to letting him do it again. But she's still curious to hear what he has to say.

Fuck, is this more than physical attraction? Did this cocky, immature asshole actually find a way to worm inside her heart?

We both look to him, waiting.

He glances between us. "Well, I can't just whip out a speech like he can," he whines.

Poppy sighs.

"What? I mean, come on, Cole's probably been practicing that in the mirror for weeks."

"That came straight from the heart," I assure her. "That's this thing that sits right about here," I add at him, tapping my chest with my fist. "The poets like to claim it's responsible for regulating things like love and other genuine human emotions."

He rolls his eyes before turning back to Poppy. "Okay, so I'll admit I don't know what the fuck I'm doing. I'm not a poet. I'm just a guy who plays hockey. And I'm not good enough for you or nice enough for you," he goes on. "You'll probably have to hide me in your closet if your parents ever come to visit. But I mean, there's something here, right?"

Poppy stiffens, saying nothing.

With no encouragement whatsoever, he charges ahead. "And I mean, sure, our default settings are sarcasm and insults, but it's fun, right? I've never had a girl serve it back to me the way you can. I've never been, I don't know, inspired? Is that the word?" He looks to me.

I raise my brow. "You really think I'm gonna fucking help you right now?"

"Fine, fuck you too," he mutters, turning back to Poppy. "I'm trying to say that you're different. And this feels different. *I* feel different."

"Different how?" she murmurs, and my heart fucking shatters.

Fuck. This is more than physical attraction. She's genuinely interested in him. Somewhere between her moving here and now, Lukas Novikov has managed to charm my girl.

"This can't happen," I hear myself say.

They both look to me. Poppy's hurt eyes are wide. "What can't?"

"You can't want us both," I declare. "I don't fucking share. You have to choose, Poppy."

Novy steps in. "Well, I'm not giving you an ultimatum, so that makes me more attractive, right?"

"This isn't an ultimatum," I counter. "This is me knowing what I want from my partner." I turn back to Poppy. "My cards are all on the table. You know where I stand. I won't press you to make a choice now."

"Colton, please don't go," she begs.

But I have to leave. I can't stand here and watch her do the calculations on which one of us she wants more.

This is my own fault. I waited too long, and now I'm somehow in competition with Lukas Fucking Novikov. I give her a weak smile, feeling utterly shattered inside. "When he breaks your heart, come find me, okay? I'll be waiting."

35
POPPY

*C*all me biased, but I'd say my first major fundraiser as head of PR for the Rays is a hit. The music is light, the drinks are flowing, and the food keeps disappearing off the plates. Most importantly, the grant for the new pediatric wing of Jacksonville General Hospital is already halfway funded. Whatever money we raise tonight, Mark Talbot has promised to match it.

Glancing across the room, I spy Rachel chatting with Mars at the silent auction table. Our giant Finnish goalie is one of the biggest draws of the night. A two-time Stanley Cup-winner, he's an all-around gorgeous enigma.

Breezing their way, I place a hand on his arm. "Mars, you can't hide in the corner all night, honey. We gotta get you mingling." He groans as I steer him away. "Oh, and Rachel, can you track down the other fellas and corral them back this way?"

She smiles. "Sure thing, Pop."

I wave over my shoulder in thanks as I lead Mars over to a group of older ladies. They host the most exclusive book club in Jax Beach. "Ladies—Angela, Donna, Marie—have you met Mars Kinnunen? He speaks four languages. *And* he has a strong affinity for reading."

They coo appreciatively. Resigned to his fate, he puts on a smile and starts in on his routine of the world's smallest talk. I stand with them for a few minutes, laughing at the ladies' jokes, until a hand brushes my shoulder.

"Hey."

Lukas stands behind me looking devastating in a custom black tuxedo, his hair slicked back. I haven't seen him since karaoke night. That was three days ago. Three days since we were all shouting at each other on that moonlit beach. Colton told me I had to choose between them, and now I feel paralyzed with indecision.

As if I don't have enough on my plate with this new job, and my sister's wedding, I've somehow found myself in the middle of a complicated love triangle with *two* of my players? No, this cannot happen. I can't have this distraction right now.

"Hey," I say, walking a few steps away from Mars and his book club.

Lukas follows. "Doc said you were looking for me."

"No, I wasn't. I mean—*yes*, I was. But I was looking for all the players. I—we just need you here in the main room to mix and mingle. You're the draw, after all. Not me. Certainly not the mini quiches," I add with a nervous smile.

He gives me a long look, his caramel eyes soft and searching. "What's wrong?"

"Would it be completely inappropriate to say I'm gonna get myself off later to the image of you in this dress?"

"Oh my—*yes*." I slap his arm, even as I laugh. "You're incorrigible."

He's not wrong though. I look dynamite in this dress. It's this spicy little red number with thin straps and a thigh-high slit. I may have picked it knowing they'd see me in it. Don't judge me. I'm an indecisive mess, but I'm still a girl, and two boys think I'm pretty.

His eyes are doing that stupid smolder thing. "You know, if you weren't freezing me out right now, I'd take you to a dark corner and impolitely ask you to smear that red lipstick all over my dick."

My heart skips as I glance around, praying no one heard him. "Heavens, is this how you're greeting all the guests tonight?"

"No, just you."

"Well, thank you."

"My pleasure. It could be yours too," he adds with a wink.

"I'm a little busy at the moment, running this event, remember?"

"But you're saying there's a chance." His gaze traces me up and down again. "At an event you're *not* running, all bets are off. Yes?"

"Why are you still standing in front of me?"

He laughs, popping one of the mini quiches in his mouth. "I'll go mingle now, yeah? Anyone in particular you want me to fleece?"

"The ladies talking to Mars." I point their way. "They're all richer than god, and they like chatting with charming young men."

"Say less." He squares his shoulders, ready to pounce.

As he turns away, I can't help myself. "Hey—have you seen Colton yet?"

Colton was signed up as one of my volunteers. I had him down to help run the silent auction table.

Lukas turns back, his smile falling. "Yeah, uhh . . . he texted that he's not gonna make it. Family emergency, I think."

Family emergency? Well, if that's not the most rote excuse in the freaking book. Is he punishing me for daring to have feelings for Lukas? If he is, I think I'm gonna scream, then cry, then eat a pint of Neapolitan ice cream.

Worse, what if that's how deeply I've hurt him? What if he can't even bear to face me now? What if I've broken his heart and shattered his dreams, and he's currently at home cursing the day he ever met me? I blink rapidly, fighting the sudden stinging in the corners of my eyes.

"Poppy . . ."

"No, that's totally fine. It's not like this was mandatory."

"Pop, I really think it was an emergency."

"Mhmm. Will you just excuse me for a second?" I step past him.

I am *not* crying over a boy right now. Blame my family drama, blame my anxiety, but I think all this pressure is finally starting to get to me. Lukas follows as I duck behind the catering curtain. We step through into the empty exhibit wing.

"Pop, come on, don't make me chase you," he calls. "Seriously, I have, like, zero tread on these damn tuxedo shoes."

"I'm fine, Lukas. Just go mingle, please."

"If you want Cole so badly, why haven't you gone to him yet? Why are you making him sweat it out?"

I groan, turning to face him. "It's not that simple."

"Oh shit." He grabs my arm. "Wait. Poppy, are you picking me?"

"No," I cry, pulling my arm free. "I'm not picking either of you!"

His eyes narrow. "Why not?"

"Because I hardly know you! I hardly know Colton either, and he's already saying he'll follow me to the ends of the freaking earth. You don't think that's a little premature? Maybe even a little crazy?"

He shrugs. "Not really."

"Why not?"

"Because he's a Leo."

I gaze up at his handsome face. "What the heck does that mean?"

"It means he's a Leo," he replies. "It's in his nature. He can't help it."

"What's in his nature?"

"To love you at first sight and stay loyal until he dies."

Well, knock me down with a feather.

"Now, take me for comparison," he goes on, hands in his pockets. "I'm a chaotic double Scorpio."

I roll my eyes. "And what does that mean?"

He grins down at me. "It means I'll *want* you at first sight and fight it until I die."

With a frustrated groan, I press a hand to my forehead. "Oh god, you're both crazy. This is all so completely crazy."

He laughs. "Hey, you picked us."

"I didn't pick *either* of you! You both just keep showing up in my pocket like a couple of bad pennies, offering me stress ulcers and orgasms!"

"Pretty great orgasms though, right? I mean, I can't speak for Cole. Maybe there's not a lot of motion happening in that ocean. But I think I delivered on my end—"

"Will you stop talking about orgasms?"

"You brought it up," he teases, flicking my long ponytail off my shoulder.

I bat his hand away. "I didn't ask for any of this. And, to own the truth, it's all starting to feel like too much to handle right now."

His pretty caramel eyes narrow. "What's all too much?"

"This," I cry, gesturing around. "Believe it or not, I didn't move to Jacksonville to start up a complicated love triangle with two hockey players. I came here for a job—one I would very much like to keep, by the way. A job that brings me happiness and fulfillment and purpose outside of any relationship I might have with a man."

"And we compromise your ability to do that job?"

"In every sense of the word, yes."

"How?"

Popping my hands on my hips, I glare up at him. "Well, I'm supposed to be running this event. Yet, here I am, arguing with you in front of the creepiest painting of a man on a horse I've ever seen."

Lukas glances up at the painting showcased in a gaudy gold frame. The man on the horse looks like his face was melted with wax, and the horse has the proportions of a sleep paralysis demon. "Jeezus," he mutters. "That shit'll haunt you till you're dead."

"I have to get back." I step around him.

"Whoa, hold on." He grabs my arm again. "Just so you know, you *can* have both, Poppy."

I go still, my heart in my throat. He can't mean what I think he means . . . can he? I won't lie and say I haven't thought about it. Stranger things have happened, right? I mean, not to me. But other people. Other women. Bolder women. And some guys can even be into it, I've heard.

But Colton and Lukas want me to pick just one of them. Which, frankly, feels impossible. They're so different. It's like picking between cake and ice cream. Colton is sweet and kind and so deeply good. He makes me feel cherished. And Lukas is funny and adventurous and wild. With him, I feel like myself. I feel like my sarcasm is a strength, not something I have to constantly keep in check. He likes my snark and my moods.

And they both make me feel sexy and confident in my own skin, something no partner before them has ever managed. Sure, they drive me a little crazy too. But typically, it's only the good kind of crazy. They spin me up and leave me panting for more.

Is it possible they could ever not make me choose?

I look up at Lukas. "What do you mean?"

"The career and the guy," he clarifies. "You can have both, Poppy. One doesn't have to compromise the other. Look at Shelby O'Sullivan. She's a child psychologist, a mother, president of the WAGs. She's awesome. Lauren Gerard is in fashion design."

I sigh. "Lukas . . ."

"I'm just saying you can be with Cole and be yourself too," he goes on. "He would never want to change you or hold you back, Pop. Hell, he's the kind of guy who would retire in a heartbeat if he thought it would somehow help make your dreams come true."

I look up at him, my gaze softening. "You care about him."

He nods. "Yeah, he's my friend. He may be, like, my *only* friend. Is that pathetic to say?"

"No, it's not pathetic. I think Tina is my only real friend," I admit.

"I mean, if I'm gonna have one, he's the one to have, right? Loyal Leo and all that." Leaning down, he kisses my forehead. "If he's who you want, I won't stand in the way. You can choose him with no hard feelings, okay? You and I can just be friends. I think I'd like to have another friend."

Damn it. Sarcastic Lukas spins me up and drives me crazy, but vulnerable Lukas tugs at my heartstrings and lures me closer. I want to know him. I want him to let me care for him. Because I get the sneaking suspicion that maybe no one else does.

Resolved, I tip up on my toes and kiss him. It's soft and quick, just a gentle pressing of lips. But there's a promise in it, a little kernel of hope. I pull away first, and he's left blinking down at me in surprise. Heavens, is he really that convinced of his own lack of worth? He must think this is a no-contest win for Colton.

He swoops down to kiss me again, but I lean away, my senses homing in on a curious sound.

"What is it—"

"*Shh.*" I put up a hand. "I thought I just heard someone crying."

He's on alert as we both listen for the sound. After a minute, we hear it again. It's not a cry . . . well, at least it's no cry of pain. His face lights up as his mouth splits into a grin. "Oh, someone is totally fucking behind that door."

He's right, the sound is coming from behind a black metal door. We tiptoe forward, a difficult feat for me in these strappy heels.

Grunting, panting, whispered words of passion—

I gasp. Those voices are unmistakable. We turn to each other at the same time. Lukas points dramatically at the door. "It's Compton!"

"And Rachel!" I mouth.

Oh god, Jake and Rachel. My player and his doctor. Oh, I just *knew* there was something happening between them! My hyperactive mind instantly goes into media crisis mode. The spin isn't impossible, but it wouldn't be painless either. She really should disclose their relationship to HR immediately. Should I let them know that I know? Maybe later . . . after they're finished.

Oh god, now I'm picturing it! I put a hand to my forehead, blinking the image away as rapidly as I can. Yeah, no definitely, this is a problem. On Monday morning, I'll start preparing our spin.

Next to me, Lukas chuckles, pulling on my arm as we slowly back away. "Those dirty dogs. Don't they know this is a museum benefit for a children's hospital?"

"Seriously? Three minutes ago, you wanted to pull *me* into a dark corner."

"So, you're still thinking about it too?" he teases. "Good. I bet we can find another stairwell. Or just use that one. Sounds like they're almost done."

"Goodnight, Lukas." Turning away, I walk back toward the party. I can't think about disappearing into a dark corner with him. I have money to raise, a pediatric hospital wing to build, and a brewing PR crisis to manage.

"See you around, Poppy," he calls after me. "Let's do a friend hang soon, yeah? Clothing optional."

I groan, not looking back. I swear, that man drives me up the wall and down the other side. What the heck am I doing even contemplating getting more deeply involved with him? It's breaking my own rules. I said, "no players," and that was for good reason. This *exact* reason, in fact. Dating the players is messy and complicated and about a thousand other adjectives that all translate to "majorly bad idea."

Besides, Colton and Lukas have made it clear that they expect me to choose one of them. In my heart, I know I don't want to choose. God help me, I want them both. I at least want a chance to see what this could be. But I fear the only responsible option, the only *fair* option, will be to walk away . . . leaving all three of us at least a little bit brokenhearted.

ame night. Rays versus the Pittsburgh Penguins, and we're fucking losing. Hard not to suck when three of our best starters are off the ice. J-Lo's been back in the dressing room the whole game, retching his guts out. Apparently, he caught a stomach bug from one of his kids. Karlsson is riding the bench with a nasty finger sprain. Then they pulled Mars from the net at intermission.

I don't know what's wrong, but Doc Price has him on the bench, and he's not happy about it. I can see him now across the ice. He's sitting there, mask off, watching stony-faced as Davidson lets in another goal to the wild cheers of the crowd.

I just shake my head, trying to keep my rage in check. Cole did his best to clear the net, but that shot went straight past him and over Davidson's shoulder.

The score is now 0-3. I swear to god, if this is a shutout, I'm gonna walk back to Jacksonville.

It's not like I can be of any fucking help. I'm trapped in the penalty box for another four minutes. Stupid, bullshit charging penalty. The ref called it a major because the guy went down hard. Now, I'm just watching my teammates chase the puck up and down the ice, trying to compensate for the hole I left in our line. All the while, rowdy Pens fans slam the glass behind my head, shouting obscenities at me.

Cole skates past the penalty box, not giving me a second look. Seriously? Is he gonna be a sour grape about this? This isn't my fault. We've all had bullshit charges called on us. He's had more than his fair share too.

No, he's still pissed about Poppy and me. It's been a week since the beach, and I don't even know if they've spoken yet. His principles are keeping him warm at night while she stresses overthinking she has to pick one of us. Meanwhile, I'm stuck in the shitty position of feeling like I'm losing two people I care about.

Maybe the *only* two people I care about.

How the hell did I get here?

I sit in the box, elbows on knees, and watch the ref drop the puck. Sully wins control and passes back to Cole. He's got great puck-handling as he works around two Pens, passing it up to Langley.

I've never really paused to consider what Cole's friendship means to me. He's been in and out of my life for a decade now, ever since we played together in the WHL. He's one of the few guys who says he'll keep in touch and then actually does. Joking on the ice whenever we play against each other, the occasional dinner, texts on my birthday. He's the kind of guy who will watch your game on his day off and text you "good play" while you're still out on the ice. More than once, I've returned to the dressing room to see a missed call from him.

Like I said: loyal fucking Leo.

And he hasn't had it easy. I know all about his heart stuff. We've all seen the scars on his chest, but I was dumb enough to ask him. He told me about his surgeries as a kid, his long road to recovery.

I know about his road to the NHL too. He didn't go first round in the draft like me, or even third round. No, he went fifth round and got sent down to the minors. He was a farm team guy for two years. He had to fight to prove himself worthy of a permanent seat on the bench.

The man is tough as nails.

And I'm trying to take away the one thing he wants.

It just so happens that the one thing Cole wants is the only thing I think I've *ever* wanted outside of playing hockey.

Poppy.

Fuck, that girl is twisting me up like nothing else. I don't even know when or how it happened. One minute, I was groaning with annoyance at the sound of her walking up behind me in those kitten heels. The next, I'm groaning into my fist in the shower every chance I get, spilling into my hand to the memory of her smile, her laugh.

It's not just the sex. Though, please god, if you're listening, let there be more sex. I feel completely untethered. The need to touch her, hold her. It's making me crazy. If Cole is feeling half of what I'm feeling, I know he's suffering too.

Before Poppy, all I ever wanted from a woman was sex. Don't even tell me your name. Just let me get lost in your body for a few stolen moments. Let me soothe the desperate ache of loneliness.

Blame my deep-seated neglect issues.

I never knew my dad, and my mom was a drug addict who left me on the front step of my grandpa's house. Anton did the best he could at first, hiring nannies to feed me. He made sure I had uniforms for school and gave me a bed to sleep in. But the older I got, the more he took his foot off the gas pedal, letting me drive my own car.

By the time I was twelve years old, I was on my own, smoking cigarettes, fucking girls, and getting in fights behind the dumpsters at school. Old Anton took the belt to me one time too many over my constant suspensions, and I finally ran.

A truancy officer caught up with me after a couple weeks and sat me down. He had evidence of a string of petty crimes—shoplifting, vandalism, underage drinking. He gave me one last chance to reform my wild ways. He thought maybe a sport would help give me an outlet for all my anger and keep me on a tighter leash.

Enter hockey.

The first time I put on those skates and flew down the ice was pure freedom. I felt like a goldfish that had been suffocating on dry land, dropped back into a bowl of water. They put a stick in my hand, told me I could hit people, and I was hooked. A few years later, a lucky encounter with a scout landed me on my first Junior League team. The rest is history.

Now here I sit, a first-round NHL draft pick at the peak of my career. Hockey is the only thing I care about. It's the only thing I'm good at. That and fucking girls. I gave up the smoking. Bad for the lungs.

Poppy and all the other PR reps like to think I'm this loose cannon. They think I'm out here playing with fire, just trying to get myself cut from the League, but nothing could be further from the truth. I know where the line is, and I'm careful not to cross it because hockey is literally all I have. No family. No life outside the ice and my teammates. Not even a pet.

Hell, my new beach house is practically empty. All I need is a bed and a fridge. It's not like I ever let anyone over or entertain. I don't need them seeing how empty my life is.

For the longest time, I convinced myself I liked it this way. Nothing holds me back. A team can call with a trade offer, and I can have my whole life moved in a day. Trust me, it's happened. More than once. I drink and I party, and I fuck a lot of girls because it keeps the feelings of emptiness at bay.

At least it did.

Now there's Poppy. I haven't touched another woman since the day she sat me down in her office and set out her plan for my stupid sex contracts. Don't get me wrong, I've had plenty of chances. Bunnies can be persistent on the road, and I have a reputation. But I've gone home alone every night. I don't want bunnies anymore. I don't want the endless disconnect.

Goddamn it, I want Poppy.

But to have her will mean I hurt Cole, one of the only other people on this earth who has ever given a damn about me.

God, this fucking sucks.

The Pens goalie starts slapping the ice with his stick, warning his guys that my penalty is ending. That hollow *thwack* fills my senses. I buckle my helmet and climb on the edge of the boards, ready to leap over. The Pens are all over us in our defensive zone. Compton is out there doing his best to guard Dave-O while the forward line fights to get the puck clear.

"Come on," I growl. "Get it out!"

A Pens forward knocks Langley down to the ice, and I see the opening Compton can't cover.

"Fuck—*no*," I bellow.

Too fucking late. Quick as a bullet, the puck slips right between Davidson's toe and the post, hitting the back of the net. The cherry goes off, and the Pens go wild.

I just cost my team two fucking goals.

My penalty ends, and I leap over the boards. Speeding across the ice, I join the Rays just as Compton is replaced with Cole. "Hey, tough game," I say at him.

He glances my way, the arena lights reflecting off his visor. "Just get over on your side, Novikov. Let's fucking finish this."

I glare as I coast backward.

Oh, we are just getting started.

37
COLTON

*I*t's after midnight, and I'm stretched out shirtless on my hotel bed, icing my knees. SportsCenter is playing on the TV, recapping the highlights of all tonight's various games. That's the good thing about sports: every sport, every day, someone wins, and someone loses.

Well, the Rays lost big-time tonight. Honestly, it was embarrassing. Thank god for Sully and that last-minute goal, or it would've been a shutout. After the game, Coach informed us that Mars will be out of the net for the next two games, at least. They're getting him checked out for a possible groin pull.

I groan, shifting the pack of ice from my left knee over to my right. Groin pulls are no joke. A third-degree pull derailed the start of my NHL career. I lost over half a season of ice time as I rehabbed it.

Knock. Knock.

Someone's at my door after midnight? I roll to my side, reaching for my phone. If it's a Ray, they usually text ahead. I don't have any missed texts or calls.

"Come on, bud. Open the door," Novy calls.

Fuck. I don't want to deal with him right now. "I'm asleep," I bark.

"No, you're not," he calls through the door. "You're watching SportsCenter recaps and icing your damn knees."

I glance from the ice pack on my knee to the TV. We always roomed together in the Juniors, so the fucker knows all my routines.

"Come on, Cole. Just let me in. I gotta piss."

Muttering a curse, I toss my ice pack on the bedside table and swing my legs off the bed. I cross over to the door and throw the bolt, pulling the door open. "What?"

He's leaning against the door wearing a pair of checkered pajama pants and an unzipped Rays hoodie. It's on inside out. The asshole isn't wearing any shoes. "For a minute there, I contemplated knocking on *that* door instead," he says, gesturing with a thumb over his shoulder. "Sounds like they're having way more fun."

I follow the line of his point. It only takes a second to catch on. The walls between the rooms must be thick because I haven't heard a peep out of my neighbors all night. The doors, not so much. "Oh shit," I mutter. "Jeez, it sounds like a porn set over there."

"Yup. Whose room is that?"

"Jake's," I reply.

"Shoulda figured. Is that Doc in there with him again?"

"Probably."

He grins at me. "Wait, you know too?"

"Yeah, I caught them kissing a couple weeks ago. It looked like it was getting carnal, so I made myself scarce."

He chuckles. "Clever having his sneaky link travel with the team—"

"Wait, shut up." I raise a hand at him.

"What?"

I point at the door. "There's a third person in there."

He glances over his shoulder. "Two girls at once? Nice. Doc didn't seem like the sharing type but—"

"No, I just heard another guy."

He raises a brow in surprise. Then, like the nosy assholes we are, we cross over to Jake's door. I flip my door latch out first to stop it from closing. Then I lean in next to Novy, my hand on his shoulder as we listen in like teenagers.

After a few seconds, he gasps. "It's *Sanny*."

The sound is muffled, but I think I can hear it. Yeah, that definitely sounds like Sanford. I grunt as Novy snags me by the arm, dragging me back across the hall. "Hey, getoff—"

"We need to talk," he says, shoving me inside my room.

I shut my door, watching him stumble over to the mini bar. "Are you drunk?"

"I *was* drunk. Now I'm just lightly toasted." He grabs a six-dollar bottle of FIJI water. Twisting off the cap, he downs half of it. "You got any food?"

"There's some jerky and peanuts in my backpack. Front pocket." I make my way over to the bed and sit, gingerly placing the ice pack on my aching knee. Novy rustles around in my bag, tugging out the big bag of granola from the main compartment. I sit up. "I said you could have the peanuts, asshole."

He digs out a handful of granola and shoves it in his mouth. After a few chews, he groans. "God, this is so fucking good." He turns to me, holding up the bag. "It's so sweet and nutty. Did you make this, bud?"

I glare at him. "Poppy made it."

He blinks twice, swallowing his mouthful. Grabbing the bottle of water, he downs the rest. It's shockingly curative. His gaze sharpens and he stops swaying like a reed. Glancing down, he plucks at his hoodie. "Is this on inside out?"

"And you have no shoes on."

He wiggles his toes on the hotel carpet. "I think I left them in my shower."

I can't help but smile. "That's a good place for them."

He plops himself on the end of my bed. "We need to talk about Poppy."

I tense, moving the ice pack from my knee up to my elbow. The icy coolness feels good against my aching joints. "I don't want to talk about her with you."

"Well, we have to talk about her because I'm not gonna do this."

"Do what?"

"Lose you."

I gaze across the bed at him. "What the hell are you talking about?"

"You were here first, Cole. You're one of the only guys in this whole league who genuinely cares about me. I mean, do you know how many people texted me on my birthday last year?" He holds up two fingers. "That's right, you and my lawn care service. But they were only offering me a coupon for five dollars off my next mow. Happy fucking birthday to me, right?"

Jesus, that's depressing.

"Well, you don't make it easy for the guys to know you," I say. "I mean, you say we're close, but I've never even seen the new place where you're living."

"You're not missing anything, trust me. It's a four-bedroom beach house with exactly three pieces of furniture: a bed, a couch, and a TV."

"Why don't you hire a decorator? A lot of the guys do."

He just shrugs. "No point. I don't care enough to decorate."

"So, you're just going to live in a big empty house with nothing but a bed and a couch? Won't you be here for, like, six years?"

"If they keep me. They could trade me away if they really wanted to. There's always a back door, an emergency valve."

"Perfect philosophy for a guy who's always on the run," I muse.

He glares at me. "Yeah, well, I've had a lot of shit worth running from in my life, Cole."

I adjust the ice pack on my elbow. "Have you ever found anything worth running *to*?"

He looks quickly away. "No."

I sigh, leaning back. "You're lying."

"Well, I can't just come out and fucking say it, can I? I told you, Coley. I don't wanna lose you. I'd rather know that the only two people I care about are together than know my selfishness drove all three of us apart. So, I'm gonna help you win her over."

"You don't have to do this—"

"I want to," he presses. "I want you both to be happy."

I raise a brow at him. "Even if it costs you your own happiness?"

He just shrugs again. "I've never been happy. Why start now?"

"Nov—"

"Wait, scratch that." He holds up a hand, deep in thought for a moment. Then he smiles and snaps his fingers. "When Canada went all the way to the gold medal stand in the 2014 Olympics. I watched every game and cried like a baby. I was happy then."

My mind hums as I take in all this new information. I've always liked Novy. He's fun and funny, and he has a great nose for sniffing out cool restaurants. He's also a damn hard worker. He'll be the first guy in the gym and the last off the ice. It's been nice to play on the same team again.

But I won't deny it shocked the hell out of me when he told me I was his emergency contact. For all the time we've spent together, it's always been at work or with the other guys. Does he really have no one else? I can't imagine not having my mom and my sisters in my life to look out for me and be ready to take that call if it came.

Well, for better or worse, I'm in Novy's life now. So long as we're both Rays, I'm his person. This bullshit with Poppy aside, I'm the one who's gonna step in and give a damn about him. My gaze softens a little as I take him in, looking so pathetic in his inside out hoodie. "What did you have in mind, Nov?"

He digs his hand back into the bag of granola. "Well, for starters, I think you need to play harder to get."

I grind my teeth. "I don't *want* to play hard to get. I want her to fucking come and get me."

He nods, swallowing the granola. "Yeah, and you can think that, and you can say it to me all you want. But you don't say that to anyone else—*especially* her."

I wave a hand in frustration. "Why can't I tell her that I want her more than anything? Why can't I tell her that she's all I fucking think about?"

He groans, zipping the granola bag shut. "God, you are too Leo to function."

"What the hell does that mean?"

"It means you're scaring her off, bud. She's not ready to hear you talk about love and babies and weddings in Aruba."

"How do you know?"

"Because she told me."

I sit up, jostling my ice pack. "When the fuck did you talk to her?"

"At the benefit. You know, the one *you* volunteered us both to attend and then boycotted?"

Yeah, that was a shitty day. Speaking of emergency contacts, I got a call from someone at the hospital in Orlando saying my mom slipped and fell, cracked her head pretty good. They discharged her with a mild concussion, but she needed someone to monitor her overnight. What was I supposed to do, not help my own mother?

"I told you I had a family emergency."

Novy snorts. "Yeah, which sounds like a flimsy fucking excuse. Pop didn't buy it."

"What do you mean she didn't buy it?"

"She ran off all upset," he replies. "I had to chase her down. It was a whole thing. But look—she wore this red dress and looked like Jessica Rabbit." He pulls his phone out and flashes me a picture.

"Fuck me," I mutter.

"Right?" He slips his phone back in his pocket. "If your excuse was legit, you should tell her. She thinks you don't want her anymore."

I sigh, adjusting the ice pack on my elbow. "Well, if she's not ready for confessions of love, then what *is* she ready for?"

"She's ready to come and get it—and by that, I mean your dick." He points to my crotch.

"Nov—"

"Hey, I am not wrong about this. Underneath the business suits, she's like a tiny blonde sex cheetah. Stop trying to wife her up and just let her get to know you. Dial back the Leo and date the girl. We're talking flowers, favorite foods, naked massages." He lists each thing out on his fingers. "And make sure she knows there are no strings attached. Just casual fun."

"Casual fun? You want me to treat her like a bunny?"

"Honestly, maybe," he says with a laugh. "She may not be ready to marry you, but she's definitely ready to keep riding your train, if you know what I mean."

"The wallpaper knows what you mean," I mutter.

"Well, the sex was working, right?" He looks my way, waiting for my response. "Oh god, please tell me the sex was working. Because if you tell me she was just okay, I'm gonna push you out that goddamn window, and wife her up myself. Our sex was fucking volcanic—"

"I don't want to hear about your sex."

Lie. I'm getting hard trying not to picture it. It's a total mindfuck.

"But it was good, right?"

I lean back against the headboard again. "It was good, Nov. God, it was so fucking good. I can't stop thinking about it. I am so completely fucked."

"That bad, huh?"

I toss my ice pack onto the bedside table. "Worse. Fantasizing about her for two years was already torture enough. Now that I've tasted the real thing? I want more, even as I know I'll never get enough. But then I had to go and shove that stupid ultimatum in her face." I groan, burying my face in my hands.

Novy's quiet for a moment. "Yeah, why did you do that?"

Dropping my hands, I glare at him. "Because I had to. She can't just date us both, right? Unlike Jake and Sanny, I don't share."

He nods. "Yeah, totally get that. Neither do I, but I've also never been in this position before."

"What position is that?"

"The position where the only woman I've ever wanted to spend more than one night with wants me, but she *also* wants the only man who wishes me a 'Happy Birthday.'"

The mood in this hotel room shifts. Suddenly, it's like a goddamn confessional. "What are you saying?"

"I'm saying, well, just listen across the hall." He waves his hand at the door. "It *can* be done, Cole. You know, with the right people. Are you really that opposed to sharing her with me? I mean, if it's what she wanted," he adds quickly. "Like, if she made it clear it would make her happy, would you still never even consider?"

"I don't share," I say again.

He nods, shifting off the bed. "Yeah. Got it. Fuck you too."

"Nov," I call at his back.

He glances over his shoulder.

"When I say I don't share, I mean to say I've *never* shared."

Slowly, his face breaks into a grin. "Well, neither have I."

"That cannot possibly be fucking true."

He chuckles. "I know, right? But I'm telling the truth."

Are we actually having this conversation? I'd be lying if I said my fucked-up head wasn't already taking me there in my dreams. I've been picturing them together for the last few weeks. While my first reaction was to growl and rage and feel like a possessive fucking caveman, there's no denying I was turned on.

Now, Lukas Novikov is standing in my hotel room with no shoes on, hoodie inside out, strongly hinting that he'd like to be in the room while I casually fuck our PR director, all of us pretending I don't want to put a ring on her finger. He says she's not ready for forever. Based on the radio silence from her this week, I'm inclined to believe him.

Maybe he's right. Maybe I need to recalibrate my approach.

And if I *had* to share her with someone, Lukas would at least be entertaining. And it's not like I haven't already seen him naked a thousand times, so there'd be no surprises . . .

"I don't want to hurt Poppy," I say.

"Good. I don't want to hurt Poppy either."

"We don't even know if this is what she wants," I go on. "Maybe she just wants to date us separately. I mean, could you handle that? Could you know I'm with her when you're not? Know I'm touching her and laughing with her and fucking her behind your back?"

He's quiet for a moment. "Honestly? Yeah, I think I could."

"Why?"

"Well, it wouldn't be behind my back, would it? And you're a good guy, Cole. She could do a heck of a lot worse than date a guy like you." His smile turns to a grin. "She could date an asshole like me." Fumbling with his hoodie, he tries to zip it up while it's still inside out. "Fuck, I'm so tired."

"Well, you can't sleep in here. Sharing my girl is crazy enough. I'm not sharing my pillows." Slipping off the bed, I follow him to the door.

He gets it open, and we both pause. Across the hall, muffled sex noises are still humming beyond Jake's closed door. Novy grins. "Sharing sounds rather lively, doesn't it?"

I sigh, giving him a push. "Goodnight, Nov. Don't walk into traffic in your bare feet, yeah?"

"This isn't over," he says as he walks away. "I have no intention of letting either of you go."

On that note, I shut my door, muffling the sounds coming from Jake's room.

To own the truth, I've had my suspicions about those three for weeks. Jake and Rachel have been obvious from the start, even before I caught them kissing. And the guys have always joked about Jake and Sanny and their "domestic life partner" situation. Is she with them both? Are they finally with each other?

I'll admit, I know nothing about threesomes. It's never interested me. I always thought I was too jealous to share my partner. Even now, if I think of Poppy with some random guy, I see fucking red. But at some point in all this, when I pictured her with Novy, my curiosity started outweighing my jealousy.

God, are we crazy for even considering this?

I bolt my door, locking myself inside the hotel room. I'm

exhausted from the game, but I'm wired too, alive with sudden and surprising possibility. Alone in my bed, I turn out all the lights, lie back, and let my imagination run wild. For the first time in weeks, I don't try to keep those mental doors shut. I walk right through them.

I come in record time, my warm release filling my fist with Poppy's sweet name like a prayer on my lips . . . and Novy's hands on my hips.

38

POPPY

Olivia Rodrigo plays on my wireless speaker as I stuff tissue paper into glittery pink gift bags. Violet's bachelorette party is this weekend, and I'm not finished prepping the gifts. Little piles of cosmetics and face masks and silky pajama sets surround me on the floor as I rush to assemble a bag for each girl.

There are some naughty gifts too. Everyone is going home with a new vibrator. And I picked up some sample packets of fruity lube and some penis candy necklaces. There's also a handful of rainbow penis confetti in each bag.

Is this all still weird and awkward and painful? Yes.

But I'm Poppy St. James, and these party favors are going to be fabulous.

I planned the bachelorette party as an overnight trip to St. Augustine. It'll be twenty-four hours stuck with my little sister and six of her brattiest friends talking about how wonderful it is that she's marrying my awful ex. The only silver lining is that Tina is coming. I know because I invited her. I don't think I'll survive this weekend without her. She texted me last week with a screenshot of the invite saying, "You fucking kidding me, bitch?" I sent back a string of twenty begging GIFs until she finally relented with, "Fine. But you're paying for my flight."

Fastest two hundred bucks I ever spent.

I have a few special gifts for her bag. Instead of a vibrator, I got her a dildo shaped like a rainbow unicorn horn. And a ball gag. And her lube is cinnamon bun flavored. I smile as I collect her little pile of gifts off to the side, away from the others.

A knock at my door has me turning. Who the heck would be here at eleven o'clock on a Thursday night? Getting to my feet, I trot over to the door and bounce up on my toes, peeking through the peep-hole. I gasp, pushing away from the door with both hands.

Colton is outside my door.

Oh god, what is he doing here? It's been two weeks since the beach, and things between us are still so tense. That night, he told me I was his endgame. Then he demanded I shut off all my feelings for Lukas like I'm a freaking faucet. *Then* he didn't show up to my charity event, even though he signed up to attend. He sent me a text later saying his mom had a fall. Something about a concussion?

Since he got back from Pittsburgh, I've been bumping into him everywhere—the practice rink, the coffee cart, even twice at the grocery store. He smiles, he engages me in conversation, he listens with his whole body, and then he walks away as if the beach never happened.

He said it, right? He told me he wanted to love me and marry me and follow me to the ends of the earth. That happened?

Oh god, I don't know if I have the strength to deal with this right now.

But I'm also too dang curious not to open the door.

My curiosity wins.

"Colton, hi."

His dark eyes widen, almost as if he's surprised I answered. He looks as good as ever, relaxed and comfortable in some Rays workout gear. He's got a five o'clock shadow that looks delicious on him. Is he growing his beard out?

"Hey, Poppy," he replies, his gaze trailing me up and down.

That's the one thing that *hasn't* changed. He can't help but look at me. It makes me shiver every time. I wish I was wearing something cuter than these kitty cat pajama shorts and my faded, slouchy "Mrs. Darcy" sweatshirt. "Need to borrow a cup of sugar?"

He smiles. "Nah, I'm good."

I wait, holding onto the door. Inviting him in feels like a colossal mistake that will just end with me naked.

"I didn't know how to do this without sending you all the wrong signals again," he finally says. "But I feel like I really need to clarify something."

Oh heavens, he wants to have a relationship talk now? Keeping a smile on my face, I crack the door open a little bit. "Do you want to come in?"

A hint of panic flashes across his face. "Uhh . . . no. I think it's best if I stay out here."

"You don't want to come in?"

He groans, stepping back to grab the handrail with both hands. "Poppy, I want to come into that apartment more than I want fucking air. But maybe you could just come out here instead. Would that be cool?"

So, this is about mutual restraint? A test of wills? "Sure." I step out, shutting the door with a soft click. "Better?"

"Yeah," he mutters, not letting go of the handrail.

I wait for him to speak, arms folded over my chest, hugging myself inside my sweatshirt.

"I just wanted to let you know that I'm sorry for what happened at the beach," he says. "I was spun up, maybe even a little drunk, and I said some shit I didn't mean. Actually, a *lot* of shit I didn't mean. If you'll let me, I'd like to take it back."

"You want to take it back?"

He nods.

"Which part?"

"All of it. Is that possible? But especially the part about the ultimatum. That was selfish and unfair. You are your own person, Pop, with your own feelings and life and romantic connections that you're free to make with whomever you choose. I don't get to have a say in what you do, and I definitely don't get to be upset about it. I was a jerk, I was wrong, and I'm apologizing."

Well, this is unexpected.

"I hope I can earn your forgiveness, maybe even gain back your trust too. And since actions speak louder than words . . . here." He slips his hand inside his pocket and pulls out a folded piece of paper. Reaching out across the breezeway, he hands it to me.

I unfold it, quickly scanning what looks like an online receipt. "What is this?"

"I had Novy place bids for me on some of the stuff at your silent auction," he explains. "I won this. It's a sunset cruise down in St.

Augustine. I was going to invite you to go with me, but now I'm just giving it to you."

"Colton—"

"I think you should take Novy."

My heart skips. "You do?"

"Yeah, he's never been on a boat, I don't think. More importantly, he's never been courted by a woman of your caliber. He's a good guy, Poppy. Under all the bravado and bullshit. He's not easy to love, but you're trying anyway, and I think that's commendable."

My mind feels fuzzy, like someone's spinning cotton candy inside it. "You think it's commendable that I'm fighting my attraction to another man?"

"Yeah," he replies. "And you don't have to keep fighting it on my account. You could do a lot worse than Lukas Novikov."

"Oh, trust me, I have," I say, folding up the paper and slipping it in the pocket of my shorts. My heart is racing as I glance up. He hasn't taken his eyes off me. "Is this you telling me you're bowing out? Do you cede victory?"

In a single step, he crosses the breezeway, backing me against my apartment door. He's so close, his woodsy scent enveloping me. But he's not touching me. My body is screaming with the need for connection, but instead he hovers, not taking what both of us so clearly want.

"I'm not bowing out of a goddamn thing," he says, his voice low.

I tip my head back, palms flat against the door. Heart on my sleeve, I say exactly what I'm thinking. "Please tell me I haven't lost you before I ever even got the chance to try for you."

His hand cups my face, thumb brushing my cheek. The moment our skin touches, a charge of electricity jolts through me. I'm magnetized by him, locked in place through this point of sacred contact. "I haven't gone anywhere," he says, kissing my brow. I arch up on my toes, seeking more contact. His hand smooths over my cheek and around until he's burying his fingers in my French-braided pigtail. "Poppy, baby, I'm right here."

My hands fist his T-shirt as I pull him closer. I drop my forehead to the middle of his chest and breathe him in. His arms wrap around me, one at my shoulders and the other at my waist, and we just hold each other. I feel moored to him. "Do you want to come in?" I say again, meaning it this time.

He groans. I feel it rumble against my chest. Then he pulls away, cupping my cheeks with both hands. His gaze is soft as he smiles down at me. "I would love nothing more . . . but you need to talk to Novy first."

I lean away, my hand wrapping around his wrist. "Why? What happened?"

He shakes his head. "Just square everything with him, then come find me. I'll still be waiting." His words echo what he said on the beach. Only this time, they hold the promise of more.

Pressing one more kiss to my forehead, he walks away.

39
POPPY

The front door slams shut as a shrill voice calls through the beach house, "Look out ladies, the fun has arriiiiived!" Of course Oliva Monroe is the last one here. I bet she'll be fashionably late to her own funeral. Seriously, this girl should come with a warning label— and a complimentary hangover IV drip.

"Gird up your loins," Tina mutters.

I grin at her, rolling my eyes. Olivia is the main reason I invited Tina. I can't possibly handle her on my own, not with the way she spins my sister up. They bring out the worst in each other, like a perfect storm of mean girl nastiness. And the more they drink, the nastier they get. Good thing Tina isn't afraid to slap a bitch.

Olivia sweeps into the kitchen, waving like she's Miss America. Her ash-brown hair is blown out, her expensive extensions nearly reaching her waist. She's wearing a hot pink bedazzled jumpsuit.

"Livy!" Violet squeals, racing around the kitchen island to wrap her arms around her best friend.

Letting her go, Olivia steps back. "Who's ready to celebrate the bride?" She pulls a bottle of Cristal from inside her designer tote.

The girls all scream again. The cork is popped, someone turns up the music, and they dance around the kitchen in their swimsuits.

We were only allowed to check into this rental at noon. Already, we've made a sizable dent in the liquor supply. Violet and her friends spent the first hour gossiping and dancing on the back porch. Then we all went down to the beach. That part I didn't mind. The ocean was cold, but the sand was warm.

Now that the party is underway, it's clear why Violet asked me to host this for her. She's using me. More accurately, she's using my attention to detail, something her ditzy friends utterly lack. Case in point, I'm the only one aside from Tina, the literal bartender, who seems capable of mixing drinks. I turn off the blender and pop the lid. Putting a smile on my face, I turn around singing, "Who wants more strawberry margaritas?"

Five glasses get shoved in my face.

I look to Tina, still wearing my fake smile. She just grins, tattooed arms crossed as she leans against the counter. Lord, help me. It's gonna be a long night.

"*POPPY* Girl, tell us about life in Florida," says Olivia, nestled on the sofa between Violet and our quiet cousin, Bianca.

All eyes turn to me.

"Well, it's pretty great," I say, taking a sip of my coconut water. I was already feeling a little green and stopped drinking hours ago. "I run PR for the NHL team here in Jax, which is fun and exciting—"

"Do you know any of the players?" squeals Lemon. Unfortunate name, I know. She's sitting next to a girl named Chutney. I wish I was making this up. Tina is wedged on the other couch between two of Violet's current DC friends, Maggie and Giselle.

I look to Lemon. "Yeah, I know them all. I kind of have to as part of my job—"

"Wait. I have an amazing idea," Olivia says over me. "We should totally invite them to come out and party with us tonight!"

"Yes!"

"I am so in."

"Oh, yes. Poppy, *please.*"

"No," I say loudly, my smile falling. "Sorry ladies, but that's not happening."

"Why not?" Lemon whines.

Why not? Because I respect my players enough to not treat them like sporty blowup dolls for a drunk bachelorette party to play with and then discard.

I think this. I don't say it.

More possessively, the thought sneaks through the back of my mind that hell will *literally* freeze over before I let Violet and her friends flirt with Colton or Lukas in front of me. Anderson she can have, and good riddance. She's not touching them.

"Sorry, ladies," I say again, the lie slipping from my lips. "I think they have a game tonight."

They grumble their disappointment. Giselle and Olivia lament that it's too far a drive to get to Miami. When I hear whispers of the word "charter jet," I glance anxiously over to Tina. Ever a clutch friend, she clears her throat. "So, Poppy, what's on the agenda for tonight?"

Flashing her a smile of thanks, I stand up. "Well ladies, I've planned out a super fun evening. We'll start the night with dinner over at O.C. White's. They have a gorgeous outdoor patio with live music and great food. Then we'll hop along a couple of the bars on St. George's Street that always do karaoke and dancing. I thought we'd end the night with a round of boozy popsicles and twinkle light carriage rides!"

"*Oooor*," sings Olivia, getting to her feet too. "We could play a fun little game of . . . Naughty Bachelorette Bingo!!" All the other girls squeal as she pulls out a stack of hot pink cards from inside her tote. She passes them around to more excited chatter.

"Maggie, did you see this one?" Giselle points to something on the card that has them both breaking into a fit of giggles.

Tina gets a card next, and I watch her eyes scan it. "Jesus," she mutters. Okay, if the edgy club-owning bartender is worried, I'm gonna go ahead and up my own anxiety level to a cool DEFCON 3.

"Oh, Livy," Lemon cries. "We are not playing this!"

"Yes, we are," says Olivia. "Listen up, ladies. First to bingo is gonna win five hundred dollars. First to double bingo wins five *thousand*!"

The girls all cheer as Olivia comes to stand in front of me. Her smile is triumphant as she holds out a bingo card. "It's okay if you don't wanna play, Poppy. We all know this kind of game isn't your idea of fun."

"Yeah, 'cause she's a stick in the mud," Violet shouts, already tipsy.

Lemon glances between us, confused. "Vi, I thought you said your sister was an insufferable prude, and that's why Anderson dumped her?"

I slowly turn to stare at my sister. Oh, is *that* the story we're going with?

Violet just laughs.

"Lem, honey, that's what it means to be a stick in the mud," Olivia teases, patting her arm.

"Yeah, Perfect Poppy would never be caught dead playing a game like this," Violet adds. "She's too good for us."

"You should lighten up," says Olivia, brushing my beach braid off my shoulder. "Life is more fun if you're willing to be just a little bit bad."

A few of the girls laugh and clink their glasses.

"Actually, I'm pretty sure Poppy's stick is in her ass," Violet teases. "Anderson said he could feel it lodged up in there while they fucked!"

Olivia cackles. Some of the others laugh too, though they have the grace to look uncomfortable about it.

"Vi, you're crazy," says Maggie.

Heart racing, I just wait and pray for this to be over soon.

Violet shrugs, sloshing her champagne. "What? Some sisters share makeup and dresses. Poppy and I share a dick. It's no big thing. Actually, well, with Anderson it *is* a big thing." She winks at me. "You remember. Right, Pop? It's got a little bend in it, like this." She curls her finger. On that charming note, she stumbles away, her champagne glass raised in the air as she bops along to the music.

"Don't worry, Poppy. You can be our DD," Olivia says, stroking my face. "You're such a thoughtful big sister."

If only my eyes had freaking lasers. I lean away from her touch, snatching the bingo card from her hand. As soon as she turns away, I start reading the challenges. "Oh my—"

If I were wearing pearls right now, they would officially be clutched. By the time I scan the third row, I think my heart is gonna give out. I look frantically over to Tina. She just shakes her head.

"Time to get ready, bitches," Olivia shouts. "Whip out your glitter and your sequins and everything pink because tonight's party theme is Barbies!"

The girls all laugh and chatter, racing to their rooms to get ready.

Clutching my coconut water, I stand by helplessly and watch as the fun, tasteful evening I had planned goes up in smoke. It's fitting, really. Because watching seven drunk women play this raunchy bingo game is about to become my own personal hell.

40
COLTON

$\mathcal{S}$tanding in the middle of Novy's empty living room, I turn a half circle. "You weren't kidding about the 'no decorating' thing."

"Right?" He leans against the kitchen island, watching me take it all in. And by *all*, I mean his sectional sofa in the middle of the floor angled toward the hundred-inch TV he has perched atop its own box.

That's it. That's all he has in this whole goddamn room.

This is our first weekend free in a month, and he invited me over tonight to watch the Bruins/Oilers game. Our takeout containers of chicken fettuccini alfredo sit on the counter, along with a case of double IPA. "You don't even have a coffee table we can set the beers on," I mutter.

"Oh, I use this." Stepping around the other side of the sofa, he picks up an overturned packing box. I can see the faded water rings dotting the surface.

I sigh. "Just show me the rest."

He takes me on a quick tour of the rest of his empty beach house. The bones of this place are great. Good natural light, lots of wall space he could use for built-ins. There's a room in the back that would make a great in-home theater. A room on the second floor would make an awesome library-slash-office.

Wait, does Novy read?

I mean, I know he *can* read. But does he *like* to read?

I realize as I'm walking around, dreaming up what this space could look like, that I really don't know much about him. He's one of the chattiest guys you'll ever meet, but it's only on reflection that I realize he doesn't ever share anything personal. It's usually just crazy stories from his travels, his parties, or the girls he wheels. He never talks about Novy. He never lets anyone in.

"And this is my room," he says, leading the way through the double doors into a large bedroom. There's a pair of king-sized mattresses stacked on the floor with no frame. The bed at least looks comfortable. He's got a fluffy comforter and a generous amount of pillows. But it's all stark white, devoid of any personality, like a hotel.

Shit, even hotels have a *little* charm.

I sigh again. "Dude, I'm sorry, but the vibes in here are wretched."

"Told you," he mutters.

"Well, you gotta decorate. You don't even have a lamp for your bedside."

"There's a light in the ceiling, bud." He points to the stationary ceiling fan.

"Yeah, but—okay, so it's late at night and you're tired, but you're not ready to fall asleep. You come in here, turn on the light, then you get in bed and then you *are* ready to sleep—"

"Why the fuck are you detailing the steps of going to sleep?"

"Well, because what do you do?" I press. "You're tired, and you wanna sleep, but instead of rolling over like a normal fucking person and turning off the lamp, you have to get *out* of bed and turn off the ceiling light?"

"No, I turn on the bathroom light."

I blink at him. "Why do you turn *on* the bathroom light?"

"Because it's closer than going and turning off the ceiling light."

"So, you sleep with the goddamn lights on?"

"No, I never turn that light on," he says, pointing up at the ceiling fan again.

"It's on now."

"Yeah, 'cause I'm giving you a fucking tour," he snaps. "I'm saying I only ever turn on the bathroom light, and *that's* the light I turn off when I go to bed. Geez, what's your problem?"

"Okay, let's go." I grab his arm, pulling him from the bedroom.

"Ouch. Where are we going?"

"Out. I'm not sitting in this empty house, eating pasta on my lap with my beer on the floor."

"I told you I didn't have any furniture—"

"Yeah, and we're gonna fix that," I say, leading the way down the stairs. We get to the kitchen and I swipe my wallet and keys off the counter.

"Where are we going?" he says again.

"Dinner and the game. We'll find a sports bar or something. I just can't sit in here. It's freaking me out. And first thing Monday, we're asking Poppy for the name of an interior decorator."

The trouble with going out to watch the game is that a lot of the regulars in the sports bars around Jax Beach have started to recognize us. Don't get me wrong, I love our fans. But there's nothing worse than trying to watch pro hockey in a bar with people who know you also play.

Novy and I get a wild hair and end up driving down the A1A highway all the way to St. Augustine. The little downtown is lousy with bars and restaurants where you can grab a bite and watch a game in peace. We find our way onto a pair of barstools in the corner of a dark Irish pub. A big TV hangs right in front of us over the bar, so it's like we're in our own little world as we watch the game.

"Look at Norris." Novy snorts into his beer, snagging a few French fries off my plate. "What a fucking fool."

We both laugh as we watch the defenseman get circled on the ice, too slow to keep up with his mark. "He's a total pylon," I say.

"Right? Outta the way, 41!" he shouts at the screen. "God, how is he starting for them still?"

I shrug. "Bribes? Hand jobs?"

"Don't tell me he's the coach's nephew."

We snort again, watching for a few more minutes as Novy eats the rest of the fries off my plate. I glance over, taking in his profile in the glow of the wall of flashing TV screens. The bridge of his nose is bent from a previous break. I wouldn't say I tend to notice the attractiveness of men, but he's not bad looking.

"Tell me something about yourself," I say.

He's distracted by the action on the TV. "What?"

"Just tell me one thing that's not about the game or the girls," I go on. "One thing about you."

He turns, one brow raised. "What the hell, Morrow? Want me to put out later too?"

"Don't last-name me anymore. To you, I'm Cole."

He blinks, leaning away. "Jeez, is this a date?"

"Call it an interview," I counter.

"An interview?"

"You think you're good enough to be with Poppy? You want to share her with me? I want to know whether you're worth the trouble."

He chuckles. "Well, A, no, I don't think I'm good enough for Poppy. B, I never technically said I'd share her with you. And C, I can save you the time now and say I'm definitely *not* worth the trouble."

I just give him a deadpan stare. "Don't do that either."

"Do what?"

"Your self-deprecating bullshit. I see through it, and so does she."

"Oh, does she?"

"She wants to know you, Nov. She wants to let you into her world and her life and her bed, and I'm gonna make sure you're the kind of man worthy of such an honor. Now, if you won't open up to her and be real without the jokes and the swagger, you're gonna do it with me. I want one real thing. Just one, and then I'll leave you alone."

His eyes narrow. "One thing?"

"Easy peasy."

"You go first," he challenges.

Swiping my beer off the bar, I take a sip. "Fine. My dad died."

His protective shields instantly lower. "Oh, shit. CJ died?" His hand drops to my thigh. "Oh, Cole. When?"

Shit, his concern is genuine. How could I have forgotten that Novy knew my dad? He knew how close we were too. I talked about him all the time. I think Novy even went to dinner with us once or twice after a game when Dad was visiting. It feels *good* to tell him, like a weight's been lifted. It's validating, like seeing his concern assures me Dad was the kind of person who deserved to be missed, to be mourned.

"He was fading for a long time," I explain. "He passed shortly after last season ended. That's why I was so late getting down here. It's why I still live in temporary housing. House-hunting didn't seem to matter when I was busy packing up the last fifty years of his life."

"Dude, I'm sorry," he says, giving my thigh a squeeze. "You

should've told me when it happened. I could have come to the funeral or something. Why didn't you?"

"I'm telling you now."

He drops his hand away. "Well, I don't think I can top that."

"I hope you can't," I reply. "But I'll take any small thing, any piece of you, Nov."

He's thoughtful for a minute. "I cry watching sheepdog herding videos."

"What?"

He shrugs. "Can't explain it. I just watch those dogs racing around, collecting all their sheep, moving them from pen to pen, and I get choked up every damn time. You ever seen it?"

I smile, my chest feeling a little lighter. "No, I can't say that I have."

"I'll send you some links. It's fucking magical." He pulls out his phone. Within moments, my own buzzes in my pocket. His eyes stay on his phone for a few more minutes while I return to watching the game.

"She's not gonna do this with us, is she?"

I glance his way again. "What?"

"Poppy." He lowers his phone and looks at me. "You told her to come to me. You told her to square things so we could take this to the next level, but she didn't. Did I somehow ruin this?"

I sigh, setting my beer down. "Nov, it's been less than twenty-four hours, and she's busy. She works harder than the both of us combined. Besides, didn't she have that bachelorette thing this weekend?"

Novy perks up. "Oh shit. Wasn't that here in St. Augustine?" He slaps my chest. "Hey, we should go find her."

I laugh, shaking my head.

"What, how hard could it be? Come on, bachelorette parties always draw attention. Wouldn't you rather go dance with our girl than sit on these damn barstools watching the Bruins win again?"

I go still, pulse humming. "Novy."

"Hey, if you think I'm gonna sit here and watch sheepdog herding videos with you, think again. I don't cry in public—well, unless it's the Winter Olympics." He snaps his fingers. "Or there's this one Cheerios commercial—"

"*Nov*," I growl, slapping his chest.

"Ow." He rubs the spot. "What?"

Grabbing him by the shoulders, I spin him around on his stool to face the door just as the bar explodes with noise. All the guys cheer and wolf whistle as a swarm of pink flamingos enters in a flurry of feathered boas and glittery sashes.

Only they're not flamingos. They're a squealing, laughing, blinking penis hat-wearing bachelorette party. And right in the front, dressed like my wet dream, is a smoky-eyed, big-haired Poppy wearing a pink beaded bra top, gold sequin miniskirt, and gold platform stilettos with thin straps that wrap up her slender calves.

"Hooooly fuck." Novy spins back around on his stool and cups my face with both hands, his own alight with excitement. "Say yes."

I lean away, distracted by Poppy as she sweeps into the room, the fringe on her beaded top teasing her bare midriff.

"*Hey*." Novy slaps my face. "Say yes, asshole."

I grunt. "Yes to what?"

"Yes to sharing her. Say you're in. All the way in. We're fucking do this."

"I thought we were playing hard to get," I challenge.

"No, we *were* playing hard to get because you're a fucking Leo and you require a goddamn leash. Now it's Scorpio time."

"What the hell does that mean?"

"It means it's time to strike," he says with a grin. "Now, are you in or out?"

Poppy turns away, flashing her bare back, and all my thinking power shifts straight down to my dick. "Yes," I manage to say, setting my beer aside. "I'm all in."

"Fuck yes." He leaps off his stool. Grabbing my arm, he tugs me off mine too. "Let's go get our girl."

41
POPPY

I don't know what Violet and her friends expected from St. Augustine's nightlife, but it's not the freaking Miami strip. We've already stumbled our way through the only two bars hosting karaoke tonight, making complete fools of ourselves singing Britney Spears and the Spice Girls. But I don't think they'll stop until we've sampled the delights of every bar in town.

I crinkle my nose as we step into a little Irish pub. It's tucked away off the main street, and I can see why. The place smells like day-old fried fish and beer. There's no music playing, no party lights, and no room to dance. A row of TVs behind the bar play five different sports, including golf.

At least the reception is warm. All the patrons hoot and holler. Some are laughing at us. And, I mean, fair. We look ridiculous. Violet forced me into this beaded bikini top, and I feel naked. I've spent half the night adjusting it, worried the girls are peeking out.

Behind me, Lemon trips on the rug, bumping into me and nearly losing her pink cowgirl hat topped with a large pink and purple blinking penis. "Oops! Sorry, Daisy," she giggles.

"It's Poppy," I remind her for the third time.

She strides into the middle of the bar in her white fringed jean shorts and red lace bustier top. Her Cowgirl Barbie look is complete with a pair of blinged-out rhinestone boots.

Okay, the boots are cute.

"Can someone turn the music up in here?" she shouts. "We've got a bride to celebrate!"

To my surprise, upbeat dance music fills the bar. The bartender flips a switch and colorful lights shine on a disco ball that slowly starts to spin. It's no Club 7, but the effect is cute. The other girls rush forward, ready to order drinks and dance.

I turn to Tina. "Set a timer for twenty minutes, and then we'll make our exit. No need to subject these folks to Bianca's "Macarena" routine for any longer than necessary."

She nods, pulling out her phone.

"Well, if it isn't my favorite flavor of sweet treat," a voice calls from behind me.

My heart leaps into my throat as I grab Tina's arm. "Oh god."

She looks from my hand to my face. "Girl, what—"

"You gonna turn around for us, Popsicle?"

Tina glances behind me, her confusion morphing into a wolfish grin. "Well, hello again. You're Poppy's devil, right?"

"One of them," Lukas replies, his tone dripping with steam.

"This one looks familiar too," she says, her gaze leveling over my right shoulder.

I turn around, nearly bumping into Colton. He puts a hand on my arm to steady me, the heat of his touch spreading up my arm like wildfire. I glance between them. God help me, they look beautiful. Popsicle is right because I'm about to melt into a puddle on the floor.

Colton holds out a hand to Tina. "Hey, Colton Morrow. I used to play for the Washington Capitals."

"That's it," she says, connecting the dots as she shakes his hand. "You and your buddies would come into my club."

"On occasion," he replies, his gaze shifting right back to me.

My heart is still racing. "What are you two doing here?"

"Oh, just dinner and a game with my best bud," Lukas replies, draping an arm around Colton's shoulders. "Kinda like a date night. We would've invited you, but you were otherwise engaged."

Tina is still grinning. "Oh, what the fuck is this?"

"Nothing," I say, fighting my blush.

"Just a little mating ritual," Lukas teases. "Let me borrow that boa, and I'll even shake my tail feathers for ya."

"Sure." She slips the pink feathered boa off her neck and wraps it around Lukas.

A few of the other girls notice and start weaving this way. My little champagne bubble of happiness pops. "Oh god." I grab their hands. "You have to leave. *Now.*"

As a conflict-avoidant, people-pleasing double Libra, there are many things in life I can tolerate with a smile on my face. For example, I'm wearing this skimpy Coachella Barbie costume while hosting my bitchy little sister's bachelorette party to celebrate her shell of a marriage to my terrible ex on my own freaking dime.

What I will *not* tolerate is Violet and her friends flirting with, dancing up on, or otherwise touching my hockey players.

"Oh, come on, Pop," Tina calls. "Let 'em stay."

"Babe, we haven't paid our bill yet," Lukas adds.

Colton steps in, a hand on my shoulder. "Poppy, what's wrong?"

"You have to go. *Please.* Before my sister gets her hands on you—"

As I say the words, Olivia and Violet saunter up, fruity drinks in hand. "Hey, who invited cocks to this hen party?" Olivia calls out. She's still in her bedazzled pink jumpsuit as Disco Barbie. Next to her, Violet is wearing a white mini dress with a veil as Bridal Barbie. Olivia settles her hungry gaze on Lukas's tattoos. "Well, hi there, handsome. Who might you be?"

If she reaches out even one hand to touch him, I'm gonna bite it off.

Sensing my distress, Lukas slips around me, away from her. Wrapping his arms around my shoulders, he pulls me in against his chest. In seconds, this man has neutralized the threat, turning me into a human shield. "I'm Poppy's boyfriend," he declares.

Pin freaking drop.

Umm, I feel like I should remember having that conversation, right? Now seems like a terrible moment to ask for clarification because Violent and Olivia look like they've just swallowed a handful of sour grapes.

Oooh, I *like* seeing Olivia Monroe jealous.

Next to her, Violet scoffs. "Yeah, right. If Poppy had a boyfriend, I would know."

If Poppy had a boyfriend, *Poppy* would know, right?

I just keep smiling.

The other girls crowd in, chatting and laughing.

"Did I hear Poppy has a boyfriend?" Maggie coos.

"Actually, we're *both* her boyfriends," Lukas clarifies to more excited chatter.

Wait, now Poppy has two boyfriends? How did I miss all this?

"I'm Lukas," he goes on. "This handsome fella is Cole. Nice to meet you, ladies. Now, which one of you is the blushing bride?"

Oh, he's smooth. He's already met Violet once before. Not to mention, we look alike. But he just glances around, pretending like he doesn't see her standing there in her veil and glittery "Bride" sash.

If there's one thing my sister can't stand, it's being ignored. Her smile flickers in annoyance as she sticks out her hand. "I'm Violet St. James, Poppy's younger sister. And we've met, actually."

"Right," he says, shaking her hand. "I guess I forgot what you looked like."

Olivia snorts into her drink. "Seriously? She looks like a taller, hotter version of Poppy."

Okay, I'm about to punch this girl right in the cunt.

"It's fine," Violet says with a simpering smile. "Names and faces must be tough for how often you get hit in the head, right?"

Lukas tightens his arm around me, keeping me from lunging.

Oblivious to the tension, Chutney leans in. "And she's wearing the 'Bride' sash, silly."

"Hmm, I didn't even notice." He relaxes his arm, stroking his hand up and down the bare skin of my shoulder. Violet watches the movement with narrowed eyes. "Coley, did you see it, bud?"

Colton weaves his fingers in with mine, smiling down at me. "Nope. I only saw Poppy."

Be still my heart. Is there anything hotter than loyalty? You get that with two boyfriends, right? Even fake ones?

"Wait, are you guys hockey players?"

Perfect. Now Lemon has entered the chat.

"We are indeed," says Lukas. "What gave us away? Was it my twice-broken nose, or all my fake teeth?"

"It was probably our hockey T-shirts," Colton teases.

"Or those rockin' bods," Giselle calls out.

Several of the girls laugh, clinking their glasses with Giselle.

"Ignore her. She's drunk," says Maggie.

"We're all drunk!"

Lemon still looks confused. "Wait, I thought Poppy said you had a game tonight, and that's why you couldn't come party with us." She looks around, hopeful. "Are there more of you?"

Lukas laughs, kissing my cheek. "Popsicle, did you lie to your sister and her friends so you could keep us all to yourself?"

Violent and Olivia glare at me. A warm feeling of triumph settles in my core as I hold their gazes. Slowly, I lift Colton's hand to my lips, giving it a gentle kiss. "Yes, I did."

Lukas laughs again. "Our kitten is a little territorial. But now that you're all here, we'd love to help the bride celebrate. Next round of drinks is on us."

The girls all squeal, making both guys jump. A few of them pull out their bingo cards.

"That's almost a bingo for me," sings Giselle, waving her card in Olivia's face.

"Me too," calls Chutney.

"Hey, ask them if they have a condom," says Maggie.

"Ask them for their number!"

Giving me one last disdainful look, Olivia points to the bar. "Drinks first, ladies. Let's leave Perfect Poppy to her pretty boy toys." She and Violet lead them away, much to my relief.

"I've said it once, and I'll say it again," Lukas says as they walk off. "Pop, your sister is a witch with a capital 'B.'"

I sigh, leaning back against his chest. "I know, but she's family."

He relaxes his hold on me. "And what's with the cards?"

"It's just a stupid game they're playing."

"A game *we're* playing," Tina says. "You're playing too, Pop. Don't forget."

"Half the stuff on my card is just doing shots. I'd be under the table in five minutes—and wait—what the heck are you wearing?" I didn't really get a good look at her before we left the beach house. I was too busy organizing the Ubers. Now that she has the boa off, I can take it all in. "Is that my blazer?" I gasp. "Tina, those are *my* clothes!"

She throws her head back and laughs. "Took you long enough!" The sneaky bitch raided my closet. She's wearing my petal pink pencil skirt, a white silky top, and my favorite fuchsia blazer. Her pink hair is curled and styled in a long ponytail.

"Which Barbie are you supposed to be?"

She's still laughing, eyes alight with mirth. "Duh? I'm *you*."

"Me?"

"Yeah, I'm PR Barbie." She strikes a pose with both hands on her hips.

Behind me, Lukas and Colton crack up.

"I want my clothes professionally laundered and returned," I shout at her. "This is *not* going to be the Great Ugg Boots Disappearance of '08!"

Still laughing, she pulls out one of the pink bingo cards. "Here, do us all a favor and help Poppy win this game already."

"Tina!" I slap at her arm, trying to get the card.

She just laughs, holding it out of my reach. "What? This is, like, the *Jumanji* of bachelorette parties. It won't stop until someone wins. With two hot hockey players on your team, you'll knock out a double bingo in ten minutes flat."

Colton reaches over me and takes the card.

"What do we get if we win?" Lukas asks. "I'm nothing if not competitive."

"Holy fuck." Colton's eyes blaze as he holds up the card. "You've been playing this?"

I huff, crossing my arms. "Please, I did, like, two of the things. I sang karaoke and traded shoes with a lady at the last bar."

Lukas glances down at my strappy gold gladiator heels. "You traded shoes with a total stranger?"

"Yeah, I was wearing these cute little white go-go boots before. They had a much more sensible heel."

"But those make you look waaay more fuckable," Tina teases.

"Facts," Colton mutters.

"Are you still here?" I say at her.

She just laughs again.

Lukas steals the bingo card from Colton. "So, what kind of game are we playing?" His eyes widen as he scans it. "Dollars?! Double bingo wins five *thousand* American dollars?"

"Yep," Tina replies.

"It's not, like, Monopoly dollars?"

"Olivia's parents are loaded," I explain. "Dropping five thousand dollars on Naughty Bachelorette Bingo is like sneezing for her."

His face lights up. "Oh, we are *so* winning that double bingo."

Tina claps her hands. "Yes! Get it, Poppy. Show these snooty bitches how it's done."

"We are *not* playing," I cry. "Lukas, did you even read half the stuff?"

"Oh, I read the whole thing. Come on." He grabs my hand and spins me around, pulling me toward the bar. "Coley, let's go! We gotta strategy sesh this out!"

He weaves us through the dancing bachelorette party girls. Pulling up at the end of the bar, he grabs Colton's arm and drags him forward too. They box me in, both of them with a hand on my bare back as they lean over me, inspecting the bingo card.

"I wanna do this one and this one," Lukas says, tapping the card. "Wait—and this one."

Colton is still just shaking his head. "It's like you can't win unless you're willing to perform a sex act."

"Why do you think I gave up after trading shoes?" I say. "Guys, I think some of this stuff is technically illegal—"

"Oh, we are *so* doing this one," Lukas goes on, tapping the square in the bottom row.

"We'd have to do the rest in that diagonal," Colton reasons.

"Well, if we combine the dick pic with this one, and the shots with this one, I think we'll have it," Lukas says, his tone bright with excitement. "Question." He raises his hand and turns to me. "Do these all have to be witnessed by someone else in the party? Like, is there a judge?"

I sigh, resigned to my fate. "Olivia is the judge. She's calling it the Dishonor System."

His grin spreads. "Oh, Popsicle, we are in for a wild fucking ride. You ready to play?"

I glance to Colton, and he smiles too, giving me a nod of encouragement.

Oh god, what is happening right now? For weeks, their signals have been all over the place. They want me, they tease me, then they make me see stars . . . then Lukas kicks me out of his hotel room, and Colton nods at me like we're strangers at the freaking coffee cart! The last time we were all together, they were literally punching each other into the sand at the idea of sharing me. Now they want to play Naughty Bachelorette Bingo? *Together?*

And don't even get me started on Lukas's little "boyfriends" comment. My gossipy sister is going to have a field day with that joke. I'm sure I've already missed a call from my mother in pieces over it.

"Come on, Popsicle," Lukas says, cupping my cheek. "We promise we'll behave."

Colton steps in at my back, his hands smoothing over my hips. "You're overthinking this," he says in my ear. "I can hear your brain ticking like a bomb."

"And I think you're both underthinking it," I say, fighting the urge to melt against him.

"We've thought it through plenty," he replies, his hands slipping under the beaded fringe on my top. "We're on the same page now, Poppy. We know what we want."

Lukas nods, his gaze heated as he watches Colton touch me. Oh god, why does he look so turned on? Both of them are touching me, and I can't think. Lukas grins, brushing his fingers through my hair. "Come on, baby. Let us show you what good teamwork looks like."

Colton's lips brush the shell of my ear. "Play with us."

Heart in my throat, I nod. "Okay."

Lukas's face lights up. "Yes?"

"Yes."

With that one little word, Colton lowers his face to my neck on a grateful groan, breathing me in like I know he's been dying to do since the moment I stepped into this bar. His hands hold possessively to my hips.

"Yes," I say again, arching my neck into the fevered press of his lips. "Play with me. Please."

Lukas silences my plea with a kiss. Then I'm free-falling into a new world of sensation as two beautiful men kiss me. My body is a live wire. I'm humming with aching need, lost in the feel of their lips and hands on me, warm bodies pressing in.

We're all trembling as we pull apart. Lukas recovers first. He gives one more glance to the bingo card before he's dropping my hand. "Right. Coley, trade tops with Poppy."

I don't even get to voice my concern before Colton strips his shirt off in the middle of the bar to the wild cheers of the crowd. Laughing, he twirls it around his head. Then he's handing it over to me, stealing a kiss as he does.

Lukas is right behind me, his hand on my hip. They're comfortable together. They're excited. God help me, I think they really want this. They want to share me. Heart on fire, I tip up on my toes and brush a quick kiss to Colton's lips. Arching back, I steal one from Lukas too, ignoring the wolf whistles and surprised squeals. "Right," I say. "Let's win this stupid thing."

"That's my girl," Lukas says. "Someone get us a pen," he shouts down the bar.

I tug Colton's old Winter Classic tee on over my head. It's still warm, hanging on me like a dress. I stretch my arms around my back inside the shirt to unhook my bra top. Once it's loose, I stuff my arms through the T-shirt holes and pull my top out through the neck. Grinning, I hand it over to Colton.

Everyone in the bar watches as he receives it gallantly, slipping the halter on over his neck. The bachelorette party goes wild as he does a little shimmy, the shiny pink beads glinting in the bar lights. The top is practically a necklace on him. "That's one," he calls out to more cheers.

"Come here, Popsicle." Lukas turns me around and holds out a pen. "Draw a dick on me."

"What?"

"That's the next easiest one in the row," he explains, tapping the bingo square. "Look, it says 'draw a penis on someone.' Well, I'm someone. So, draw."

Smiling, I take the pen. "I'm not much of an artist," I warn.

"I don't think that matters in this game," Colton says at my back. He slips his hands up under his shirt, palming my bare skin. Every touch sets me aflame.

I fight a shiver, searching Lukas's colorful ink. He's got so many large pieces, and they all connect—a reaper crowned in flowers, a dagger piercing a heart, an inky black scorpion. "There's no spot for it," I say, twisting his arm around.

"Do it over here." He lifts his other arm and taps on a blank space on the outside of his forearm alongside an Anubis figure.

With very poor precision, I freehand a cock and balls, even adding a few sprinkles to the ball sac for cartoonish hair. "There," I say, capping the pen. "I think I did at least as well as a twelve-year-old boy."

They both laugh, and I toss the pen down on the bar. "That's two," I call out.

The bachelorette girls cheer some more.

"Yeah, Poppy!"

"Look at you go!"

Lukas brushes a kiss to my forehead. "Now we really get to have some fun."

Stuffing all my anxiety in a box, I jump into the game with both feet. "Let's do it."

"Yeah?"

"Yeah," I say on a laugh, gasping as Colton's hands sweep up to cup my breasts. "God." I arch into him, pushing his hands down. "Let's just do the next thing before I burst into flames."

"Way ahead of you." Lukas finally loses the pink boa and pulls his shirt off, tossing it down on a bar stool. Turning to the crowd, he cups his mouth and shouts, "Body shots!"

Apparently, we're combining bingo squares. "Tequila shots" and "Do a shot off a guy's abs" are now a two-for-one special. Lukas hops onto the bar as the crowd presses in behind us, eager to watch. The bartender hands him a lime wedge as he lies back, flexing those delicious ab muscles.

"Have you ever done a body shot before?" Colton says in my ear.

"No. Are you kidding me?"

"She needs some salt," he calls over to the bartender. Then he's pushing me forward. "Lick his neck."

My body is one raw nerve as I bend over the bar and lick Lukas's neck. The bartender dusts salt on the spot.

"Let's do this," Lukas calls, popping the lime wedge in his mouth.

The bartender pulls out a bottle of tequila and pours a measure of the amber liquid into Lukas's naval.

"Lick the salt, drink the shot, then take the lime," Colton explains, giving me a little push.

"Get it, Poppy!"

"Suck him good!"

I smile down at Lukas. He's grinning like the devil around his wedge of lime. Flicking my hair back, I sweep it up with both hands, holding it away from my face. I keep one hand on my fistful of hair as I brush my other up his leg from knee to thigh. Bending over the bar, I lick the salt off his neck. Then I slide down and suck the tequila from his skin, teasing him with my tongue. It's a riot of flavor, all sweet and sharp.

Lukas groans, trying to hold still as I let my hand slip a little higher up his thigh.

"Now the lime," Tina shouts. "Yeah, get it girl!"

Brushing my lips over his abs, I lower my face to claim the lime from his mouth. As soon as the tart wedge touches my teeth, I give it a squeeze, letting a burst of citrus coat my tongue. Standing up straight, I pop the lime wedge into my hand, laughing as I wipe the drippy juice from my chin.

Lukas sits up in a flash and hops off the bar. Cupping my face with both hands, he pulls me forward, burying his tongue in my mouth. I'm lost to his kiss as he steals every last taste of the tequila shot from my lips. The room is spinning as we break apart.

"That's two more," Colton calls out to the room. Then he grabs my hand. Walking backward, he moves with the music in a little shuffle step. He's still wearing my beaded pink top like a necklace, which lets his dark skin shine under the flashing lights. He leads me over to where some of the others are dancing. Maggie and Olivia found themselves partners while Violet dances with Bianca, Lemon, and Giselle. Chutney is making out with a man in the corner. I glance over to the bar to see Tina watching me, a smile on her face, beer in hand.

Turning my attention back to Colton, I wrap my hands around his neck, swaying with him. "What are we doing now?" I call out.

Lukas folds himself in against my back, his shirt back in place. "Next bingo square says you have to dance with a couple."

I laugh, swaying my hips to the beat as they both put their hands on me. "I think the game makers had a different kind of couple in mind."

"Well, playing by the rules of dishonor, this still works," Lukas says, nipping at my earlobe.

Oh, yeah. This works.

I lose myself to the music and the feel of their roving hands as the first notes of Dua Lipa's "Dance The Night" fade in. All around us, the bachelorette party girls erupt with excited cheers. Colton takes my hand and steps back, spinning me under and in. I land against him with a laugh, palms flat on his bare chest.

"I can't dance in these crazy shoes," I say, praying I don't step on his foot.

"Just move the rest of your body, then." Hands on my hips, he bends at the knees, rocking with me. I keep one hand on his bare chest, wrapping the other around Lukas's neck to reel him in closer. I want the feel of them both sharing my skin. I don't want air. I don't want space. I just want *them*. I want more of this, and I never want it to stop.

Lukas tucks himself in behind me, rocking with us until I can feel his hard cock grinding against my ass. He sweeps my hair aside, kissing my neck. "You ready to win this game?"

I shiver, looking into Colton's dark eyes. They glitter with the light of the twirling disco ball. "What do I have to do?"

"Get a dick pic," he replies. "Which can be accomplished while you give a hand job."

I shake my head, unable to stifle my laugh. "If you think I'm gonna do that right here in the middle of this dance floor, you're both crazy. Olivia can keep her money."

Lukas cups my breasts over the shirt, pinching my nipples until I gasp. "We have a fix for any more public displays of indecency."

"And what's that?"

"The last box to check," he teases. "The only other one you need for double bingo."

I turn in their arms, facing Lukas. "And which one is that?"

His smile is blinding as he leans in. "Three minutes in heaven."

I go still, heart racing. Are we really doing this?

Hell yes.

Feeling like a powerful goddess, I take their hands and lead them away from the dancers, angling toward the bathroom. I make a quick stop by Tina at the bar.

"Having fun?" she calls over the music.

"Tons," I reply, adrenaline flooding me.

"And just where are you three going?"

I hold her gaze and grin. "To win double bingo. Give me your purse."

She slides it over. It takes me all of two seconds to find what I'm looking for. Pulling out a sample packet of cinnamon bun-flavored lube, I hold it up between two fingers. "I'm taking this."

She smiles from ear to ear. "Yeah, you are. Go get some."

I hand her back her purse. "Cunt block the others while I'm gone, yeah? No one is winning bingo tonight but me."

Tina shakes her head, smiling like a proud mama bear. "Who are you, and what have you done with Poppy St. James?"

"Don't worry about what I've done," I tease. "Just be jealous of what I'm about to do."

"You're my hero," she calls as I walk away, my guys hot on my heels.

43
POPPY

I step into the tiny pub bathroom, crossing to the far wall in two strides. Lukas and Colton crowd in behind me, squishing together to get the door shut. The dance music is instantly muffled. Colton throws the lock, and they turn as one, shoulders brushing in the tight space as they stare hungrily down at me.

My smile falters as I take them in. Now that we're alone, all the questions and confusion I've been trying to keep trapped in a box are starting to leak out. I'm not this girl. I'm not "offers hand jobs in a bathroom" girl. I'm "panics about her feelings and stress runs five miles" girl. Two beautiful men are standing here, wanting me. My heart is racing, my palms feel clammy, and all I can think is, "What the heck are we doing?"

Okay, so I guess I don't think it. I just go ahead and say it out loud.

"We're playing three minutes in heaven," Lukas replies with a grin. "It'll be a busy three minutes because we have to manage a dick pic and a hand job. If we wanted to go for a Triple bingo, you could give us a lap dance too—"

"I meant what are *we* doing!" I gesture frantically between the three of us. "What the heck is this?"

"We thought that was obvious," he replies with a shrug.

"Obvious? Lukas, you just hard-launched our love triangle to my sister and all her friends! Without telling me first! Do you have any idea the shitstorm that little joke is gonna swirl me in? As if I didn't have enough on my plate with this new job, and this stupid, awful wedding, now I'm gonna have to field questions from my mother about why two hockey players are calling themselves my boyfriends."

His smile falls. "Hey, come on. Your sister needed to be put her in her place—"

"My sister needed to be kept in the dark!" I snap. "Now she's gonna turn this into the scandal of the century. Poppy the chaos monster strikes again. She can't make up her mind, so now she's stringing *two* men along—oh god." My PR brain is already spinning out the likely scenarios.

Colton looks confused. "Poppy, what scandal? It's not like we're doing anything illegal here. We're all consenting adults."

"I'm sorry, but clarifying that we're 'consenting adults' won't ease people's minds," I reply. "In fact, don't be surprised if my mother shows up in town with Pastor John to try to force an exorcism on me."

"So, I'll just take it back," Lukas offers. "I'll tell your sister it was a joke—"

"No," I cry. "Oh my—do you wanna make it worse? Pathetic Poppy had no boyfriends, then she had two, and now she has none again?"

He groans. "Then what the hell do you want, Poppy?"

"I wanted this all kept quiet!"

He glares, arms crossed. "You want us to be your dirty little secrets? Poppy St. James is too good to be seen on the arm of a tatted-up hockey player, right?"

I shake my head. "That's not fair. I wanted us *private*, not secret. We don't even know what we are to each other yet, Lukas. I mean, ten minutes ago, I thought we were all going our separate ways."

Colton's eyes narrow. "Why did you think that?"

"Seriously?" I glance between them. "Do you not remember the beach? Oh, and Claribel told me about your little tortilla wrestling match too," I add, hands on my hips. "You tease me, you chase me, you *fuck* me . . . but ever since Pittsburgh, you've both been so weird and polite and distant—"

"We've been busy," Lukas counters. "You have too. I mean, Jeezus, Pop. We're professional athletes in the middle of a new season. I hardly have time to wash my own socks, let alone manage a complicated three-way. And Cole and I had some shit to sort out first."

My eyes well with tears as I slowly nod. "See, and here's me twisting into a ball of nerves knowing I'm the 'shit' you're sorting out. But you're doing it without me. How is that fair? How am I supposed to know you've both changed your mind if you don't *tell* me?"

"We just didn't have time yet!" Lukas shouts.

"And then you go and tell me in front of my sister!"

"Enough," Colton shouts over us. He puts a hand on Lukas's shoulder. "Nov, that's enough." To my surprise, Lukas relaxes, giving Colton a nod. Colton turns to me, his hand still on Lukas's shoulder. "Poppy, what are you scared of?"

I suck in a breath of surprise. "What?"

"So what if your sister knows? Fuck her. Fuck anyone who's not in this room. If you're that afraid of what other people think, you should leave now." He steps to the side, gesturing to the door.

When I make no move to leave, he goes on. "Because we're not afraid of this, Poppy. You're right. We handled our shit away from you because our jealousy is not your burden to carry. We worked it through, and we decided that we *want* this. We want *you*. If you want to date us separately, that's fine. If you want us together, we'll try that too. We've never done it, but we're willing to try. For *you*. But we're only willing under the condition that *this*"—he gestures between the three of us— "is exclusive. Understood?"

Heart in my throat, I nod.

Emboldened, Colton steps forward, cupping my face with both hands. My hands go to his bare chest, instantly warming under the heat of his skin. His voice is low and fevered as his hands smooth down the column of my neck to brace my shoulders. "You want this kept quiet while we all figure out what we are to each other? We'll be quite as the fucking grave. You want to sign the paperwork with HR and start wearing our jerseys to our games? I'll buy a house and move you into my bed tomorrow. All options are on the table here. All eventualities. Have us together, have us apart, it's whatever the fuck you want. But you *will* have us, Poppy. Because not having you is no longer a fucking option."

"Colton . . ."

He lowers his face closer to mine, breathing me in before saying, "So what do you wanna do here, Poppy? We need to hear you say it."

Lost in the sensation of having him so close, I recite the words already carved into the walls of my heart. "Colton, please, I want you so badly."

He claims my confession with a searing kiss. Digging his hands into my hair, he teases with his tongue, sinking it deep into my mouth. I cling to him, weak and breathless as he takes what he wants from my lips, leaving me with nothing.

He breaks the kiss first. Pulling me by the hair, he turns me to face Lukas. Pressing his front to my back, he speaks in my ear, his breath hot on my skin. "What about Lukas? Do you want him?"

Lukas stands there, gazing down at me with such longing.

"Yes," I say on a breath. "I want him too. So much."

"Then *show* him." Colton gives me a little push forward, sending me stumbling in these wobbly heels into Lukas's chest.

Lukas catches me, his arms going around my waist. "Look, Pop, I know I'm not the kind of guy you typically go for but—"

"Don't." I place my fingers over his lips, silencing his self-criticism. "Lukas, you *are* the guy I go for. I'm standing right here."

He shakes his head, suddenly nervous as he holds me. "I don't know what the fuck I'm doing with you."

I grin up at him, smoothing my hands over his chest. "If all else fails, we'll always have sex and sarcasm, yeah?"

He grins. "Sex and sarcasm? Really? Is that all I offer—"

"Just shut up and kiss me." Tipping up on my toes, I wrap my hands around his neck and pull him down to my lips, kissing him quiet.

Colton's kisses are soul-searing and searching, like plunging into deep water. I feel moored to him, anchored and safe. Lukas's kisses are the flashes of sunlight sparkling on a sun-kissed sea. There's something wild in the way he kisses, something playful and free.

With a groan, he kisses down my neck, his fingers buried in my hair. Lips parted on a breath, I open my eyes to see Colton watching us. Intensity rolls off him. He's not angry or jealous. God help me, he's turned on. He watches us with hungry eyes.

Feeling daring, I hold out a hand to him. "I want you both. Now."

Without hesitation, he steps in next to Lukas and unbuckles his belt, opening the top of his jeans. As Lukas teases my pulse point with his tongue, Colton takes my hand by the wrist, slipping it inside his pants. I moan low in my throat at the joint sensation of being kissed by Lukas as I wrap my hand around Colton's hard cock. "Oh god."

Lukas pulls away with a satisfied smile. "You ready to finish our three minutes in heaven?"

I blink, remembering why we even came in here. "I—"

"Wait." Colton squeezes my wrist to stop me from stroking him. "She has to agree first."

I glance between them. "Agree?"

"Say you're ours," he commands. "Call it secret, call it private, call it a fucking fever dream, I don't care. But so long as Lukas and I are satisfying your every need, you don't look at another man. You don't touch another man. You're *ours*. Say it, Poppy."

Holding Colton's fierce gaze, I trail my free hand down Lukas's chest until I'm palming his hard dick over his jeans. He groans, moving his hips against my pressure. "I'm yours," I say with a smile. "And these are *mine*."

Colton's eyes flash with triumph.

I smooth my hands up and down their shafts together—Lukas through his jeans, Colton against his warm, silky skin. Nothing makes me feel more powerful than to feel them harden under my hands. "Olivia dared to look at you like she stood a chance. Does she?"

Colton's fingers tangle in my hair as he brushes his lips against mine. "Who the fuck is Olivia?"

I smile, kissing him back. *Good answer.*

He leans away and Lukas grins, cupping my cheek. "You are so fucking ruthless, babe. You're a wildcat."

"I'm a *queen*," I counter, slipping my hand inside his jeans to wrap a needy hand around him too. "And this belongs to me."

He nods, still grinning. "I mean, sure. He seems to like you." I give him a little squeeze, making him gasp. "Fine—*fuck*—he's yours. I'll tattoo your name on him if you want."

I soften my touch, stroking my thumb around his head, smearing his precum. "I don't think that will be necessary." Then I turn to Colton.

"It's yours," he says without hesitation or jest.

I smile. "Good."

Power and control course through me. I've never felt this way during sex with anyone, like I could be in control, like it's *fun* to be in control, like the man could willingly *cede* control. Now I have two men putting me in the driver's seat. It's intoxicating. I chase the feeling as I smile up at them, stroking them in tandem. "I know it's been more than three minutes, but we have a game to finish. Are you both still in?"

"Fuck, yes," Lukas grunts, moving his hips with the stroke of my hand.

"I'm in," Colton says, jaw clenched tight.

Smiling, I glance between them. "Can I tell you what I want?"

"Of course," says Colton.

"Anything," Lukas echoes.

This intoxicating feeling of power surges through me as I let myself say exactly what I desire, knowing they'll make it happen. "You're mine, and I'm yours, and I don't want to stop at a silly little hand job."

Lukas's pretty caramel eyes flash with interest. "What *do* you want, Popsicle?"

I hold his gaze, brushing my thumb over his tip again. "They already know we came in here. I want to leave them in no doubt of what happened. I want to smear my pink lipstick all over your pretty dicks. I want to claim you both, mark you as mine." I turn to Colton. "And I want your cum in my mouth. I want to swallow it down like a greedy little whore who just can't get enough."

"Fuck," he says on a breath, his hand tightening around my wrist.

I smile. "In this moment, I'm not afraid of anything except how much I want you." Slipping my hands from their pants, I sink down to my knees. Gazing up at them, seeing the way they look at me, so much hope and longing blooms in my chest. "Give yourselves to me."

As one, they work their jeans the rest of the way open, tugging them down around their muscled thighs until two perfect cocks spring hard and ready in front of my face. Lukas sheds his shirt in a one-handed pull. He offers it to me. "For those pretty knees."

I take it with a smile, tucking it under my knees. As I do, I arch forward and suck his tip into my mouth. He groans, fisting my hair. The second I get a little salty taste of his precum on my tongue, I pop off. "Let's get the pic out of the way, yeah?"

Colton fishes in his pocket for his phone and hands it out to me with the camera on. "It gets deleted the moment the game is over."

"Duh." I turn my face to lick and suck on his dark tip too.

He grunts, flexing his hips away. "Fucking hell. Just take the phone, you goddamn troublemaker."

I take the phone with a grin. Leaning back on my heels, I snap a pic of them standing together, fisting their hard cocks. Their heads are cut off, nothing visible above the chest or below the knee, but I would have no trouble knowing it's them.

"For the Christmas card," I tease, handing him the phone. Colton slips it back in his pocket, trading me for the little packet of lube I stole from Tina. I tear into it with my teeth, squeezing the generous helping into my palm.

"Is that flavored?" Lukas asks.

I smear the lube between my hands. "Yeah, cinnamon bun. Is that okay?"

He laughs, brushing my hair back. "You are fucking precious."

Reaching out with both hands, I stroke their dicks in one long pull, coating them in lube.

"Oh, fuck me," Lukas mutters, his hand going up to rest on Colton's shoulder.

Colton keeps his eyes on me, his gaze heated, body tense.

I work my hands up and down, luxuriating in the feel of them, hard and greased beneath my palms. Touching them at the same time is like a drug. I'm fascinated. I'm high. I can't look away. I stroke and tease, swirling my thumbs around their tips, watching with pleasure as they both leak more precum. "Tell me if you want something different."

"Are you kidding?" Lukas says on a laugh.

"It's perfect," says Colton. "Just don't stop."

I'm desperate and turned on, but I'm not crazy. And Lukas and I haven't crossed this particular bridge yet. My gaze darts between them. "Is there anything I should know before I put my mouth back on these cocks and swallow your cum?"

Colton grunts, his hips moving in rhythm with each pull of my hand. "No. You know I'm clean."

I look to Lukas.

He exhales through parted lips. "I'm clean, Pop. And I've never touched a girl without a condom until this moment."

"Not even for a blowjob?" I say, unable to hide the tone of surprise from my voice.

"Trust is hard for me," he replies. "Even now, I'm kind of panicking in my head a little."

My hand stills. "I can stop."

"Don't you fucking dare," he says, wrapping his hand around mine. "Poppy, I want this. Want *you*. I trust you. Trust you both," he adds, squeezing Colton's shoulder.

Heart overflowing with relief, I lean forward and suck his tip back into my mouth. The taste of the cinnamon bun lube is sickly sweet, but I don't care. I work Colton with my fist as I hollow my cheeks and sink down on Lukas, taking him deeper into my mouth. The feel of them watching me is overwhelming, my core is a burning flame of want and desire. The lube mixes with my lipstick, smearing the color pink down Lukas's shaft.

"So fucking good," he mutters, his hand in my hair.

I let him go, turning my attention to Colton. I circle his tip with my tongue, the sweet lube smearing more of my lipstick. I suck him down, humming with pleasure at this feeling of holding them both in my hands.

Someone pounds on the door with a heavy fist. "Hurry up!"

I gasp, popping off him, my eyes wide.

"In a minute," Colton shouts, his voice deep and harsh.

Lukas groans. "I think we need to make this a speed round. Babe, I am right fucking there. You can finish me with a few more flicks of that tongue."

"Suck him dry, then use his cum as lube on me," Colton commands.

My stomach flips as I gaze up at him, eyes wide.

Lukas turns to him too. He just said trust is hard for him. He's never trusted an intimate partner before, but he trusts us. Colton means to show him that his trust is returned. He wants to share this with us, connect us all in this intimate way.

"Well, alrighty then," Lukas says on another laugh. "Pops, you heard the man."

Excitement shivers through me as I put my mouth back on Lukas, kissing and licking down his shaft, returning to his head to suck and tease. I fight my gag reflex, moaning around him as I try to take him deeper. Colton wraps a hand around my wrist. "Both hands on Novy, queen. Give him your full attention."

With a whimper, I drop my hand away, moving it over to double-fist Lukas. I focus on sucking his tip, working both hands with a twist and pull.

"I'm right there," Lukas pants. "Babe, I'm right—*ahhh*—" I hold my hands still, applying enough pressure to create a tight squeeze he can rut into. He comes on a groan, his warm seed spilling into my mouth. "Show me," he pants. "Show me. Open your mouth."

I lean away, mouth open as the last of his cum shoots out of his tip, coating my lips and tongue. He's never let another woman have this before. No one but me. It fills me with a sense of such primal power. This man is *mine*.

"God," he groans. "Oh god." He sags back, his dick glistening with lube and my saliva. "Finish Cole, baby. Wanna watch you get face fucked with a mouth full of my cum."

I'm a blazing inferno as I turn to Colton. He nods down at me, both hands diving into my hair to hold it back. "You own me," he says. "Take what's already yours."

Crowing with confidence, I sink my mouth around him. The swirl of Lukas's cum in my mouth feels strange as I use it help me pleasure Colton. Both men groan. I can feel their eyes on me as I wrap my hands around Colton's thick shaft and begin to stroke.

"No—" Colton grabs my wrists. "Nov, take her hands. Hold them behind her back. I only want her perfect fucking mouth."

I'm trembling as Lukas steps in behind me, straddling my legs as he grabs me by the wrists, gently pulling my hands behind my back. The movement arches me forward. I feel almost limp, like I can sink into my own weight, knowing Lukas will hold me. He'll never let me fall. I'm just a mouth, taking what I want, letting Colton guide my lips around his cock again. I make a mess as I play with him, swallowing some of Lukas's cum and spilling the rest as I drown in the sensation of sucking my second cock.

"Please," I murmur, looking up at Colton. "Please, baby, give me your cum. Let me have it. I need it."

His hands tighten in my hair as he finally gives me what I want. There's no more gentleness as he fucks my face, pushing me right up to the edge of what I can take. When I gag and pull back, he lets me go, allowing me to recover a breath before he goes again.

"Right fucking there," he says on a breath. "Poppy, don't stop. Take it all."

Lukas squeezes my wrists and Colton holds my head still as he releases, his hot cum filling my mouth. I cry out, an inch from coming myself from the adrenaline rush alone.

"Swallow it," Colton commands, cupping my chin with his hand. "Such a good fucking girl. A queen on her knees. You're *ours*. Branded with our cum. We'll take such good care of you."

I swallow everything he gives me, and Lukas releases my wrists. I'm left swaying on my knees between them, my mouth smeared with lipstick, lube, and cum. Lukas drops down to one knee behind me, kissing my shoulder. He brushes my hair aside, whispering in my ear. "Cancel your plans, babe. You're ours for the rest of the night."

44

POPPY

Three minutes later, I lead the way out of the bathroom. Colton and I traded our tops back. The beaded fringe sways against my tummy as I walk. My eye makeup is deliciously smudged, and there was no saving my smeared lipstick. Smiling at my boys in the mirror, I wiped it off.

I may look like Thoroughly Debauched Barbie now, but I keep my head high as I march back into the bar. I grab my bingo card and walk right over to where Olivia and Violet are chatting up two surfer-looking guys. I slap the card down on the bar top table. "And that's a double bingo. Pay up, Olivia."

Violet lets out a laugh. "Oh, as if. Perfect Poppy would never play a game that required performing lewd acts in public."

I narrow my eyes at her. "Perfect though I may be, I *did* play your silly little game. And I won. I'd like to claim my prize now."

Our conversation has caught the attention of the other girls in our group. They crowd in behind Violet and Olivia. "Wait, what happened?" asks Giselle.

"Did Poppy win?" asks Maggie.

"OMG! Poppy, seriously?" Chutney squeals.

Olivia holds up her hand for quiet. "Poppy *says* she won," she calls out to the group. "But she has yet to prove it. The Court of Dishonor is now in session. Judge Olivia is presiding."

"Oh, Judge, put me on the stand," Lukas says with a wave of his hand. Reaching around me, he taps the card. "We can prove it. Look—we just did this row and this diagonal."

Olivia and Violet put their heads together, reading each of the boxes he pointed out.

Violet gasps, looking up at me. "Poppy, you did *not* just give a hand job?"

Crossing my arms in this stupid beaded top, I hold her gaze. "Actually, I gave two."

"Dude, awesome," says one of the surfer bros.

"I can confirm, it was totally awesome," says Lukas with a grin. To Olivia's mortification and my delight, he bumps fists with her surfer.

"Does that win me triple bingo?" I tease.

Olivia purses her lips. "And the dick pic?" Her gaze heats as she looks behind me to my men. "I won't deny I'm curious to see what two professional hockey players are packing in those padded pants."

Colton steps in before I can commit violence, placing a hand on my arm. "We'll only show the pic to Tina," he declares. "And only if she agrees. No need to scar her for life unnecessarily."

All the girls turn to her. Arms crossed, Tina just shrugs. "Eh, you've seen one, you've seen 'em all. Nothing can shock me at this point."

The girls all giggle as she steps around the table to come stand by Colton. He takes out his phone and makes a show of covertly flashing her the picture. She purses her lips, nodding like an art critic. "Mhmm. Okay. Yep." She looks to Olivia and Violet. "Well, ladies, those are two healthy-looking dicks. Poppy, well done," she adds, giving my shoulder a fond pat.

I turn back to my sister and her friend. "Well? This means Perfect Poppy wins the game, right?"

I can tell it kills her to say it, but Olivia smiles. "Yeah, Poppy, you win. You're our most dishonorable Maid of Honor. Congratulations."

"And the prize?" I say with a raised brow.

Reaching into her bag, she pulls out a small red-banded stack of hundred-dollar bills. "As promised." She holds it up, waving it dramatically in the air. "Our sweet, precious Poppy just won double bingo!"

The bachelorette party girls all cheer, congratulating me. I don't take my eyes from Olivia as I pluck the cash from her hand. Then I turn to Violet. "You can find your way back to the beach house, right?"

She huffs, crossing her arms. "Seriously? This is *my* party, Poppy. You have to stay and help me host it."

I step back from the table. "You know, I think I've done all the hosting I'm gonna do tonight. You don't need me, Violet. You never have. In fact, I imagine you'll have more fun without me. So here." I slip one of the hundred-dollar bills out of the stack and set it on the table. "This should cover the Ubers. Have a good night."

Turning on my heel, I hand the rest of the cash to Colton and take Lukas's hand. Colton peels away to pay their tab as Lukas guides me over to the door. "Where to next? Wanna see if we can find a limbo contest? Maybe a challenging game of charades?"

I look up at him, adrenaline still humming through my veins. "You know what I want."

He laughs, brushing my hair back. "Yeah, but it's fun to hear you say it."

Colton joins us, and I take his hand too. "Orgasms," I say. "I want lots and lots of orgasms."

Lukas presses a kiss to my forehead. "It will be our absolute fucking pleasure."

FIFTEEN minutes later, I'm standing with Lukas in the front room of a little bed and breakfast, while Colton checks us in.

"Babe, look," Lukas says, pointing at a sign. "This place actually comes with breakfast. They do scones. God, I love a good scone."

I smile, glancing around this chintzy parlor. A dozen floral patterns clash spectacularly—from the wallpaper to the sofa to the cream lace curtains. All the dark wood furniture looks antique, the china cabinets stuffed with teetering piles of teacups. A silver tray on the table boasts a large, beaded milk glass vase, overflowing with a spray of fall flowers.

Lukas takes a step away from me, inspecting the knickknacks on the shelf. "Aw, babe, look," he says again. "Little lighthouse salt and pepper shakers."

I feel like my heart grows two sizes as he holds them out to me, a happy smile on his face. I did that. I put that smile there. This isn't his teasing smile, or his competitive smile, or even the fake one he wears when he's talking to the press. No, this is just . . . Lukas. This is a man I could love. This is a man I could build a life with. Why does he always hide himself away?

Crossing the carpet over to him, I wrap my hands around his neck and pull him down to me, kissing him. He's surprised for a moment, the lighthouse salt and pepper shakers still in his hand, but he recovers with a hungry groan, wrapping his arms around me.

"You two," Colton calls. "Let's go."

Lukas and I break apart, smiling. His eyes are bright as he takes me in.

"*Now*," Colton barks.

I hurry to follow him out the door, Lukas hot on my heels. We have to weave around the side of the sprawling old Victorian house. Not two blocks away, St. George's Street is still bustling with Saturday night life. I hear the jazzy notes of someone busking with a saxophone. Somewhere close by, a horse and carriage clip-clops over the cobblestones.

The guys duck under a trellis of vines as we follow a stone foot path to a private set of stairs that lead up to a third-story room. Colton works the key into the door, swinging it open to admit me first.

I step in and click on a lamp, looking around at the pristine white walls and lace curtains. A walnut-stained four-poster bed takes up most of the room, decorated with a white quilt and frilly pillows. There's an antique-looking washstand in the corner complete with a round marble top, and a chest of drawers with aged gold hardware. Peeking into the bathroom, I spy a large lion-foot soaking tub. A thriving pothos plant hangs from a ceiling hook by the window, trailing bright green vines down to the floor.

"This was all they had available," Colton says from the door.

I turn around, taking in the way he stands there, keys in hand. Is he nervous? Is he regretting taking this step? Why is he always so difficult to read? "Please tell me what you're thinking," I blurt.

He raises a dark brow. Slowly, he sets the keys down on top of the dresser. "I'm thinking I want you naked on that bed," he replies, his voice low. "And I want to sit in that chair, with my dick in my hand,

and watch as Lukas devours your cunt." He points to the upholstered chair next to the dresser.

Lukas stops his inspection of the minibar, glancing between us. "Well, fuck me, Coley. You're really leaning all the way into this sharing thing, eh?"

"I do nothing by halves," he replies, his gaze still hot and heavy on me. "Neither Lukas nor I have ever shared a partner before."

My eyes go wide. "What? Never?"

"Never," he replies.

"Not even close," Lukas adds. "I mean, I think once my roommate and I both had girls in the room at the same time, but he was in his bed, and I was in mine and—why am I talking about this?" He fades into silence, a sheepish look on his face while Colton and I level glares at him.

"I have absolutely no idea," I say.

Colton steps away from the door, sitting down on the chair. "If the bathroom proved anything to me, it's that I have an unexplored voyeur kink. I want to watch . . . if you'll both let me."

I raise a brow. "But you'll join in eventually?"

He holds out his hand.

Stepping forward, I place my hand in his. He reels me in and pulls me down onto his knee. One hand goes to my nape as the other takes my hand and places it over his hardening cock. I bite my bottom lip, fighting the urge to melt into him.

"Feel what you do to me? Can you feel how hard you make me?"

I nod, smoothing my hand down his shaft. "Yes."

"I don't even have to touch you. The thought of you alone does this to me, Poppy. Call me a masochist, but I crave the feeling of wanting you almost as much as I've come to crave this miserable fucking ache of not having you. Now, I want to sit in this chair and watch him fuck you until the desperate, burning need to claim you makes me get up, shove him aside, and bury myself in you. I won't stop until my cum is dripping down your legs. Understand?"

I nod again, the heat of lust burning in my chest.

"Perfect," he croons. "Now, be our good girl and go lie on the bed. Lukas is going to pleasure that sweet little pussy until you scream."

*P*oppy slips off my lap in her wobbly heels, the fringed beads of her top softly clicking as she walks over to the bed and sits down on the edge. Lukas comes over and places a hand on my shoulder. "You're sure?"

I nod. "This is what I want."

"If you're sure," he says, giving my shoulder a squeeze. He follows Poppy over to the bed, dropping down to one knee on the carpet in front of her. All her attention is on him as he reaches out and smooths his hands up her calves, brushing his fingers over the thin gold laces of her strappy heels. He leans down, kissing the tops of her knees as he works the laces loose.

I only know the Novy that chugs beers and slams guys into the boards. The Novy who would spit out his own teeth and keep skating to deliver a hard hit. The Novy who jokes and chirps and wears the name "asshole" like a badge of honor.

This Novy is a revelation. He's gentle with her. Fuck, he's tender. Loving, even. He doesn't say anything personal about himself, but if you really look, you can read it all in his body language. Right now, he's shouting it from head to toe. He's in love with her. Religiously. Hopelessly.

Join the fucking club.

Poppy reaches out, flipping his hat off his head to the floor. Her fingers sift through his hair as he unwraps the gold laces from her leg, slipping the shoe off and tossing it aside. Taking her leg by the ankle, he holds it up, peppering kisses up her calf to her knee, showering her with affection like only a queen deserves.

Hunger and need coil in my gut. The third beast is jealousy. I let myself sink into that feeling, loving the burning ache that accompanies it. I'm jealous of Lukas, there's no denying it. I'm jealous of his easy way with her, how he makes her laugh and distracts her with jokes. I'm jealous of the way she watches him, on and off the ice. She likes to watch him when she knows he can't see her.

I've seen it all. The voyeur. I've known almost from the start that my path to her wasn't clear. I was kidding myself pretending it was. They'd be the last to admit it, but they've been circling each other for weeks, always one good argument away from fucking in a hallway. She wants me, but she wants him too.

I have to see it. I have to understand what they have together.

He gets her other shoe off, tossing it aside. Leaning down, she kisses him, unable to wait a second longer for more. God, she's insatiable. In her business role, she's always so buttoned up and professional. But that tension and stress have to go somewhere. She has to have a release valve. For me, it's always been hockey. For Poppy, it's sex.

But I get the feeling her partners haven't always been generous. Her need for praise and reassurance is troubling, as if she's always half-doubting whether I'm enjoying myself. She dances on the edge of subspace with wild abandon. When she's worshipped, she can get so overwhelmed that she dissociates. She leaves her body and becomes a raw nerve of pleasure, begging and desperate and willing to do anything for release.

I love the sound of her begging, but I want her to know the roles can be reversed too. I want my queen to take her pleasure as much as she wants. I want her to stay present in her body, claim control, and demand her satisfaction. That's my long game. For now, we're playing the short game. Our girl wants orgasms, and she's going to get them.

She breaks her kiss with Lukas, pulling at his shirt. "Take this off," she pants. "God, I need to touch you. Need to feel your skin."

I drop my hand to my dick as I watch them undress each other. Eager to join them, I undress down to my boxer briefs, my dick hard and heavy, aching in my lap. I fight a groan as Lukas gets her little beaded top off. From his knees, he's in the perfect position to lean forward and suck her sweet tit into his mouth.

Tipping her head back, that tumble of blonde hair touches the quilt as she moans out her pleasure. "God, it feels so good," she whimpers. "Lukas, please. Baby, come on."

He lets her go, claiming her mouth instead. Then he pulls her up standing. Out of her heels, she barely reaches the middle of his chest. They look beautiful together, strong and confident. They vibrate with passion, like two magnets desperate to connect.

Lukas drops his jeans and boxers to the floor as Poppy shimmies out of her little gold sequined miniskirt. They chase with lips and hands, bared to each other as he pushes her down onto the bed. My dick leaks precum. It drips onto my leg as I watch him hoist her up the bed, making room for himself between her spread thighs.

"Oh my god," she cries, arms over her head as she arches back, freeing herself from the tangle of her hair.

Lukas is all power, those colorful tattoos swirling up his arms and over his rounded shoulders. He drops his face between her legs and takes his first taste of her cunt. She squeals, her hands dropping down to his head as she spreads wider, relaxing her hips. "Yes—baby, please. Don't stop."

I don't touch myself. Not yet. I just sit in this roiling ache, letting it build in my gut and bloom like a weed up into my chest. I want it to fester. I want it to fucking burn. It will feel all the sweeter when the balm of her touches wash it all away.

"Are you a needy girl?" Lukas teases, giving her cunt a little slap that has her jolting. "Are you a good little whore who likes to get fucked by two men?"

"Yes," she cries, squirming under his mouth. "Yes—*god*, I fucking love it. Colton is watching us, and I'm dying. I want you both. Want him watching you fuck me."

This has me sitting up in the chair, dick twitching.

"He can look, but he can't touch," Lukas taunts. "This pussy is all fucking mine." He licks her again, groaning into her cunt as she writhes. "This body," he goes on, smoothing his hands up her naked sides. "These perfect fucking tits." He cups her with both hands, pinching her nipples tight until she moans.

"Imagine if I had another pair of hands to help me fuck you," he goes on. Shit, this asshole likes to talk. I'm embarrassed to admit how well it's working for me. I don't know if I've ever been this hard in my life. "Imagine if Cole got off his lazy ass and helped me pleasure this greedy fucking cunt."

I glare at him. He doesn't even bother looking over at me, but I can see his smirk from here.

She whines, moving her hips under him as she chases her release. "Lukas, please. Baby, please—"

"God, you're so wet." He groans. "Come for me. Gonna make you soak yourself before you get a taste of my dick. *Come*." He shoves his fingers up inside her, working her clit with his mouth until she shatters. It starts in her toes. They point as her orgasm shoots up her leg, making it shake. When it hits her center, she detonates, her flat little tummy going taut as she curls forward on a cry.

He teases her through it, not taking his mouth off her clit until she's weak and trembling and begging him to stop. He crawls over top of her, roughly cupping her face. "You're mine. *Say* it."

"Yours," she echoes dreamily. "God, baby, you fuck me so good."

I'm losing control of my patience. I need to touch her. I need her saying those words to *me*. Need to feel her beneath me, trembling as she takes my cock one greedy little inch at a time.

"Get up," Lukas growls. "Hands and knees. I'm not done with you."

She rolls herself over. From this new angle on the bed, she's looking right at me. Fuck me, her pretty blue eyes are alight with lust. She looks drunk with it, high on sex like some woodland nymph who sees visions of her god only through physical communion. She holds my gaze as Lukas gets in position behind her. Then they're both looking at me, and I'm frozen to this goddamn chair. They keep their eyes on me, their expressions heating with desperation as he slides into her tight cunt.

"Oh, my fucking god," he groans, his eyes shutting.

"What's wrong?" she pants, glancing over her shoulder.

He shakes his head, not moving. All the muscles across his chest and down his arms are tight. "I've never taken a woman bare before," he admits. "I'm just—Poppy, you feel so fucking good. This wet silk, this raw fucking heat. Baby—I'm sorry, I'm not gonna last."

"Then don't," she urges, pushing back against him. "Lukas,

please, fuck me. I've missed you inside me. I need your cum. I want it. Please—*ah!*" She cries out, her back arching as he slams in to the hilt, burying his dick inside my girl with no rubber in his way.

I know exactly what she feels like. I dream of it. I know how perfectly she squeezes a dick, how she trembles. I have to have her. I have to get my taste. My balls ache, heavy and warm between my thighs as I tug my briefs down. I pull out my dick, wrapping my fist around it. I smear my precum around my head, groaning with need as Lukas starts to move inside her.

Poppy grips to the comforter, shoulders down, meeting him thrust for thrust. Lukas holds onto her hips as he pounds into her, riding her closer toward the edge of another orgasm. I rise from the chair, and her gaze sweeps down my body, landing on my hand stroking my dick. She smiles, lost to her lust. "Is that for me?"

"It's all for you," I reply, speaking my presence into the room. We all know I never left, but speaking makes me take up new space.

Lukas has all his attention on her as his rhythm starts to stutter. Fuck, he's gonna come inside her. Leaping into action, I cross over to the bed and grab her under the arms, pulling her right out from under him. "No—fuck," he shouts, glaring at me like he's going to tear off my fucking head.

I crow with power and Poppy cries out. Her arms go around my neck as I hoist her up my body, my hands wrapping under her thighs. I press her against the post of the bed, finding her center with the tip of my dick. Holding her gaze, I sink in.

"Oh god, oh god," she cries, her pussy pulsing around me as I press in deeper. She fits me like a fucking glove. The squeeze is so tight as she fights to relax around my girth.

This is heaven. She clings to me, giving me her body, claiming my lips in a kiss as she begins to move on her own, desperate to take all of my dick. Holding her in my arms, I move her off the bed post and over to the dresser. I set her down on top of the white lace doily and begin to piston my hips into her, taking her all the way to the hilt.

Her nails grip my shoulders as she shifts her hips forward, her heels digging into my ass. "Don't you dare fucking stop," she pants.

We rattle the dresser against the wall as I barrel toward the edge of my own release. I have to fill her. I need my girl full up of me, dripping with my cum. Only then can Lukas have her back. He can come anywhere he wants—her mouth, her cunt, her tight little ass. But he'll come after me.

"God, help me," she cries out, her rhythm hitching.

Reaching up, I wrap a hand around her throat, applying careful pressure. She gasps, her eyes flashing with desperation as I slam my hips against hers. "Come on this dick, Poppy. Lukas can have you when I'm finished. Our good girl is gonna take all our cum. You want it?"

"I want it," she whimpers, arching her neck to offer more for me to squeeze. God, she's fucking cosmic.

"You want me dripping out of you when Lukas slides back in? You want to be our filthy, cum-filled whore?"

"I'm yours," she chants. "Yours—*god*—fucking fill me."

"Such a dirty fucking mouth when you're getting fucked," I tease, slapping her tit. She squeals, rocking her hips harder into me. "Where's this mouth when you're selling season tickets to our games, huh?"

I swear to god she growls like a little hellcat, her eyes burning through to my goddamn soul. She grabs my jaw, her grip firm, nails biting. "I'm not waiting another second. Come inside me or I'll—*ahh*—"

She lets go at the same time I do. I slam into her with three more hard thrusts as the heat of my release rockets through me. I burn up, letting go in a stream of muttered promises and curses. My body curls around hers, aching with peace to feel the way she trembles and clings to me. With a groan, I haul her up in my arms, keeping my dick buried in her as I walk her the three steps over to the bed.

Lukas is standing now, watching with his dick in his hand. I lay Poppy out on the bed, pulling out of her. She's boneless as she sinks onto the mattress, her blonde hair fanning out around her head like a halo. I take in her every curve, the peak of her rosy pink nipples, the faint lines of a swimsuit tan that leave her little breasts creamy white. I let my gaze travel down her toned stomach to her bare pussy lips.

She pants, breathless, eyes closed.

"Open your legs," I say.

Biting her bottom lip, she stifles a little moan. Her legs drop open, exposing her used pussy to us. She's wet and glistening with her own release. I lean over the bed, parting her pussy lips with my fingers. "Squeeze your cunt. Show Lukas what you did, my perfect good girl."

She whines again, lost in her orgasm haze, thrilled by my praise as she squeezes those tight inner muscles. My cum leaks out of her, white and runny, dripping down onto the bed.

"Holy fuck," Lukas mutters.

Inside, I roar with delight. She's mine. She's claimed.

Lukas steps in, his gaze intense as he looks from Poppy to me. "Can I taste it?"

46
LUKAS

*P*oppy and Cole look at me with wide eyes. I just shrug, still fisting my dick. "What? This is a night of firsts, right? I mean, I'll try anything once. Including eating out my girl while her pussy is full of cum."

"Oh god." She sinks back onto the bed.

I slide my fist up and down my dick. "It sounds fucking dirty when I say it out loud, right? God, it's turning me on more than I already am," I admit with a soft laugh. "Which feels fucking impossible."

"It's fine with me," Colton says, smoothing his hand down her thigh.

I look to him. "Seriously?"

He nods. "Anything between the three of us is allowed."

Shit. I don't know if I'm quite ready to waltz through *that* door. But I look to Poppy. Slowly, she nods too. "I'm yours. So long as you're worshipping only me, my body is your temple to use as you wish. Just . . . don't hurt me," she adds tentatively. "And please don't say mean things."

Colton crawls up the bed, stretching out beside her, cupping her face as he tenderly kisses her. "My love, never. I will *never* say mean things."

Watching Cole fuck Poppy was a thrill I didn't expect. He moves so well with her. He knows exactly how to spin her up. Is he that good with all the ladies, or is this just . . . *us*? I swear, there's some kind of magic in the air in here.

He's used her and filled her and now I just have to know. As they kiss, I sink down onto the edge of the bed, spreading her thighs apart. She whines against his mouth as I kiss up her inner thigh. Fuck me, her scent has changed. It's mingled with his now. It's warmer and headier than before. Some kind of hindbrain effect kicks in, and suddenly I feel like the shark in *Finding Nemo*. Need takes over me. I have to get a taste.

Taking two fingers, I sink them up inside her, smoothing them along the front wall of her pussy. I press my thumb down on her clit, heart racing as I watch more of Cole's cum leak out around my fingers. They keep kissing, but I feel the way Poppy shifts her hips under me, making room for me. Her free hand drops down to my head, her fingers weaving into my hair. She wants me where I am. She wants me to taste them together.

I tease her for a few more seconds with just my fingers before I add my mouth. Sucking on her clit, I get the first taste of them. I groan, swallowing them down. It's tangy and sweet. It tastes like raw hedonism. It tastes like the first crash of a wave hitting your body, like the blinding lights of a karaoke stage, like hearing the first few chords of your favorite song on the radio.

I lean into her, feeling my need to come growing tighter in my gut. A soft tingling creeps up my spine as I move my fingers and replace them with my tongue. Poppy cries out, fisting my hair tight as I suck all my friend's cum from her stretched little pussy.

Desperate for more, I crawl up her body and slide my dick back inside her. Taking her bare is euphoric. I sink in deep, right to the hilt as she moans, her arm going around my shoulders. Colton is on his side, still pressing kisses to her lips as I rut on top of her, fucking her hard and fast. There's no gentleness left in me tonight.

"Oh god—don't stop," she begs. "Lukas, please—"

Colton cups her face, keeping her eyes on him. "You want his cum?"

She nods. "I do."

"Is he making you feel good?"

"Yes—so good—"

"Do you feel like a queen?"

"I do," she whines.

"Do you feel cherished, Poppy? Fucking adored?"

"I feel so full. I wanna feel you both. *God*—I just want you both. I want you touching me. I want you *in* me."

I groan, dropping down to suck her tit into my mouth.

"You'll have us both," he promises her. "Next time we fuck you, I'm taking your sweet little ass. Lukas will fill your cunt, and you'll ride two cocks at the same time until you fucking shatter."

"Oh my god," she cries, her pussy squeezing me tight.

"You want that?" I tease, biting her breast. "You want us to fill both your tight holes?"

"I'm gonna come," she cries. "Lukas—"

"Take his cum," Colton growls. Reaching a hand down between us, he works her clit as I pound into her tight cunt. His fingers set her off and she bursts in a flurry of weak cries and trembling limbs, clinging to me, trying to pull me in deeper.

Groaning with exhausted relief, I release inside her. I shut my eyes tight, my body folding over hers as I hold her to me, letting myself savor this moment of coming inside a woman for the first time. *This* woman. My Poppy.

I don't even realize that I'm saying her name, chanting it into her hair. I don't want to crush her, so I pull out, dropping down to the bed on her other side. The three of us lie there, naked and panting. After a moment, Poppy starts to giggle.

"What?" I say, brushing my hand down her arm.

When a laugh leads to a snort, she covers her mouth, the sound shaking her shoulders.

Cole pushes up on his elbow, staring down at her intensely. "What is it?"

She just shakes her head, those pretty eyes wide. Slowly, she lowers her hands. "I mean, are y'all freaking kidding me? Is this what I've been missing all these years?"

Colton's brown furrows. "What?"

"Before us, she hadn't had sex in, like, three years," I explain.

"No," she cries. Slipping down between us, she all but stumbles off the bed. We both sit up, watching as she keeps laughing, her shoulders shaking. Her blonde hair is a beautiful mess, trailing down her shoulders.

"Poppy, you gotta fill us in, babe," I say. "Laughing after sex is kind of a major turnoff. You're gonna give Cole a complex thinking he did something wrong."

She turns around, smiling from ear to ear. She stands there without a scrap of clothing on. God, she looks beautiful. She's glowing, like someone lit a candle under her skin. "You don't get it," she says. "I've never felt so wanted before, so . . . *alive*." Dropping her hands to her side, she rolls her shoulders back, resolve shining on her face. "This is the best sex I've ever had." She points between us, still smiling. "You two gave me the best sex I have *ever* had."

Warmth blooms in my chest at her praise.

She hurries forward, crawling back onto the bed. With one hand on me and one on Cole, she leans in, giving us each a quick kiss. "I don't work tomorrow. Come over to my place? I'll make us dinner, and we'll do this again."

It's official, I'm an addict. It's been a week, and I simply cannot get enough of these men. If I'm not busy working, baking, or running (or dodging calls from my mother), they're inside me. Sunday night was a marathon of sex unlike anything I've ever experienced in my life. They took turns fucking me in every room of my apartment, every surface. I didn't know it was even possible to orgasm that many times.

Then they were gone for two days for an away game. When they came back, I was ravenous. They barely got in the door before I had their clothes off. After that round of sex, we made a pact that our hookups would only happen in the privacy of my home. We all have important jobs to do, professional reputations to protect.

Okay, maybe it's happened a few times at work too.

Addict, remember?

Two days ago, Lukas pulled me into that little mop closet where we argued and fingered me against the door until I came. Twice. Yesterday, I was daydreaming about the naughty things Colton whispers in my ear when he appeared in my doorway as if summoned. We fucked on my desk, knocking my phone to the floor with a loud clatter. It's fine. Not like it works anyway.

Now I'm standing in line at the coffee cart, waiting to get my caffeine fix for the day, and I can feel their eyes on me. I hear them too. They're chatting, but it's a ruse. I know they're only here to watch me.

I don't turn around. Not yet. That would ruin the game. Oh god, I can feel them undressing me with their eyes. Colton's heavy gaze feels like a weighted rope, an anchor sinking deep. Lukas's attention sizzles over my skin, lighting a fire in my belly. How am I supposed to do this? How do I function as a professional person with them looking at me? God help me, how do I stop wanting them every minute of the day?

I bite my lip, fighting the urge to squirm. We need a room. *Now*. Just make it any room with a door and a lock. I'll be able to breathe again if I can just have a taste.

Next to me, Claribel raises a dark brow. "Boss? You okay?"

"What? Oh—yeah, I'm fine. Fit as a fiddle."

She eyes me suspiciously. "What the heck are you thinking about right now?"

Three-way sex.

"Nothing."

She grins. "You're blushing."

"Yeah, well it's hot in here," I say, fanning myself.

"It's an ice rink, boss."

I lower my hand. "Drop this now, and I'll buy your coffee."

She chuckles, turning her attention back to her phone.

We get our coffees and biscotti. I pay, of course. We turn to leave, and I have no choice but to look at them. They're standing four people back in line. Fresh off a practice, they're both showered. Lukas's longer hair is still wet at the nape and over his ears. Enlivened by the exercise, they look strong and relaxed and so freaking beautiful.

"Coming, boss?"

I glance to Claribel, flashing her a quick smile. "Mhmm. Yep, I'm ready."

We walk past them and Colton nods. Lukas utters a simple, "Good morning, Poppy."

Oh my god, why the heck was that so hot? It felt like some kind of forbidden moment in one of my Regency romance novels where the dashing gentleman dares to acknowledge his lady in the ballroom. I think I *do* need a fan because my body is burning from the inside out.

Claribel leads the way over to the main practice rink. It's become our little habit to take our coffee break in here and strategize before each home game. For being understaffed, her team is crushing it. She doesn't really need my input, but it's still nice to chat. Claribel is funny when she wants to be, and she's been a good listener as I've unloaded a little of my family drama.

The fallout from the bachelorette party hasn't been as intense as I expected. Thanks to the NDAs we all signed, no videos of me doing shots off a half-naked Lukas have been leaked online. The NDAs weren't actually my idea this time. Turns out Maggie and Giselle both clerk for the Supreme Court. The social media gag order was their idea.

No, the main fallout has been restricted to my family.

I think I've always made excuses for Violet's behavior because she was never quite as toxic as our mother. Violet isn't an image-obsessed narcissist, she's just insecure. And that insecurity leads to feelings of jealousy. That jealousy has to go somewhere, so she becomes petty and vindictive. Case in point, she spent the first half of this week threatening to uninvite me to the wedding for "abandoning her in a bad part of town." As if St. Augustine is some dystopian slum. It's a quaint little downtown with ice cream shops and tarot card stands.

Her threat was music to my ears. Frankly, I'd love nothing more than an excuse not to go to this wedding. But if I'm not there to look sad and pathetic, holding her bouquet while she steals all my dreams, then she doesn't win.

Realizing her error, she instantly changed her tune, reminding me of the duties of a maid of honor, and asking me a dozen questions about shoes and makeup and hairstyles. She also overnighted a bouquet of flowers and some chocolates from one of my favorite DC chocolatiers as a "thank you" for hosting the bachelorette party.

If she thinks I can't see through her scheming, she's delusional . . . but the chocolates are delicious. I had to hide them from Lukas.

The more pressing worry is my mother. Of course Violet told her I'm dating two of my players. That apple was too ripe not to pluck and smash with a hammer. Mom has tried to call me every day, leaving long-winded voicemails asking what she did to deserve a daughter who would embarrass her like this. She's accusing me of trying to upstage my little sister. She's calling this a desperate bid for attention. She's threatening to take away my trust fund. She thinks it's a cruel prank, a cry for help, and a sign that I'm not getting enough vitamin B12 in my diet.

I haven't taken one of her calls yet, but I can't freeze her out forever. I mean, she's family, right? She's my mother. This is the woman who birthed me, and raised me, and went to all my cross country meets. She took me on my first shopping trip to Paris. She helped me pick out my wedding dress. Under all the hurt feelings, I still love her. I just wish she could understand me better. I really don't want the first time we speak again to be at Violet's wedding. That will be a surefire way to make a terrible day worse.

No, I'll call her soon. Maybe.

Oh god, I don't want to call her!

I sink down onto the bleacher seat, setting my coffee and the bag of biscotti to one side. Things are going so well with Colton and Lukas, and I don't want her to ruin it. I don't want her negative voice in my head spinning me up and scaring me into thinking this can't work. I have enough anxiety as it is. My PR brain literally never shuts off. I'm constantly running through long lists of worst-case scenarios. It doesn't matter if I'm dealing with a legitimate crisis at work, or just shopping for groceries. My stupid brain is always an inch away from, "What if they don't have shallots? I can't just substitute red onion; they have an entirely different flavor profile."

Case in point, I've been spinning myself up for a week about the fact that I know Colton and Lukas want to have anal sex with me. I won't lie, the vision in my mind is thrilling. Both of them inside me? Sharing me? Filling me? God help me, I could melt into that popsicle puddle right here next to the ice rink.

But then there's the *other* side of my mind. The dark side. The side that can't substitute red onion for shallots. That side of my mind has been secretly trolling the internet every night. Because here's the thing: I've never actually had anal sex. I tried once in college but got so freaked out that I made him stop. Then I cried, and he left. Then I threw up in my roommate's closet. It was all around just a bad night.

Since then, I've always just said it's something I don't do. It wasn't long after that I started dating Anderson anyway. He pressured me for it a lot, but I always had excuses, or I could distract him with a half-hearted blowjob. For Colton and Lukas, I'm willing to try . . . or at least I was. Go deep enough down any rabbit hole on the internet, and you'll eventually be convinced you're dying. My carefully deleted search history of "how to do anal sex" has me panicking over words like infection, fissure, and perforation. Have you ever heard of a fistula?

I don't know how to quiet the dark side of my mind that won't let me just try a new position with my boyfriends. You really think I want to add my mother's cruel opinions about our unconventional relationship into the mix? Who needs the threat of hemorrhoids when I have her?

"Did you hear a word I just said?"

I blink, confused for a moment to find I'm sitting at an ice rink watching ten-year-old hockey players do speed drills. I turn to Claribel in confusion.

She's looking up at me from a row down, coffee and phone in hand. "Okay, seriously. What is going on inside that head?"

I consider her for a moment. Claribel is a vault. I can ask this without feeling judged or crazy or worry that it'll spread through the rest of the team and haunt me until I die. Taking a deep breath, I let it out with a quick, "Have you ever had anal sex?"

Her mouth parts slightly. Then she grins. "Poppy St. James, are you propositioning me at work?"

"What—no," I cry.

"You're my superior. This is technically harassment—"

"Oh god, stop! Forget I asked. Seriously, just toss me out on the ice, and let the Zamboni run me over."

I get up to leave and she pulls on my arm. "Hey, come on. Sit. I had to tease you a little. I did, and now I'm done."

I sit back down, snatching up my coffee.

"You asked me a question," she goes on.

"No, I didn't."

"And my answer is yes. I've had anal sex. Why do you ask?"

"No reason." I burn my lips on this hot coffee, but I don't care. "So, home game. Tomorrow. You're ready with our schedule of events—"

"Poppy, if you think I'm gonna talk to you about hockey right now, you're dreaming. Ask me about anal sex. You're considering it? You tried it but don't like it? Or you want to be the one penetrating, and you'd like recommendations for pegs and straps?"

My eyes go wide as I stare at her. "We live very different lives."

She snorts. "Thank god for that. Your life is entirely too pink for me."

I glance down at my rose-pink Michael Kors wrap dress and my matching Gianni Bini ankle strap heels. "I guess I just wanted to talk to someone about it," I hedge. "You know, instead of searching on the internet..."

She nods. "Oh yeah, research anything too long and you'll be convinced you're dying."

"Exactly," I say, already feeling a little lighter.

She checks her phone. "Alright, I can give you twenty minutes before I'm due in the locker room. Ask me anything."

An hour later, Claribel and I finally leave the practice rink. She takes the rest of my biscotti, and I take her list of recommendations for toys, lubes, and best positions for optimal comfort. I may be an anxious, overthinking mess, but you can't deny that I'm well-organized. And I am *always* prepared.

48
COLTON

My microwave beeps, and I take out my steamer bag of green beans. When I'm home and cooking for myself, I eat, like, two of these bags a day. They serve one family of three, or one hockey player. Tonight, I'm eating them with two grilled chicken breasts and a loaded double-baked potato. I dump the green beans into a mixing bowl I have prepped with some salt and pepper and a chunk of butter. I'm swirling them with a fork when someone knocks on my door.

It can't be Poppy. We had dinner plans she had to cancel when she was called in to deal with a PR crisis. A drunk rookie drove his car into a goddamn sand dune. I guess he thought he could drive *over* the dune to get to the beach. The trouble is that the dunes are all protected here in Florida. You face a major fine for damaging one. This is serious. We're talking police presence, threats of jail time, and Poppy contacting lawyers.

Fucking rookies. Not only am I losing the chance to see my girl before I leave for another two days, but now I have to eat by myself.

Whoever it is knocks again with a heavy fist.

"I'm coming," I shout.

Why do I already know who this is just based on the annoying sound of his knock?

"What?" I say at Lukas, swinging the door open.

It's been a week since the bachelorette party, and things are going really well. Sharing a woman with this asshole has proved to be a lot easier than I thought it would be. Granted, we're in the middle of a messy set of home and away games that has us traveling or on the ice every other day, so there hasn't been a lot of time to do any deep relationship-building.

But the sex is going great. They were both over here last night.

We took turns fucking her on my couch before we both came on her chest. Then we watched TV and ate popcorn with her snuggled between us. I got to hold her and pet her hair while she fell asleep on me, her legs stretched out across Nov. It was pretty fucking perfect.

My eyes widen as I take in the two large suitcases at his feet. "Nov, what—"

"This is all your fault," he snaps, shoving past me to wheel the first bag inside.

I step back. "What the hell happened?"

"*You* told Poppy I needed an interior decorator," he replies, dragging in his other bag. "Now Janice is redoing all my floors because apparently, we want to achieve 'floorplan flow.' Whatever the fuck that means."

I grin. "It just means your floorplan was all chopped up with different floorings."

He narrows his eyes at me. "What?"

"Like, you had tile in the kitchen, wood in the living room, and carpet down the hall. It was going to be my first recommendation too."

"Well, that's just fucking perfect." He steps past me into my little apartment kitchen. Walking right over to my cabinets, he takes out a second plate. "I have to be out of my house while she demos the kitchen and all the floors, so I'm staying here."

"You're redoing the kitchen?"

"Yeah. She didn't like the outdated layout."

Honestly, I didn't either. Something more modern and open would fit the space great. He should upgrade to a double oven and an industrial fridge too. I wonder if he's considering bookshelf built-ins for that sunny second-floor bedroom . . .

As I watch, he uses my own damn fork to stab one of my garlic lemon pepper chicken breasts, plopping it onto his plate. Then the asshole dares to take half of my perfectly dressed potato. A lesser man would knife him for it. "You know, I had actually planned to eat all that myself," I say, crossing my arms.

"Yeah, and *I* planned to live in my own damn house. We've all got problems." He picks up the little mixing bowl of green beans and frowns. "This isn't nearly enough for us to share."

With a sigh, I toss my kitchen towel onto the counter. "There's another bag in the fridge."

"Well, if you think I'm making them, you're dead wrong." Stealing the whole bowl of green beans for himself, he takes all his pilfered food and wanders past me into the living room. "Hey, you wanna keep watching *Sons of Anarchy*?"

Did I just say this was going well?

49
LUKAS

"**P**oppy, where are we going?" I ask for a third time.

She's in the driver's seat, smiling as she bops her head to the music. "Honey, what part of 'it's a surprise' do you not understand?"

"Yeah, come on," Cole teases from the front seat. "Live a little."

"Do *you* know where we're going?" I challenge.

"Nope."

She laughs, glancing over her shoulder to switch lanes. "I promise you're both gonna love it."

She picked us up from the apartment thirty minutes ago, looking like a dream in a yellow sundress and black cat-eye sunglasses. We only just got back in town from our away game this afternoon. We barely had time to set our stuff down before she was knocking on the door.

Now I'm wedged in the backseat of her little sports car. We flipped a coin and Cole won, so he gets to hold her hand like a greedy asshole. God, he's so needy for affection. Any moment spent not touching Poppy makes him irritable. It's obnoxious.

Okay, fine. Any moment I'm not touching Poppy makes me irritable too. Resigned, I reach out my hand and set it on her shoulder, my thumb brushing down the insanely soft fabric of her little white cardigan. "What fabric is this?" I say, enthralled by how soft it is.

"Cashmere," she replies, flashing me a smile in the rearview mirror.

Fuck, I want more of this. I want this on pillows, blankets. I want to wrap her in this. I lean through the seats. "Hey Cole, tell Janice—"

"Already did," he says, holding up his phone. I can see on the screen an open text thread he has going with my interior decorator.

She's been hassling me all week, asking me endless questions about fabrics and wood stains and if I'm comfortable with "fashion over function." I was feeling so overwhelmed, I shoved the phone in Cole's face, demanding that he talk to her before I set the house on fire. He's been dealing with her ever since. I don't care what goes in the house, I just want it done.

And now I want a cashmere blanket to wrap Poppy in.

She drives us another twenty minutes south on the A1A until we're back in St. Augustine. But she doesn't head downtown. She drives us over to a marina, parking in a lot by a little fish camp restaurant.

"Are we going to dinner?" I say, ready to pull up the restaurant on my phone and check reviews. I'm a religious Yelper.

"We can," she says, slipping out of the car. "If you're both still hungry after."

"After what?" I say, unfolding my massive body from this tiny backseat. It was sweet of her to drive, but in future, I think I'm gonna have to insist we take my truck or Cole's SUV.

Cole steps around the car, taking her hand. "Babe, you didn't."

She smiles up at him, looking radiant as the setting sun shines in the reflection of her glasses. "Of course I did."

"It was for two people."

She shrugs. "I changed the reservation to three."

Smiling, he cups her face and kisses her, his free hand snaking around to grab her ass, making her giggle and swat at his hand.

I roll my eyes. "And while this is charming to watch. Clearly, you both know something I don't. One of you better fill me in before I walk off the edge of the pier and get eaten by a manatee."

They break apart, Poppy laughing. "Manatees are herbivores."

"Yeah, they eat mostly seagrass," Cole adds.

Oh, that's another thing about them that drives me fucking crazy. They love watching animal documentaries. Do you know how many hours of bug shows I've watched this week? Okay, it was, like, one . . . but one is a lot. We could've been having sex instead.

Poppy tips up on her toes, kissing Colton's cheek again, holding his hand in both of hers. With the row of sailboats behind them, they look like a damn Nautica ad. Unable to help myself, I slip my phone from my pocket and snap a picture of them.

"Lukas, honey, will you get the cooler from the trunk while I get us checked in?" Poppy calls.

I open the trunk to find a striped soft-sided beach cooler. I zip it open. She's packed fruit, meats, cheeses, sliced bread—everything you need for a picnic. Two bottles of wine stick out from a side compartment.

"Come on," Cole calls, waving me over. He's standing at the edge of the dock.

Slinging the picnic bag on my shoulder, I close the trunk and head over to where he's waiting. "What the hell are we doing?"

He smiles. "Remember that sunset cruise I had you bid on at the silent auction?" He gestures down the row of boats. There at the end, a big white one sits waiting for us. Poppy is standing on the dock, laughing and talking with her hands at a pair of shirtless guys in board shorts and sunnies.

I smile too, feeling a lightness growing in my chest. Of course I fucking remember. I felt like a saint standing there bidding on it for him, knowing I was shipping them off on a love boat without me. "But that was for two people."

He wraps an arm around my shoulders, leading the way down the dock. "Now, it's for three."

50
POPPY

Our sailboat races over the choppy water, a spray of sea air hitting my sunglasses as I laugh, flipping them up into my hair. The weather is perfect for a sunset cruise. Perhaps a little chilly out on the open water, but Steve and Mike, our deck crew, provided me with a big striped beach towel to drape over my legs.

Colton and Lukas sit to either side of me, laughing and talking. I haven't felt this relaxed in ages. We ate all the snacks I brought, and now we're just stretched out on the blue canvas deck cushions, enjoying this time together.

I've felt protective of what we have, like I want us safe and hidden inside a little shell. Hard-sided and resilient, it will keep the world out and just let us be . . . whatever it is that we are. No mothers with strong opinions, no sisters with biting jokes, no strangers with narrowed looks.

Out here on this open ocean, I feel completely free.

"Let's take a picture," I say, pulling out my phone. The boys lean in and Colton takes the phone to snap a few selfies. They get increasingly obnoxious, starting with kissing my cheek, and ending with Lukas licking my face. "*Ugh*—stop it," I cry, wiping my cheek as he laughs. "Can you be serious for two seconds, please?"

He snatches my phone, taking a look at the photos. "Oh yeah, this one's a keeper." He shows me the last picture—my face of alarm as he squeezes my cheek, his tongue out, mid-lick, Colton's face next to mine, laughing.

"Erase that one," I cry as Colton says, "Send it to me."

"Already sent it," says Lukas, handing me back my phone.

He behaves as we take a few more pictures, even offering to take the camera so I can get a few of just me and Colton. Then Colton takes the camera but keeps cutting Lukas out of all the shots. They fight until they nearly send my phone over the side, and I have to tuck it away for safekeeping.

We settle back against the deck cushions, and I smooth my hands down their thighs. Turning to Colton, I smile. "Are you having a good time?"

He tucks my wind-whipped hair back from my face, kissing my cheek again. "This is great, baby. I needed the fresh air."

"We both did," says Lukas, stretching out with his arm around my shoulders, ankles crossed, feet bare. "Sometimes it feels like the only place I exist is on the ice, in the gym, or on the seat of a damn plane."

Their schedules really are grueling. I see how hard it is on the families too. The players with kids miss so much—birthdays, doctor's visits, recitals. Walsh had to attend his girlfriend's first baby wellness check from a bus this week. Lukas said he video-chatted in, showing them all the live sonogram. They get the summer to recover, but during the season, these men are living and breathing hockey 24/7.

"I'm glad we could do this together," I say, snuggling in a little closer to Lukas to give him another kiss. I just can't help myself.

Colton scoots into the space I've made, tucking me in tighter between them. He snakes his hand around me, cupping my breast, and I gasp, grabbing his hand. "Col—they'll see us." I glance over my shoulder to where Steve and Mike stand at the helm, still chatting.

"So?" says Lukas, stealing another kiss, his own hand roaming as he slips it under the large, striped beach towel.

I let their petting go just a minute too long—Colton's tongue is in my mouth, and Lukas is kissing my shoulder with his fingers brushing over my panties—when Steve comes padding over in his flip-flops. "We'll be anchoring here in a minute to watch the sunset," he calls out.

The three of us break apart, Lukas dropping his hand away from me under the blanket.

"Don't stop on my account," Steve says with a chuckle. He's a young guy with a beachy Matthew McConaughey vibe. "Y'all poly?"

I blink, heart suddenly racing. Oh god, the sandy-toed, sun-kissed boat captain wants to know the parameters of our relationship. I can literally feel the walls of our protective clamshell snapping shut as Colton says, "Yeah, we are."

"It's new," Lukas adds, his hands still on me. "Just consider us a trio of sea explorers."

"These be strange tides," Steve says with a wink.

Oh my god, what is happening right now?

"I've dabbled myself," he goes on, readying to drop the anchor as the boat slows. "Love is love is love, am I right?"

"Definitely," Colton replies, his hand brushing down my arm.

"We'll stay here about thirty minutes," Steve goes on, hands on his hips as he glances around at the blue patch of water. Off in the distance, you can still see the shore. "That sun'll go down quick. Then it'll be back to the marina. You love birds have a nice time," he adds, walking away. "Mikey and I will make ourselves scarce. If this boat's a'rockin,' we won't come knockin.'"

On that note, he leaves, Colton and Lukas laughing to either side of me.

"What the heck was that?" I hiss, sitting up.

"What was what?" says Lukas.

"You just told Steve that we're in a relationship."

Lukas glances to Colton, confused. "Is that not what this is? I mean, I don't have all the words for it, but I'm pretty sure the term 'poly' applies to a 'two guys, one girl' situationship, right?"

"Neither of us is French-Canadian," Colton adds. "So, I don't think we can use 'ménage à trois' without sounding like assholes."

Lukas snorts. "Yeah, I'm not calling us that."

My heart is racing so fast as I glance between them. "Well . . . what *would* you call us?"

Lukas narrows his eyes, his smile turning to a smirk. "Uh-oh. Brace yourself, Coley. Poppy wants to have the talk. You realize it's only been, like, a week, right?" he teases at me.

Is that how time works? I've been so swept under in all this that it wouldn't surprise me in the least if you told me I'd been with these two for a decade.

Colton crosses his arms, his pretty dark eyes locked on me. "What are we allowed to say here that won't scare you off?"

"What do you mean?"

"I mean, I've been told I'm too Leo to function," he replies to another laugh from Lukas. "I'm not saying anything that might risk sending you running."

"Yeah, please don't," Lukas urges. "I mean, you're a literal angel, Pop, but I doubt you can run on water."

I roll my eyes at him, turning my attention back to Colton. These boys like to tease, and they *love* games. Fighting a smile of my own, I hold his gaze. "Truth or dare, Colton."

"Oh shit," Lukas mutters, sitting up.

Colton smirks. "Dare."

I was ready for this. "I dare you to label us. Tell me what we are."

He's quiet for a moment, considering. Then he takes my left hand, slowly turning it over, his fingers brushing featherlight over mine in the softest, most tantalizing caress. "At the moment? You're my girl-friend." He glances to Lukas and grins. "You're his girlfriend too. If anyone asks me outright, I won't lie and I won't hide. You're ours, Poppy."

My whole body is humming as I lose myself in the intensity of his attention.

"If you're asking me where this is going . . . then I'll say it's going here." He holds my hand up by the wrist, his finger stroking down my ring finger. "I won't speak for Lukas, but for me it's going right here." Leaning forward, he kisses the tip of my ring finger. Then he lets me go. His gaze is fire as he turns to Lukas. "Truth or dare, Nov?"

Lukas groans, glancing between us. "Guys, I hate this game."

"Yeah, because you know you have to be real with us," Colton challenges.

He sighs. "Fine, but I'm only going once. Truth."

Colton smiles. "If you could have a beer with any hockey great, who would it be and why?"

Lukas opens his mouth, then shuts it, like a fish. "I—wait, what?"

I turn to Colton. "Yeah, what?"

"You're my partner in this too," he says at Lukas. "I know you well enough to know that you don't like being expressive with your feel-ings verbally. And I *respect* you enough, that I would never force that on you. I'll be the Leo, loud with all his feelings. You be a Scorpio, and just keep showing us with actions, yeah?"

Slowly Lukas nods. "Okay, yeah."

"And when you're ready to talk, we'll both listen," Colton adds, his hand absently trailing down my back.

"Fine." Lukas sits back. Then he looks to me. "Truth or dare, Popsicle?"

"Truth," I say, ready for anything.

He opts for a softball question. "Tell us something we don't know about you."

Honestly, I'm grateful for the question. I smile, ready to steer this conversation away from the choppy waters of relationship labels and back toward sexy fun. "Well, funny you should ask," I say, perching up on my knees.

They both raise a brow, intrigued by my sudden change in tone.

I flash them a devilish smile. "Something neither of you know is that I've been wearing a butt plug all afternoon . . . and tonight, if it's okay, I'd like to try having anal."

51
POPPY

I t turns out it's impossible to announce to your two sex-crazed boyfriends that you're wearing a butt plug, and then expect them to sit quietly to watch a sunset. They had their hands all over me. Their lips too, whispering naughty words, spinning me up tighter than stripes on a candy cane. As the sun sank below the horizon, Lukas slipped his hand under the beach towel to massage my clit while Colton dirty-talked me to orgasm.

I'll never be able to look at Steve and Mike without blushing again.

When we got back to the marina, it was dark, and the parking lot was full. Lukas pressed me up against the side of my car, hands on my hips as he leaned over my shoulder. "You know, I've been thinking about it, Popsicle . . . and I think you're a little liar. I don't think you've been sitting on a butt plug for us all night."

Widening my stance in the gravel, I pressed my hands to the car, pushing into Lukas with my hips. "Don't believe me? Check."

With a hungry groan, he flipped up my dress, his hand slipping under the hem of my little white cotton panties. I shivered as his finger trailed between my cheeks, pausing on the jeweled head of the plug. "Oh, fuck me." He pressed his teeth to my shoulder in a desperate growl.

Colton boxed me in and smoothed his hand over my ass cheek before he felt it too. Grabbing my hair in a fist, he jerked my head back, making me gasp. "Who gets to take you here tonight?"

I smiled. "If we play right, you both can. I hope you do."

Now we're back home, and my apartment door shuts with finality. Lukas turns the lock. "Get naked and get on the goddamn bed." He marches toward me, and I hold up a hand.

"Wait—" I'm nervous, but Claribel assured me honesty is always the best policy. "I may have told a white lie before."

They look down at me, puzzled. "What?" asks Colton.

"Well, it's not so much that I *told* a lie," I clarify. "More like I lied by omission."

"Poppy, what—"

"I've never actually had anal before."

They glance at each other, then back to me. Colton speaks first. "That's okay—"

"Yeah, only, it's hard for me to try new things in the bedroom because I've never really had partners who made me feel adventurous or sexy," I admit. "And you both know how I tend to overthink things. And if you dive deep enough down any rabbit hole on the internet, you'll be convinced you're dying. So, I guess I've always just been too anxious to try it, you know what I mean? But you both said you wanted it, and I want to be adventurous for you, and I want it to be so, *so* good for you. So, I went to Claribel, and she explained what to do, and that made me feel like I won't die. But I'm still nervous, and I'm sorry, and I just had to get that all out there before we start . . . and I understand if I've ruined this, and you don't want to do it anymore . . . and now I'm done."

They just keep staring at me.

"Talking," I add. "I'm done talking."

Slowly, the boys glance at each other again. "Did you get all that?" asks Lukas.

"About half," Colton replies. "She's never tried anal, and the internet has convinced her it will kill her."

Lukas nods. "Right, well, should we just watch TV instead?"

Colton snaps his fingers. "We could make granola."

"Yesss," says Lukas. "I fucking love granola."

They turn away from me, as if they're actually about to head into my kitchen to bake. "Guys—what are you doing?"

Lukas glances over his shoulder. "Wanna come help us?"

I just shake my head, eyes wide. "No, I wanna have sex. What is happening right now?"

Smiling, Colton crosses over to me first. Cupping my face, he kisses me deep, letting our lips linger before he pulls away. "Poppy, you are more than your body. We're not here just to have sex with you. Do you understand?"

Lukas steps in at his shoulder, his smile teasing. "Don't get him wrong, the sex is fucking fantastic. More sex, I say."

"But we would never pressure you to do something you don't want to do," Colton goes on. "Your body is a gift. You tell us what's allowed, and we'll thank you for it."

I glance between them, heart in my throat. "I wanna try. Guys, I want this. I want to feel you both inside me. God, I feel like I'm buzzing with the need to be with you. I can't get enough." I take Colton's hand and press it to my chest. "Do you feel my heart racing?"

He nods, his warm hand splayed against my skin.

I look to Lukas, putting all my trust in his hands. "Will you take control again? Tell me what to do. I don't want to think anymore. I don't want to worry. Just make me feel."

Lukas steps in, pressing a kiss to my lips. "Get naked," he says again. "And get on the bed."

Taking a step back, I slip off my cardigan, dropping it to the floor. Then I unzip the side of my sundress, letting it fall off my shoulders and down in a circle of butter yellow fabric. I'm left standing in a little strapless bra and my white cotton panties. They watch me as I work open the back clasp of my bra and toss it aside. Last, I slowly drag my panties down my thighs until they drop. I'm left naked, my windswept hair caught up in a messy ponytail.

Swallowing my nerves, I let them watch me walk naked into my bedroom. They follow, Colton turning on the lamp in the corner as I stretch out on the bed.

"Coley, warm her up," Lukas commands. "We want her wet and relaxed and begging for it."

I fight a shiver as Colton strips off his shirt and walks over to the side of my bed. He's so beautiful, the scars that crisscross his chest showing the inner strength that matches his outer strength. He sinks onto the bed over me, his hands smoothing up my bare skin from hip to shoulder as he claims my mouth in a deep kiss. Dropping his hand between us, he fingers my clit, pressing in as if he means to turn me on with the push of a button.

I smile. Honey, I'm already turned on. I've been turned on for hours.

His fingers dip down, and he groans against my mouth. I know he can feel how wet I am. Kissing down my body, he keeps his fingers in me, teasing me. "I can feel the plug," he says, adding a third finger.

I was a nervous wreck as I followed all Claribel's instructions to put it in. Now that it's in, and my body has relaxed around it, I've hardly noticed it. But Colton adding a third thick finger changes the game. "Oh god," I whimper. He presses down on the toy with his fingers as he sucks my nipple into his mouth. I cry out, my hands going to his shoulders. "Oh—don't stop—"

Lukas stands at the end of the bed, slowly stripping out of his clothes. "Poppy, where's your lube?"

"Side table," I pant, already teetering on the edge of orgasm.

Colton removes his fingers, replacing them with his mouth, and I arch into him, one hand on his head as I fling the other back to grip the comforter. My orgasm comes quick, teased out by the gentle sucking of his mouth on my clit. It pulses under his tongue until I can't take it. I let out a sharp breath, pushing on his head. "Enough," I beg. "Let me breathe a sec."

He kisses his way back up my body, pausing to tease my nipples again. They feel oversensitive already, and I gently push him off again. "God, it's too much," I whine. "Baby, come here." I wrap my arms around him and claim his mouth instead. I can taste myself on his lips, which turns me on even more.

"You said you want to take us both together," he says, kissing my neck as he grinds into me with his hips. He's still wearing his pants. His belt digs into the naked skin of my hip. "Do you want to know what it feels like with the toy first? I imagine it's smaller than our cocks."

I nod. "Yes. I wanna feel it."

Colton kisses me once more before he slips off the end of the bed. Lukas is already naked, stroking his lubed dick as he steps around Colton, replacing him on the bed. "I'm gonna show you how tight it will be," he warns. "You say 'stop,' and it all stops."

I nod again, reaching for him. "I'm ready."

He settles himself over me, shifting my hip to make room between my legs. His tip prods at my entrance, and I'm already trying to sink down on him. He smiles, giving me a quick kiss. "Take it slow, baby. Keep your eyes on me so I know if it's too much."

I can't look away, lost in his caramel eyes as he pushes in against the tightness of the toy. "Oh my—"

"You okay?" he asks, holding himself still.

I squeeze his shoulders, nodding. "Yeah. I'm good."

He sinks all the way in, adjusting his hips in the cradle of my legs as he lets out a groan. "Fuck, baby, you are so tight like this. What a fucking dream." He kisses me, tongue prodding as he starts to move his hips, his cock gliding along the toy until we're both moaning.

"Luk—*ahh*—I'm gonna come," I squeal, my orgasm building inside me lightning fast. I cry out, my pussy trembling as my ass clenches down on the toy.

Lukas shouts, pulling out of me. "Fuck—" He's gasping, hovering over me in push-up position. "I'm not gonna last if you squeeze me like that, baby." He slides off the bed, leaving me lying here, spread-eagle, waiting for more.

I'm still trembling as the afterglow recedes. I blink my eyes open to see them both standing by the bed, voices low as they exchange something in their hands. "What are you doing?" I shift up on my elbows, legs still spread.

"Strategizing," Lukas replies. "Cole is going to take your ass first, and I'm gonna pull out the toy. Is that okay?"

I nod, trying to stop my nerves from settling in.

He climbs onto the bed next to me, brushing my hair back as he kisses my forehead. "We're gonna wear condoms, okay?"

I nod again.

"Good girl. Up for me. Hands and knees."

I roll over onto my tummy, getting on my hands and knees for him. He shifts down the bed to sit behind me, his hands smoothing over the globes of my ass as he lightly parts my cheeks. "Of course it's pink," he says with a soft chuckle, swatting my butt.

I gasp, rocking into the sting. I feel it like a slap to my clit too. I bite my lip, humming. "God—honey, do that again."

"Insatiable," Lukas growls, rubbing his hand in a circle before he gives me another slap, harder this time.

I clench around my little toy, dropping down to my elbows. I want him to do it again, but I'm afraid to ask.

Reading my mind, Colton says, "You want another one, don't you?"

I nod, feeling sleepy and hazy and so warm and wet. "Mhmm . . . please."

"Baby, all you have to do is ask," Lukas says, smoothing his hand over my cheek for a third time. He gives me a slap hard enough to sting, and I cry out, squeezing my little toy once more.

"Take it out," I pant. "God, Lukas, please. I want a cock. Take the toy out."

He chuckles again, smoothing both hands over my ass as he reaches for the toy, pinching it between his fingers. "Take a deep breath and relax for me, okay?"

I nod, keeping my face pressed to the crook of my elbow. I wince, trying to relax as Lukas pulls the toy free. It leaves me feeling aching and empty. His weight leaves the bed, replaced quickly with Colton. He folds himself over me, his delicious, woodsy scent like a little slice of heaven as he wraps his hands around my hips, dipping one down to finger my clit.

"I'm gonna lube you up, then slide in. You tell me when to stop. We'll take this slow, okay?"

"Okay."

He kisses my shoulder. "Good girl."

I gasp at the first wet press of his lubed fingers at my hole. "*Mmph*—keep going."

His fingers penetrate, and I'm afraid I'll bite a hole through my bottom lip. But under the strangeness and the vulnerability, it feels good. No stretching. No pain. Then he's pulling out and both hands are on my hips. "You ready?"

I nod.

"Words, Poppy," Lukas commands.

"Yes," I say on a breath.

Colton gets himself in position. "Just take the tip and see how you feel."

I brace myself for a feeling of being cut in half or cored like an apple, but it doesn't come. Instead, it's just deep, warm pressure. I groan, fighting the urge to tremble and push him out as Colton slides in a little deeper.

"Fuck me, Pop. You're so goddamn tight."

My nerves spiral as I glance over my shoulder. "Is that—"

"It's a good thing," he says, moving his hips a little to work his dick in and out, stretching me, adding more lube.

"How does it feel?" Lukas asks.

"Like pressure," I say on a breath. "So much pressure."

"Do you want us to stop?"

"No, I want more," I admit. "Colton, go deeper." His hands tighten on my hips. I try to stay relaxed as he sinks in a little more. "Oh god—okay, stop," I pant.

"Good girl," Lukas says coming around the bed. He tips my chin up, stealing a kiss. "Tell us what feels good. We can't know what you're feeling. Read your own body, baby."

I nod. "More. Col, keep going."

Colton takes his time, thrusting slowly, letting me take more and more of his cock. By the time he's all the way in, his hips pressed against my ass, I'm on the verge of another orgasm. "Please," I whimper. "Please, let me come again. I have to feel it—feel you so deep—"

Colton wraps his hand around me, teasing my clit as he rocks into me, his deep groaning telling me how much he likes what he feels. Heat and pressure fill me. It's like a stone weight sits in my gut as he thrusts, his movements slow and deliberate.

"Oh—right there," I cry, pushing up on my hands.

"Fuck," he growls, rutting a little faster. "Poppy, I'm gonna—"

"Don't come," I shout. "God—Lukas, I need you too. Wanna feel you both."

Colton groans. "Nov, get on the bed."

"But—"

"Get on the fucking bed."

Lukas gets on the bed, shifting himself under me as Colton holds me up, his cock buried deep in my ass.

"Spread your legs, baby," Colton says at me, helping me widen my stance so Lukas can slide under me.

We've never done anything like this before. It's thrilling. I'm flying and falling, so desperate for them both. "Take the condom off," I tell Lukas. "No barrier. I wanna feel you in my pussy, baby—want your cum—please, fill my pussy with cum—"

He takes it off, muttering a curse as I start to sink my weight on top of him. "Let me guide you down," he says, his fist gripping his dick as he cups me with the other hand, feeling for my entrance. "You tell us if this is too much," he commands, his eyes locked on me.

I nod, whimpering as I feel his fingers sink into my wet pussy.

"Hurry up," Colton groans.

"Patience is a fucking virtue," Lukas replies, his fingers sinking deep. I think he's scared they're gonna break me.

"Not right now," I say on a breath. "Please, baby. I'm ready. Need to feel you both. God, I'm dying for it."

He kisses my lips as he slips his fingers out of my pussy, replacing them with the tip of his cock. "Slow," he says. "Nice and slow."

I sink down on his cock, the pressure of them both filling me enough to have me ready to burst into tears.

"Oh god," Colton groans. "Fuck—Nov, I feel you."

Lukas keeps his hands on my hips as I sink him in deeper. "Keep going."

I settle on his hips, his cock buried to the hilt inside me. Then Colton adjusts, pressing in behind me. "I feel you," he says again.

"I know," Lukas replies, eyes closed. "This is a fucking mind trip. This is . . ."

"Everything," Colton mutters, kissing my shoulder, his hands cupping my breasts.

The three of us hold each other there in that moment of perfect union. Their cocks are together inside me. They feel each other as much as they feel me. Not for the first time, we feel like *us*. The three of us. This is meant to feel just like this. I'm theirs completely. I'm filled and claimed in a way I never dreamed possible.

I can't hold back the tears. I start to cry as I beg them to move, beg Lukas for his cum. I transcend my body as they make love to me, moving together in a tandem of thrusts that has me coming on a wave of cries. I collapse onto Lukas as he thrusts up into me, finally coming on a groan. I feel him warm and wet between my legs, dripping from me. Colton folds himself over me, pressing in deep as he comes too.

The first time we had sex, Lukas teased that he was going to rewrite my DNA. God help me, he did. This feels like a second transformation, a rewriting of Poppy St. James. Being here with them, the three of us together, I know deep in my soul that nothing will ever be the same . . . for any of us.

51
COLTON

*P*ractice ends, and I make my way with the rest of the team into the dressing room. The guys are all feeling rowdy today, laughing and joking. We're riding a wave of wins, and moods are high. I'm trying to share in their enthusiasm, but instead I'm all in my head. The team may be playing great, but this is shaping up to be one of my worst seasons since my groin pull. Nothing is outright injured, but something definitely feels off.

As a former heart patient, I'm deeply in tune with all my body's functions—recovery time between shifts, pulse and heart rate, muscle aches and pains. I'm fast, and I'm strong, and I'm making all my passes and taking the hits. My stats would show that I'm still a solid player, worthy of my spot on this team.

But the sensation lingers, growing stronger. I feel out of sync on the ice, like I'm constantly catching up to the action instead of driving it . . . and I fucking hate this feeling. Is this all just my mental game affecting my physical performance?

Hockey is such a demanding sport. So much pressure, so many games, so much travel. It can grind you down if you let it, body and soul. Not for the first time, I wish I still had my dad. He was someone in my corner who helped me catch my breath. His pep talks helped me align the physical with the mental.

If you can't accept losing, you can't win.
You can only control your own performance.
Keep your mind in the game, Colton.

He was always good for a little sports psychology.

It's easy to focus on hockey when hockey is all you have. But my life is changing. I have more now. I *want* more. My loyalties feel divided. Do I chase the happiness I feel on the ice, the power, the purpose? Or do I embrace the happiness I have off it, the love and comfort, the unexpected feeling of family I've found?

What if I want it all? Do I have to choose? Is one person allowed to be that happy?

I get my first skate off as Lukas drops down on the bench next to me. Phone to his ear, voice gruff, he argues with someone on the other line. "Listen, I don't know what the fuck you're talking about. Why are you even at my house?" After a minute, he groans. "Oh, really?" He stiffens, his tone changing. "Will you hold for a second, please?" He covers the phone with his hand, dropping it to his lap. One brow is raised as he turns and glares at me. "I'm putting in a home theater system?"

Shit, was that today? "Yeah, in the back room. Why? What's wrong?"

"What's wrong?" His brows shoot even higher. "What's wrong, asshat, is that someone is trying to deliver twenty-thousand dollars' worth of furniture to my house, but no one is there to sign for it." He holds up his phone. "Now this nice gentleman is saying they'll be charging a second delivery fee for the furniture I didn't know I fucking ordered."

I just shrug, tossing my other skate aside. "I'll cover the fee."

"Oh, you'll cover all of it, you cheap fuck," he snaps at me, raising the phone back to his ear. "That's officially *your* home theater room now."

He exchanges a few more clipped words with the guy, arranging a new delivery time, and I can't help but smile. My master plan is coming together nicely.

We're saved from any more argument when Poppy comes marching into the dressing room in her heels and red dress, toting a big colorful box in her arms. Some of the guys hoot and call out.

"Hey, we're indecent!"

"Boys only, Poppy!"

She doesn't care. Her expression is wild, and her curls look extra voluminous as she slams the box down on one of the gear boxes. "Stop sending popsicles up to my office!"

The guys all laugh as, next to me, Lukas gets a smug look on his face. "Gotta call you back," he mutters, hanging up.

Jake walks forward, still in his skates. "What happened, Poppy?"

She huffs, hands on her hips, impatiently tapping her foot. Fuck, why is this turning me on? "This is the *third* box of popsicles delivered to my office this week, and I *know* it's one of you," she shrieks, waving her hand at the box.

I shake my head, glaring at Lukas.

The smug asshole just crosses his arms, leaning back against his stall. "Why would someone send you popsicles?" he asks, innocent as a fucking schoolboy.

She slow turns to glare at him too. "I don't know," she replies, her tone level. "But if the culprit doesn't stop, I may have to take drastic measures of my own."

Half the guys "ooh" and laugh as the others look around, pretending they don't know it's him. Ryan Langley walks up to the box, flipping back the lid. "Are these for anyone?"

She huffs, waving her hand again. "Take them, Ryan. Free of charge."

"Score." Ryan snatches out a blue one.

The other guys crowd around, passing out the popsicles as Poppy marches back out of the room.

"Seriously?" I say at Lukas the moment she's gone.

He shrugs, accepting a banana-flavored popsicle from Jake. "What?"

I hold my stare.

He just chuckles. "Look, I may have turned over a few new leaves recently, but I'm still the same guy. If I can't prank, I can't live. And this one is harmless," he adds, unbuckling his pads.

I turn away to hear him add, "Just wait until she realizes I've glued her shoes to the floor . . . God, I hope she spanks me."

53
LUKAS

How do you know if you're falling in love? I've never been in love before. Frankly, I've never even been in like. I'm twenty-six years old, and all the human interactions I've had for the last fourteen years have been transactional. Coaches? They give me instruction. Teammates? I play with them. Opponents? I play against them. You hit me, I hit you, and the Zamboni smooths over the ice. Sexual partners? Well that one's obvious. We're both just there to get off. It's a good time. But in an hour, maybe if you're lucky by the morning, the transaction ends, and we both move on.

Nothing about Cole has ever felt transactional. Poppy's right, he's just a nice guy. He's the guy who invites the awkward rookies out to the movies. He picks up tabs left and right. He'll order in food for the whole team just because he wanted to.

Now that I'm living with him, he does things for me all the time with no expectation of return. He'll collect my dishes and wash them as we talk about our day. He folds my laundry and sets it in a clean pile on the end of my bed. He gets green apples at the store because he knows I prefer them to red.

But the Novy who keeps receipts wants a balanced ledger. You get me green apples? Boom, I get you bananas for your morning oatmeal. You fold my laundry? I vacuum the floor. In the first week, he was running me ragged with this tit for tat, until he finally grabbed me by the shoulders and said right in my face, "Will you just let me take care of you?"

Talk about an awkward moment. We held eye contact for a second too long, and then he was wandering off saying something about going for a run.

It's official, I think I'm in like with Colton Morrow.

And don't even get me started on Poppy.

I think she's falling in love with me. God knows what I did to deserve it. I'm still the same asshole who pranks too often and jokes too much. At least twice a day, she says, "Do you take *anything* seriously?"

But at least twice a day she's kissing me. She's always touching me. She likes to hold hands. She likes when our fingers are laced, my thumb on top. I'll stand in her kitchen, pouring her a glass of wine, and her hand will slip under my shirt to stroke her fingertips up my spine. She *has* to touch me. She has to soothe and caress.

What she's not saying in words yet, she's saying in action. She loves me.

And I'm fucking terrified.

I don't know what I'm doing. I don't know how not to mess this up. I could never deserve her. I don't deserve either of them. As friends, as lovers, it just doesn't make sense. Lukas Novikov is the kid from the street who the other kids can't bring home for dinner. He's the guy on the team who sleeps on the assistant coach's couch because no family would billet him.

Unwanted.

Unloved.

You harden yourself to the reality that everything is a transaction, and it makes it all easier. It numbs the pain. I put in my hours, I make the hits, I score the goals.

But Cole and Poppy don't work that way. They won't let *me* work that way.

And I'm scared.

I don't know if I can change. I don't know if I *want* to change.

Taking a deep breath, I knock on Poppy's door. Cole wasn't in the apartment, so I have to assume he's over here. I wait for one minute. Two. Huffing, I knock on the door again, harder this time.

"I said, I'm coming, asshole," Cole barks from within. He unlocks the door and jerks it open to reveal himself in a pair of basketball shorts, his hard dick barely concealed beneath the fabric.

"Am I interrupting something?" I say with a smirk.

"We're getting you a fucking key," he growls, pulling me in by the shirt.

I follow him down the hall into the kitchen just as Poppy comes walking out of her bedroom wearing nothing but his T-shirt. It hangs off her like a dress, hitting her at mid-thigh. Fuck, she looks good in our clothes. We practically share a wardrobe, so I can just flip the switch in my head that changes "his" to "ours."

Her hair is done up in a messy braid over one shoulder, and her cheeks are pink. Her lips look thoroughly kissed. She looks goddamn delectable. My sweet Popsicle, tart like a cherry, sugary like a peach.

"Whatcha guys doing in here?" I tease, slinging my bags of sushi up onto the counter.

"Nothing," Poppy says as Cole says, "Fucking." He stands by the stove with his arms crossed over his bare chest, glaring at me.

I grin. "Well, I scored a shit ton of discount sushi at the store." I dig into the bags, pulling the containers out and setting them on the counter. "California rolls, shrimp tempura, spicy crab and avocado, an eel roll for Pops. There are some dumplings in here too we can pan fry up quick. And a seaweed salad."

They glance at each other before looking to me.

I pretend I don't see it, determined to make them break first. "Yeah, I figured we could get it all set up in front of the couch and watch one of your stupid nature documentaries," I go on. "Maybe, if we're feeling crazy, we can even walk down the beach a few blocks and get some ice cream—"

"Lukas," Poppy whines, one hand on her doorframe.

My grin spreads as I glance between them. The tension in this room is about to boil over. "Or, you know, we can shove this all in the fridge, and fuck till we're dead?"

"Thank you," she cries, hurrying back into her room.

I laugh out loud as Cole steps in, grabbing half the sushi. Together, we throw it all in the fridge. Then I'm shoving him into the cabinets for good measure, racing him to the bedroom. I stop in the doorway, eyes wide, to see Poppy already naked in the middle of her bed, fumbling with the latch on a little leather handcuff.

"I can't get the other one back on without help," she says.

My dick feels fucking spring-loaded for how fast it hardens. "Oh, what the fuck were you two doing in here?" I turn to glare at Cole. "Is this why it took you so long to answer the goddamn door?"

"Yes," he replies, shoving past me. He moves to the bed. Leaning over, he kisses Poppy, taking her free hand. He presses kisses up her arm as he wraps the other cuff around her wrist, buckling it.

Poppy is smiling, her knees demurely folded over to one side, while her goddamn wrists are chained to her headboard. She looks over at me. "Do you wanna play?"

Well, fuck me dead.

I strip my shirt off and drop my shorts in two seconds flat, fisting my hard cock as I walk over to the bed. "Baby, I will play with you every day for the rest of forever."

She's shining. She's incandescent. That's a word, right? Fuck, I don't even care. The word feels right.

"Taste her," Cole commands, sinking down on the bed beside her.

I raise a brow at him.

"I want to watch," he replies to my unasked question. We're developing a good shorthand, as good as anything we have on the ice. We like the tag team. He fucks her to the edge of orgasm and then leaves her for me to finish. Then we switch.

And she's such a fucking champ. She's literally up for anything. Our girl is a powerhouse of sexual charisma.

I drop down onto my knees on the edge of her bed with a groan of relief. It's not like I haven't been inside her in the last twelve hours. But I swear to god, there is no enough. I crawl up the bed, bypassing her sweet cunt to get a taste of her mouth first. The feel of her soft skin, the scent of her, rosemary and mint and floral body soap—it fills my senses. *Home*. This is my home. This is where I want to live, right here in the cradle of her thighs.

I cup her breasts, sinking my tongue in her mouth. She hums her joy against my lips. Her wrists rattle the chains as she gives the cuffs a tug. "More," she pants.

She's right, I need all parts of me touching her. Dropping a hand between us, I angle my dick for her entrance and test her with my tip. Fuck, she's so wet and ready. I don't know what Coley did to her, and I don't care. He made my girl ready to take this dick.

We both groan with relief as I sink in, burying myself between her legs.

"How does she feel?" asks Cole. He's still sitting on the edge of the bed, his presence calm and controlling as he strokes his fingers down her arm, gazing down at her lovingly.

"Like heaven," I pant, thrusting into her tight pussy. "Baby, you feel so fucking good."

She whimpers, her legs around me as her arms strain against the cuffs. "Love your big cock in me. Fuck, you have such a pretty cock. Want your cock in my ass. Please, baby—"

I grip her jaw hard with one hand as I keep thrusting. "I fucking love your little porn star mouth." I press a biting kiss to her lips that has her gasping. "The second we get our dicks in you, our sweet little glass of peach iced tea turns into a straight shot of whiskey."

She hums with delight, her heels digging into my thighs as she rocks with me. "You boys make me feel so free—want your cocks in me every night—want your cum on my skin—"

"Fuck," I shout, trying to hold back my release.

"She said she wants a dick in her ass," Cole directs. "Are you gonna do it, or am I? Don't leave her waiting."

Okay, fuck me, director Cole is such a fucking turn on too.

"Get the lube," I pant, pulling out of her cunt.

Colton reaches over to where the lube is already waiting on the bedside table. He hands it to me. Popping the top, I dribble some onto my fingers and rub them over her tight little hole. She whimpers, straining against her cuffs.

"Spread your legs wider and relax," I say, soothing her with my free hand on her thigh. I brush up and down with slow strokes, changing my energy from feral to focused. She's so goddamn responsive. You slap her tits a little, and she'll claw your back like a wildcat. Rock into her slow, and she hums out a rolling wave of orgasms. Pet her, like I am now, and she turns to jelly.

"Please, baby," she coos, her eyes bright as she looks at me.

I sink a finger past her tight ring of muscle, and she bites that bottom lip, arching her back. I play with my fingers, adding lube, and stretching her out. Cole hands me a condom, but I shake my head. "I wanna come in her tight little ass. I want her to feel my heat inside her. My cum is gonna drip out of her hole tonight."

She sinks back against the pillow. "Oh god."

I grab her legs and roll her hips back, prodding my dick at her entrance. "Nice and slow. Take me, baby."

She relaxes, letting me sink my tip in.

"Such a good fucking girl," I croon. Oh, that's the other thing. Our girl will do almost anything for praise. Cole and I can all but get her off just with our words. "Look at you taking my thick cock in your sweet little ass."

She whimpers, pulling on her cuffs. "Please—"

I sink in deeper, thrusting in and out of her tight heat nice and slow. "Give me a toy," I say at Cole. "We're gonna fill all her holes tonight."

He wastes no time snagging a pink vibrating dildo from her drawer. Lubing it up for me, he slides it into her pussy as I lean back.

"Fuuuck me," I groan. This tightness is beyond anything. I press back in to the hilt, holding myself there as Cole turns the little toy on.

"Oh—*god*—" she shrieks, jerking hard on the chains as she comes. The vibrations from the toy buzz along my cock, straight up into my goddamn chest. Her ass clenches around me, and I thrust, riding her orgasm as she bears down.

"Cole, get in her fucking mouth," I grunt. "Fill her. Our fucking queen."

He's already on the move. Using her headboard as leverage, he balances overtop her in a crouch. "Take this fucking cock," he commands. "That's my good girl. Look at you. Choke on it, baby. That's it . . ."

She arches up, mouth open, desperate for him. The sound of her gagging sends me spiraling. I drop my hand between us and grip the base of the vibrating toy. I move it with my thrusts, finding a rhythm that has her trembling, overwhelmed by her orgasm. I feel like some kind of mythical, two-dicked monster, pleasuring my girl in both her tight holes.

"I'm coming," I shout. She cries out, clenching around me as the heat of my release fills her.

"Swallow what I give you," Cole pants. "Such a good girl. Swallow it."

She's gasping, her whole body wrung out. She squirms around me, and I know the toy is too much. I slowly pull it out, dropping it glistening and vibrating onto the bed. Cole stands, his feet planted to either side of her head on the firm mattress. She looks down at me dreamily between his legs. Some of Cole's cum is smeared on her chin. Her arms are still chained to the headboard.

Slowly, I pull out of her. Keeping her legs in the air, I look down, watching as I drip from her tight little hole. "Perfect," I mutter, my heartbeat quickly returning to its resting rate. I trail my gaze back up her body to her beautiful blue eyes. All my walls are down. No more transactions, no receipts. I give her my words because I want to. I give them to her because she deserves them. "Poppy, you're perfect."

54
POPPY

Isn't it ironic that the moment your life starts to feel just a little too perfect, chaos inevitably descends. I woke up naked in bed, nestled between my two beautiful boyfriends . . . feeling sick as a dog. I stumbled to the bathroom and barely got the door shut before I was puking into the sink.

Note to self: Don't eat day-old sushi. Lukas brought, like, eight boxes of it home from the store because it was on sale. After a marathon of amazing sex, we ate it on the couch watching *Night on Earth*. It tasted good at the time, but now I'm fisting a bottle of Pepto as I argue with Julie in VIP services.

This day has officially gone to hell in a freaking hand basket. It's a home game tonight, Rays versus the Kraken, and I'm expected at the arena in two hours. But a glitch in our computer system means we've oversold our behind-the-scenes "Meet the Rays" tickets by more than double. All the notifications have already gone out, and neither Todd in ticketing nor Julie seem to know what the heck we do about it.

Oh, and Bryson, the rookie who drove his car into a sand dune, was just handed two hundred hours of community service and a felony misdemeanor charge. The news already broke on all the networks. My contact over at the police department was apparently trying to warn me all morning, but my office phone *still* doesn't work!

Did I mention my "check engine" light came on this morning?

See what I mean? Chaos.

Oh, and in a total bitch move, Violet just took away my "plus one" invite to the wedding. She says it's because they had some last-minute asks for more invites. And since I'll be *so* busy with my maid of honor duties, I don't need a date there feeling bored and alone.

I swear, she is so freaking transparent. This really is my absolute limit. She just wants me there looking sad and pathetic. How can I do that if I'm dancing in the arms of my gorgeous NHL boyfriends? I get limiting me to one guest, but now she's saying I can't bring *either* of them? Who's going to hold me back from cunt-punching Olivia when she says my dress looks unflattering on my body type?

Pushing back from my desk, cell phone to my ear, I keep arguing with Julie. "No—I'm telling you we'll just have to postpone them to a later game." I stuff my feet into my heels. "Because we don't have permission to move that many people behind the scenes, Julie. I have approval for fifty people, not two hundred and fifty. Security will have a field day if we—*ahh*—"

A hissing sound in the ceiling is all the warning I get before the emergency sprinklers activate. I throw my hands over my head as icy cold water sprays down, drenching me, my laptop, all my paperwork.

"What the hell is happening?" I scream.

Moving fast, I sweep as much as I can off the desk and into my bag. I stumble out of my office into the hallway. Several other people have come out too, looking scared, confused, and very wet.

"Is there a fire?" asks Brandi.

"No alarms are going off," says Greg, looking around.

"Does anyone smell smoke?"

"Greg, honey, call 911," I say. "We'll let the fire department figure out what the heck is happening. In the meantime, let's all pretend it's a fire. Not like we can work in hurricane conditions anyway."

"I swear, this place is cursed," Brandi mutters, following me toward the stairs.

We reach the first floor, our shoes squeaking, clothes dripping wet, and who should be waltzing toward me but Lukas, double fisting coffees? His smile falls as he takes us all in. "I swear, I did *not* do this," are the first words out of his mouth.

"Okay, fire department says they've got no alerts for an actual fire," says Greg, holding the phone away from his ear. "Looks like it's just a faulty sprinkler. They say they're en route."

"Thanks, Greg. Hey, why don't you all take an early day?" I say to the rest of the group. "I'll stay here and deal with this."

"Are you sure?" asks Brandi. "There's still so much to do."

"Well, take a break at minimum," I reply. "Everyone, the coffee cart is open. No charge. And I'll get one of the equipment guys to bring a stack of towels to the atrium."

With muttered words of thanks, all my wet staffers wander away, leaving me with Lukas. "I came to invite you to lunch, but—Babe, what the hell happened?"

I take the coffee from him. "The sprinklers on the fourth floor are faulty. They just went off while I was in the middle of a phone call and—" I groan, glancing at my phone. I've missed two calls and four texts from a confused Julie and Todd. "Here—" I hand Lukas back the coffee. "I have to return this call. We oversold our VIP tickets and—"

"Well, wait. Just hold on a sec and talk to me."

"I don't have a sec, hon."

He shifts his weight, blocking me from ducking around him. "Jesus, you're not a surgeon being called in for life-saving brain surgery, Pop. It's just some tickets—"

I scoff. "Oh really? I'll have you know this is about two *hundred* tickets. It's a security nightmare and—"

"Poppy!"

I blink, stepping back. "Lukas, what? Come on, I have to go and deal with this—"

"No, you have to stop for two seconds and deal with *me*."

"But this is my job—"

"Yeah, it's just a fucking job!" he shouts, finally breaking through my crazy fog of stress, adrenaline, and hyper productivity. "Poppy, this is a job that you're grossly overqualified for and, frankly, it's a job that has been treating you like complete dog shit."

"That's not true—"

"It *is* true! Poppy, you're the director of public relations for a major international sports team. You coordinate multi-million-dollar brand deals before breakfast. You organize press junkets for Olympic team trials. You set up fundraisers that raise seven figures for pediatric cancer research. I mean, Jesus, you *literally* keep our asses out of jail. And Mark Talbot has you overworked and under-freaking-paid."

"My salary is actually competitive for the market."

"Pop, he shoved you in a shitty fucking office with no windows, no phone, and no fucking internet."

"The internet got fixed," I say in a small voice.

He just glares down at me. I can see it's all he can do not to crush the piping hot coffees in his hands. "You are dripping on the goddamn floor right now. You are *mine*, and you deserve better. No one gets to treat you this way and fucking breathe."

His words sink like an arrow through my chest. "These are just growing pains. The building is new—"

"Stop making excuses," he shouts. "Stop making excuses for Mark. Stop making excuses for your mother, for your shitty fucking sister—"

"This isn't about them," I cry.

"Yes, it is! Because it's all about *you*!" He steps in closer, eyes blazing. "Poppy, this is about you constantly lying down and allowing shitty things to happen to you, and I'm telling you it's enough. Stop accepting less when you *know* you deserve more."

Tears trail down my face, and he holds out the coffee cup again. "Will you please fucking take this so I can touch you?"

I take the coffee and his warm hand instantly cups my face.

"Look at me."

I glance up, eyes watery.

His caramel eyes lock on me. His touch is like a lifeline. "You deserve the world," he says. "Poppy, you deserve *everything*. I won't sit back and watch you struggle. Fight for yourself, or I'm gonna fight for you, and I fight dirty. Do you understand?"

I swallow, giving him a nod.

He steps in closer, pressing a kiss to my forehead.

I smile, my free hand brushing down the colorful tattoos of his arm. "I like possessive Lukas. He makes me feel so safe . . . so loved."

He stiffens and leans away, glaring down at me. "You think my violence is a virtue? You really think you understand what I'm capable of?"

Holding his darkening gaze, my heart drops. His walls are lowering. He was just a little too vulnerable and it scared him, so now he's going to deflect. My hand circles his wrist, ready to hold him to me. "I know you, Lukas—"

He twists away from my grip, stepping back, his shoulders tense. "No you don't. Not really. How could you?"

"Lukas—"

"I mean, look at you," he says, gesturing to me up and down. "You're so polished and poised. So fucking perfect."

It's my turn to stiffen and lean away. Last night he said those exact words like a prayer. *Poppy, you're perfect.* Now he's lobbing them at me like a curse. "Lukas, please don't—"

"Don't what? Warn you away from me? Someone has to, before I ruin this. I was raised on the fucking streets, Poppy. I've been on my own since I was twelve years old, fighting for the right to fucking exist in a world that didn't see me, didn't fucking care."

"I care—"

"Sure, you took me in and gave me a warm bed to sleep in at night. But I am the same fucking monster who was always too aggressive, too angry, and too out of control to do anything but put on a pair of skates and slam grown men into the boards. I am good at what I do, and what I do is *hurt* people. I hit them over and over, until they can't get back up. *That's* what I am."

"You're not," I say, grabbing his shirt. "Lukas, honey, it's just a game. You play it so well, but your ability to be a good defenseman on the ice is just one piece of you. You are so beautiful and complicated—"

"Stop."

"No," I cry. "I won't stop complimenting you and telling you that you matter. I won't stop coming home to you at night. Lukas, I will always come home to you because I *love* you."

He goes still, his expression a riot of emotions—anger, fear, frustration, longing. So much deep, aching longing. I want to hold him to my chest, his ear against my heart, so he can hear and feel how it beats for him. "What did you just say?"

"I said, I love you. Lukas, I am so in love with you—"

He drops his hand away as if I burned him. "Take it back."

I hold my position, unwavering. "No."

"Poppy, take it back."

I shrug. "I can't. It's done."

He steps in, grabbing me by the back of the neck. "You still don't get it. I wanna march up those stairs and *kill* Mark for upsetting you. I'm violent, Poppy. My thoughts are so fucking dark. I wanna set your sister's hair on fire. I wanna hit her shitty friends with my fucking car. *No one* hurts you and gets away with it. That's who you wanna love? That's who you want in your bed? That's a man of *fucking* virtue?"

I hold his gaze. "You won't do it."

He growls, lowering his face to mine. "You think I fucking won't?"

"You won't," I repeat, my voice trembling. "You won't because I'm asking you not to. You are mine, Lukas, and I love you, and if you do *anything* to jeopardize my ability to be with you, I will hound you to the ends of the earth. Do you understand me?"

He drops his hand away. "This is a mistake. I should've let you go."

"Too late."

"No. I'll ruin this. I'll—Poppy, let me go."

"Never." I extend my hand, silently asking him to take the coffee. His hand wraps around it, our fingers brushing. "You have a game to prep for, and I have to go hunt down Mark. We'll finish this later."

Turning away, I leave him standing there. I've said what I need to say. Now he needs space to retreat and panic and wrestle with his own feelings. I know he loves me too. He shows me every day. The words will come eventually.

I step into the stairwell, letting the door close behind me. My whole body feels like it's humming. I'm angry, I'm tired, I'm so freaking stressed. But I'm alive, and I'm fighting, and he's right, I am *done* accepting less than what I deserve.

And what I deserve is Lukas. With all his flaws, all his feelings of unworthiness. I deserve Colton too. I deserve the beautiful life the three of us can build together. I *want* that life. I want the house, and the high-powered jobs, and the adorable babies. I want my men rubbing sunscreen on my shoulders as our kids play at the beach. I want sunset sailing and cozy nights on the couch. I want a family who loves me, friends who make me laugh, and a job that respects me.

And, god help me, I'm going to get it.

55
POPPY

$\mathcal{S}$quaring my shoulders, I march into Mark Talbot's executive suite. I haven't stopped to look in a mirror, so I have no idea what I look like, but I know I'm still dripping water on the floor. "Is Mark in? I need to speak to him."

His personal assistant takes me in with wide eyes. "Did you fall in the fountain?"

"Is that seriously the most plausible explanation you could come up with for why the director of public relations is standing at your desk dripping wet?" I retort. "You think I tripped and fell ass-over-tits into a fountain?"

Slowly, she glances over her shoulder.

"It's not raining outside," I shout, making her jump. "Is Mark available, yes or no?"

"Poppy?" Mark pushes his own door open. "I thought I heard you out here—whoa." He chuckles. "You got caught in the little sprinkler mishap too? I just got off the phone with—"

"Mark, we need to talk," I say over him. "In private, if you please."

He steps back, gesturing for me to enter. "Hold my calls, Nadine."

I sweep past him, my toes squelching in my shoes as I cross from tile to a nice carpet. The far wall of his office is windows looking out over the Jacksonville skyline. I take in his cluttered walls of sports memorabilia—a pair of boxing gloves signed by Muhammad Ali, signed baseballs, pictures of Mark with quarterbacks and golf pros.

I spin around, hands on my hips, and take in the man himself. Mark is tall, late forties, with a head of salt and pepper hair. He looks like he's a better fit for a Silicon Valley tech presentation than a Hockey Hall of Fame dinner.

"Well, it looks like your office is bone dry," I say.

He steps around to sit behind his desk. "Yeah. You know, these little hiccups are to be expected when—"

"Let me stop you right there," I say, holding up a hand. "If you don't mind, Mark, I'm gonna go ahead and speak, and I'd like for you to listen. And if I cry, please know it's not because I'm too weak or too emotional to be a working professional capable of running your PR department. It's just that crying is a stress response to the amount of *anger* currently coursing through my body."

I pause, eyes wide. Standing here, soaking wet, in the middle of Mark's swanky office, a truth hits me. Oh my god, it's so obvious. It's been floating right in front of my face for days, weeks. All the signs were there, and I completely freaking missed it? I blink back tears as I look to Mark. "Also, I may be realizing in this exact moment that I'm pregnant, and you're the first person I'm telling, and I'm *definitely* feeling pretty emotional about that too."

Mark clears his throat. "Um . . . congratu—"

"Don't you dare," I say with a shake of my head. "And I'm still speaking."

"Fine. The floor is all yours, Poppy."

I take a deep breath. "Right then. Mark Talbot, I accepted this job because you promised to roll out a golden carpet for me. 'State of the art,' you said. 'Top of the line,' you said. Virtually unlimited expenses, the power to hire in my own team, control over the direction of philanthropy efforts. Do you know what I've received so far? A tiny little cupboard of an office with no window, no phones, no internet, and a lingering smell of Funyuns."

"Okay, well I can address a few of those—"

"Still talking," I say, raising my voice. "You have lights that flicker, elevators that break, generators that stall out, and sprinklers on the fritz. The house is crumbling, Mark. Fix the freaking house! And I am at least three people short to run my department effectively. I've put in the requests to hire, and they're still languishing in HR. Because of my lack of a functioning office space, and my short-handed staff, I am dropping plates left and right and center. I am missing calls. I'm getting information late. I'm chasing my freaking tail for you, Mark. All of this leaves me feeling *completely* incompetent when we both know I am anything but. I'm tired, I'm stressed . . . and I deserve better."

He watches me, waiting.

"And I'm done," I say. "Talking, I mean. Not, like, with the job. I'm not quitting . . . yet."

Slowly, he nods again. "Right, well I get the feeling an apology at this moment would be—"

"I don't want you to *say* you're sorry, I want you to *show* you're sorry," I say over him.

He's quiet for another minute, processing. "What exactly do you want, Poppy? Be specific."

I cross my arms. "Well, for starters, I want a better office, with a proper suite, where I can actually entertain sponsors and donors and members of the press. I want to be able to have a meeting with more than four people without having to reserve the conference room."

"Done. What else?"

"I want to hire three more people—"

"Done. What else?"

I narrow my eyes at him. "I want a fifteen percent raise, effective immediately. And I want an extension on my one-year contract. I want three years minimum, with an option to renegotiate salary based on performance, to include yearly scheduled raises."

He smirks. "Done. Anything else?"

I consider for a moment. "Yes. I want the night off. There's shitstorm brewing between ticketing and VIP services, and they're trying to make it my problem. But there's a monsoon in my office, and I need to go take a pregnancy test, and I haven't sat down to watch the Rays play a game once this entire season. So, I would like to make the ticketing issue *your* problem . . . just for tonight. I'll be back at work tomorrow."

He's quiet for a moment. Slowly, he reaches into his pocket and pulls out a wad of cash.

I glare down at it. "What's that for?"

"For the concession stand," he replies. "We overcharge the hotdogs. Makes us a killing, but it's reason two-thousand four-hundred and sixteen why I'm definitely going to hell."

My frown deepens.

"Take the cash, Poppy. Go home. Dry off. Go to the game tonight, and just have fun. And please know your work is appreciated. I hear you, and I value you. Give me a chance to do better before you take one of the dozens of offers I'm sure you're already fielding for a new job."

"Fine." Stepping forward, I pluck the cash from his hand. I pretend to count it, flicking through the hundred-dollar bills. "I wanted popcorn too."

Smirking, he fishes in his wallet, pulling out a few more bills. "You drive a hard bargain."

"I know my worth," I say, taking five hundred more dollars from his hand.

"That's good, Poppy. I wish that was a lesson I'd learned at your age. Took me a bit longer, I'm sorry to say."

"And I'm sorry I yelled at you," I say, stepping back.

"Don't be," he replies with a shrug. "You'll get everything you asked for. Now, get out of here. Go have fun tonight, I mean it."

I move over to the door.

"And Poppy," he calls as I reach for the handle.

I glance over my shoulder.

"Can I say, 'congratulations' now?"

I smile, nodding. "Thanks, Mark. Fix the sprinklers."

He nods. "Will do."

THIRTY minutes later, I'm standing at the sink in a Walgreens bathroom, staring down at a pregnancy test. I was too anxious to make it all the way back to my apartment. I have to know. I mean, I feel like I already know . . . but I need to *know* know.

The signs have been everywhere if I was bothering to look. My irregular cycle should've clued me in. But, as a former DI cross country runner, I've always struggled in that department. There was a solid two years at the peak of my running when I don't think I had a single cycle. I thought it was just stress and poor diet making me miss a period this month.

Then there's all the other little signs: nausea at the bachelorette party, tender breasts too sensitive to touch, getting sick on sushi, these high/low mood swings. Each of these things separately could mean anything. But when you add them up together, they form one big, blue plus sign.

The timer on my phone goes off and I reach for the test. Slowly, I turn it over, glancing down. Of course it's positive. I'm pregnant. How far along I am, I can't be sure.

Tears in my eyes, I place a hand over my belly, a calming sense of rightness filling me. I should be freaking out, right? As a chronic overthinker, finding out you're pregnant in a Walgreens bathroom while you're still wearing a damp business suit should be cause for at least a little panic.

I glance up at my reflection, still holding the test. My makeup is smudged around my eyes, hair slicked back. "I'm in love with two men that I'm secretly dating. Now I'm having their baby, and I don't know which one of them is the father."

I wait . . .

Come on, Poppy, really? No freak out? Not even a little one?

I take a deep breath, trying again. "I have to tell my mother that I'm pregnant out of wedlock."

Okay, now I'm just grinning . . . and I'm craving peanut butter. Maybe I'll get a king-sized Reese's Cup when I pay for this test I just peed on.

And now I'm laughing, tears of happiness rimming my eyes. I rub my hand over my flat stomach. "Well, you're just a little chaos monster, aren't you?" I say at the surprising little life growing inside me. "Should you tell your daddies, or should I?"

Tucking my popcorn bucket under my arm, I grab my Diet Coke, waving my thanks to the sweet redhead with glasses working the concession stand. As I turn, I see Rachel standing over by section 107 waiting for me. She's looking double cute in tall, skinny boots and an oversized Rays jersey.

"Hey, honey," I call out, weaving through this busy crowd.

I was so glad when she said she'd come to the game with me. I feel like I have a hive of bees buzzing inside my chest. I'm pregnant, and Mark Talbot is the only one who knows. There'll be no telling my guys until after the game. Even then, part of me wants to sit on the news a little longer. There's something sacred about it. Right now, this life-altering secret is just for me and my little chaos monster . . . and Mark.

Oh god.

I brush it off, smiling as I come to stand by Rachel. "Oh, girl, you look amazing! Kinnunen is just gonna die that you're wearing his jersey tonight."

It's his first night back on the ice after his injury, and everyone's watching to see what he'll do. The Finnish hockey scouts are in town, eyeing him for a starting position on their Olympic team. News like that is the perfect thing to help overshadow Bryson and his sand dune escapades.

"This is so exciting," I go on. "You know, this is my first game I've gotten to watch as a spectator? I've been running myself ragged this season."

"Same," she replies, taking a handful of popcorn from the top of my bucket.

We chat for another minute before Caleb Sanford comes weaving through the crowd carrying a big soda and a heaping tray of nachos. The thought of those salty chips has me salivating. "Hey, Caleb," I call out to him. "Ooh, nachos! Why didn't I think of that?"

Like Rachel, he's wearing a Rays jersey. Suddenly, I'm feeling left out. I'm just in a Rays polar fleece zip-up and yoga pants with my little white Adidas tennies. How do you pick a jersey to wear if you're dating *two* of the players? I think they make those cute "house divided" jerseys. Do those come in the love triangle variety?

The three of us chat as we make our way down to our section. Leo in ticketing got us great seats one row back from the glass. I glance around, taking in the charged atmosphere. It's so strange to see it all from this angle. I'm usually up in the boxes, schmoozing all the VIP guests. From these seats, you can actually smell the ice, the buttery popcorn, the frothy beer. It's enchanting. I can't stop smiling.

We've missed warmups, so I settle in next to two bear-sized men with big beards and painted faces. Apparently, they're brothers who run a construction business. And they're season ticket holders. We exchange some laughs until the lights go out.

My heart does a backflip as the pregame music starts. This is my favorite part of the night. Jumping up and down, I grab Rachel's hand, both of us cheering. Suddenly, the lights come up, and it's like the ice has been transformed into a coral reef. I'm grinning ear to ear as the lights and music work together, creating a spectacle like we're stingrays racing through the reef.

By the time the smoke machine starts, and the lights in the eyes of the mechanical stingray start to glow, I'm hoarse from screaming. The Rays are announced, and the starting six come shooting out. Our forwards, Ryan, Henrik, and Josh, race onto the ice first. My smile widens as they call Lukas next, followed by Jake. Ilmari is the last to take the ice. He doesn't rush. He steps calmly onto the ice, and the crowd surges with excitement, thrilled to have him back in the net.

The main lights come back up, and the support team works quick to clear the ice for game start. The Rays are at our end of the rink, finishing their warmup. I can't take my eyes off Lukas as he skates past once, twice. Can he see me? Does he know I'm here?

"Hey, 42," Caleb shouts, his hands cupping his mouth. "You suck!"

I jump, eyes wide, as Jake slides to a stop, glancing over his shoulder at Caleb. Then he's barreling over toward us, and Rachel is chanting "make it stop." He slams both his gloved fists on the glass. "What the fuck, Seattle?" he shouts, glaring at Rachel.

"Compton, what are you doing?" I cry.

Are they seriously having a lover's tiff *now* in the middle of a freaking game? Oh god, I knew this would happen. What a disaster. All around us, people are flashing pictures. Is anyone recording? Please say no—

"Take it off," Jake shouts at Rachel.

"Maybe if you play really well tonight, she'll wear *your* jersey on Saturday," Caleb jeers.

Jake leans away, dropping his hands from the glass as those around us start to laugh. His eyes narrow. If looks could kill, Caleb would be dead. Frankly, I'm not convinced I wouldn't help hold him down.

"I'm sorry," Rachel calls, daring to look contrite.

"She's totally not," Caleb jabs, flinging his arm around her. "Go skate, douche canoe! Try not to embarrass her!"

Oh god. More camera flashes, more laughter. There's no way people aren't recording.

Lukas has caught on that something's wrong too. He skates up to Jake and mutters something. Following Jake's gaze up into the stands, he locks eyes with me. Heavens, how can one man look so beautiful and so angry all at the same time? Is my loving him really so hard for him to accept? Despite the chaos of how we started, we're so good together.

I brace my hand over my stomach. For the first time today, doubt creeps in. If he's this resistant to the idea of me loving him, what will he do when I tell him I'm pregnant and there's a 50/50 chance the baby is his? Will he fight for us? Will he love us as we love him? Or will he cut and run, too broken and too scared to make a home with us?

Holding my gaze, he skates away, pulling Jake back with him. I'm distracted by Caleb jostling me. He throws his arm around Rachel again, pretending to give her a big sloppy kiss on the cheek as the guys in the front row laugh and point. I follow this new chaos to where Ilmari is standing at the net, mask up, glaring at them.

"Oh, my goodness, what is happening right now?" I shout. "We don't want our boys upset before a big game!"

Caleb just laughs, dropping his hand away from Rachel. "Don't worry, Pop. It's just a little team-building exercise."

I shake my head, a million fresh questions running through my mind. The last thing I knew, Rachel was still hooking up with Jake in closets. Caleb is Jake's best friend. He has to know, right? And Rachel sits with Ilmari on the plane, but that's just about his lucky charm thing, right? A lot of these players have weird superstitions. Lukas plays with two different kinds of gloves. Colton only has one brand of undershirt he'll wear under his uniform.

I have to assume this is some kind of game. Caleb *wants* Jake upset. He wanted Mars to see Rachel in his jersey. Does he think they'll play better or something?

My last question is answered as soon as the puck is dropped. In seconds, Jake makes his first hard hit, sending his mark sprawling down to the ice to the rabid cheers of the fans.

I look to Rachel. More importantly, I look to the sea of people around us, still eagerly snapping pictures and pointing. I've been working in PR long enough to sense some serious trouble brewing.

Oh girl, what have you done?

I t's 5 a.m., and the cauldron of trouble Rachel and Caleb stirred at the game last night is officially starting to boil over. I mean, what did she expect? Her father has been one of the most famous faces in global music for four decades. She grew up under a blinding international spotlight—features in magazines, paparazzi at her school, drones flying over beaches on family vacations.

And celebrity fans are crazy, nothing like hockey fans. They'll home in on your favorite flavor of cereal if they think it will make them feel closer to you. She can't go making moon eyes at a young, hot NHL player and not expect people to notice that too.

By the second period, even the freaking media team knew something was going on. I'm officially going to kill Jimmy and Tad. Did they have to pan the camera over to us so many times? Each time the Jumbotron zoomed in on Rachel, the crowd would cheer, she'd wave, and then Jake would hit someone harder.

My phone pings on my side table with message after message. Then it starts buzzing.

"Turn it off," Colton grunts. His hand is splayed over my naked breast. He pulls me in closer as I lean away, reaching for the phone.

"I have to get this," I whisper. "Just go back to sleep."

Lukas's side of my bed is empty. I decided last night that I'd give him exactly one night to continue freaking out about the thought of our happily ever after. Tonight, I'll reel him back in. For now, I'm doing my job.

I reach for the phone, answering it before it can go to voicemail. "This is Poppy St. James."

TWO hours later, I'm buzzing with a caffeine headache as I weave my way through the Rays gym equipment. I know the books all say a little caffeine won't hurt baby, but I'm not willing to risk it.

I see Rachel over in the corner chatting and laughing with Ryan on a massage table. "Rachel," I call out. "Rach! Girl, I need to talk to you."

Rachel turns toward me with a smile. "What's up?"

I hurry the rest of the way over to her. My scoop neck Rays T-shirt slips off one shoulder as I nearly trip over a dumbbell.

Rachel keeps massaging Ryan's shoulder, oblivious to the shit-storm she's in. "What do you need?"

I look to Ryan, still trying to catch my breath. "Get lost for a minute, honey."

"But we're in the middle of—"

"Yeah, that's great," I say, tugging him off the table. "Tell your story walking. We'll let you know when we're done talking."

He wanders off, muttering under his breath. I'll apologize to him later.

Rachel looks to me. "Poppy, what—"

"Not here," I say, shooing her backward into her little office. As soon as the door shuts, I spin around, dropping my heavy bag to the floor. "My phone has been ringing off the hook all morning."

Rachel glances up to the clock on the wall, "Pop, it's barely 7:30—"

"You don't think I know that? The calls started coming in at 5 a.m. It was all I could do to make myself presentable and get in here and find you." I pull my phone from the pocket of my coral pink yoga pants. Flicking with my finger, I show her my missed call history.

She looks mortified. "Just tell me."

"They're all about you," I say. "Asking about last night."

She lets out a deep breath. "Show me."

I step over and show her the phone. The headlines just get more ridiculous:

Rachel Price in Secret Tryst with NHL Player(s)

Rachel Price's Love Triangle Explained

Fire on the Ice: Inside the Secret Love Affair of Rachel Price

Rachel Price: Too Horny for Hockey?

She's currently the trending topic on most of the celebrity gossip sites, as well as the Ferrymen fan sites, and some of the hockey gossip sites. The footage is on all the social media channels. Videos from several different angles show the moment Jake came skating up to the glass, pounding his fists and telling her to take Ilmari's jersey off.

"And these are just the short video clips that went viral," I explain. "People have questions, Rachel. They think they know what they're seeing. I'm trying to stay ahead of it for you, but I need to know if what I know is the thing I think I know."

She hands me back my phone with a confused frown. "The thing you—what?"

I toss my phone down on the counter. Hands on my hips, I glare at her. "Rachel Price, did you spurn Jake Compton and take Caleb Sanford as your lover?"

"What—*no*," she cries, "No spurning—"

I raise a brow. "Did you spurn Jake Compton and take Mars Kinnunen as your lover?"

She sighs, shaking her head. "I haven't spurned Jake, Poppy."

I do her the courtesy of faking my own surprise. "So, you *are* with Jake Compton. Why, you sneaky little minx. I didn't suspect a darn thing. How long?"

She sighs again. "Poppy . . ."

"Well, what was this then?" I cry, frustrated that she won't just let me in. "You're just teasing him? Wearing Kinnunen's jersey to get a rise out of him? And what was Caleb doing involved? I thought they were friends."

"They *are* friends, Pop. It's—god, it's complicated."

"Oh, my good gravy, is it a love triangle? Is Caleb the spurned lover? Are they trying to make you choose? Have you decided—"

Rachel grabs me by the shoulders. "Girl, pull yourself together. No one, and I mean *no one* is getting spurned here. I wouldn't even know how to spurn something." She drops her hands away from me. "Last night was an inside joke between friends, okay? We all work together, and it was a joke. That's the official story, alright? No romance, no spurning, no broken hearts."

I search her face and the realization hits: she's scared. I was trying to rile her up with my crazy line of questioning, but I know what I saw last night. And I know the look in her eyes now. She's hiding. I think she has reason to hide. This isn't just about keeping her and

Jake a secret. She's with all of them. Rachel is dating multiple players too. What we're doing may be socially unacceptable, but for her, as their treating physician, it even crosses the line into unethical.

Oh, this is a disaster. This is going to blow up in spectacular fashion. How long can I sit on this lid?

"An inside joke between friends?" I repeat.

"Between colleagues," she corrects. "We're all working on the same team, and the three of us had a fun night out in the stands, right? We ate our weight in junk food, and we got to watch our friends play."

Friends, lovers, fathers of my child. Who can keep track?

"Caleb and I played a little prank on the players where we wore their jerseys," she goes on. "Good clean fun, alright?"

Yeah, the kind of fun that gets you fingered on a yacht and pregnant.

I nod, feeling like the world's biggest freaking hypocrite. "Yeah, good clean fun."

Taking a deep breath, I turn my attention to my phone. Rachel needs to buy more time, and I'm going to buy it for her. It's what I would want in her position. It's what I *do* want. Colton, Lukas, and I aren't ready for the eyes of the world on us either. I don't want them shoved under a microscope and dissected, all the messy details of their lives picked apart as people judge us, judge our child.

Oh god, the baby . . .

My little chaos monster doesn't deserve any of this. I can feel the walls of my shell closing in, ready to protect us from the eyes of the world. This is *exactly* why you don't get involved with the players! Because in no time at all, you go from managing the story to being the freaking headline! What will our headlines say?

I close my eyes, taking a deep breath.

No.

I'm not going to make this about me. This is about Rachel and her guys and doing the best job I can to protect them. I can freak out about my own secret threesome on my own time. For now, I am Poppy St. James, and I have a crisis to manage.

58
COLTON

"**W**e need to talk." Lukas appears at the shower door like he fucking teleported there. I must not have heard him come in over the sound of my music.

"Jesus—fuck—" Dropping my hands away from my dick, I turn and hit the wall with my elbow. "*Ow—*"

"Did you see the screenshots I sent you this morning?"

I groan. The nice little vision I had of Poppy in here with me, her slick body rubbing up on me, fizzles. "Nov, I'm in the shower. Will you get the fuck out?"

"You think I care that you're stroking your dick in there? Want me to get in and finish you off?"

"How did you get in?" I growl, keeping my back turned as I wait for my dick to go down. We're in Poppy's fucking apartment, and the last I checked he didn't—

"I have a key."

I glare over my shoulder through the steam-coated glass. "How the hell did you get a key?"

"I took her key and duplicated it," he replies with a shrug. "Hey, if you think I'm gonna let you have access to her without me, you're fucking dreaming. I'm not going anywhere, Cole."

I turn fully around, not caring that my dick is still half-hard. "If you care so much about access, where were you last night—"

He waves his hand. "Not important. We've got bigger fish to fry."

"Fine. Get out so I can finish."

"Sure, and by 'finish' you mean you'll come into her loofa, right? I bet you used her body wash on your dick too. Anything to get a little hit—"

"What the fuck is your problem?"

He smirks, glancing down at my dick. "Looks like this angry foreplay is working for you there, bud. Want me to keep slinging insults, and you can just unload right here on her shower glass?"

I raise a brow, heat coiling in my gut. "You want to watch me jerk myself off onto the glass?"

"If it gets you out of there faster," he teases.

Well, I'm in no mood to be fucking teased. Poppy left me alone in bed this morning, meaning I didn't get to start my day inside her. I'm on edge, and I'm calling his bluff. I wrap my hand around my dick and give it a slow pull. Blood rushes back to it, leaving me breathless. I reach out, bracing my hand palm-flat against the steamy glass.

Novy's eyes are wide, his lips parted with the joke he's not telling.

Yeah, if he keeps teasing me, I'll shut him up with my dick in his mouth—

Fuck, that just made my balls twitch. Am I into this? Do I like him watching me like this, even without Poppy here? He's not leaving, and he's not telling any more jokes. Does he like watching me? I groan, the sound deep in my throat as I rub my soapy thumb all around my thick head. "Fuuuck."

"Don't stop," he says.

I keep stroking myself, luxuriating in the silky wetness, the heat of my hand. Don't get me wrong, I'll always prefer Poppy's hands on my dick, but there's no shame in self-pleasure either. I know what I like, and I know what makes me come hard and fast.

Lukas steps away, and I pause. "What are you—"

"I said, don't fucking stop."

I watch him walk over to the sink, taking his shirt off as he goes. He tosses it to the floor and pumps some of Poppy's lotion into his hand. Then he returns to stand in front of me. Slipping his shorts down with his other hand, they drop to his ankles, exposing his dick. He stands there naked and wraps his lotioned-up hand around his hard length, giving it a stroke.

My dick twitches at the sound of his desperate groan. I fist myself tighter, matching his rhythm as he fucks into his hand. My senses fill with the smell of Poppy's body wash as I add more, lathering myself with it.

"I'm close," he mutters, his breathing labored.

"Put your hand on the glass."

He reaches out with his free hand, pressing it palm-flat against mine, aligning our splayed fingers. Fuck, why is this so hot?

"I'm right there," I grunt.

"Me too. Don't fucking stop. Come on the glass. I wanna see it."

I groan, moving my hand faster over my dick, squeezing at the base as I roll my palm over my tip.

"Look at me, Cole."

I blink, lifting my gaze away from our hands to meet his eyes through the glass.

"Don't stop," he pants.

"I'm coming—"

"Fuck," he shouts, stepping closer to the glass as he comes too.

I lean in, the heat of release building inside me until I'm roaring out my climax. My cum shoots from my tip, hitting the glass. I keep stroking my dick, gliding with my thumb on the underside of my shaft until I spurt again.

"Oh, fuck," Lukas cries. "Col—I'm coming so fucking hard."

"I know," I say on a low hum. "Me too."

I give my dick one more long, slow pull. Then I drop my hand away, leaving my dick twitching as the warm shower washes it clean. I look at Lukas through the glass just as the asshole dares to say, "Next time, I'm catching it in my mouth."

TWENTY minutes later, we're dressed, Poppy's shower glass is clean, and we're rolling into the parking garage of the practice arena. Lukas parks his truck in his assigned spot.

Grabbing the bag of granola we've been munching on, I get out. "So, how do you wanna do this?"

"We just need to be straight with them," he replies. Pausing in his steps he grins and adds, "Well . . . you know what I mean."

I know he's joking again, but it is an interesting conundrum. I've always considered myself to be a straight man. I've only ever been attracted to women. I've only dated women. I've only fucked women. That means I'm straight . . . right?

Well, now I feel like I'm straight plus Novy.

Is that a thing?

Sharing Poppy like we do, I can't help but also be interested in sharing more with him. When the three of us are together, it's hard not to let hands and mouths wander. I'd like to know it's not a problem if occasionally my hands touch him . . . maybe they wrap around his dick . . . maybe my mouth does too . . . maybe I lick her climax off his shaft when he's done with her—

Fuck.

I have to stop, or I'll get hard again, and you can see everything in these damn workout shorts.

We all saw the little jersey-swapping game Rachel and Sanny played last night, first during the actual game, then again at the press conference. Jake was practically squirming in his chair over it. The big reveal was Sanford wearing Jake's jersey like he was a goddamn WAG.

Now the gossip is everywhere. When I got out of the shower, that's what Nov showed me on his phone. He's still in a couple group chats with some of the guys on the Pens and the Bruins, and they were asking him to confirm whether Jake and Sanny are finally out as gay.

But they don't know what Novy and I know. It's possible no one else does. Jake and Sanny are sharing our team doctor. They're together. The three of them. They're in the same goddamn position as us . . . and now they're getting dragged for it. That's what pulled Poppy out of my bed at 5 a.m. She's been over here dealing with the PR "crisis" that is three consenting adults choosing to be together.

It's a fucking mind trip, like we're getting to watch the world's craziest game of "What if" happen before our eyes:

What if Lukas and I came out as dating Poppy?

What if we came out saying we want to live together, share our girl, and grow fucking old together?

Would the League accept us? Would our teammates? Would the fans?

We get inside the practice arena and head up to the gym floor looking for Jake or Sanny. We step into the gym and Novy sticks out his arm, stopping me in my tracks.

Mars Kinnunen is standing in the middle of the floor in a fucking rage, yelling at DJ Perry. "And what gives you the right to think you get to have an opinion?"

"Jeez, Mars. I only said—"

"What Compton and Sanford do outside this gym is no business of yours or *any* other person on this team!"

Shit, looks like we're too late.

Novy grabs my arms and pulls me into the gym, going over to where Langers is watching, eyes wide. "What the fuck happened?"

"Avery started chirping about Jake and Sanford being gay," he explains, pointing over to where our head of PT stands, arms folded, smirking. I fucking hate him. "And that got Dave-O going, and then Perry joined in," Langers goes on. "I guess some of the guys got pings to their group chats about it all. The Pens, the Kings . . ."

"Fuck." Nov glances warily over to me.

Mars is still on a fucking tear. "—and I will not stand silently by as members of *my* team are derided by the likes of a no-talent fourth line forward who doesn't know his ass from his goddamn elbow!" We all lean away as he switches to Finnish. He strides forward, all six-foot-five of him. Towering over Perry, he pounds his fist into his hand as he continues to shout.

"DJ's gonna piss himself," Langers says, clearly in awe of the goalie.

"Come on." Novy pulls on my arm, dragging me out of the gym.

"You don't want to see how that ends?"

"Perry's already crying. You wanna stick around? Come on, we gotta go find Compton. This is fucking bad."

"Well, what do you want us to say?"

"I don't know. What would *you* wanna hear?" He pauses, glancing over his shoulder at me.

I shrug. "I don't know, Nov. I'm not in the hot seat."

"Yet."

I nod. It's only a matter of time, really . . . if we keep doing what we're doing. I hold his gaze. "Are we fucking crazy here?"

It's his turn to shrug. "Does it matter at this point?"

No. It really doesn't.

WE finally find Sanford lurking in the laundry room. "Hey, Sanny," Novy calls, stepping into the room first.

"Aww, what happened to Snuffy?" I tease. Some of the guys still call him that from when Doc Price thrashed that blonde bunny at the club. "I liked that nickname," I add.

Sanford just rolls his eyes. He's standing behind a large folding table, ironing jerseys for tomorrow's game. "What do you need, Nov?"

"Not a thing," Novy replies, taking a handful of the granola and popping it in his mouth. "Compton still around?"

"How should I know?"

"Uh . . . maybe because you live together," Novy says with a laugh.

"And you carpool into work all the time," I add. Novy flashes me another and I just shake my head. Yeah, we've started carpooling too.

"And you've got your weird DLP-ESP," he adds.

Sanny just chuckles, flipping over the jersey he's ironing. "That hasn't been officially diagnosed yet. We're still on the waitlist for that study at Mayo."

While Novy laughs, I snag the bag of granola from his hand. This is my favorite batch we've made so far. Poppy added a little honey water drizzle over the oat and pistachio clusters after the bake. I move around the side of the table as he mutters a curse at me.

"Give it back," he growls.

There's nothing worse than a hangry Lukas, so I seal the bag shut and toss it back to him.

Sanny just shakes his head at our antics. "I've been down here since I got in," he says, moving the iron slowly back and forth over Sully's jersey. "I don't know anything happening outside this room."

Nov and I exchange another look. There are so many ways this could be done. Ways this probably *should* be done. But we can't wait around and watch as this blows up further. We have to be ready to act, ready to protect them the way Mars seems so prepared to do. It's what we hope they'll all do for us too.

He narrows his eyes at us. "What is it?"

Novy takes another handful of granola, shoving it in his mouth, and I know that's his fucking cue to make me talk first.

"What?" Sanny says again. "Come on, guys. I got a shit ton to do, so if you're not gonna—"

"Are you with him?" I ask.

Across the table, Novy groans. "Dude, come on. You're not supposed to just ask a guy if he's gay like that. That's like, breaking the rules. Right?" He looks to Sanny too.

Sanford is annoyed. "What are you assholes talking about?"

"You haven't seen it then?" asks Nov.

"You haven't heard?" I add, one brow raised.

He groans, dragging both his hands through his hair. "Fuck, guys. Drop the suspense, before I go looking for Colonel Mustard holding a candlestick. Now, what the hell are you talking about?"

Novy sighs. "Aw, shit. It's everywhere, man. The guys are all chirping with it online."

"Chirping with what?"

"That you and Compton are together," I explain. "You know, like . . . *together*. Like a gay thing."

He glares at me. "Yeah, I get what 'together' means."

Diving in with both feet, we explain everything that's happened in the last twelve hours, first with all the footage going viral from last night, which spilled over to the team chats. Neither Sanny nor Rachel has any social media, so I'm not surprised they're in the dark.

Sanny acts totally surprised by the news that the team is chirping them too. We tell him about Asshole Avery and Mars coming to the rescue.

"He needs to learn his place, or the guys are gonna turn on him," I say about Avery. "I don't want my head of PT ribbing my teammates in front of me. That's not gonna fly."

"And hey, Sanford . . ." Novy steps around the table, going to stand at his side. "The point here is that if you ever *do* want to tell us anything, you can. You or Compton. Because this is a team. It might be a new team, but the way we see it, we'd like to stick around a while." I don't miss the way he covertly looks to me as he's speaking.

"Yeah, totally," I hear myself say. "Team means family."

Novy smiles. "We want a good atmosphere here. We don't want bullshit and drama. Jokes are one thing. We all love jokes. Chirping on a guy for being gay is another." He looks back to Sanny. "You just tell us which end is up, and we'll make sure the next guy who chirps you is the last guy."

Slowly, Sanny nods. He's always been a man of few words.

"So . . . you telling us anything right now?" Novy asks.

Come on, man. Just tell us.

"No," he says. "There's nothing. Jake and I are just friends." I can actually hear the disappointment in his tone. Hiding their relationship is fucking killing him.

I glance over at Nov, my heart twisting as I think of our sweet Poppy in the middle of a shitstorm like this. I want to protect them at all costs. I'll stay silent as long as they need . . . but hiding our relationship is killing me too.

59

POPPY

"**Y**ou wanna say that again?"

My gynecologist smiles, adjusting the vaginal wand with one hand as she points up to the tiny circle in the middle of the black and white monitor. "I said, judging by the size of the embryo, it looks like you're about six weeks pregnant."

I lie back, one arm over my head, and stare up at the popcorn ceiling panels. *Holy crap.* I'm six weeks pregnant? I've known for all of two days, and here it's been half a freaking trimester. My little chaos monster has already seen and done so much. He went sailing, played bingo, sang karaoke, ate bad sushi.

Wait—*six* weeks?

I grab my phone, and flip through my calendar, counting back the days. "Oh my . . ."

I lie back again. That was the week I was in DC. That was the week the elevator broke.

"Everything okay?" the nurse asks with a kind smile.

I snort, trying to hold in my laugh. "No, I'm fine. It's just that this baby was either conceived due to a broken condom up against the side of a hotel ice machine . . . or on the floor of a busted elevator."

"Oh." My gynecologist removes the vaginal wand. "Well, that sounds adventurous."

I nod up at the ceiling. "Yep, that's me. I'm just one big thrill-seeker." I push up on my elbows, glancing between them. "Did I mention it was with two different men? Yeah, there's literally *no* telling which of them is the culprit. I'd say it was Colton, since Lukas and I used a condom, but I was on the pill. So, it should be neither of them, right? This should be divine conception."

They both offer me patient smiles.

"Pills aren't one hundred percent effective," the doctor cautions. "Especially if you miss any or take them at irregular times—"

"Oh, trust me, I know. I've watched literally every romcom ever created. And I've read about a thousand more. I know how this works, doc."

She pushes back in her wheelie chair. "Well, it was a bit too early to see any cardiac activity this time. But everything looks like it's going very well."

I nod, sitting up.

"We'll be sending you home with the sonogram images today. And I want you to get with Shelia to book an appointment to return in another few weeks, okay?"

I nod again. "Yep."

"For now, I want you to just take it easy," she adds, patting my knee. "Rest as much as you can. Relax, and just let your body adjust to its strange new reality."

I fight another laugh. Rest? Relax?

When?

This is possibly the most stressed I've ever been. As I was lying here, I've missed eight calls and gotten eleven texts. I'm in the middle of this Rachel Price media storm, I'm trying to navigate a major pet adoption promo, and I *still* have reporters calling me about the damaged freaking sand dune.

Not to mention we have another home game tonight. I only just slipped away from the office before I have to be over to the arena to meet with the Finnish Olympic scouts. They're still in town to watch Kinnunen play again, and I'm supposed to entertain them. Have you ever tried to entertain members of the Finnish Ice Hockey Association? I mean, really, where is Lemon when you need her?

By the time I'm dressed back in my teal sheath dress and strappy black heels, the nurse practitioner knocks and steps back in the room. "Here's that sonogram printout for you." She hands me a thin strip of photo booth-style images. "Baby is the size of a lentil," she chimes.

I take the photo strip from her, staring down at the top one that has a little white arrow pointing to my occupied embryonic sac. A lentil. That seems a lot nicer than calling him my chaos monster. "Well, Lentil? Any clever ideas? How the heck are we gonna tell your daddies?"

60
LUKAS

This game is a goddamn fucking gong show. The Leafs defense-men are always hard hitters, taking their cues from veteran grinder, Brett Durand. I've played against this guy since the Juniors, and he's a menace. He's built like a linebacker, making him slow on his skates, but he hits like a freight train.

Coley and I are paired up this game, and it's all we can do to keep Durand away from our forwards. I'm pouring sweat, sides heaving between each shift as I wait on the bench.

There's a Finnish forward playing on the Leafs. The Olympic scouts are here watching him too. Compton informed the whole D-line that we have to stop him from making a goal. Mars wants Mäkinen to prove his worth to the scouts. I can respect that, but damn if it isn't making me tired. Mäkinen is so fucking fast. And every time I turn around, there's Durand in my face.

We're into the first minutes of the second period, Rays are up 2-1, when all fucking hell breaks loose. I'm on the bench with Cole, watching as Compton and J-Lo scrap it out around our net, trying to clear the puck. Mäkinen takes a shot. Mars deflects, sending the puck over to Langers, but he's just a bit too far ahead of it. Durand lands a nasty hit, sending Langley sprawling down to the ice.

Compton and J-Lo scramble to cover Mars as he skates out past his crease. Our forwards slip out of sync as Sully is knocked off balance. At the same time, J-Lo trips on a stick, falling in slow motion to the side of the goal. It leaves Mars totally unguarded, and he's too far out.

Mars leaps backward, his body slamming down to the ice as he flattens out, stretching from fingers to toes to block the net. The Leafs forward gives Mars a full face of snow as he skates in too fast, doing a pirouette to avoid a goalie interference penalty. Mars blocks the shot, but it costs him. He's flat out on the ice like a limp fucking fish.

"Get up," I shout, one leg already over the boards.

"Come on, Mars!" says Cole at my side.

Durand skates in from the side too fucking fast as Mars is getting up to his knees. He slams into Mars, crashing into the back of the net, knocking the whole damn thing loose. It's a hard fucking hit, with Mars bent back at the knees, overextending his hips as the full weight of Durand lands on him. His pads are good, but the human body can only bend so far.

"Mars!" Cole shouts again.

I'm seeing fucking red, my rage boiling over. Mars is down, and he's not getting up. White spots dance at the corner of my vision. Rule number one in hockey? *Never* touch the fucking goalie.

But I'm not out on that ice. I'm stuck watching from the boards as Compton goes barreling in. I can hear his primal shout of rage as he crashes into Durand. Dropping his gloves, Compton tackles him to the ice and starts wailing on him. He's punching Durand with both fists, pinning him down with his hips as he screams.

"Jake, no!" Doc cries from behind me, her hands on my shoulders as she boosts herself up onto the bench. "Stop it—he'll kill him!"

"He really is gonna kill him," says Coley, one gloved hand on my arm to keep me on the boards.

The crowd is on its feet, screaming for more bloodshed as whistles blow and the refs start pulling guys apart. It takes Sully and a lineman to drag Compton off Durand. Even from here, I can see the blood on the ice. The lineman tries to pull Compton over to the box, but he's still shouting insults back and forth with Durand.

What the fuck? I have *never* seen Compton so violent on the ice.

"God—Jake, stop," Rachel screams.

Durand says something that makes Compton Hulk-out again. He breaks free of Sully's hold, and it takes Sully and Langley to pull him back. The ref calls it, booting Compton from the game. They finally get him back over to our bench, and Cole and I hop off the boards, ready to replace him. J-Lo has a hand on him too, dragging him back. Compton only has eyes for Mars. He shouts across the ice, trying to get his attention.

"He's fine," J-Lo soothes, pushing him against the boards.

I look myself to see that Mars is back up on his knees. His mask is up and he's talking to the linesman. He's okay for now. I glare across the ice toward the penalty box. Durand is dabbing at his bleeding face as Rays fans hammer the glass with their fists behind his head. He better be happy he's in there for five fucking minutes. Otherwise, he'd be dead.

I skate into position, ready to take advantage of the hole Durand left in his line. The puck is dropped, and I'm throwing elbows left and right, slamming Leafs into the boards wherever I can.

At the shift change, I hop over the side, downing a pair of mustard packets to help with my leg cramps. The sharp, tangy taste hits my tongue, and I groan. It's fucking disgusting, but players swear by it. I know some guys who drink pickle juice by the jar for the added sodium and electrolytes.

In under two minutes, Coach calls for the shift change, and Cole and I each swing a leg over the boards, waiting for J-Lo and Woody to skate up. Once they hop off, we hop on, skating like a pair of sharks into the fray. The puck is down at the Leafs' end for a change, so Cole and I are left playing cleanup, keeping the puck in the zone.

Karlsson takes a shot, and the damn puck goes missing. It hasn't crossed the line, and the goalie doesn't have possession. It's a fucking scramble as the forwards get it out from the back corner of the net. Cole and I are pulled in closer, staying in position for a rebound or to catch a stray. My mark is all over me, throwing elbows and grunting like a horse in heat.

"Get the fuck off me," I growl, giving him a hard check with my shoulder.

But his stick pulls through my legs, tripping me up. I go down hard, hitting both knees before I'm rolling to my side. The puck shoots loose, whizzing pasts me down the ice toward Mars, and everyone skates my way. The Leafs forward tries to avoid tripping as he leaps over me. Only he doesn't leap *over* me so much as he steps *on* me.

Blinding fucking pain.

White lights dancing in my vision.

Screaming.

Who the fuck is screaming?

Oh, it's me.

"Novy!"

"Nov!"

I can taste my own blood in my mouth. Fucker just stepped on my fucking face with his goddamn fucking skate blade. I blink, eyes burning. Oh god, is that sweat or blood? I can't open my right eye. It stings.

Wait—I can't open my fucking eye? No, no, no. This is a career-ender. You can't play hockey with one fucking eye.

Cole drops to his knees by my side, his hand on my shoulder. "You're okay, Nov. Don't fucking move."

It's bad. I can hear the panic in his tone. It has to be bad, right? Colton John Morrow III doesn't panic. He's the steady rock on which my life is now built. He knows everything about cabinets, and escrow payments, and accessorizing your wardrobe. He's the reason I have lamps, and now he's panicking.

I reach up, trying to unbuckle my helmet, but I'm fumbling, still wearing my damn gloves.

"I said don't move," he cries, grabbing my wrist. "Leave it on. Doc is coming."

"My eye," I mutter. "Cole—my eye—"

The other guys talk over my head.

"Fuck, he's bleeding so much."

"Oh god, I'm gonna be sick—"

"Did it get his neck?"

"Wait for the medic—"

"Apply pressure if it's his neck—"

"He could fucking bleed out!"

"It's not his neck, just his face," Cole assures them.

The ref's face floats in my vision. "Hold on, Novikov. EMTs are right here."

My wound has its own pulse, pumping all my red-hot blood out of my body, all over my face and neck, dripping down onto the ice. "Coley . . . my eye," I say again.

He's down on all fours, his gloved hands pressed to the ice as he puts his face right by mine. "It's not your eye. Okay, bud? The cut goes up along your jaw to your ear. You're split open real good, and the blood is getting in your eyes because of how you're lying. Just be still. Doc is here now—"

"Novy, don't move," comes Doc's panicked voice. Her face replaces Cole's in my limited vision. "We're gonna get you to the hospital, okay? A plastic surgeon is gonna fix you up real nice and pretty."

"Good," I mutter, words slurring as I give in to this drop of adrenaline. "I want Poppy to think I'm pretty."

"**O**ut of the way," I shriek, racing down the escalator as fast as these stupid heels will carry me. "Move, before I run you down!"

I watched Lukas's hit from my box seat, wedged between the two reps from the Finnish Ice Hockey Association. I think they could hear my scream from the International Space Station. I certainly put in the effort. My glass of iced tonic water with lime shattered at my feet as I leapt up at the sight of Lukas's blood spilling down his face.

Now I'm racing to get down into the tunnels. They're taking him off the ice on a stretcher. *My* Lukas. He's currently being strapped down and transported to a hospital. How badly is he hurt? Oh god, I think I'm gonna be sick—

"Move, move, move," I chant, flashing my badge at one of our regular security guards.

"Oh, Poppy, I hope he's okay," she calls as I rush down the last escalator.

He better be okay . . . or I'm gonna freaking *kill* him. God, why did I give him a second night to panic on his own? I was trying to be a good girlfriend, trying to give him space, knowing he'd come to me when he was good and ready.

Now I just watched him get partially decapitated, and he hasn't told me that he loves me too? Oh, this is *not* happening.

My heels click on the concrete, jarring my calves with each step I take. "Where are they taking Lukas?" I shout at the first polo shirt I see.

A young guy holding a handful of hockey sticks looks wide-eyed at me. "Who?"

"Novikov," I shriek. "Where the hell is he?"

"Ambulance bay," he says, pointing over his shoulder, nearly dropping his bundle of sticks.

I see the stretcher, and I wanna die. At least they have it propped up a little. They keep it flat when you're dead, right? Oh god, I watch romcoms and nature documentaries, not true crime!

"Lukas!" I fly down the last twenty feet of the hallway until I'm practically stumbling into the ambulance bay. The truck is already running, and the EMTs are hurrying around, exchanging quick words with Rachel and the medical intern.

"Lukas—wait—" His jersey is soaked in blood, as is the sheet he's lying on. It's in his hair, down his neck. "Oh my god," I cry, tears falling. "Lukas." I take his hand, squeezing it.

"Hey, Pop," he mutters. They already have his jersey sleeve rolled up with an IV jammed in his arm.

"What is that?"

"Just an antibiotic cocktail," Rachel replies, squeezing my shoulder. "We want to fight infection as fast as we can. An ice skate is not the most hygienic of surgical cutting tools."

"Oh, Lukas, I saw the whole thing. It was so awful."

"M'okay," he mutters, his hand going slack in mine.

"What's wrong with him? Is he passing out?"

"Probably," one of the EMTs replies. "He's lost quite a bit of blood, and the shock is wearing off. We're ready to go here," she adds at Rachel.

"Right." Rachel turns to Lukas. "I'll come check on you after the game, okay? You're in good hands—"

"What?" I cry. "You're going with him, right?"

"Pop, I'm needed more here," she replies.

"Rachel Price, you are a doctor, and he is your patient, and you are going with him to that hospital," I shriek. "I cannot have it out there that we send our unconscious players off with strangers to perform medical procedures on them! He needs an advocate!"

He needs *me*. He needs his family.

But our relationship is still safe and private in our little shell. We're not ready for the eyes of the world. We need more time. He's not even ready to admit he loves me to *me*. Meanwhile, I'm over here keeping the world's biggest secret from him because *I'm* not ready to cause him more emotional panic. You think we need to be mutually panicking while @hockeybro122 posts a viral cutting diatribe about how we're both going to hell for our lifestyle?

"Don't worry," Rachel assures me. "We'll notify his emergency contact."

I blink back my tears. "Colton is his emergency contact, and he's otherwise engaged. It has to be you, Rachel. *Please*. Do this for me. Go with him."

With a sigh, Rachel hands off her medical bag to the intern. "Tell Tyler where I've gone. I'll be back as soon as I can."

Lukas's limp hand slips from mine as they wheel his stretcher away, loading him into the back of the ambulance. Once the EMTs are in, Rachel climbs in too, and the doors are shut. The ambulance makes a *woop-woop* sound as it pulls out of the bay, lights flashing.

I'm left standing in the empty bay with a hand over Lentil, heart racing like I just ran a marathon.

Rest, the doctor said. *Relax*.

Great idea. I'll get right on that.

I step into the lobby of the Jacksonville General Hospital ICU, and head over to the nurse's station. The Leafs game is finally over. We won, and I don't even fucking care. Lukas is hurt. I had to watch him get wheeled away on a stretcher, leaving behind a pool of blood on the ice.

I tried to find Poppy before I left, but she went missing, and now she's not answering her damn phone. I pray to god she beat me here.

Something's off between them. Lukas hasn't come over for the past two nights. He made a lame excuse about needing to focus for the game, but I don't buy it. I swear, if he's about to sabotage what we have, I'm gonna finish what that Leafs player fucking started.

"Hey, I'm looking for Lukas Novikov," I say at the nurse.

"Are you next of kin?"

"I'm his emergency contact. If you check his file, I should be listed. Colton Morrow."

She taps a few keys on her keyboard, glancing at the screen over her sparkle-framed readers. "He's in room 2D. Have you spoken to the doctor yet?"

"No, I literally just got here."

"You can go in. If he's asleep, please let him rest."

"Thank you," I say, already on the move down the hall.

I find the right room and step through the open door. Lukas is dressed in a hospital gown, blankets pulled up to his chest. All his hockey gear is piled in clear plastic bags on the floor. I can see the blood-stained jersey they probably had to cut off him. There are no bandages on his face to let the wound breathe. A row of stitches trails along the bottom of his cheek from the edge of his jaw up into his hairline by his ear.

My stomach twists in a knot. "Jesus, Nov."

"Hey," he mutters.

"You're awake?"

"Barely."

This room is quiet as a tomb. The only sound is the slow beep of his heart rate monitor. It's a jarring change coming from the screaming of sixteen thousand fans. He's got a pulse monitor on his finger, the tip glowing red. An IV sticks out of his arm, leading up to a double bag of fluids and antibiotics. As I step closer, I see that it's not bruising or discoloration on his cheek, it's just Betadine. I sink down into the chair by his bedside, taking his hand in mine. "So, how many stitches is that?"

"One hundred and twenty," he replies, eyes closed.

I squeeze his hand. "Well, I think that's a record. You may even have Frankenstein beat, bud."

He smiles, but it turns into a wince as it pulls on his stitches.

"How long are they gonna keep you caged in here?"

"Just overnight. They'd let me go now, but they want at least one more round of IV fluids in me. Turns out I was dehydrated and possibly low on iron."

"Well, we'll just get you some vitamins. I can swing by the store on the way home."

"Was Poppy here? Did I miss it?"

I glance around the room, looking for any sign. Knowing her, she'd bring him a basket packed with slippers and a toothbrush and homemade snickerdoodle cookies. "I don't think so . . . things were pretty crazy after the game, bud. She had those Finnish scouts here—"

"It's fine. She probably won't come."

"Why would you say that?"

"Because she's mad at me."

I sigh. "Why is she mad at you? What did you do?"

"I didn't do anything," he replies with a shrug. "And that's the fucking problem."

"What do you mean?"

"She told me she loved me, and I didn't do anything. I didn't say anything. Well, actually, I told her to take it back, and when she said no, I walked the fuck away."

"Fucking hell," I mutter. "What prompted her to say that she loved you?"

"We were arguing."

"Naturally."

"I told her to stop accepting shitty things, and to fight for what she wants, and that made her mad. Then I got mad and told her if she didn't fight, I was gonna fight for her. So, she told me she loved me and said I better *not* fight for her, or she'll hound me to the ends of the earth."

I fight a smile, picturing the chaos of that moment perfectly in my mind. God, she's so beautiful and fierce. It doesn't bother me at all that she told him she loved him before she said the words to me. I know exactly how Poppy feels about me. That woman loves with her whole being. To be loved by Poppy is to be wrapped up body and soul in her goodness, her light.

I love her too. I'd say it every hour of the day if she'd let me. But I'm going to appreciate her timing here. She'll say it when she's ready. Once she does, there'll be no holding me back.

In the meantime, I get to watch these two circle each other like sexy cats in a bag, which is highly entertaining.

"She loves you, Nov."

"I know. Fuck me if I know why." He glances my way. "Do you think I can get her to stop?"

"Do you really want her to stop?"

He looks away. "I don't know how to do this. I don't know how to be this guy."

"What guy?"

"Mr. Dependable. I don't know how to be the guy who answers the phone and remembers the detergent and always minds his manners."

I chuckle. "I'm sorry, did she tell you that she loves you, or did she ask you to get a personality transplant?"

He glares at me. It looks extra menacing with that face full of gnarly stitches. "What the hell are you talking about?"

I sigh. Seriously, of all the defensemen she could've picked, I'm yoked to this one forever? "Nov, she loves *you*. This shitty version of you right here." I gesture at him lying in the hospital bed. "The version who steals all my food like a feral raccoon, can't appreciate the benefit of lamps, and buys new clothes instead of doing laundry. This imperfect, annoying, selfish person. She's not asking you to change."

He narrows his eyes at me. "I appreciate your lamps, asshole."

I smile. "I'm not asking you to change either . . . though the clothing habit is wasteful. I've already scheduled a laundry service for you."

He looks up at the ceiling. "She deserves better than this."

I tense. "Better than what?"

Slowly he turns to look at me again. "You've been watching all this bullshit unfold the same as me. You really want to put her in the middle and let people say that shit about her, about *us*?"

"What are you saying?"

"I'm saying if I back off, then the two of you can come out as dating and just be a free, normal couple. No media hassle, no bullshit, no wacko keyboard warriors saying you're going to hell."

"We were bound to get some of that anyway," I say with a shrug.

"What? Why?"

"Racism is still alive and well. Not everyone supports interracial dating."

"That is so fucked up," he mutters.

"I couldn't agree more." I lean forward in my chair. "But I'm not going to let you pull away from this—"

"I'm not gonna hurt her."

I drop his hand and lean away with a glare. "Pulling away will fucking hurt her. And I warned you weeks ago what I would do to you if you hurt her."

"Cole—"

He doesn't get another word out before Poppy's clicking heels in the hall announce her imminent arrival. She comes around the corner in her teal dress and sexy black heels. Her hair that was down is now tossed up in a ponytail. Her makeup looks smudged, like she's been crying, and her cheeks are pink.

She looks from me to Lukas before bursting into tears. "I'm sorry," she cries, hurrying into the room, dropping her heavy bag to the floor by the door. "Honey, I'm so sorry." She stands on the other side of

Lukas's bed, taking his hand. Her other hand goes to his hair, brushing it back as she kisses his brow through her tears.

The asshole leans into her touch, his whole body turning like a plant seeking the sunlight.

Yeah, this is a man ready to take two big steps back.

"I'm sorry I couldn't get here sooner," she says, lifting his hand and kissing that too, careful not to dislodge the pulse monitor. "I had the Finnish scouts, and the press conference, and then Rachel and—oh—Mars is going to the Olympics!"

"That's awesome," I say. "It'll be fun to watch."

Her smile falls as she glances between us. "It's out. It's all coming out."

My heart skips. "What's coming out?"

"You didn't hear it from me, but Rachel was just suspended tonight for unethical conduct."

I lean forward. "What?"

"Because of Compton?" Novy echoes.

She shakes her head. "No, it turns out they've had all the HR relationship forms signed since the beginning. And she hasn't been treating him. No, it's because of Ilmari."

"His injury?" I ask.

"No, they're together," she says. "It all came out tonight. It was just awful. I had to be there to witness the whole thing with Vicki and the coaching staff. Rachel and Jake I knew about, but apparently Caleb has also been involved."

"Well, we knew that," Nov says with a shrug.

Poppy's eyes go wide. "What?"

"Yeah, we caught them fucking at the hotel. They've been sneaking around for weeks."

She sinks down onto the bed. "Seriously? Weeks? And neither of you said anything?"

I shrug. "It didn't really seem like our business. We didn't want them in our business either."

"Well, hold onto your hats because she's been seeing Mars too. And Jake and Caleb were literally caught in the closet tonight."

"No," Novy gasps. "Man, we *just* asked the assholes to fess up, like, two days ago. Seriously?"

"And now they all wanna come out. They say they're done hiding. Full press releases, the works. They want to get ahead of it as best they can. Rachel Price, America's rock'n'roll princess, is in a loving, polyamorous relationship with our equipment manager, our Olympic-bound goalie, and one of our star defensemen. So, my life just got infinitely more complicated. I now get to coordinate a four-way coming out with the PR reps for Hal Freaking Price."

"No," Novy gasps again. "Do you get to meet him?"

"Well, y'all have a game in LA next weekend, and I've been asked to fly out for it." She glances between us, her shoulders slumping a little. "Honeys, I'm sorry, but this is gonna take up a lot of my time this week. It's gonna be a mess. My phone is already ringing—"

"Poppy, we're not gonna stop you from doing your job," Lukas says.

"I know, but you're injured. You're in the hospital."

"I'm fine."

"You have a face full of stitches—"

"Proof that I'm fine," he says over her. "Besides, you're not my emergency contact. Cole is. He's the one legally obligated to bring me ice chips and a change of underwear and help me hobble out to the car—"

"Oh—underwear," she cries. "I came straight from the game, and I didn't even stop to get you anything you might need. But I was already making a list and—"

"Poppy." He grabs her hands in both of his. "I am fine. I'm happy you're here, but I don't *need* you here. You have your own life with your own job to do. In my job, injuries happen. This isn't my first, and it won't be my last. I'm doing my job. You can go do yours without any hard feelings."

She blinks back her tears. "Yeah, but we really need to talk. There's so much to say . . ."

I glance over to Lukas, waiting. Is he going to say the only thing she needs to hear? The asshole covers his silence by reaching out a pathetic, pulse monitor-clad hand for his cup of water, taking a sip.

"We have time," I say, covering for him. "We're not going anywhere, baby. And Lukas is right. If you have a job to do, you go do it."

She looks between us again as we all hear her phone buzzing

in her bag. Leaning down, she gives Lukas a kiss, just a quick press. Stepping around his bed, she comes to me. Hand on my shoulder she leans down, kissing first my forehead, then my lips. I can't help but skate my hands up her thighs. I take in a deep breath, filling my senses with her—her warmth, her scent, her closeness.

She pulls away, her hand still on my shoulder, looking down at me with watery eyes.

"I'll stay with him tonight," I say.

"Thank you."

I smile, tucking her hair back behind her ear. "No thanks needed. This is family, yeah?"

She sniffs back her tears. "Yeah, it is."

Turning away, she collects her stuff off the floor, pausing by the door to give us both one last look, like she's trying to commit us to her memory. I can't help but realize I'm doing the same thing, watching as my future smiles and walks away.

63
POPPY

I thought coordinating a benefit for a children's hospital was stress-ful. But that has nothing on coordinating the international media storm that is a four-way coming out press tour. I have never jug-gled so many PR balls in my life. And not one of these balls can be dropped or mishandled.

First there's navigating Jake Compton coming out as queer and in a relationship with his longtime best friend—former NHL player, and Rays equipment manager—Caleb Sanford. Yeah, that's a big flaming ball of fire. The hockey world has been taking most of that heat. I helped the boys coordinate a few public dates to show them together and happy—at the beach, getting coffee, walking the dog. We had trusted people take pictures and post them to the right sites, doing our best to control headlines and keep all the gross trolls away.

Then there's the delicate glass ball that is Ilmari Kinnunen's Olympic news. At least I've had help there, with his agent and my new contacts at the Finnish Ice Hockey Association handing press on their end.

But then there's Rachel Price. She's not so much a ball as she is one of those medieval things that hangs on the chain with all the spikes. She's heavy and she's prickly, and she's swinging around making a freaking mess. I've been doing damage control in three different directions. First, there's dealing with the news of her sus-pension for ethical misconduct.

Some of this has been out of my hands as the Rays stage their own internal coup against Todd Avery, our current head of Physical Therapy. As his own misconduct has come to light, the team has ral-lied around Rachel, demanding that Mark lift her suspension and give her Todd's job. I've been coordinating press releases, and helping the guys write letters of support for Rachel. Ryan Langley left me a seven-minute soliloquy on my now-working voicemail, asking if someone in my office would type it up for him to sign.

Second has been dealing with the reveal itself. Rachel Price is consensually dating and living with, not one, but *three* men . . . and two of those men are also dating. That news has blown up most widely on all the celebrity gossip sites. Every rag at the grocery store checkout has pictures of her face on them.

Most of the gossip is trying to paint her as some kind of sexual deviant . . . or a sinister mastermind, playing three men, and pitting them against each other. Whore. Slut. Floozy. Tease. Trash. The cruel names are endless. People don't believe three men could ever *choose* to share one woman. No, they must be bamboozled. They're under her spell. It must all be a lie.

There's little I can do to control that narrative for now, as she's currently in hiding at her family's media-proof compound in LA. I can't leak photos of her happy with all three of her guys because she's not currently *with* her guys.

I know the feeling well. I've been so busy this week, I've hardly had the chance to see or speak to Lukas and Colton.

I step through Jake's kitchen, pausing at the open lanai door, watching as my friend Janine from ESPN interviews the guys on the couch. I was careful to craft the perfect image for this, wholesome and family friendly. Jake, Caleb, and Ilmari are seated on the couch, Jake and Caleb holding hands. There's just enough beach touch with the natural light and the woodgrain furniture. A pitcher of iced tea and glasses sit staged on the table in front of them, complete with lemon curls.

This was actually their idea. It's the third prong of our public relations strategy: rehabilitating Rachel's image. I've done my best to silence the trolls, but there's no denying there's a lot of nastiness out there. I can't imagine being her guys and having to sit back and watch the world say heinous things about the woman they love. Of course they want to protect her. Now that they're not trying to hide, it's clear they're crazy about her.

And she's a good person. She's kind and she's funny. She's

a talented doctor. I think she just got caught up in the chaos. Everything moved so fast with Ilmari and the injury. She was in the middle before she even knew she'd begun.

I brush a hand over my belly. This morning in the shower was the first time I noticed a change. I now have the smallest little sign of a bump. In truth, Rachel and I are no different. We were both in the middle before we realized we'd begun. I'm in love with two men I met at work. I fought it, and I lost. Sometimes the world just brings people together.

Will this be us soon? Will my boys have to beg the world to see me for who I am, a good person with a strong heart, who they're proud to know and love?

I know Colton loves me, and I know he wants to say it. I think he's waiting for me to say it first. I know Lukas loves me too . . . but I'm getting anxious worrying that he'll *never* be ready to say it. I look at the quiet strength of Ilmari on that couch, so poised as he refuses to let the press penetrate his hard shell. I look at Jake and Caleb, ready to defend Rachel and profess their love for her and each other.

What would Lukas do on that couch? He says he wants to fight for me, but I don't need him to physically fight. I don't need him championing my character to ESPN. I just need to know he'll emotionally fight for me. Gosh darn it, I need to hear him say he loves me. Colton might be okay with only action, but I need words too. I need that validation. Without it, I feel frozen. Like I can't move forward with either of them. I need us all on the same page.

Until then, I can't tell them about the baby. I won't use the news of a child as leverage to force an emotional confession. But the longer Lukas waits to say anything, the more likely this little chaos lentil will be the one to tell them both how things have changed.

God, why is this all so hard? Why are we even put in these impossible positions? Why can't people just let others live? I'm in love with two men, and I want to grow old with them, and be happy with them, and raise their children without the trolls of the world telling us we're terrible people.

Blinking back tears, I step out onto Jake's front porch, breathing in the fresh beach air. Placing a hand on my belly, I take comfort in talking to Lentil. "Don't you even worry about all the mean-spirited people in the world. They're just jealous of us. They know we're happy, and jealous people will always try to make happy people less happy. But we're not gonna let them win, are we? I'm a fighter, and so are your daddies. We're gonna fight for our happiness, okay? You just stay in there. I'm gonna make sure everything is okay."

Well, color me impressed. Maybe I should start taking PR lessons from my own players because, in under a week, Jake, Ilmari, and Caleb just flipped the script on bad press. I'm standing in one of our team's boxes at the LA arena, looking out at a sea of "Price" jerseys. Fans are waving signs and cheering, going crazy for Rachel and her guys.

Again, it was all their idea. I hardly had to do a thing except approve some promo materials and order some travel packages for flights and hotels to the game. In a show of solidarity, Jake, Caleb, *and* Ilmari are all legally changing their last names to Price. It's already been changed on their jerseys. Jake and Mars are down there now, playing a shutout game against the Kings. Nothing is getting past our goalie tonight. He's made some truly spectacular saves.

I'm smiling from ear to ear as I feed off the joy and exuberance of the crowd. After a hellish week being torn apart by the media, this is what Rachel needed to see. She needed to see the joy again. She needed to know it could all be okay.

Heck, I needed to know it too.

I watch Lukas and Colton hop the boards, tagging out Jake and Jean-Luc. Lukas is playing with a full cage to protect the cut on his face. I begged him to wait another week to heal, but the man can't be stopped. We're deep into the third period now, and the Rays are up. My guys work as a team, moving the puck out of the defensive zone. They're so beautiful together. So strong and good.

I have to tell them. I want them to know about the baby. I want them to know how much I love them both. I don't want it to be a secret anymore. I want everyone to know.

My phone buzzes in my pocket. I pull it out and see it's a text from

Rachel. She's sitting down right on the ice with the rest of her family. I tap the screen and read:

RACHEL: Just FYI, the boys and I made a bet. If this is a shutout game, we're getting married tonight.

"What?" I shriek, gripping to the phone with both hands.

RACHEL: And no, this is not a joke. I'm marrying Ilmari, and Caleb is marrying Jake. Tonight.

I'm gonna have to ask Mark for another raise. We'll call it the Price Family Bonus.

I look to the game clock. Less than three minutes left. That's not enough time for the Kings to win this game. We're up by too many points. But it's enough time for them to score a point. Apparently, we're holding out until the last second here because if Mars lets even one puck in that net, he's not marrying Rachel tonight. With one look at our dialed-in goalie, I know that's not happening. Nothing is going to stop this man from getting what he wants, and what he wants is Rachel Price.

WE won. It was a shutout game.

And the Prices are now married.

It's well after midnight, and all the guests are still celebrating. Needing a minute of peace and quiet, I escape outside into Hal Price's sweeping back garden. Behind me, a path lit by a string of Edison bulb lights leads back up to the house. I hold Colton's suit coat around my shoulders with one hand, warding off the mid-December chill as I take in the lights of Hollywood.

It was a beautiful wedding. Caleb and Jake got married first, declaring vows to each other that made me cry like a baby. Then it was Rachel and Ilmari's turn. One look in his eyes as she came walking down the aisle was all it took to break me again.

He loves her. He says it out loud. He declares it in multiple languages. He takes her hand before god and man and vows to love her forever. *Aina*, he said. It means always. He will always love her.

Watching them marry each other did more than emotionally break me. It broke something in my brain too. It cracked a truth wide open. Oh god, why did I never think of this before now—

"Hey."

I glance over my shoulder to see Colton coming down the lit path, holding two glasses of champagne. He hands me one, and I take it wordlessly. Tears fill my eyes as I look down at it. He doesn't know. How could he when I haven't told him?

He clinks his glass with mine and takes a sip. "Crazy night, huh?"

I make no move to drink my champagne. "Yeah . . . crazy."

"What's wrong?"

I smile up at him, knowing it doesn't meet my eyes. "What makes you think anything's wrong?"

He tips his head to the side, letting his eyes savor the look of me in my glittery gold dress and his suit jacket. "Because I know you. I know you from your pretty blonde hair down to your polished pink toes."

"My toes are purple right now."

"I stand corrected. I'll go walk into Hal Price's pool now." He moves as if to brush past me, and I reach out a hand.

"Don't."

He chuckles. "Come on, Poppy. Talk to me." He brushes his fingertips over my cheek. "Is it just all the stress of this week? You haven't been sleeping . . . I've hardly seen you. I mean, I know it's been fucking awful, but it's over now. They're married. Hard to keep gossiping about how it'll never last when they've all signed on the dotted line—"

I spin away, not wanting him to see the tears start to fall.

"Hey." He takes me gently by the shoulder and turns me back around. "What is this? I thought you'd be happy for them. A win for them is a win for us too."

"We are not the same," I whisper. "Their story can't be our story."

He frowns. "Well . . . no. I mean, if anything, our story will be a bit easier to write. We have nothing like their fame, or their baggage."

"Colton . . ."

"Babe, you can check any of my closets," he goes on. "Give me a scrub-down, or whatever you call it in the biz. The most you'll find is, like, three parking tickets and a handful of speeding tickets. Sure, Novy has a juvie record, but most of that gets expunged when you become an adult."

Squaring my shoulders at him, I hold his gaze. "Colton, on the yacht you told me exactly what you wanted. You held up my hand, and stroked my ring finger, and said *that's* where you wanted this to go. You want us to get married, right?"

His eyes widen a little, looking for the trap. "Of course I want to marry you. Poppy, I've been clear on that from the beginning—"

"But I *can't* marry you."

He goes still, glaring down at me. "Why not?"

Oh god, this is coming out all wrong. "Colton—"

Before I can respond, Lukas comes waltzing down the path, holding a glass of champagne and a bottle of beer. "There you two are. I was looking everywhere. Hey, who wants to bet me a thousand bucks that Langers marries that redhead he's dancing with?"

He comes to stand next to Colton, the golden lights of the patio casting shadows on the swollen, raised cut on his cheek. He looks down at the untouched glass of champagne I'm holding. "When you're done with that one, I'm ready with number two." He holds up the glass in his hand, taking a swig from his beer bottle. Sensing the mood, he glances between us. "What happened? What did I miss?"

"Poppy just said she won't marry me," Colton replies.

My heart squeezes tight. "That's not what I was trying to say."

Lukas steps in, glaring at Colton. "Wait, you just proposed? A heads up would've been fucking nice. Where the hell's the ring, asshole?"

"I didn't propose," Colton replies. "She didn't give me a chance. She's already said no."

"I *have* to say no," I reply, voice breaking. "Not because I don't love you. Because I *do*, Colton. You know I do. I love you so much, honey. But seeing them all get married tonight just made me realize I can never have that," I say with a shrug. "*We* can never have that. The three of us."

"Why can't we have that?" says Colton.

"Honey, because it's illegal. Look at what the Prices just had to do. His and Hers marriages? I can't imagine marrying one of you and not the other."

"So, then we just don't get married," he says with a shrug.

"But you *want* to get married," I cry. "You want the wedding and the house and the babies. And you want to call me your wife. You want all of those traditions. I know you, Colton. And you *deserve* all those things. Maybe once, I could've been the woman to give them to you, but I'm not that woman anymore."

"And I'm not that guy anymore," he replies, his tone heating. "You changed me. *This* changed me." He points between the three of us. "Poppy, this is what I want now. This right here is all I will ever need. I love you, and I love him, and I want the three of us to be together. I mean, we're happy, right? Aren't you happy?"

"I was so happy," I whisper, blinking back more tears.

"Was," he echoes, his expression closing off. "Meaning you're not now. Can I ask what the fuck happened?"

"Everything happened," I cry. "This awful week happened. Watching people around the world tear a woman apart for loving more than one man happened. I have spent the last seven days buried up to my neck in some of the worst vitriol I've ever experienced in my life. And I'm a PR manager. I *manage* the crises; I don't take center stage in them!"

"Good to know you see loving us as a fucking crisis," he snaps.

"You have no idea what it's been like," I go on. "Even now, I have a team of people actively blocking comments and requesting media takedowns of the most cruel and insensitive content. All because a woman is daring to do the same thing I'm doing and love more than one man. What happens when there are children involved? How will we protect them from the hate of this world?"

"Babe, there are no fucking kids," Colton shouts. "We're just three adults living a life."

"But there *will* be kids. It's what you want, right? It's what I want too. Are you really ready to bring them into this kind of chaos? Are you ready for them to face censure and cruelty for being part of a polyamorous union?"

"Can I interject here?" Lukas's gaze is steely as he glances between us. "Love how you're both making declarations and planning out my whole goddamn future without me right now, but I *never* agreed to kids. I don't want kids. So, if that's happening . . ." He shrugs, making a show of taking a large step back.

The pieces of tape holding me together all start to break.

"Why don't you want kids?" Colton asks for me, glaring at Lukas.

Lukas glances between us with an incredulous look on his face. "Are you fucking kidding me? You've met me, right? You know me, you know my life story. And you're still asking me that?"

"Lukas you are not your life story," I say as gently as I can.

"No, but my life story still plays a pretty big motivating factor in why I will *never* have a fucking kid," he shouts. "You think I'm gonna risk messing up a kid as badly as I was messed up? You think I can be someone's daddy? I've never had one, so what the fuck do I know about it? I just had a sad drunk of a grandpa who beat me with a belt for eating too many soda crackers when I was fucking hungry. No, I can be the fun uncle at best. I can teach them how to pull pranks, and shoot pucks, and put on a condom. Otherwise, I have no interest in being a goddamn parent."

A long moment of silence stretches between us. The only sounds are the jazzy notes coming from the band inside.

"I have to go," I whisper. Turning away, I take three steps before Colton is calling out.

"Poppy . . . stop."

I stop.

"Turn around."

Slowly, I turn.

Colton's eyes are obsidian in this darkness, his jaw clenched tight. He points to the glass still clutched in my hand. "Drink that champagne."

Heart in my throat, I pinch the slender stem with two fingers, making no move to bring the glass to my lips. Instead, I defiantly hold his gaze.

More unbearable silence.

"Poppy, drink the goddamn champagne."

Next to him, Lukas finally catches on. His expression falls. That look of horror on his face is all I need to see. "Oh . . . fuck."

"Poppy!" Colton shouts, taking a step forward.

Flinching, I step back and raise the glass a little. Then, holding it out to the side, I tip it over, pouring the bubbly drink onto the patio tiles. My glass empty, I turn and walk away.

They don't follow me.

65
LUKAS

"**W**hat do you mean you're fucking leaving?" Cole shouts, following me around his apartment as I collect my crap. "Lukas!"

We're three days back from LA, and things are a goddamn mess. Poppy is pregnant and hiding out from us. Cole keeps trying to get me to open up about my past. I'm fucking sick of it. I can't take another second. As if lying on his couch and crying into a tub of ice cream will fix the fucked-up-ness in my head that is sending me running for the hills.

I can't do this. He's right, I never fucking could. It's all just feeling like too much for me. Too much pressure, too much commitment. I'm not the guy who stays. I'm not the boyfriend. You don't bring me home to mom. You certainly don't raise a fucking kid with me.

You flirt with me at the bar, fuck me in the bathroom, and let me pay for your Uber home.

"Look, this was always supposed to be temporary anyway," I say. "Just until my house renos were done."

He stands in the hallway, blocking me from getting back to my room. "You mean *my* house renos?"

I glare at him, laptop and a pair of trainers in hand. "It's my fucking house, Cole."

"Yeah, your house that I've spent the last month decorating. Why do you think I did that?"

I dare to give him an asshole smirk. "Because you like interior design."

He just shakes his head, the disappointment flowing off him. "That house is fucking perfect for us. For the *three* of us!"

"There is no us," I say, feeling dead inside.

His expression cracks just a little to show me the turmoil brewing underneath. Oh, he's fucking mad. Maybe, if I push a little harder, I can get him to punch my goddamn lights out. At least then I'll feel something as I sit alone in that empty house, icing my jaw.

"Come on, Coley. I'm giving you what you wanted. With me out of the way, you can have her all to yourself. You can marry her, buy her a house—hell, buy *my* house. I'll give you a good price for it. You can raise your babies, get a dog, and live the perfect little life together."

"And what if the baby is yours?"

I go still. "Then I know you'll be the standup guy you are, and you'll step in and do the job I can't."

He just stands there, arms crossed. "And what the hell will you do while we're living our dream life in your house?"

I shrug. "Fuck bunnies and drink until my liver gives out? That's always been my dream."

He narrows his eyes in disgust. "If you touch another woman besides Poppy, I'll cut off your goddamn hands. Try playing hockey then, asshole."

"Hey, I'm a free agent. I'll put my hands *and* my dick wherever the fuck I want."

"You belong to Poppy," he counters. "I was there in that bar bathroom when she wrapped her hand around your dick and fucking claimed you. I've been right next to you as you've come inside her, burying your face in her hair as you groan out her name. I watched you in the hospital, Lukas. You latched onto her touch like you were both made of goddamn magnets."

I groan, turning away.

"You love her," he shouts, following me back into the little apartment living room. "Say it!"

"There's nothing I need here enough to stay and deal with you," I say over my shoulder. "I've got my laptop. I'm fucking leaving."

"And what about me!"

I slip my feet into my slides by the door, checking my pockets for my keys. Grabbing my hat, I put it on, reaching for the handle.

Cole comes up behind me, slamming his hand flat on the door, closing it. He boxes me in, his front pressing against my back. "What about me, Lukas?"

I don't dare turn around. I cling to my laptop and my trainers and my fist of keys, letting those jagged bits of metal dig into my palm. "What about you?"

"You don't just belong to Poppy. Not anymore. I'm in this, Lukas. I'm *all* the way in."

I let out a shallow breath, closing my eyes. "I'm not interested."

He leans in closer, his warm chest brushing against my back, his breath like a caress on my ear. "Yeah . . . except you've tasted my cum. I watched you whimper for it like a desperate fucking whore. You were on your knees between our queen's legs, sucking my seed from her cunt."

"Stop," I say, praying that he won't, praying he'll just grab me by the throat, pull me back to his bedroom, and chain me to the god-damn bed. That's the only way I'm staying in this apartment. My bolting instincts are too well-honed.

"You came to me in that bathroom, remember?" he goes on. "You dropped your shorts and showed me that hard dick. Then you stroked it for me, dreaming it was my hand, fucking *praying* I would come out of the shower and get on my knees and take it. You want me to do it now?"

I groan, every muscle coiled tight as blood rushes to my dick.

"Turn around, Lukas," he coaxes. "Stay here, and fight for us. Say you want me, like I want you, and I will drop to my knees and suck your hard cock into my mouth. I will gag on you, baby. I will choke on your cum, spit it into my hand, and use it as lube to blow my own load on your chest."

"Fuck." I lean forward, pressing my forehead against the cool metal of the door.

"Say you're not hard. Say you're not aching for it. You fucking piece of shit, say you're not mine in all the ways I'm yours."

I reach for the door handle again. "I'm not yours. I'm not anyone's. I'm nothing."

He gave me a choice. Now that it's made, he's done. Colton Morrow doesn't beg. "Get the fuck out."

I pull open the door and slip out, leaving everything I own inside that goddamn apartment. I can hardly think past the pain in my dick as I do the only thing I've ever been good at. I fucking run.

66
COLTON

Three Weeks Later

"Are you ready to hear the heartbeat?" The doctor smiles up at us from her place at the end of the exam table.

It's the day after New Year's, and Poppy and I are at her ten-week wellness check. It's amazing to see the changes three weeks can bring. She's finally starting to look pregnant. She's hiding it easily at work with open blazers and the cut of her clothes. But when she's at home in her ratty cross county tee, I can see the little curve of her tummy.

I take her hand and nod. "Yeah, we're ready."

Poppy lies back, one arm stretched over her head as Doctor Renner glides the wand through the jelly and turns up the sound on the monitor. A strange *womp-womp-womp* fills the room that sounds more like the first encounter with alien life than a human baby's heartbeat.

I kiss Poppy's hand as I watch the sound waves flash on the monitor. The baby sits in the middle of the screen, floating like a little peanut.

Poppy smiles up at me. "Pretty cool, right?"

I nod, tears in my eyes. "Yeah . . . can we get a copy of this?" I ask the doctor.

"Of course," she replies. "We can provide you with an audio file as well."

I let out a shaky breath, eyes locked on the monitor. Hearing the heartbeat is making me way more emotional than I expected. But, hey, I'm a heart guy. Hearts and their functioning have been my life for so long. My obsession, my hill to endlessly climb.

You need a good heart in your chest. That's why the news of this pregnancy rattled me as deeply as it did. I wasn't ready to have my dream shift into a reality. I definitely wasn't ready for the crippling fear that would creep in with my joy. Those dark thoughts that whisper to you in the quiet moments. Genetic abnormalities. One in a million chance. I won the bad heart lottery, and I don't want this child to suffer like I did. I want our baby to have such a good, strong heart.

"And everything's okay?" I say, looking from the monitor to the doctor.

"Mhmm. The fetus is measuring just as it should—"

"With the heart," I say over her.

Poppy wraps her other hand around mine, giving it a gentle squeeze.

"Everything seems fine," the doctor assures us. "No irregularities in rhythm. Poppy told me heart health is a major concern. As things progress, we'll be sure to monitor closely. Starting in the second trimester, I think it may be best to have biweekly check-ins, just so we're not missing anything."

Poppy asks a few questions about diet and exercise as I turn my attention back to the monitor. The last three weeks have been a total blur. We've had so many games, so much travel. I feel like I've pretty much been living out of a suitcase. I spent the only few days I had off at Christmas down in Orlando with my mom and my sister Jasmine's family. Poppy came with me, rather than go home to her family in DC and risk breaking the news that she's pregnant.

We're not ready to tell people . . . not with things still so up in the air.

But it was a good weekend. My mom and sister are in love with her, obviously. The morning we left, Mom pulled me aside and gave me her old engagement ring. Colton from three months ago would be leaping at the chance to plan some elaborate proposal, desperate to put that ring on Poppy's finger. Now it's sitting in a box in my sock drawer, untouched.

Then, to celebrate our first year in the League, the Rays were put into the Winter Classic, which means we had to work over New Year's Eve. It's just an exhibition game, but it can be a ton of fun. The atmosphere is usually pretty festive, especially when it's hosted in New York City. Poppy even traveled up to help run a few pre-game events.

New Year's Eve in the Big Apple with my girl and my . . .

Well, it *could* have been fun.

Instead, Poppy spent the night watching Hallmark movies alone in her hotel room, and I spent half the night in the hospital with Langley. He took a hard hit on the ice and banged up his knee. We just got back yesterday, and I drove him over to Mars's bungalow where he's gonna recover for a few weeks.

Now, I'm holding Poppy's hand, looking at our baby for the first time, feeling like a goddamn ghost. I know she feels it too. It's like we're stuck in limbo. Can't move forward. Can't focus on the past. We just . . . *are*.

How can one person go from being all but a nonfactor in your life one moment, to carving out the center of it in the next?

It's not like I haven't seen Novy. We both see him all the goddamn time. I skate with him. We workout together. We still share a bench in the dressing room. He sits in my row on the plane. He sits behind me on the bus. He's fucking everywhere.

I'm not the goddamn ghost. *He* is. He's haunting me, haunting my life . . . the life we could have shared. Does he miss us? Is he hurting like we are? Will he ever come back?

I watch him as best I can. He's smiling and laughing, putting on a good show. But he's not chirping. He's not pulling pranks. He's like Novy in 2D. An artist's abstract interpretation of Lukas Novikov. This version lacks all vibrancy, all the color and life that made him so goddamn obnoxious . . . and likable.

Hell, who am I kidding? He's lovable. I don't know how he did it, but that shitty little prank-loving, French fry-eating asshole has wormed his way into my life and into my heart. I love him. As a friend, as a partner. I love what we had together. I love how he loved Poppy. God, he can make her laugh like nothing else.

I mean, I can tell a joke too. But Nov gets this glint in his eye, like he's reeling you in. He knows when he has you hooked. You can see it in the subtle curl of his mouth. Then, when he lands the punchline, and you laugh, his eyes flash with a secret. He locks each laugh away, like he knows something essential about you.

Watching him do it to Poppy is intoxicating.

"Colton? Honey, you okay?" I glance down to see Poppy, the doctor, and the nurse all looking up at me.

My heart starts racing. "I . . . don't—"

No, I'm not fucking okay.

Shit, am I having a panic attack?

"Could you give us a minute?" Poppy says, sitting up on the exam table.

The others clear out, and I finally suck in a shaky breath. "Ohhh fuck."

Poppy keeps hold of my hand, her other rubbing up and down my arm. "Honey, it's okay."

"Fuck—no, I'm sorry," I say on a breath. "I'm fine."

"You're not fine," comes her soft voice. "Neither of us is fine."

I shake my head, looking back up to the monitor, where the image of our baby is still frozen. "He's missing so much, and I'm just . . . I'm so fucking frustrated."

"He *wants* to miss it," she says gently.

"Oh, and you fucking believe him? You really think he's happy without us?"

She just shrugs, tears in her eyes. "It's not about whether he's happy. He doesn't want children, Colton. He's made that clear, and we have to respect it. As much as I love him, I would never push a child on someone who didn't want one with their whole heart. We can love him, and miss him, and wish him well."

"It's fucking killing me," I admit.

It's the first time I've said it out loud, even to myself. I've been trying so hard to just keep it together, keep us moving forward.

She's quiet for a moment. "Have you talked to him about it?"

I glance down at her. "About the baby?"

"About any of it."

I shake my head. "No. Not since he left."

He never even came back for his stuff. It's all still just shut up in the guest room like a fucking time capsule. I've all but moved myself into Poppy's apartment, but I go back occasionally for clothes and random crap. Seeing that door closed in my face makes it feel like it's a vault I can't access.

"If you're this upset, maybe you should talk to him," she offers.

I glance down at her again. "And you're not upset? Are you over it then? Have you suddenly moved on without telling me?"

She blinks back her tears. "Please don't be mean. You know I haven't."

I sigh and kiss her forehead. I *do* know. I catch her crying all the time. Sometimes she still sleeps in his shirts. We're a pair of love-struck fools, hopelessly pining after an emotionally unavailable wannabe playboy who walked away from us and didn't look back.

Actually, he ran. Like he was on fucking fire.

I frown, my mind humming as it tries to latch onto something, some glimmer of an idea.

"Colton?" Poppy takes my hand. "What is it?"

"What if we're going about this all wrong?"

"Going about what?"

"Lukas. What if respecting his wishes, and giving him space, and waiting for him to come to us is the wrong tactic?"

She squeezes my hand. "Honey, we can't force him to want to be with us. He knows how we feel. We both told him. Repeatedly. And, frankly, it would hurt my heart too much to keep trying and get shot down. A girl can only take so much, you know?"

"Yeah . . . but what was it that he said at that benefit? The silent auction thing?"

A smile flits across her mouth. "He always says rather a lot . . . usually it's inappropriate."

"You told me he said something about Leos and Scorpios."

Now she really smiles. She looks up at me. "He said Leos love at first sight and stay loyal until they die . . . which seems to be true."

"And Scorpios?"

She sighs. "That they'll want you at first sight, and fight it till they die."

Oh, fucking hell—

"Babe, I have to go."

"What?" She slips off the exam table. "Col, you were my ride here."

I groan. "Fine, I'll drop you off at home. But then I really need to go. I might not be back for a little while."

"What are you doing?"

I brace my hands on her shoulders. "I don't know," I admit. "Something . . . maybe something crazy. Possibly even illegal. But it feels right."

Anxiety flashes in her eyes. "Oh god . . . Colton, what are you gonna do?"

I smile, set on my course. Bending down, I give her a quick kiss. "I'm gonna go be a Leo."

My doorbell rings. Groaning, I roll over in my bed, reaching for my phone to check the time. It's only ten minutes after eight. God, I'm so fucking pathetic. Lukas Novikov in bed before nine o'clock at night?

Yep, this is my new normal. I wake up, play hockey, eat, go to sleep, repeat. Hey, hockey players love a good routine, right? If I'm not traveling, eating, or playing hockey, I only want to be sleeping. Why would I stay awake, when my reality is a fucking nightmare worse than anything my subconscious mind could ever conjure?

My life now is just one long horizon of endless fucking loneliness. I feel like Matt Damon's character in *The Martian*, only that guy got to say he went to Mars.

Emptiness. Isolation. A primal, raw ache.

I did this to myself. I didn't just walk away from the two best things that ever happened to me, I fucking *ran*. I bolted. I bailed. It's what I always do when things get just a little bit tough. For me, the fear of losing something I want has always felt so much scarier, so much harder to bear, than the pain I feel at choosing to let that thing go.

After a lifetime of this shit, I've perfected the art of self-sabotage. The rationalizations come so easy now. All my usual standbys play on a loop in my mind:

I was no good for them anyway.

They don't need me.

I bet they're happier without me.

I only break things.

Why would anyone ever love me?

It sucks now, but this pain will eventually fade. Someday, I'll be able to fucking breathe again without it hurting. Can you imagine if I was in any deeper when I started to pull away?

My doorbell rings again.

Fuck.

Rolling out of bed, I click on my bedside lamp. That's right, I have two now, one for each side of the bed. And my bed is on a frame. And my walls are painted, and I have curtains. Janice and her team have been hard at work these last few weeks putting all the finishing touches together on the house. It actually looks like someone lives here now. Hopefully all the new built-in features and the kitchen renovation will help me sell it faster.

I sure as fuck can't live here. Not when Cole installed a library on my second floor and ordered eight boxes of books to fill the shelves for Poppy. Half the book covers are pink. The asshole took the smallest bedroom off the master and converted it into a walk-in closet for her. He added an industrial fridge in the kitchen. What's a single guy who never cooks gonna do with an industrial-sized fridge? Check it now, and the only thing you'll find is beer, takeout containers, and half a bottle of ketchup.

I pause halfway down the stairs as I hear my front door open.

Oh, fuck.

Did someone just break into my fucking house? My heart starts to race as I consider my options. I left my phone up by the bed, and it's not like I own a gun. I think there's a hockey stick in the laundry room. I'm pretty deadly with that. How do I get to it? I definitely should've put on a fucking shirt and some pants.

The door slams shut. "Honey, I'm home!"

Oh, you are fucking kidding me. I jog down the stairs in my boxers and socks, practically sliding on my new hardwood floors into my living room.

Cole is standing over by my front door, two suitcases and a backpack at his feet, a fistful of grocery bags in his hand. "Hey. Did you not hear me ringing the doorbell?"

"Did you just break into my fucking house?"

He brings the groceries into the kitchen. "Don't be dramatic. It's not breaking and entering if I have a key. Whoa—" He pauses, glancing around at the kitchen and all the new furniture in the living room. Then he grins. "Bud, this looks fucking amazing. You love the dark cabinets, right?"

"Wait, but you *don't* have a key," I shout, following him.

"You have a hide-a-key rock in your potted plant. I just used that."

"So, you don't *have* a key so much as you *stole* a key," I reason, pressing my hands flat to the granite island countertop. "And then you used that stolen key to come into my house in the middle of the fucking night?"

He chuckles. "It's not even eight thirty, Nov. We have games that start later than this. What's the big deal?"

"The big deal is that you weren't invited!"

He hefts his shopping bags onto the island and starts unpacking them. "What, like I'm a vampire? You gonna rescind my invitation like you're Sookie Fucking Stackhouse?"

"Yes!"

He pauses in his unpacking, two containers of oatmeal in his hands. "No."

"Yes," I say again. "God, just get *out*, Cole. Don't you understand? I can't fucking have you here."

He tips his head to the side in that way he does. "Why not?"

Groaning, I drag both my hands through my hair. "You know why."

"I'm sure that I don't." He pulls a few more groceries from the bag—eggs, milk, a package of shredded cheese. "I have absolutely no idea what goes on inside that toxic head of yours. But I can imagine it's a lot of really terrible shit that sounds something like 'I'm not worthy' and 'No one will ever love me.'"

I cross my arms over my bare chest. "Don't make light of my personal fucking baggage."

"I'm not," he replies. "I'm acknowledging that you engage in self-destructive behaviors as a coping mechanism for managing your deep fear of abandonment."

I blink twice, letting his words sink in. Then I glare at him. "So what, you're my fucking shrink now?"

"No, I just know you," he replies. "I know you better than anyone, Nov. Because I'm your person, remember? Before Poppy was ever even in the picture, you picked *me*."

"Yeah, to be my emergency contact," I say on a forced laugh. "It was just some form they made me fill out."

He's not laughing. "We both know I mean more to you than that."

I suck in a breath, hands dropping to my sides. "Please, don't do this."

He arches a dark brow. "Do what? Chase you? Someone has to. If your default is to bolt every five seconds, your partners better like running. Lucky for you, Poppy and I are both athletes. Have you seen how sexy she looks when she runs?"

I shake my head. "Cole—"

His gaze hardens to iron as he points across the island at me. "Don't 'Cole' me in that shitty fucking tone. I've been letting you handle this your way for three fucking weeks now. I gave you time to run, but now you're done."

"Oh, am I?"

"Yes." He turns that finger around and taps his own chest. "*I'm* in charge now."

My stomach flips at the sound of command in his tone. "What are you gonna do, huh? Gonna drag me back to Poppy on my knees?"

"Nah." He pulls my favorite cereal from the shopping bag, setting it on the counter. "When you're ready to face her on your own, we both know you're gonna fucking crawl."

Fuck, why is this turning me on?

"Then what are you doing here?"

"I'm moving in." He turns away to put the milk, eggs, and cheese in my pathetically empty fridge.

"You're . . . what? But Poppy—"

"Is perfectly fine," he says over me. "Hell, she might even enjoy having me out of her hair for a bit. That's a small fucking apartment. She's set with three cartons of Thai food, two Hallmark Christmas movies, and a month's supply of bath products. If she needs anything, she'll call me. And she knows I'll come running."

Ignoring the rest of the groceries, he slowly starts prowling around the island, all his attention focused on me. "Because that's what I do, Lukas. I'm a Leo, and I chase after the things I want. I hunt them down, I hold them in my claws, and I shred them the fuck open until I get to their tender beating hearts . . . and then I *devour* them.

I take them inside me until they become part of me. Her heart is *my* fucking heart now." He presses his hand to his chest, fingers splayed. "It beats in my chest. You wanna feel where yours beats?"

I swallow my nerves, not moving. Desperate to make this stop, I say the only thing sure to send him away. "Nothing's changed, Cole. I still don't want kids."

"Let's just take this one step at a time, yeah?" He sounds like a physical therapist outlining a rehab regimen. "Because you're right, how could you ever risk loving a child and letting it love you in return when you believe, to your core, that you're unlovable?"

"Fuck, I'm not doing this." Panic rising, I turn away, racing for the stairs.

"You're not ready to tell Poppy you love her, and that's fine," he calls after me. "You're not ready to tell me either, and that's also fine. God knows you're not ready for a big happily ever after with commitment, and babies, and that chocolate lava cake in Aruba! But I'm gonna get you ready because I'm an insufferable fucking asshole who's too Leo to function, and I love you, Lukas Novikov!"

His words chase me up the stairs and into my bedroom. Slamming the door, I try to block him out. I can't do this. I can't let him in. I can't let him care about me. A few days of this, and he'll get tired and frustrated and go crawling back to Poppy, and then I win. My freedom will be restored. I can survive having him here. I can resist the urge to fall at his feet and beg him not to leave me.

After all, it's just a few days . . .

IT'S been four days, and I'm totally fucked. The asshole shows no signs of letting up. Cole is like this six-foot-three parasite that's crawled into my house and infested every part of my life—my fridge, my DVR, my laundry pile, my fucking bed.

Yeah, on the first night, he gave me an hour to cool off before he came tiptoeing into my bedroom. I was laying there with the lights off, wide awake. I told him to leave, and he told me to shut up. Then he stripped down to his boxers, got in my bed, and fell asleep in under five minutes.

He hasn't touched me. Hasn't even tried.

Frankly, I don't know what I want here. So long as he keeps not touching me, I get to feel this exquisite squirming, aching, bleeding kind of pain of desperation that is really pairing well with my crippling doubt and self-loathing.

But if he does touch me . . . well, then I'll get to shatter like a glass Christmas ornament, fall at his feet, and beg him to fuck me. Knowing Cole, if I beg prettily enough, he'll do it.

But so far nothing. Not even a casual handshake.

What he *is* doing is saying he loves me a hundred times a day. He'll ask me for the remote, I'll hand it to him, and he'll say, "Thanks. You know I love you, right?" I finished the last of the milk and put the carton back in the fridge (just to piss him off), and he just tossed it in the trash with an, "It's fine. I still love you." He crawls into my bed at night and turns off his lamp with an "I love you so fucking much."

I'm gonna break. This is harassment, right?

Did I mention the pictures?

Yeah, I think one whole suitcase he brought over was just pictures of us. He blew them up from phone pics and slapped them in IKEA frames, staging them all over the house. He put a picture of Poppy and me right on my bedside table. It's the two of us snapped from behind in her kitchen. He must have taken it when we were making granola. She looks so good in her little silky pink shorts, her blonde hair in a messy braid over her shoulder. She's looking up at me like I hung the moon, and I'm laughing down at her like she's the funniest goddamn person I know.

Yeah, seeing that picture was a punch right to the chest.

He hung more pictures in the hallway. There's a large one of the two of us, an action shot from the ice a few weeks ago. The asshole even found some old pics from our Thunderbirds days. I was in a bleached hair phase. It was awful.

He put the framed yacht selfie of the three of us in Poppy's library room near the cozy reading chair. Pictures from karaoke night—me on the stage, Poppy too. I opened my underwear drawer this morning and got a nice little jump scare. Our dick pic. He printed it out and framed it like a total fucking lunatic.

He can't mean this, right? Or maybe he means it for now. But shit like this can't last. No one can ever be this happy. The other shoe always drops. People lose interest. They find another shiny object. They fade away.

Okay, *most* people fade away. Apparently, Leos don't.

I make my way down the hall to the bedroom to find Cole is already there. He's sitting shirtless on the bed in a pair of shorts, eyes on his phone, one foot propped up on a bunch of pillows. His heart stuff means he sometimes deals with swelling in his ankles. Most nights, if he's not icing his knees, he's propping up his feet.

He was gone most of the night, having dinner with Poppy since we leave tomorrow for a quick away. Thinking of them together, laughing and happy without me, was a perfect kind of torture. Did they fuck? Does she miss me?

As if in answer to my question, Cole glances over his phone. "Poppy says hi."

"She can say it her own damn self," I mutter. "We still work together." I step into the bathroom and flip on the light to brush my teeth.

"You could be living together," he calls over the sound of the running water. "She could be sitting in that tub soaking in a salt bath right now. She could get out, towel off, and crawl between these sheets and fall asleep with your cock in her hand."

I spit into the sink, putting my toothbrush away. "Don't be a dick."

"Don't keep her waiting much longer."

I go still, hands on the hem of my T-shirt. "She's waiting for me?"

He rolls his eyes, focusing his attention back on his phone. "Yeah, 'cause she's not the asshole I am. She still thinks you deserve space and time to process your feelings on your own. Childhood trauma is complex, Nov, and she respects that. But she's ready to start being happy again. She wants to be happy with *you*."

My heart drops with my shirt to the floor. "She's not happy?"

"Half her heart is missing," he replies with a shrug. "Are you happy?"

I just sit on the bed, leaning back against my stack of pillows.

"Wanna hear something cool?" he says after a minute.

"Sure."

We do this at night. We scroll on our phones and read out funny headlines and share cool animal facts. I'm expecting him to show me footage of some deep-sea jellyfish. Instead, he plays an alien sound. It's this weird *womp-womp-womp* heartbeat-sounding thing—

"Oh shit." I glance his way. "Is that . . ."

He nods. "Yeah. That's the heartbeat."

We're both quiet for a moment as we listen to it.

He shuts it off, a tense silence filling the empty space between us on the bed. "I've been trying really hard to keep it all together for Poppy, and just be there for her, and be excited . . . and be hopeful." He turns to look at me, tears in his eyes. "But the truth is that I am so fucking scared, Nov."

I take his hand. "What? Why?"

"I want it to be yours," he says, squeezing my hand. "I want it to be yours so fucking badly."

"Why?" I say again.

"Because you don't have my heart conditions. Nov, what if I hurt him? What if I set him up to fail? You can't get far on a weak heart. Trust me, I know."

"Hey." I roll up to my knees and grab his face in both my hands. "*Stop*. Do you hear me? Enough. Have the doctors given you any cause for concern?"

He shakes his head. "No. They say development looks normal."

"So then cling to that," I say, my tone firm. "Do you have a picture?"

He nods.

"Show me." Anything to calm him down and get his mind out of the bad place. I let him go, and he shows it to me. It's just a black image with a little white thing floating in the middle that looks like a peanut. "Is that it?"

"That's him," he replies with another nod.

My heart stops. "Him?"

He smiles. "Yeah, it's a boy. We'll have the full anatomy scan in a few weeks, but the doctor is like seventy percent sure. Poppy calls him Lentil."

"Well, we're changing that," I mutter, my eyes locked on the phone screen.

Poppy's having a boy, and Cole wants it to be mine. Another Novikov, with her pointy chin and my bad attitude? Oddly enough, I can picture it, a preppy little kid wearing Oshkosh and talking with his hands on his hips, just like his mom. He'll be a terror. He'll break my stuff and steal my car keys and talk his way out of everything because he'll have her blue eyes.

Fuck.

"Nov . . ."

I glance up at Cole, seeing the depth of his anxiety etched on every line of his face. "What?"

He groans, dropping the phone to his lap. "I don't know how to . . . I don't want to cross this line or push you. I mean, there's pushing you, and then there's *pushing* you—"

"Just say it." I wait, heart in my throat.

"Will you hold me?" he whispers. "Just for a minute. I just wanna try it out."

"Yeah," I say on a breath. "Yeah, Coley, I'll hold you."

We turn off our lamps, set aside our phones, and lie down on the bed. Unsure of exactly what he wants, I slide over across the middle of the bed onto his side. He rolls over, making space for me at his back. I slot myself in as the big spoon, wrapping one arm around his waist as I tuck the other up under the pillow.

We settle into each other, Cole, weaving our fingers together and tucking my hand up against his chest. We lie there, the heat of our skin transferring until it feels like we're a human furnace. I'm not asleep, and I know he's not either.

Brushing my lips to his shoulder, I whisper the words sitting heavy in my fragile, skittish heart. "I miss you so goddamn much."

Lifting my hand to his lips, he kisses my knuckles. "I didn't know I was looking for you until I found you. Now that I have, I'm not letting you go."

I breathe a sigh of relief, nestling my face at the nape of his neck. His comforting scent surrounds me, and I shut my eyes tight. For the first time since I bolted in LA, I don't try to crash into the oblivion of sleep. I stay present. I hold him in the dark, and I let myself imagine the possibility that someone could stay. I imagine that someone could really want me . . . love me.

Feeling bold, I imagine I could let them.

I stand under the shower's hot spray, eyes closed, mentally preparing for game day. This will be a quick away trip. I take stock of my body, doing my pre-game damage report. Shoulders feel tight, but a massage should help. My left knee is still aching from a hard hit earlier this week. I worry another bad over-extension might tear something. That's the last thing we need right now. We've already got Langers out with a knee injury.

My music plays from my phone on the counter as I turn, letting the water hit my front. I rub my face with a tired groan.

The music stops.

Leaning out of the spray, I open my eyes. Lukas is standing by the counter dressed in a backward hat, hockey tee, shorts, and socks with tennis shoes. Did he go for a run on game day? I fell asleep in his arms last night and woke up in an empty bed. The water keeps pouring down, hitting my chest and shoulder as I peer at him through the glass. "What?"

He opens his mouth and closes it again. Curling his hands into fists at his sides, he bobs once on the balls of his feet, swaying forward, then back.

I narrow my eyes. "Jeezus, you look like you're trying to do long division in your head. What?"

"I have something to say."

Silence stretches between us as I wait.

"I'm listening," I finally say.

He opens his mouth. Then he closes it and groans, cursing under his breath. This man is such a goddamn disaster. How is it possible I love him so much?

"Lukas—"

"No, I'm doing it," he shouts, one hand pressed to his forehead like feeling his feelings is physically hurting his brain. "Just give me a fucking second, alright? Jeez, you impatient fuck."

"Okay. Take your time—"

He drops his hand to his side with an irritated huff. "Fine. I love you, okay?"

The words hang in the air between us. I swallow back my smile, heart pounding as I look through the shower glass at him. His eyes are wide, like a cat who just swallowed a bug and now doesn't know what to do about it. "And?" I say.

His eyes narrow in frustration. "And what? You need more? Need me to recite you a goddamn poem? I'm not that guy, Cole. I'm *this* guy. I said it. That's what you wanted, right? That's what you've been waiting for? You wanted me to break. You wanted to move in here, and drive me crazy, and make me fucking desperate enough to confess how I feel." He shrugs, flapping his arms like an angry penguin. "Well, now I have, and you win. Alright? I didn't even last a week. You fucking win, Cole. Now, can you please stop torturing me?"

"How am I torturing you by just standing here?"

"By breathing!" He storms right up to the glass. "You're in my house, Cole. You're in my bed, and my kitchen, and my fucking shower! You're in *here*," he shouts, pointing at his temple with two fingers. "And I can't get you out. I miss you so goddamn much. You're standing right in front of me, and I miss you. You're right, I'm not happy, and it's not enough. It's like I can't even *breathe* without you and Poppy in my life. I'm angry all the time. I don't sleep. I'm losing weight. It's affecting my game, Cole. I haven't gotten an assist in three fucking weeks. Did you notice?"

"I noticed," I reply. "I notice everything about you. I never look away."

He lets out a breath with his whole chest, a flicker of relief passing across his face. "How do I fix this? How do we just go back?"

"We don't go back," I reply. "We go forward. No going back, Lukas."

"Just tell me what to do," he pleads. "I want you. I want Poppy. I want you both here in this house."

Heart racing, I search his face. "And the baby?"

He groans, rocking on his heels again. "Alright, I'll admit I'm still fucking terrified. I have no idea what the fuck I'm doing. But then, I have no idea what the fuck I'm doing most of the time," he adds with a shrug. "Hockey is the only thing I've ever been good at. It's the only thing I've ever fully understood. I don't know how to let people love me, and I definitely don't know how to handle a kid—and doing both those things scares me to death."

"You're allowed to be scared," I say. "I'm scared too. But you have to stay in the room. You can run circles inside it all you want. Hell, I'll buy you a treadmill. Then you can run all goddamn day. Just *stay* with us. That's all we want. Don't change. Don't become a whole new person. You're fine as the shitty mess that you are. Just *stay*."

Slowly he nods.

I can hardly breathe. God, is this happening? Did this actually work? Did I just fix us through the power of Leo obstinance and breaking and entering?

"So . . . what now?" he asks, looking so completely helpless.

I glare at him. "Are you fucking serious?"

"Will you please just tell me what to do before I burst through my fucking skin?"

I smile, feeling victorious. "Get in here."

He lets out a groan of relief before he's stepping around the open shower glass. He walks right into the shower with all his clothes on, and then he's in my arms. He steps under the spray with me, one arm around my shoulder and one around my waist as he kisses me. The shower soaks him in seconds, his gray T-shirt clinging to his broad shoulders.

I've never kissed a man before. The first thing I notice is his height. At six-foot-three, I'm usually the taller one in the equation. Poppy is a whole foot and change shorter than me. But Lukas is my height. There's no bending required to meet his lips. It's actually kind of nice.

He presses in, mouth slanting to taste me. Heart in my throat, I open for him, kissing him back. He's fully dressed and soaking wet, but I'm naked. Anywhere his hands touch, they're touching all of me. I'm fighting a shiver, even under the hot water.

"I don't know what I'm doing," he says against my lips, pressing his forehead to mine with his hands on my shoulders. "Cole, what do I do?"

"I don't know either," I admit, my hands at his waist over his wet T-shirt. "Do you wanna stop?"

He pulls away, searching my face. "I don't wanna stop. Do *you* wanna stop?"

I take a breath, the water pounding on my neck and back. "I don't wanna stop."

"What do I do?"

I smile. "Why don't you start with taking your clothes off."

He blinks, as if he's only just realized he walked in here with them on. He flips off his hat and kicks off his shoes, hopping like a flamingo on one leg to peel off his wet socks. Next to go is the shirt. It slops down to the shower floor, leaving him with all his colorful ink on display up his arms and over his shoulders. He has other ink too—over his ribs, along his side, down his hip.

He tucks his thumbs into the top of his shorts, about to tug them down, when I stop him.

"Wait."

He looks up at me, concern and rejection blooming on his face. "What—"

"Lukas, what the fuck is this?" I grab his arm and pull it to the side of the shower spray, tilting it up. There, wedged between a standing figure of Anubis and a pinup girl, is a small, cartoonish drawing of a hairy cock and balls.

He grins. "Oh, that."

I rub my thumb over it. "Lukas, this is fucking permanent. Is this a goddamn tattoo?"

"Yeah."

I stare at him. "You got a tattoo of a cock and balls on your arm?"

Still smiling, he just shrugs. "So? I liked it. Poppy drew it, and I was feeling nostalgic . . . and maybe a little vulnerable."

"How did you do it?"

"I showed a picture to the artist." He covers it with his hand. "Do you really hate it?"

Shaking my head, I cup his face in my hands. I'm gentle with the all-but-healed cut, pulling him back to me. "You're fucking crazy, and

I love you. Now, get on your knees, and show me how much you like a real one."

Grinning, he tugs his shorts to the floor and kicks them aside. Now we're just two coulda-fooled-me straight men naked in a shower. I let my gaze trail down his muscled chest to his abs, to the cut "V" of his waist. The man is completely hairless. I've never really paused to notice before. "Do you wax?"

"Duh. Why don't you?"

I skim a hand over the sparse coils of black hair on my chest, my fingers brushing over my raised sternotomy scar. "I don't know that my chest hair is gonna get in the way of you sucking my dick . . . unless you're just really bad at this."

Chuckling, he drops to his knees, his hands on my hips, my hard cock in his face. "This is the first dick I've ever sucked. Buckle in, bud. We could find out I have a rare lockjaw condition."

Stopping him with a hand under his chin, I tip his face up, my back blocking him from getting a face full of shower spray. "This is the *only* dick you suck."

"First and only," he says with a grin. Then his mouth is on my tip, and I'm bracing my hand against the goddamn shower glass. He's not as finessed as Poppy, but we're giving him an "A" for enthusiasm. He wraps a hand around my base, keeping one at my hip, and starts teasing the underside of my shaft with his tongue.

Okay, fuck me—no, this is good.

He pulls back with a slurp, looking up at me. "Good?"

I groan, the sound low in my throat. "Mhmm. Don't stop." I put a hand on the back of his head and direct him back on my dick, my other hand still pressed against the shower glass. I apply pressure, guiding him to go deeper as I make little thrusts with my hips.

When he groans, the vibration goes down my dick and straight to my gut, warming me up inside. Fuck, I'm already close. He groans again, pushing back into the pressure of my hand. "Go harder," he commands.

"Harder?"

"Come on, I've watched you face fuck Poppy a dozen times. If I'm gonna suck a dick, I'm sucking this dick. Make me choke—*fuck*—"

He laughs as I drag him over to the shower wall, pressing him back against it. With his head hitting the tile, I grip his hair and feed him my tip.

"Fucking take it," I growl. "Such a good boy on your knees for me. Swallow this cock."

He groans again, his hands wrapping around to grip my ass. He hollows his cheeks, pulling me in deeper until I feel him gag.

"Right fucking there," I pant. "You ready?"

He pushes on my hips, taking a breath, then I'm pushing right back, my dick tapping his throat as I thrust. "Fuck," I shout, feeling my climax coming. "Oh, fuck—I'm gonna come—"

He grips my hips tight, letting me pound his throat as I release with a torrent of muttered curses. He gags on my cum and I ease up, slipping out till just the tip is in his mouth. Gripping my dick, I stroke, rolling with my thumb up my shaft as a last spurt of cum hits his lips.

He groans again, licking it up, eyes closed as he sags against the shower wall. Reaching down, I rub my thumb all over his lips, working my cum in before the shower can wash it away. "Look at you," I croon, heart hammering. "You wear my cum so well. Gonna put you on your knees every damn day. Away travel just got a lot more interesting."

He grins, opening his eyes. "You gonna leave me aching down here, bud?" His hard dick is wet and dripping from the shower.

I pull on his shoulders. "Stand up." He gets to his feet, and I press an open-mouthed kiss to his lips, unafraid to taste myself on his tongue. "Turn around. Hands on the fucking wall."

He narrows his eyes at me. "If you think I'm gonna rock this bottom energy every time, think again. I've jerked off more than once to the image of me bending you over a locker bench and pounding your ass."

"We'll try that next time," I tease. "For now, you came into *my* shower, so it's my turn on top."

"Technically, it's my shower," he says as he dutifully turns around.

I press myself against him, wrapping a hand around his throat. I pull him to me. "Tell me the color of this tile, and I'll tattoo your name on my dick."

He groans, hands flat against the wall. His Adam's apple shifts under my hand as he swallows. "Tell me how to get Poppy back, and I'll tattoo both your names on mine."

I pin him with my hips and squirt some body wash into my palm. Wrapping my arm around his hip, I fist his dick, coating it in the silky soap.

"Oh, fucking god—" He drops his forehead to the wall of dark blue tiles (Smoke Blue, to be exact) and presses his hips against me.

I stroke him good, pretending his dick is mine. I know just how I like it. I work him slow, rocking my hips with his as he fucks into my hand.

"You're a fucking hand job wizard," he groans. "I want one of these every day. Fuck, why don't guys give more hand jobs to each other?"

"Right?" I tease. "You just enjoy, baby. Come into my fist when you're ready. I'll take my time. Want a finger in your ass?"

He groans, choking on a laugh as I circle my thumb over his tip. "I mean, I'll try anything once. I should probably start with a finger before I try a dick, right?"

"*My* dick," I growl, dropping my free hand down to smack his wet ass.

He sucks in a breath, his dick twitching in my hand. I lean in, smacking him again. "There's no *a* dick where you're concerned. Never the fuck again. You refer to my dick with the proper fucking pronouns."

He laughs, arching his body as he presses into the slow stroking of my hand. "Fuck me, you're so good at this."

"Show me how much you like it. Come for me. Can you come on command?"

"I'm usually the one giving commands—*ah*—"

I grip his shoulder tight and start stroking him hard and fast. "*Come.*"

"Oh, holy fuck," he cries, pressing his body against mine as his entire being becomes one raw, aching nerve of pleasure.

"Come for me, right the fuck now, you desperate fucking whore," I growl in his ear.

Elation has me soaring and power has me trembling as I feel him rock into me and come, no ass play needed. He drops a hand down around mine, gripping my fist tight as he unloads on the shower wall. I stroke him through it, not stopping until he's slumped against the wall and batting my hand away.

"We'll do the finger in the ass next time," I tease, giving his ass one last wet smack because I can. "Maybe Poppy can do the honors while I suck you down."

He just groans, still slightly incoherent. Slowly, he rolls with his shoulder, turning to face me. There's a look of bliss on his face. I smile because I know I put it there. Reaching out, I stroke his face. His parted lips brush my palm.

"I don't know how to keep this quiet around the other guys," he admits. "I don't want to."

"I know. I don't want to either. But we have to be whole first. We need Poppy."

His head is tipped back against the wall, eyes shut tight. "She hates me."

"She loves you more than her own life," I counter. "It's the only way she knows how to love."

"She's mad at me."

"She's hurt, and she's scared, and her trust in you is shaken. It's reparable."

He shakes his head. "She'll never trust me with this kid. Not after I told her I don't want one."

"You'll show her you're ready. You'll do what you do best."

He frowns, opening one eye to squint at me. "Play hockey?"

I sigh, giving his half-hard dick a tap. He winces, shifting away with a muttered curse. "I meant you'll be you," I say. "Be a chaotic double Scorpio and show her with action. You love her, right?"

He rolls his head to glare at me. "Don't be a dick."

I sigh. "Okay, well, show her with action, but at least *once* you're gonna need to say those three little words, Nov."

He rubs his hand absently over his new cock and balls tattoo. "Fuck, why is this so hard?"

I give his shoulder a reassuring squeeze. "Welcome to an adult relationship. Now, clean your jizz off my shower tiles. And get ready quick. We're gonna be late for the plane."

69
POPPY

Listen, there are no guarantees in public relations. You can think a story angle is compelling, and pray it brings you some good press, only for it to fall flat. You can post an innocent picture of a player standing by a balloon arch, and have that picture become a banner cry for environmental reform. Social media is a hellscape. Fans choose violence every day.

In the midst of this chaos, there is one true and good thing left on this earth. Cute animals. It doesn't matter who you are—your religious affiliation, your stance on rainbow-colored tape on hockey sticks. Everyone loves cute baby animals.

So, when the Jacksonville Humane Society approached me, asking if the Rays would like to be an official sponsor, I jumped at the chance. Today, we're shooting our first promo. All the animals featured will be available for adoption at tomorrow's home game.

Working with Claribel and our media team, we get everything set up for an on-ice commercial spot. We've got the banners set, the carpet is all laid out, the animals are ready. Now, where the heck are my hockey players?

"You told them all eleven o'clock, right?" I say at Claribel.

A few of the dogs yip excitedly in their cages.

"I told them eleven," she replies.

I groan, pulling out my phone. It's almost 11:30 a.m. I don't have any missed texts or calls. "Who all volunteered?"

"Morrow, Jake Price—Woody was in, but he had to leave," Claribel reads out from her phone.

"I guess I can see if any more players are hanging around. Otherwise, you're gonna have to pick up that Chihuahua and say 'cheese.'" I turn around and groan with relief. Colton is walking toward me, a smile on his face. My own smile falls to see who is walking at his side.

Oh god, has Lukas gotten more beautiful in the time we've been apart? How is that possible? How is it fair? It's not like I haven't seen him around, but I've been doing my best to keep my distance. I don't let myself get too close. Certainly not this close. The wanting is just too painful.

My eyes immediately fix on the thin red line along his jaw. The cut ends at his hairline right above his ear. Heavens, it could've been so much worse. An inch or two lower or higher ...

I swallow, pushing that fear down deep. The doctors did an amazing job. It should heal up well, leaving hardly any scar.

"Look who I found," Colton says in greeting, a hand on Lukas's shoulder. "He heard we were doing a pet adoption, and he just couldn't volunteer fast enough."

Claribel glances between the three of us with a smirk. She may have caught me kissing Colton last week.

"You're late," I say, nerves on fire.

Why is Lukas looking at me like that?

"You said 11:30," Colton replies.

"No, I said—" I let out a breath. "It doesn't matter. I'm just glad you're here." I wave forward our Human Society rep. "Okay, so Wendy is gonna get you set up with your animals, while Claribel and I go track down a few more warm bodies."

"Pop—" Colton calls after me as I spin away.

Oh goodness, what is happening right now? I mean, Colton's kept me informed over the past few days as he's been camped out over at Lukas's house. I think the idea is mad and, frankly, a little invasive. I mean, if I made it clear I wanted out of a relationship, if I made it clear I didn't want the child that was the product of that relationship, I think I'd be pretty upset if my ex-partner then moved himself into my freaking house.

Colton assures me it's the right plan of action, and that he's "helping him get out of his own way." I'm personally less convinced. I love Lukas, and I want him with us, but he has to want to be with us. He's right, I'm done accepting anything less than what I deserve, and I deserve to not have to beg him to love me.

I spy Ryan Langley sitting in the stands at the other practice rink. Oh, he's perfect. With that baby face and the green eyes and the floppy blond hair? Shove a puppy in his hands, and you have PR gold. Waving him down, I call out. "Yoo-hoo, Ryan!"

He looks like a bunny who just got his name called by the Big Bad Wolf. Behind me, Claribel snorts. Am I really that scary?

I step up into his bleacher row and walk toward him. "Hi, Ryan. You got a minute?"

"What's up, Poppy?" he says in welcome, giving Claribel a nod.

"We're looking for one more Ray to help us with this commercial spot, and you're perfect. Come on."

"Well—wait—"

I glance back.

"I—" He groans, shifting his weight as he gestures out to the ice where the other forwards are skating. "Well, I can't just leave. Coach wants me watching practice."

"This will only take a few minutes," I say. "Now, come on, handsome. The camera crew is waiting."

He follows us down the bleachers. "What are we doing?"

"We've partnered with the Jacksonville Humane Society to shoot a pet adoption promo," I explain as we turn the corner. "I found one," I call out with a wave to our waiting camera crew.

I try not to let my heart flip at the sight of Lukas and Colton laughing and holding dogs. Well, Colton is laughing. He's holding the cutest little Labrador mix. The yellow puppy licks his chin and I think my ovaries are going to explode.

Too late. I'm already pregnant.

"Nov, look," he says as the puppy squirms. "Look, I think he likes me."

I glance at Lukas and fight a smile. He looks miserable. He's holding the ugliest dog I've ever seen. It's a little Chinese Crested, with a poof of white hair on his head. Otherwise, his speckled pink skin is completely hairless. I smirk at Wendy. Did she do this on purpose? The poor thing looks more miserable than Lukas.

"Come on, this is bullshit," Lukas says at me. It's the first words he's spoken to me in eight days. "You know I'm allergic to dogs."

"Which is why I gave you the hypoallergenic one," I reply, flashing a wink at Wendy.

"Dude, I told you, that's not a dog," says Colton. "It looks like that thing that sits on Jabba the Hutt in *Return of the Jedi*."

"Ryan, come take your pick," I call. "We've got a cute little bulldog over here, a few kitties—oh, sweet heavens—look at the way she's looking at me." My heart is suddenly fit to burst as I take in a fluffy gray and white kitten with big green eyes peering out through the bars of her cage. The little thing puts her white paws up, mewing at me like I'm her momma. I stick out a finger, brushing it over her soft little toes. She sniffs my finger and I wanna die. "Claribel, tell me I don't need a cat," I whine, feeling like my heart will break if they take this kitten away from me. Screw love at first sight between humans. This right here is the purest kind of love.

"You don't need a cat," Claribel says at my shoulder.

"Can we hurry this up?" Lukas calls out. "This thing is hairless, and this is an ice rink. I think it's getting frostbite."

Pulling my finger away from the precious fur baby, I huff, flicking my ponytail off my shoulder. "Hold your horses. And it's not a *thing*, Lukas," I add, feeling raw and vulnerable under his heavy stares. "It's a dog. A very rare breed of dog called a Chinese Crested."

"It's shivering, and it can smell my fear," he says with a scowl.

Okay, who spit in his cereal? Why did he even come?

Ryan is the perfect distraction, stepping in with his big body to block me from Lukas. "So, uhh, what's the deal here?"

"We're shooting a short commercial for the Humane Society," I explain. "It will go on all our socials too. Just pick an animal and take the card on top of their cage. Then you read out what's on the card in front of the camera."

"You, uhh . . . you want me to read what's on the card?"

"Mhmm." I take one off the top of the bulldog's cage. "So, this one says her name is Gracie, and she's a five-year-old American Bulldog. She's house trained, loves kids, blah, blah, blah. Just read the card." Slapping the card to his chest, I turn, taking a deep breath. "Colton, you're up first."

He's still standing with Lukas, tickling his puppy's tummy. "Dude, I swear, I'm gonna adopt this little guy myself."

"At least yours has fur," says Lukas. "I feel like I'm holding a raw chicken."

Colton snorts as they both follow me over to the camera spot. Lukas steps in at my back. "Hey—can we talk after this?"

Down the other end of the rink, the goalies still haven't finished their practice. "Hey, can you stop slapping pucks for five minutes," I shout. "You can stay in the shot, but we need some quiet for this."

Eric glares at me. "You realize this is a hockey rink, and this is a hockey practice!"

"I reserved this rink for 11:30," I call back. "You were supposed to be done a half hour ago. Now, clear off my ice, or I'll drag you *all* in front of the camera. Yes, I mean you too, Eric!"

He knows I don't actually mean it. Eric is tough as nails as a coach, but a big softie once he steps off the ice. A box of my homemade toffee nut cookies will smooth this over easily.

Lukas isn't deterred by my pathetic dodge. He's right there at my back, still cradling that poor little dog like it's a pit viper. "I'd like to talk to you," he says again, "After this—like, not now. Not holding this," he adds at the shivering dog.

"Lukas, I have an impossible day—"

"Five minutes of your time," he pleads.

"Hear him out," Colton says.

I glance between them. "Please don't do this here," I whisper, knowing the camera man is approaching. "Please. I'm barely holding it together."

With a stiff nod, Lukas steps away.

It only takes them a few minutes each to shoot their spots. Colton goes first, charming the cameras with his little rundown of "Pepper" the puppy. The camera angle is perfect for when the excited puppy starts to pee, and we all laugh.

Lukas is also a natural. He sells the hell out of that little hairless dog. I can't help but smile as I watch him. A picture flashes in my mind of him holding our baby like that, laughing and smiling as he swings him toward the camera, just to make him squeal. The image feels so real, it makes my heart physically hurt. I have to step away.

"Okay, Ryan," I call out. "You're up. Did you pick your animal? Let's go, honeybun. We don't have all morning."

Ryan is distracted talking to Mars. The goalie towers over him in his full kit.

"Ryan," I call again.

"We're coming," he says. "Mars and I are gonna shoot the spot together."

"Oh ..." I glance between them, confused. Mars Kinnunen Price *never* volunteers to help with this kind of thing. It's usually all we can do to get him to sit for press conferences to talk about hockey. "Oh, that's wonderful," I say, hurrying over.

Ryan steps over to the row of cages and pulls out the tiny gray and white kitten.

My heart squeezes tight again. "Oh, my goodness, that kitten is double cute."

He holds it close to his chest, and I step in, unable to help myself from giving her a few pets, wiggling my finger under her chin. She turns her little face up, purring like she's got a box of marbles in her chest. How can such a big sound come from such a tiny animal?

"You're just the sweetest thing," I coo at her. "Yes, you are. Yes, you are." Ducking down, I give her a few kisses. She flicks her fluffy tail in my face and my heart literally bursts. This cat is now my child. I'm convinced.

"Uhh ... Pop?"

Realizing I have my hands on Ryan's arms and my face nuzzled into his chest, I stiffen. Slowly, I right myself, flashing him a smile. I'm a working professional, and yes, I'm going to pieces over a cat. Let me live. "Are we ready then, gentlemen?" I glance from Ryan to Mars, who is still in his full hockey kit, sweaty hair tied up in a messy bun. Honestly, the aesthetic works. "You got the card?"

"Got it," he says, holding it up.

I just can't help myself. I have to know. It's a fate thing. The dice are rolling, and the lives of one cat and one pregnant woman now hang in the balance. "What's the kitten's name?"

Mars glances down at the card and frowns, shooting a glare over at Ryan. "Miss Princess."

Be still my freaking heart. I turn back to Ryan, desperate to pet her again. The mother-child bond is nearly complete. "Oh, it's perfect," I squeal. "She is *such* a little princess."

I can feel Lukas and Colton watching me. The pressure of their eyes is enough to have me ready to melt onto this ice. But I can't focus on them right now. This is my job. We're at work. I can't run to Lukas and shake his shoulders, begging him to tell me all the deep dark secrets of his heart. I can't crash through these cameras and announce to the world that I'm pregnant and in love with two men.

What I *can* do is run this commercial shoot . . . and hopefully adopt this kitten.

TO LUKAS

In all the chaos of the pet adoption, Poppy found a way to slip my damn net. I blame the forwards. They finished their practice and came over to our rink, and then it was a free-for-all. Sully, Karlsson, and Jonesy all wanted to pet the animals and pose with them too.

Poppy was a swirl of lavender, getting us all in front of the camera, trading out dogs for cats. There was even a rabbit that Sully decided to adopt for his kids. At one point, the bulldog got loose and went slipping across the ice. Then the Humane Society rep tried to take a snake out of a box, and that pretty much ended things. Mars was the only one brave enough to hold it for the camera.

Cole had to duck out for a PT checkup, so I'm left alone to find Poppy. I walk down the wall of the rink, searching for any sign of her lavender pantsuit. I pass the equipment room where they keep the Zamboni and some ice shovels and sweepers. That's when I hear a soft little sound that has me turning. There in the corner, Poppy is sitting on an overturned bucket, phone in hand, crying.

Rage fills my chest as my first thought is vengeance. Who made my Poppy cry? I look all around, searching for the culprit as I stalk into the room. "What happened?"

She looks up at me, blurry tears in her eyes. "I was denied."

I drop down on one knee, my hand brushing her arm. She stiffens, and it breaks my fucking heart. I did this. I made my girl wanna pull away from me. Swallowing my frustration, I say, "What are you talking about?"

"My application," she says, her voice all soft and weepy.

Wait, she's sending out job applications? Is she leaving? Did Cole fucking know and not tell me? Oh god, did she get fired? If she got fired because of us, I'm gonna march straight up to Mark's office and—

Calm down. Ask first.

"Poppy, did you get fired?"

She blinks up at me, eyes wide with confusion. "What? God—*no*," she cries. "I'm talking about my pet adoption application."

"You're trying to adopt one of the animals?"

She nods, sniffing back her tears.

"Which one?"

"Miss Princess," she replies, her bottom lip trembling.

I try to think back. "The cat?"

Please say it wasn't the fucking snake.

"Yeah, the sweet little gray and white kitty. I put in an application, but it turns out I can't have pets at the apartment. It's in the lease agreement I signed. The units are owned by the team, and there's a 'no pet' policy."

"Well, that's fucking dumb," I say. "Just don't tell anyone you have it. The thing is like the size of a cotton ball. Hide it in a teacup if the pet police come knocking. That's what Sanny did with Poseidon."

She just shakes her head. "Caleb already had his dog. The shelter called the apartment complex as part of the reference check. They know it's not allowed, and they denied my application. Which means I'm gonna lose her."

Okay, I was really hoping this would go differently. I wanted to sweep her off her feet with a bold declaration and kiss her senseless. That's how they do it in all her movies. But now she's a crying, snotty mess. I rock back on my heels, thinking fast. "I'll adopt it."

She goes still. "What?"

"Sure," I say with a shrug. "I'll adopt the cat."

She huffs, digging in her pocket for a tissue. "Lukas, you hate cats."

"So?"

"So, you're not adopting a cat you're gonna hate, just to hold some kind of weird emotional leverage over me. I can't do that with you. It's too much. It's too hard."

My gut squeezes tight and I take her hand. "Poppy, no. That's not what I—"

She gasps, eyes wide as she points down at my arm with her free hand. "Lukas, what is *that*?"

I follow her point down to my newest tattoo. Right. She hasn't seen it yet. "Okay, so—"

She tugs me forward to inspect it. Just like Cole, she rubs a thumb over it, praying that will smear the ink. "Lukas, is this permanent?"

I can't help but chuckle. "Well, yeah. It's a tattoo—"

She chokes on a shriek as she shoves my arm away and stands, nearly tripping over the bucket. "Lukas Novikov, tell me you did *not* permanently brand your body with a cartoon doodle of a penis!"

Slowly, I stand too, facing her. My heart is fucking racing. This is the moment, right? This is the moment I tell her? "I didn't *not* do it."

"Oh my god, you are *so* irresponsible."

"What? It's just a tattoo. I have like fifty others—"

"Yeah, tasteful, beautiful pieces of art," she cries, waving at the rest of the tattoos on my arms. She's seen them all, inspected them, asked for stories about them. The memories of her, warm and soft and naked in my arms while I took her on a tour of my tattoos, is something I hold deep in my chest, buried with whatever part of me holds my soul.

I cross my arms, making sure the cock and balls tattoo is visible. "Well, this is art to me. *You* drew it."

She shakes her head, arms crossed, mirroring my stance. "You walk away without a second look. For weeks, you freeze me out, freeze Colton out. And then you do *this*? I wanna know why! Why would you get that as a freaking tattoo?"

"Because I fucking missed you! I was sad, and alone, and feeling like my entire life was caving in on me. I was so fucking desperate, feeling like the only thing I could do to make the pain stop hurting was to go numb. And the only way I've ever been able to go numb before was through drinking or sex. Well, I couldn't drink because I had a game."

Her eyes go wide as she steps away from me, the walls of her heart slamming shut.

Oh, fuck.

"No, no," I say quickly, raising my hands toward her. "Poppy, I just *thought* about doing it. Old habits die hard, right? I thought I'd lost you both forever. I wanted to die—"

"What were you going to do?" she says through her tears.

I shake my head, my tone firm. "I didn't do it."

"What were you going to do, Lukas?" she asks again.

She's not gonna stop until I say it. "I didn't go out and fuck someone else, Poppy. I swear on my fucking life, I haven't been with *anyone* since I walked away from you." But then I'm groaning. "Well, I mean, *technically*, I have. But—"

"Goodbye, Lukas." She darts around the other side of the Zamboni.

"Poppy, *no*! It's not like that. Just wait—"

"Just get away from me, Lukas."

I grab her arm, pulling her to a stop. "It was Cole."

She tries to pull away from me. "Let me go—"

"I was with Cole," I say again, and she stops struggling.

Panting, she searches my face, tears in her eyes. "You and Cole?"

I nod. "Me and Cole. We fucked yesterday. We figured you wouldn't mind, seeing as you want us all to be together anyway. Cole isn't cheating, he's *ours*." My voice breaks with the depth of my emotion. I cup her face, stepping in. "Poppy, I would *never* cheat on you. I got this stupid tattoo as a reminder that I'd have to be a dick to ever think there would be a woman who comes after you. It's only ever gonna be you, me, and Cole."

"And the baby," she says, her tone quiet, distant. "Which you've made clear you don't want."

I let her go, taking a deep breath. "Okay, listen—"

Before I can get another word in, she's going stiff and pulling away from me. I turn to see Shelby and Sully wandering up, arms around each other.

"Hey, guys," Shelby chimes. "You two coming to the party tonight?"

I groan. Shelby has a birthday party tonight, and we all said we'd go.

Poppy takes a step back, trying to wipe under her eyes. Shelby notices. "Everything okay here?" she asks, glancing between us.

"We're fine," I say.

We're not fine. This was a disaster, and Cole's officially gonna kill me. Forget me running this time. He's gonna shove me head-first into a cannon, and light the fuse. Maybe I should've tried sarcasm. That always tends to work better for me with her. I bait her a little, she rises to it, then I swoop in with the charm. Why the hell did I go for sincere?

"Party starts at seven," says Sully, also glancing between us.

"I don't think I'll make it," says Poppy. "Sorry, Shelbs. I'm just not feeling very well."

"Oh, that's too bad," says Shelby, reading through the lie. She looks suspiciously over at me.

Fuck me. What does a guy have to do to get a little privacy in the workplace to confess his undying love to his pregnant secret ex-girlfriend?

"Excuse me," says Poppy, using the O'Sullivans as human shields to escape me.

I have no choice but to watch her walk the fuck away.

"What the hell was that about?" Sully says, glaring at me.

Feeling desperate, I turn to them. "I need your help."

Shelby still looks wary. "What do you need?"

"I want to adopt a cat for Poppy, but I don't know how. Will you help me?"

She narrows her eyes at me. "Why would you adopt a cat for Poppy?"

"Aren't you allergic to cats?" Sully adds.

Taking a deep breath, I finally say those three little words . . . I just say them to the wrong fucking person. "Because I love her. I am so in love with her that it's physically hurting me. And she wants that cat, but she can't have that cat, so I'm gonna get her that fucking cat, or die trying. Do you understand me? I will die to get her that cat, Shelby. Now, I ask again. Will you help me?"

11

LUKAS

To their credit, the O'Sullivans only ask a few pointed questions before they take pity on me. Shelby helps me adopt the cat, while Sully runs interference. He makes my excuses to the rest of the guys. Apparently, they're all hanging out at the beach before Shelby's party. But I don't have time to hang out. I need a plan . . . and a litter box.

With the kitten in a carrier, I drive over to the nearest pet store. Pathetic mewing sounds squeak from the carrier as I walk up to the first person I see. She's a tiny redhead who looks like she's fifteen. But she's wearing a badge, which makes her more competent than me.

"Yeah, hi. I just adopted this cat for my girlfriend, and I need help." She eagerly helps me collect the basics.

Cole calls while I'm in the cat treat aisle. With a groan, I answer. "What?"

"Where the hell did you go?"

"It's complicated," I reply, tossing two bags of treats into the cart.

"Well, where is Poppy? Did you talk to her?"

"I'm putting together my grand gesture as we speak. Tomorrow morning, I need you to get Poppy, and bring her over to the house, okay? We'll show her the library with all the books, the walk-in closet, and the room for the nursery. I have Janice and her team coming over in an hour to get started."

"You're putting a nursery in?"

I huff, hand on my hip as the kitten glares at me through the mesh of her carrier. "Well, where the hell else is the baby gonna sleep, Cole? The roof? The fucking garage, like he's a goddamn scooter?"

"Well, where are you?"

"Pet store," I reply.

He groans. "You realize you shop for baby supplies at a *baby* store, right? Not a pet store. Do I need to come over there and help you?"

"Shut up. I adopted a cat." I push the cart down the toy aisle, eyes wide as I take in the bright feathers, lasers, and crinkly balls.

"But you fucking hate cats."

"I know I hate cats, but Poppy loves this thing. She wanted to adopt it, but they wouldn't let her, and she was freaking out. I tried to calm her down, but that backfired, so I adopted the cat."

"What do you mean it backfired?"

I stop the cart. "Listen, I'm not gonna do this with you, okay? We hit a little speed bump, but I'm fixing it. We'll both stay outta the house tonight to let Janice work. We'll go to Shelby's party, make an appearance, and tomorrow morning, we'll pounce. Grand gestures, okay? Love and family and chocolate lava cake in Aruba."

He's quiet for a moment. "Fine. I trust you."

Fuck me, those three little words almost sound sweeter than the "L" word.

As if the asshole can read my mind, he adds, "And I love you, Lukas."

My heart skips as I let out a breath. "Yeah."

"Say it back, or I'm not hanging up."

I roll my eyes, smiling like an idiot. "I love you too, Colton."

"Of course you do. I'm a damn catch." With that, he hangs up.

Slipping my phone in my pocket, I smirk down at the cat. "See? I don't need your validation. You can keep making that mad face all you want because Cole loves me." I pause for a second. It can't harm to practice a little more, right? "And I love Poppy." I take the cat out of the carrier and let her sniff the toys. "Now, will you pick something you want, so we can get out of here?"

Driving back from the pet store, the cat quiet in her carrier, I can't get my mind to stop humming. I mean, it's kind of handy, right? Not only do they have everything you could ever need for a pet in there, but they have grooming services, training classes, a vet, books on animals.

And if a store can have all that stuff for a cat, then they definitely have it for human babies too, right? I mean, it might sound dumb, but this is sort of a revelation for me. I've been sitting here spinning my wheels for weeks thinking I would be the worst thing that ever happened to a kid. I don't know anything about being a parent. It's not like I ever had one. I've never even held a baby. But I wasn't born playing hockey either. I learned how to skate, then I learned how to handle the puck, then I learned the rules of the game. One step at a time. I was never alone. I always had a team there to show me how to do things better.

Poppy, Cole, and me—we can be a team. I really think we can do this. And I'm not gonna be the weak side here. I'll get the books; I'll go to the classes. If this kid is mine, I'm not gonna abandon him the way I was abandoned. I'm not gonna make him someone else's problem.

What the hell am I saying? Of course the kid is mine. Even if he's Cole's, he's mine too. I'm in this, right? That's what I want. I want the three of us together . . . soon to be the four of us.

A team. A *family*.

Holy fuck. Just saying it inside my own head is so fucking scary. When it comes to hockey teams, there's always a trade clause. There's always a way to make me someone else's problem. But not with this. There's no trades on this team. There's no walking away. If I join, I'm in it for the long haul.

I take a deep breath, both hands on the wheel as I gaze out through the windshield. My truck coasts up the bridge over the intracoastal waterway, the bright blue of the water almost blinding in its beauty.

Fuck me, am I about to cry?

I let out a shaky breath. I want this. I want *them*. Poppy, Cole, the baby. Our son. God, he's gonna be so beautiful. Holy shit, it's a whole other person. And I want all of it. For once in my life, I want to belong somewhere and know it's not temporary. I want to go home.

God, please let Poppy still want me too.

JANICE and her team spend the afternoon remodeling the bedroom upstairs, while I spend most of it on the floor of my bathroom, trying to get Miss Princess to eat or drink something. It's gonna be a great show of my parenting skills if I can't even keep a cat alive for one fucking night.

By seven o'clock, I'm scrambling to leave. Fuck, I'm so late for this stupid party. I don't even want to go, but now I feel like I owe Shelby and Sully. I mean, it's a costume birthday party for a grown-ass adult. We're supposed to come as our favorite fictional character.

I pick up Cole at Langley's place. Both of them are fresh off the beach, looking sandy and salty as they force me into my costume. The three of us are dressed as bikers from *Sons of Anarchy* with jeans, white T-shirts, and fake leather biker vests.

"Everything good?" Cole says as we get in the truck.

I nod. "Yeah, Janice just texted. They're still working."

"And you went with the ocean explorer theme?"

"I sent her all your mood boards," I assure him. I don't know the first thing about decorating any room, let alone a nursery, so Cole put together some ideas. All I know is I saw a lot of blue paint and a large stuffed octopus.

We roll up to the party, and it's already in full swing. Dance music pulses and colored lights flash in the windows. As we're crossing the lawn, Coley cries out, nearly knocking Langers over. "Jesus," he shouts. "Dude, what the fuck?"

We all turn to see a grim reaper-looking fucker wander out of the shadows.

"Who the fuck is that?" Cole shouts. "Who are you?"

"Dude, chill," comes a deep voice. "It's me." Dave-O pulls back his hood and the three of us sigh with relief. "Pretty cool, huh?" he says, gesturing to the costume.

"It's not a haunted house, asshole," Coley snaps. "It's a birthday party."

I just grin. Cole doesn't like horror movies. He's worse than Poppy when it comes to jump scares.

"Yeah, but this was left over from Halloween," Dave-O says with a shrug.

They keep bickering as I lead the way inside. We hit the front entry, and J-Lo and Lauren are there wearing bright blue and pink wigs. Lauren's pink dress is covered with flowers, and J-Lo is in robes of black, a little skull pinned to his chest.

I grin. *Hercules* happens to be one of my favorite movies. "Whoa, cool costume, J," I say. "Hades, right?"

"And his darling wife, Persephone," Lauren chimes, throwing an arm around his shoulders.

Just then, Teddy the PT intern goes dancing past between us, moving like he's got noodles for legs.

"Who are you supposed to be?" Langers says with a laugh.

Teddy turns, double fisting his beers. He's wearing a long blue bathrobe that has silver stars stapled to it. And he has a Santa beard strapped to his chin. "I'm Merlin," he says, swaying toward me. "Aw, damn. Where's my hat?" He looks all around. "It makes more sense with the hat."

With a sigh, I slip one of the beers out of his hand and pass it to Langers. Then I snag the other one as Teddy goes stumbling off. "This party is gonna get messy," I mutter, taking a sip of the beer.

Wishing I was anywhere else, I lead the way toward the kitchen. We can't leave until Shelby and Sully see us—

Fuck.

I stop, fisting tight to my beer. Standing at the other end of the hall, holding a red Solo cup adorned with fruit and a little pink umbrella, is my Poppy. Oh fuck, she's not supposed to be here. She said she wasn't coming. I had hours yet. The house isn't even ready. Janice texted when we arrived that she's still doing paint touchups. Why is she here?

Cole stops too, glancing between us. Langers nearly knocks into me. "Guys—what?"

What the hell is she wearing?

She's in a long dress, and she's done something with her hair to pin curls around her face like a bunch of grapes.

"You said you weren't coming," I say.

She stiffens.

Great. Smooth. Just fucking perfect. Now tell her the cat won't eat.

"Well, obviously, I changed my mind," she replies.

This is all out of order. She can't be here now. Everything is planned for tomorrow. You can't just change the plans on a hockey player. We crave the structure of routine. "But you said—"

"Cool it," says Cole, placing a hand on my arm. He knows I'm spiraling. Do I tell her now? Right here in this hallway in front of

Langley and the drunk PT intern dressed as half a Merlin? "Not here," he says, and I breathe a sigh of relief.

No, that's good. We wait. I can do this.

"Guy's what's up?" says Langley, pushing his way between us.

Poppy's eyes go wide, as if she didn't even notice he was there. "Oh—hi, Ryan. Nice costumes." Hiding her nerves, she takes a sip from her cup.

"Hey, Poppy," says Langley, all bright and cheery. "Who are you supposed to be?"

She sighs. "Honestly, I should've just made a sign and worn it around my neck. I'm Elizabeth Bennett." She gestures down her costume with a flourish.

The three of us glance confused at each other, and she huffs, hand on her hip. That defiant posture stirs my dick awake. Wait, is she annoyed with me right now? Sad and upset are one thing. Those emotions scare me. But angry and annoyed? Hell, that's one small step away from sex as far as we're concerned.

"Elizabeth Bennett?" she repeats with a raised brow, that attitude shining through. "Only one of the greatest romantic heroines of all time? From *Pride & Prejudice*?"

"That's a movie?" Cole asks.

Surprising the hell out of me, tears spring to her eyes as she glares between the three of us, but mostly she glares at me. "This is why you boys only attract the likes of puck bunnies! Cause any woman of class, taste, and sense knows to steer clear!"

I barely have time to process the words before she storms right through us and marches away. Cole is pressed back against the wall, and Langers just looks supremely confused. So . . . maybe she's a step past angry? I'm trying to mentally recalibrate. Fuck, why are feelings so hard? Oh god, this is bad, right?

Langers is looking at me like I have all the answers, when all I really have is a tongue that suddenly feels like it's too big for my fucking mouth. "Ignore her," I say. "She's just upset because she couldn't adopt that cat."

He nods, but I can tell he doesn't buy my dodge. Meanwhile, Cole is gonna burn holes into the back of my head with his laser eyes. I'm on autopilot as I turn away, moving deeper into the house. My mind is racing. This changes everything. I can't possibly wait until tomorrow, right? Poppy's here, and she's mad, and this can't fucking wait.

But then Shelby is smiling at me and all the people in the kitchen start waving me forward.

"Guys, I found Shelbs," I say over my shoulder.

Cole comes up right behind me, his hand on my neck, giving it a squeeze. I feel it like a fucking brand. His silent command is heard loud and fucking clear. *Fix this.*

We say hello to Shelby and Sully. I think I even ask a question. Something about her costume. I don't even fucking know. I don't care. We have to find Poppy. It's Cole who peels away first, and then I'm chasing after him, grabbing his arm in the hallway. "What the fuck do we do?"

He rounds on me, eyes blazing. "Fix this now, or I swear to fucking god, it'll be *you* who sleeps in the garage like a goddamn scooter."

I groan. "But I had a plan. Tomorrow we were gonna—"

"Plans change," he says over me. "Hell, *all* my plans have changed, thanks to you. I was finally ready, Lukas. I had the career, my health, the life of my dreams, and I finally had the fucking girl. Poppy is the dream I've been chasing for two goddamn years. She's my future, and I had her in my hands. I was done. I was set. She was the one."

"Cole, I—"

He leans in, jabbing a finger at my chest as he lowers his voice. "But then *you* skated into my life with that stupid fucking shit-eating grin, and your pranks, and your bad attitude. You got between me and Poppy and drove me fucking crazy . . . until you stayed between me and Poppy and drove me even crazier."

"Bud, I'm sorry—"

"Now here I am, completely uninterested in the life I'd imagined," he says over me. "You have ripped that future from me, and fucking shredded it, Lukas." He lets out a breath, his gaze softening as he looks at me. "And in its place, you've handed me a new picture framed in gold."

My heart fucking stops.

He steps in, his hand going to my waist. "There's an engagement ring sitting in a box that I will never give to the woman I love. Do you understand? Because I would never put her in the position of having to choose between us—and there *is* an us, Lukas. The three of us. I'm not choosing between you, so why should she? Poppy wants us both, she loves us both, and she deserves us both." He steps in closer, mouth against my ear. "Now, get your head out of your goddamn ass, and go get our girl back."

Taking a deep breath, I let it out. "Right. Let's do this."

He steps away and nods. "Let's fucking do this."

I lead the way as we search the house looking for her. We check all the rooms on the first floor before making our way up the stairs. I'm starting to panic, thinking she left, when I open the door to one of the bedrooms and find her sitting on the bed, clutching a princess crown pillow to her chest.

Taking in the determined look on my face, she clutches tighter to the pillow and slowly stands. Fuck, she's so beautiful, with her bright blue eyes, and that pointed chin.

I'll never deserve her, and I know that. If I were a better man, I'd walk away and never look back. I'd free her of the burden of having to love me and put up with all my bullshit. But this woman is mine, and I'm hers, and Cole is ours, and I'm going to make her understand that I am never leaving again.

"Lukas, please," she says on a breath.

Squaring my shoulders, I hold her gaze. "Poppy, I love you."

I cling to this little sparkly crown pillow like it's a life saver as Lukas comes blasting into the room professing his love. "Don't do this," I plead, my hope mingling with my fear. "Please, not here."

"No, we're doing this right the fuck here," he replies. "Because I can't go on for another second without you."

Colton steps in behind him, shutting the door. They're blocking my only exit . . . unless I want to flee out the window and shimmy down the rain gutter. In a show of solidarity, Colton steps around Lukas and crosses the room to my side. I sigh with relief as his hand goes to my shoulder. He gives it a gentle squeeze and I go still.

Wait . . . is he here for me, or for Lukas?

I look up at him, pleading.

"Hear him out," he says.

Slowly, I turn back to Lukas, heart hammering in my chest. He looks so nervous. He's clenching his fists and swallowing, jaw tight. He licks his lips, once, parting them as if to speak, but nothing comes out.

Next to me, Colton sighs. "Nov—"

"No, I'm doing it," he snaps at him. "I'm just coming up with the right words. I thought I had more time, you know? I had this all planned out for tomorrow."

"Tomorrow?" I glance between them.

"Yeah, Cole was gonna bring you over to the house, and we were gonna show you what we've been working on."

"What have you been working on?"

"Renovations," he replies. "For you. For the family. Cole worked with the interior designer you suggested, and he added a whole walk-in closet for you, Pop. And there's a library. There are so many books, baby. And this cool, cozy chair, and I put a cashmere blanket in there for you too."

Oh god, I'm gonna cry again. "Lukas . . ."

"And I have the team over there right now finishing the nursery." He pulls his phone from his pocket and flashes me a picture of a Pinterest board of a nautical-themed nursery. "It's right across the hall from the main bedroom, and it'll have monitors, a changing table, everything." He slips his phone back in his pocket. "I mean, if you hate it, we can change it, obviously. But Cole picked the design, and everything he picks is cool, so I think he'll like it."

"He?" I whisper.

He nods, his gaze trailing down my body. "Yeah, the baby." He looks back up at me. "It's a he, right? We're having a boy?"

I nod, tears in my eyes. "Yeah, we are."

He lets out a shaky breath, dragging a hand through his hair. "Okay, and I'm not saying I'm not still freaked out," he goes on. "Because I am. I have no idea what to do with a kid, Pop. I don't know how to be a parent. I never had one. But I figure you two do," he adds, gesturing between us. "Or you have more of a clue than me. So, maybe I can learn something new. I can figure it out. And I wanna figure it out because goddamn it, I need you. I need you, and I need Cole, and I need us to be together."

He takes a step closer. "More than that, I *want* to do this." He looks down at my baby bump, and I fight the urge to cover it with my hands. "I was abandoned, Poppy. I know what that feels like. I know what it feels like to wish *one* person cared about you. Just one." He holds up a finger. "Well, how lucky could this kid be to say he has three, right? I mean that's . . . that's a really lucky kid. And I could be part of that for someone. I could make someone feel wanted. I'll figure out the other stuff like feeding it and holding it. But the wanting it? I *know* I can do that," he says with a firm nod, tears in his eyes.

My heart is racing as I toss the glittery pillow aside. "Lukas—"

"No." I hear the desperation in his tone. Oh god, he thinks I'm going to turn him away. Even now, he doubts I can love him. He drops to his knees, raising both hands out to the sides. "Cole said that when I was ready to face you on my own, I would crawl to you. And goddamn it, that's what I'm gonna do."

Cole keeps me standing, his grip steady on my shoulder as Lukas inches forward on his knees. Heart in his hands, he bleeds for me. "I love you, Poppy. I love you so much that it scares me. And when I get scared, I run. To say I can't help it feels like a cop out, but it's true. At first, I ran to keep from getting physically hurt. Then I ran from my emotions. I figured no one can hurt me if I just keep running."

I swallow back my tears as he comes on his knees, his hands reaching out for me. As soon as they touch my hips, I'm crying, melting toward him. "But you're hurting yourself," I say. "And I can't bear it."

"I know," he groans, pulling me in tighter. He wraps both arms around my waist, pressing his face to my stomach. "I can't run from you anymore. It's tearing me apart. I can't—"

"Then don't," I beg him, smoothing my hands over his shoulders, clinging to him. "Just stop. Lukas, honey, come home to me."

He breathes me in deep as I stroke my hands up his neck to his hair, weaving my fingers through it. "Don't hurt me," he begs, his face pressed against me as he cries. "Please, baby. You gotta let me love you. And I need you to love me too. I need you to try to not hurt me—"

"I do," I whisper. "Lukas, you know I do. I love you both so much."

He pulls back, eyes wet as he searches my face. "I'm sorry." The words shatter my walls like a hammer on glass. "I hurt you, Poppy, and I'm sorry."

I cup his face, brushing my thumb over his lips. "I just want to love you."

He nods, turning to Colton. Reaching out, he grips him by the front of his shirt. "I'm sorry, Cole. God, I'm so fucking sorry."

Cole reaches out too, cupping the other side of Lukas's face. We hold him like that, claimed between us. "You stay with us now," he says, his voice low. "You are wanted. You are fucking cherished, Lukas."

He nods, turning his face to press kisses to our palms.

My whole body is trembling as I wrap a hand into the leather of his vest and pull. "Stand up."

Lukas stands, his large body towering over mine. He looks down at me with such hope and fear in his eyes. I smooth a hand down his chest, swallowing back my nerves. Holding his gaze, I ask for what I want. "Kiss me."

He doesn't hesitate. Our lost, broken spirits collide as he smashes his lips against mine, groaning as he kisses away all these weeks of pain.

"I love you," we're saying over each other, our hands desperate to map the other. "Baby, I love you so fucking much," he says against my lips.

I pull away, gasping for air, my hands on his shoulders. "You're not alone anymore. You're mine," I say on a panting breath. "Lukas Novikov, you belong to me."

He nods, his hand smoothing down the column of my neck.

Colton steps in, wrapping a hand around each of us, pulling us to him. "This is it, understood? This is where I wanna be. I want you both. We don't run from this, and we don't hide. Together. The three of us, no matter what. Family."

"Family," Lukas echoes with a nod.

I'm glowing on the inside, thinking of these two beautiful men at my side, boldly telling the world I'm theirs. Loving me, protecting me, treating me like a queen. My need for them spirals higher. We need to reconnect. We need to be one unit again. How have we waited this long?

I look between them. "I need you both. Now."

Lukas looks desperate, but Colton raises a wary brow. "What, here? In this kid's bedroom?"

I don't care where we are. We could be in the rice and beans aisle of the grocery store, and I'd still have to have them. They always appreciate action, so I shimmy the long skirt of my floral maxi dress up and tug my panties down around my ankles. They watch, wide-eyed, as I hold the dress up and slip my own fingers through my wetness. I pull them away with a whimper, showing how they glisten with my desire.

With a growl, Lukas grabs my wrist, and sucks my fingers into his mouth, licking them clean. The feel of his warm mouth sets me on fire. I arch up, kissing his neck, flicking with my tongue until he groans, letting me go.

Colton leans in, claiming Lukas in a fierce kiss, tasting me off his lips. I lean away, watching as they kiss each other. Oh my god, seeing them like this has my core turning volcanic. I'm practically crying out with need as Lukas works my skirt up for himself, burying his fingers in my pussy. He breaks his kiss with Colton and kisses me again, all but bending me back as his fingers move inside me. His thumb swirls over my clit and I feel zapped. I arch in his arms, panting for breath. "Right there—baby, don't stop."

They each claim a side of my neck, licking and sucking as I whimper, coming on Lukas's fingers. He works me through it, teasing with his thumb on my pulsing clit. With one hard press to my lips, he's turning me. "Face Cole."

I brace my hands on Colton's shoulders, smiling up at him in bliss as Lukas gets himself in position behind me. I hear the zip of his jeans coming open. He shifts in closer. "Hold this up," he says, making me drop a hand to help him bunch up my dress. I'm grinning at the image of Elizabeth Bennett getting pinned between two leather-clad bikers. Feeling bold, I look up at Colton's smiling face. "Baby, I want your cock in my mouth. Please, give me both at once. Don't make me wait."

He cups my face, dropping his other hand to sink his fingers inside me. Then he lifts them, gliding them over my lips. "You want my cock in this pretty mouth?"

I nod, shifting my stance as Lukas taps my hip. I widen for him, tipping up on my toes. Lukas works his hard dick between my legs, groaning into my shoulder as he strokes his silky shaft through my wetness.

"Fuck, I need you so bad," he says into my neck.

"Take me," I beg. "Lukas, I'm yours. I'm—"

We both groan as he sinks in. One hand is on my hip and the other wraps around, splayed across my chest. He rocks into me, pushing in deeper, filling me. "God help me," he pants.

Colton watches us with such hunger in his eyes, his hand dropping down to feel where Lukas is inside me. He presses in with two fingers, stretching me, making me gasp. "Keep going," he orders. "Fuck my fingers in her cunt."

Lukas thrusts, his slick cock sliding inside me along the ridges of Colton's fingers.

"Please," I beg, dropping a hand to cup Colton's hardness. "I want you both. Put your dick in my mouth. Claim me, and never let me go. Please—"

He drops his hands to his belt, hurrying to open his pants and jerk them down, freeing his hard cock. "Take it," he says, fisting a hand tight in my hair. "You're such a fucking queen. You own us. Take anything you want."

Opening my mouth, I pull on his hip and he steps in, letting me have what I'm aching for. I moan with relief as I take both my men inside me, feeling complete for the first time in weeks. Colton rocks against my face, his hands in my hair gentle but direct, urging me to take him deeper. I suck on him, teasing with my tongue as Lukas thrusts into me from behind.

"You look so beautiful sucking his cock," he croons at me, wrapping a hand around to tease my clit. "I'm gonna come inside this cunt, and then Cole's gonna lick my dick clean."

I whine, pressing back with my hips as Colton makes me choke. Oh god, this is euphoria. I'm dizzy, and I'm drowning, and I never want it to stop.

Clinging to them both, dancing on the edge of orgasm, I hardly notice when the door busts open. Both Lukas and Colton freeze, their hands holding me protectively.

"Whoa—ohmygod," a woman shrieks.

My heart drops out, even as Lukas keeps thrusting into my pussy, working my clit until I'm choking on a scream. "Get the fuck out," he barks.

Gasping, I push back against him, taking my mouth away from Colton's dick. Holding to his hips, I glance over my shoulder.

Standing in the doorway are Rachel's pretty friend Tess, dressed as the devil, and Ryan Langley, carrying what looks like a passed-out teenager dressed as Cleopatra. "Oh my god," I cry. Lukas wraps a protective arm around me, pulling me up against his chest as Colton steps in.

"Oh *my* god," Ryan shouts back, his wild gaze bouncing between the three of us, mouth open in confused horror.

Tess recovers first. Leaning around him, she jerks the door shut with a quick, "Sorry, carry on!"

The three of us stare at the closed door, Lukas's cock still buried deep inside me. He recovers first, giving my ass a slap. "I was almost finished. With the way you were squeezing me with your tight little cunt, you were too. Coley, you good?"

Colton rubs the back of his neck. "Lemme lock the door first, Jesus Christ."

I grab his leather vest as he tries to step back. "No."

He looks down, one brow raised.

"Pop?" Lukas teases, giving me a little press with his hips.

I hum, wiggling against him. "Leave it unlocked," I say. "Colton, give me that pretty dick. I wasn't finished."

"Fuck yes," Lukas grunts, his hands going to my hips as he starts winding me up again. I'm laughing as he pushes on my shoulder, bending me over to take Colton's hard dick in my mouth.

"Speed round," Colton says, fisting his hands in my hair. "Then we're taking you home, so we get you naked and take our time."

Home.

I'm already there. This is home. Wherever the three of us are is all the home I need.

13
POPPY

God, I don't know if I've ever been so turned on. Lukas drove us home, and I couldn't wait to chase more of this feeling. Heart on fire, I pulled up my dress up and started fingering myself right there in the backseat, moaning at the exquisite ache as I swirled Lukas's cum over my clit.

When they noticed what I was doing, they went feral. Lukas pressed the gas, trying to watch me in the rearview mirror. At the first stop light, Colton unbuckled and crawled between the seats. As Lukas cursed in the driver's seat, Colton pressed me up against the truck door and devoured my pussy, making me scream out an orgasm before we pulled into the drive.

We barely get in the door before their hands are on me, stripping me out of my clothes. I'm down to my underwear before I'm turning and stumbling away on a laugh. "Nice house," I tease, pulling the pins from my hair to loosen the little Regency curls I had framed around my face. "Can I get a tour?"

"Yeah, this is the living room," says Lukas, swooping in to claim my mouth in another hungry kiss.

Behind him, Colton kicks off his shoes and pulls off his shirt, tossing them aside.

Lukas picks me up and hauls me into the kitchen, setting me down on the large island. "And this is the kitchen," he says, biting at my nipple through my lace bra.

I hiss, pushing him away. "Gentle with the boobs, honey. They're a little sensitive."

He leans away, his gaze trailing over my chest and down to the little pronounced bump at my belly. It looks larger when I'm sitting. He puts a protective hand over it. Taking a deep breath, he lets it out.

Moving more slowly, he unhooks my bra and tosses it aside, revealing my breasts. He cups them reverently, smoothing his calloused thumbs over my skin. Leaning down, he takes each one in his mouth, licking without sucking, swirling his tongue around each nipple, until I'm arching into him.

"Better?" he asks.

I nod, my hand smoothing up his shoulder to tangle in his hair.

Colton steps in behind him, brushing his nose along his neck to nip his ear. Lukas shivers, his eyes still on me, hands on my breasts.

I lean back, bared except for my panties, and watch them. Colton smooths his hands down Lukas's sides, reaching for the hem of his shirt. He slowly pulls it up, forcing Lukas to raise his arms. Colton pulls the shirt off and tosses it away, one hand wrapping around Lukas's chest as the other goes to cup his cock through his jeans.

Lukas groans, pressing back against him.

I can hardly breathe. They want this. They crave it with each other. It's the most beautiful thing I've ever seen. So unexpected, but it brings me nothing but joy. I smile through my tears as I watch Colton kiss along Lukas's shoulder, up to his neck. "Do you love him?" I ask Lukas.

He nods, his gaze so warm and relaxed.

Colton rewards him by slipping his hand inside his jeans, teasing until he groans.

"And do you love me?" I ask.

Lukas nods again, groaning as he gives in to his pleasure.

Smiling, I lean back on the counter, dropping down to my elbows. "I like you in the middle," I say. "I like seeing you pinned from behind, unable to escape."

"I'm not going anywhere," he says, helping me strip my panties off. He tosses them aside, spreading my legs as Colton starts undoing his jeans. My heart skips when Colton drops down. Circling between Lukas and the island, he sinks his mouth around Lukas's cock. Lukas groans out a curse. Bending forward, he crashes into me, his mouth dropping to my pussy.

I lie back on the counter, staring up at the underside of a modern driftwood chandelier lighting fixture as Lukas eats me out while Colton sucks his cock. In no time, I'm crying out a little release, pushing on his head. He leans back, lips glistening, a hand on Colton's head pushing him off too.

I sit up, breathless. "Show me more of the house."

We don't even make it halfway up the stairs before Lukas and I get Colton stretched out. He sits naked on the middle stair, arched back to let me ride his face. Below him, Lukas is between his legs, sucking his cock and fingering his ass. I cling to the stairs, grinding against his chin as he hums a curse against my clit.

It's all I can do to hold back another release as we break apart, stumbling our way up the stairs. This feels like a ritual. There's no speaking. We have no room left for words. We can only feel what we are together. We stoke these flames, fucking and kissing and touching until I find myself lying on my back in the middle of an extra wide king bed. Lukas is balanced over me, his pretty caramel eyes glassy with need as Colton presses in behind him.

"That good?" Colton asks, breaking the sacred silence as he works his fingers deeper inside Lukas's ass.

Lukas nods, letting out a breath. "Yeah, it feels really fucking good." Ducking down, he kisses my breasts, teasing with his tongue, gentle but claiming.

I brush my hand through his hair, heart beating with contentment.

"You're gonna fuck Poppy's cunt while I fuck your ass," Colton directs. "We are gonna claim you from the inside out. Love you so hard. Ruin you for anyone else. You're *ours*."

Lukas groans as he drops lower over me. Cupping my thigh with his strong hand, he lifts my leg, making room to slide in. I arch back, letting him take me again. The slide home is so easy. I'm wet and ready and aching for more. I'll never get enough of them, of this feeling of us.

He kisses me, teasing my mouth open, his breath catching as Colton pushes in behind him.

"Take my tip and we'll stop," Colton warns. "You don't like it, and we—"

"Don't fucking stop," Lukas begs. "Cole, please. I need this. Need you. Please, don't stop."

I hum, shifting my hips as Colton presses in deeper. He applies lube, working slowly, thrusting in and out until Lukas is trembling.

"I can't," Lukas pants. Colton stops and Lukas groans, all but pulling out of me to push back into Colton. "Please, baby, don't stop. Fucking fill me up. Give me all of your cock."

Colton rocks forward, sinking fully in. His weight presses down on Lukas, which sinks him deeper into me.

"Yes," I pant, holding Lukas's shoulders. "Colton, honey, do it again."

Colton takes over, moving into Lukas so that he moves into me. My emotions are a riot, swirling inside me as I let my men claim me and each other, binding us together. I reach a state of effervescence as I cry out my orgasm. My pussy clenches tight, the sensations hitting me in deep waves, body and soul aching to pull these men in deeper, love them harder, keep them longer.

Lukas is a trembling mess as he buries his face in my hair and releases. Atop him, Colton pistons with his hips, grunting out his own desperate release, filling Lukas with his cum.

"Oh my god," Lukas groans, the weight of his sweaty body pressing me into the mattress.

"Fuck me," Colton says after a minute, the fog of climaxes slowly lifting. "That was . . ."

None of us have a word for it. There isn't a word to describe the feeling of three souls touching.

Colton moves first, sliding carefully out of Lukas and dropping down beside me on the bed. He's a heap of bones. There's nothing left after our marathon of sex. I think Lukas would just sleep right where he is, all two hundred plus pounds of him squashing me into the mattress.

I tap his shoulder, kissing his neck. "Honey, let me up."

Lukas slips out of me, and I feel that exquisite pooling of his cum as it drips out of my spent pussy. God, it's dirty and so freaking divine. Honestly, before these two, sex was something I endured more than anything. I tried to have a good time. I always tried to make sure my partner had a good time. But until Lukas and Colton, I didn't know what it felt like to have an attentive partner actually focus on *my* good time.

These two read my body like a book. They make my pleasure their own. They listen and learn and adjust to meet my needs. They *care.* They care about me, about my body and my pleasure and the joy they want me to find in them. I'd say it's a gift, but it's not. Everyone deserves this. Everyone deserves to find a partner who can make them feel the way they make me feel.

How can there be anything wrong in this? Anything deviant or taboo? It's perfect. Apart, we were three lonely people, living our lives in quiet isolation. Together, we're a family. A communion of souls flourishing best together.

"I love you," I say, rolling on my side to kiss Colton's shoulder.

"Love you," he murmurs, his hand brushing down my arm as I turn away.

"And I love you," I say, kissing Lukas's sweaty cheek.

He turns his face, claiming a quick one for his lips as well. "I love you, baby."

I shimmy down the bed between them, slipping off the end. Padding barefoot over the soft rug, I head to the bathroom. Opening the door, I flick on the light. I shriek as something gray scampers across the dark tile floor, disappearing behind the toilet.

"What is it?" Colton calls.

"I think I just saw a mouse," I cry.

On the bed, Lukas groans. "Oh shit—no, it's not a mouse."

Hand to my naked chest, cum literally dripping down my leg, I stare wildly around, taking note of the litter box, a food dish, a pink water bowl.

Lukas and Colton are off the bed, pressing in behind me.

I turn around. "Lukas, why do you have a litter box in here?"

He rubs the back of his neck with a groan. "So, uhh . . . that was part of the surprise meant for tomorrow. I think she hates me though because she wouldn't eat or drink anything earlier."

I gasp. "You didn't." Dropping to my knees, not caring that I'm naked, I crawl over to the toilet and peek around it. "Lukas, tell me you didn't adopt that cat for me!"

He leans his naked hip against the sink. "I didn't *not* do it."

There, sitting on a folded hand towel, is a very cranky-looking Miss Princess.

14
COLTON

"**A**nd have you been experiencing any feelings of breathlessness, fatigue, dizziness?"

I stiffen in my chair. "No, why?"

My cardiologist looks over his tablet. "Any trouble exercising?"

"I'm a professional hockey player," I reply with a forced laugh. "My life is exercising."

"What about nausea and vomiting?"

Fuck, did someone tell him? I have been getting sick more often lately. The last three games, I threw up behind the bench. I thought it was just stress and a particularly grueling string of shifts. I must give something away in my face because he jots it down.

"And what about swollen feet and ankles?"

"Like I said, I play hockey. A lot of stuff swells." I lean forward in my chair. "Doc, what is this about? I just had my yearly checkup and, next thing I know, you're calling me in, asking for a follow-up. What's going on?"

He nods, setting the tablet aside. "I'm concerned, Mr. Morrow. You're showing some signs of left-side weakness. And your ejection fraction is lower than I'd like it to be for the level of physical activity you do. Have you felt any palpitations?"

"Nothing out of the ordinary," I admit.

"And your heart rate, your breathing? Are they recovering on their own in a timely manner while you're out on the ice?"

"It's been a tough season . . ."

"Let's not do that," he replies, taking off his glasses, and tucking them in the pocket of his coat. "You've been a heart patient for long enough now. We don't diminish, and we don't sweep symptoms under the rug."

I sigh. "Okay, well, so what do we do here? What's the best course of action?"

"In my professional opinion? The best course of action is that you retire from playing professional hockey—"

"No." I stand up. "No, I'm not ready. Doc, I have to play."

"Well, you can't play dead. And with the way you're overworking this heart, it's only a matter of time."

I glare at him. "That's some shitty fucking bedside manner you have there."

"Would you respond better to a sweet sugary coating?" he asks with a raised brow. "You have a weak heart, Mr. Morrow. You know this. Given all it's been through, your path to playing at the top of a professional sport has been nothing short of miraculous. But there's no denying that the rate at which you push your heart to perform is taking its toll."

A weak heart. Is this man really daring to say that I, Colton Morrow, have a weak heart?

The heart is just a muscle. It pumps and regulates. It's nature's perfect machine. And I've always known the truth: my machine is weak. We patched it up and changed out a few parts over the years until it ran like new. I've accomplished so much with this battered, broken-down pump. It's taken me around the world and back again. It brought me to the height of a professional sports career.

But now it's growing tired. I'm working it too hard, asking for too much. Because my *heart* is strong. The spirit inside me, the will to live this life to the fullest—*that* heart beats hard and fast in my chest. I am a tower of strength. I am bold and decisive. I'm passionate and proud and fierce. A fiery heart, that's what I have. A loyal heart. A lion's heart.

But a *weak* heart?

No, I've never been weak.

I can practically hear my dad inside my head, serving up more sports psychology gold.

Winners never quit.

Nothing will work unless you do.

"Give me more time," I say at the doctor. "Tell me what to do, and I'll do it, just keep me on the ice."

He sighs, checking over the notes on his tablet again. "Well, at a minimum, we need to look at changing up some of your medications. I also want us to look at how we can improve your ejection fraction. You can't play if your heart can't fill, and your blood can't oxygenate."

I nod. "Okay. I'll try anything."

"And I want you monitoring your heart rate more closely," he goes on. "We need you tracking any dysrhythmias. It's not me being alarmist to say a pacemaker could be on the horizon for you, Mr. Morrow."

My stomach fills with lead. "Please, doc. You put a pacemaker in me, and I'm done. My hockey career will be over."

He nods, his gaze somber. "True . . . but if retirement and a pacemaker could buy you *twenty* more years with the people you love? Would it not be worth at least considering?"

I leave the doctor's office. I can't even tell you how I got to my car. Before I know it, I'm pulling up inside the practice arena parking garage. I make my way inside, and head up to the fourth floor. The elevator on the left pings, and the doors slide open.

I can't help but smile as I step in. This is the elevator where Poppy and I got stuck. It was right on the floor of this elevator that we may have made a baby together. My son. He's growing inside her right now. Every minute. Every second. There's a clock ticking in my head, counting down the days until I get to meet him.

Fuck, is this really happening? Hockey is my life, right? It's all I've ever wanted. I have to keep playing. I *want* to keep playing . . . right?

Maybe it *was* my life.

I let out a shaky breath, my eyes focused on that spot on the floor where I first made Poppy mine. Fuck, who are we kidding? She made me hers. What is hockey compared to a longer life loving her, loving Lukas, watching our child grow?

The elevator dings and the doors open. But I don't go straight to Poppy's office. I have a stop to make first.

"HEY, honey," Poppy says brightly, waving me in with her phone to her ear.

Stepping in, I close the door, and glance around her new office. It has a wall of windows. My little pothos sits in a place of honor in a pink pot on the sill. This office is large enough for a couch and two chairs around a coffee table. She still has room for an executive desk too.

The walls are adorned with shots of the Rays in action. I smile as I take in the one in the middle. It's Lukas and I, arms around each other, skating away from the camera. You can see our numbers large on our backs, 22 and 3. I have my stick in the air because I just scored my first goal as a Ray.

Poppy finishes up her phone call, a smile on her face. "Well, aren't you a sight for sore eyes. Come here, sweets."

I step around her desk and give her a lingering kiss.

"Mmm, better than coffee," she teases. "Did I know you were stopping by? You didn't have a workout today, right?"

"No, I didn't."

Fuck me, now that I'm actually here, I don't want to say anything. I don't want to risk popping this perfect bubble we're all in.

"For dinner tonight I was thinking that place over by the beach with the really good fried green tomatoes," she says, shuffling things around on her desk. "You know, the one with the goat cheese and that spicy remoulade?"

"Sounds perfect."

Something in my tone must give me away because she pauses. "What is it? What do you got there?" She glances down, finally noticing the manilla folder in my hand.

Taking a deep breath, I open the folder. "I stopped by Vicki's office and picked these up." Pulling out all three contracts, I set them down on her desk.

She slides them over. "And what are these?"

"The love contracts we each have to fill out to make our relationship official with HR. I've already filled mine out and left a copy with Vicki," I add, tapping the one filled in with blue ink.

She looks up, eyes wide. "Colton—"

"We don't have to come out to anyone else," I assure her. "Not until we're all ready. But I want this cleared with HR. I want no question that I'm in a committed relationship with you both. And I updated my emergency contact," I add. "I put you first, Lukas second ... please don't tell him."

She smiles. "I won't. Should I update mine to you?"

I brush her hair back with my fingers. "I'd like that."

"Well, okay," she says with a flap of her arms. "Seriously, what is going on?"

Steeling myself, I dive forward. "If the baby isn't biologically mine, I want to adopt him. And I want the same for Lukas. I want all three of us to be named the legal parent with full rights."

"Of course," she says tears filling her eyes. "Honey, please just tell me what's wrong."

I drop down to one knee behind her desk and grab her chair by the arms, wheeling her closer to me. I wrap my arms around her and breathe in her perfect floral scent, burying my face at her shoulder.

Her hands go around me, smoothing over my shoulders. "Colton . . . you're scaring me."

I lift my head away from her, and cup her cheek. "If I retired from hockey, would you care?"

"Of course not—"

"I never went to college," I warn her. "I got drafted and went straight to the minors. I've never even had a job outside of school and hockey."

"That's okay," she replies. "You could go now if you want. It's never too late. Will you please just tell me what's bothering you?"

I have to tell her. She has to know. I can't sit on this alone.

"I saw my cardiologist today."

Her eyes go wide, and her bottom lip instantly starts trembling. "Colton—"

"No," I say quickly, cupping her face with both hands. "Poppy, no. There are some symptoms we're going to be monitoring closely, that's all."

She wraps her hands around my wrists. "What symptoms?"

Like the doctor said, there's no way to sugar-coat this. "Symptoms of heart failure."

She sucks back a sob as she falls forward against my chest, clinging to me.

"Hey—baby, look at me," I say, pushing back on her shoulders, and tipping her chin up to meet my gaze. "It's a scary word, I admit. They call it heart failure if the heart is weak and unable to pump blood effectively. But I'm not dying," I assure her, kissing her forehead. "I have so many options open to me, from new medications, to monitoring devices. I don't want you to worry, okay?"

"Fat freaking chance," she cries, making me smile.

"I know," I soothe, kissing her forehead again. "We may need to be ready to accept that this might be my last season playing professional hockey."

She leans away, tears still falling. "Oh, honey . . ." Now it's her turn to cup my face. Her expression takes on such a look of deep tenderness. "I am so sorry."

"Don't be," I say, turning my face to kiss her wrist. "There are always new dreams to chase. I expect you, and Lukas, and Lentil will run me ragged for a good long while." I place my hand on her stomach, and she quickly covers it with both of her own, holding me to her, to them.

Tears sting my eyes as I look up. Fuck, I could get lost in her pretty blue eyes. "Nothing comes before my family, do you understand?"

She nods, brushing her thumb over the back of my hand.

"I'm not even close to throwing in the towel," I assure her. "But I want you and Lukas and the baby to have everything you need. I want HR contracts and legal safety nets. I want adoptions and powers of attorney. I will never ask you to marry me, Poppy St. James, but I mean to tie the three of you to me in every other way . . . starting with those forms," I add, nodding at the contracts on the desk.

She nods, her breathing calmer. "Okay."

I smile. "Good. 'Cause this is it for me."

"Colton, you're it for me," she whispers. "Baby, I love you so much."

"Good. Now, kiss me."

Flinging her arms around me, she kisses me. We hold each other, mouths seeking and claiming as we leave our marks. I pant against her lips, and she pulls away, shoulders stiff. "Wait—" She searches my face as if looking for a sign I'm about to keel over.

"Babe, I'm not dead," I assure her. "One of the loves of my life is in my arms, and for as long as this broken heart still beats, I'm gonna fuck you." She gasps as I pick her up, slinging her onto the desk. I'm kissing her again, my hands working feverishly to get her pleated skirt up and her panties down. "I'm gonna love you," I pant against her mouth, freeing my hard dick from the top of my shorts.

She slants her hips back, one hand pressed flat to the desk as I push my tip in at her entrance. "Love you so much," she says on a breath as I start to slide in.

"Gonna worship you," I groan, sinking myself deeper into her hot, wet pussy.

She clings to my shoulders, her legs around me. "Yes. *Please—*"

"Fucking cherish you." My hand cups her breast over her shirt as I start to rock into her. "My queen. My fucking salvation."

"Oh god, take me," she sighs, moving with me, her pussy squeezing me so tight. "I can't not have you. Please, baby."

"Gonna come inside this cunt, brand you as mine."

"Do it."

"I love you so much."

"Colton—*god*, I fucking love you."

I pound into the side of her desk with my thighs, burying myself in her cunt again and again as we each chase our climax. In a few more thrusts, I'm groaning into her neck, heart racing as I come inside my queen. She trembles around me, swallowing her scream as her pussy clamps down so beautifully, coating my dick in her wet release.

I pull out, one hand flat on the desk as I catch my breath.

She settles on the desk, her hands brushing down my arms as she searches my face. "Are you okay?"

I laugh, tucking my wet dick back inside my shorts. I don't want to clean her off me yet. Leaning forward, I kiss her parted lips. "I may have a weak heart, but pray to god it's always strong enough to do that."

She rolls her eyes, shimmying her panties back up her legs.

"Aren't you gonna clean yourself up a little?"

She just shrugs. "No. I'm fine just as I am." She slips off her desk and drops back into her chair, brushing her hair back from her face.

Grinning, I lower my hands down to the arms of her chair and spin her to face me. "Oh, so you're just gonna sit here with my cum leaking out of your cunt, taking phone calls and ruling the hockey PR universe?"

She smiles right back. "Yep, pretty much."

I shake my head and grab her around the middle, dragging her back onto the desk.

"Colton—oh my—I have to actually work today!"

"This *is* work," I tease, nipping her ear as I snake my hand back up under her skirt. "You're gonna work for this dick, sweet girl. Now, turn around, and put your hands on the desk. We don't stop until you're dripping wet."

Smiling, she slowly turns around, and puts her hands on the desk.

"**H**ello?" I set my stuff down in the laundry room, kicking off my shoes. "Cole? Pop?"

Poppy's car is parked outside, but Cole's SUV is gone. They said they were out running some errands, but that was hours ago. I figured they'd be home by now. I wander through the house, flipping on lights. I turn on the TV, flicking it off the Hallmark channel and back to SportsCenter. I go to grab a beer from the fridge, tossing my hat on the kitchen island.

Squish.

"Oh—what the—*fuck*—" I lift my foot. The sensation of stepping on a squished banana makes me want to gag. Only it's not a squished banana. It's brown squishy cat vomit.

"Fuck!" Hobbling on one foot, I sling my entire leg into the sink and jerk the water on. "Are you fucking kidding me with this?"

I don't care what Poppy says, that cat is a menace. The thing weighs like half a pound, and yet she eats, shits, and pukes more than a goddamn rookie. And she destroys everything—shoelaces, charging cords, headphone wires. Funny how she only seems to target me and my shit.

But Poppy just fawns over her, taking her everywhere. She has this sweater she wears around the house, and she puts that damn kitten in her pocket. She talks to it all day. You'd think they had a bond like that kid with E.T.

I rinse my foot off. Then I'm climbing out of the damn sink to look at the mess on the floor. Grumbling, I jerk a few paper towels off the roll and wipe up the puke, trying not to gag as I toss it in the trash. "Fucking hell," I mutter, slamming the trash door shut.

Good mood soured, I glance around suspiciously. Usually, the little shit likes to appear just in time to watch me clean up one of her messes.

Nothing.

I walk into the living room. "Here, kitty," I call. "Princess?"

Groaning, I abandon my plans of beer and sports highlights, and instead go looking for the cat. There's obviously a lot Poppy will forgive me for, but killing this cat definitely doesn't make the list. "Here puss, puss, puss," I call up the stairs, feeling like a goddamn idiot. "Come on out. I just wanna see that you're alive."

I move down the hall to the main bedroom. "Come on, cat. Please?" I drop down to my knees and check under the bed, letting out a breath of relief. She's there, lying on her side. "Hey, fuzzball. Come on out." I rub my fingers together the way Poppy and Cole do.

She doesn't move.

With a groan, I flatten out on my chest, wedging myself under the bed frame. I wrap a hand around her and pull her out. "Please don't be dead."

She's not moving. Her little belly looks distended and she's listless.

"No, no, no." I pull out my phone, panicking. I can't call Poppy. She'll freak out and cry and blame me. I can't call Cole. He's *with* Poppy. Then they'll both freak out and blame me. Cursing, I race downstairs and get the cat carrier out of the garage. "It's okay fuzzball," I say, gently placing her into the carrier.

As I hurry back down the stairs, I search on my phone for the nearest animal hospital. It's after hours, so the only one is an emergency vet fifteen minutes away. I get in the truck, buckling her carrier in the front seat. Then my truck is roaring to life. As soon as I get on the A1A, I make a quick call to the only person I think will help me and not be a dick about it.

He answers on the third ring. "Hey, what's up?"

"Hey, I'm sending you an address. I need you to meet me there right now, before I freak the fuck out and ruin my goddamn life."

I don't even wait for a response before I'm sending the address and tossing the phone in the cup holder. "You better not die," I say at the little gray cat. "Do you understand me? I have big plans for my life now, and for better or fucking worse, you're in them."

TWENTY minutes later, Langley comes busting through the doors. "Dude, what the fuck?"

"They just took her back," I say, rising out of my chair. "I don't know what's wrong."

He looks around, confused. "Wait—why are we at a vet? What the hell is going on?"

"Poppy's cat is sick," I explain. "And I cannot let this cat die. She's bonded to this thing, man. If it dies, I'm gonna be in so much trouble—"

"Poppy has a cat?"

"Well, technically it's my cat," I say. "I'm on all the paperwork. Poppy couldn't adopt it because of the rules at the apartments so—"

"Hold on," he says, holding up a hand. "You called me saying I had to come to this address."

"Yeah."

"You said you were about to ruin your goddamn life."

"Yes."

He frowns. "But I'm here for a cat?"

Okay, now I'm confused. "The address I sent you was for a vet. How are you fucking confused?"

He huffs, crossing his arms. "I didn't read what the address said, I just followed the damn GPS. Nov, I didn't even tie my shoes." He points down at his untied shoelaces.

Okay, that's commitment. I smile at him, feeling a little better. But then my smile falls. "Wait—what did you think you were coming here to do?"

"I don't know." He waves an arm. "You said you were freaking out and about to ruin your life. I just assumed you and Poppy were eloping. I thought maybe this was a courthouse or something."

"You thought I called you in a panic, wanting you to come watch me marry Poppy?"

"Watch it, stop it." He shrugs again. "I figured I'd feel out the vibe when I got here."

I glare at him, arms crossed. "Why would I want you to stop my wedding to Poppy?"

"Seriously?" He huffs a laugh. "Maybe because it's you, Mister 'My Longest Commitment Is With My Bauer Nexus Geo.'"

"Oh, and you're so wise with relationships? Propose to the red-head yet?"

"Nope," he replies, totally nonchalant. "I don't think we'll ever get married."

"She kicked you to the curb already?"

"Nope," he says again, grinning wider. "Actually, we're happy and in love, thanks for asking. Tess is my forever. She's perfect for me, and I'll follow her anywhere. I love that woman more than my own life. It's done."

My shoulders drop a little. He said it so openly, so freely. He loves a woman, and he's telling me about it. No fear, no shame. Nerves buzz in my chest. It can be this easy, right? Oh god, I'm doing this. The HR forms are signed. We can't get in trouble letting people know. "Look . . . about what you saw at Shelby's party—"

He holds up a hand. "Hey, man, I didn't ask. And I didn't tell," he adds. "Tess didn't either. Your secret is safe."

I take a deep breath. "Well, that's just the thing . . . I don't want it to be a secret anymore."

He raises a brow at me.

I square my shoulders at him, hands on my hips as I stare him down. "Langers, I want you to be the first to know: I'm in love with Poppy St. James. I love her so goddamn much, and I nearly lost her because of my bullshit fear of commitment. But now I got her back, and I am never losing her again. That's why I'm freaking out about the cat," I go on. "I needed someone here with me because if this cat dies, I need a witness that I did *everything* I could to save it. I am not above giving a cat mouth-to-mouth. Hell, I'll give it a piece of my kidney."

"Why don't we just wait and see what the vet says."

"Well, when Poppy packs my bags, maybe you could tell her how desperate and pathetic I was," I go on. "You could even add that I cried a little. Because I will do anything for that woman, Langers. Literally anything."

"Jesus," he mutters, eyes wide. "Okay, so you've definitely got it bad."

"Oh, I'm not even finished," I say, heart racing. "I think you should also know that I'm in love with Cole."

He blinks. "Morrow?"

"What Cole do you think I mean, asshole? We don't have another one on the team."

"I'm just checking," he says, both hands raised.

"Well, yeah, it's Cole Fucking Morrow. I love him, and he loves me. And we love Poppy. And we're together. The three of us."

"Wow," he mutters. "Seriously, wow. And it's . . . good? You're happy and it's all working?"

I smile. Even with Cole's news about his heart health, we're all in good spirits, ready to plan our future. "Bud, I quite literally cannot help myself," I say. "It's so fucking good."

He smiles. "Well, I'm happy for you—"

"Oh, there's more."

His eyes go wide again. "What?"

"She's pregnant."

"Whoa."

"Yeah, whoa. Could be mine," I say with a shrug. "Could be Cole's. There's literally no way to tell until he comes out."

"He?"

"Yeah, it's a boy. I'm gonna be a father in like six months. That will be another occasion when you can race to the hospital with your shoes untied."

He laughs. "Noted." He's quiet for a minute. "Nov . . . why did you tell me all this? I mean, like, why me first?"

"Because I'm really fucking happy," I admit. "And when I considered who would hear my news and only be happy for me, and not, like, judgmental or rude, I thought of you. I knew you'd let me just be happy."

I can see my words have blindsided him. He recovers, clearing his throat. "Well, this is fucking dumb. Come on, we're hugging it out."

I put up a hand. "Not necessary."

"No, it's happening." He steps in. "We're having a tender moment." He wraps his arms around me, giving me a firm hug. "That's right, just let it happen."

"I fucking hate this," I mutter.

"Hug me back, or I'll recite this whole conversation to every player on the team. And as you requested, I'll throw it in that you were crying. A lot."

I wrap my arms around him, patting his back.

Just then the vet tech comes out. "Which one of you is here with Princess Novikov?"

Langers stiffens in my arms. We break away, and he tries to hide his goddamn smirk.

Sighing, I raise my hand. "That would be me."

It turns out that, after seven-hundred dollars' worth of cat X-rays, our little Miss Princess was suffering from bloating in her intestines. That's right, I paid almost a thousand dollars in emergency vet bills, and outed myself to Ryan Langley, only to be told that the cat who hates me simply needed to fart.

This is my life now.

And goddamn it, I am still so fucking happy.

76

POPPY

"**P**oppy, you listen to me now. You cannot do this, honey," Mom says into the phone.

I sigh, crossing my legs in my reading chair. "Mom, it's already done. I'm fourteen weeks pregnant. The baby is the size of a kiwi. And he's a boy. You're gonna have another grandson—"

"No, I do not accept that," she says over me. "Honey, you're not even married yet."

I nod, stroking Miss Princess on my lap. After her little health scare, I've been extra vigilant. "I told you, Momma, we won't be getting married. Unless it becomes legal for me to marry both my partners, we're not—"

"Oh, and what is this nonsense about 'partners?' You're not opening a law firm or playing doubles tennis. You are a lady, Poppy St. James. Someday, I hope you'll become someone's wife. And when you do, that man will be your *husband*."

"Well, what if I don't marry a man?"

"Don't be ridiculous."

I groan. What did I think would happen telling my mom I was pregnant? It's not possible she could just be happy for me; I knew that going in. But after Colton's heart update, the three of us made an action plan. Part of that plan involves coming out to our families. We don't want there to be any questions or confusion as to exactly what we are and what our wishes are.

I mean, god forbid something happens to me, and my mother swoops in trying to take my child away from his fathers. I don't know that I believe in ghosts, but I would haunt that woman to the grave and beyond if she so much as looked at my child without his fathers' consent.

Meanwhile, Lukas has no family to tell, and Colton's family has been a literal dream. His mom Cynthia is wonderful, so warm and welcoming. I met her at Christmas, along with his oldest sister Jasmine and her three kids. His middle sister Gloria is married to a woman named Kelly, and they have two daughters. Cynthia cried when we showed her the ultrasound pictures, and Jasmine and Gloria want to plan us a baby shower after the hockey season ends.

I wish my own family could be as understanding . . .

"It's not ridiculous, Mom," I try to reason. "Queer people exist. They fall in love, and get married, and have families, and live perfectly well-adjusted lives."

"Well, you answer me this," Mom huffs. "What are we supposed to tell people, Poppy? What do I tell our friends, our family, our pastor?"

"Tell them your daughter is happy and flourishing in a job she loves," I reply patiently. "Tell them she's in love with two wonderful men, and she's having her first child this summer."

"And that's another thing," she says, ready with the redirect. "I can't believe you would choose to do this now when Deidre has waited so long to get pregnant again. This is just like a slap in the face. How are we supposed to take the time to properly celebrate *her* when we're all suddenly worried about *you*?"

I blink back my tears. "You don't have to worry about me, Momma. That's what I'm trying to tell you. I am so freaking happy—"

"Don't curse. Honestly, you'd think I raised you in a barn. What would your Nana say?"

I place my hand on my growing baby bump, fighting the urge to scream. "I'm happy, Mom. I wish you could see how happy I am. I swear, I'm not trying to upstage Violet or steal Deidre's thunder. I'm just living my life. I fell backward into this, and now I'm here. I want this baby, and I love my partners. And if you'll let me, I'd like to bring them to the wedding. I want you and Daddy to meet them."

"Lord rue the day your own baby girl calls you and tells you that she has not one, but two, gentleman callers. I swear, this is like hearing the plot of *The Scarlet Letter* has up and come to life, and your own precious child is playing the lead role of Hester Prynne!"

"Wow," I murmur, shifting the cat off my lap. "Mom, I have to go—"

"Well, just wait a minute now," she says. "I think we need to talk about Nana's money first."

Heaven help me, not this again. "What about it, Mom?"

"Well, I'm still the guarantor of her estate," she replies. "Which means it falls to me to see that her money is spent in a way that would do her memory honor."

"I know, Momma. And I loved, Nana," I'm quick to say. "She was my dearest friend in the family—"

"Well, how do you think she would feel knowing you're setting yourself up for a lifetime of ridicule?" she says over me. "How do you think she'd feel knowing you're gonna push that on an innocent baby, confusing them and making them stand out to their peers? Bullying is real, Poppy. I mean, did you think about *any* of this?"

Tears burn sharp and painful. It's like she's reading aloud from the pages of my anxiety journal. All my darkest fears and worries are breathed to life in her poisoned words. "I've thought about it a lot, Mom. But at the end of the day, I think what matters most is that my children will know they are loved and happy and cared for by parents who cherish them."

"Well, I just don't see how Nana could support this lifestyle choice," she says. "And yes, Poppy, you are making a choice here. You are *choosing* to put your own selfish desires over the needs of a child. I mean, who does that? Such behavior cannot be rewarded, honey, I'm sorry."

"So, what?" I say. "Are you gonna cut me off and cut me out because I won't break up with my boyfriends? Are you gonna take all the money my precious Nana left me, money that should be going to my son?"

"I don't see that you're leaving me a choice."

I sit forward in my chair, jostling the cat. "What are you gonna do, Mom? Give it to Violet and Anderson, your perfect match made in heaven?"

"Well, now, that's not a bad idea—"

"He doesn't even love her!" I cry. "He's just using her to get to Daddy and to climb the ladder."

"Poppy, why would you say such an awful thing?"

"Because, Mom, he told me so. Because he is the same person he was three years ago. He is spoiled and selfish and self-serving.

He doesn't love her, he admitted it. And, by the way, she doesn't love him either," I add. "She's just sick and tired of being treated like she's good-for-nothing. She wants to do you proud, so she's marrying someone *you* would choose, regardless of her own feelings."

"Now you're just being cruel again."

"No, I'm being honest. They are not a match made in heaven, Mom. They are a pair of desperate, lonely schemers destined for a living hell if you make them marry each other."

"Once again, you are just jealous of your sister—"

"Oh my god," I cry.

"*Yes*, you are jealous," she says over me. "And you're broken-hearted, and vulnerable, and you're acting out. But here's how it's gonna be, Miss Poppy Girl. You are coming to your sister's wedding, do you understand me? And you will not embarrass us with this mess of your 'partners' and your secret love child. You will show up, you will stand up, and you will smile and watch our sweet Violet marry into the Montgomerys. And I am telling you, honey, if you mess up this chance for her, I will guarantee that you never see a dime of Nana's money. Do you understand me? And don't think I won't get your daddy involved if I have to."

"And what the heck does that mean?"

She doesn't reply. She knows whatever my brain can conjure up is worse than any other threat she could make. My dad is a powerful man with powerful friends. Righteous anger surges inside as I grip the arm of my chair with one hand. "Momma, you listen to me now. If you or Daddy do *anything* to negatively impact the careers of my men, or interfere in our lives in any way, I will never forgive you. You get between me and my family, and I will *rage* on you."

"Don't be ridiculous—"

"Daddy taught me everything I know about PR," I say over her. "Don't think I don't know how to sell and spin a story that would ruin you both."

She huffs. "And now you're threatening your own mother?"

"You threatened me first."

"I did no such thing—"

"You threaten my men, you threaten me," I shout, my rage ready to boil over.

We're both quiet for a minute, like a pair of tired bears circling each other before they land another blow.

She breaks the silence. "Well, it looks like the ball is in your court, Poppy. You know what I want. I want to get through this wedding without any more obscene outbursts from you. I want you present and smiling and holding your flowers like a dutiful sister. You do that, and maybe we'll talk about Nana's money."

"I want to bring them," I say before she can hang up.

"Not possible."

"Mom, I am bringing my partners to my sister's wedding. Just this once, I'll tell everyone they're my colleagues. But you will say yes to them coming, or I will announce my pregnancy on a table at the rehearsal dinner. You can keep Nana's money. Set it on fire for all care."

I'm bluffing, and we both know it. But that money is about so much more than the dollar value. It's about the legacy of a life lived, a life I cherished. It's about knowing best what my Nana would've wanted for me. More than anything, she wanted me to be happy. She would *never* have kept this money from me.

"Fine. Bring them," she says. "But if you embarrass me, you know what I'll be forced to do."

"Mom, I have to go," I say, feeling broken and so very tired.

"I have to go too."

As I hang up, I hear the sounds of Lukas and Colton returning from the store. I wipe under my eyes, praying they don't look red and puffy as I hear them climbing the stairs.

"Babe? We're home!"

"In here," I call out.

"We gotta go in like an hour," Lukas calls up the stairs. "We have that turtle thing tonight. You still wanna go, right?"

"Yeah," I call back, checking the time. Shoot, I have to get ready.

Lukas pops his head in the room, holding out a fresh bag of salted, shelled pistachios. I've been craving them like crazy. Colton is behind him, offering me a cold bottle of lemon iced tea.

"What happened?" says Lukas, his smile falling.

At his shoulder, Colton looks stricken.

I force a smile. "You're both invited to a wedding."

"Wait, you told Ryan about us? Lukas—" I grab his arm before he can step under the bright lights of the beachside supper club.

For once, I get to attend a gala I'm not hosting. This is all the work of Mars and Tess and their little turtle team at Out of the Net. Colton is already inside. He got roped into helping Ryan with setup. Lukas and I are unfashionably late because I wasted a good forty minutes trying on every dress I own, praying one would properly conceal the bump. I ended up picking a flouncy lilac number with a full tulle skirt.

Lukas turns, devastating me in his dark blue suit. "You said we were done hiding." His eyes flash with anger and frustration.

I know it's not directed at me. I told them about the phone call with my mom, and they've been in a rage ever since. Colton thinks we should go "no contact" with my entire family. Lukas wants us to go to the wedding, but only so we can "fuck on the altar like fucking rabbits."

I don't feel ready to pursue either of those options. "I'm not saying we can't tell anyone," I assure him for the tenth time. "I'm just saying we don't go full blast 'this is us' and make it front page news until *after* the wedding. Come on, that's only, like, two months away."

He groans.

"I know, if I can just deal with this in person, I can fix it," I go on, my PR brain in hyperdrive. "I can smooth it over, manage it. Daddy is reasonable. I'll talk to him. You two can talk to him too, show him how great you are—"

"Hey, if you inheriting your Nana's money is hinging on me making a good impression with your fucking parents, then you can just light it on fire now."

I step back. "So, you're not even willing to try?"

"Oh, I'll try," he replies. "But this is what they're gonna get," he adds, gesturing down at himself. "I'm a know-nothing hockey player from Thunder Bay with a juvie record, too many tattoos, and a swearing problem. I can't talk about racehorses or stock portfolios or whatever else the fuck it is that your people are into. And I'm telling you right now, your mom is just gonna use this as an excuse to try to drive a wedge between us."

His words sink deep, hitting their mark. "I know she will." Stepping in, I take his hand. "But she'll fail, Lukas. And I told you both, this isn't about the money."

"Good, because we don't fucking need it. We know you love your job, and you make good money all on your own. But work, don't work. It doesn't matter to us. We take care of you now, not some trust fund. Even if Cole retires, we'll still be fine."

I nod, leaning into his hand. God, why can't things just be easy? Why do I have this bone-aching need to be seen and respected by my family? I should walk away. If people show a pattern of disrespecting you and your values, if they seek only to manipulate and control, you walk away, right? I would walk away from a job that treated me that way. I would certainly walk away from a romantic partner. Heck, I already did. Anderson was all of those things and more.

So why can't I walk away from this? Why do I keep crawling back to them time and time again, desperate for their validation? And now I'm asking Colton and Lukas to crawl with me? I'm angry at myself. I'm angry at the stupid heart beating in my chest, telling me to keep trying, telling me this time will be different. Mom will love me for me. She'll understand. She won't put conditions on her love. She won't threaten and manipulate me.

Lukas steps in, brushing a kiss to my forehead. "I'm not mad at you, I'm mad *for* you," he assures me, saying what I need to hear.

I nod again, pressing myself to his chest.

"Come on," he says after a minute. "If we're any later, the only food left will be the tray garnishes."

We make our way inside, and he splits off, heading over where all the other Rays are congregated. I put on my best smile and work the crowd a bit, saying "hello" to Tess and Mars, congratulating them on the event. Colton wanders past, handing me a tray of appetizers with a wink. He piled on all my favorites—shrimp cocktail, cubed cheese, veggies with hummus. There's even something that looks like little Mac and Cheese cups.

Ten minutes later, I'm stuck in a corner with the ladies from the Jax Beach book club. They call themselves a book club, but they're really more of a gossip and social club. These are some of the wealthiest women in the city. Their money in the right pockets can effect real change. Sure, I'll talk up the turtles, but I have my own schmoozing agenda too.

Monica Graham-Ives has me by the arm, telling me all the gossip about her sister's daughter's salacious divorce. "Oh—and did I mention my nephew, Cabot?"

"I'm not sure that you did," I say with a smile. Women like Monica are always trying to play matchmaker. I grew up with Annmarie St. James, so I know the game inside and out.

"Oh, Poppy, honey, you just have to meet him. Cabot is an engineer for Boeing. He recently got out of a long relationship, college sweethearts," she adds. "But he's just the kind of guy who would be perfect for you. Let me set you up."

"Sure," I say, knowing it's the only way this will end. "Why don't I take his number from you?" Classic dodge. I get his number, then promptly lose his number.

Monica reaches excitedly for her phone as an elbow brushes at my back. I hear the muttered, "'scuse me," and my heart freaking stops. I glance over my shoulder to see Lukas walking away.

God. Of course he heard *that* and not Monica recounting her recent mole removal.

She taps her phone with one finger. "Okay, now let me see—"

"Actually, can you excuse me for teensy second?" I say, darting away. I follow after Lukas, weaving through the crowd. "Lukas," I call out.

He doesn't stop.

"Hey—" I catch up with him as he walks through the doors into the unused event room. It's dark, stacks of chairs piled in the corner. "Lukas, come on, you didn't hear what you—"

As soon as I'm through the door, he's turning around. In his hands are a bottle of beer for him and a tonic water with lime for me. He drops both to the floor, letting them smash as he grabs me with both hands. I gasp as he reels me in, claiming my lips in a fierce kiss. A groan sits low in his throat as he walks me backward, slamming my shoulders into the wall.

Golden lights pools at our feet next to us, shining in through the glass doors. A sea of people laugh and chatter just beyond.

Lukas nips my neck, his mouth pressing in at my ear. "Who the fuck is Cabot, huh? And why are you taking his goddamn number?"

I smile, turned on by his jealousy as he works a hand up under the layers of tulle in my skirt. "Oh, he's just a highly eligible bachelor," I tease. "He's an engineer for Boeing—"

"He's dead," he growls against my lips, working his hand under my panties.

"He's nothing," I say, holding his gaze as I ride his fingers. "He's no one."

He grins. "You remember the first time we ever fucked? I pressed you up against the goddamn ice machine and made you mine."

"I remember."

"We are gonna fight and fuck, scream and screw, until we're old and gray, do you hear me? God—you're *mine*, Poppy."

"Yes," I moan, kissing him again. I need him. I need this release. All the toxicity building up inside me from that awful phone call has to come out. "Please, god," I beg.

A shadow of someone passing right in front of the glass doors has us both going still. I'm panting, pressed against the wall, Lukas's fingers teasing my wet pussy. My lipstick is on his lips, my fingers messing his hair.

He looks around, eyes narrowed. "Come on."

Grabbing my hand, he leads me to the corner of the empty banquet room, pushing his way into the bathroom. A row of three high windows along the top of the wall let in a stream of silver moonlight. Just outside this building, the sand stretches over the dunes down to the beach.

"I'm still mad about that goddamn phone call," he admits.

"I know. I am too."

"She hurt you."

"She does that," I reply with a shrug.

"I'm afraid of going to the wedding." He drags a hand through his hair. "I'm afraid of what I'll do, what I'll say. I can't stand by and watch people hurt you, Poppy. But I'm afraid if I do anything, I'll make it worse."

"Just be there," I say, cupping his cheek. "Let me handle the rest?"

Stepping in, he smooths his hands over my bare shoulders. "I have to have you. Can't fucking think, can't calm down. Take the edge off, so I can go back out there and talk about the goddamn sea turtles."

Smiling, I turn around, pressing my hands against the wall. "I remember our first time," I say again, glancing over my shoulder at him. "I remember you got so deep, rode me so hard. I felt you for days, Lukas. I ached with it."

He groans, working up my layers of tulle. "I've never stopped feeling you. You're in my blood, in my head, in my fucking bones."

"In my DNA," I pant, spreading my legs for him as he reaches between my thighs, lining himself up at my entrance. We both sigh as he sinks in, adjusting his feet to take some of my weight. "In my heart," I say, hands splayed as he begins to thrust.

He kisses my neck, his breath warm in my ear. "In my fucking soul."

We fuck hard and fast, finding our rhythm as we each take what we need. He needs a quick recentering, reassurance that I'm his. I need comfort and the protection of his body. His love is like a shield, cloaking me and keeping me safe. We can do this. We can be together, and be happy, and all the pieces of my life can fall perfectly into place.

TEN minutes later, I make my way back into the party, cheeks flushed, the cum Lukas wouldn't let me clean away sticky between my legs. I hurry over to the table where Rachel and Tess are standing. Rachel looks dynamite in a silky black dress, while Tess looks like a mermaid in blue. "Hey, y'all, what did I miss?" I snatch a carrot stick off Tess's plate. "Anything good?"

Both women give me a once over. "Poppy . . ." Rachel glances behind me. "Where did you just come from?"

"The bathroom," I reply, stealing another carrot stick.

"Don't lie to me," she teases. "Were you just hooking up with someone?"

Great, so I'm that freaking transparent? Oh god, I can't lie to save my life. And Lukas is right, I don't want to lie. I hate this. Turning to Rachel, I take my frustration out on her, "Why don't you just scream your foul accusations to the high heavens?"

Next to me, Tess snorts. "You're as bad as this one," she says, jabbing a thumb at Rachel.

"Hey, I've been good all night," Rachel replies. "The gala host's wife isn't allowed to sneak off into coat closets, right?"

"I don't know what you two are talking about," I feign. "I stepped out for five minutes to take a phone call and use the bathroom."

As I speak, Lukas, walks right past us, straightening his tie as he winks at me. "Evening, ladies."

I go still as Rachel and Tess exchange a quick glance.

"Poppy," Rachel gasps the second he passes. "You and Novy—"

"*Shhh.*" I wave a hand in her face. "Will you hush up?"

"You horny little horndog," Tess teases. "In front of the turtles, Poppy?"

Seriously? This woman caught me getting Eiffel-towered in a child's bedroom last week. "Oh please, if you two aren't the pot calling the kettle black. First, there's you, Miss I Married Three Hockey Players," I say at Rachel. Tess laughs, and I round on her. "And don't think we don't see the way you look at Langley like you wanna climb him like a tree."

"Actually, it's the other way around," she teases. "He was the one climbing me when we first got here. I may have given him a lil' taste in the storage room."

I snatch a glass of wine off a passing tray as Rachel leans over with a cheeky little smile on her face. "So, uhh, how long have you two been . . . you know?"

"That is absolutely none of your business," I say, taking a sip of the fruity wine. The second it touches my tongue, I spit it back in the glass. "*Blegh*—will someone take this away from me?"

Rachel and Tess watch in slow motion, their eyes going wide.

"Wait—are you pregnant?" asks Tess.

I freeze like a deer in the headlights. *Whoops.*

"Oh, Pop." Rachel reaches out, squeezing my hand. "It's Novy's isn't it? Does he know?"

God, do I just tell them? Do I let it out? I search their faces, my anxiety making me choke on the words. "I . . ."

Rachel searches my face, confused. "Wait, it's not his?"

"Ohmygod," Tess says from my other side. "She's not sure."

I take in the looks of surprise on their faces.

"You're not, are you?" Tess presses. "You're not sure."

Slowly, I shake my head.

"This is a lot of information to digest at the turtle gala," says Rachel. After a moment, she gives my hand another squeeze. "Well, are you—I mean—is it *two* guys on the team?"

Heart racing, I reach for the wine glass again, desperate for anything to do with my hands. "Oh, for Pete's sake," I mutter, shoving it away again. "No, okay? I don't know who the father is." Every awful, toxic thing my mother unloaded on me swirls in my head as I glare between my friends. "And yes, they're both on the team. And *yes*, I know I'm a mess. So why don't you just slap the scarlet *A* on my chest, and tie me to the stake already? Because this wanton hussy has *two* gentleman callers."

They lean back, eyes wide.

"And you know what?" I go on, righteous indignation surging through me. "I'm not picking. You didn't have to pick, so why should I?" I say at Rachel. I know she's just a stand-in for my mother at this point, but she's here, and she asked, and now she's getting all my deflected rage. Distracted, I pick up the wine glass for a third time. The glass touches my lips, and I all but fling it over to Tess with a shrieked, "Gosh darn it!"

She rescues me from the wine, setting it aside on the next table over.

"It's Morrow," says Rachel. "You've started something with Novy and Morrow. Right?"

I take her hand. "Please, Rach, you can't say anything. I'm not ready for people to know. I'm not—we're not like you, okay?" I'm stumbling all over my words as my head wars with my heart. "We're—this hasn't been easy for us the way it seems to be so easy for you. The boys are— it's just not easy to fall into something like this . . ." Not when you have a family who doesn't support you. Not when you have a lifetime of personal and professional training that has made you conflict-avoidant to a fault. Not when you have the added burden of wanting to protect the peace and security of a child.

Rachel squeezes my hand. "I won't say anything, Pop. It's not my business. It's not anyone's business."

I sniff back my tears, letting go of the rest of my anxiety before it eats a hole through my insides. "I just—*god*, I never meant for any of this to happen. And now it just keeps happening. Four months ago, I was arguing with Lukas in an Uber. Now, I'm meeting him in empty bathrooms at charity events like we're a pair of horny teenagers." Echoing his words, a smile flits across my lips. "If we're not screamin', we're screwin', and I don't know how to stop."

I don't want to stop.

"And Morrow?" Rachel asks.

Looking out across the party, I see him standing with Lukas and some of the other defensemen. They're both laughing, Lukas relaxed now that he's had a taste of me. As I watch, he brushes a hand down Colton's back. The others don't notice. The others don't care.

But I notice. I care. It's not the touch of a teammate or a friend. It's the claiming, reassuring touch of a lover, a life partner, a soul mate.

Calmness settles in my chest for the first time since the phone call. "I don't know how to stop," I say again.

I'll never stop. Lord, help me, I will *never* stop loving these men.

78

COLTON

Two Months Later

Lukas and I walk side-by-side through the lobby of this swanky South Carolina hotel. Large potted palms tower in all the corners. Everything is marble and gold, dripping in elegance. It's wedding weekend, and we have our game faces on. Literally. The moment the wheels of our team plane touched down in Jacksonville, we were getting in my car, and driving the four hours straight up to Charleston.

Poppy's already been here for two days without us. Yesterday, she had to co-host a bridal shower, and then there was a "family only" dinner. Our grueling game schedule means this was the soonest we could get away. We've already missed out on the "guys and gals" events this morning. Apparently, the groom and his party went to play a round of golf, while the ladies headed to the spa.

Lukas and I are here just in time to check into our room, change our clothes, and head back downstairs for the start of the rehearsal dinner. He's still got his shades on, a hint of stubble on his face. I trace my gaze down the thin pink scar on his jaw.

"Okay, now what are we gonna do?" I say, putting a hand on his shoulder.

I can see him roll his eyes at me behind his shades. "We're gonna be polite to her family."

I nod. "And what are we *not* gonna do?"

He sighs. "We're not gonna punch the groom in the face."

"And?" I press.

Now he's scowling. "We're not gonna fuck like rabbits in the church."

"Very good," I say, squeezing his shoulder.

There's a small line at the check-in desk, so we drop our bags down and wait.

"Did you tell her we're here?" he asks, eyes on his phone.

"I told her the moment we arrived," I assure him.

As an added little "fuck you" from Poppy's mom, she booked us in a separate room. Apparently, Poppy spent thirty minutes arguing with the hotel staff until she got us moved into adjoining rooms. Lukas pulls up the reservation on his phone.

Laughter has me glancing over my shoulder. A troop of about ten white men in a rainbow of matching pastel golf shirts and khaki shorts comes strolling in through the large glass doors. Jesus, they look like carbon copies of each other. Two of the men look a little older, graying at the temples. But most are young, ranging in age from sixteen to mid-thirties.

I know the guy in the middle in the mint green golf tee. I recognize his face. It's the groom. He notices me and Lukas, and, for a brief moment, his carefree smile falls. He quickly replaces it with something that looks more eager, like a dog with a bone.

Lord, here we go.

I tap Lukas in the chest.

"Gentlemen," Anderson calls out, holding his arms out as he walks up.

Lukas turns, his expression going stony. We already thought this guy was a douche based on his social media profile. We hate him for what he did to Poppy. But he's somehow so much worse in person. He oozes wealth and sophistication, but the stronger scent wafting off him is bullshit. Yeah, he's about to come over here and shovel it on thick.

"Rule two," I mutter at Lukas.

No punching the groom in the face.

"You're the hockey guys, right?" Anderson holds out a hand.

Lukas reaches for him first. "Yeah, and you're Andy, right? Lukas Novikov."

"It's Anderson," he replies. "But you knew that," he adds with a smirk.

"Hey, I'm Colton Morrow," I say, offering my hand.

Anderson shakes it. "And you two are Poppy's friends . . . or is it coworkers? We're all a little confused about that."

"Sure," Lukas replies.

"We're friends, and we're coworkers," I add.

And, you know, soul mates . . . if you believe in that sort of thing.

We're finally out to everyone on the team. That's what happens when you can't keep your hands off each other, and you just keep getting caught. Lukas and I were messing around in the storage closet the other day, when Jake and Sanny came busting in, looking to do the same thing. They dared to get offended, and said it was their storage closet. We stood there like a bunch of assholes playing rock, paper, scissors to decide who stayed and who left.

"That Poppy, I tell ya," Anderson says. "She's a little spitfire, isn't she?" Why is he still holding my hand? "When will one of you step up, and lock that girl down, put a ring on her finger?"

"Poppy's perfectly content as she is," I reply.

Seriously, he's still shaking my fucking hand.

"She's not looking for a ring," Lukas adds.

Anderson huffs a laugh, finally letting me go. "Have you met these St. James girls? My advice? Wife her up, or she'll be moving on. Maybe someday the right guy will finally get her down that aisle. Lord knows I tried. Looks like you two are fumbling the ball too."

"Yep, that's us," Lukas replies, his tone flat. "Pair of butterfingers over here."

Oh, fuck me, I wanna leave. I want to walk out those doors and just fall head-first into the goddamn pool.

"Whoever he is, I hear he'll have to be okay with becoming a stepdaddy," he goes on. "Shame about all that. She was really going places."

I feather a touch over Lukas's hand, keeping him at my side.

Another man steps in behind Anderson. I know his face too. I know it because it's Poppy's face, or at least a version of it. It's a bit rounder and more masculine, but he has the same blond hair and blue eyes. "Hey, are these the hockey guys?"

"These are the hockey guys," Anderson replies. The way they both say it, you'd think we were a pair of phone salesmen who play beer league hockey on the weekends, not two of the top-ranked defensemen in the world, worth a combined fifty million dollars.

The blond steps in. "Hey, I'm Rowan St. James, Poppy's brother. Hey, Dad—" he calls, before either of us can introduce ourselves.

One of the older men glances our way, lured in by his son's waving hand. He's built like a damn house. I think Poppy mentioned he played some American football in college. I can see a glimmer of her in his features. His blond hair has all but gone silver.

"These are the hockey guys," Rowan calls out.

"Seriously, should we get shirts made or something?" Lukas mutters at me.

Her dad's eyes narrow at us as he steps over. I feel like I'm getting x-rayed as he offers out a hand. "Hello, I'm Hank St. James, Poppy's father."

Poppy says his nickname in DC is "the Kingmaker." He's some super high-powered political lobbyist who sits in the shadows and launches political careers. That's the main reason Anderson is so interested in marrying into the family. The asshole fancies himself the next JFK. He's just out here desperate to find his perfect Jackie. Who better than the daughter of the Kingmaker himself? Turns out Anderson isn't picky about which daughter, much to my goddamn relief.

"Hey, how you doing?" I say. "I'm Colton Morrow, this is Lukas Novikov."

Lukas holds out his hand and Hank shakes it too. Looking down, he takes in Lukas's colorful ink. I groan as he turns his arm slightly. "Son, is that a hairy johnson tattooed on your arm?"

"Uhh . . . yeah," Lukas replies.

Behind Hank, some of the guys laugh, including Rowan and Anderson.

"It's a long story," Lukas adds.

"I hope you were drunk," Hank replies, dropping Lukas's hand.

"If only, sir." Lukas looks to me for help, but what the hell am I supposed to do? He's the one with the goddamn cock and balls tattoo.

"Poppy says you boys are having a good season," Hank goes on.

"We are," I reply.

"You headed for the playoffs?"

I laugh. "Well, you know, we don't count anything out. We're a new team, so it's been more about restructuring this year—"

"Hey." Rowan snaps his fingers, pointing at Lukas. "Weren't you the guy that got in all that trouble for punching out a ref last season?"

"He swung first," Lukas replies. "It's on video. The review committee cleared me with a minor fine." He's trying so damn hard right now. He deserves a medal for not chirping this guy into tears.

"Right . . . well, a fight video is small potatoes," Rowan goes on. "Not like all the videos of you partying it up with blondes that aren't my sister."

Okay, seriously? Fuck Rowan.

Next to his son, Hank just frowns. "That's enough, Rowan."

Yeah, eat a dick, Rowan.

I think it, I don't say it. Instead, I wrap an arm around Lukas, pulling him a step back. "Well, it was great to meet you all, but we gotta get checked in. We'll see you at dinner, yeah?"

"You're gonna cover the dick tattoo, right?" Anderson calls after us. "This is a nice hotel, and we're nice people."

Could've fucking fooled me.

"I'll make sure he puts on long sleeves," I say, still pulling Lukas back. We turn away to the sound of their laughter, nearly tripping over our bags in the process.

Their voices fade away as they all walk off toward the elevators.

Lukas ducks down, grabbing the strap of his weekender bag, and slinging it over his shoulder. "Hey, Coley, be a pal and check. Is there blood coming out of my goddamn ears?" He tips his head to the side.

"No, why?"

"Okay, cool. So, it just *felt* like all the vessels in my head were exploding."

I know the feeling. "Man, fuck Rowan, eh?"

Lukas just grinds his teeth, walking up to the empty check-in counter. "That fucking weasel's gonna eat my fist if he comes at me again, I swear to fucking god."

I grab the back of his shirt. "Hey—rules one *and* two."

"I'll be nice to him if he's nice to me," he growls. "And rule two only applies to the groom."

"This is for Poppy," I remind him. "She wants us to make a good impression."

"Coley, they made up their minds about us long before we ever walked through that door."

I know, he's right. This is a total lost cause. But I'll be damned if I'm gonna do anything to add stress to Poppy's waking nightmare of a weekend. "Come on," I beg him. "We said we would do this. We love her. She's worth it, right?"

He sighs. "Yeah, she's fucking worth it."

I smile, patting his back. "That's the spirit. Hey, maybe before the rehearsal dinner, we can go get His & His eels shoved up our asses?"

He snorts a laugh.

We then spend the next twenty minutes getting checked in and finding our room, exchanging ideas of all the things we'd rather be doing than attending this goddamn wedding.

"**O**h, thank god," I cry, opening the door of my hotel room to find my guys lounging on the bed. They leap up as I hurry in. I kiss Colton, then Lukas. Arms around their waists, I just breathe them in.

"That bad, huh?" Colton teases, his hand smoothing down my back.

"Worse," I say. "Tell me why I agreed to do this again?"

"Hell if we know," Lukas mutters.

Colton brushes my hair back from my face. "What happened, babe?"

"Oh, you know, my mom is still upset because I showed up looking so pregnant." I gesture down at my super obvious baby bump. "I don't know what she expected, seeing as I'm twenty-two weeks along, and I'm only five-foot-two and one hundred and ten pounds. I mean, the baby has to go somewhere."

I step between them, moving over to the vanity. "And my aunt Tilly thinks I need fillers in my forehead. Oh, and if Lemon calls me 'brave' one more time for having this baby 'all on my own,' I'm gonna find an actual lemon and choke her with it."

"Cool. I'll hold her down," says Lukas. "In other news, we met your fucking ex."

I spin around. "Where? Oh god, you know I wanted to be there to referee all interactions with the 'A' word—and yes, I mean 'Asshole.'"

"Downstairs in the lobby," says Colton.

"Yeah, we met your dad too," Lukas adds with a glare. "And Rowan. You were sure keeping *that* wild card close to the chest."

I wince. "Was my brother rude?"

"Babe, scientists are already investigating the masterclass that was his dickholery," he replies.

"I know," I admit with a tired nod. I've been dealing with his snide comments and cutting stares for two days. "For a while, I thought it was just typical older brother meanness. But I really think working for Daddy takes a toll on him. He can never stick up for himself, so he copes by bullying others. It's childish. I just try to ignore him."

Lukas sighs. "Yeah, well, rules one and two mean I just had to stand there and take it, like I was a goddamn goalie with my arms taped to my sides."

I glance over my shoulder, hairbrush in hand. "What are rules one and two?"

"Rule one: we have to be polite to your family," he replies, holding up a finger. "Rule two: we can't punch your ex in the face."

"Seriously? What do you get if you win?"

They both smirk.

"What do you get?" I say again.

"We don't wanna say," says Lukas.

Now I'm smiling. "Well, what do you get if you *both* win?"

"We both get to win," says Colton, his gaze heating.

I raise a brow, curious. "And if you lose?"

"Eh, I'll owe him fifty bucks," Lukas says with a shrug.

"What—fifty? That's it? Can we up that please?"

"No way. The chances of us losing are too freaking high," he replies.

I glance between them again. "Well, are those the only two rules?"

"Nope," Lukas replies.

I narrow my eyes at them. "Well, what are the other rules?"

"Only one more," says Colton. "No fucking like rabbits in the church."

I giggle. "Well, that one should be easy, at least."

They both toss a heated look my way.

"Okay, enough," I cry. "Get out of here." I wave at the open door connecting our rooms. "Go back in there and leave me to get ready."

AN hour later, the three of us make our way downstairs to the restaurant Daddy bought out for the night. My guys look divine in suit and tie, Lukas in charcoal, Colton in a pretty, dark green. I'm wearing a black Banana Republic dress that wraps around my neck, falling to the floor in pleats. There's enough fabric, and the color is dark enough, that from the front, at least, you'd have to squint to tell I'm pregnant. From the side? Well, honey, there's just no sucking this in.

I paired the neutral dress with a bold red lip, full curls, and a pair of absolutely gorgeous opal stud earrings, a gift from Colton last month.

The dining room is already filling as we make our way inside. I smile and wave as I walk past people I know, cousins and old friends of the family. I laugh out loud as I see who's standing at the bar. I hurry over to her, knowing the guys are following right behind. "Bitch, who invited you?" I tease, throwing an arm around Tina.

She laughs, hugging me back. She's changed up her hair, opting for a deep fade along the sides. Her petal pink hair on top is done up in curls and pinned like a faux hawk. "I thought it was you."

I just shake my head. "You didn't say a word."

"Yeah, cause I thought it was *you*," she repeats.

"It was me."

We both turn as Violet walks up. She doesn't look like her normal self. She hasn't all weekend. She looks like "Wedding Weekend Violet," all done up in my mother's makeup choices and clothing styles. Her white sheath dress hugs her curves, and her blonde hair is styled in a big Annmarie-approved blowout.

"You invited her?" I say.

She just shrugs, as if it means nothing that she let my friend come to her wedding. "She came to the bachelorette, and she brought cool gifts. I figured I could squeeze another couple hundred bucks out of her."

"Fuck you too," Tina teases.

A smile flickers across Violet's face. Then she's turning, offering out a hand to my men. "You both came."

"We were invited," says Lukas, shaking it.

"I know, I invited you too," she replies, shaking Colton's hand. "I'm glad you're here," she adds, shocking the heck out of me. She's quickly called away by her friends, leaving me with the only friendly faces at the party.

"It's good to see you again, Devil One, Devil Two," says Tina, stepping in for a hug.

"Hey, come on, I'm an angel," Colton teases.

"Well, I'm not. Devil in the streets *and* the sheets," says Lukas, hugging her next.

She just rolls her eyes. She knows everything about us, and she's been so supportive. She already sent Lentil a box of goodies, including the breast pump and bottle-cleaning kit I put on my registry. She called it "Baby's First Mixology Set."

"Now it makes sense," Rowan says, wandering up with a pregnant Deidre on his arm. "The freakazoid got you roped into the alternative lifestyle, right, Pops?" He nods at Tina. "Hey, Tuna, how's it going?"

Tina stiffens. We both hate that nickname. "Rowan. Don't you have a pile of ants you can go burn with a magnifying glass?"

He chuckles. "Nope, but I do have a couple deals I can close. Those should bring in a cool million each by close of business LA time."

"Spare us," I say with a sigh.

"What would you know about it, Pops?"

Before I can speak, Lukas steps in. "Actually, Poppy just helped me close an endorsement deal with Under Armour. It's worth a cool *two* million."

Next to him, Colton smirks.

Rowan takes a sip of his beer. "Hmm. That surprises me. With that ugly scar, I bet it's hard to put your face on the posters."

"Actually, women love a guy with scars," Lukas replies. "Turns out they're attracted to strength and resiliency. But you wouldn't know anything about that, would you?"

Colton groans, and I put a hand on Lukas's arm. "Deidre, I love your hair," I say loudly, inching in front of him.

Deidre smiles. "Thank you. It's—"

"Actually, I *would* know a thing or two about strength," Rowan counters.

"God, are you still here," Lukas deadpans.

Tina chuckles, but Rowan bristles, trying to make himself taller than his five-foot-nine next to Lukas's six-foot-two. "You listen to me, asshole. My family built this country—"

"Lemme stop you right there," Lukas says, putting up a hand. "See, I'm Canadian. So, all your posturing 'America rules' political bullshit is gonna go right over my head."

"Hey, don't blame Canada for why you're so unintelligent," Rowan snaps. "Blame the NHL for not giving you dumb jocks better protective headgear."

"Rowan, that is enough," I finally say. "You're just embarrassing yourself."

"Oh, *I'm* the embarrassment? Come on, Popcorn, what did you expect? Did you really think we'd welcome these guys with open arms? That we'd just look the other way when you show up pregnant with no ring on your finger? These guys are obviously trash. No real man would treat you this way—"

"I will *not* let you speak to them like that," I all but shout. Colton and Lukas each have a hand on my arm now, holding me back.

Tina steps forward, arms crossed. "The only trash here is *you*, Rowan. Your sister is fucking amazing. She's a girl-bossing queen that is so all-powerful, she deserves *two* kings. You couldn't hold a candle to these guys, and you fucking know it. So just go crawl back over to King Daddy and suck your own tiny dick."

"Goodness, I do hope nothing's the matter over here."

I squeeze both my guys' hands in warning as I slowly turn.

Mom comes gliding up in a silver dress, her hair perfectly styled, thick black pearls around her neck. She's clutching her usual glass of pinot grigio with a practiced hand. She peers around at all of us, looking the longest at Colton and Lukas, before her gaze settles on Tina.

"Mom, you remember Tina," I say, still keeping myself between Lukas and Rowan.

Of course she remembers. Tina only lived over our garage for years. She swam in our pool and rode our horses. She used to climb our fence and trip the alarms to go hang out with her stoner friends at the park.

"Christina," Mom says. "Did I know you were coming, dear?"

"Violet invited me, ma'am."

Oh, she just called my mom "ma'am." I am so teasing her about that later. As if she can read my mind, she shoots daggers at me with her eyes.

"Hmm." Mom takes in all Tina's piercings and tattoos. "What is it with you young people feeling the need to desecrate your bodies with all this ink and metal?"

"It's called body modification," Tina replies. "And it's actually a practice as old as humanity. They've found tattoos on human remains that are over three-thousand years old."

Mom grimaces. "Well . . . isn't that a fun little anecdote for a wedding."

"I think it's cool," Lukas says with a shrug. When all eyes turn to him, he tenses. "Oh—Lukas Novikov, ma'am. I'm your daughter's—"

She raises a warning brow at him.

"I'm . . . Lukas," he finishes lamely, holding out his hand.

She shakes it as if his hand were a wet fish, and angry tears sting the corners of my eyes. She's not even trying. In fact, she's deliberately *not* trying.

"And which one are you?" she says at Colton.

"That's Colton, Mom," I say. "If Lukas has already introduced himself, you know he must be Colton. You know their names."

"Do not raise your voice to me, Miss Poppy."

I take a deep breath, turning to Tina with a pleading look.

"You know, Annmarie, that is such a pretty dress," she says, trying to buy me an out.

"Thank you, Christina." She smooths her hand over the sparkles of her silver dress. "If only my sweet girl thought to dress for a wedding, instead of a funeral. She brings down the entire mood, sulking over here in the corner."

"Okay, look—" I spin around, but Lukas pulls on my arm, tucking me in at his side with a muttered, "Rule number one."

Wait, now *I* have to be polite to my family? Fat freaking chance. Not if they're all gonna act like this. I can't bear it.

"Why don't we find our seats for dinner?" Colton says, his hand on my back as he tries to lead me away. "Mrs. St. James, it was a real pleasure meeting you—"

"Poppy, honey, you're up at the top table with the rest of the bridal party," Mom says over him. With one last look, she turns and walks away.

I let out a shaky breath as they both groan.

"Fuck, I think my feet are sweating," Colton mutters.

"Your mom is scarier than my high school hockey coach," Lukas adds. "That guy hunted elk with a bow and arrow."

I squeeze both their hands. "Sit with Tina, and I'll find you when this is all over."

"Hey, yeah—and just a heads up, if you can't find Rowan, I killed him and hid him under the table," says Lukas.

Tina steps in too, draining her glass of wine. "Nothing is fucking worth this. I'm outta here—"

"No—Tina, *please*," I beg. "We need you. The team needs you. Go with Lukas and Colton, and keep them from stuffing Rowan in a toilet."

"Fine," she mutters. "But I make *no* promises I won't stuff him in there myself."

THIS is torture. Literal torture. As the maid of honor, they sat me on the other side of Anderson, next to his best man, his little brother Cody, whose entire personality is car racing. Oh, and he once tried to feel me up at a family Christmas party.

Every time Anderson speaks to me, he leans in, like he's telling me a secret. Which means I've been leaning away from him all night, practically crawling into Cody's lap. My guys have been watching me squirm in my chair for over an hour. When I can't take it for another second, I leave the rest of my chicken uneaten on my plate and make my way back over to the bar.

Sensing my distress, Lukas, Colton, and Tina join me. "I swear to fucking god, if he tried to touch you one more time," Lukas growls.

"I'm fine," I say, my hand on his arm. "It's fine."

"Pops, this is totally fucked," Tina says. "Why did you even come?"

I feel the tears burn again. "Because I wanted to try, okay? Before I walked away for good, I wanted to know I did *everything* I could to try to make my family see me, to make them respect me, and understand what makes me happy."

Tina gives me a sympathetic smile. "Honey, some people are just blind to what's right in front of them. You gotta be able to let that shit go."

"We've been telling her this for months," says Lukas.

"We knew being here would only hurt you," Colton adds.

"Say the word, and we'll leave," Lukas assures me. "The car is outside, and our bags are already packed. We'll just shove Rowan's body over a bit and—*fuck*—"

Feedback from the microphone has all of us wincing and turning. My eyes go wide as I see a tipsy Olivia tugging on the mic, her arm around Lemon. "Excuse me, everyone," she says, the mic squeaking. "I know it's not time for speeches, but I just have something to say about our beautiful bride . . . my best fucking friend in the whole world . . . Violet."

The dining crowd quiets down, confused.

"Oh no," I whisper, the doom already spreading.

From across the room, Mom shoots a glare over at me, like this is all my fault. Is this another maid of honor duty? I'm sorry, but I packed my butterfly net and my tranquilizers in my *other* dress.

Olivia breathes onto the mic saying, "When Violet first told me she was fucking her sister's fiancé, I was like 'whaaaat?' 'Cause that's just crazy, right?"

A gasp shivers over the room as I feel my heart drop from my chest. Half the guests slowly turn, their eyes locking on me. The other half of the room looks to Violet and Anderson. They sit there, hands held on the table, eyes wide.

Tina drains her third glass of wine. "Fuck, here we go."

"Yeah, we all thought this was just like a fun thing," Lemon adds into the mic.

"None of us *ever* thought she would actually go through with marrying him," Olivia goes on to the horror of the crowd. "I mean, we all understand marrying rich, but god at what cost?"

Violet shakes her head as Anderson shifts his hand away, cheeks reddening. Mom looks apoplectic as Dad stands, gesturing to the emcee. At the other side of their table, Anderson's mom is frozen with shock.

Olivia boldly goes on, one hand clutching her chest. "In my heart, I know this is wrong. You don't even love him. Violet, *please*," she cries, making the microphone pop again. "We've been through so much. And I know now that we're meant to be together. Violet, I lo—"

The mic cuts out before Olivia can finish her drunken confession of love. Then the emcee is taking over on another mic. "Alright, folks. We're gonna hold off on the rest of the speeches until after dessert. Who needs another refill? Just hold up your glass!"

A pair of waiters shuffle Olivia and Lemon away from the mic, while this graveyard silence is suddenly filled with the cheery staccato of Rosemary Clooney's "Batch-A-Me."

"What the fuck?" Lukas mutters.

Tina turns, grinning like it's Christmas. "Can we go push Rowan in the pool now?"

She can laugh, but I feel like I've stepped out of my own body. I'm floating above the room, watching the chaos. Dad argues with the emcee. Mom is trying to reassure Connie Montgomery. All the guests buzz with gossip. Half of their faces are still turned my way. Did part of me always know? Is that why I called it off when I did?

Across the party, I see Violet and Anderson exchanging heated words. Then Violet is tossing her napkin onto the table and getting up. Anderson follows her, shoving back his chair.

"Pop," Colton says, his hand on my back.

Lukas leans in. "Are you okay?"

I set my Shirley Temple down on the bar. "No," I say in a faraway voice. "I'm not okay. Will you please excuse me?" Fueled by adrenaline, I feel half the eyes of the room watching me as I follow in the direction Violet and Anderson disappeared.

"Poppy," my mom hisses, grabbing my arm as I pass. "Don't follow them—"

I jerk my arm free. "Did you know?"

She dares to give me that confused look, hand clutching her literal pearls. "Know what?"

I glare at her. "About their sordid little affair lasting even before Anderson and I broke up? Did you know?"

She glances around, putting on her fakest smile. Dad is now behind her, talking to the furious Montgomerys. "Poppy, dearest, let's not discuss this here," she says, reaching for me again.

I back away. "Oh, so I'm 'dearest' to you now? I thought I was the family disappointment? I thought I deserved a scarlet letter? Selfish, you called me. Irrational, hysterical. That's me, right?"

Her smile turns wooden. "Poppy Aurora, if you make this any worse—"

"How can it get worse?" I cry. "You've lied to me, and manipulated me, and bullied me for years, Mom. You knew my own fiancé was cheating on me and said nothing. God, you almost let me marry him!"

She huffs. "You're being ridiculous."

Blinking back my tears, I shrug helplessly. "Well, no one can ever say I didn't try. No one can say I didn't do *everything* in my power to earn your approval." I take a deep breath, resolve settling in my chest. "But now I'm done."

"Poppy . . ."

"Nana, if you're listening, you know I love you, but you can keep your freaking money," I call to the heavens.

"Oh, you are just being spiteful," Mom hisses. "Please, can we just not do this here?"

"You know what, Mom? No," I say, raising my voice. "I want to do this here. I wanna do it *right* here!"

Dad, and the Montgomerys, and several other faces turn my way. The whole restaurant quiets.

"Poppy," Mom begs. "Don't—"

"Look closely, folks!" I call out, putting both hands on my stomach. "My prudish mother doesn't want y'all to know that I'm knocked up out of wedlock, but this is no Christmas ham stuffed under my freaking dress!"

A few gasps go around the room, and my mom looks like she's going to either faint or morph into a snarling beast.

"That's right, I'm pregnant with my partners' child," I go on. "And that's partners plural because I have *two*. Give a wave, honeys!"

Eyes wide, Colton and Lukas wave their hands.

Lukas recovers first shouting, "Ice machine sex. It's a ten out of ten, I'm telling' ya!"

"Yep, your precious little Poppy Girl is riding two dicks at once!" A wild thrill rushes through me as I finally let this all out. "And if anyone has a problem with that, you can alllll take it up with Christina Renoux." I point at her in the corner. "Because *she's* the one who gave me the faulty condoms that likely got me pregnant!"

"You're my hero," she shouts over the crowd.

"Poppy," Mom cries, angry tears in her eyes. "That is *enough*."

"Yeah." I nod, a deep sense of calm filling me. "You're right, that is enough. I've had enough. You and me? We're done."

"Poppy—"

Turning on my heel, I go in search of Violet and Anderson.

I walk out into the manicured hotel garden, complete with climbing trellises and boxwoods. Several yards away, a fountain bubbles in the middle of a square glowing with twinkling lights. Violet and Anderson stand just beyond the fountain, arguing.

"No—I can't do this anymore," Violet cries.

"We had an agreement. Goddamn it, I am not going to be made a fool of again."

"I'll pay you back," she says with tears in her eyes.

"You already signed the contract. We're going through with this, Vi."

My heart is racing as I cross the square over to them. Every cruel and cutting word I was about to lob at my sister fizzles like fire on water as I take in the desperate look on her face.

"Please, Anderson. Just let this be enough—"

"No," he says, grabbing her arm.

"Hey, is everything okay?" I call out, my heels clicking on the large paver stones.

Anderson drops his hand away from Violet, and she covers the spot with her hand. Tears well in her eyes. "Poppy, I'm so sorry—"

"Don't." I raise a hand to her. "Not now." I turn back to Anderson. "I asked if everything is okay."

"No, everything's not okay," he snaps. "Your stupid fucking sister thinks she can make a fool of me the same way you did, and I'm reminding her that's not how this is gonna go."

Violent flinches, stepping away from him.

"What's the agreement between you?" I ask, looking to Violet.

"We have a prenup—"

"Shut up," he growls at her. "She doesn't get to know our business."

"Violet?" I press, only looking at her.

"He was paying me," she explains as he curses under his breath. "A third when we got engaged, a third when we marry, and the last third when Daddy helps him win his first election."

I fold my arms over my bump. "So, he's buying you then? You're selling yourself as his political trophy wife? Seriously, Vi?"

"Come on, Pop. Don't make it sound so tawdry," says Anderson. "Prenups are a standard practice. I had one with you too, if you remember."

"I remember everything," I reply flatly. I look to my sister. "How much?"

"Ten million."

My heart stops. "But you'll get that from Nana."

She just shakes her head, lip trembling. "Not anymore. Mom took it from me six months ago . . . right before I agreed to marry Anderson."

I drop my hands to my sides, all the pieces falling together in my mind. "Why?"

Tears fill her eyes. "Because I'm a disappointment to the family, and Nana wouldn't want me to have the money. Mom said I don't deserve it, since all I do is party and waste my life away. She said she was giving it to *you*."

Well, shit. No wonder Violet's been so extra bitchy to me lately.

"I went from thinking I'd be set for life to having nothing," Violent admits with a teary shrug.

This is the core difference between Violet and me. I've always worked hard to make it so I didn't need Nana's money. But Violet went another way. It's hard not to dream when our siblings are able to do things like take expensive holidays in Vale and rent apartments in Paris. Violet sees Nana's money as the answer to a life problem, while I only ever saw it as a gift.

Violet steps toward me. "Popcorn, I'm so sorry. Anderson and I have just been one big mistake from the start. I think I was feeling rebellious at first . . . and then I kept crawling back, even when you warned me away—"

"I'm standing right here," he huffs.

"Anderson asked me to marry him again and again, and I always said no," she goes on. "I know he's only after me for Daddy and his own career, but then Mom took everything from me, my whole future. So, the next time Anderson asked, I heard myself say yes."

He moves around the fountain toward us. "You fucking bitch. You really think that's how it played out?"

"That's exactly how it played out," she says over her shoulder. "You've only ever cared about this obsession with your stupid political destiny. But it takes more than a square jaw and pockets full of cash to win the hearts of the public. You're pathetic, Anderson!"

"And it takes more than a pair of tits and the St. James name to bag a man," he jeers. "Look at you both: beauty on the outside, but rotten to the fucking core."

Violet steps closer, taking my hand.

"I'm the only man who has *ever* given you a chance—either of you," he adds at me with a glare. "No other man fucking wants you. Hank should've been paying more attention at home. Maybe then he would've noticed his hired help raised a pair of sloppy whores."

Violet flinches. But my rage crackles like a holy fire. "Anderson, this is over. You need to go."

He dares to take an imposing step closer to us. "I'm not going anywhere. Violet and I still have a deal. She owes me three million dollars. I don't leave until I get every dime back."

Violet looks to me, panicking. "I don't have it," she whispers.

My heart sinks as I squeeze her hand. "You'll get your money back, Anderson. You know we're good for it. I promise—"

"Your promise doesn't mean *shit* to me," he shouts. "You promised to love me and marry me and give me the future I've always wanted. The future I fucking *deserve*! You made a goddamn fool out of me, and I'll be damned if I let your spoiled little sister do the same thing." He grabs her arm and jerks her away from me, both of us crying out.

"Anderson, don't," I beg.

He grabs her by the shoulders, shaking her as she cries. "We're getting married tomorrow, and you're going to keep your word and deliver *everything* we agreed on. Do you understand?"

"Let her go," I cry.

"Poppy!" Lukas rushes to my side, Colton just behind him.

They both get their hands on me, pulling me to safety.

"Stop this," I say on a breath. "Please, stop him."

Colton's hands clamp down like bands of iron on my arms.

"Permission to break rule number two?" Lukas asks.

I nod, heart racing as they still argue. "Please—"

"Then where's my money?" Anderson shouts, his hands squeezing Violet's arms.

"I said I don't have it," she cries.

"Give me back my fucking money!"

"Anderson, please, just stop this!"

Lukas storms up with a holy vengeance. "Get your fucking hands off her!"

Anderson balks at Lukas's approach, shoving my sister away. She cries out, stumbling down to the paver stones as Lukas lunges, slugging Anderson in the jaw. It's a K.O. punch that sends Anderson falling backward like a sack of flour. He drops to the ground and doesn't move.

"Ohmygod, is he dead?" Violet shrieks, crawling on her hands and knees over to him.

Lukas drops to one knee, feeling for his pulse. "Nah, he's alive," he assures us.

I let out a shaky breath of relief, tears falling. Colton presses in behind me.

"He's just out cold," Lukas adds. "A doc should check if I broke his jaw. I sure tried hard enough."

"Well, that was a fucking assault!" Rowan shouts, striding toward us.

Lukas stiffens and turns, ready to face my brother.

"Don't fucking move, asshole! I'm calling the police right now. I saw what you did."

Ignoring him, Lukas stands. "What you saw was me protecting your sister. It was Anderson who did the assaulting!"

Violet is still on her knees, mascara running down her cheeks. "Ro, it's true."

"What the hell is happening out here?"

I take a deep breath as our dad appears, striding down the path behind Rowan. He steps past my brother and surveys the scene. His gaze is murderous as he looks from Anderson's prone body to Violet on her knees to Lukas, still panting. Slowly, Daddy turns to me. "Poppy, explain."

"Violet and Anderson were arguing—"

"I didn't see an argument," says Rowan. "I saw one of your boyfriends punch Anderson's damn lights out!"

"Because you're a day late and a dollar fucking short," Lukas shouts. "He had his hands on your sister!"

Daddy turns to me. "Go on, Poppy."

Next to him, Rowan huffs, arms crossed as he glares at Lukas.

"She wanted to call off the wedding," I go on. "But he didn't. Apparently, they have a financial agreement. He said he wouldn't walk away until he got his money back."

Daddy looks to Violet. "Is this true?"

She nods.

"How much?"

She rises shakily to her feet, the knees of her pristine white dress now stained and ruined. "Daddy, I'm sorry—"

"How much, Violet?" he shouts.

She flinches back, lip trembling. "Ten million in total. He paid me 3.3 million already. I was going to get another 3.3 when we married tomorrow . . ."

"Jeezus," Rowan mutters. "And let me guess, you already spent it all?"

"Quiet, Rowan," Dad warns.

Rowan bristles but crosses him arms again.

"And the last third?" Dad asks with a raised brow.

She's quiet for a moment, embarrassed to own the truth right to his face. "When you helped him win his first election. He wanted to run for Senate next year."

Dad sighs. "Lord have mercy. Anderson has all the potential of a state senator, maybe a mayor, but the town's gotta be small . . . and solidly red." He rubs a tired hand across his brow. "What a goddamn mess."

I step forward. "Well . . . if you have no faith in his political career, then why did you try to pair us both with him? Why did you push so hard for these marriages?"

"I didn't," he shouts. "You think I wanted any of this? I want my girls happy. That's all I've ever cared about. I don't know what either of you ever saw in this turkey bird," he adds, waving at Anderson's prone form. "But I was willing to put on the tux and pay for the wedding. Twice," he adds with a glare. "If it made you happy, and your mother assured me it did, then I was gonna suck it up and do it."

My heart shatters all over again. "So, this really has been all about Mom and her vision for our futures."

"Your mother is a complicated woman, Princess."

"Oh Daddy, please. She's a narcissistic 'queenmaker' with a god complex!"

"Hey," he says, tone firm. "Don't talk about your mother that way."

"Daddy, she ruined our freaking lives! She forced us both into thinking Anderson was a good match. I *never* would've picked him for myself if she wasn't in my ear from the age of ten telling me the best I could ever hope to achieve in life was becoming a politician's wife. I'm supposed to be the woman behind her man, raising him up and helping him shine."

"That's ridiculous," he counters. "We sent you both to the best schools. You have a top-tier business education. Violet has a law degree. Pops, you're a goddamn director in your field."

"I know," I cry with a wave of my hand. "I did all that *despite* her, not because of her. She's been dragging me down and hating on my choices my whole freaking life because they weren't *her* choices."

He sighs, shaking his head. "I didn't know."

"You didn't care," I clap back, hands on my hips. "You've never paid attention to what was happening to us at home, what she was doing to us. Daddy, do you know she took Violet's trust fund away? Just took it. Poof." I snap my fingers.

He looks to Violet with a raised brow. "She did?"

Violet nods. "She said she was giving it to Poppy."

"And the only reason I'm even here is because she was threatening to do the same thing to me," I go on. "You heard her, Dad. At the Lafayette. Were you even listening? She hates my choices, even though they've made me the happiest I've ever been in my freaking life, and she's punishing me for it. She was so determined to see Violet married off, she just recycled my bad pick. I mean, it's madness! And it has to freaking stop."

Daddy's quiet for a moment. "I'm sorry. Girls, I'm so sorry. This is all . . ." He just shakes his head. He looks to Violet. "What do we do here, sugar bean? What do you want?"

"I don't want to marry him," she replies. Panting, she wiggles the huge engagement ring off her finger and drops it down to the paving stones next to Anderson's limp body. "Daddy, *please.*"

"But you owe him money? There's a contract involved?"

She nods.

"Right. Well, I'll have my people deal with that first thing in the morning." He turns to me. "And what do you want?"

Heart racing, I hold his gaze. "Nothing," I reply. "The only thing I've ever wanted was the respect and genuine love of my family. Since I can't have that, there's really nothing left."

Daddy's eyes narrow at me. "You think I don't love you?"

Tears sting my eyes. "You may love me, Daddy. But you don't respect me. You don't respect any of us. You and Mom, you both just trample and control—you with Rowan, and Mom with us. And I'm telling you, it has to stop. You need to open your eyes and see that we are our own people with our own goals and dreams. I may not have followed the path you set out for me, but that doesn't make what I do beneath your notice or your respect."

He takes a step closer. "You think I'm not impressed by your career? You think I don't talk up your accomplishments to my friends and colleagues? You think I don't watch hockey games, hoping for a glimpse of you?" Closing the space between us, he cups my face.

Tears fall as I lean into it, pressing his hand to my cheek.

"You are so strong," he says down at me. "Every day, you make me proud. Never change."

Taking a deep breath, I hold my dad's steely blue gaze. "You're right. I am strong." Reaching up, I brush his hand away and take a step back. "I'm strong enough to know I deserved better from you. We all did."

His eyes narrow as his shoulders tense. "Poppy—"

"All my life, I just wanted you to see me. I wanted you to care. I wanted you to protect me from her . . . but you didn't."

He sighs. "I'm so sorry, honey."

I nod, reaching blindly for Colton's hand. His touch is like a lifeline, giving me strength. "And maybe someday I can forgive you, but you need to know that I will never forget. This is what it took to make you see us." I gesture around. "Your indifference brought us here as swiftly as Mom's constant meddling. If you ever want to earn my respect back as your daughter, you will fix this."

Dad's expression is impossible to read. Resolved, he looks to Colton. "Will you please see my girls safely inside? I'll deal with Anderson."

"Daddy, no," Violet cries. "You can't kill him."

He just chuckles. "I'm not gonna off the man. I'm gonna splash some water on his face to get him conscious. Then I'll tell him in no uncertain terms that the next time he comes sniffing around a St. James, he's gonna get his nose stomped with the heel of my goddamn boot."

Lukas steps forward. "Sir, I can't have him pressing charges—"

"Should've thought of that before you knocked him out cold," Rowan counters.

"Rowan, enough," Dad snaps. He looks to Lukas. "We have witnesses that he was attacking Violet, yes?"

"Yes," I say with a fervent nod.

"We both saw it too," Colton assures him.

"That's good enough," Dad replies. "As I said, leave Anderson to me. The day he presses charges on you will be the day his life goes up in smoke."

"Thank you, sir." Lukas steps over and offers out his hand.

Daddy shakes it. "By the way, I like the tattoo."

Lukas grins. "Thanks. Your daughter drew it."

"Oh god," I mutter as Colton laughs.

"Did she now?" Dad looks at me. "Always full of surprises." He drops Lukas's hand. "Now, y'all head on inside. I'd prefer not to have a witness to the threats I'm about to levy on this man's soul."

Lukas takes Violet's hand, leading her over to us. I take her other hand, and the five of us start walking back toward the golden lights of the hotel. The music grows louder as we approach the restaurant.

"Well, that was embarrassing," Rowan mutters. "Are you two capable of doing anything but bringing shame to the damn family?"

"Oh, Rowan, will you shut up already?" I snap. "If we can survive our mom, you can surely survive dad. Or if you can't, do what I did and walk away. The door is always open to a new life."

He huffs. "Sure. Why don't I just go see if a few football players can knock me up too?"

Next to me, Colton groans. "Permission to break rule number one?"

"Be my guest," I say with a wave of my hand.

Rounding on my brother, Colton grabs him by the shoulders and shoves him up against the nearest boxwood. "Ouch—*fuck*—get your hands off me," Rowan cries.

"Listen to me, you literal fucking shit stain," Colton growls in his face. "Say one more bad word about your sisters, and I will personally put my fist so far down your throat, it'll massage your prostate. Do you understand me?"

Rowan's eyes go wide. Then he squirms, fighting Colton's hold. "I don't think you know who you're talking to—"

"I know *exactly* who I'm talking to," Colton shouts. "And your sister is an angel sent to this earth to fucking redeem me. She is the best person I know, and I will tear your heart out if you hurt her feelings again. So much as look at her sideways, Rowan, I goddamn dare you."

Rowan opens his mouth, but then closes it again.

"Good boy," Colton sneers. Pulling him from the bush, he gives him a shove. "Now, get the fuck out of here."

Rowan stalks away, cheeks pink with embarrassment, muttering under his breath.

"Okay, you're my new favorite," Violet says at Colton.

"Wow," Lukas says with a dramatic nod of his head. "You're welcome for saving your life, by the way."

She smiles at him. "You're my favorite too."

"Better." He leads the way in the opposite direction Rowan just disappeared.

Over by the restaurant, Tina is leaned up against the wall, puffing on her vape. She takes in the state of Violet's ruined dress and our makeup-smeared faces. "Do I even wanna know?"

"The wedding is off," I reply. "You came all this way for nothing."

She shrugs. "Eh, it was a nice drive."

I smile, an idea forming. Squeezing Violet's hand, I glance to Tina. "Wanna do me a favor?"

"Depends," she replies.

"Get Violet out of here? Take her home before my mom notices she's gone?"

It was Tina who supplied me with my getaway car when I left Anderson. It's only fitting she should help another St. James girl in need. She grins, nodding. "Life is a freaking circle, isn't it?" She holds out her hand. "Come on, Vi."

Violet looks to me, all the words unspoken lingering between us. "Poppy . . ."

"Go," I say, giving her a nod. "Really, it's okay." At her wary look I add, "Okay, it's very much *not* okay . . . but maybe it could be again. The door on my side is still open, yeah?"

Slowly she nods, giving my hand one last squeeze. "Yeah."

She walks away with Tina, leaving me standing in the light of the restaurant. Inside, I can see that the guests have all but cleared out. Another Rosemary Clooney song plays as waiters clean up the plates.

"Well . . . that was memorable," says Lukas, wrapping his arms around me.

I let out a shaky breath, leaning against him. "That was a disaster."

Colton steps in, and they both nuzzle me, exchanging kisses. We're still whole, and that's all that matters.

"I've thought about it," I say, rubbing my hands down both their arms. "And I'd like permission to break rule number three."

They both look down at me.

"Babe, the wedding is off," Colton says. "No wedding, no church."

I just shrug. "So, we find one. Maybe this hotel has a chapel."

"That's how you wanna spend the rest of your sister's ruined night?" says Colton. "Fucking like rabbits in a hotel chapel?"

I feel oddly light as I grin. "Let's try to steal some tiramisu too."

"On it." Lukas ducks away from us to slip inside the restaurant.

I turn in Colton's arms. "What were we going to win if we didn't break the rules this weekend?"

He smiles down at me. "Whoever won got to take you to Aruba."

My eyes go wide, but my smile is wider. "Can we do it anyway?"

He kisses me with a laugh. "Of course. I already bought the tickets."

81
COLTON

Four Months Later

I wander down the hall toward the kitchen, pausing as I hear Lukas singing what sounds like Queen's "Don't Stop Me Now." Only he's changed the words to make it a song for the damn cat.

"Princess says meow," he sings, swaying with her in his arms. "Feed me right now ... 'cause we're having some pâté—*Jesus*—" His shoulders stiffen as he turns and sees me leaning against the doorway. "Dude, what the fuck. Lurk much?"

Princess mews in his arms, squirming to be put down.

I just grin. "Did you rewrite a Queen song for the cat?"

"No." He sets her down.

"How many verses have you done?"

"Well, that's none of your goddamn business," he replies, stroking her tail as she leads the way over to her food dish.

"So, all of them then," I tease, stepping into the kitchen.

After months of simmering resentment on both sides, Princess and Lukas have finally struck an accord. He feeds her. She can't hate the hand that feeds her, right? At least, not forever. He peels open the can of food, tipping it into her pink bowl.

"You about ready?" I say at him.

"Do you think she's lonely?" he replies, scratching her butt.

I lean against the island with my hip. "No, I think she's spoiled rotten. I think she has three humans who feed her, brush her, and call her precious 24/7. She lives better than any of us. If she's bored, we'll get her another cat tower to climb."

"I didn't say bored, I said lonely," he replies. "I think she needs a friend."

"Well, she's about to have a new human friend here in a couple weeks. Let's just focus on that."

He nods, giving her one last pat. "Yeah, okay."

I give his shoulder a shove. "Come on. We can't be late, or Pop'll kill us."

"No, she won't," he says with a laugh. "We're too damn pretty."

"Just get your shit, and let's go."

Poppy and her team have been working on this little project for months. Most of the NHL teams run hockey camps in the summer for youth. Under Poppy's guidance, the Rays are hosting their first camp this week, and all the participants have full scholarships, which includes a gifted pair of skates, a stick, and a cool tie-dyed camp tee.

Lukas and I are both already wearing the tees. We're camp counselors, along with a few other Rays. We'll be working with the kids on drills, and at the end of the week we'll play a game.

Growing up in Canada, playing hockey is just a normal option for a kid. It's as normal as saying you want to play basketball or soccer. But here in Florida, hockey is rare. It feels good to know we can spread the joy of the sport in our own backyard.

We make our way to the practice rink, laughing and joking as we get ready. Today's just about footwork drills and stick handling, so we don't bother with pads or helmets. Lukas and I are both in long pants and camp tees. Down the bench, Jake and Sanny get ready too, wearing their matching tie-dyed tees.

"Look at us," Jake jokes. "Who'd a thought, huh?"

I sit back with a groan, rubbing my chest. That damn breakfast burrito smothered in ranchero sauce is giving me indigestion. "It surprises you that we all volunteered to be camp counselors?"

"I'll have it stated that I did *not* volunteer," Lukas says with a raise of his hand. "Poppy forced me on pain of no sex so . . ."

"No, it surprises me that we're all *here*, living the life, you know?" Jake glances around.

"What life?" asks Sanny.

"The queer life," Jake replies. "Guys, we're sitting here wearing tie-dyed shirts, head-over-skates in love with our own teammates. It's pretty cool, right? I mean, this was never on my bingo card, but I'm so fucking happy."

Lukas and I exchange a grin. "Yeah, that bingo'll get you every time," he replies.

Jake snaps his fingers. "We should all do Pride. The parade, I mean. When is that?" He looks to Sanny.

"It already passed," he replies, tying his skate laces. "It's at the beginning of June."

"Well, next year, we're doing it," Jake says, getting to his feet. "I mean all of us, the whole team, the girls too. We'll even bring the dog. Wouldn't that be fun?"

"Sure," Sanny replies. "Now, if you're done waxing poetic about the joys of being queer in hockey, there are fifty terrors out there waiting for us to show them how to handle a stick."

Jake just laughs. "Oh, we *alllll* know how to handle a stick."

I step past him in my skates, giving his shoulder a pat. "Come on, man, you gotta save something inappropriate for the kids."

He follows me out to the ice, Lukas and Sanny right behind.

For the first hour, it's a circus. The kids race around, waving their sticks in the air. After a brutal trip incident that ends with a bloody nose, we lay down some ground rules and talk about the penalties for slashing, spearing, and high-sticking.

Now, Lukas and Sanny are leading a cone drill, while Jake and I watch, keeping the other kids corralled.

"Hey, honey!"

I turn to see Poppy walk up behind the plexiglass. Fuck, she looks so goddamn beautiful. Her blonde hair is up in a ponytail, her makeup minimal. Her baby bump is huge, stretched tight under a teal Rays jersey. "Babe, what are you wearing?" I say with a grin.

"Isn't it sooo cute? Caleb and the equipment managers made it for me." She turns, showing me the shoulders that have a number twenty-two and a number three. "And did you see the back?" She turns fully around, showing me the big number one and her first name: POPPY.

"You're number one, huh?" I tease.

She turns back around, shrugging. "Well, yeah. There's only one Poppy. St. James."

"I love it," I reply with a laugh.

She looks out anxiously at the ice. "How's it going?"

"Uhh, you know, we're getting there," I say, rubbing the back of my neck.

"Well, don't forget, we're doing some interviews as they come off the ice today, and I want to include you guys. Claribel is setting it up now."

"Got it," I reply with a nod. "Whoa—hey—hold on." I skate off as I see a small fight break out between a couple of the bigger boys waiting in the back of the queue. They're picking on a small kid with glasses.

"Stop it," he cries. "It's mine—"

"I just wanna hold it for a second," the big kid teases, waving the stick up high.

Two of the other bigger kids laugh goonishly.

"Hey, come on, fellas. Knock it off," I say, skating in.

Jamal, the little kid with glasses, lunges. "Give it back!"

They wrestle with the stick as I get up behind them. "Enough," I shout, glaring at the big kid. I think his name is Jeremy. He lets the stick go, and Jamal loses his balance. I don't have time to react before Jamal is sharply butt-ending me with his stick right in the goddamn chest.

I mutter a curse as the motion glides me back a few feet.

"I'm sorry," he cries, his eyes going wide behind his glasses.

"Hey, what's going on over here?" Jake calls out.

I blink twice, taking a deep breath as a nauseous feeling coils in my gut. Oh, you gotta be fucking kidding me.

The kids all scramble to explain to Jake, but I don't hear a thing. My heart is fluttering in my chest like a bird trapped in a cage. It's in dysrhythmia. Fuck, this is not good. I rub a hand over my chest, taking a breath, praying my heart paces itself out.

"Dude, you okay?" Jake asks, one hand on my shoulder.

I grunt, dropping down to one knee.

"Cole—whoa—" Jake grabs my arm.

"My heart," I get out on a breath. "The pacing is off." I still try to breathe through it. In through the nose, out through the mouth. Slow, controlled. Recover. Breathe.

Jake's face swims in my vision. "What do you need? What can I do?"

Lukas skates up, sliding to a stop. "What happened?"

I look up from my knees, hand on my chest, and shake my head.

I watch as Lukas's soul drops from his body. I know, if he could, he'd rip his own heart from his chest in this moment and give it to me. "Call 911," he says at Jake. Dropping to his knees, his stick clattering down, he takes me by the shoulders.

"Is he okay?" Jamal asks, his face stricken with worry.

Shit. Poor kid. This isn't his fault. It's not anyone's fault.

I have a weak heart.

"Call fucking 911!" Lukas shouts.

I'm fading out. Feels like my heart is skipping in my chest. "Lukas—" I hold tight to his arm.

"Hold on, baby. Just breathe. You fucking stay with me. Breathe."

Somewhere, Poppy screams.

"Colton!" I cry, pounding my hands on the plexiglass.

He's on his knees, one hand on his chest, shoulders slumping.

Lukas skates in fast, shouting a few questions. I can see his face as it goes white as a sheet. "Call 911," he shouts, dropping to his knees to support Colton.

"Ohmy—Colton," I cry again, racing down the wall of glass toward the door.

"Call fucking 911!" Lukas shouts again.

There's a flurry of activity as the other volunteers spring into action, clearing the kids down to the other end of the ice, leaving Jake and Lukas with Colton. I grab for the handle, rattling it with a trembling hand as I try to get it open.

"Poppy!" Claribel comes up beside me. "Wait—"

"I have to get out there! I have to go to him—"

"The medics are already here," she assures me. "We had them on staff for the event remember? Look, there they go." She points out to the corner of the ice as our EMTs race out.

"It's his heart," I cry. "Oh god, he took that stick right to the chest!" As I watch, Lukas goes down with him, trying to control the speed of his fall as Colton slumps back onto the ice, his body limp.

I'm screaming, Claribel's arms are around my shoulders, keeping me from going to him. Kids are crying, and the volunteers are trying to get them off the ice.

"Let me go—"

"No," she growls, her hands tight on my shoulders. "I am not letting my nine-months pregnant boss out onto a sheet of ice to slip and fall in a race to do the job the paramedics are already doing. Now, come on." She pulls on me, wrestling me farther down along the glass.

"Oh god, is he dead?" I sob. "Claribel, if he's dead—"

"Hey—" She grabs me by the face, forcing me to look at her. "We're not gonna do this, okay? We're holding it together. We're breathing, and we're calming down. Breathe with me, boss." She takes a deep breath in, pushing it out through her lips.

I try to copy her, but I just suck in the breath, choking on it as a spasm pierces my side like a lance. "*Ahh*—" I bend, grabbing my side, pressing against the pain.

Claribel leans away. "Oh shit—are you seriously going into fucking labor right now?"

"No, it's too soon," I cry, heart racing. "I still have three more weeks—*ahh*—" Another sharp pain has me wincing.

"Fuck, you are. Come on." She pulls on me again.

"No, it's probably just Braxton-Hicks. I'm fine. Just let me go check on Colton." I look back out to the ice. They have him on a stretcher, an oxygen mask over his face. Lukas is holding his hand, saying words I can't hear.

"Poppy, please," Claribel urges. One arm is around my shoulder and the other grips tight to my hand. "Do you really wanna have this baby right here on the bleachers?"

That image penetrates my fog of panic and now my feet are moving. She leads me down to the corner of the ice as pressure pushes in at all sides of my abdomen.

"Oh god, I think this is a contraction," I cry.

"I know," she says. "Trust me, I come from a big Catholic family. I'm one of eight kids."

"Wow, eight is a lot," I say on a breath, delirious as she takes me to where they're wheeling Colton off the ice.

Lukas is already on a bench, furiously untying his skates, kicking them off. He follows after the stretcher in socked feet.

"Lukas!"

Hearing me, he turns, his face stricken. He takes in my posture, both my hands gripping to my belly, and races to my side. "Poppy— oh shit, are you—"

"Is he alive?"

He nods. "Yeah. he's alive. He says he's having dysrhythmias. Poppy, I think he might—"

"Don't say it." Another contraction hits and I cry out, doubling over.

"Oh—*fuck*," Lukas shouts, panicking as he looks from me to where they're loading Colton into an ambulance.

"Go with him," I say, panting through the pain. "Lukas, you have to go."

"But you're having our goddamn baby!"

I just shake my head. "If something happens to him, and one of us isn't there—"

"If something happens to *you*, he'll wish he was fucking dead either way. So, you tell me what I'm supposed to do!"

"I've got her," Claribel assures him. "I have Poppy. Lukas, you go with Colton. Go. She'll be fine."

I nod, squeezing his hand. "Go, baby. Please."

With a groan, he kisses my hand and races off in his socked feet, hopping into the back of the ambulance just before they close the doors. The ambulance takes off, lights and sirens on, and I'm left standing by this hockey rink wearing a pair of wet pants.

I let out a shaky breath. "Claribel?"

"Yeah?"

"I think my water just broke."

Her arm tightens around my shoulders. "Come on, I'll take you to the hospital. We'll follow right behind them, okay? It's fine," she assures me. "This is all gonna be fine."

83
LUKAS

They take Cole away from me through a pair of big double doors, and I'm left pacing in this goddamn waiting room like a tiger in a cage. How many minutes has it been? Five? Ten? An hour? I have no clue. Time has no meaning. I just pace. When he went through those doors, he was still alive. His pulse was thready, his heart rate was erratic, but he was still breathing. He better be fucking breathing when they're done with him too.

I drag both hands through my hair, trying to get air in my lungs as I groan. God, this is so completely fucked! I'm standing here with no fucking shoes on. One love of my life is in active heart failure, while the other is in labor with our baby.

Where is Poppy? Why did I leave her? Who fucking does that?

My phone rings in my pocket, and I scramble for it. It's Jake. I tap the green button. "What?"

"We have Poppy," he assures me.

I breathe a heavy sigh of relief, sinking down onto the nearest empty chair. "Oh, thank fucking god. Where?"

"We're here in the hospital. Third floor. They took her right up to labor and delivery to get her checked out. Her water broke, but she's got some time."

I nod, my head sinking as I drop it between my knees, trying to get air.

"We won't leave her side, man. Claribel's here too. We have her, okay? You deal with Cole. Any update?"

I lean back, head against the wall as I hold back my tears. "No. Nothing."

"No news is good news," he assures me. "It means they're still working. I'll text you any updates from here as I get them."

"Can you put her on the phone?" I need her. I have to hear her voice. She'll tell me it will all be okay.

"Nah, they're doing a pelvic exam now. Figured you'd appreciate me stepping out of the room for that one."

Before I can say another word, a nurse comes through the doors, looking around. She's the same nurse who first took Cole. Seeing me, she waves me over.

"Oh fuck, I gotta go." I don't even wait for Jake's response before I'm out of my chair and walking over to her.

"You came in with Mr. Morrow, correct?"

"I did," I reply with a nod.

"He says you're family?"

Oh god, he *said* something. He spoke. I heave a deep breath. "Fuck—Yeah, I'm family. We're—he's mine. We're partners. He's my best fucking friend, please—"

"Okay," she assures me. "We have a few minutes while they prep the OR, and he asked if you can come back. Would you like to come this way?"

I nod, following after her in my socked feet.

"This is the ICU, so I'm gonna ask that you put on this protective gear." She hands me a mess of shoes covers and a paper robe and a mask and gloves, before she's leading me into exam room three.

Cole is lying there on the bed, shirtless, oxygen mask on, tubes coming out of both arms. Machines are beeping. Nurses monitor everything, adjusting the equipment. He's still breathing. I can see the cresting of his heart beeping on the machine.

"We only have minutes," the nurse urges. "Please be quick."

I nod, moving over to his bedside. I take his hand in mine, giving it a squeeze. "Coley?"

He blinks his eyes open, looking up at me. "They can't—stop—the dysrhythmia," he says on each exhale. "I'm not—responding—to meds."

"Okay." I sink down on the side of his bed, putting his hand in my lap.

"They're putting in—a pacemaker."

I nod again. "Well, we thought that might happen eventually. We were ready for it, yeah?"

He holds my gaze, tears in his eyes. "My career. It's over."

Tears burn hot and heavy as I give his hand another squeeze. "Hey, you know, that's okay, bud. You weren't that good anyway. Really, it's not much of a loss."

He just smiles, leaning back against the pillows.

I bend over, kissing his hand. "I fucking love you so much."

"I love you," he says. "Poppy?"

Fuck, I have to tell him. "Yeah, she's here too."

He searches the room for her, seeking out the warmth of her light.

"No, she's here in the hospital."

He looks to me, confused.

Fuck, just tell him. "Bud, she's in labor."

His eyes go wide as his heart rate spikes on the machines.

"No, no, no," I say as the nurses surge forward to check his leads.

"Sir, just try to breathe."

"Mr. Morrow?"

I stand and look down at him. "Okay, don't fucking do that. Calm down, bud. She's fine."

"Go to her," he says on a breath, his eyes turning fierce.

"Your problems are a bit more pressing—"

"Fuck that. You go—be with Poppy."

"I'll go," I assure him. "I'm going right after this. You two are gonna drive me fucking crazy, I swear."

"It's too early," he says, squeezing my hand tight.

"She's thirty-seven weeks. That's good, right?" I glance around at the nurses. "Is that good? Our girl is in labor at thirty-seven weeks."

"Thirty-seven weeks is good," one of them quickly assures us.

"Yeah, that's practically full term," says another.

"If I die—you have to stay," he says at me.

My stomach flips as I glare down at him. "What did you fucking say?"

"You'll be such—a good father. I want you to promise me."

"Cole—"

"Use my ring. It's in—my sock drawer."

"Stop," I growl. "You're just getting a pacemaker implanted. That's a goddamn outpatient procedure."

He shakes his head. "You take care of them. Sign the papers. If he's mine, adopt him—"

"Stop," I say again, my tears falling. "Cole, *please . . .*"

"Don't make him play hockey—if he doesn't want to."

I cup his face, careful not to jostle the oxygen mask. "You are *not* dying, do you understand me? I am not done loving you, Cole. Poppy's sure as shit not done. And our son hasn't even fucking started. You *live*, do you hear me?"

"Don't let her name him—after a plant—or a fruit," he says on another labored breath. "No Lime. No Oak or Twig."

"Yeah, and no flower names. I got it."

"Okay, we need to go," the nurse calls out. "They're ready for us in the OR."

I kiss his brow. "Name him now. Cole, name our son. Before they take you back."

He looks to me, tears in his eyes as they start rattling up the rails of his bed, readying him for transport.

I brush a gloved hand over his hair. "Cole, baby, please. Name our son."

He pulls the oxygen mask away from his mouth. Licking his lips, he says our son's name. Then they take him away from me, bringing him to a place I can't follow.

84
POPPY

"**C**an someone *please* tell me what's happening with my partner?" I ask for the twentieth time, pacing the room in my hospital gown and nubby socks. "Colton Morrow. He was brought into the cardiac ICU an hour ago, and we've heard nothing since."

"Let me ask at the nurse's station again," says the nurse, leaving the room.

I look to Claribel. "Will you please go check?"

"And leave you here alone?" she says with a raised brow.

"I will fire you," I cry, pointing a shaking finger at her. "This is insubordination!"

She shrugs, looking back at her phone. "Go ahead."

I cry out to the heavens in frustration, both hands on my belly. I've never done very well with feeling this helpless. I'm Poppy St. James. I always have a plan. I'm organized. I have lists. Of course I had a baby bag all packed and ready. Of course the nursery is set, and my birthing playlist is sync'd on all our phones. I knew exactly how this would go. I'd wear the robe I handpicked, and my hair would be braided, and Lukas would rub my feet while Colton held my hand. I wanted to feel ready to become a mother. I wanted to feel calm, and centered, and freaking prepared!

Instead, I'm pacing like a wild animal with my ass hanging out in this thin hospital gown. It's a lurid shade of yellow, with little bunnies all over it. And I don't have my soft arch-support slippers. I have these ugly maroon hospital socks. I don't even have my baby bag. Oh god—I don't have a diaper, a onesie, a freaking carrier. How will I even take this baby home?

Worst of all, I don't have my loving, supportive partners. I have Claribel on her phone and Jake Price is standing like a bouncer in the hallway. Colton might be dying with active heart failure a floor away. And where is Lukas?

Emotions crash in at me on all sides, making me feel like a rag doll tossed in the waves. "Right, here's what we're gonna do," I say, pacing back over to the window. "He's just gonna stay in."

"What?" Claribel looks up over her phone.

I glance down at my belly, feeling the baby kick into my spleen. "Do you hear me in there? You are not coming out. Not today. No way. So, just stop kicking me, and take a freaking nap."

"Poppy, you're already at seven centimeters—"

"Who freaking asked you," I shout at her.

She just holds my stare. "They are not going to let you leave when your waters have broken and you're at seven centimeters. You are having this baby today, boss. It's happening. Make your peace with it."

I shake my head, tears welling. "I'm not ready."

She sets her phone aside. "Are you serious?"

"What if I can't do it? What if I'm a terrible mother? What if I raise him to hate me, and cut me out, and loathe every time the phone rings with my call?" I should freaking know. It's been four months since I last took one of my own mother's phone calls. We haven't spoken since the wedding. It's certainly not for her lack of trying.

"Not possible," Claribel says gently. She crosses over to me and tucks my messy hair back behind my ear. "Poppy, you are literal sunshine. It's annoying how positive and wonderful and upbeat you are. Truly. Working for you has been the bane of my existence."

I smile. "Really?"

"Really," she deadpans. "You're gonna be a great mom, and this kid is gonna love you."

"You think so?" I say on a sniffle.

"Yeah, you're gonna be the kind of mom who bakes cookies from scratch, and loves to finger paint, and pick up shells at the beach."

"I *do* love to bake," I murmur.

"See, there you go."

I groan, breathing through the pain of another contraction as the door bursts open.

"I found him," Jake cries, one arm on Lukas as he pulls him into the room.

The second we lock eyes, we both break into tears. My heart shatters. "Oh *god*—"

"No—" Lukas catches me before I can sink to the floor. "Baby, no. He's alive. Look at me." He cups my face. "Cole is alive. His heart wasn't responding to any of the medications to stop his dysrhythmia. We were out of options. They're taking him back for a pacemaker surgery now. Okay? He's alive."

"He's alive?"

"He's still alive, baby." He kisses my brow. Then he steps away, taking me in from head to toe. "Now, what about you? What's happening? Where are we?"

Fresh tears well as I cling to him. "I'm sorry. Lukas, honey, I really tried. But he won't stay in."

His eyes go wide in confusion. "Well, that's a good thing, right? We wanted him to come out eventually. So, he's a little early." He shrugs, glancing from Claribel to Jake. "Probably means he's a Morrow, not a Novikov. You know how I always like to be fashionably late."

I give a weak laugh.

"Come on, babe. We can do this," he assures me.

"Colton was supposed to be here," I whimper. "I don't want him to miss it."

He nods. "Yeah, I know. But Cole's busy taking care of his own business now. This is gonna be just you and me. But I'm here, and I'm in this. Game time. We are gonna have this baby, and when Cole gets out of surgery, he's gonna get to meet him, and he's gonna be so fucking happy. Yeah?"

I hold his gaze, losing myself in the depths of his pretty caramel eyes. "Yeah . . . we can do this." I take his hands in both of mine, giving them a squeeze.

"We can do this," he echoes, his tone steady and sure. "We're ready."

Reassured, I nod. Lukas is my family now. Colton and Lukas and this baby. And we are going to share such a beautiful life together.

He smiles, hope and love shining on his face. "Let's meet our son."

85
COLTON

My tongue feels dry. That's the first thought I have as I wake in the ICU. I don't have to open my eyes to know where I am. I know the sounds of a cardiac intensive care unit better than any person ought. There's that sterile smell hospitals have, and the gentle whir, hum, and beep of all the machines. An oxygen hose wraps around my face.

I don't want to move. I know what they did to me. I know what sits in my chest, just beneath the skin. And I'm so goddamn grateful. Like the doctors said, with my heart, it was only a matter of time. A pacemaker gives me *more* time. Who knows, with advancements to devices and new medications, I could live to be a hundred.

Ten years, a hundred years, I'll take them all. Every day with my loved ones is a gift I won't be taking for granted.

Part of me wants to feel angry about it all. My career is over. My last game was my last game, and I didn't even know it. But I think maybe it's better this way. There were no tears, no long speeches from the guys. No one had to live with being the one who ended my career with a hard hit. This was such a freak thing. An accident—

Oh shit.

Jamal. That's his name, right? Skinny kid with glasses. I'll have Poppy get in touch with him for me. He doesn't need to carry this. It's not his fault.

I just have a weak heart.

"Cole?"

I smile. Lukas's voice is like a balm on my weary soul.

"Hey, bud. I saw you starting to move a bit. You just relax, okay? I'm here."

"Poppy," I manage to say, not feeling ready to open my eyes.

He takes my hand, squeezing it. "She's good. She's upstairs. Claribel is still with her. Poppy made me come down here and sit with you. You've been terrific company by the way," he adds. "I haven't been bored at all."

I open my eyes. It could be day or night. I can't tell because there are no windows in this room. Lukas is sitting at my bedside. This is still the ICU, so they've got him in the protective clothing—mask, gown, gloves. "Hey," he says. "How do I look?"

"Better than me," I mutter.

"Not possible. You're a sexy beast."

"What time is it?"

"Almost midnight."

I pause for a moment, readying myself for the worst. "How bad is it?"

He shrugs. "You'll understand more of the jargon than me, but they said the implantation went well, and your heart seems to be responding so far. Normal rhythm. Given the emergent nature of the incident, they wanna hold you at least overnight—"

"Wait—she's upstairs?" I try to sit up but fall back with a groan.

Lukas puts a hand on me. "Whoa, easy there. Let's not move just yet, yeah?"

Things still feel a little fuzzy and I'm so tired. "The baby—what's happening?"

Even through the mask, I can see that he's smiling.

"Oh god . . ."

"He's perfect," he says. "He was born around 6 p.m."

I sigh with relief. Closing my eyes, I send up a prayer of thanks.

"He's a little nugget," Lukas goes on. "He only weighs, like, six pounds. I can't remember the length. But he has ten fingers, two tails, and the cutest little flippers for feet, just like we wanted."

I smile, opening my eyes again. "And Poppy?"

"Bud, she was a total champ. She cursed like a sailor and nearly broke my hand, but we got there in the end. She's doing great. No complications. And Little Bud is happy and healthy. Wanna see?"

I nod.

He pulls his phone from his pocket and dials Poppy. "Here, lemme try to do a video call."

She picks up immediately. "Hi, honey," she says, her voice filling this room.

"Hey," Lukas says through his mask. "I'm here with Coley. He's awake."

"Oh, thank god," she says, the relief evident in her tone. "Let me see him."

Lukas stands and leans over the side of my bed, keeping the camera facing us so I can see Poppy. She's propped up in her own hospital bed, a pile of pillows behind her. Her hair is in a messy bun on top of her head, and a silky floral robe is tucked around her shoulders. She looks beautiful. I take in my own tired features before my eyes are right back on her.

"Hey, honey," she says at me. I know from her tone that she's trying not to cry. "How are you feeling?"

"Tired," I admit. "You?"

"Oh, you know, the same."

"Can I see him?"

She nods. "Yeah, Claribel was just changing his diaper. She's bringing him over now." There's a bit of jostling as she moves the camera back. Then I see Claribel's shoulder in the shot as she hands my son back to his mother. He's swaddled in a little white blanket dotted with anchors. "Can you see him?" Poppy asks.

I nod, tears in my eyes. "You both look so beautiful, baby."

"Here, hold on—" Poppy reaches for the phone one-handed. She jostles it again as she gets the camera turned around. Then she's holding it up over our sleeping son, showing me a closeup of his face. One hand is out, clutching to the blanket. I can see tiny little fingernails on each finger. His eyes are closed. His head is dusted with dark, baby soft hair, and his skin . . .

Oh god.

Lukas leans in. "We can do a DNA test if you want, but the kid looks just like you, bud." He kisses my brow through his mask. "Looks like sex in the elevator won this time."

I'm so fucking happy. This doesn't feel real.

"Lukas said you gave him a name?" says Poppy, her smile as radiant as the sun.

"Yeah, I did," I reply, shifting a little. I want to get closer. I want to reach through the phone and touch them. "If you're both okay with it, I want to call him Bennett. It means 'blessed.'"

And we are. God, we're so fucking blessed. So goddamn lucky. I blink back my tears.

"It's perfect." Lukas squeezes my shoulder. "No Colton John Morrow IV? You're sure?"

I just smile. "Colton is a fine name. But growing up, I always wanted a name that was just mine. A name with no weight to it, no expectation. Bennett is a gift, a blessing all his own."

"I love it," Poppy echoes.

"Bennett St. James?" Lukas asks with a raised brow. "We can break with tradition entirely."

Poppy flips the camera, her face back in view. "Oh no, my babies will have their daddies' last names. Bennett Morrow."

"Well, look at you, Miss Old Fashioned," he teases.

She laughs. "Yeah, I'm nothing if not traditional."

"What about a middle name?" Lukas asks, looking at me.

I'm quiet for a moment. "I was thinking maybe Anton."

He goes still. "But that's my middle name."

I smile. "I know, that's why I picked it."

He lets out a shaky breath. "Look, I love you, and I'm flattered, but Anton was my grandpa's name, and I fucking hated that asshole. If it's all the same to you, I'd like to just skip using any of my names altogether."

"Lukas—"

"No, I'm serious," he says, over Poppy. "Babe, if you and I ever have a kid, I want them to be Morrows too. Morrow to me means family. You're a Morrow, you know you're wanted and loved. You know you belong."

She nods. "Okay, Morrow it is. But Mister Bennett still needs a middle name."

We're all quiet for a moment.

"Let's go with John," says Lukas.

I raise a brow. "John?"

He shrugs. "Yeah, it's your middle name. It's a good, strong name. And not all traditions have to end. Four generations of Morrow men with the middle name 'John' seems fitting to me."

"Is that your name, baby?" Poppy turns the phone back around to show us his sleeping face. "Is your name Bennett John Morrow?"

Seeing his face again, all the emotions of the day hit me like a wave, and I start to cry. The sobs cause a sharp pain around the bruising in my chest, but I can't stop.

"Okay, whoa." Eyes wide, Lukas leans away from the bed. "What's wrong, bud? Are you—is this like a heart thing? Are you in pain?"

"I just wanna hold him," I pant, unable to catch my breath. "Wanna hold them both."

"Yeah, only they can't come down to the ICU," Lukas warns.

"Will you please do something, Lukas?" Poppy cries through her own tears.

He looks around wildly. "Okay, umm . . . here—" He takes my hand and curls my fingers around the phone. "You're holding them, okay? Just hold them just like that."

I hold the phone in both hands as he moves around the other side of my bed. Rattling the rail down, he climbs onto the bed, wrapping his arms around me as best he can. Clutching the phone, I press my face to his chest and let go of all the fear, grief, and anxiety weighing down my chest. Lukas holds me, whispering soothing words of love, telling the three of us about the beautiful life we'll share together.

When Bennett fusses, Poppy sets the phone down where I can still see them both and offers him her breast. Lukas holds me as I watch her hold my son. She hums softly as she rocks him, letting him feed. My breathing finally calms as I realize she's humming the Jonas Brothers song I sang to her at karaoke a few months ago. A smile tips the corner of my lips.

We stay like that, the four of us, locked in this quiet moment, until the only emotion left in my still-beating heart is peace.

THE END

EPILOGUE
POPPY

Six Years Later

"**M**ommy! Mom, watch! Are you watching?"

"I'm watching, sweets," I call out. Sitting in the shade of a large beach umbrella, I mime raising a hand over my eyes, and watch as Bennett floats on his colorful boogie board, waiting for the surf to swell and sweep him back in for the hundredth time.

At six years old, my sweet boy is already so tall and lanky. And he lives for the beach. Any minute not spent in the water is a minute wasted. All he wanted for his birthday were surfing lessons. I blame us still living in Florida, but I think my guys are slowly resigning themselves to a future of early morning surf meets instead of hockey practice.

The wave sweeps in, and Bennett is ready, rising up off his knees to try to stand. He's wobbly, but he gets there, his arms windmilling to keep his balance as he rides the board right onto the sand and hops off.

"Good job, Benny!" I shout, clapping my hands.

He stands in the sand like a superhero, his chest puffed out in his blue life vest. Hands on his hips, he flashes me his daddy's confident smile. My heart hums as I see a glimpse of a young Colton in his eyes. The board taps his ankles as the surf tugs it back out. He gets himself untangled from the cord and hurries back out to join the others.

Colton helps him back on his board, while Lukas keeps a close eye on Emma and Grace. At four years old, Grace isn't as daring as her brother. She prefers playing in the sand under the shade of the umbrella. Even now, she won't leave Lukas's side. He holds her, dunking her in the water, and helping her chase the others around, splashing them with her feet.

Emma is five years old and has a more adventurous spirit; not surprising seeing as she's Tess Langley's clone. She's riding her own board, cruising in on her tummy. She laughs as Lukas and Grace chase her, slipping off the side of the board like a little seal to paddle in her puffy life vest over to Colton.

This is our last full day of family vacation in Aruba. It's become our end-of-summer tradition. We've been coming for a week every year since Bennett was an infant. It's one perfect week to completely unplug and just enjoy the surf and sun.

Sometimes, guys from the team join us with their families. The O'Sullivans and the Gerards came last year. This year, we've got Tess and Ryan in the bungalow next to us. It works out well because we all take turns watching the kiddos, giving the adults a break. I think Tess and Ryan are over at the main resort right now getting a couple's massage.

Or, you know, back at their bungalow . . . doing the other thing.

Actually, knowing them, it's *definitely* the other thing.

But I'm not gonna judge because they're taking our kiddos tonight so my guys and I can enjoy a little candlelit dinner. I fully intend for the three of us to *also* do the other thing.

The sun is starting to dip lower, the blue of the sky slowly turning a hazy yellow-orange. I check the time. "Honeys, we should probably get going," I call out.

Lukas nods that he heard me as Colton plops a squealing Emma back onto her boogie board for one last ride. Lukas strides out of the surf, setting Grace safely in the sand. She hurries over to me, her cheeks bright pink from the sun.

"Did you have fun?" I coo, helping her out of her life vest.

"Yeah!" She digs with sandy fingers in the beach bag for a snack. "Mommy, I'm hungry."

I reach over her and take out a banana, peeling it for her.

If Emma is Tess's clone, Christina Grace is mine. Her blonde hair is a tangled mess from the salt water. It'll take me forever to detangle it. She's got my pointed chin and my sassy attitude too. But then she looks up, cheeks full of banana, flashing me those hazel eyes. I like to think they're a mix of my baby blues and Lukas's salted caramel.

"Benno, let's go," Lukas shouts, striding after him as Bennett's wave drifts him a little too to the far left.

Colton walks out of the water with Emma in his arms, her board dragging in the surf behind him. "Water feels great," he calls out to me. "Sure you don't wanna do a quick swim?"

I lounge back in the shade of my umbrella, my hands folded over my growing baby bump. "I'm fine right where I am, thank you very much."

"You *are* fine," he teases, plopping Emma on the beach blanket next to Grace. "Look at you, my sandy-toed sun queen."

I smile up at him, rubbing my hands over my bump. He watches the motion with a possessive glint in his eye. I purse my lips. Yeah, I know my man. He loves the sight of me pregnant. He better soak it in while he can because this is the last baby I plan on having.

Baby number three was a bit of an oops. We certainly weren't trying. I'm pleased, but I'm anxious too. After Grace, it's been harder for me to get back into the routine of work. Lukas is still as busy as ever playing for the Rays. Now, he's an alternate captain under Jake Price. And Colton is about to start his fourth year as part of the Rays media team providing live commentary. He has a ton of fun, and it keeps him close to the action, but it means he's traveling just as much as Lukas.

I won't deny that it wears on me. These grueling hockey schedules wear on everyone, family or no family. This week in Aruba is my last taste of normal. During the summer months, I have both my men with me to help with snacks and naptimes and stocking the fridge. All three of us sleep in the same bed at night.

Starting next week, we'll be juggling five different schedules again. Adding a sixth is really feeling like a lot. So, you better believe I'm gonna sit here like a shell on the beach and soak up the privilege of having both my men here to chase our kids in the surf.

TWO hours later, the babies are nestled safely in the Langley bungalow for the night, and my guys and I are enjoying a private dinner catered on our candlelit porch. There's fresh fruit salad, grilled red snapper with creole sauce, rice and beans, and an Aruban favorite called pastechis. They're like empanadas, made with a cornmeal crust, and stuffed with a variety of fillings. The kids love them too. We usually order a few around lunchtime to snack on at the beach.

The moon is out tonight, nearly full. It glows silvery white, sitting low on the horizon. The sounds of the ocean echo from yards away across the sand. From somewhere down the beach, a live band plays upbeat Caribbean dance music. The notes of drums and trumpets float toward us on a sea breeze. It's enchanting. My little slice of heaven.

The guys talk quietly about the preseason schedule, while I finish the last of the fruit salad. We've nicknamed this baby Kiwi because it's all I seem to be craving right now. As they chat, our chef lays out the dessert course. There's a sampling of cheeses with dried fruit and nuts, a few pieces of cocada (an Aruban grated coconut candy we all love), and a generous slice of Dutch chocolate cake, decorated with edible flowers.

I smile as I look down at the cake. There are no rings hiding in it. I already have those on my finger. Three years ago, I found Cynthia's engagement ring tucked away in Colton's sock drawer. Feeling a little daring, I slipped it on my right ring finger, and waited to see how long it would take for him to notice.

It took approximately 2.5 seconds.

Let's just say he was very pleased with its placement, and demanded that I never take it off.

But then Lukas took one look at the ring, turned around, and walked out of the house. He returned three hours later, flashing me a black ring box with a cheeky wink. Then he "hid" it in his sock drawer. I made him sweat it out for a week before I "found" it. I had the rings soldered together, and now they never leave my finger.

They aren't wedding rings because this isn't a marriage. At least, it's not the kind of marriage I was ever led to believe I deserved. It'll never be formalized on paper, but Colton, Lukas, and I share such a beautiful life. Our days are full of so much laughter and joy. Sure, we still fight and scream and drive each other crazy some days, but life with these two is beyond anything I could have ever dreamed.

"What are you thinking about over there, all quiet?" Lukas asks, refilling my water glass.

"You," I reply honestly. Turning to Colton, I add, "And you."

Colton smiles. "What about us?"

I turn back to Lukas. "You predicted all this. Do you remember? In my office?"

"You mean the coffin?" he says with a grin. "I wouldn't say I predicted exactly this."

Colton takes my hand. Turning it over on the table, he brushes his fingers in circles on my palm.

"You predicted that Colton and I would get together," I go on. "You predicted love and babies and chocolate cake in Aruba."

Lukas's grin softens into a proper smile. "I did."

"You just never predicted we'd drag you along for the ride," Colton teases, his fingers gently twisting the rings on my finger.

Lukas raises a curious brow. "Would we call it dragged?" He reaches out too, tucking a loose strand of my hair behind my ear. Then he lets his finger trail down to my shoulder and along my collarbone. "If my memory serves, I believe I crawled to you."

His touch and his words send a shiver through me. I smile, glancing over my shoulder through the glass wall into the beach house. Our chef is still in the kitchen, washing dishes.

Reading my mind, Colton stands from the table. "Why don't I go hurry her along?"

I turn to Lukas, taking in the soft glow of the candlelight on his face. I smile at the lump on the bridge of his nose. The scar from the skate blade is now a thin white line trailing from his chin, along his jaw, disappearing over his ear. He's had more injuries over the years. Three broken fingers, a groin pull, a hairline fracture in his foot. Yet still he plays. Hockey remains his only love outside his family.

He holds out a hand to me. I rise from my chair, and he pushes back from the table, setting me down on his knee. I place my hands on his shoulders as his arm snakes around my waist. His gaze heats as he brushes the knuckles of his other hand down my breastbone. "You keep looking at me like that, and I'll have no choice but to strip you out of this dress, bend you over the table, and pound my dick into your sweet little cunt."

I smile. This man doesn't do subtle. He never has.

And I live for it.

Taking a page from his book, I weave my fingers into his hair and tug, forcing him to look at me. "I think we should get in the shower."

He raises a brow, his hands now eagerly exploring, winding me up with gentle touches. "Oh, yeah?" He drops his head, kissing along my shoulder and up my neck to that spot that makes me melt. "Am I a dirty boy, Popsicle? You wanna clean me up?"

"No," I reply, holding him to me as he kisses lower, moving the little triangle of fabric aside to suck on my nipple. I hum, fighting the urge to squirm. I feel each flick of his tongue like a pinch to the clit.

"No?" he teases. "You don't wanna scrub me down?"

I pull on his hair, making him look at me again. "No. I want to make you filthy."

He grins. Lowering his face again, he flicks my nipple until I gasp. "That's my fucking girl. Keep going. Tell me what you want. What have you been dreaming about? Don't think we didn't notice you squirming in your chair all through dinner."

At that moment, Colton returns, his hand smoothing over my hair as he leans down and kisses my check. "What did I miss?"

"Poppy was just about to tell us all the way she wants to get fucked tonight," Lukas replies.

"Excellent." Colton steals my chair, pulling it forward. I squirm on Lukas's knee, pinned between them as they peel the little straps of my black sundress down, exposing my breasts to the ocean air. They've grown two cup sizes thanks to the babies. My guys each take one, sucking and teasing until I'm crying out, my pussy fluttering in desperation.

"Oh my—stop," I whine.

Lukas pulls away, searching my face. "You want us to stop?"

"No—I meant *don't* stop," I pant, already feeling bubbly. "God help me, never stop." I kiss him, cupping his face with my hand. Our tongues tease as Colton kisses along my shoulder. When I break for air, Colton has his hand around Lukas's neck, pulling him closer.

Even after six years of sharing a life, their kisses are still playful and seeking.

Lukas breaks first, turning back to me. "Now, Poppy. What was this about a shower?"

I smile, glancing between them. "Well, you know the shower has that handy little bench—oh, also, I think we should remodel our shower to add one—"

"I'll text Janice the moment we get home," Lukas assure me, kissing my jaw. "But you were saying?"

I brush my hands down their chests, glancing between them. I settle my gaze on Lukas. "I was just imaging how fun it would be to ride Colton's cock on that bench while we both suck your dick."

Before he can respond, I slip off his lap and step back toward the wall of glass, holding up my dress so I don't trip. They both groan, rising to their feet, their hungry gazes locked on me. The straps of my dress are already off my shoulders. The silky black fabric pools around my waist. I let the whole thing drop, leaving me standing naked under the Aruban moon.

Colton's dark eyes take in all my curves. "Fuck."

"Agreed," says Lukas.

Smiling, I cup my breasts, tweaking my nipples. I take a step back, loving how they mirror me with an eager step forward. "Do you know how good it feels, knowing I'm claimed by you? Knowing no other man will ever have me?"

"You're goddamn right no man can have you," Lukas growls, stepping closer. "You're ours, Poppy. You ride our dicks, and wear our cum, and grow our goddamn babies."

I crow with happiness, feeling like a queen as I let my fingers trail down my body, over my growing baby bump. Dropping my hand low, I tease my clit. "I'm yours, and you're mine. You belong to me." I tease my fingers inside myself, loving the feel of their eyes on me. Need burns between us. "Say it," I plead, already dancing on that edge. "Tell me who I am."

"The woman of my dreams," says Colton, tugging off his shirt and tossing it aside.

"Mother of my children," Lukas adds, doing the same.

I take another step back.

"Love of my fucking life," says Colton, his pants dropping to the deck.

"Queen of our goddamn universe."

Lifting my fingers to my lips, I suck them into my mouth, tasting my own desire. God help me, I pray I *never* stop craving these men. Turning on my heel, I lead the way into our little beach house. Lukas and Colton follow.

I smile. They'll follow me anywhere.

THE sun peeks in through the windows of our bungalow, making it glow. I stretch out naked on the bed like a happy house cat. Colton is on his side facing me, his brow furrowed in sleep. Lukas is star-fished on his back, his lips parted in a silent snore.

I slip the sheet off and scoot down the end of the bed, wrapping myself in a fluffy white bathrobe. Padding into the kitchen on bare feet, I pluck a kiwi from the fruit bowl and peel it. I'm slicing a banana when a bleary-eyed Colton comes wandering out of the bedroom, my phone in his hand. "Your phone keeps ringing."

I pop one of the banana slices in my mouth. "So? We're still in Aruba for, like, three more hours. No real life until we touch down in Jacksonville, remember?"

He crosses the living room. "I think it's serious, babe. It's Henrik."

I go still, another slice of banana halfway to my lips. "Karlsson?"

He flashes my phone screen at me, and the name is right there, including a roster picture of the handsome Swedish forward. I didn't even know I had his number saved. Six years with this team, and I've never had an occasion to communicate with him directly. He's certainly never gone out of his way to call me three times in a row.

Curious, I take the phone and answer the call. "This is Poppy St. James."

"Hello, Poppy." I recognize his voice instantly, his accented English smooth and proper. "This is Henrik Karlsson calling from Sweden."

I set my paring knife down. "Hey, Henrik. This is sure a surprise. What can I do for you?"

"I need your help. It's rather urgent."

I place one hand flat on the counter as my PR brain instantly starts spinning out worst-case scenarios. I knew he was going to Sweden to deal with a family emergency. I believe it had something to do with a sudden death. It all happened right before we left for Aruba, so I'm a little out of the loop. "Hen, honey, what happened?"

He groans into the phone. I can picture him dragging a hand through that stylish, sandy blond hair. "I may have done something rather reckless last night."

Colton looks at me wide-eyed, and I just shake my head, my anxiety blooming like a weed. "How reckless are we talking?"

He got into a bar fight. He murdered someone. He stole a kidney. My brain spins out crazy ideas until I finally hear him say, "I got married."

Okay, well this just doesn't compute at all. In the six years I've known Henrik, I don't think he's ever been in a relationship. The man lives and breathes hockey. No scandals. No drama. No clingy bunnies. "Did I know you were even seeing anyone?" I ask. But then I'm gasping. "Oh god—don't tell me you married, like, Swedish royalty or something! Henrik Karlsson, did you marry a freaking princess?"

He lets off a soft chuckle. "No, I married Teddy."

My brow furrows in confusion. I'm pretty sure I only know one Teddy. He was a physical therapy intern for us several years ago. Lukas raved about his massages so much that Colton got a teensy bit jealous. Of course, once Lukas knew Teddy was a trigger, he just couldn't help but taunt him. I got to watch it blow up in a shouting match that ended with Lukas under Colton, moaning his name. Honestly, it was a pretty memorable night.

Last I heard, Teddy is now a full doctor of physical therapy. I think he's coming back to the team to fill in while Rachel Price takes maternity leave. But Henrik can't mean *that* Teddy, right?

I shuffle the phone to my ear as I walk around to the other side of the kitchen island, pulling out a stool. "You wanna say that name again, sweets? I'm not sure I heard you right."

He sighs. "Poppy, last night I married Teddy O'Connor."

Yep, it's that Teddy.

"But this doesn't make any sense. Aren't you in Sweden for a family emergency?"

"Yes. He came with me."

"I am so confused right now," I admit, sinking down onto the stool as Colton brings me my bowl of fruit.

"And we'll fill you in, I promise," Henrik assures me. "For now, we need your help."

"Sure, honey. What help do you need? Want me to write up a formal press announcement?"

He's quiet for a moment. "No, I want you to help me defraud the Swedish and American governments."

I nearly drop the bowl of fruit as Colton hands it to me.

Defraud the—oh, I do *not* get paid enough for this!

Setting the fruit aside, I slide my laptop over and flip it open. Switching the phone to speaker, I set it on the bar. "Okay, Henrik. Why don't you just start at the beginning?"

Want to find out what happened in Sweden?

The next book in the Jacksonville Rays Universe is *Pucking Strong*. This story features the slow-burning, swoony romance of Rays physical therapist Teddy O'Connor and Swedish left winger Henrik Karlsson.

If you want to be the first to know when the preorders for *Pucking Strong* are available, join my newsletter.

THANK YOU

This story is all Amanda's fault. From the earliest days of drafting *Pucking Around*, I knew Poppy would get her own book. I had this image in my head of the infamous "ice machine" scene. From that scene, an enemies-to-lovers plot unfolded for Poppy and Novy that would include an unplanned pregnancy.

Enter Amanda.

That lil genius told me it would be a good idea to enrich the plot with an angsty "who's your daddy" love triangle by throwing Morrow into the mix. This book is the result. Amanda, I hope you like it. If the rest of you hate it, take it up with her.

Okay, let's thank some people. To my intrepid beta team—Sam, Rachel, Alex #1, Alex #2, Amanda, and Nicole. You were a dream to work with. You helped make this book shine.

To my amazing teams at Kensington, Penguin Michael Joseph, and Tantor, thank you for being so organized and efficient. This hybrid publishing machine can be chaotic at times, and I'm so grateful to all of you for helping me roll this beast of a series forward.

To my agent, Susan, you've been such a support for me as I've made pretty much every mistake trying to figure out how to do this whole "being a hybrid author" thing.

To Ashley, you treasure, we did it again. We wrote another book. I'm not saying "I" anymore. *We* did this. You know how valuable your insights are to me.

To my readers, thank you so much for your patience and your loyalty as you waited for this book. The wheel of life was determined to churn me into butter this year. I'm so deeply grateful to all of you for waiting for me to write a story worth telling.

I want to say a special word of thanks to the heart patients in my life who gave their time and their insights to inform Colton's story. Your fortitude is an inspiration.

Continue reading for an excerpt of

North Is the Night

INSPIRED BY FINNISH FOLKLORE,
INTERNATIONALLY BESTSELLING AUTHOR
EMILY RATH PRESENTS A NEW FANTASY
DUOLOGY WITH ADVENTURE, INTRIGUE, AND
TWO YOUNG WOMEN WHO DEFY THE GODS

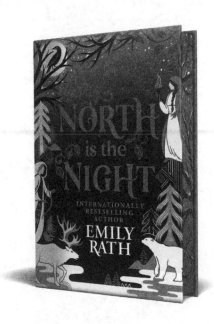

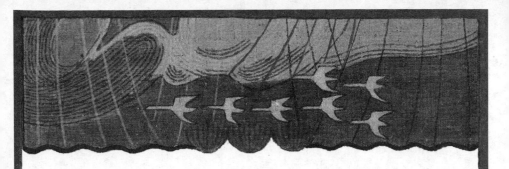

Siiri

A CHILL AUTUMN WIND whips at my face as I stand on the lakeshore, hands on my hips. Aina waits dutifully at my side. Together, we watch as my father calls out to us in greeting. He pulls in his oars just as the bottom of our wooden boat crunches against the pebbly beach. Flipping my braid off my shoulder, I wade in shin-deep and hold the boat steady for him. The water is icy cold, soaking through my socks and the hem of my woolen dress. I bite my lip against the pain. Father hops out, and we grip the sides, giving the small boat two sharp tugs.

"A good catch today," he says proudly.

We give the boat one more heave, pulling it fully up onto the beach.

I peer inside. It *is* a good catch. And thank the gods for that. We need more fish if we're to survive the winter. Father managed to fill a whole basket with perch. The other basket is a mix. Zander, a skinny pike, a handful of roach. A few of these will be set aside and given to Mummi, my grandmother, for tonight's supper, but the rest must be salted and stored in the njalle for winter.

Father wipes his hands on his breeches. "Your brothers will stay out a bit longer. Help them bring in their catch too. Understood?"

"Yes, Isä," I reply.

Glancing up at the sky, he judges how much daylight is left. There are still more chores to do before nightfall. "Remember not to stay out too late, Siiri. You, too, Aina. Get yourselves home well before dark."

We nod, and he leaves us with the baskets.

I don't fault him his curt manner. Everyone in the village is on edge. A few days ago, some of the menfolk returned from the southern market with chilling news: More young women have been going missing up and down the lakeshore. Strange tales of screams heard in the dark woods, creatures with eyes that glow red, a lingering stench of death in the air. People always talk of such things, but never so close to us, never here. And none of the girls have been found.

These are dark times. If Father could spare me, he would probably make me stay nearer the house with Mummi and my little sister. But winter is coming, and I have two strong hands. We both know he needs me. There's no time for worry, not when our worries seem endless now.

Once, these forests were a safe haven. The gods give of their bounty, and we Finns take. We *must* take. And that which is taken is always shared. When the harsh winter comes, and the long, cold night sets in, we sit by our fires and warm each other with good food and stories of summertime. I have golden memories of sitting on my mother's lap as she told us stories of the old gods—Ukko and the making of his stone hammer, Ahti the seafaring warrior, the clever shaman Väinämöinen and his magical kantele. Summer is the time for hard work and sacrifice. Winter is for stories and family and a quietly lived life.

That was before.

Before the gods went quiet, abandoning us here in these woods. Before bards stopped strumming kanteles and singing the songs. Before Swedish settlers arrived on our shores, stealing farmland across the south, uprooting thousands of us, including my family. We left my mother there, buried in the cold ground outside Turku. No one remains to tend to her grave. No flowers. No songs.

And that was before the whispers of a new god whistled darkly through the woods. Every day, the Christians grow bolder, challenging our gods and threatening our way of life.

In a few short years, the Swedes have turned these forests from a haven into a hell. Powerful men in robes of white now call out from their great stone houses in the south, offering gold and silver to any Finn who would provision them— meat, fur, timber, grain. Our forests are full of thieves who dare to take more than they need, leaving little enough for the rest of us. Each summer, the fight for land becomes bloodier. They slash and burn large swaths of acreage for their cattle. They thin our herds of free-roaming deer and elk. They claim the best of the farmland for their wheat and barley.

Before long, they'll take even the mushrooms. We Finns will be left with nothing but the brambles in the fens and the bark on the trees.

I gaze down at the baskets in my father's boat. The Swedes may be trying to claim everything, but Ilmatar hear me, they will not have our small, regular haul of fish. Lifting my hands, I close my eyes and offer up a blessing to the sea goddess. "Vellamo, righteous in beauty, thank you for your bounty."

Next to me, Aina offers up her own quiet blessing.

"You don't have to help me." My tone is half-apologetic,

half-hopeful. As much as I know we need these fish to survive the winter, I hate salting them. It's probably my least favorite chore. With a heavy sigh, I pick up the first basket.

Aina just smiles, taking the other basket. "I don't mind. You're always helping me with my chores."

I lead the way over to our salting station. A few of the older women are seated together, gossiping quietly as they work. They nod in welcome, their expressions worried, if a little curious too.

Aina frowns, the basket of fish still balanced on her hip. "It's as if they expect one of us to be taken next."

"Ignore them," I mutter, giving the women a fake smile and a wave. "They're just jealous, because they know no man wants a catty old fishwife with salty fingers in his bed." I drop down onto a stump and select a crock, preparing it with a base of salt. This is the worst part. The salt finds every scrape and blemish on my skin, burning and stinging so sharply, my eyes water. I hiss, waiting for the sting to numb, as I pick up the first fish, roll it in salt, and layer it in the bottom of the crock.

We'll have to repeat this whole process in a few days. Once the fish are all repacked, they'll last for up to nine months. Come winter, we'll stay warm by our fires eating stews of perch with barley and dried mushrooms.

I try to hold my breath as I work, because the briny smell of the fish makes me gag. Also, I hate the feel of their slippery bodies as I roll them in the salt. On the stump next to me, Aina laughs. When I cast her a glare, she flicks a little salt my way with her fingers. "Don't," I mutter, in no mood to be teased.

"You're such a goose. You like to eat fish, right?"

"Of course."

"Well, you won't be eating anything this winter if you don't salt these first."

I grimace, packing a layer of salt over the first row of perch. "What does it look like I'm doing?"

She turns her attention back to her own work. After a few minutes of silence, she glances my way. "What if these girls aren't really missing? Perhaps they simply chose to leave."

My shoulders stiffen. "Why would someone do that? Just disappear like smoke in the wind without a word to anyone? All because you fancy a new life for yourself?"

She huffs, rolling another fish in salt. "Well, I wouldn't, but other girls might. Not everyone has a mother as kind as mine . . . or a mummi as protective as yours."

True.

I smile, thinking of my grandmother, of her warm hands and her cold glare. That woman was born with iron in her spine. She protects her grandchildren with the ferocity of a mother bear, and she loves us just as fiercely. And there really is no kinder woman than Aina's mother . . . except perhaps Aina herself.

"You've made this point already," I tease. "More than once."

"Well, it's as true now as it was this morning," she counters. "We've heard these stories for years. Women go missing, Siiri. Too many women die in childbirth, and that leaves too few of us unmarried women left. And men get lonely—"

I snort, peering out at the boats. "Oh, do they? You wouldn't know it from Aksel."

She follows my gaze. We both know how decidedly *not* lonely my brother is, most nights. If my father catches him with a girl in the barn again, he's likely to strap Aksel's hide clean off.

"Fine, *some* men get lonely," she clarifies. "And then they get desperate. I'm not saying it's right," she adds quickly. "I'm only saying I bet if someone went out and looked, they would find every one of those missing girls scattered somewhere along the lakeshore, adjusting to her lot as a lonely man's wife."

Now my grimace has nothing to do with the salt burning my hands. "Gods, why does your theory sound even more horrifying than the one about witches and blood sacrifice?"

She purses her lips, trying to hide her smile. "Perhaps because you are singularly opposed to even the idea of marriage? For you, a woman choosing to marry is as disturbing as being kidnapped by a witch or fed to a stone giant."

I snort. "Surely I'm not that bad?"

"You are worse, and you know it. No man will ever be good enough for you, Siiri. You're smarter than they are, funnier than they are."

"True," I joke.

"Not to mention you always best them in every contest of will. It's quite maddening, I assure you."

"Maddening? For whom?"

"For them."

"How can you know how they feel about it?"

"Because they *tell* me so," she replies with a laugh. "Repeatedly. They call you the pickled herring."

I laugh, too, puffing a little with pride. "Well, perhaps they should try harder to impress me."

"And since no man is good enough for *you*," she says over me, "you've decided no man can possibly ever be good enough for *me,* either. You've scared away my last three suitors—"

"Stop right there." I waggle a salt-crusted finger in her face. "If you call that duck-brained Joki your suitor one more time, gods hear me, I'll marry you to him myself. See how well you like it when a year from now he's still telling you the same story of the time he *nearly* felled a ten-point stag."

She laughs again despite herself, tossing another fish down

on her bed of salt. Leaning over, she gives my knee a gentle squeeze. "Be at peace. I don't want to marry Joki."

The tension in my chest eases a bit at her admission.

"But I will eventually marry someone," she adds, turning back to her work.

Her words stifle the air like a blanket tossed over a fire. I can't look at her, can't let her see my face.

"I want a family," she says, her tone almost apologetic. "I want a home of my own. Gods willing, I'll have children."

"Gods willing, you'll survive it," I mutter. Too few women do. We lost our dear friend Helka just last month. Her and her baby. That's three mothers and three babies this summer alone. Just another one of the curses plaguing our land. I swear, sometimes it feels like the gods are laughing at us . . . if they bother to see us at all.

Maybe my brother Onni is right. Maybe our gods really are dead. What else could account for this cruel, senseless suffering?

But my sweet Aina is ever hopeful. "I'll have children and a husband who loves me," she goes on. "A home of my own. A family. A purpose. Don't you want that for me, Siiri? Don't you want it for yourself?"

I stare down at my fingers, red and stinging and swollen with salt. *A family and a home of my own.* That's supposed to be the dream, right? Children. A warm fire and full bellies. My own njalle stocked with provisions to last us the long winter. A man in my bed to warm my back and keep the wolves at bay.

I shake my head. All my life, I've tried to see that future for myself. It's what my mother wanted for me . . . before she died bringing my little sister into this world. It's what my grandmother wants for me. Now, it's what Aina wants for us both.

But what do I want? What do I see when I close my eyes and dream of my happiest self?

I take a deep breath, gazing out across Lake Päijänne, my home for the last fourteen years. The days are getting shorter, the nights colder. I can taste autumn in the air, that crisp smell of drying leaves. The lake is changing too. In summer, she's as bright as the blue of a jaybird's wing. In autumn, the lake darkens as the fish sink to her depths. She grows quiet and secretive as she waits for spring.

Watching the boats bob, the truth unravels itself inside me like a spool of golden thread. I want to live the life I already have. I want long summer days running through the forest, hunting deer and snaring rabbits. I want quiet winter nights in Aina's hayloft, cracking walnuts and laughing until we fall asleep. I want to swim naked in the lake, my hair loose and tangled around my arms. I want us to stay just like this, happy and free forever.

"Siiri?" Aina's hand brushes my arm. "Are you well?"

Sucking in a sharp breath, I turn to face her. Bracing myself with both hands on her shoulders, I search her face. Her lips part in silent question, her brows lowered with worry.

"Aina, I want you to be happy," I say at last, giving her shoulders a squeeze. "That's what I want. Tell me what will make you happy, and I'll get it for you. If you want to marry Joki, the fish-faced farm boy, I will be the first to light a candle in the great oak tree."

She rolls her eyes with a soft smile.

"If you want to leave our village and go on that adventure in search of a new love, I will leave with you—"

She leans away. "Siiri—"

"I *will*," I say in earnest. Taking her salty hands in mine, I hold them fast. "Aina, you are my oldest and dearest friend. I don't care about finding myself a good man and settling down. I am perfectly content being my own good man. What I cannot bear is the thought of losing you or making you unhappy. So please, just tell me what you want, and I'll get it for you."

She blinks, eyes brimming with tears as she searches my face. I fear what she might see in me. She's always seen too much—the parts I hide, the parts I pretend not to have. My weaknesses, my fears. She knows me better than any person living or dead.

Slowly, she sighs, shaking her head. "I guess . . . I wish there was just some way you really could be happy for me if I pick a life you wouldn't pick for yourself."

I drop her hands. "What do you mean?"

"I mean . . . " She groans. "Gods, you know, I wish I knew whether there was even *one* person out there who you thought was good enough for me. I could never marry without your blessing, Siiri, so I need to know. Is there no man living you could bear to see me wed?"

I consider for a moment, heart in my throat. Does she want me to say Joki? The poor man is duller than lichen on rocks. My brothers are both clever enough, I guess, but they're all wrong for her. They're both too independent. Aina needs someone who really sees her, someone who listens, someone who *needs* her.

She watches me, waiting, still searching my face. I can't sit here and have her looking at me with such hope in her eyes. Taking a deep breath, I hold her gaze. "You want a name? Fine. Let it be Nyyrikki."

She blinks. After a moment, she laughs. It bubbles out of her like foam off a stream. Before long, she's gripping her sides with salty fingers. I join her, and we both laugh, tears filling our eyes.

"Nyyrikki?" she says on a tight breath. "God of the hunt

and prince of the forest? That's where I must set my standard of matrimony?"

"You said any man living. And you'd never be hungry," I add with a shrug. "There would always be game for your table. And he's supposed to be of famed beauty, with a head of flowing hair . . . and he lives in a forest palace with gates of wrought gold. You could do worse, Aina."

She laughs. "Well, next time I stumble across his palace in the woods, I'll just give those golden gates a knock, shall I?"

"We'll both knock," I tease, catching her gaze again. Aina has the most beautiful eyes, bright like new blades of spring grass. She has freckles too, though not so many as me. Hers are soft and small, scattered over her pointed nose. Wisps of her nut-brown hair frame her face, tugged loose by this wind. I want to tuck the strands behind her ear. I want to touch her face. I want to brush my fingertips over the freckles on her nose.

"What is it?"

Looking at her now, I can see the truth so clearly: I don't want things to change between us. And marriage *will* change her. It always does. It's the way of things. Once children come, they will be her world, and I'll lose her. I'll lose everything. Call me selfish, but I'm not ready. Not yet. I want just one more summer of being the first in her affections.

I curl my salted fingers until the tips of my nails bite into the meat of my palms.

"Siiri?"

"It's nothing," I mutter, turning away.

She drops her hand from my thigh, reaching for another fish. "And . . . who shall we find for you, then?" She keeps her tone light, trying to move us past my awkwardness. "I don't believe Nyyrikki has a brother . . . "

"I don't need to marry."

"Ilmarinen could spin gold for you," she offers.

I huff. "So can the moon goddess. And she'd likely darn her own stockings. Clean up her own messes too. Now, no more talk of god-husbands. Let's just get this done."

Before long, I'm packing the last perch into the top of my crock. Aina is crouched over at the water's edge, washing her hands. She stands, shielding her eyes with her hand, as she gazes out across the lake. The setting sun is casting a glare.

"What are they doing?" she asks.

I glance up, squinting. My brother Aksel is perched in the front of our other fishing boat, waving at us. "Maybe they caught a massive pike," I say with a shrug. It doesn't make me happy. It's just more work.

"They'll have the boat over if they keep rocking it like that," Aina warns.

I look up again. Aksel isn't so much waving as gesturing frantically. Cupping his mouth, he shouts across the water. Meanwhile, Onni faces the opposite way, rowing as hard as he can. I rise to my feet. "What the . . . "

"Run!"

I join Aina at the water's edge. What is he saying?

"Siiri, run!"

Screams erupt behind us. Up and down the beach, the others scatter. My heart leaps into my throat. On the shore, not fifteen feet from me, stands a woman. No . . . a *monster*. She has the body of a woman, draped in heavy black robes. The cloth is soiled and torn, dragging on the ground, hanging off her skeletal frame. Her face is painted—a band of mottled white across her eyes and nose—while her forehead and exposed neck are smeared with what looks like dried, flaking blood. Perched on her head is a set of curling black ram's horns.

She looks at me with eyes darker than two starless skies.

They dare me to leap into their depths. Sucking in a breath, I blink, breaking our connection. Her mouth opens, showing broken, rotting teeth. She hisses, taking a step forward, and one thought fills me.

Run.

Grabbing Aina by the hand, I take off down the beach.

She asks no questions. She just holds my hand, and we sprint. Our feet crunch against the pebbles. I chance a look over my shoulder as I pull her towards the trees. The creature slowly turns and raises her tattooed hand, pointing right at us. In a swirl of black smoke, a monstrous wolf appears at the creature's side. The jaws of the beast open wide as it pants, exposing rows of sharp white teeth. The glowing red eyes track us like prey. With a growl, it leaps from its mistress's side.

The chase is on.

"Ilmatar, help us," I cry to the heavens. "Aina, *run.*"

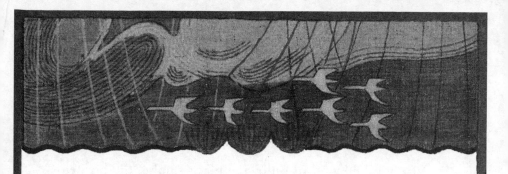

Siiri

"WHAT IS THAT CREATURE?" Aina cries as soon as we slip under the cover of the trees.

"My guess is that's the thing stealing girls," I pant. "Not some lonely fisherman and not a scurrilous Swede."

I pull us deeper into the forest, Aina's hand clasped firmly in mine. It's darker here. Too dark. We should have been home already. Behind us, I can still hear the screams of the people on the beach. The men will soon be out in droves, bows and axes at the ready. They'll come for us. They'll help. We just have to find a place to hide.

"You're faster than me, Siiri." Aina pulls on my hand. "I can't keep up. Just go—"

"Not a chance."

Through the dim trees, the underbrush rustles and twigs snap. As we burst into a clearing, I stop and drop Aina's hand, still holding tight to my little filleting knife. Chest heaving, I put a protective arm up in front of her. Something is coming, and Aina's right, we can't keep running. Better to stand and catch my breath. Better to die facing my foe.

"That thing is here for one of us. Siiri, you need to *go*." She gives me a shove. "Keep running."

Too late.

In another swirl of billowing black smoke, the horned woman appears before us on the other side of the clearing. Her head tips to the side at an impossible angle, more owl than human, and those black eyes gauge us, as if she's deciding which of us to kill first.

"Stay behind me," I rasp, stepping in front of Aina.

She clings to my hips with both hands. I can feel the warmth of her breath on my neck.

The creature's mouth opens wide, and I can't help but gag. Once, when I was hunting with Onni, we came across a dead deer washed up on the beach. The carcass was bloated and rotting, bugs eating away its eyes. The waves slowly pushed it back and forth against the pebbles. The smell of that mangled, bloated deer carcass emanates out of this creature's cavernous mouth. Moist decay, sour rot. I can't breathe. Can't think. My eyes sting. My nose and throat burn. Behind me, Aina makes a choking sound.

A low growl comes from behind us both, and I know what I'll see if I turn around. That monstrous wolf will be there, those glowing red eyes watching me. With one hand on Aina, I adjust my stance so I can face both monsters at once.

"Stay back," I shout, swiping the air with my little knife.

The horned woman steps closer, so close her shadow towers over us. She makes no sound when she moves. Not a single whisper or crunch over the fallen leaves. That rune-marked, skeletal hand extends towards me.

"I said stay back," I cry, swinging wildly with my knife. The blade connects with the meat of the creature's palm, and she pauses. Next to her, the wolf growls, flicking his serpent-like tail. A sickening smile spreads across the woman's face, as if she's surprised and delighted to see I would dare attack her. With a sweep of her arm, she launches me off my feet. Her hand doesn't even touch me, and yet I'm breathless, my vision spinning as I fly through the air and slam against a tree. I crumple, body aching.

"Siiri," Aina cries out, somewhere to my right. "Don't hurt her," she screams at the monster. "Take me. *Please*, take me instead!"

Never.

Darkness creeps in from the corners of my vision as I scramble to my knees. That creature is not taking Aina away from me. Warm blood oozes from my cut brow and down my cheek, dripping onto the fallen leaves. My breaths come short and fast as I paw at the ground, desperate to find my knife. I grasp a small rock. The fingers of my other hand wrap around the sharp metal of my knife blade. Stumbling to my feet, I throw the rock. It strikes the horned woman on the side of the head. She turns to face me, letting out an unearthly hiss.

"Aina, run," I shout.

But Aina is rooted to the spot.

With a feral cry, I throw my knife. It spins through the air, handle over blade, landing hilt-deep in the chest of the horned woman. "Now, Aina," I call. "Run!"

She shakes her head, tears slipping down her cheeks. "Not without you."

The monster doesn't even blink as the knife pierces her heart. Slowly, she raises her hand and jerks it free. With her haunting gaze locked on mine, she drops the knife to the ground at her feet. Still looking at me, she steps to the side and reaches out, her rune-marked fingers gripping Aina's exposed forearm.

Aina's scream rips through me, stealing the air from my lungs.

Torches bob around us in the night, flashes of golden yellow. Men run towards her screams. The monster gives me one last lopsided smile before disappearing in a swirl of black smoke, drawing Aina with her.

"Siiri—" Aina's cry is cut short, lost to the shadows.

"Aina!"

As the smoke dissipates, the giant wolf lunges, crossing the clearing in one leap. It follows Aina and the creature into dark oblivion. I stumble forward, waving my hand through the wisps of shadow, but they're gone.

I sink to my knees, heart thudding in my chest. My eyes are fixed on the point where Aina just disappeared. She could have run, but she wouldn't leave me. Given the choice between her and me, she let the monster take her.

The black void that swallowed her whole fills me, growing, growing inside me. My heart pounds as the truth sinks into my chest, coiling around my very bones. Aina is gone. I couldn't protect her. I failed her. She sacrificed herself to the monster to save me.

I collapse on the forest floor, the moss now a pillow for my aching head. *It's my fault Aina's gone, so let me die here in these woods.* I close my eyes, my cold hand pressed against the soil. "Take me," I whisper to the ground. "Ilmatar, take me with her. I am nothing without her."

The All-Mother answers my prayer as blessed darkness overtakes me.